TALES OF ADVENTURE

Robert Louis Stevenson (1850–94), was born and educated in Edinburgh. He was a sickly child, and most of his adult years were to be spent travelling in search of a climate which would do least damage to his lungs. Following the family tradition in civil engineering, he went to Edinburgh University in 1867. More interested in literature and the bohemian life, he changed to law and qualified as an advocate in 1875. Thereafter he gave himself to his creative ambitions, with frequent visits to London and to France, where he met Fanny Osbourne, a married American woman who was to become his future wife.

Stevenson began with essays, short stories and travel writing, most notably *Travels with a Donkey in the Cevennes* (1879). He went to California to marry Fanny in 1880. The journey nearly killed him, but he wrote of his experiences in *Across the Plains* (1892), *The Amateur Emigrant* (1895) and *The Silverado Squatters* (1883). He is, perhaps, best rememberd for his first novel *Treasure Island* (1883), and his early reputation was made with this and other examples of adventure fiction, not least *Dr Jekyll and Mr Hyde* which appeared as a paperback thriller in 1886. The great Scottish novels followed, with *Kidnapped* (1886), *The Master of Ballantrae* (1889), and *Weir of Hermiston* (1896), which was left unfinished at his death. *Catriona* (1893), was always planned as the immediate sequel to *Kidnapped*, but had been delayed in the writing.

Stevenson spent seven years in the South Seas, settling for the last five on the island of Upolu in Samoa, where he died suddenly from a cerebral stroke at the age of forty-four.

Robert Louis Stevenson

TALES OF ADVENTURE

Introduced by F. R. Hart

THE BLACK ARROW
TREASURE ISLAND

The Treasure of Franchard
The Sire de Malétroit's Door
Will o' the Mill

The House of Eld
The Song of the Morrow

CANONGATE
Edinburgh · London · New York · Melbourne

First published as a Canongate Classic in 1997,
by Canongate Books Ltd,
14 High Street, Edinburgh, EH1 1TE

Introduction copyright © Francis Russell Hart, 1997

Cover illustration reprinted with the permission of
Atheneum Books for Young Readers, an imprint of
Simon and Schuster Children's Publishing Division
from Treasure Ireland by N. C.Wyeth
Copyright © Charles Scribner's Sons;
copyright renewed 1939, N. C.Wyeth

The publishers gratefully acknowledge general
subsidy from the Scottish Arts Council towards
the Canongate Classics series and a specific
grant towards the publication of this title

British Library Cataloguing-in-Publication Data
A catalogue record for this book is available on
request from the British Library

ISBN 978 0 86241 687 4

Typeset in 10pt Plantin
by Hewer Text Ltd, Edinburgh

www.canongate.tv

Contents

Introduction   vii

The House of Eld   1

Will o'the Mill   9

The Sire de Malétroit's Door   37

TREASURE ISLAND   61

The Treasure of Franchard   277

THE BLACK ARROW   339

The Song of the Morrow   597

Stevenson: The Two Sindbads

'R.L.S.', notes his most recent biographer Ian Bell, 'wrote tales of adventure. That is true enough, but not the whole truth.' Far from it. But the ideas of adventure and of the adventurer haunt his fiction in many guises. The highly unusual collection of stories in this volume shows us the young tale-teller experimenting, trying out his craft. It includes two short fables, three longish short stories, and two long stories which, for want of a better term, we will call 'novels'. They are printed here in the chronological order of composition, so that, should you be so inclined, you can speculate about his artistic development. But such speculation is risky with R.L.S. His restless impulse to strike out in new directions and his habit of returning later to get unfinished work 'unstuck' have frustrated scholars in search of coherent development. Some vent their frustration by faulting him for uncertainty or frivolity. Others impose models that are too conceptual to contain his impulsive genius and that depreciate his early writing.

Storytelling surrounded Stevenson from childhood, and he was dictating stories to his mother and his nurse 'Cummie' before he was ten. At thirteen, he was editing a schoolboy magazine, and before he was twenty, he was writing stories about the Scottish covenanters. But the discovery of Scotland as his subject was far off in the future. His early published tales reflect foreign interests.

The fable as a form appealed to him through his career; indeed, Jenni Calder, the author of my favourite study of Stevenson, thinks all of his fiction tends toward fable. 'The House of Eld' and 'The Song of the Morrow' may have been drafted in 1874, though their final versions came only twenty years later. 'Will o' the Mill', a tale of an

Alpine village, was written in summer, 1877. 'The Sire de Malétroit's Door', a sketch arising out of the young scholar's immersion in late medieval France, followed a few weeks later. *Treasure Island,* which carries us from the south English coast to a remote tropical isle, was begun at Braemar in summer, 1881, and after a delay when (characteristically) he got 'stuck' in Chapter Sixteen, was finished to meet serialisation deadlines in November in Switzerland. 'The Treasure of Franchard', an ironic idyll of a French town familiar to him as an artists' colony, came a year later. *The Black Arrow,* an anti-romance of war-torn fifteenth-century England, was tossed off as a serial sequel to *Treasure Island* in 1883. Stevenson was then thirty-three. In 1884 at Bournemouth he settled down to serious reflection on fiction, and the 'mature novelist' emerged.

So, these stories belong to his first decade as a man of letters, when he was also publishing essays, travel books, biographical and historical studies, lay sermons, and critical reviews. He was experimenting tirelessly, seeking his form, style and matter. The variety is astonishing; versatility was Stevenson's Delilah. His friend and admirer Henry James said:

it is a delight to read him, and . . . he renews this delight by a constant variety of experiment . . . It is just because he has no speciality that Mr Stevenson is an individual . . . It is easy to believe that if his strength permitted him to be a more abundant writer he would still more frequently play this eminently literary trick – that of dodging off in a new direction.

Less genial and pluralistic critics, wedded to the norm of consistency, have found this 'dodging' habit a symptom of immaturity or frivolity. James is the better guide.

Certainly the young writer was 'eminently literary', passionately committed to learning *how* to write. *What* to write, on what subject, in what form, followed after. In the 1870s and 1880s, his options were unsettling, overabundant; the choices hard to make. The literary world he entered was stirred by four currents.

First, the great practitioners of the mid-Victorian novel were dead or dying, and their mode – realistic, domestic, psychological – seemed restrictive, sterile. A taste arose for non-realistic modes, poetic, fabulous, which Stevenson the aesthetic theorist would later promote under the heading of 'romance'. The term we adopt for this collection, 'tale', with its connotations of the exotic and the quasi-legendary, recalls that current.

Second, contemporaneous with, possibly related to the current of romance, was a programme to cultivate prose as an art, to elevate prose to the level of poetry. Its prominent spokesman was Walter Pater. And of the documents generated by this 'cult of prose style', Travis Merritt singles out Stevenson's essay 'On Style in Literature' as 'far and away the most important . . . and most amazing' for its 'sheer concentration on verbal method, for specific interest in the texture of language'. Stevenson was fascinated by style, and he freely admitted he had trained himself by playing 'the sedulous ape' to an array of past stylists. 'Before all things he is a writer with a style', wrote James, 'a model with a complexity of curious and picturesque garments'. His denigrators accused him of being a mere mannerist, an 'eminently literary' poseur.

In our tales you will find a variety of accomplished styles. To be fair to Stevenson the artist in prose, let me gather here a few samples and let them serve as a first introduction to the tales. We can turn then to the more solemn matters beloved of scholastic interpreters, genre and meaning. But linguistic surface is not to be overlooked. As T.S. Eliot once wrote of Tennyson, his 'surface, his technical accomplishment, is intimate with his depths . . . By looking innocently at the surface we are most likely to come to the depths.'

In 'Will o' the Mill', the style of quasi-allegorical romantic panorama:

Year after year went away into nothing, with great explosions and outcries in the cities on the plain: red revolt springing up and being suppressed in blood, battle swaying hither and thither, patient astronomers in observatory towers picking out and christening new stars, plays being performed in lighted theatres, people being carried into hospitals on stretchers, and all the turmoil and agitation of men's lives in crowded centres.

In 'The Sire de Malétroit's Door', the style of the surreal grotesque:

His countenance had a strongly masculine cast; not properly human, but such as we see in the bull, the goat, or the domestic boar; something equivocal and wheedling, something greedy, brutal, and dangerous. The upper lip was inordinately full, as though swollen by a blow or a toothache; and the smile, the peaked eyebrows, and the small, strong eyes were quaintly and almost comically evil in expression.

In *Treasure Island*, the elegantly simple Augustan style of generalised image and antithesis:

I followed him in, and I remember observing the contrast the neat, bright doctor, with his powder as white as snow, and his bright, black eyes and pleasant manners, made with the coltish country folk, and above all, with that filthy, heavy, bleared scarecrow of a pirate of ours, sitting far gone in rum, with his arms on the table.

In 'The Treasure of Franchard', the style of parodic, playfully inflationary satire:

So he rattled on, copiously greasing the joint of his inconsistency with words . . . The Doctor sang, the Doctor whistled, the Doctor talked. He spoke of the woods, and the wars, and the deposition of the dew; he brightened and babbled of Paris; he soared into cloudy bombast on the glories of the political arena.

In *The Black Arrow*, the style of pathetic naturalistic impressionism (in striking counterpoint to the pseudo-archaic dialogue):

The words died in Richard's throat. He saw, through tears, the poor old man, bemused with liquor and sorrow, go shambling away, with bowed head, across the snow, and the unnoticed dog whimpering at his heels, and for the first time began to understand the desperate game that we play in life; and how a thing once done is not to be changed or remedied, by any penitence.

And finally, in the fables – in this case 'The House of Eld' – the scriptural mythical style of incantatory repetition:

The blood ran backward in his body and his joints rebelled

against him for the love he bore his father; but he heaved up the sword, and plunged it in the heart of the appearance; and the appearance cried aloud in the voice of his father; and fell to the ground; and a little bloodless white thing fled from the room.

The precocious new stylist raised high expectations among men of letters in London, not always to his advantage.

The third current of the '70s and '80s was the growth of the institution known as 'men of letters', professional writers supported by a spate of magazines and reviews, who played multiple cultural roles as refined entertainers, arbiters of tastes, shapers of opinion, even lay moralists for a literate middle-class public that (as John Gross writes) 'hungered for intellectual guidance'. In 1873, new friendships brought twenty-three-year-old Stevenson into a London coterie of men of letters. It was a mixed blessing. True, his new friends brought him status and income. But they also held their own high expectations as to what the promising protégé should write. This proved especially troublesome for Stevenson, whose chameleon-like temperament made him peculiarly susceptible to friendly influences. On at least one occasion, he angrily rebelled. His friend Henley had reported that some of their refined circle were distressed to see the gifted R.L.S. serialising 'hackery' in a magazine called *Young Folks*. Stevenson fired back at 'those who ask me (as you say they do) to do nothing but refined, high-toned be-jay be-damn masterpieces . . . Let them write their own damn masterpieces. Let me alone.' The hackery in question was *Treasure Island*.

In this story of adventure, written 'for boys' and thus freed of the need for 'psychology or fine writing', he had found the freedom he needed. Not many 'boys' were enthused, but a surprising number of older men, including Stevenson's engineer father, were enthralled. The late nineteenth century – and this was the fourth current – saw a great revival of taste for adventure. Perhaps it offered an escape from the growingly repressive, grey utilitarianism of bourgeois culture. Perhaps it served as a romantic propaganda for the imperialism of the day. Certainly it constituted a key impulse in the late Victorian cult of childhood. Whatever the causes, Stevenson rode the wave of adventure.

What is 'adventure'? Everyone knows, intuitively, vaguely. I like Paul Zweig's evocative definition:

The cat's paw of chance hovers tantalizingly, and suddenly the simplest outcome seems unpredictable. For a brief moment, we are like warriors, charged with the energies of survival, reading every detail of the scene as if it were a sign revealing what was to come . . . excursions of excitement . . . 'vacations' from our actual selves.

I would add Antoine de Saint-Exupery's:

. . . by the grace of an ordeal in the night which stripped you of all that was not intrinsic, you discovered a mysterious creature born of yourself. Great was this creature, and never shall you forget him. And he is yourself.

Paradoxes! 'Adventure' means 'that which comes' – but comes how? By chance, yet somehow fated? It joins peril and possibility in a brief, intense 'island in life', an ordeal, a thrilling challenge. Its opposite is stability, routine, home.

Adventure is a kind of *experience*, not a kind of story, and yet in it experience takes on the qualities of story. Adventure is the aboriginal stuff of which stories have been made, at least since the earliest Sindbad the sailor came home to enchant the homebound Sindbad with his fearful quests, encounters, dangers, and escapes. Adventure was Stevenson's *donnée*. What he made of it and in what various moods is a more complex matter.

Our selection hints at the variety. In *Treasure Island*, Jim Hawkins's home life is suddenly invaded by piracy and violence. A treasure map is found, the ship sails to a desert island, the pirate crew mutinies, and Jim must find extraordinary skill and nerve to outwit the Bad Guys and save his grown-up companions. In *The Black Arrow*, young Dick Shelton is caught up in a world of war and treachery and survives through all the game-like ordeals of adventure: flight and pursuit, hide and seek, tunnels and mazes, disguises and escapes. He 'proves' himself a warrior and saves his fair maiden. In 'The Treasure of Franchard', kindly, pedantic Doctor Desprez and his contented wife lead a bucolic existence until the doctor chances on lost treasure in the woods. Their minds fill with eager visions of opulent, adventurous life in Paris. The treasure vanishes, their house and fortune are lost, the treasure reappears, and the chastened couple contentedly stays home. In the two fables, an innocent young person leads a constricted home life, protected in a pleasant castle or fettered by a mysterious gyve. Chance breaks in: a walk in the woods or on the beach; a chance encounter with an unfettered dancing boy or a prophetic old crone. The young boy and girl rebel; the rebellion proves illusory and tragic. The boy discovers guilt; the girl falls into time. Such can be the price of adventure.

Will o' the Mill, in his quiet mountain home, awakens to a desire for the intense, crowded life of the cities on the plain. After an encounter with a disillusioned, fat young man, he chooses not to pay the price, stays home, and even retreats from marriage to the girl he loves. His is a story of adventures that never happen – until the end. The young cavalier of 'The Sire de Malétroit's Door' must pay the price or die. His story is of the essence of adventure. Surrounded by enemies in a strange town, he visits a friend and becomes lost in a dark maze of narrow streets: 'It is an eerie and mysterious position to be thus submerged in opaque blackness in an almost unknown town. The silence is terrifying in its possibilities.' A 'chapter of accidents' ensues to 'make this night memorable above all others in his career'. Trapped in a lane, he backs through the door and finds himself locked in a noble house, where he is 'expected' by the proud, evil Sire. It is a 'mistake', but the Sire doesn't care, and the young man learns that his only escape from death is through marriage to the Sire's lovely, lovable niece. He accepts his fate. His evil new uncle chuckles.

What are we to make of this? Would he indeed, as we are told at the start, 'have done better to remain beside the fire or go decently to bed', as Will would have done? Are we to seek any meaning? Is this simply a case of 'the strangest oddities and revolutions in our sublunary things'? Is this that elusive thing some critics call 'pure story'? If not, what kind of story is it?

These problems – and they are connected – have nagged critics ever since R.L.S. first puzzled them with his shifts in mode and seeming evasions of consistent meaning. 'Will o' the Mill' offers an intriguing case study. Its first publisher felt reservations about 'the story's indeterminate hovering between realism and allegory'. David Daiches, the wise pioneer of modern Stevenson studies, calls it 'pure allegory' and complains, 'The charm of the situation interested Stevenson as much as its meaning, with the result that the picture of rustic living is filled out in idyllic detail until the shape of the allegory is almost lost.' (Daiches perceives the same problem – if it is one – in 'Franchard'.) But what indications are there that 'Will' began with a 'purely allegorical' intention? And isn't the charm of Will's situation essential to the meaning?

Jenni Calder finds 'Will' a 'puzzling story, part fable, part impression of an unfulfilled existence'. Why not both? The American critic Robert Kiely is not puzzled: 'Will' is one of Stevenson's 'finest short stories', a 'fable' with a complex moral about living death and self-deceptive illusion. Henry James believes in puzzlement: 'Will' is an 'exquisite little story' with 'that most fascinating quality a work of imagination can have – a dash of alternative mystery as to its meaning, an air (the air of life itself), of half inviting, half defying you to interpret.' James is the safest guide for a reader who wonders what and how much Stevenson's tales of adventure 'mean'.

What of *Treasure Island*? Shall we accept and celebrate it as 'sheer story', 'pure adventure', or praise it for transforming 'mere adventure' into something of thematic complexity? Must we find either no meaning or too much? At one extreme are those like Kiely for whom the book is 'unhampered' or 'unencumbered' by symbolic burden or moral pattern: 'To try to speak seriously of good or evil in *Treasure Island* is almost as irrelevant as attempting to assign moral value in a baseball game.' At the other extreme are those for whom it is a parable replete with archetypes of mutilated fathers, thematic explorations of power, loyalty and duty, and of course dominated by that persistent phantom of Stevenson interpretation, the lovable, glittering scoundrel in the shape of Long John Silver. For such zealous exegetes, the story is *remembered* for its complex bond between Silver and Jim.

And here is an interesting problem in the reading of *Treasure Island*, akin to the problem of reading Stevenson's other best *remembered* story, *Jekyll and Hyde*. These two have long since passed into that public domain of world story, half myths, half youthful memories, in the minds of countless people who 'know' them from some forgotten source, version or hearsay, and who have, in the mysterious workings of memory, transformed them into personal fables. No mere 'introduction' can, or perhaps should, dislodge such fables. I would simply urge that the story itself deserves a close, fresh look. Please pause and take your own look before even considering mine.

My *Treasure Island* begins with the perception of the Spanish philosopher Fernando Savater (in *Childhood Regained*) that the story's 'most disconcerting' character is Jim Hawkins. He is not a 'good boy', nor does he 'play at pirates'. He is a creature of impulse, of reckless 'notions' he can't account for and was wrong to follow, but which, as he often brags, result in the salvation of his friends. His most common emotions are terror, horror, disgust and sadness at adventures in which seventeen men are killed in the quest for treasure that does no one much good. From the start, his involvement with pirates causes him 'monstrous nightmares' and 'abominable fancies'. Only once, early on, does he indulge in daydreams of adventure, 'but in all my fancies, nothing occurred to me so strange and tragic as our actual adventures'. At first sight he 'hates the very thought of Treasure Island.' After accidentally (?) shooting the pirate Israel Hands, he has 'horror . . . on my mind', but it is mitigated now by the habit of tragedy. 'Horror' and 'black despair' return. The only emotion sometimes stronger than fear is his curiosity. His 'notions' carry him away. His only pure, extended adventure is Part V, when he is on his own and sets out in a coracle, commandeers the ship with bravura, hides it, and then is overwhelmed with desire to get back to the stockade and boast. He is truly a young Odysseus.

What of his bond with Silver? When, hidden in a barrel, he overhears Silver's plans, he thinks him an 'abominable old rogue' whom, 'if I had been able to I would have killed'. Later he grudgingly admires Silver's skill and nerve and feels pity at the thought of the 'dark gibbet' that awaits him. Jim's only extended interaction with Silver is Part VI – the last, and hence most easily remembered – when he equals Silver in the deal-making of sea lawyers. The bond between them is one of mutual protection. Jim's Silver is a clever, brave imposter, 'hypocrite, murderer, and traitor', whose only ambition is to get rich, become more 'genteel', go home, and set up as a gentleman with a coach and a seat in parliament, no worse than many another ex-colonial imperialist desperado.

For all of Jim's boasting, it is Doctor Livesey who makes the deal that saves them, who risks his life to care for sick and wounded pirates, and who would remain behind on the island if he thought the marooned pirates were ill. And 'Ben Gunn, the half-idiot maroon, was the hero from beginning to end' in setting up the climactic trap. After the homecoming, we learn from Jim only that Silver 'has at last gone clean out of my life' and that Jim retains of the adventure only his 'worst dreams' of 'that accursed island'.

But of course, *our* story is not the same as Jim's horrific adventure. He is Sindbad the sailor, and we are the landbound Sindbads enthralled safely at home. And my text can never quite be anyone else's. One hallmark of a true classic is that it can sustain and survive many 'readings' and still claim a consensus that it is a 'supreme and deathless story', one of the best ever told, loved by Gladstone, 'about the only book' Yeats's seafaring grandfather 'ever found any satisfaction in reading', and for a student of mine, a tough, literal-minded cab-driver, 'the best book I ever read'. I was fortunate – or unfortunate? – never to have read it as a boy, never read it until I was a jaded English professor, and then found it spellbinding, and still do.

The Black Arrow has no such reputation, if it has any reputation at all. Critics usually ignore it, quoting R.L.S. himself, often his own most deprecatory judge, that it is 'Tushery, by the mass! Ay, friend, a whole tale of tushery.' He wrote it fast, hence perhaps could not trust it, and could not bring himself to read it. Yet, its *Young Folks* readers preferred it to *Treasure Island*; it raised circulation 'by many hundreds of copies a week'; and a later printing in America, reports the editor McClure, 'brought in more money than any other serial novel we ever syndicated'. Some astute contemporaries thought it his best book so far, and the historian G.M. Trevelyan praised it as a 'good historical novel' which 'reads like the outcome of an eager and imaginative study of the Paston letters', the correspondence of a fifteenth-century Norfolk family, a favourite book of Stevenson's. *The Black Arrow* is his sole sustained novel of history, set in the socially brutal, politically chaotic, morally anarchic century which Stevenson had long studied and which had likewise intrigued and repelled Walter Scott in *Quentin Durward*. The difference is that Stevenson viewed history chiefly as tragic farce. In no other book is what he called 'the profound underlying pessimism' of the Stevensons, 'their sense of the tragedy of life', more apparent.

The first-time reader should at least try to read *past* the pseudo-Shakespearian style of the dialogue and overlook the hasty lapses in plotting. Stevenson had trouble remembering what he had written. And appropriately, his young protagonist Dick Shelton is so often oppressed by the memory of his adventures that he survives by forgetting and repeatedly running away from them. Escapism, yes. The escapism of moral desperation.

The intricate plot, no doubt all in all for the Young Folks, is a headlong dramatic enactment of 'dark and dubious' battles, bloody ambushes, terrified flights, catastrophic follies (notably Dick's), swithering loyalties, and betrayals of trust. Dick is helplessly implicated with four adventurers, four variations on John Silver: his opportunistic guardian Brackley; his protector Duckworth, the 'Robin Hood,' who is as piratical and oppressive as Brackley; his drunken ally Will Lawless, who admits, 'If my bottle were empty and my mouth dry, I would rob you, dear child, as sure as I love, honour, and admire your parts and person!'; and climactically, the brilliant, ruthless Diccon Crookback, on his way to becoming Richard III. All four are unabashedly candid about their self-serving cynicism. Not surprisingly, Dick's moods and responses fill increasingly with moral perplexity, helpless pity, remorse, and bitter regret. The ebullient adolescent of the start – 'Give me to hunt and to fight and to feast and to live with jolly foresters' – becomes the ambivalent partisan, 'plunged in gloom', who confesses his crimes and follies: 'I am unfit for life.' His confessor, a sprightly, ironic girl, laughs and forgives him. The story closes with acts of forgiveness.

The only clear 'lessons' of *The Black Arrow* are identical with those of Stevenson's *Prince Otto* – not surprising, since *The Black Arrow* was turned out in a two-month 'vacation' from his long labours on *Otto*. In their worlds, Dick and Otto both learn, 'nobody does right'. The only salvation is forgiveness, of others, of ourselves. The only stability for Dick is his love for Joanna, the girl companion whose rescue and protection are Dick's only true goals throughout the story. It is surprising to find romantic love at the centre of Stevensonian adventure. Women were generally excluded. Stevenson knew he could not deal frankly with romantic passion; on the pages of Victorian magazines, only mums and maidens were welcome:

With all my romance, I am a realist and a prosaist, and a most fanatical lover of plain physical sensations plainly and expressly rendered; hence my perils. To do love in the same spirit as I did (for instance) D. Balfour's fatigue in the heather [in *Kidnapped*]; my dear sir, there were grossness – ready made!

So Dick and Joanna are permitted only a loving presexual friendship. But the idea – love, friendship, forgiveness as the only trustworthy code – is nonetheless central.

The rest of adventure is now seen simply as 'the desperate game we play in life'. But not for the first time. My lasting impression of Stevenson the tale-teller of adventure is of the radical ambivalence he felt for his subject. There were two Sindbads in him: one the restless sailor; the other the landsman, who would stay home if only he could find the home to stay in, safely distant, like Dick and Joanna in their greenwoods, from the desperate game. Thus, it seems fitting to place Jim Hawkins and Dick Shelton in the strange company of the unadventurous Will, the amiable pedant of mediocrity Doctor Desprez, the hapless rebel of 'The House of Eld', and the princess who learns that 'the song of the morrow' simply turns her into the crone on the beach. She had better have remained home in her Lady of Shalott cloister, like those ambivalent lotus-eaters Will and Desprez. Yet, had the young cavalier stayed home, gone decently to bed, and not backed through the Sire de Malétroit's door, he would not have found his love.

In the face of this ambivalence at the heart of adventure, we are left with the wicked Sire's enigmatic chirp and chuckle, with the caustic Casimir's equally enigmatic '*Tiens!*' at the end of 'Franchard', and with Henry James's amiable evocation of the author, 'half inviting, half defying you to interpret.'

Francis Russell Hart

The House of Eld

The House of Eld

so soon as the child began to speak, the gyve was riveted; and the boys and girls limped about their play like convicts. Doubtless it was more pitiable to see and more painful to bear in youth; but even the grown folk, besides being very unhandy on their feet, were often sick with ulcers.

About the time when Jack was ten years old, many strangers began to journey through that country. These he beheld going lightly by on the long roads, and the thing amazed him. 'I wonder how it comes,' he asked, 'that all these strangers are so quick afoot, and we must drag about our fetter?'

'My dear boy,' said his uncle, the catechist, 'do not complain about your fetter, for it is the only thing that makes life worth living. None are happy, none are good, none are respectable, that are not gyved like us. And I must tell you, besides, it is very dangerous talk. If you grumble of your iron, you will have no luck; if ever you take it off, you will be instantly smitten by a thunderbolt.'

'Are there no thunderbolts for these strangers?' asked Jack.

'Jupiter is long-suffering to the benighted,' returned the catechist.

'Upon my word, I could wish I had been less fortunate,' said Jack. 'For if I had been born benighted, I might now be going free; and it cannot be denied the iron is inconvenient, and the ulcer hurts.'

'Ah!' cried his uncle, 'do not envy the heathen! Theirs is a sad lot! Ah, poor souls, if they but knew the joys of being fettered! Poor souls, my heart yearns for them. But the truth is they are vile, odious, insolent, ill-conditioned, stinking brutes, not truly human – for what is a man without a fetter? – and you cannot be too particular not to touch or speak with them.'

After this talk, the child would never pass one of the unfettered on the road but what he spat at him and called him names, which was the practice of the children in that part.

It chanced one day, when he was fifteen, he went into the woods, and the ulcer pained him. It was a fair day, with a blue sky; all the birds were singing; but Jack nursed his foot. Presently, another song began; it sounded like the singing of a person, only far more gay; at the same time there was a beating on the earth. Jack put aside the leaves; and there was a lad of his own village, leaping, and dancing and singing to himself in a green dell; and on the grass beside him lay the dancer's iron.

'Oh!' cried Jack, 'you have your fetter off!'

'For God's sake, don't tell your uncle!' cried the lad.

'If you fear my uncle,' returned Jack, 'why do you not fear the thunderbolt?'

'That is only an old wives' tale,' said the other. 'It is only told to children. Scores of us come here among the woods and dance for nights together, and are none the worse.'

This put Jack in a thousand new thoughts. He was a grave lad; he had no mind to dance himself; he wore his fetter manfully, and tended his ulcer without complaint. But he loved the less to be deceived or to see others cheated. He began to lie in wait for heathen travellers, at covert parts of the road, and in the dusk of the day, so that he might speak with them unseen; and these were greatly taken with their wayside questioner, and told him things of weight. The wearing of gyves (they said) was no command of Jupiter's. It was the contrivance of a white-faced thing, a sorcerer, that dwelt in that country in the Wood of Eld. He was one like Glaucus that could change his shape, yet he could be always told; for when he was crossed, he gobbled like a turkey. He had three lives; but the third smiting would make an end of him indeed; and with that his house of sorcery would vanish, the gyves fall, and the villagers take hands and dance like children.

'And in your country?' Jack would ask.

But at this the travellers, with one accord, would put him off; until Jack began to suppose there was no land entirely happy. Or, if there were, it must be one that kept its folk at home; which was natural enough.

But the case of the gyves weighed upon him. The sight of the children limping stuck in his eyes; the groans of such as dressed their ulcers haunted him. And it came at last in his mind that he was born to free them.

There was in that village a sword of heavenly forgery, beaten upon Vulcan's anvil. It was never used but in the temple, and then the flat of it only; and it hung on a nail by the catechist's chimney. Early one night, Jack rose, and took the sword, and was gone out of the house and the village in the darkness.

All night he walked at a venture; and when day came, he met strangers going to the fields. Then he asked after the Wood of Eld and the house of sorcery; and one said north, and one south; until Jack saw that they deceived him. So then, when he asked his way of any man, he showed the bright sword naked; and at that the gyve on the man's ankle rang, and answered in his stead; and the word was still *Straight on*. But the man, when his gyve spoke, spat and struck at Jack, and threw stones at him as he went away; so that his head was broken.

So he came to that wood, and entered in, and he was aware of a house in a low place, where funguses grew, and the trees met, and the steaming of the marsh arose about it like a smoke. It was a fine house, and a very rambling; some parts of it were ancient like the hills, and some but of yesterday, and none finished; and all the ends of it were open, so that you could go in from every side. Yet it was in good repair, and all the chimneys smoked.

Jack went in through the gable; and there was one room after another, all bare, but all furnished in part, so that a man could dwell there; and in each there was a fire burning, where a man could warm himself, and a table spread where he might eat. But Jack saw nowhere any living creature; only the bodies of some stuffed.

'This is a hospitable house,' said Jack; 'but the ground

must be quaggy underneath, for at every step the building quakes.'

He had gone some time in the house, when he began to be hungry. Then he looked at the food, and at first he was afraid; but he bared the sword, and by the shining of the sword, it seemed the food was honest. So he took the courage to sit down and eat, and he was refreshed in mind and body.

'This is strange,' thought he, 'that in the house of sorcery there should be food so wholesome.'

As he was yet eating, there came into that room the appearance of his uncle, and Jack was afraid because he had taken the sword. But his uncle was never more kind, and sat down to meat with him, and praised him because he had taken the sword. Never had these two been more pleasantly together, and Jack was full of love to the man.

'It was very well done,' said his uncle, 'to take the sword and come yourself into the House of Eld; a good thought and a brave deed. But now you are satisfied; and we may go home to dinner arm in arm.'

'Oh, dear, no!' said Jack. 'I am not satisfied yet.'

'How!' cried his uncle. 'Are you not warmed by the fire? Does not this food sustain you?'

'I see the food to be wholesome,' said Jack; 'and still it is no proof that a man should wear a gyve on his right leg.'

Now at this the appearance of his uncle gobbled like a turkey.

'Jupiter!' cried Jack, 'is this the sorcerer?'

His hand held back and his heart failed him for the love he bore his uncle; but he heaved up the sword and smote the appearance on the head; and it cried out aloud with the voice of his uncle; and fell to the ground; and a little bloodless white thing fled from the room.

The cry rang in Jack's ears, and his knees smote together, and conscience cried upon him; and yet he was strengthened, and there woke in his bones the lust of that enchanter's blood. 'If the gyves are to fall,' said he, 'I must go through with this, and when I get home I shall find my uncle dancing.'

So he went on after the bloodless thing. In the way,

he met the appearance of his father; and his father was incensed, and railed upon him, and called to him upon his duty, and bade him be home, while there was yet time. 'For you can still,' said he, 'be home by sunset; and then all will be forgiven.'

'God knows,' said Jack, 'I fear your anger; but yet your anger does not prove that a man should wear a gyve on his right leg.'

And at that the appearance of his father gobbled like a turkey.

'Ah, heaven,' cried Jack, 'the sorcerer again!'

The blood ran backward in his body and his joints rebelled against him for the love he bore his father; but he heaved up the sword, and plunged it in the heart of the appearance; and the appearance cried out aloud with the voice of his father; and fell to the ground; and a little bloodless white thing fled from the room.

The cry rang in Jack's ears, and his soul was darkened; but now rage came to him. 'I have done what I dare not think upon,' said he. 'I will go to an end with it, or perish. And when I get home, I pray God this may be a dream, and I may find my father dancing.'

So he went on after the bloodless thing that had escaped; and in the way he met the appearance of his mother, and she wept. 'What have you done?' she cried. 'What is this that you have done? Oh, come home (where you may be by bedtime) ere you do more ill to me and mine; for it is enough to smite my brother and your father.'

'Dear mother, it is not these that I have smitten,' said Jack; 'it was but the enchanter in their shape. And even if I had, it would not prove that a man should wear a gyve on his right leg.'

And at this the appearance gobbled like a turkey.

He never knew how he did that; but he swung the sword on the one side, and clove the appearance through the midst; and it cried out aloud with the voice of his mother; and fell to the ground; and with the fall of it, the house was gone from over Jack's head, and he stood alone in the woods, and the gyve was loosened from his leg.

'Well,' said he, 'the enchanter is now dead, and the fetter

gone.' But the cries rang in his soul, and the day was like night to him. 'This has been a sore business,' said he. 'Let me get forth out of the wood, and see the good that I have done to others.'

He thought to leave the fetter where it lay, but when he turned to go, his mind was otherwise. So he stooped and put the gyve in his bosom; and the rough iron galled him as he went, and his bosom bled.

Now when he was forth of the wood upon the highway, he met folk returning from the field; and those he met had no fetter on the right leg, but, behold! they had one upon the left. Jack asked them what it signified; and they said, 'that was the new wear, for the old was found to be a superstition.' Then he looked at them nearly; and there was a new ulcer on the left ankle, and the old one on the right was not yet healed.

'Now, may God forgive me!' cried Jack. 'I would I were well home.'

And when he was home, there lay his uncle smitten on the head, and his father pierced through the heart, and his mother cloven through the midst. And he sat in the lone house and wept beside the bodies.

MORAL

Old is the tree and the fruit good,
Very old and thick the wood.
Woodman, is your courage stout?
Beware! the root is wrapped about
Your mother's heart, your father's bones;
And like the mandrake comes with groans.

Will o'the Mill

Will o' the Mill

THE PLAIN AND THE STARS

THE Mill where Will lived with his adopted parents stood in a falling valley between pine-woods and great mountains. Above, hill after hill soared upwards until they soared out of the depth of the hardiest timber, and stood naked against the sky. Some way up, a long grey village lay like a seam or a rag of vapour on a wooded hillside; and when the wind was favourable, the sound of the church bells would drop down, thin and silvery, to Will. Below, the valley grew ever steeper and steeper, and at the same time widened out on either hand; and from an eminence beside the mill it was possible to see its whole length and away beyond it over a wide plain, where the river turned and shone, and moved on from city to city on its voyage towards the sea. It chanced that over this valley there lay a pass into a neighbouring kingdom, so that, quiet and rural as it was, the road that ran along beside the river was a high thoroughfare between two splendid and powerful societies. All through the summer, travelling-carriages came crawling up, or went plunging briskly downwards past the mill; and as it happened that the other side was very much easier of ascent, the path was not much frequented, except by people going in one direction; and of all the carriages that Will saw go by, five-sixths were plunging briskly downwards and only one-sixth crawling up. Much more was this the case with foot-passengers. All the light-footed tourists, all the pedlars laden with strange wares, were tending downward like the river that accompanied their path. Nor was this all; for when Will was yet a child a disastrous war arose over a great part of the world. The newspapers were full of defeats

and victories, the earth rang with cavalry hoofs, and often
for days together and for miles around the coil of battle
terrified good people from their labours in the field. Of all
this, nothing was heard for a long time in the valley; but at
last one of the commanders pushed an army over the pass by
forced marches, and for three days horse and foot, cannon
and tumbril, drum and standard, kept pouring downward
past the mill. All day the child stood and watched them
on their passage – the rhythmical stride, the pale, unshaven
faces tanned about the eyes, the discoloured regimentals
and the tattered flags, filled him with a sense of weariness,
pity, and wonder; and all night long, after he was in bed,
he could hear the cannon pounding and the feet trampling,
and the great armament sweeping onward and downward
past the mill. No one in the valley ever heard the fate of
the expedition, for they lay out of the way of gossip in those
troublous times; but Will saw one thing plainly, that not a
man returned. Whither had they all gone? whither went
all the tourists and pedlars with strange wares? whither all
the brisk barouches with servants in the dicky? whither
the water of the stream, ever coursing downward and
ever renewed from above? Even the wind blew oftener
down the valley, and carried the dead leaves along with
it in the fall. It seemed like a great conspiracy of things
animate and inanimate; they all went downward, fleetly
and gaily downward, and only he, it seemed, remained
behind, like a stock upon the wayside. It sometimes made
him glad when he noticed how the fishes kept their heads
up stream. They, at least, stood faithfully by him, while all
else were posting downward to the unknown world.

One evening he asked the miller where the river went.

'It goes down the valley,' answered he, 'and turns a power
of mills – six-score mills, they say, from here to Unterdeck –
and it none the wearier after all. And then it goes out into
the lowlands, and waters the great corn country, and runs
through a sight of fine cities (so they say) where kings live all
alone in great palaces, with a sentry walking up and down
before the door. And it goes under bridges with stone men
upon them, looking down and smiling so curious at the
water, and living folks leaning their elbows on the wall

and looking over too. And then it goes on and on, and down through marshes and sands, until at last it falls into the sea, where the ships are that bring parrots and tobacco from the Indies. Ay, it has a long trot before it as it goes singing over our weir, bless its heart!'

'And what is the sea?' asked Will.

'The sea!' cried the miller. 'Lord help us all, it is the greatest thing God made! That is where all the water in the world runs down into a great salt lake. There it lies, as flat as my hand and as innocent-like as a child; but they do say when the wind blows it gets up into water-mountains bigger than any of ours, and swallows down great ships bigger than our mill, and makes such a roaring that you can hear it miles away upon the land. There are great fish in it five times bigger than a bull, and one old serpent as long as our river and as old as all the world, with whiskers like a man, and a crown of silver on her head.'

Will thought he had never heard anything like this, and he kept on asking question after question about the world that lay away down the river, with all its perils and marvels, until the old miller became quite interested himself, and at last took him by the hand and led him to the hill-top that overlooks the valley and the plain. The sun was near setting, and hung low down in a cloudless sky. Everything was defined and glorified in golden light. Will had never seen so great an expanse of country in his life; he stood and gazed with all his eyes. He could see the cities, and the woods and fields, and the bright curves of the river, and far away to where the rim of the plain trenched along the shining heavens. An overmastering emotion seized upon the boy, soul and body; his heart beat so thickly that he could not breathe; the scene swam before his eyes; the sun seemed to wheel round and round, and throw off, as it turned, strange shapes which disappeared with the rapidity of thought, and were succeeded by others. Will covered his face with his hands, and burst into a violent fit of tears; and the poor miller, sadly disappointed and perplexed, saw nothing better for it than to take him up in his arms and carry him home in silence.

From that day forward Will was full of new hopes and

longings. Something kept tugging at his heartstrings; the running water carried his desires along with it as he dreamed over its fleeting surface; the wind, as it ran over innumerable tree-tops, hailed him with encouraging words; branches beckoned downward; the open road, as it shouldered round the angles and went turning and vanishing faster and faster down the valley, tortured him with its solicitations. He spent long whiles on the eminence, looking down the rivershed and abroad on the flat lowlands, and watched the clouds that travelled forth upon the sluggish wind and trailed their purple shadows on the plain; or he would linger by the wayside, and follow the carriages with his eyes as they rattled downward by the river. It did not matter what it was; everything that went that way, were it cloud or carriage, bird or brown water in the stream, he felt his heart flow out after it in an ecstasy of longing.

We are told by men of science that all the ventures of mariners on the sea, all that counter-marching of tribes and races that confounds old history with its dust and rumour, sprang from nothing more abstruse than the laws of supply and demand, and a certain natural instinct for cheap rations. To any one thinking deeply, this will seem a dull and pitiful explanation. The tribes that came swarming out of the North and East, if they were indeed pressed onward from behind by others, were drawn at the same time by the magnetic influence of the South and West. The fame of other lands had reached them; the name of the eternal city rang in their ears; they were not colonists, but pilgrims; they travelled towards wine and gold and sunshine, but their hearts were set on something higher. That divine unrest, that old stinging trouble of humanity that makes all high achievements and all miserable failure, the same that spread wings with Icarus, the same that sent Columbus into the desolate Atlantic, inspired and supported these barbarians on their perilous march. There is one legend which profoundly represents their spirit, of how a flying party of these wanderers encountered a very old man shod with iron. The old man asked them whither they were going; and they answered with one voice: 'To the Eternal City!' He looked upon them gravely. 'I have sought it,' he said, 'over the most part of the world. Three such pairs as I now carry on my feet have I worn out upon this pilgrimage, and now the fourth is growing slender underneath my steps. And all this while I have not found the city.' And he turned and went his own way alone, leaving them astonished.

And yet this would scarcely parallel the intensity of Will's feeling for the plain. If he could only go far enough out there, he felt as if his eyesight would be purged and clarified, as if his hearing would grow more delicate, and his very breath would come and go with luxury. He was transplanted and withering where he was; he lay in a strange country and was sick for home. Bit by bit, he pieced together broken notions of the world below; of the river, ever moving and growing until it sailed forth into the majestic ocean; of the cities, full of brisk and beautiful people, playing fountains, bands of music and marble palaces, and lighted up at night from end to end with artificial stars of gold; of the great churches, wise universities, brave armies, and untold money lying stored in vaults; of the high-flying vice that moved in the sunshine, and the stealth and swiftness of midnight murder. I have said he was sick as if for home: the figure halts. He was like some one lying in twilit, formless pre-existence, and stretching out his hands lovingly towards many-coloured, many-sounding life. It was no wonder he was unhappy, he would go and tell the fish; they were made for their life, wished for no more than worms and running water, and a hole below a falling bank; but he was differently designed, full of desires and aspirations, itching at the fingers, lusting with the eyes, whom the whole variegated world could not satisfy with aspects. The true life, the true bright sunshine, lay far out upon the plain. And O! to see this sunlight once before he died! to move with a jocund spirit in a golden land! to hear the trained singers and sweet church bells, and see the holiday gardens! 'And O fish!' he would cry, 'if you would only turn your noses down stream, you could swim so easily into the fabled waters and see the vast ships passing over your head like clouds, and hear the great water-hills making music over you all day long!' But the fish kept looking patiently in their own direction, until Will hardly knew whether to laugh or cry.

Hitherto the traffic on the road had passed by Will, like
something seen in a picture: he had perhaps exchanged
salutations with a tourist, or caught sight of an old
gentleman in a travelling-cap at a carriage window; but
for the most part it had been a mere symbol, which
he contemplated from apart and with something of a
superstitious feeling. A time came at last when this was
to be changed. The miller, who was a greedy man in his
way, and never forewent an opportunity of honest profit,
turned the millhouse into a little wayside inn, and, several
pieces of good fortune falling in opportunely, built stables
and got the position of post master on the road. It now
became Will's duty to wait upon people, as they sat to
break their fasts in the little arbour at the top of the
mill garden; and you may be sure that he kept his ears
open, and learned many new things about the outside
world as he brought the omelette or the wine. Nay, he
would often get into conversation with single guests, and
by adroit questions and polite attention, not only gratify
his own curiosity, but win the goodwill of the travellers.
Many complimented the old couple on their serving-boy;
and a professor was eager to take him away with him, and
have him properly educated in the plain. The miller and his
wife were mightily astonished and even more pleased. They
thought it a very good thing that they should have opened
their inn. 'You see,' the old man would remark, 'he has a
kind of talent for a publican; he never would have made
anything else!' And so life wagged on in the valley, with
high satisfaction to all concerned but Will. Every carriage
that left the inn-door seemed to take a part of him away
with it; and when people jestingly offered him a lift, he
could with difficulty command his emotion. Night after
night he would dream that he was awakened by flustered
servants, and that a splendid equipage waited at the door
to carry him down into the plain; night after night; until
the dream, which had seemed all jollity to him at first,
began to take on a colour of gravity, and the nocturnal
summons and waiting equipage occupied a place in his
mind as something to be both feared and hoped for.

One day, when Will was about sixteen, a fat young

man arrived at sunset to pass the night. He was a contented-looking fellow, with a jolly eye, and carried a knapsack. While dinner was preparing, he sat in the arbour to read a book; but as soon as he had begun to observe Will, the book was laid aside; he was plainly one of those who prefer living people to people made of ink and paper. Will, on his part, although he had not been much interested in the stranger at first sight, soon began to take a great deal of pleasure in his talk, which was full of good-nature and good-sense, and at last conceived a great respect for his character and wisdom. They sat far into the night; and about two in the morning Will opened his heart to the young man, and told him how he longed to leave the valley and what bright hopes he had connected with the cities of the plain. The young man whistled, and then broke into a smile.

'My young friend,' he remarked, 'you are a very curious little fellow, to be sure, and wish a great many things which you will never get. Why, you would feel quite ashamed if you knew how the little fellows in these fairy cities of yours are all after the same sort of nonsense, and keep breaking their hearts to get up into the mountains. And let me tell you, those who go down into the plains are a very short while there before they wish themselves heartily back again. The air is not so light nor so pure; nor is the sun any brighter. As for the beautiful men and women, you would see many of them in rags and many of them deformed with horrible disorders; and a city is so hard a place for people who are poor and sensitive that many choose to die by their own hand.'

'You must think me very simple,' answered Will. 'Although I have never been out of this valley, believe me, I have used my eyes. I know how one thing lives on another; for instance, how the fish hangs in the eddy to catch his fellows; and the shepherd, who makes so pretty a picture carrying home the lamb, is only carrying it home for dinner. I do not expect to find all things right in your cities. That is not what troubles me; it might have been that once upon a time; but although I have lived here always, I have asked many questions and learned a great deal in these last years, and certainly enough to cure me of my old fancies. But you would not have me die like a dog and not see all that is to be seen, and do all that a man can do, let it be good or evil? you would not have me spend all my days between this road here and the river, and not so much as make a motion to be up and live my life? – I would rather die out of hand,' he cried, 'than linger on as I am doing.'

'Thousands of people,' said the young man, 'live and die like you, and are none the less happy.'

'Ah!' said Will, 'if there are thousands who would like, why should not one of them have my place?'

It was quite dark; there was a hanging lamp in the arbour which lit up the table and the faces of the speakers; and along the arch, the leaves upon the trellis stood out illuminated against the night sky, a pattern of transparent green upon a dusky purple. The fat young man rose, and, taking Will by the arm, led him out under the open heavens.

'Did you ever look at the stars?' he asked, pointing upwards.

'Often and often,' answered Will.

'And do you know what they are?'

'I have fancied many things.'

'They are worlds like ours,' said the young man. 'Some of them less; many of them a million times greater; and some of the least sparkles that you see are not only worlds, but whole clusters of worlds turning about each other in the midst of space. We do not know what there may be in any of them; perhaps the answer to all our difficulties or the cure of all our sufferings: and yet we can never reach them; not all the skill of the craftiest of men can fit out a ship for the nearest of these our neighbours, nor would the life of the most aged suffice for such a journey. When a great battle has been lost or a dear friend is dead, when we are hipped or in high spirits, there they are unweariedly shining overhead. We may stand down here, a whole army of us together, and shout until we break our hearts, and not a whisper reaches them. We may climb the highest mountain, and we are no nearer them. All we can do is to stand down here in the garden and take off our hats; the starshine lights upon our heads, and where mine is a little bald, I dare say you can see it glisten in the darkness. The mountain and the mouse. That is like to be all we shall ever have to do with Arcturus or Aldebaran. Can you apply a parable?' he added, laying his hand upon Will's shoulder. 'It is not the same thing as a reason, but usually vastly more convincing.'

Will hung his head a little, and then raised it once more to heaven. The stars seemed to expand and emit a sharper brilliancy; and as he kept turning his eyes higher and higher, they seemed to increase in multitude under his gaze.

'I see,' he said, turning to the young man. 'We are in a rat-trap.'

'Something of that size. Did you ever see a squirrel turning in a cage? and another squirrel sitting philosophically over his nuts? I needn't ask you which of them looked more of a fool.'

THE PARSON'S MARJORY

After some years the old people died, both in one winter, very carefully tended by their adopted son, and very quietly mourned when they were gone. People who had heard of his roving fancies supposed he would hasten to sell the property, and go down the river to push his fortunes. But there was never any sign of such an intention on the part of Will. On the contrary, he had the inn set on a better footing, and hired a couple of servants to assist him in carrying it on; and there he settled down, a kind, talkative, inscrutable young man, six feet three in his stockings, with an iron constitution and a friendly voice. He soon began to take rank in the district as a bit of an oddity: it was not much to be wondered at from the first, for he was always full of notions, and kept calling the plainest common sense in question; but what most raised the report upon him was the odd circumstance of his courtship with the parson's Marjory.

The parson's Marjory was a lass about nineteen, when Will would be about thirty; well enough looking, and much better educated than any other girl in that part of the country, as became her parentage. She held her

head very high, and had already refused several offers of
marriage with a grand air, which had got her hard names
among the neighbours. For all that she was a good girl,
and one that would have made any man well contented.

Will had never seen much of her; for although the church
and parsonage were only two miles from his own door, he
was never known to go there but on Sundays. It chanced,
however, that the parsonage fell into disrepair, and had
to be dismantled; and the parson and his daughter took
lodgings for a month or so, on very much reduced terms,
at Will's inn. Now, what with the inn, and the mill, and the
old miller's savings, our friend was a man of substance; and
besides that, he had a name for good temper and shrewdness
which make a capital portion in marriage; and so it was
currently gossiped, among their ill-wishers, that the parson
and his daughter had not chosen their temporary lodging
with their eyes shut. Will was about the last man in the
world to be cajoled or frightened into marriage. You had
only to look into his eyes, limpid and still like pools of
water, and yet with a sort of clear light that seemed to
come from within, and you would understand at once
that here was one who knew his own mind, and would
stand to it immovably. Marjory herself was no weakling
by her looks, with strong, steady eyes and a resolute and
quiet bearing. It might be a question whether she was not
Will's match in steadfastness, after all, or which of them
would rule the roast in marriage. But Marjory had never
given it a thought, and accompanied her father with the
most unshaken innocence and unconcern.

The season was still so early that Will's customers were
few and far between; but the lilacs were already flowering,
and the weather was so mild that the party took dinner
under the trellis, with the noise of the river in their ears and
the woods ringing about them with the songs of birds. Will
soon began to take a particular pleasure in these dinners.
The parson was rather a dull companion, with a habit of
dozing at table; but nothing rude or cruel ever fell from
his lips. And as for the parson's daughter, she suited her
surroundings with the best grace imaginable; and whatever
she said seemed so pat and pretty that Will conceived a

great idea of her talents. He could see her face, as she leaned forward, against a background of rising pinewoods; her eyes shone peaceably; the light lay around her hair like a kerchief; something that was hardly a smile rippled her pale cheeks, and Will could not contain himself from gazing on her in an agreeable dismay. She looked, even in her quietest moments, so complete in herself, and so quick with life down to her finger-tips and the very skirts of her dress, that the remainder of created things became no more than a blot by comparison; and if Will glanced away from her to her surroundings, the trees looked inanimate and senseless, the clouds hung in heaven like dead things, and even the mountain-tops were disenchanted. The whole valley could not compare in looks with this one girl.

Will was always observant in the society of his fellow-creatures; but his observation became almost painfully eager in the case of Marjory. He listened to all she uttered, and read her eyes, at the same time, for the unspoken commentary. Many kind, simple, and sincere speeches found an echo in his heart. He became conscious of a soul beautifully poised upon itself, nothing doubting, nothing desiring, clothed in peace. It was not possible to separate her thoughts from her appearance. The turn of her wrist, the still sound of her voice, the light in her eyes, the lines of her body, fell in tune with her grave and gentle words, like the accompaniment that sustains and harmonises the voice of the singer. Her influence was one thing, not to be divided or discussed, only to be felt with gratitude and joy. To Will, her presence recalled something of his childhood, and the thought of her took its place in his mind beside that of dawn, of running water, and of the earliest violets and lilacs. It is the property of things seen for the first time, or for the first time after long, like the flowers in spring, to reawaken in us the sharp edge of sense and that impression of mystic strangeness which otherwise passes out of life with the coming of years; but the sight of a loved face is what renews a man's character from the fountain upwards.

One day after dinner Will took a stroll among the firs; a grave beatitude possessed him from top to toe, and he kept smiling to himself and the landscape as he went. The river ran between the stepping-stones with a pretty wimple; a bird sang loudly in the wood; the hill-tops looked immeasurably high, and as he glanced at them from time to time seemed to contemplate his movements with a beneficent but awful curiosity. His way took him to the eminence which overlooked the plain; and there he sat down upon a stone, and fell into deep and pleasant thought. The plain lay abroad with its cities and silver river; everything was asleep, except a great eddy of birds which kept rising and falling and going round and round in the blue air. He repeated Marjory's name aloud, and the sound of it gratified his ear. He shut his eyes, and her image sprang up before him, quietly luminous and attended with good thoughts. The river might run for ever; the birds fly higher and higher till they touched the stars. He saw it was empty bustle after all; for here, without stirring a foot, waiting patiently in his own narrow valley, he also had attained the better sunlight.

The next day Will made a sort of declaration across the dinner-table, while the parson was filling his pipe.

'Miss Marjory,' he said, 'I never knew any one I liked so well as you. I am mostly a cold, unkindly sort of man; not from want of heart, but out of strangeness in my way of thinking; and people seem far away from me. 'Tis as if there were a circle round me, which kept every one out but you; I can hear the others talking and laughing; but you come quite close.—Maybe this is disagreeable to you?' he asked.

Marjory made no answer.

'Speak up, girl,' said the parson.

'Nay, now,' returned Will, 'I wouldn't press her, parson. I feel tongue-tied myself, who am not used to it; and she's a woman, and little more than a child, when all is said. But for my part, as far as I can understand what people mean by it, I fancy I must be what they call in love. I do not wish to be held as committing myself; for I may be wrong; but that is how I believe things are with me. And if Miss Marjory should feel any otherwise on her part, mayhap she would be so kind as shake her head.'

Marjory was silent, and gave no sign that she had heard.

'How is that, parson?' asked Will.

'The girl must speak,' replied the parson, laying down his pipe. 'Here's our neighbour who says he loves you, Madge. Do you love him, ay or no?'

'I think I do,' said Marjory, faintly.

'Well then, that's all that could be wished!' cried Will, heartily. And he took her hand across the table, and held it a moment in both of his with great satisfaction.

'You must marry,' observed the parson, replacing his pipe in his mouth.

'Is that the right thing to do, think you?' demanded Will.

'It is indispensable,' said the parson.

'Very well,' replied the wooer.

Two or three days passed away with great delight to Will, although a bystander might scarce have found it out. He continued to take his meals opposite Marjory, and to talk with her and gaze upon her in her father's presence; but he made no attempt to see her alone, nor in any other way changed his conduct towards her from what it had been since the beginning. Perhaps the girl was a little disappointed, and perhaps not unjustly; and yet if it had been enough to be always in the thoughts of another person, and so pervade and alter his whole life, she might have been thoroughly contented. For she was never out of Will's mind for an instant. He sat over the stream, and watched the dust of the eddy, and the poised fish, and straining weeds; he wandered out alone into the purple even, with all the blackbirds piping round him in the wood; he rose early in the morning; and saw the sky turn from grey to gold, and the light leap upon the hill-tops; and all the while he kept wondering if he had never seen such things before, or how it was that they should look so different now. The sound of his own mill-wheel, or of the wind among the trees, confounded and charmed his heart. The most enchanting thoughts presented themselves unbidden in his mind. He was so happy that he could not sleep at night, and so restless that he could hardly sit still out of her company. And yet it seemed as if he avoided her rather than sought her out.

One day, as he was coming home from a ramble, Will found Marjory in the garden picking flowers, and as he came up with her, slackened his pace and continued walking by her side.

'You like flowers?' he said.

'Indeed I love them dearly,' she replied. 'Do you?'

'Why, no,' said he, 'not so much. They are a very small affair, when all is done. I can fancy people caring for them greatly, but not doing as you are just now.'

'How?' she asked, pausing and looking up at him.

'Plucking them,' said he. 'They are a deal better off where they are, and look a deal prettier, if you go to that.'

'I wish to have them for my own,' she answered, 'to carry them near my heart, and keep them in my room. They tempt me when they grow here; they seem to say, "Come and do something with us"; but once I have cut them and put them by, the charm is laid, and I can look at them with quite an easy heart.'

'You wish to possess them,' replied Will, 'in order to think no more about them. It's a bit like killing the goose with the golden eggs. It's a bit like what I wished to do when I was a boy. Because I had a fancy for looking out over the plain, I wished to go down there – where I couldn't look out over it any longer. Was not that fine reasoning? Dear, dear, if they only thought of it, all the world would do like me; and you would let your flowers alone, just as I stay up here in the mountains.' Suddenly he broke off sharp. 'By the Lord!' he cried. And when she asked him what was wrong, he turned the question off, and walked away into the house with rather a humorous expression of face.

He was silent at table; and after the night had fallen and the stars had come out overhead, he walked up and down for hours in the courtyard and garden with an uneven pace. There was still a light in the window of Marjory's room: one little oblong patch of orange in a world of dark blue hills and silver starlight. Will's mind ran a great deal on the window; but his thoughts were not very lover-like. 'There she is in her room,' he thought, 'and there are the stars overhead: –

a blessing upon both!' Both were good influences in his life; both soothed and braced him in his profound contentment with the world. And what more should he desire with either? The fat young man and his counsels were so present to his mind, that he threw back his head, and, putting his hands before his mouth, shouted aloud to the populous heavens. Whether from the position of his head or the sudden strain of the exertion, he seemed to see a momentary shock among the stars, and a diffusion of frosty light pass from one to another along the sky. At the same instant, a corner of the blind was lifted up and lowered again at once. He laughed a loud ho-ho! 'One and another!' thought Will. 'The stars tremble, and the blind goes up. Why, before Heaven, what a great magician I must be! Now if I were only a fool, should not I be in a pretty way?' And he went off to bed, chuckling to himself: 'If I were only a fool!'

The next morning, pretty early, he saw her once more in the garden, and sought her out.

'I have been thinking about getting married,' he began abruptly; 'and after having turned it all over, I have made up my mind it's not worth while.'

She turned upon him for a single moment; but his radiant, kindly appearance would, under the circumstances, have disconcerted an angel, and she looked down again upon the ground in silence. He could see her tremble.

'I hope you don't mind,' he went on, a little taken aback. 'You ought not. I have turned it all over, and upon my soul there's nothing in it. We should never be one whit nearer than we are just now, and, if I am a wise man, nothing like so happy.'

'It is unnecessary to go round about with me,' she said. 'I very well remember that you refused to commit yourself; and now that I see you were mistaken, and in reality have never cared for me. I can only feel sad that I have been so far misled.'

'I ask your pardon,' said Will stoutly; 'you do not understand my meaning. As to whether I have ever loved you or not, I must leave that to others. But for one thing, my feeling is not changed; and for another, you may make it your boast that you have made my whole life and character something different from what they were. I mean what I say; no less. I do not think getting married is worth while. I would rather you went on living with your father, so that I could walk over and see you once, or maybe twice a week, as people go to church, and then we should both be all the happier between whiles. That's my notion. But I'll marry you if you will,' he added.

'Do you know that you are insulting me?' she broke out.

'Not I, Marjory,' said he; 'if there is anything in a clear conscience, not I. I offer all my heart's best affections; you can take it or want it, though I suspect it's beyond either your power or mine to change what has once been done, and set me fancy-free. I'll marry you, if you like; but I tell you again and again, it's not worth while, and we had best stay friends. Though I am a quiet man I have noticed a heap of things in my life. Trust in me, and take things as I propose; or, if you don't like that, say the word, and I'll marry you out of hand.'

There was a considerable pause, and Will, who began to feel uneasy, began to grow angry in consequence.

'It seems you are too proud to say your mind,' he said. 'Believe me that's a pity. A clean shrift makes simple living. Can a man be more downright or honourable to a woman than I have been? I have said my say, and given you your choice. Do you want me to marry you? or will you take my friendship, as I think best? or have you had enough of me for good? Speak out for the dear God's sake! You know your father told you a girl should speak her mind in these affairs.'

She seemed to recover herself at that, turned without a word, walked rapidly through the garden, and disappeared into the house, leaving Will in some confusion as to the result. He walked up and down the garden, whistling softly to himself. Sometimes he stopped and contemplated the sky and hill-tops; sometimes he went down to the tail of the weir and sat there, looking foolishly in the water. All this dubiety and perturbation was so foreign to his nature and the life which he had resolutely chosen for himself, that he began to regret Marjory's arrival. 'After all,' he thought, 'I was as happy as a man need be. I could come down here and watch my fishes all day long if I wanted: I was as settled and contented as my old mill.'

Marjory came down to dinner, looking very trim and quiet; and no sooner were all three at table than she made her father a speech, with her eyes fixed upon her plate, but showing no other sign of embarrassment or distress.

'Father,' she began, 'Mr Will and I have been talking things over. We see that we have each made a mistake about our feelings, and he has agreed, at my request, to give up all idea of marriage, and be no more than my very good friend, as in the past. You see, there is no shadow of a quarrel, and indeed I hope we shall see a great deal of him in the future, for his visits will always be welcome in our house. Of course, father, you will know best, but perhaps we should do better to leave Mr Will's house for the present. I believe, after what has passed, we should hardly be agreeable inmates for some days.'

Will, who had commanded himself with difficulty from the first, broke out upon this into an inarticulate noise, and raised one hand with an appearance of real dismay, as if he were about to interfere and contradict. But she checked him at once, looking up at him with a swift glance and an angry flush upon her cheek.

'You will perhaps have the good grace,' she said, 'to let me explain these matters for myself.'

Will was put entirely out of countenance by her expression and the ring of her voice. He held his peace, concluding that there were some things about this girl beyond his comprehension – in which he was exactly right.

The poor parson was quite crestfallen. He tried to prove that this was no more than a true lovers' tiff, which would pass off before night; and when he was dislodged from that position, he went on to argue that where there was no quarrel there could be no call for a separation; for the good man liked both his entertainment and his host. It was curious to see how the girl managed them, saying little all the time, and that very quietly, and yet twisting them round her finger and insensibly leading them wherever she would by feminine tact and generalship. It scarcely seemed to have been her doing – it seemed as if things had merely so fallen out – that she and her father took their departure that same afternoon in a farm-cart, and went farther down the valley, to wait, until their own house was ready for them, in another hamlet. But Will had been observing closely, and was well aware of her dexterity and resolution. When he found himself alone he had a great many curious matters to turn over in his mind. He was very sad and solitary, to begin with. All the interest had gone out of his life, and he might look up at the stars as long as he pleased, he somehow failed to find support or consolation. And then he was in such a turmoil of spirit about Marjory. He had been puzzled and irritated at her behaviour, and yet he could not keep himself from admiring it. He thought he recognised a fine, perverse angel in that still soul which he had never hitherto suspected; and though he saw it was an influence that would fit but ill with his own life of artificial calm, he could not keep himself from ardently desiring to possess it. Like a man who has lived among shadows and now meets the sun, he was both pained and delighted.

As the days went forward he passed from one extreme to another; now pluming himself on the strength of his determination, now despising his timid and silly caution. The former was, perhaps, the true thought of his heart, and represented the regular tenor of the man's reflections; but the latter burst forth from time to time with an unruly violence, and then he would forget all consideration, and go up and down his house and garden or walk among the fir-woods like one who is beside himself with remorse. To equable, steady-minded Will this state of matters was intolerable; and he determined, at whatever cost, to bring it to an end. So, one warm summer afternoon he put on his best clothes, took a thorn switch in his hand, and set out down the valley by the river. As soon as he had taken his determination, he had regained at a bound his customary peace of heart, and he enjoyed the bright weather and the variety of the scene without any admixture of alarm or unpleasant eagerness. It was nearly the same to him how the matter turned out. If she accepted him he would have to marry her this time, which perhaps was all for the best.

If she refused him, he would have done his utmost, and might follow his own way in the future with an untroubled conscience. He hoped, on the whole, she would refuse him; and then, again, as he saw the brown roof which sheltered her, peeping through some willows at an angle of the stream, he was half inclined to reverse the wish, and more than half ashamed of himself for this infirmity of purpose.

Marjory seemed glad to see him, and gave him her hand without affectation or delay.

'I have been thinking about this marriage,' he began.

'So have I,' she answered. 'And I respect you more and more for a very wise man. You understood me better than I understood myself; and I am now quite certain that things are all for the best as they are.'

'At the same time—' ventured Will.

'You must be tired,' she interrupted. 'Take a seat and let me fetch you a glass of wine. The afternoon is so warm; and I wish you not to be displeased with your visit. You must come quite often; once a week, if you can spare the time; I am always so glad to see my friends.'

'Oh, very well,' thought Will to himself. 'It appears I was right after all.' And he paid a very agreeable visit, walked home again in capital spirits, and gave himself no further concern about the matter.

For nearly three years Will and Marjory continued on these terms, seeing each other once or twice a week without any word of love between them; and for all that time I believe Will was nearly as happy as a man can be. He rather stinted himself the pleasure of seeing her; and he would often walk half-way over to the parsonage, and then back again, as if to whet his appetite. Indeed, there was one corner of the road, whence he could see the church-spire wedged into a crevice of the valley between sloping fir-woods, with a triangular snatch of plain by way of background, which he greatly affected as a place to sit and moralise in before returning homewards; and the peasants got so much into the habit of finding him there in the twilight that they gave it the name of 'Will o' the Mill's Corner'.

At the end of the three years Marjory played him a sad trick by suddenly marrying somebody else. Will kept his countenance bravely, and merely remarked that, for as little as he knew of women, he had acted very prudently in not marrying her himself three years before. She plainly knew very little of her own mind, and, in spite of a deceptive manner, was as fickle and flighty as the rest of them. He had to congratulate himself on an escape, he said, and would take a higher opinion of his own wisdom in consequence. But at heart, he was reasonably displeased, moped a good deal for a month or two, and fell away in flesh, to the astonishment of his serving-lads.

It was perhaps a year after this marriage that Will was awakened late one night by the sound of a horse galloping on the road, followed by precipitate knocking at the inn-door. He opened his window and saw a farm servant, mounted and holding a led horse by the bridle, who told him to make what haste he could and go along with him; for Marjory was dying, and had sent urgently to fetch him to her bedside. Will was no horseman, and made so little speed upon the way that the poor young wife was very near her end before he arrived. But they had some minutes' talk in private, and he was present and wept very bitterly while she breathed her last.

DEATH

Year after year went away into nothing, with great explosions and outcries in the cities on the plain: red revolt springing up and being suppressed in blood, battle swaying hither and thither, patient astronomers in observatory towers picking out and christening new stars, plays being performed in lighted theatres, people being carried into hospitals on stretchers, and all the usual turmoil and agitation of men's lives in crowded centres. Up in Will's valley only the wind and seasons made an epoch; the fish hung in the swift stream, the birds circled overhead, the pine-tops rustled underneath the stars, the tall hills stood over all; and Will went to and fro, minding his wayside inn, until the snow began to thicken on his head. His heart was young and vigorous; and if his pulses kept a sober time, they still beat strong and steady in his wrists.

He carried a ruddy stain on either cheek, like a ripe apple; he stooped a little, but his step was still firm; and his sinewy hands were reached out to all men with a friendly pressure. His face was covered with those wrinkles which are got in open air, and which, rightly looked at, are no more than a sort of permanent sunburning; such wrinkles heighten the stupidity of stupid faces; but to a person like Will, with his clear eyes and smiling mouth, only give another charm by testifying to a simple and easy life. His talk was full of wise sayings. He had a taste for other people; and other people had a taste for him. When the valley was full of tourists in the season, there were merry nights in Will's arbour; and his views, which seemed whimsical to his neighbours, were often enough admired by learned people out of towns and colleges. Indeed, he had a very noble old age, and grew daily better known; so that his fame was heard of in the cities of the plain; and young men who had been summer travellers spoke together in *cafés* of Will o' the Mill and his rough philosophy. Many and many an invitation, you may be sure, he had; but nothing could tempt him from his upland valley. He would shake his head and smile over his tobacco-pipe with a deal of meaning. 'You come too late,' he would answer. 'I am a dead man now: I have lived and died already. Fifty years ago you would have brought my heart into my mouth; and now you do not even tempt me. But that is the object of long living, that man should cease to care about life.' And again: 'There is only one difference between a long life and a good dinner: that, in the dinner, the sweets come last.' Or once more: 'When I was a boy, I was a bit puzzled, and hardly knew whether it was myself or the world that was curious and worth looking into. Now, I know it is myself, and stick to that.'

He never showed any symptom of frailty, but kept stalwart and firm to the last; but they say he grew less talkative towards the end, and would listen to other people by the hour in an amused and sympathetic silence. Only, when he did speak, it was more to the point and more charged with old experience. He drank a bottle of wine gladly; above all, at sunset on the hill-top or quite late at night under the stars in the arbour. The sight of something attractive and unattainable seasoned his enjoyment, he would say; and he professed he had lived long enough to admire a candle all the more when he could compare it with a planet.

One night, in his seventy-second year, he awoke in bed, in such uneasiness of body and mind that he arose and dressed himself and went out to meditate in the arbour. It was pitch dark, without a star; the river was swollen, and the wet woods and meadows loaded the air with perfume. It had thundered during the day, and it promised more thunder for the morrow. A murky, stifling night for a man of seventy-two! Whether it was the weather or the wakefulness, or some little touch of fever in his old limbs, Will's mind was besieged by tumultuous and crying memories. His boyhood, the night with the fat young man, the death of his adopted parents, the summer days with Marjory, and many of those small circumstances, which seem nothing to another, and are yet the very gist of a man's own life to himself – things seen, words heard, books misconstrued – arose from their forgotten corners and usurped his attention. The dead themselves were with him, not merely taking part in this thin show of memory that defiled before his brain, but revisiting his bodily senses as they do in profound and vivid dreams. The fat young man leaned his elbows on the table opposite; Marjory came and went with an apronful of flowers between the garden and the arbour; he could hear the old parson knocking out his pipe or blowing his resonant nose. The tide of his consciousness ebbed and flowed; he was sometimes half asleep and drowned in his recollections of the past; and sometimes he was broad awake, wondering at himself. But about the middle of the night he was startled by the voice of the dead miller calling to him out of the house as he used to do on the arrival of custom. The hallucination was so perfect that Will sprang from his seat and stood listening for the summons to be repeated and as he listened he became conscious of another noise besides the brawling of the river and the ringing in his feverish ears. It was like the stir of the horses and the creaking of harness, as though a carriage with an impatient team had been brought up upon the road before the courtyard gate. At such an hour, upon this rough and dangerous pass, the supposition was no better than absurd; and Will dismissed it from his mind, and resumed his seat upon the arbour chair; and sleep closed over him again like running water. He was once again awakened by the dead miller's call, thinner and more spectral than before; and once again he heard the noise of an equipage upon the road. And so thrice and four times, the same dream, or the same fancy, presented itself to his senses: until at length, smiling to himself as when one humours a nervous child, he proceeded towards the gate to set his uncertainty at rest.

From the arbour to the gate was no great distance, and yet it took Will some time; it seemed as if the dead thickened around him in the court, and crossed his path at every step. For, first, he was suddenly surprised by an overpowering sweetness of heliotropes; it was as if his garden had been planted with this flower from end to end, and the hot, damp night had drawn forth all their perfumes in a breath. Now the heliotrope had been Marjory's favourite flower, and since her death not one of them had ever been planted in Will's ground.

'I must be going crazy,' he thought. 'Poor Marjory and her heliotropes!'

And with that he raised his eyes towards the window that had once been hers. If he had been bewildered before, he was now almost terrified; for there was a light in the room; the window was an orange oblong as of yore; and the corner of the blind was lifted and let fall as on the night when he stood and shouted to the stars in his perplexity. The illusion only endured an instant; but it left him somewhat unmanned, rubbing his eyes and staring at the outline of the house and the black night behind it. While he thus stood, and it seemed as if he must have stood there quite a long time, there came a renewal of the noises on the road: and he turned in time to meet a stranger, who was advancing to meet him across the court. There was something like the outline of a great carriage discernible on the road behind the stranger, and, above that, a few black pine-tops, like so many plumes.

'Master Will?' asked the new-comer, in brief military fashion.

'That same, sir,' answered Will. 'Can I do anything to serve you?'

'I have heard you much spoken of, Master Will,' returned the other; 'much spoken of, and well. And though I have both hands full of business, I wish to drink a bottle of wine with you in your arbour. Before I go, I shall introduce myself.'

Will led the way to the trellis, and got a lamp lighted and a bottle uncorked. He was not altogether unused to such complimentary interviews, and hoped little enough for this one, being schooled by many disappointments. A sort of cloud had settled on his wits and prevented him from remembering the strangeness of the hour. He moved like a person in his sleep; and it seemed as if the lamp caught fire and the bottle came uncorked with the facility of thought. Still, he had some curiosity about the appearance of his visitor, and tried in vain to turn the light into his face; either he handled the lamp clumsily, or there was a dimness over his eyes; but he could make out little more than a shadow at table with him. He stared and stared at this shadow, as he wiped out the glasses, and began to feel cold and strange about the heart. The silence weighed upon him, for he could hear nothing now, not even the river, but the drumming of his own arteries in his ears.

'Here's to you,' said the stranger, roughly.

'Here is my service, sir,' replied Will, sipping his wine, which somehow tasted oddly.

'I understand you are a very positive fellow,' pursued the stranger.

Will made answer with a smile of some satisfaction and a little nod.

'So am I,' continued the other; 'and it is the delight of my heart to tramp on people's corns. I will have nobody positive but myself; not one. I have crossed the whims, in my time, of kings and generals and great artists. And what would you say,' he went on, 'if I had come up here on purpose to cross yours?'

Will had it on his tongue to make a sharp rejoinder; but the politeness of an old innkeeper prevailed; and he held his peace and made answer with a civil gesture of the hand.

'I have,' said the stranger. 'And if I did not hold you in a particular esteem, I should make no words about the matter. It appears you pride yourself on staying where you are. You mean to stick by your inn. Now I mean you shall come for a turn with me in my barouche; and before this bottle's empty, so you shall.'

'That would be an odd thing, to be sure,' replied Will, with a chuckle. 'Why, sir, I have grown here like an old oak-tree; the devil himself could hardly root me up: and for all I perceive you are a very entertaining old gentleman, I would wager you another bottle you lose your pains with me.'

The dimness of Will's eyesight had been increasing all this while; but he was somehow conscious of a sharp and chilling scrutiny which irritated and yet overmastered him.

'You need not think,' he broke out suddenly, in an explosive, febrile manner that startled and alarmed himself, 'that I am a stay-at-home, because I fear anything under God. God knows I am tired enough of it all; and when the time comes for a longer journey than ever you dream of, I reckon I shall find myself prepared.'

The stranger emptied his glass and pushed it away from him. He looked down for a little, and then, leaning over the table, tapped Will three times upon the forearm with a single finger. 'The time has come!' he said solemnly.

An ugly thrill spread from the spot he touched. The tones of his voice were dull and startling, and echoed strangely in Will's heart.

'I beg your pardon,' he said, with some discomposure. 'What do you mean?'

'Look at me, and you will find your eyesight swim. Raise your hand; it is dead-heavy. This is your last bottle of wine, Master Will, and your last night upon the earth.'

'You are a doctor?' quavered Will.

'The best that ever was,' replied the other; 'for I cure both mind and body with the same prescription. I take away all pain and I forgive all sins; and where my patients have gone wrong in life, I smooth out all complications and set them free again upon their feet.'

'I have no need of you,' said Will.

'A time comes for all men, Master Will,' replied the doctor, 'when the helm is taken out of their hands. For you, because you were prudent and quiet, it has been long of coming, and you have had long to discipline yourself for its reception. You have seen what is to be seen about your mill; you have sat close all your days like a hare in its form; but now that is at an end; and,' added the doctor, getting on his feet, 'you must arise and come with me.'

'You are a strange physician,' said Will, looking stead-fastly upon his guest.

'I am a natural law,' he replied, 'and people call me Death.'

'Why did you not tell me so at first?' cried Will. 'I have been waiting for you these many years. Give me your hand, and welcome.'

'Lean upon my arm,' said the stranger, 'for already your strength abates. Lean on me heavily as you need; for though I am old, I am very strong. It is but three steps to my carriage, and there all your trouble ends. Why, Will,' he added, 'I have been yearning for you as if you were my own son; and of all the men that ever I came for in my long days, I have come for you most gladly. I am caustic, and sometimes offend people at first sight; but I am a good friend at heart to such as you.'

'Since Marjory was taken,' returned Will, 'I declare before God you were the only friend I had to look for.'

So the pair went arm-in-arm across the courtyard.

One of the servants awoke about this time and heard the noise of horses pawing before he dropped asleep again; all down the valley that night there was a rushing as of a smooth and steady wind descending towards the plain; and when the world rose next morning, sure enough Will o' the Mill had gone at last upon his travels.

The Sire de Malétroit's Door

The Sire de Malétroit's Door

DENIS DE BEAULIEU was not yet two-and-twenty, but he
counted himself a grown man, and a very accomplished
cavalier into the bargain. Lads were early formed in that
rough, warfaring epoch; and when one has been in a
pitched battle and a dozen raids, has killed one's man
in an honourable fashion, and knows a thing or two of
strategy and mankind, a certain swagger in the gait is
surely to be pardoned. He had put up his horse with
due care, and supped with due deliberation; and then,
in a very agreeable frame of mind, went out to pay a
visit in the grey of the evening. It was not a very wise
proceeding on the young man's part. He would have done
better to remain beside the fire or go decently to bed. For
the town was full of the troops of Burgundy and England
under a mixed command; and though Denis was there on
safe-conduct, his safe-conduct was like to serve him little
on a chance encounter.

It was September, 1429; the weather had fallen sharp;
a flighty piping wind, laden with showers, beat about the
township; and the dead leaves ran riot along the streets.
Here and there a window was already lighted up; and the
noise of men-at-arms making merry over supper within,
came forth in fits and was swallowed up and carried away
by the wind. The night fell swiftly; the flag of England,
fluttering on the spire-top, grew ever fainter and fainter
against the flying clouds – a black speck like a swallow in
the tumultuous, leaden chaos of the sky. As the night fell
the wind rose and began to hoot under archways and roar
amid the tree-tops in the valley below the town.

Denis de Beaulieu walked fast and was soon knocking at
his friend's door; but though he promised himself to stay

only a little while and make an early return, his welcome
was so pleasant, and he found so much to delay him, that
it was already long past midnight before he said good-bye
upon the threshold. The wind had fallen again in the
meanwhile; the night was as black as the grave; not a star,
nor a glimmer of moonshine, slipped through the canopy
of cloud. Denis was ill-acquainted with the intricate lanes
of Chateau Landon; even by daylight he had found some
trouble in picking his way; and in this absolute darkness
he soon lost it altogether. He was certain of one thing only
– to keep mounting the hill; for his friend's house lay at the
lower end, or tail, of Chateau Landon, while the inn was up
at the head, under the great church spire. With this clue to
go upon he stumbled and groped forward, now breathing
more freely in open places where there was a good slice of
sky overhead, now feeling along the wall in stifling closes. It
is an eerie and mysterious position to be thus submerged in
opaque blackness in an almost unknown town. The silence
is terrifying in its possibilities. The touch of cold window
bars to the exploring hand startles the man like the touch
of a toad; the inequalities of the pavement shake his heart
into his mouth; a piece of denser darkness threatens an
ambuscade or a chasm in the pathway; and where the
air is brighter, the houses put on strange and bewildering
appearances, as if to lead him farther from his way. For
Denis, who had to regain his inn without attracting notice,
there was real danger as well as mere discomfort in the
walk; and he went warily and boldly at once, and at every
corner paused to make an observation.

He had been for some time threading a lane so narrow
that he could touch a wall with either hand, when it began
to open out and go sharply downward. Plainly this lay no
longer in the direction of his inn; but the hope of a little
more light tempted him forward to reconnoitre. The lane
ended in a terrace with a bartisan wall, which gave an
outlook between high houses, as out of an embrasure,
into the valley lying dark and formless several hundred
feet below. Denis looked down, and could discern a few
tree-tops waving and a single speck of brightness where the
river ran across a weir. The weather was clearing up, and

the sky had lightened, so as to show the outline of the heavier clouds and the dark margin of the hills. By the uncertain glimmer, the house on his left hand should be a place of some pretensions; it was surmounted by several pinnacles and turret-tops; the round stern of a chapel, with a fringe of flying buttresses, projected boldly from the main block; and the door was sheltered under a deep porch carved with figures and overhung by two long gargoyles. The windows of the chapel gleamed through their intricate tracery with a light as of many tapers, and threw out the buttresses and the peaked roof in a more intense blackness against the sky. It was plainly the hotel of some great family of the neighbourhood; and as it reminded Denis of a town house of his own at Bourges, he stood for some time gazing up at it and mentally gauging the skill of the architects and the consideration of the two families.

There seemed to be no issue to the terrace but the lane by which he had reached it; he could only retrace his steps, but he had gained some notion of his whereabouts, and hoped by this means to hit the main thoroughfare and speedily regain the inn. He was reckoning without that chapter of accidents which was to make this night memorable above all others in his career; for he had not gone back above a hundred yards before he saw a light coming to meet him, and heard loud voices speaking together in the echoing of the lane. It was a party of men-at-arms going the night round with torches. Denis assured himself that they had all been making free with the wine-bowl, and were in no mood to be particular about safe-conducts or the niceties of chivalrous war. It was as like as not that they would kill him like a dog and leave him where he fell. The situation was inspiriting but nervous. Their own torches would conceal him from sight, he reflected; and he hoped that they would drown the noise of his footsteps with their own empty voices. If he were but fleet and silent, he might evade their notice altogether.

Unfortunately, as he turned to beat a retreat, his foot rolled upon a pebble; he fell against the wall with an ejaculation, and his sword rang loudly on the stones. Two or three voices demanded who went there – some in French, some in English; but Denis made no reply, and ran the faster down the lane. Once upon the terrace, he paused to look back. They still kept calling after him, and just then began to double the pace in pursuit, with a considerable clank of armour, and great tossing of the torchlight to and fro in the narrow jaws of the passage.

Denis cast a look around and darted into the porch. There he might escape observation, or – if that were too much to expect – was in a capital posture whether for parley or defence. So thinking, he drew his sword and tried to set his back against the door. To his surprise, it yielded behind his weight; and though he turned in a moment, continued to swing back on oiled and noiseless hinges, until it stood wide open on a black interior. When things fall out opportunely for the person concerned, he is not apt to be critical about the how or why, his own immediate personal convenience seeming a sufficient reason for the strangest oddities and revolutions in our sublunary things; and so Denis, without a moment's hesitation, stepped within and partly closed the door behind him to conceal his place of refuge. Nothing was further from his thoughts than to close it altogether; but for some inexplicable reason – perhaps by a spring or a weight – the ponderous mass of oak whipped itself out of his fingers and clanked to, with a formidable rumble and a noise like the falling of an automatic bar.

The round, at that very moment, debouched upon the terrace and proceeded to summon him with shouts and curses. He heard them ferreting in the dark corners; and the stock of a lance even rattled along the outer surface of the door behind which he stood; but these gentlemen were in too high a humour to be long delayed, and soon made off down a corkscrew pathway which had escaped Denis's observation, and passed out of sight and hearing along the battlements of the town.

Denis breathed again. He gave them a few minutes' grace for fear of accidents, and then groped about for some means of opening the door and slipping forth again. The inner surface was quite smooth, not a handle, not a moulding, not a projection of any sort. He got his finger-nails round the edges and pulled, but the mass was immovable. He shook

it, it was as firm as a rock. Denis de Beaulieu frowned and
gave vent to a little noiseless whistle. What ailed the door?
he wondered. Why was it open? How came it to shut so
easily and so effectually after him? There was something
obscure and underhand about all this, that was little to
the young man's fancy. It looked like a snare; and yet who
would suppose a snare in such a quiet by-street and in a
house of so prosperous and even noble an exterior? And
yet – snare or no snare, intentionally or unintentionally –
here he was, prettily trapped; and for the life of him he
could see no way out of it again. The darkness began to
weigh upon him. He gave ear; all was silent without, but
within and close by he seemed to catch a faint sighing,
a faint sobbing rustle, a little stealthy creak – as though
many persons were at his side, holding themselves quite
still, and governing even their respiration with the extreme
of slyness. The idea went to his vitals with a shock, and
he faced about suddenly as if to defend his life. Then, for
the first time, he became aware of a light about the level of
his eyes and at some distance in the interior of the house
– a vertical thread of light, widening towards the bottom,
such as might escape between two wings of arras over a
doorway. To see anything was a relief to Denis; it was like
a piece of solid ground to a man labouring in a morass; his
mind seized upon it with avidity; and he stood staring at it
and trying to piece together some logical conception of his
surroundings. Plainly there was a flight of steps ascending
from his own level to that of this illuminated doorway; and
indeed he thought he could make out another thread of
light, as fine as a needle and as faint as phosphorescence,
which might very well be reflected along the polished wood
of a handrail. Since he had begun to suspect that he was
not alone, his heart had continued to beat with smothering
violence, and an intolerable desire for action of any sort
had possessed itself of his spirit. He was in deadly peril,
he believed. What could be more natural than to mount
the staircase, lift the curtain, and confront his difficulty at
once? At least he would be dealing with something tangible;
at least he would be no longer in the dark. He stepped slowly
forward with outstretched hands, until his foot struck the

bottom step; then he rapidly scaled the stairs, stood for a moment to compose his expression, lifted the arras and went in.

He found himself in a large apartment of polished stone. There were three doors; one on each of three sides; all similarly curtained with tapestry. The fourth side was occupied by two large windows and a great stone chimney-piece, carved with the arms of the Malétroits. Denis recognised the bearings, and was gratified to find himself in such good hands. The room was strongly illuminated; but it contained little furniture except a heavy table and a chair or two, the hearth was innocent of fire, and the pavement was but sparsely strewn with rushes clearly many days old.

On a high chair beside the chimney, and directly facing Denis as he entered, sat a little old gentleman in a fur tippet. He sat with his legs crossed and his hands folded, and a cup of spiced wine stood by his elbow on a bracket on the wall. His countenance had a strongly masculine cast; not properly human, but such as we see in the bull, the goat, or the domestic boar; something equivocal and wheedling, something greedy, brutal, and dangerous. The upper lip was inordinately full, as though swollen by a blow or a toothache; and the smile, the peaked eyebrows, and the small, strong eyes were quaintly and almost comically evil in expression. Beautiful white hair hung straight all round his head, like a saint's, and fell in a single curl upon the tippet. His beard and moustache were the pink of venerable sweetness. Age, probably in consequence of inordinate precautions, had left no mark upon his hands; and the Malétroit hand was famous. It would be difficult to imagine anything at once so fleshy and so delicate in design; the taper, sensual fingers were like those of one of Leonardo's women; the fork of the thumb made a dimpled protuberance when closed; the nails were perfectly shaped, and of a dead, surprising whiteness. It rendered his aspect tenfold more redoubtable, that a man with hands like these should keep them devoutly folded in his lap like a virgin martyr – that a man with so intense and startling an expression of face should sit patiently on his seat and contemplate people with an unwinking stare, like a god, or a god's statue.

His quiescence seemed ironical and treacherous, it fitted so poorly with his looks.

Such was Alain, Sire de Malétroit.

Denis and he looked silently at each other for a second or two.

'Pray step in,' said the Sire de Malétroit. 'I have been expecting you all the evening.'

He had not risen, but he accompanied his words with a smile and a slight but courteous inclination of the head. Partly from the smile, partly from the strange musical murmur with which the Sire prefaced his observation, Denis felt a strong shudder of disgust go through his marrow. And what with disgust and honest confusion of mind, he could scarcely get words together in reply.

'I fear,' he said, 'that this is a double accident. I am not the person you suppose me. It seems you were looking for a visit; but for my part, nothing was further from my thoughts – nothing could be more contrary to my wishes – than this intrusion.'

'Well, well,' replied the old gentleman indulgently, 'here you are, which is the main point. Seat yourself, my friend, and put yourself entirely at your ease. We shall arrange our little affairs presently.'

Denis perceived that the matter was still complicated with some misconception, and he hastened to continue his explanations.

'Your door . . .' he began.

'About my door?' asked the other, raising his peaked eyebrows. 'A little piece of ingenuity.' And he shrugged his shoulders. 'A hospitable fancy! By your own account, you were not desirous of making my acquaintance. We old people look for such reluctance now and then; and when it touches our honour, we cast about until we find some way of overcoming it. You arrive uninvited, but believe me, very welcome.'

'You persist in error, sir,' said Denis. 'There can be no question between you and me. I am a stranger in this countryside. My name is Denis, damoiseau de Beaulieu. If you see me in your house, it is only—'

'My young friend,' interrupted the other, 'you will permit

me to have my own ideas on that subject. They probably differ from yours at the present moment,' he added with a leer, 'but time will show which of us is in the right.'

Denis was convinced he had to do with a lunatic. He seated himself with a shrug, content to wait the upshot; and a pause ensued, during which he thought he could distinguish a hurried gabbling as of prayer from behind the arras immediately opposite him. Sometimes there seemed to be but one person engaged, sometimes two; and the vehemence of the voice, low as it was, seemed to indicate either great haste or an agony of spirit. It occurred to him that this piece of tapestry covered the entrance to the chapel he had noticed from without.

The old gentleman meanwhile surveyed Denis from head to foot with a smile, and from time to time emitted little noises like a bird or a mouse, which seemed to indicate a high degree of satisfaction. This state of matters became rapidly insupportable; and Denis, to put an end to it, remarked politely that the wind had gone down.

The old gentleman fell into a fit of silent laughter, so prolonged and violent that he became quite red in the face. Denis got upon his feet at once, and put on his hat with a flourish.

'Sir,' he said, 'if you are in your wits, you have affronted me grossly. If you are out of them, I flatter myself I can find better employment for my brains than to talk with lunatics. My conscience is clear; you have made a fool of me from the first moment; you have refused to hear my explanations; and now there is no power under God will make me stay here any longer; and if I cannot make my way out in a more decent fashion, I will hack your door in pieces with my sword.'

The Sire de Malétroit raised his right hand and wagged it at Denis with the fore and little fingers extended.

'My dear nephew,' he said, 'sit down.'

'Nephew!' retorted Denis, 'you lie in your throat;' and he snapped his fingers in his face.

'Sit down, you rogue!' cried the old gentleman, in a sudden harsh voice, like the barking of a dog. 'Do you fancy,' he went on, 'that when I had made my little

contrivance for the door I had stopped short with that?
If you prefer to be bound hand and foot till your bones
ache, rise and try to go away. If you choose to remain a free
young buck, agreeably conversing with an old gentleman –
why, sit where you are in peace, and God be with you.'

'Do you mean I am a prisoner?' demanded Denis.

'I state the facts,' replied the other. 'I would rather leave
the conclusion to yourself.'

Denis sat down again. Externally he managed to keep
pretty calm; but within, he was now boiling with anger, now
chilled with apprehension. He no longer felt convinced that
he was dealing with a madman. And if the old gentleman
was sane, what, in God's name, had he to look for? What
absurd or tragical adventure had befallen him? What
countenance was he to assume?

While he was thus unpleasantly reflecting, the arras that
overhung the chapel door was raised, and a tall priest in his
robes came forth and, giving a long, keen stare at Denis,
said something in an undertone to the Sire de Malétroit.

'She is in a better frame of spirit?' asked the latter.

'She is more resigned, messire,' replied the priest.

'Now the Lord help her, she is hard to please!' sneered
the old gentleman. 'A likely stripling – not ill-born – and
of her own choosing, too? Why, what more would the
jade have?'

'The situation is not usual for a young damsel,' said the
other, 'and somewhat trying to her blushes.'

'She should have thought of that before she began the
dance. It was none of my choosing, God knows that: but
since she is in it, by our Lady, she shall carry it to the end.'
And then addressing Denis, 'Monsieur de Beaulieu,' he
asked, 'may I present you to my niece? She has been waiting
your arrival, I may say, with even greater impatience than
myself.'

Denis had resigned himself with a good grace – all he
desired was to know the worst of it as speedily as possible;
so he rose at once, and bowed in acquiescence. The Sire
de Malétroit followed his example and limped, with the
assistance of the chaplain's arm, towards the chapel door.
The priest pulled aside the arras, and all three entered. The

building had considerable architectural pretensions. A light groining sprang from six stout columns, and hung down in two rich pendants from the centre of the vault. The place terminated behind the altar in a round end, embossed and honeycombed with a superfluity of ornament in relief, and pierced by many little windows shaped like stars, trefoils, or wheels. These windows were imperfectly glazed, so that the night air circulated freely in the chapel. The tapers, of which there must have been half a hundred burning on the altar, were unmercifully blown about; and the light went through many different phases of brilliancy and semi-eclipse. On the steps in front of the altar knelt a young girl richly attired as a bride. A chill settled over Denis as he observed her costume; he fought with desperate energy against the conclusion that was thrust upon his mind; it could not – it should not – be as he feared.

'Blanche,' said the Sire, in his most flute-like tones, 'I have brought a friend to see you, my little girl; turn round and give him your pretty hand. It is good to be devout; but it is necessary to be polite, my niece.'

The girl rose to her feet and turned towards the new comers. She moved all of a piece; and shame and exhaustion were expressed in every line of her fresh young body; and she held her head down and kept her eyes upon the pavement, as she came slowly forward. In the course of her advance, her eyes fell upon Denis de Beaulieu's feet – feet of which he was justly vain, be it remarked, and wore in the most elegant accoutrement even while travelling. She paused – started, as if his yellow boots had conveyed some shocking meaning – and glanced suddenly up into the wearer's countenance. Their eyes met; shame gave place to horror and terror in her looks; the blood left her lips; with a piercing scream she covered her face with her hands and sank upon the chapel floor.

'That is not the man!' she cried. 'My uncle, that is not the man!'

The Sire de Malétroit chirped agreeably. 'Of course not,' he said; 'I expected as much. It was so unfortunate you could not remember his name.'

'Indeed,' she cried, 'indeed, I have never seen this person

till this moment – I have never so much as set eyes upon
him – I never wish to see him again. Sir,' she said, turning
to Denis, 'if you are a gentleman, you will bear me out.
Have I ever seen you – have you ever seen me – before this
accursed hour?'

'To speak for myself, I have never had that pleasure,'
answered the young man. 'This is the first time, messire,
that I have met with your engaging niece.'

The old gentleman shrugged his shoulders.

'I am distressed to hear it,' he said. 'But it is never too
late to begin. I had little more acquaintance with my own
late lady ere I married her; which proves,' he added with
a grimace, 'that these impromptu marriages may often
produce an excellent understanding in the long run. As
the bridegroom is to have a voice in the matter, I will
give him two hours to make up for lost time before we
proceed with the ceremony.' And he turned towards the
door, followed by the clergyman.

The girl was on her feet in a moment. 'My uncle, you
cannot be in earnest,' she said. 'I declare before God I will
stab myself rather than be forced on that young man. The
heart rises at it; God forbid such marriages; you dishonour
your white hair. Oh, my uncle, pity me! There is not a
woman in all the world but would prefer death to such a
nuptial. Is it possible,' she added, faltering, 'is it possible
that you do not believe me – that you still think this' – and
she pointed at Denis with a tremor of anger and contempt
– 'that you still think *this* to be the man?'

'Frankly,' said the old gentleman, pausing on the threshold, 'I do. But let me explain to you once for all, Blanche
de Malétroit, my way of thinking about this affair. When
you took it into your head to dishonour my family and
the name that I have borne, in peace and war, for more
than three-score years, you forfeited, not only the right to
question my designs, but that of looking me in the face. If
your father had been alive, he would have spat on you and
turned you out of doors. His was the hand of iron. You may
bless your God you have only to deal with the hand of velvet,
mademoiselle. It was my duty to get you married without
delay. Out of pure goodwill, I have tried to find your own

gallant for you. And I believe I have succeeded. But before God and all the holy angels, Blanche de Malétroit, if I have not, I care not one jackstraw. So let me recommend you to be polite to our young friend; for upon my word, your next groom may be less appetising.'

And with that he went out, with the chaplain at his heels; and the arras fell behind the pair.

The girl turned upon Denis with flashing eyes.

'And what, sir,' she demanded, 'may be the meaning of all this?'

'God knows,' returned Denis gloomily. 'I am a prisoner in this house, which seems full of mad people. More I know not; and nothing do I understand.'

'And pray how came you here?' she asked.

He told her as briefly as he could. 'For the rest,' he added, 'perhaps you will follow my example, and tell me the answer to all these riddles, and what, in God's name, is like to be the end of it.'

She stood silent for a little, and he could see her lips tremble and her tearless eyes burn with a feverish lustre. Then she pressed her forehead in both hands.

'Alas, how my head aches!' she said wearily – 'to say nothing of my poor heart! But it is due to you to know my story, unmaidenly as it must seem. I am called Blanche de Malétroit; I have been without father or mother for – oh! for as long as I can recollect, and indeed I have been most unhappy all my life. Three months ago a young captain began to stand near me every day in church. I could see that I pleased him; I am much to blame, but I was so glad that anyone should love me; and when he passed me a letter, I took it home with me and read it with great pleasure. Since that time he has written many. He was so anxious to speak with me, poor fellow! and kept asking me to leave the door open some evening that we might have two words upon the stair. For he knew how much my uncle trusted me.' She gave something like a sob at that, and it was a moment before she could go on. 'My uncle is a hard man, but he is very shrewd,' she said at last. 'He has performed many feats in war, and was a great person at court, and much trusted by Queen Isabeau in old days. How he came to suspect me I cannot tell; but it is hard to keep anything from his knowledge; and this morning, as we came from mass, he took my hand in his, forced it open, and read my little billet, walking by my side all the while. When he had finished, he gave it back to me with great politeness. It contained another request to have the door left open; and this has been the ruin of us all. My uncle kept me strictly in my room until evening, and then ordered me to dress myself as you see me – a hard mockery for a young girl, do you not think so? I suppose, when he could not prevail with me to tell him the young captain's name, he must have laid a trap for him: into which, alas! you have fallen in the anger of God. I looked for much confusion; for how could I tell whether he was willing to take me for his wife on these sharp terms? He might have been trifling with me from the first; or I might have made myself too cheap in his eyes. But truly I had not looked for such a shameful punishment as this! I could not think that God would let a girl be so disgraced before a young man. And now I have told you all; and I can scarcely hope that you will not despise me.'

Denis made her a respectful inclination.

'Madam,' he said, 'you have honoured me by your confidence. It remains for me to prove that I am not unworthy of the honour. Is Messire de Malétroit at hand?'

'I believe he is writing in the salle without,' she answered.

'May I lead you thither, madam?' asked Denis, offering his hand with his most courtly bearing.

She accepted it; and the pair passed out of the chapel, Blanche in a very drooping and shamefast condition, but Denis strutting and ruffling in the consciousness of a mission, and the boyish certainty of accomplishing it with honour.

The Sire de Malétroit rose to meet them with an ironical obeisance.

'Sir,' said Denis with the grandest possible air, 'I believe I am to have some say in the matter of this marriage; and let me tell you at once, I will be no party to forcing the inclination of this young lady. Had it been freely offered to me, I should have been proud to accept her hand, for

I perceive she is as good as she is beautiful; but as things are, I have now the honour, messire, of refusing.'

Blanche looked at him with gratitude in her eyes; but the old gentleman only smiled and smiled, until his smile grew positively sickening to Denis.

'I am afraid,' he said, 'Monsieur de Beaulieu, that you do not perfectly understand the choice I have to offer you. Follow me, I beseech you, to this window.' And he led the way to one of the large windows which stood open on the night. 'You observe,' he went on, 'there is an iron ring in the upper masonry, and reeved through that, a very efficacious rope. Now, mark my words; if you should find your disinclination to my niece's person insurmountable, I shall have you hanged out of this window before sunrise. I shall only proceed to such an extremity with the greatest regret, you may believe me. For it is not at all your death that I desire, but my niece's establishment in life. At the same time, it must come to that if you prove obstinate. Your family, Monsieur de Beaulieu, is very well in its way; but if you sprang from Charlemagne, you should not refuse the hand of a Malétroit with impunity – not if she had been as common as the Paris road – not if she were as hideous as the gargoyle over my door. Neither my niece nor you, nor my own private feelings, move me at all in this matter. The honour of my house has been compromised; I believe you to be the guilty person; at least you are now in the secret; and you can hardly wonder if I request you to wipe out the stain. If you will not, your blood be on your own head! It will be no great satisfaction to me to have your interesting relics kicking their heels in the breeze below my windows; but half a loaf is better than no bread, and if I cannot cure the dishonour, I shall at least stop the scandal.'

There was a pause.

'I believe there are other ways of settling such imbroglios among gentlemen,' said Denis. 'You wear a sword, and I hear you have used it with distinction.'

The Sire de Malétroit made a signal to the chaplain, who crossed the room with long silent strides and raised the arras over the third of the three doors. It was only a moment before he let it fall again; but

Denis had time to see a dusky passage full of armed men.

'When I was a little younger, I should have been delighted to honour you, Monsieur de Beaulieu,' said Sire Alain; 'but I am now too old. Faithful retainers are the sinews of age, and I must employ the strength I have. This is one of the hardest things to swallow as a man grows up in years; but with a little patience, even this becomes habitual. You and the lady seem to prefer the salle for what remains of your two hours; and as I have no desire to cross your preference, I shall resign it to your use with all the pleasure in the world. No haste!' he added, holding up his hand, as he saw a dangerous look come into Denis de Beaulieu's face. 'If your mind revolts against hanging, it will be time enough two hours hence to throw yourself out of the window or upon the pikes of my retainers. Two hours of life are always two hours. A great many things may turn up in even as little a while as that. And, besides, if I understand her appearance, my niece has still something to say to you. You will not disfigure your last hours by a want of politeness to a lady?'

Denis looked at Blanche, and she made him an imploring gesture.

It is likely that the old gentleman was hugely pleased at this symptom of an understanding; for he smiled on both, and added sweetly: 'If you will give me your word of honour, Monsieur de Beaulieu, to wait my return at the end of the two hours before attempting anything desperate, I shall withdraw my retainers, and let you speak in greater privacy with mademoiselle.'

Denis again glanced at the girl, who seemed to beseech him to agree.

'I give you my word of honour,' he said.

Messire de Malétroit bowed, and proceeded to limp about the apartment, clearing his throat the while with that odd musical chirp which had already grown so irritating in the ears of Denis de Beaulieu. He first possessed himself of some papers which lay upon the table; then he went to the mouth of the passage and appeared to give an order to the men behind the arras; and lastly he hobbled out through the door by which Denis had come in, turning upon the threshold to address a last smiling bow to the young couple, and followed by the captain with a handlamp.

No sooner were they alone than Blanche advanced towards Denis with her hands extended. Her face was flushed and excited, and her eyes shone with tears.

'You shall not die!' she cried, 'you shall marry me after all.'

'You seem to think, madam,' replied Denis, 'that I stand much in fear of death.'

'Oh no, no,' she said, 'I see you are no poltroon. It is for my own sake – I could not bear to have you slain for such a scruple.'

'I am afraid,' returned Denis, 'that you underrate the difficulty, madam. What you may be too generous to refuse, I may be too proud to accept. In a moment of noble feeling towards me, you forgot what you perhaps owe to others.'

He had the decency to keep his eyes upon the floor as he said this, and after he had finished, so as not to spy upon her confusion. She stood silent for a moment, then walked suddenly away, and falling on her uncle's chair, fairly burst out sobbing. Denis was in the acme of embarrassment. He looked round, as if to seek for inspiration, and seeing a stool, plumped down upon it for something to do. There he sat, playing with the guard of his rapier, and wishing himself dead a thousand times over, and buried in the nastiest kitchen-heap in France. His eyes wandered round the apartment, but found nothing to arrest them. There were such wide spaces between the furniture, the light fell so badly and cheerlessly over all, the dark outside air looked in so coldly through the windows, that he thought he had never seen a church so vast, nor a tomb so melancholy. The regular sobs of Blanche de Malétroit measured out the time like the ticking of a clock. He read the device upon the shield over and over again, until his eyes became obscured; he stared into shadowy corners until he imagined they were swarming with horrible animals; and every now and again he awoke with a start, to remember that his last two hours were running, and death was on the march.

Oftener and oftener, as the time went on, did his glance settle on the girl herself. Her face was bowed forward and

covered with her hands, and she was shaken at intervals
by the convulsive hiccup of grief. Even thus she was not
an unpleasant object to dwell upon, so plump and yet
so fine, with a warm brown skin, and the most beautiful
hair, Denis thought, in the whole world of womankind.
Her hands were like her uncle's; but they were more in
place at the end of her young arms, and looked infinitely
soft and caressing. He remembered how her blue eyes had
shone upon him, full of anger, pity, and innocence. And the
more he dwelt on her perfections, the uglier death looked,
and the more deeply was he smitten with penitence at her
continued tears. Now he felt that no man could have the
courage to leave a world which contained so beautiful a
creature; and now he would have given forty minutes of
his last hour to have unsaid his cruel speech.

Suddenly a hoarse and ragged peal of cockcrow rose to
their ears from the dark valley below the windows. And
this shattering noise in the silence of all around was like
a light in a dark place, and shook them both out of their
reflections.

'Alas, can I do nothing to help you?' she said, looking up.

'Madam,' replied Denis, with a fine irrelevancy, 'if I
have said anything to wound you, believe me, it was for
your own sake and not for mine.'

She thanked him with a tearful look.

'I feel your position cruelly,' he went on. 'The world
has been bitter hard on you. Your uncle is a disgrace to
mankind. Believe me, madam, there is no young gentleman
in all France but would be glad of my opportunity to die in
doing you a momentary service.'

'I know already that you can be very brave and generous,'
she answered. 'What I *want* to know is whether I can serve
you – now or afterwards,' she added, with a quaver.

'Most certainly,' he answered with a smile. 'Let me sit
beside you as if I were a friend, instead of a foolish intruder;
try to forget how awkwardly we are placed to one another;
make my last moments go pleasantly; and you will do me
the chief service possible.'

'You are very gallant,' she added, with a yet deeper

sadness . . . 'very gallant . . . and it somehow pains me. But draw nearer, if you please; and if you find anything to say to me, you will at least make certain of a very friendly listener. Ah! Monsieur de Beaulieu,' she broke forth – 'ah! Monsieur de Beaulieu, how can I look you in the face?' And she fell to weeping again with a renewed effusion.

'Madam,' said Denis, taking her hand in both of his, 'reflect on the little time I have before me, and the great bitterness into which I am cast by the sight of your distress. Spare me, in my last moments, the spectacle of what I cannot cure even with the sacrifice of my life.'

'I am very selfish,' answered Blanche. 'I will be braver, Monsieur de Beaulieu, for your sake. But think if I can do you no kindness in the future – if you have no friends to whom I could carry your adieux. Charge me as heavily as you can; every burden will lighten, by so little, the invaluable gratitude I owe you. Put it in my power to do something more for you than weep.'

'My mother is married again, and has a young family to care for. My brother Guichard will inherit my fiefs; and if I am not in error, that will content him amply for my death. Life is a little vapour that passeth away, as we are told by those in holy orders. When a man is in a fair way and sees all life open in front of him, he seems to himself to make a very important figure in the world. His horse whinnies to him; the trumpets blow and the girls look out of windows as he rides into town before his company; he receives many assurances of trust and regard – sometimes by express in a letter – sometimes face to face, with persons of great consequence falling on his neck. It is not wonderful if his head is turned for a time. But once he is dead, were he as brave as Hercules or as wise as Solomon, he is soon forgotten. It is not ten years since my father fell, with many other knights around him, in a very fierce encounter, and I do not think that any one of them, nor so much as the name of the fight, is now remembered. No, no, madam, the nearer you come to it, you see that death is a dark and dusty corner, where a man gets into his tomb and has the door shut after him till the judgment day. I have few friends just now, and once I am dead I shall have none.'

'Ah, Monsieur de Beaulieu!' she exclaimed, 'you forget Blanche de Malétroit.'

'You have a sweet nature, madam, and you are pleased to estimate a little service far beyond its worth.'

'It is not that,' she answered. 'You mistake me if you think I am so easily touched by my own concerns. I say so, because you are the noblest man I have ever met; because I recognise in you a spirit that would have made even a common person famous in the land.'

'And yet here I die in a mouse-trap – with no more noise about it than my own squeaking,' answered he.

A look of pain crossed her face, and she was silent for a little while. Then a light came into her eyes, and with a smile she spoke again.

'I cannot have my champion think meanly of himself. Anyone who gives his life for another will be met in Paradise by all the heralds and angels of the Lord God. And you have no such cause to hang your head. For . . . Pray, do you think me beautiful?' she asked, with a deep flush.

'Indeed, madam, I do,' he said.

'I am glad of that,' she answered heartily. 'Do you think there are many men in France who have been asked in marriage by a beautiful maiden – with her own lips – and who have refused her to her face? I know you men would half despise such a triumph; but believe me, we women know more of what is precious in love. There is nothing that should set a person higher in his own esteem; and we women would prize nothing more dearly.'

'You are very good,' he said; 'but you cannot make me forget that I was asked in pity and not for love.'

'I am not so sure of that,' she replied, holding down her head. 'Hear me to an end, Monsieur de Beaulieu. I know how you must despise me; I feel you are right to do so; I am too poor a creature to occupy one thought of your mind, although, alas! you must die for me this morning. But when I asked you to marry me, indeed, and indeed, it was because I respected and admired you, and loved you with my whole soul, from the very moment that you took my part against my uncle. If you had seen yourself, and how noble you looked, you would pity rather than despise me. And now,' she went on, hurriedly checking him with her hand, 'although I have laid aside all reserve and told you so much, remember that I know your sentiments towards me already. I would not, believe me, being nobly born, weary you with importunities into consent. I too have a pride of my own: and I declare before the holy mother of God, if you should now go back from your word already given, I would no more marry you than I would marry my uncle's groom.'

Denis smiled a little bitterly.

'It is a small love,' he said, 'that shies at a little pride.'

She made no answer, although she probably had her own thoughts.

'Come hither to the window,' he said, with a sigh. 'Here is the dawn.'

And indeed the dawn was already beginning. The hollow of the sky was full of essential daylight, colourless and clean; and the valley underneath was flooded with a grey reflection. A few thin vapours clung in the coves of the forest or lay along the winding course of the river. The scene disengaged a surprising effect of stillness, which was hardly interrupted when the cocks began once more to crow among the steadings. Perhaps the same fellow who had made so horrid a clangour in the darkness not half-an-hour before, now sent up the merriest cheer to greet the coming day. A little wind went bustling and eddying among the tree-tops underneath the windows. And still the daylight kept flooding insensibly out of the east, which was soon to grow incandescent and cast up that red-hot cannon-ball, the rising sun.

Denis looked out over all this with a bit of a shiver. He had taken her hand, and retained it in his almost unconsciously.

'Has the day begun already?' she said; and then, illogically enough: 'the night has been so long! Alas! what shall we say to my uncle when he returns?'

'What you will,' said Denis, and he pressed her fingers in his.

She was silent.

'Blanche,' he said, with a swift, uncertain, passionate

utterance, 'you have seen whether I fear death. You must know well enough that I would as gladly leap out of that window into the empty air as lay a finger on you without your free and full consent. But if you care for me at all do not let me lose my life in a misapprehension; for I love you better than the whole world; and though I will die for you blithely, it would be like all the joys of Paradise to live on and spend my life in your service.'

As he stopped speaking, a bell began to ring loudly in the interior of the house; and a clatter of armour in the corridor showed that the retainers were returning to their post, and the two hours were at an end.

'After all that you have heard?' she whispered, leaning towards him with her lips and eyes.

'I have heard nothing,' he replied.

'The captain's name was Florimond de Champdivers,' she said in his ear.

'I did not hear it,' he answered, taking her supple body in his arms and covering her wet face with kisses.

A melodious chirping was audible behind, followed by a beautiful chuckle, and the voice of Messire de Malétroit wished his new nephew a good morning.

TREASURE ISLAND

TO
THE HESITATING PURCHASER

If sailor tales to sailor tunes,
　　Storm and adventure, heat and cold,
If schooners, islands, and maroons
　　And Buccaneers and buried Gold,
And all the old romance, retold
　　Exactly in the ancient way,
Can please, as me they pleased of old,
　　The wiser youngsters of to-day:

– So be it, and fall on! If not,
　　If studious youth no longer crave,
His ancient appetites forgot,
　　Kingston, or Ballantyne the brave,
Or Cooper of the wood and wave:
　　So be it, also! And may I
And all my pirates share the grave
　　Where these and their creations lie!

To
S. L. O.,
AN AMERICAN GENTLEMAN,
IN ACCORDANCE WITH WHOSE CLASSIC TASTE
THE FOLLOWING NARRATIVE HAS BEEN DESIGNED,
IT IS NOW, IN RETURN FOR NUMEROUS DELIGHTFUL HOURS,
AND WITH THE KINDEST WISHES,
Dedicated
BY HIS AFFECTIONATE FRIEND,
THE AUTHOR.

Contents

PART I
THE OLD BUCCANEER

I	The Old Sea-dog at the 'Admiral Benbow'	71
II	Black Dog Appears and Disappears	77
III	The Black Spot	84
IV	The Sea Chest	89
V	The Last of the Blind Man	95
VI	The Captain's Papers	101

PART II
THE SEA COOK

VII	I Go to Bristol	109
VIII	At the Sign of the 'Spy-glass'	114
IX	Powder and Arms	119
X	The Voyage	124
XI	What I Heard in the Apple Barrel	130
XII	Council of War	136

PART III
MY SHORE ADVENTURE

XIII	How My Shore Adventure Began	143
XIV	The First Blow	148
XV	The Man of the Island	153

PART IV
THE STOCKADE

XVI	Narrative Continued by the Doctor: How the Ship was Abandoned	161
XVII	Narrative Continued by the Doctor: The Jolly-boat's Last Trip	166

XVIII	Narrative Continued by the Doctor: End of the First Day's Fighting	171
XIX	Narrative Resumed by Jim Hawkins: The Garrison in the Stockade	176
XX	Silver's Embassy	182
XXI	The Attack	187

PART V
MY SEA ADVENTURE

XXII	How My Sea Adventure Began	195
XXIII	The Ebb-tide Runs	201
XXIV	The Cruise of the Coracle	206
XXV	I Strike the Jolly Roger	212
XXVI	Israel Hands	217
XXVII	'Pieces of Eight'	225

PART VI
CAPTAIN SILVER

XXVIII	In the Enemy's Camp	233
XXIX	The Black Spot Again	240
XXX	On Parole	246
XXXI	The Treasure Hunt – Flint's Pointer	253
XXXII	The Treasure Hunt – The Voice Among the Trees	259
XXXIII	The Fall of a Chieftain	265
XXXIV	And Last	271

PART I
THE OLD BUCCANEER

CHAPTER ONE

The Old Sea-dog at the 'Admiral Benbow'

SQUIRE TRELAWNEY, Dr Livesey, and the rest of these gentlemen having asked me to write down the whole particulars about Treasure Island, from the beginning to the end, keeping nothing back but the bearings of the island, and that only because there is still treasure not yet lifted, I take up my pen in the year of grace 17—, and go back to the time when my father kept the 'Admiral Benbow' inn, and the brown old seaman, with the sabre cut, first took up his lodging under our roof.

I remember him as if it were yesterday, as he came plodding to the inn door, his sea-chest following behind him in a hand-barrow; a tall, strong, heavy, nut-brown man; his tarry pigtail falling over the shoulders of his soiled blue coat; his hands ragged and scarred, with black, broken nails; and the sabre cut across one cheek, a dirty, livid white. I remember him looking round the cove and whistling to himself as he did so, and then breaking out in that old sea-song that he sang so often afterwards:—

Fifteen men on the dead man's chest—
Yo-ho-ho, and a bottle of rum!

in the high, old tottering voice that seemed to have been tuned and broken at the capstan bars. Then he rapped on the door with a bit of stick like a handspike that he carried, and when my father appeared, called roughly for a glass of rum. This, when it was brought to him, he drank slowly, like a connoisseur, lingering on the taste, and still looking about him at the cliffs and up at our signboard.

'This is a handy cove,' says he, at length; 'and a pleasant sittyated grog-shop. Much company, mate?'

My father told him no, very little company, the more was the pity.

'Well, then,' said he, 'this is the berth for me. Here you, matey,' he cried to the man who trundled the barrow; 'bring up alongside and help up my chest. I'll stay here a bit,' he continued. 'I'm a plain man; rum and bacon and eggs is what I want, and that head up there for to watch ships off. What you mought call me? You mought call me captain. Oh, I see what you're at – there;' and he threw down three or four gold pieces on the threshold. 'You can tell me when I've worked through that,' says he, looking as fierce as a commander.

And, indeed, bad as his clothes were, and coarsely as he spoke, he had none of the appearance of a man who sailed before the mast; but seemed like a mate or skipper, accustomed to be obeyed or to strike. The man who came with the barrow told us the mail had set him down the morning before at the 'Royal George'; that he had inquired what inns there were along the coast, and hearing ours well spoken of, I suppose, and described as lonely, had chosen it from the others for his place of residence. And that was all we could learn of our guest.

He was a very silent man by custom. All day he hung round the cove, or upon the cliffs, with a brass telescope; all evening he sat in a corner of the parlour next the fire, and drank rum and water very strong. Mostly he would not speak when spoken to; only look up sudden and fierce, and blow through his nose like a fog-horn; and we and the people who came about our house soon learned to let him be. Every day, when he came back from his stroll, he would ask if any seafaring men had gone by along the road. At first we thought it was the want of company of his own kind that made him ask this question; but at last we began to see he was desirous to avoid them. When a seaman put up at the 'Admiral Benbow' (as now and then some did, making by the coast road for Bristol), he would look in at him through the curtained door before he entered the parlour; and he was always sure to be as silent as a mouse when any such was present. For me, at least, there was no secret about the matter; for I was, in a way, a sharer in his alarms. He had taken me aside one day, and promised me a silver fourpenny on the first of every month if I wold only keep my 'weather-eye open for a seafaring man with one leg', and let him know the moment he appeared. Often enough, when the first of the month came round, and I applied to him for my wage, he would only blow through his nose at me, and stare me down; but before the week was out he was sure to think better of it, bring me my fourpenny piece, and repeat his orders to look out for 'the seafaring man with one leg'.

How that personage haunted my dreams, I need scarcely tell you. On stormy nights, when the wind shook the four corners of the house, and the surf roared along the cove and up the cliffs, I would see him in a thousand forms, and with a thousand diabolical expressions. Now the leg would be cut off at the knee, now at the hip; now he was a monstrous kind of a creature who had never had but the one leg, and that in the middle of his body. To see him leap and run and pursue me over hedge and ditch was the worst of nightmares. And altogether I paid pretty dear for my monthly fourpenny piece, in the shape of these abominable fancies.

But though I was so terrified by the idea of the seafaring man with one leg, I was far less afraid of the captain himself than anybody else who knew him. There were nights when he took a deal more rum and water than his head would carry; and then he would sometimes sit and sing his wicked, old, wild sea-songs, minding nobody; but sometimes he would call for glasses round, and force all the trembling company to listen to his stories or bear a chorus to his singing. Often I have heard the house shaking with 'Yo-ho-ho, and a bottle of rum'; all the neighbours joining in for dear life, with the fear of death upon them, and each singing louder than the other, to avoid remark. For in these fits he was the most overriding companion ever known; he would slap his hand on the table for silence all round; he would fly up in a passion of anger at a question, or sometimes because none was put, and so he judged the company was not following his story. Nor would he allow anyone to leave the inn till he had drunk himself sleepy and reeled off to bed.

His stories were what frightened people worst of all. Dreadful stories they were; about hanging, and walking the plank, and storms at sea, and the Dry Tortugas, and wild deeds and places on the Spanish Main. By his own account he must have lived his life among some of the wickedest men that God ever allowed upon the sea; and the language in which he told these stories shocked our plain country people almost as much as the crimes that he described. My father was always saying the inn would be ruined, for people would soon cease coming there to be tyrannised over and put down, and sent shivering to their beds; but I really believe his presence did us good. People were frightened at the time, but on looking back they rather liked it; it was a fine excitement in a quiet country life; and there was even a party of the younger men who pretended to admire him, calling him a 'true sea-dog,' and a 'real old salt,' and suchlike names, and saying there was the sort of man that made England terrible at sea.

In one way, indeed, he bade fair to ruin us; for he kept on staying week after week, and at last month after month, so that all the money had been long exhausted, and still my father never plucked up the heart to insist on having more. If ever he mentioned it, the captain blew through his nose so loudly, that you might say he roared, and stared my poor father out of the room. I have seen him wringing his hands after such a rebuff, and I am sure the annoyance and the terror he lived in must have greatly hastened his early and unhappy death.

All the time he lived with us the captain made no change whatever in his dress but to buy some stockings from a hawker. One of the cocks of his hat having fallen down, he let it hang from that day forth, though it was a great annoyance when it blew. I remember the appearance of his coat, which he patched himself upstairs in his room, and which, before the end, was nothing but patches. He never wrote or received a letter, and he never spoke with any but the neighbours, and with these, for the most part, only when drunk on rum. The great sea-chest none of us had ever seen open.

He was only once crossed, and that was towards the end,

when my poor father was far gone in a decline that took him off. Dr Livesey came late one afternoon to see the patient, took a bit of dinner from my mother, and went into the parlour to smoke a pipe until his horse should come down from the hamlet, for we had no stabling at the old 'Benbow.' I followed him in, and I remember observing the contrast the neat, bright doctor, with his powder as white as snow, and his bright, black eyes and pleasant manners, made with the coltish country folk, and above all, with that filthy, heavy, bleared scarecrow of a pirate of ours, sitting, far gone in rum, with his arms on the table. Suddenly he – the captain, that is – began to pipe up his eternal song:—

> Fifteen men on the dead man's chest—
> Yo-ho-ho, and a bottle of rum!
> Drink and the devil had done for the rest—
> Yo-ho-ho, and a bottle of rum!

At first I had supposed 'the dead man's chest' to be that identical big box of his upstairs in the front room, and the thought had been mingled in my nightmares with that of the one-legged seafaring man. But by this time we had all long ceased to pay any particular notice to the song; it was new, that night, to nobody but Dr Livesey, and on him I observed it did not produce an agreeable effect, for he looked up for a moment quite angrily before he went on with his talk to old Taylor, the gardener, on a new cure for the rheumatics. In the meantime, the captain gradually brightened up at his own music, and at last flapped his hand upon the table before him in a way we all knew to mean – silence. The voices stopped at once, all but Dr Livesey's; he went on as before, speaking clear and kind, and drawing briskly at his pipe between every word or two. The captain glared at him for a while, flapped his hand again, glared still harder, and at last broke out with a villainous, low oath: 'Silence, there, between decks!'

'Were you addressing me, sir?' says the doctor; and when the ruffian had told him, with another oath, that this was so, 'I have only one thing to say to you, sir,' replies the doctor, 'that if you keep on drinking rum, the world will soon be quit of a very dirty scoundrel!'

The old fellow's fury was awful. He sprang to his feet, drew and opened a sailor's clasp-knife, and, balancing it open on the palm of his hand, threatened to pin the doctor to the wall.

The doctor never so much as moved. He spoke to him, as before, over his shoulder, and in the same tone of voice; rather high, so that all the room might hear, but perfectly calm and steady:—

'If you do not put that knife this instant in your pocket, I promise, upon my honour, you shall hang at the next assizes.'

Then followed a battle of looks between them; but the captain soon knuckled under, put up his weapon, and resumed his seat, grumbling like a beaten dog.

'And now, sir,' continued the doctor, 'since I now know there's such a fellow in my district, you may count I'll have an eye upon you day and night. I'm not a doctor only; I'm a magistrate; and if I catch a breath of complaint against you, if it's only for a piece of incivility like to-night's, I'll take effectual means to have you hunted down and routed out of this. Let that suffice.'

Soon after Dr Livesey's horse came to the door, and he rode away; but the captain held his peace that evening, and for many evenings to come.

CHAPTER TWO

Black Dog Appears and Disappears

IT was not very long after this that there occurred the first
of the mysterious events that rid us at last of the captain,
though not, as you will see, of his affairs. It was a bitter
cold winter, with long, hard frosts and heavy gales; and it
was plain from the first that my poor father was little likely
to see the spring. He sank daily, and my mother and I had
all the inn upon our hands; and were kept busy enough,
without paying much regard to our unpleasant guest.

It was one January morning, very early – a pinching,
frosty morning – the cove all grey with hoar-frost, the
ripple lapping softly on the stones, the sun still low and
only touching the hilltops and shining far to seaward. The
captain had risen earlier than usual, and set out down
the beach, his cutlass swinging under the broad skirts
of the old blue coat, his brass telescope under his arm,
his hat tilted back upon his head. I remember his breath
hanging like smoke in his wake as he strode off, and the
last sound I heard of him, as he turned the big rock, was
a loud snort of indignation, as though his mind was still
running upon Dr Livesey.

Well, mother was upstairs with father; and I was laying
the breakfast table against the captain's return, when the
parlour door opened, and a man stepped in on whom I had
never set my eyes before. He was a pale, tallowy creature,
wanting two fingers of the left hand; and, though he wore
a cutlass, he did not look much like a fighter. I had always
my eye open for seafaring men, with one leg or two, and I
remember this one puzzled me. He was not sailorly, and
yet he had a smack of the sea about him too.

I asked him what was for his service, and he said he would
take rum; but as I was going out of the room to fetch it he

sat down upon a table, and motioned me to draw near. I paused where I was with my napkin in my hand.

'Come here, sonny,' says he. 'Come nearer here.'

I took a step nearer.

'Is this here table for my mate, Bill?' he asked, with a kind of leer.

I told him I did not know his mate Bill; and this was for a person who stayed in our house, whom we called the captain.

'Well,' said he, 'my mate Bill would be called the captain, as like as not. He has a cut on one cheek, and a mighty pleasant way with him, particularly in drink, has my mate, Bill. We'll put it, for argument like, that your captain has a cut on one cheek – and we'll put it, if you like, that that cheek's the right one. Ah, well! I told you. Now, is my mate Bill in this here house?'

I told him he was out walking.

'Which way, sonny? Which way is he gone?'

And when I had pointed out the rock and told him how the captain was likely to return, and how soon, and answered a few other questions, 'Ah,' said he, 'this'll be as good as drink to my mate Bill.'

The expression of his face as he said these words was not at all pleasant, and I had my own reasons for thinking that the stranger was mistaken, even supposing he meant what he said. But it was no affair of mine, I thought; and, besides, it was difficult to know what to do. The stranger kept hanging about just inside the inn door, peering round the corner like a cat waiting for a mouse. Once I stepped out myself into the road, but he immediately called me back, and, as I did not obey quick enough for his fancy, a most horrible change came over his tallowy face, and he ordered me in, with an oath that made me jump. As soon as I was back again he returned to his former manner, half fawning, half sneering, patted me on the shoulder, told me I was a good boy, and he had taken quite a fancy to me. 'I have a son of my own,' said he, 'as like you as two blocks, and he's all the pride of my 'art. But the great thing for boys is discipline, sonny – discipline. Now, if you had sailed along of Bill, you wouldn't have stood there to be spoke to twice

– not you. That was never Bill's way, nor the way of sich as sailed with him. And here, sure enough, is my mate Bill, with a spy-glass under his arm, bless his old 'art to be sure. You and me'll just go back into the parlour, sonny, and get behind the door, and we'll give Bill a little surprise – bless his 'art, I say again.'

So saying, the stranger backed along with me into the parlour, and put me behind him in the corner, so that we were both hidden by the open door. I was very uneasy and alarmed, as you may fancy, and it rather added to my fears to observe that the stranger was certainly frightened himself. He cleared the hilt of his cutlass and loosened the blade in the sheath; and all the time we were waiting there he kept swallowing as if he felt what we used to call a lump in the throat.

At last in strode the captain, slammed the door behind him, without looking to the right or left, and marched straight across the room to where his breakfast awaited him.

'Bill,' said the stranger, in a voice that I thought he had tried to make bold and big.

The captain spun round on his heel and fronted us; all the brown had gone out of his face, and even his nose was blue; he had the look of a man who sees a ghost, or the evil one, or something worse, if anything can be; and, upon my word, I felt sorry to see him, all in a moment, turn so old and sick.

'Come, Bill, you know me; you know an old shipmate, Bill, surely,' said the stranger.

The captain made a sort of gasp.

'Black Dog!' said he.

'And who else?' returned the other, getting more at his ease. 'Black Dog as ever was, come for to see his old shipmate Billy, at the "Admiral Benbow" inn. Ah, Bill, Bill, we have seen a sight of times, us two, since I lost them two talons,' holding up his mutilated hand.

'Now, look here,' said the captain; 'you've run me down; here I am; well, then, speak up: what is it?'

'That's you, Bill,' returned Black Dog, 'you're in the right of it, Billy. I'll have a glass of rum from this dear child here, as I've took such a liking to; and we'll sit down, if you please, and talk square, like old shipmates.'

When I returned with the rum, they were already seated on either side of the captain's breakfast table – Black Dog next to the door, and sitting sideways, so as to have one eye on his old shipmate, and one, as I thought, on his retreat.

He bade me go, and leave the door wide open. 'None of your keyholes for me, sonny,' he said; and I left them together, and retired into the bar.

For a long time, though I certainly did my best to listen, I could hear nothing but a low gabbling; but at last the voices began to grow higher, and I could pick up a word or two, mostly oaths, from the captain.

'No, no, no, no; and an end of it!' he cried once. And again, 'If it comes to swinging, swing all, say I.'

Then all of a sudden there was a tremendous explosion of oaths and other noises – the chair and table went over in a lump, a clash of steel followed, and then a cry of pain, and the next instant I saw Black Dog in full flight, and the captain hotly pursuing, both with drawn cutlasses, and the former streaming blood from the left shoulder. Just at the door, the captain aimed at the fugitive one last tremendous cut, which would certainly have split him to the chine had it not been intercepted by our big signboard of Admiral Benbow. You may see the notch on the lower side of the frame to this day.

That blow was the last of the battle. Once out upon the road, Black Dog, in spite of his wound, showed a wonderful clean pair of heels, and disappeared over the edge of the hill in half a minute. The captain, for his part, stood staring at the signboard like a bewildered man. Then he passed his hand over his eyes several times, and at last turned back into the house.

'Jim,' says he, 'rum;' and as he spoke, he reeled a little, and caught himself with one hand against the wall.

'Are you hurt?' cried I.

'Rum,' he repeated. 'I must get away from here. Rum! rum!'

I ran to fetch it; but I was quite unsteadied by all that

had fallen out, and I broke one glass and fouled the tap, and while I was still getting in my own way, I heard a loud fall in the parlour, and, running in, beheld the captain lying full length upon the floor. At the same instant my mother, alarmed by the cries and fighting, came running downstairs to help me. Between us we raised his head. He was breathing very loud and hard; but his eyes were closed, and his face a horrible colour.

'Dear, deary me,' cried my mother, 'what a disgrace upon the house! And your poor father sick!'

In the meantime, we had no idea what to do to help the captain, nor any other thought but that he had got his death-hurt in the scuffle with the stranger. I got the rum, to be sure, and tried to put it down his throat; but his teeth were tightly shut, and his jaws as strong as iron. It was a happy relief for us when the door opened and Doctor Livesey came in, on his visit to my father.

'Oh, doctor,' we cried, 'what shall we do? Where is he wounded?'

'Wounded? A fiddle-stick's end!' said the doctor. 'No more wounded than you or I. The man has had a stroke, as I warned him. Now, Mrs Hawkins, just you run upstairs to your husband, and tell him, if possible, nothing about it. For my part, I must do my best to save this fellow's trebly worthless life; and Jim, you get me a basin.'

When I got back with the basin, the doctor had already ripped up the captain's sleeve, and exposed his great sinewy arm. It was tattooed in several places. 'Here's luck,' 'A fair wind,' and 'Billy Bones his fancy,' were very neatly and clearly executed on the forearm; and up near the shoulder there was a sketch of a gallows and a man hanging from it – done, as I thought, with great spirit.

'Prophetic,' said the doctor, touching this picture with his finger. 'And now, Master Billy Bones, if that be your name, we'll have a look at the colour of your blood. Jim,' he said, 'are you afraid of blood?'

'No, sir,' said I.

'Well, then,' said he, 'you hold the basin;' and with that he took his lancet and opened a vein.

A great deal of blood was taken before the captain opened

his eyes and looked mistily about him. First he recognised
the doctor with an unmistakable frown; then his glance fell
upon me, and he looked relieved. But suddenly his colour
changed, and he tried to raise himself, crying:—

'Where's Black Dog?'

'There is no Black Dog here,' said the doctor, 'except
what you have on your own back. You have been drinking
rum; you have had a stroke, precisely as I told you; and
I have just, very much against my own will, dragged you
head-foremost out of the grave. Now, Mr Bones—'

'That's not my name,' he interrupted.

'Much I care,' returned the doctor. 'It's the name of a
buccaneer of my acquaintance; and I call you by it for the
sake of shortness, and what I have to say to you is this: one
glass of rum won't kill you, but if you take one you'll take
another and another, and I stake my wig if you don't break
off short, you'll die – do you understand that? – die, and
go to your own place, like the man in the Bible. Come,
now, make an effort. I'll help you to your bed for once.'

Between us, with much trouble, we managed to hoist
him upstairs, and laid him on his bed, where his head fell
back on the pillow, as if he were almost fainting.

'Now, mind you,' said the doctor, 'I clear my conscience
– the name of rum for you is death.'

And with that he went off to see my father, taking me
with him by the arm.

'This is nothing,' he said, as soon as he had closed the
door. 'I have drawn blood enough to keep him quiet a while;
he should lie for a week where he is – that is the best thing
for him and you; but another stroke would settle him.'

CHAPTER THREE

The Black Spot

ABOUT NOON I stopped at the captain's door with some cooling drinks and medicines. He was lying very much as we had left him, only a little higher, and he seemed both weak and excited.

'Jim,' he said, 'you're the only one here that's worth anything; and you know I've been always good to you. Never a month but I've given you a silver fourpenny for yourself. And now you see, mate, I'm pretty low, and deserted by all; and Jim, you'll bring me one noggin of rum, now, won't you, matey?'

'The doctor—' I began.

But he broke in cursing the doctor, in a feeble voice, but heartily. 'Doctors is all swabs,' he said; 'and that doctor there, why, what do he know about seafaring men? I been in places hot as pitch, and mates dropping round with Yellow Jack, and the blessed land a-heaving like the sea with earthquakes – what do the doctor know of lands like that? – and I lived on rum, I tell you. It's been meat and drink, and man and wife, to me; and if I'm not to have my rum now I'm a poor old hulk on a lee shore, my blood'll be on you, Jim, and that Doctor swab;' and he ran on again for a while with curses. 'Look, Jim, how my fingers fidges,' he continued, in the pleading tone. 'I can't keep 'em still, not I. I haven't had a drop this blessed day. That doctor's a fool, I tell you. If I don't have a drain o' rum, Jim, I'll have the horrors; I seen some on 'em already. I seen old Flint in the corner there, behind you; as plain as print, I seen him; and if I get the horrors, I'm a man that has lived rough, and I'll raise Cain. Your doctor hisself said one glass wouldn't hurt me. I'll give you a golden guinea for a noggin, Jim.'

He was growing more and more excited, and this alarmed me for my father, who was very low that day, and needed quiet; besides, I was reassured by the doctor's words, now quoted to me, and rather offended by the offer of a bribe.

'I want none of your money,' said I, 'but what you owe my father. I'll get you one glass, and no more.'

When I brought it to him, he seized it greedily, and drank it out.

'Ay, ay,' said he, 'that's some better, sure enough. And now, matey, did that doctor say how long I was to lie here in this old berth?'

'A week at least,' said I.

'Thunder!' he cried. 'A week! I can't do that: they'd have the black spot on me by then. The lubbers is going about to get the wind of me this blessed moment; lubbers as couldn't keep what they got, and want to nail what is another's. Is that seamanly behaviour, now, I want to know? But I'm a saving soul. I never wasted good money of mine, nor lost it neither; and I'll trick 'em again. I'm not afraid on 'em. I'll shake out another reef, matey, and daddle 'em again.'

As he was thus speaking, he had risen from bed with great difficulty, holding to my shoulder with a grip that almost made me cry out, and moving his legs like so much dead weight. His words, spirited as they were in meaning, contrasted sadly with the weakness of the voice in which they were uttered. He paused when he had got into a sitting position on the edge.

'That doctor's done me,' he murmured. 'My ears is singing. Lay me back.'

Before I could do much to help him he had fallen back again to his former place, where he lay for a while silent.

'Jim,' he said, at length, 'you saw that seafaring man today?'

'Black Dog?' I asked.

'Ah! Black Dog,' says he. '*He's* a bad 'un; but there's worse that put him on. Now, if I can't get away nohow, and they tip me the black spot, mind you, it's my old sea-chest they're after; you get on a horse – you can, can't you? Well, then, you get on a horse, and go to – well, yes,

I will! – to that eternal doctor swab, and tell him to pipe
all hands – magistrates and sich – and he'll lay 'em aboard
at the "Admiral Benbow" – all old Flint's crew, man and
boy, all on 'em that's left. I was first mate, I was, old Flint's
first mate, and I'm the on'y one as knows the place. He gave
it me at Savannah, when he lay a-dying, like as if I was
to now, you see. But you won't peach unless they get the
black spot on me, or unless you see that Black Dog again,
or a seafaring man with one leg, Jim – him above all.'

'But what is the black spot, Captain?' I asked.

'That's a summons, mate. I'll tell you if they get that.
But you keep your weather-eye open, Jim, and I'll share
with you equals, upon my honour.'

He wandered a little longer, his voice growing weaker;
but soon after I had given him his medicine, which he
took like a child, with the remark, 'If ever a seaman wanted
drugs, it's me,' he fell at last into a heavy, swoon-like sleep,
in which I left him. What I should have done had all gone
well I do not know. Probably I should have told the whole
story to the doctor; for I was in mortal fear lest the captain
should repent of his confessions and make an end of me.
But as things fell out, my poor father died quite suddenly
that evening, which put all other matters on one side. Our
natural distress, the visits of the neighbours, the arranging
of the funeral, and all the work of the inn to be carried on
in the meanwhile, kept me so busy that I had scarcely time
to think of the captain, far less to be afraid of him.

He got downstairs next morning, to be sure, and had
his meals as usual, though he ate little, and had more,
I am afraid, than his usual supply of rum, for he helped
himself out of the bar, scowling and blowing through his
nose, and no one dared to cross him. On the night before
the funeral he was as drunk as ever; and it was shocking,
in that house of mourning, to hear him singing away at his
ugly old sea-song; but, weak as he was, we were all in the
fear of death for him, and the doctor was suddenly taken up
with a case many miles away, and was never near the house
after my father's death. I have said the captain was weak;
and indeed he seemed rather to grow weaker than regain
his strength. He clambered up and downstairs, and went

from the parlour to the bar and back again, and sometimes put his nose out of doors to smell the sea, holding on to the walls as he went for support, and breathing hard and fast like a man on a steep mountain. He never particularly addressed me, and it is my belief he had as good as forgotten his confidences; but his temper was more flighty, and, allowing for his bodily weakness, more violent than ever. He had an alarming way now when he was drunk of drawing his cutlass and laying it bare before him on the table. But, with all that, he minded people less, and seemed shut up in his own thoughts and rather wandering. Once, for instance, to our extreme wonder, he piped up to a different air, a kind of country love-song, that he must have learned in his youth before he had begun to follow the sea.

So things passed until, the day after the funeral, and about three o'clock of a bitter, foggy, frosty afternoon, I was standing at the door for a moment full of sad thoughts about my father, when I saw someone drawing slowly near along the road. He was plainly blind, for he tapped before him with a stick, and wore a great green shade over his eyes and nose; and he was hunched, as if with age or weakness, and wore a huge old tattered sea-cloak with a hood, that made him appear positively deformed. I never saw in my life a more dreadful looking figure. He stopped a little from the inn, and, raising his voice in an odd sing-song, addressed the air in front of him:—

'Will any kind friend inform a poor blind man, who has lost the precious sight of his eyes in the gracious defence of his native country, England, and God bless King George! – where or in what part of this country he may now be?'

'You are at the "Admiral Benbow," Black Hill Cove, my good man,' said I.

'I hear a voice,' said he – 'a young voice. Will you give me your hand, my kind, young friend, and lead me in?'

I held out my hand, and the horrible, soft-spoken, eyeless creature gripped it in a moment like a vice. I was so much startled that I struggled to withdraw; but the blind man pulled me close up to him with a single action of his arm.

'Now, boy,' he said, 'take me in to the captain.'

'Sir,' said I, 'upon my word I dare not.'

'Oh,' he sneered, 'that's it! Take me in straight, or I'll break your arm.'

And he gave it, as he spoke, a wrench that made me cry out.

'Sir,' said I, 'it is for yourself I mean. The captain is not what he used to be. He sits with a drawn cutlass. Another gentleman—'

'Come, now, march,' interrupted he; and I never heard a voice so cruel, and cold, and ugly as that blind man's. It cowed me more than the pain; and I began to obey him at once, walking straight in at the door and towards the parlour, where our sick old buccaneer was sitting, dazed with rum. The blind man clung close to me, holding me in one iron fist, and leaning almost more of his weight on me than I could carry. 'Lead me straight up to him, and when I'm in view, cry out, "Here's a friend for you, Bill."' If you don't, I'll do this;' and with that he gave me a twitch that I thought would have made me faint. Between this and that, I was so utterly terrified of the blind beggar that I forgot my terror of the captain, and as I opened the parlour door, cried out the words he had ordered in a trembling voice.

The poor captain raised his eyes, and at one look the rum went out of him, and left him staring sober. The expression of his face was not so much of terror as of mortal sickness. He made a movement to rise, but I do not believe he had enough force left in his body.

'Now, Bill, sit where you are,' said the beggar. 'If I can't see, I can hear a finger stirring. Business is business. Hold out your left hand. Boy, take his left hand by the wrist, and bring it near to my right.'

We both obeyed him to the letter, and I saw him pass something from the hollow of the hand that held his stick into the palm of the captain's, which closed upon it instantly.

'And now that's done,' said the blind man; and at the words he suddenly left hold of me, and, with incredible accuracy and nimbleness, skipped out of the parlour and into the road, where, as I still stood motionless, I could hear his stick go tap-tap-tapping into the distance.

It was some time before either I or the captain seemed to gather our senses; but at length, and about at the same moment, I released his wrist, which I was still holding, and he drew in his hand and looked sharply into the palm.

'Ten o'clock!' he cried. 'Six hours. We'll do them yet;' and he sprang to his feet.

Even as he did so, he reeled, put his hand to his throat, stood swaying for a moment, and then, with a peculiar sound, fell from his whole height face foremost to the floor.

I ran to him at once, calling to my mother. But haste was all in vain. The captain had been struck dead by thundering apoplexy. It is a curious thing to understand, for I had certainly never liked the man, though of late I had begun to pity him, but as soon as I saw that he was dead, I burst into a flood of tears. It was the second death I had known, and the sorrow of the first was still fresh in my heart.

CHAPTER FOUR

The Sea Chest

ᶦ LOST no time, of course, in telling my mother all that I knew, and perhaps should have told her long before, and we saw ourselves at once in a difficult and dangerous position. Some of the man's money – if he had any – was certainly due to us; but it was not likely that our captain's shipmates, above all the two specimens seen by me, Black Dog and the blind beggar, would be inclined to give up their booty in payment of the dead man's debts. The captain's order to mount at once and ride for Doctor Livesey would have left my mother alone and unprotected, which was not to be thought of. Indeed, it seemed impossible for either of us to remain much longer in the house: the fall of coals in the kitchen grate, the very ticking of the clock, filled us with alarm. The neighbourhood, to our ears, seemed haunted by approaching footsteps; and what between the dead body of the captain on the parlour floor, and the thought of that detestable blind beggar hovering near at hand, and ready to return, there were moments when, as the saying goes, I jumped in my skin for terror. Something must speedily be resolved upon; and it occurred to us at last to go forth together and seek help in the neighbouring hamlet. No sooner said than done. Bare-headed as we were, we ran out at once in the gathering evening and the frosty fog.

The hamlet lay not many hundred yards away though out of view, on the other side of the next cove; and what greatly encouraged me, it was in an opposite direction from that whence the blind man had made his appearance, and whither he had presumably returned. We were not many minutes on the road, though we sometimes stopped to lay hold of each other and hearken. But there was no unusual sound – nothing but the low

wash of the ripple and the croaking of the inmates of
the wood.

It was already candle-light when we reached the hamlet,
and I shall never forget how much I was cheered to see
the yellow shine in doors and windows; but that, as it
proved, was the best of the help we were likely to get in
that quarter. For – you would have thought men would
have been ashamed of themselves – no soul would consent
to return with us to the 'Admiral Benbow.' The more we
told of our troubles, the more – man, woman, and child
– they clung to the shelter of their houses. The name of
Captain Flint, though it was strange to me, was well enough
known to some there, and carried a great weight of terror.
Some of the men who had been to field-work on the far
side of the 'Admiral Benbow' remembered, besides, to have
seen several strangers on the road, and, taking them to be
smugglers, to have bolted away; and one at least had seen a
little lugger in what we called Kitt's Hole. For that matter,
anyone who was a comrade of the captain's was enough
to frighten them to death. And the short and the long of
the matter was, that while we could get several who were
willing enough to ride to Dr Livesey's which lay in another
direction, not one would help us to defend the inn.

They say cowardice is infectious; but then argument is,
on the other hand, a great emboldener; and so when each
had said his say, my mother made them a speech. She
would not, she declared, lose money that belonged to her
fatherless boy; 'if none of the rest of you dare,' she said,
'Jim and I dare. Back we will go, the way we came, and
small thanks to you big, hulking, chicken-hearted men.
We'll have that chest open, if we die for it. And I'll thank
you for that bag, Mrs Crossley, to bring back our lawful
money in.'

Of course, I said I would go with my mother; and of
course they all cried out at our foolhardiness; but even
then not a man would go along with us. All they would do
was to give me a loaded pistol, lest we were attacked; and
to promise to have horses ready saddled, in case we were
pursued on our return; while one lad was to ride forward
to the doctor's in search of armed assistance.

My heart was beating finely when we two set forth in the cold night upon this dangerous venture. A full moon was beginning to rise and peered redly through the upper edges of the fog, and this increased our haste, for it was plain, before we came forth again, that all would be as bright as day, and our departure exposed to the eyes of any watchers. We slipped along the hedges, noiseless and swift, nor did we see or hear anything to increase our terrors, till, to our relief, the door of the 'Admiral Benbow' had closed behind us.

I slipped the bolt at once, and we stood and panted for a moment in the dark, alone in the house with the dead captain's body. Then my mother got a candle in the bar, and, holding each other's hands, we advanced into the parlour. He lay as we had left him, on his back, with his eyes open, and one arm stretched out.

'Draw down the blind, Jim,' whispered my mother; 'they might come and watch outside. And now,' said she, when I had done so, 'we have to get the key off *that*; and who's to touch it, I should like to know!' and she gave a kind of sob as she said the words.

I went down on my knees at once. On the floor close to his hand there was a little round of paper, blackened on the one side. I could not doubt that this was the *black spot*; and taking it up, I found written on the other side, in a very good, clear hand, this short message: 'You have till ten to-night.'

'He had till ten, mother,' said I; and just as I said it, our old clock began striking. This sudden noise startled us shockingly; but the news was good, for it was only six.

'Now, Jim,' she said, 'that key.'

I felt in his pockets, one after another. A few small coins, a thimble, and some thread and big needles, a piece of pigtail tobacco bitten away at the end, his gully with the crooked handle, a pocket compass, and a tinder box, were all that they contained, and I began to despair.

'Perhaps it's round his neck,' suggested my mother.

Overcoming a strong repugnance, I tore open his shirt at the neck, and there, sure enough, hanging to a bit of tarry string, which I cut with his own gully, we found the key. At this triumph we were filled with hope, and hurried upstairs, without delay, to the little room where he had slept so long, and where his box had stood since the day of his arrival.

It was like any other seaman's chest on the outside, the initial 'B.' burned on the top of it with a hot iron, and the corners somewhat smashed and broken as by long, rough usage.

'Give me the key,' said my mother; and though the lock was very stiff, she had turned it and thrown back the lid in a twinkling.

A strong smell of tobacco and tar rose from the interior, but nothing was to be seen on the top except a suit of very good clothes, carefully brushed and folded. They had never been worn, my mother said. Under that, the miscellany began – a quadrant, a tin canikin, several sticks of tobacco, two brace of very handsome pistols, a piece of bar silver, an old Spanish watch and some other trinkets of little value and mostly of foreign make, a pair of compasses mounted with brass, and five or six curious West Indian shells. I have often wondered since why he should have carried about these shells with him in his wandering, guilty, and hunted life.

In the meantime, we had found nothing of any value but the silver and the trinkets, and neither of these were in our way. Underneath there was an old boat-cloak, whitened with sea-salt on many a harbour-bar. My mother pulled it up with impatience, and there lay before us, the last things in the chest, a bundle tied up in oilcloth, and looking like papers, and a canvas bag, that gave forth, at a touch, the jingle of gold.

'I'll show these rogues that I'm an honest woman,' said my mother. 'I'll have my dues, and not a farthing over. Hold Mrs Crossley's bag.' And she began to count over the amount of the captain's score from the sailor's bag into the one that I was holding.

It was a long, difficult business, for the coins were of all countries and sizes – doubloons, and louis-d'ors, and guineas, and pieces of eight, and I know not what besides, all shaken together at random. The guineas, too, were about the scarcest, and it was with these only that my mother knew how to make her count.

When we were about half-way through, I suddenly put my hand upon her arm; for I had heard in the silent, frosty air, a sound that brought my heart into my mouth – the tap-tapping of the blind man's stick upon the frozen road. It drew nearer and nearer, while we sat holding our breath. Then it struck sharp on the inn door, and then we could hear the handle being turned, and the bolt rattling as the wretched being tried to enter; and then there was a long time of silence both within and without. At last the tapping recommenced, and, to our indescribable joy and gratitude, died slowly away again until it ceased to be heard.

'Mother,' said I, 'take the whole and let's be going;' for I was sure the bolted door must have seemed suspicious, and would bring the whole hornet's nest about our ears; though how thankful I was that I had bolted it, none could tell who had never met that terrible blind man.

But my mother, frightened as she was, would not consent to take a fraction more than was due to her, and was obstinately unwilling to be content with less. It was not yet seven, she said, by a long way; she knew her rights and she would have them; and she was still arguing with me, when a little low whistle sounded a good way off upon the hill. That was enough, and more than enough, for both of us.

'I'll take what I have,' she said, jumping to her feet.

'And I'll take this to square the count,' said I, picking up the oilskin packet.

Next moment we were both groping downstairs, leaving the candle by the empty chest; and the next we had opened the door and were in full retreat. We had not started a moment too soon. The fog was rapidly dispersing; already the moon shone quite clear on the high ground on either side; and it was only in the exact bottom of the dell and round the tavern door that a thin veil still hung unbroken to conceal the first steps of our escape. Far less than half-way to the hamlet, very little beyond the bottom of the hill, we must come forth into the moonlight. Nor was this all; for the sound of several footsteps running came already to our ears, and as we looked back in their direction, a light tossing to and fro and still rapidly advancing, showed that one of the new-comers carried a lantern.

'My dear,' said my mother suddenly, 'take the money and run on. I am going to faint.'

This was certainly the end for both of us, I thought. How I cursed the cowardice of the neighbours; how I blamed my poor mother for her honesty and her greed, for her past foolhardiness and present weakness! We were just at the little bridge, by good fortune; and I helped her, tottering as she was, to the edge of the bank, where, sure enough, she gave a sigh and fell on my shoulder. I do not know how I found the strength to do it at all, and I am afraid it was roughly done; but I managed to drag her down the bank and a little way under the arch. Farther I could not move her, for the bridge was too low to let me do more than crawl below it. So there we had to stay – my mother almost entirely exposed, and both of us within earshot of the inn.

CHAPTER FIVE

The Last of the Blind Man

MY curiosity, in a sense, was stronger than my fear; for I could not remain where I was, but crept back to the bank again, whence, sheltering my head behind a bush of broom, I might command the road before our door. I was scarcely in position ere my enemies began to arrive, seven or eight of them, running hard, their feet beating out of time along the road, and the man with the lantern some paces in front. Three men ran together, hand in hand; and I made out, even through the mist, that the middle man of this trio was the blind beggar. The next moment his voice showed me that I was right.

'Down with the door!' he cried.

'Ay, ay, sir!' answered two or three; and a rush was made upon the 'Admiral Benbow,' the lantern-bearer following; and then I could see them pause, and hear speeches passed in a lower key, as if they were surprised to find the door open. But the pause was brief, for the blind man again issued his commands. His voice sounded louder and higher, as if he were afire with eagerness and rage.

'In, in, in!' he shouted, and cursed them for their delay.

Four or five of them obeyed at once, two remaining on the road with the formidable beggar. There was a pause, then a cry of surprise, and then a voice shouting from the house:—

'Bill's dead!'

But the blind man swore at them again for their delay.

'Search him, some of you shirking lubbers, and the rest of you aloft and get the chest,' he cried.

I could hear their feet rattling up our old stairs, so that the house must have shook with it. Promptly afterwards, fresh sounds of astonishment arose; the window of the captain's room was thrown open with a slam and a jingle of broken glass; and a man leaned out into the moonlight, head and shoulders, and addressed the blind beggar on the road below him.

'Pew,' he cried, 'they've been before us. Someone's turned the chest out alow and aloft.'

'Is it there?' roared Pew.

'The money's there.'

The blind man cursed the money.

'Flint's fist, I mean,' he cried.

'We don't see it here nohow,' returned the man.

'Here, you below there, is it on Bill?' cried the blind man again.

At that, another fellow, probably him who had remained below to search the captain's body, came to the door of the inn. 'Bill's been overhauled a'ready,' said he, 'nothin' left.'

'It's these people of the inn – it's that boy. I wish I had put his eyes out!' cried the blind man, Pew. 'They were here no time ago – they had the door bolted when I tried it. Scatter, lads, and find 'em.'

'Sure enough, they left their glim here,' said the fellow from the window.

'Scatter and find 'em! Rout the house out!' reiterated Pew, striking with his stick upon the road.

Then there followed a great to-do through all our old inn, heavy feet pounding to and fro, furniture thrown over, doors kicked in, until the very rocks re-echoed, and the men came out again, one after another, on the road, and declared that we were nowhere to be found. And just then the same whistle that had alarmed my mother and myself over the dead captain's money was once more clearly audible through the night, but this time twice repeated. I had thought it to be the blind man's trumpet, so to speak, summoning his crew to the assault; but I now found that it was a signal from the hillside towards the hamlet, and, from its effect upon the buccaneers, a signal to warn them of approaching danger.

'There's Dirk again,' said one 'Twice! We'll have to budge, mates.'

'Budge, you skulk!' cried Pew, 'Dirk was a fool and a coward from the first – you wouldn't mind him. They must be close by; they can't be far; you have your hands on it. Scatter and look for them, dogs! Oh, shiver my soul,' he cried, 'if I had eyes!'

This appeal seemed to produce some effect, for two of the fellows began to look here and there among the lumber, but half-heartedly, I thought, and with half an eye to their own danger all the time, while the rest stood irresolute on the road.

'You have your hands on thousands, you fools, and you hang a leg! You'd be as rich as kings if you could find it, and you know it's here, and you stand there skulking. There wasn't one of you dared face Bill, and I did it – a blind man! And I'm to lose my chance for you! I'm to be a poor, crawling beggar, sponging for rum, when I might be rolling in a coach! If you had the pluck of a weevil in a biscuit you would catch them still.'

'Hang it, Pew, we've got the doubloons!' grumbled one.

'They might have hid the blessed thing,' said another. 'Take the Georges, Pew, and don't stand here squalling.'

Squalling was the word for it, Pew's anger rose so high at these objections; till at last, his passion completely taking the upper hand, he struck at them right and left in his blindness, and his stick sounded heavily on more than one.

These, in their turn, cursed back at the blind miscreant, threatened him in horrid terms, and tried in vain to catch the stick and wrest it from his grasp.

This quarrel was the saving of us; for while it was still raging, another sound came from the top of the hill on the side of the hamlet – the tramp of horses galloping. Almost at the same time a pistol-shot, flash and report, came from the hedge-side. And that was plainly the last signal of danger; for the buccaneers turned at once and ran, separating in every direction, one seaward along the cove, one slant across the hill, and so on, so that in half a minute not a sign of them remained but Pew. Him they had deserted, whether in sheer panic or out of revenge for his ill words and blows, I know not; but there he remained behind, tapping up and down the road in a frenzy, and groping and calling for his comrades. Finally he took the wrong turn, and ran a few steps past me, towards the hamlet, crying:—

'Johnny, Black Dog, Dirk,' and other names, 'you won't leave old Pew, mates – not old Pew!'

Just then the noise of horses topped the rise, and four or five riders came in sight in the moonlight, and swept at full gallop down the slope.

At this Pew saw his error, turned with a scream, and ran straight for the ditch, into which he rolled. But he was on his feet again in a second, and made another dash, now utterly bewildered, right under the nearest of the coming horses.

The rider tried to save him, but in vain. Down went Pew with a cry that rang high into the night; and the four hoofs trampled and spurned him and passed by. He fell on his side, then gently collapsed upon his face, and moved no more.

I leaped to my feet and hailed the riders. They were pulling up, at any rate, horrified at the accident; and I soon saw what they were. One, tailing out behind the rest, was a lad that had gone from the hamlet to Dr Livesey's; the rest were revenue officers, whom he had met by the way, and with whom he had had the intelligence to return at once. Some news of the lugger in Kitt's Hole had found its way to Supervisor Dance, and set him forth that night in our direction, and to that circumstance my mother and I owed our preservation from death.

Pew was dead, stone dead. As for my mother, when we had carried her up to the hamlet, a little cold water and salts and that soon brought her back again, and she was none the worse for her terror, though she still continued to deplore the balance of the money. In the meantime the supervisor rode on, as fast as he could, to Kitt's Hole; but his men had to dismount and grope down the dingle, leading, and sometimes supporting, their horses, and in continual fear of ambushes; so it was no great matter for surprise that when they got down to the Hole the lugger was already under way, though still close in. He hailed her. A voice replied, telling him to keep out of the moonlight, or he would get some lead in him, and at the same time a bullet whistled close by his arm. Soon after, the lugger doubled the point and disappeared. Mr Dance stood there, as he said, 'like a fish out of water,' and all he could do was to despatch a man to B— to warn the cutter. 'And that,' said he 'is just about as good as nothing. They've got off clean, and there's an end. Only,' he added, 'I'm glad I trod on Master Pew's corns;' for by this time he had heard my story.

I went back with him to the 'Admiral Benbow,' and you cannot imagine a house in such a state of smash; the very clock had been thrown down by these fellows in their furious hunt after my mother and myself; and though nothing had actually been taken away except the captain's money-bag and a little silver from the till, I could see at once that we were ruined. Mr Dance could make nothing of the scene.

'They got the money, you say? Well, then, Hawkins, what in fortune were they after? More money, I suppose?'

'No, sir; not money, I think,' replied I. 'In fact, sir, I believe I have the thing in my breast-pocket; and, to tell you the truth, I should like to get it put in safety.'

'To be sure, boy; quite right,' said he. 'I'll take it, if you like.'

'I thought, perhaps, Dr Livesey—' I began.

'Perfectly right,' he interrupted, very cheerily, 'perfectly right – a gentleman and a magistrate. And, now I come to think of it, I might as well ride round there myself and report to him or squire. Master Pew's dead, when all's done; not that I regret it, but he's dead, you see, and people will make it out against an officer of his Majesty's revenue, if make it out they can. Now, I'll tell you, Hawkins: if you like, I'll take you along.'

I thanked him heartily for the offer, and we walked back to the hamlet where the horses were. By the time I had told mother of my purpose they were all in the saddle.

'Dogger,' said Mr Dance, 'you have a good horse; take up this lad behind you.'

As soon as I was mounted, holding on to Dogger's belt, the supervisor gave the word, and the party struck out at a bouncing trot on the road to Dr Livesey's house.

CHAPTER SIX

The Captain's Papers

WE rode hard all the way, till we drew up before Dr Livesey's door. The house was all dark to the front.

Mr Dance told me to jump down and knock, and Dogger gave me a stirrup to descend by. The door was opened almost at once by the maid.

'Is Dr Livesey in?' I asked.

No, she said; he had come home in the afternoon, but had gone up to the Hall to dine and pass the evening with the squire.

'So there we go, boys,' said Mr Dance.

This time, as the distance was short, I did not mount, but ran with Dogger's stirrup-leather to the lodge gates, and up the long, leafless, moonlit avenue to where the white line of the Hall buildings looked on either hand on great old gardens. Here Mr Dance dismounted, and, taking me along with him, was admitted at a word into the house.

The servant led us down a matted passage, and showed us at the end into a great library, all lined with bookcases and busts upon the top of them, where the squire and Dr Livesey sat, pipe in hand, on either side of a bright fire.

I had never seen the squire so near at hand. He was a tall man, over six feet high, and broad in proportion, and he had a bluff, rough-and-ready face, all roughened and reddened and lined in his long travels. His eyebrows were very black, and moved readily, and this gave him a look of some temper, not bad, you would say, but quick and high.

'Come in, Mr Dance,' says he, very stately and condescending.

'Good-evening, Dance,' says the doctor, with a nod. 'And good-evening to you, friend Jim. What good wind brings you here?'

The supervisor stood up straight and stiff, and told his story like a lesson; and you should have seen how the two gentlemen leaned forward and looked at each other, and forgot to smoke in their surprise and interest. When they heard how my mother went back to the inn, Dr Livesey fairly slapped his thigh, and the squire cried 'Bravo!' and broke his long pipe against the grate. Long before it was done, Mr Trelawney (that, you will remember, was the squire's name) had got up from his seat, and was striding about the room, and the doctor, as if to hear the better, had taken off his powdered wig, and sat there, looking very strange indeed with his own close-cropped, black poll.

At last Mr Dance finished the story.

'Mr Dance,' said the squire, 'you are a very noble fellow. And as for riding down that black, atrocious miscreant, I regard it as an act of virtue, sir, like stamping on a cockroach. This lad Hawkins is a trump, I perceive. Hawkins, will you ring that bell? Mr Dance must have some ale.'

'And so, Jim,' said the doctor, 'you have the thing that they were after, have you?'

'Here it is, sir,' said I, and gave him the oilskin packet.

The doctor looked it all over, as if his fingers were itching to open it; but, instead of doing that, he put it quietly in the pocket of his coat.

'Squire,' said he, 'when Dance has had his ale he must, of course, be off on his Majesty's service; but I mean to keep Jim Hawkins here to sleep at my house, and, with your permission, I propose we should have up the cold pie, and let him sup.'

'As you will, Livesey,' said the squire; 'Hawkins has earned better than cold pie.'

So a big pigeon pie was brought in and put on a side-table, and I made a hearty supper, for I was as hungry as a hawk, while Mr Dance was further complimented, and at last dismissed.

'And now, squire,' said the doctor.

'And now, Livesey,' said the squire, in the same breath.

'One at a time, one at a time,' laughed Dr Livesey. 'You have heard of this Flint, I suppose?'

'Heard of him!' cried the squire. 'Heard of him, you

say! He was the bloodthirstiest buccaneer that sailed. Blackbeard was a child to Flint. The Spaniards were so prodigiously afraid of him, that, I tell you, sir, I was sometimes proud he was an Englishman. I've seen his top-sails with these eyes, off Trinidad, and the cowardly son of a rum-puncheon that I sailed with put back – put back, sir, into Port of Spain.'

'Well, I've heard of him myself, in England,' said the doctor. 'But the point is, had he money?'

'Money!' cried the squire. 'Have you heard the story? What were these villains after but money? What do they care for but money? For what would they risk their rascal carcases but money?'

'That we shall soon know,' replied the doctor. 'But you are so confoundedly hot-headed and exclamatory that I cannot get a word in. What I want to know is this: Supposing that I have here in my pocket some clue to where Flint buried his treasure, will that treasure amount to much?'

'Amount, sir!' cried the squire. 'It will amount to this; if we have the clue you talk about, I fit out a ship in Bristol dock, and take you and Hawkins here along, and I'll have that treasure if I search a year.'

'Very well,' said the doctor. 'Now, then, if Jim is agreeable, we'll open the packet;' and he laid it before him on the table.

The bundle was sewn together, and the doctor had to get out his instrument-case, and cut the stitches with his medical scissors. It contained two things – a book and a sealed paper.

'First of all we'll try the book,' observed the doctor.

The squire and I were both peering over his shoulder as he opened it, for Dr Livesey had kindly motioned me to come round from the side-table, where I had been eating, to enjoy the sport of the search. On the first page there were only some scraps of writing, such as a man with a pen in his hand might make for idleness or practice. One was the same as the tattoo mark, 'Billy Bones his fancy;' then there was 'Mr W. Bones, mate.' 'No more rum.' 'Off Palm Key he got itt;' and some other snatches, mostly single words and unintelligible. I could not help wondering who it was that had 'got itt,' and what 'itt' was that he got. A knife in his back as like as not.

'Not much instruction there,' said Dr Livesey, as he passed on.

The next ten or twelve pages were filled with a curious series of entries. There was a date at one end of the line and at the other a sum of money, as in common account-books; but instead of explanatory writing, only a varying number of crosses between the two. On the 12th of June, 1745, for instance, a sum of seventy pounds had plainly become due to someone, and there was nothing but six crosses to explain the cause. In a few cases, to be sure, the name of a place would be added, as 'Offe Caraccas;'or a mere entry of latitude and longitude, as '62° 17' 20" 19° 2' 40".'

The record lasted over nearly twenty years, the amount of the separate entries growing larger as time went on, and at the end a grand total had been made out after five or six wrong additions, and these words appended, 'Bones, his pile.'

'I can't make head or tail of this,' said Dr Livesey.

'The thing is as clear as noonday,' cried the squire. 'This is the black-hearted hound's account-book. These crosses stand for the names of ships or towns that they sank or plundered. The sums are the scoundrel's share, and where he feared an ambiguity, you see he added something clearer. "Offe Caraccas," now; you see, here was some unhappy vessel boarded off that coast. God help the poor souls that manned her – coral long ago.'

'Right!' said the doctor. 'See what it is to be a traveller. Right! And the amounts increase, you see, as he rose in rank.'

There was little else in the volume but a few bearings of places noted in the blank leaves towards the end, and a table for reducing French, English, and Spanish moneys to a common value.

'Thrifty man!' cried the doctor. 'He wasn't the one to be cheated.'

'And now,' said the squire, 'for the other.'

The paper had been sealed in several places with a

thimble by way of seal; the very thimble, perhaps, that I had found in the captain's pocket. The doctor opened the seals with great care, and there fell out the map of an island, with latitude and longitude, soundings, names of hills, and bays and inlets, and every particular that would be needed to bring a ship to a safe anchorage upon its shores. It was about nine miles long and five across, shaped, you might say, like a fat dragon standing up, and had two fine land-locked harbours, and a hill in the centre part marked 'The Spy-glass.' There were several additions of a later date; but, above all, three crosses of red ink – two on the north part of the island, one in the south-west, and, beside this last, in the same red ink, and in a small, neat hand, very different from the captain's tottery characters, these words: – 'Bulk of treasure here.'

Over on the back the same hand had written this further information:—

Tall tree, Spy-glass shoulder, bearing a point to the N. of N.N.E.

Skeleton Island E.S.E. and by E.

Ten feet.

The bar silver is in the north cache; you can find it by the trend of the east hummock, ten fathoms south of the black crag with the face on it.

The arms are easy found, in the sand hill, N. point of north inlet cape, bearing E. and a quarter N.

J.F.

That was all; but brief as it was, and, to me, incomprehensible, it filled the squire and Dr Livesey with delight.

'Livesey,' said the squire, 'you will give up this wretched practice at once. To-morrow I start for Bristol. In three weeks' time – three weeks! – two weeks – ten days – we'll have the best ship, sir, and the choicest crew in England. Hawkins shall come as cabin-boy. You'll make a famous cabin-boy, Hawkins. You, Livesey, are ship's doctor; I am admiral. We'll take Redruth, Joyce, and Hunter. We'll have favourable winds, a quick passage, and not the least difficulty in finding the spot, and money to eat – to roll in – to play duck and drake with ever after.'

'Trelawney,' said the doctor, 'I'll go with you; and, I'll

go bail for it, so will Jim, and be a credit to the undertaking. There's only one man I'm afraid of.'

'And who's that?' cried the squire. 'Name the dog, sir!'

'You,' replied the doctor; 'for you cannot hold your tongue. We are not the only men who know of this paper. These fellows who attacked the inn to-night – bold, desperate blades, for sure – and the rest who stayed aboard that lugger, and more, I dare say, not far off, are, one and all, through thick and thin, bound that they'll get that money. We must none of us go alone till we get to sea. Jim and I shall stick together in the meanwhile; you'll take Joyce and Hunter when you ride to Bristol, and, from first to last, not one of us must breathe a word of what we've found.'

'Livesey,' returned the squire, 'you are always in the right of it. I'll be as silent as the grave.'

PART II
THE SEA COOK

CHAPTER SEVEN

I Go to Bristol

IT was longer than the squire imagined ere we were ready for the sea, and none of our first plans – not even Dr Livesey's, of keeping me beside him – could be carried out as we intended. The doctor had to go to London for a physician to take charge of his practice; the squire was hard at work at Bristol; and I lived on at the Hall under the charge of old Redruth, the gamekeeper, almost a prisoner, but full of sea-dreams and the most charming anticipations of strange islands and adventures. I brooded by the hour together over the map, all the details of which I well remembered. Sitting by the fire in the house-keeper's room, I approached that island in my fancy, from every possible direction; I explored every acre of its surface; I climbed a thousand times to that tall hill they call the Spy-glass, and from the top enjoyed the most wonderful and changing prospects. Sometimes the isle was thick with savages, with whom we fought; sometimes full of dangerous animals that hunted us; but in all my fancies nothing occurred to me so strange and tragic as our actual adventures.

So the weeks passed on, till one fine day there came a letter addressed to Dr Livesey, with this addition, 'To be opened, in the case of his absence, by Tom Redruth, or young Hawkins.' Obeying this order, we found, or rather, I found – for the gamekeeper was a poor hand at reading anything but print – the following important news:—

'*Old Anchor Inn, Bristol,*
'*March* 1, 17—.

'DEAR LIVESEY, – As I do not know whether you are at the Hall or still in London, I send this in double to both places.

'The ship is bought and fitted. She lies at anchor, ready

for sea. You never imagined a sweeter schooner – a child might sail her – two hundred tons; name, *Hispaniola*.

'I got her through my old friend, Blandly, who has proved himself throughout the most surprising trump. The admirable fellow literally slaved in my interest, and so, I may say, did everyone in Bristol, as soon as they got wind of the port we sailed for – treasure, I mean.'

'Redruth,' said I, interrupting the letter, 'Doctor Livesey will not like that. The squire has been talking, after all.'

'Well, who's a better right?' growled the gamekeeper. 'A pretty rum go if squire ain't to talk for Doctor Livesey, I should think.'

At that I gave up all attempt at commentary, and read straight on:—

'Blandly himself found the *Hispaniola*, and by the most admirable management got her for the merest trifle. There is a class of men in Bristol monstrously prejudiced against Blandly. They go the length of declaring that this honest creature would do anything for money, that the *Hispaniola* belonged to him, and that he sold it me absurdly high – the most transparent calumnies. None of them dare, however, to deny the merits of the ship.

'So far there was not a hitch. The workpeople, to be sure – riggers and what not – were most annoyingly slow; but time cured that. It was the crew that troubled me.

'I wished a round score of men – in case of natives, buccaneers, or the odious French – and I had the worry of the deuce itself to find so much as half a dozen, till the most remarkable stroke of fortune brought me the very man that I required.

'I was standing on the dock, when, by the merest accident, I fell in talk with him. I found he was an old sailor, kept a public-house, knew all the seafaring men in Bristol, had lost his health ashore, and wanted a good berth as cook to get to sea again. He had hobbled down there that morning, he said, to get a smell of the salt.

'I was monstrously touched – so would you have been – and, out of pure pity, I engaged him on the spot to be ship's cook. Long John Silver, he is called, and has lost a leg; but that I regarded as a recommendation, since he lost it in his country's service, under the immortal Hawke. He has no pension, Livesey. Imagine the abominable age we live in!

'Well, sir, I thought I had only found a cook, but it was a crew I had discovered. Between Silver and myself we got together in a few days a company of the toughest old salts imaginable – not pretty to look at, but fellows, by their faces, of the most indomitable spirit. I declare we could fight a frigate.

'Long John even got rid of two out of the six or seven I had already engaged. He showed me in a moment that they were just the sort of fresh-water swabs we had to fear in an adventure of importance.

'I am in the most magnificent health and spirits, eating like a bull, sleeping like a tree, yet I shall not enjoy a moment till I hear my old tarpaulins tramping round the capstan. Seaward ho! Hang the treasure! It's the glory of the sea that has turned my head. So now, Livesey, come post; do not lose an hour, if you respect me.

'Let young Hawkins go at once to see his mother, with Redruth for a guard; and then both come full speed to Bristol.

'JOHN TRELAWNEY.

'*Postscript.* – I did not tell you that Blandly, who, by the way, is to send a consort after us if we don't turn up by the end of August, had found an admirable fellow for sailing master – a stiff man, which I regret, but, in all other respects, a treasure. Long John Silver unearthed a very competent man for a mate, a man named Arrow. I have a boatswain who pipes, Livesey; so things shall go man-o'-war fashion on board the good ship *Hispaniola*.

'I forgot to tell you that Silver is a man of substance; I know of my own knowledge that he has a banker's account, which has never been overdrawn. He leaves his wife to manage the inn; and as she is a woman of colour, a pair of old bachelors like you and I may be excused for guessing that it is the wife, quite as much as the health, that sends him back to roving.

'J.T.

'P.P.S. – Hawkins may stay one night with his mother.
'J.T.'

You can fancy the excitement into which that letter put
me. I was half beside myself with glee; and if ever I despised
a man, it was old Tom Redruth, who could do nothing
but grumble and lament. Any of the under-gamekeepers
would gladly have changed places with him; but such was
not the squire's pleasure, and the squire's pleasure was
like law among them all. Nobody but old Redruth would
have dared so much as even to grumble.

The next morning he and I set out on foot for the 'Admiral
Benbow,' and there I found my mother in good health and
spirits. The captain, who had so long been a cause of so
much discomfort, was gone where the wicked cease from
troubling. The squire had had everything repaired, and the
public rooms and the sign repainted, and had added some
furniture – above all a beautiful arm-chair for mother in
the bar. He had found her a boy as an apprentice also, so
that she should not want help while I was gone.

It was on seeing that boy that I understood, for the first
time, my situation. I had thought up to that moment of
the adventures before me, not at all of the home that I
was leaving; and now, at the sight of this clumsy stranger,
who was to stay here in my place beside my mother, I
had my first attack of tears. I am afraid I led that boy a
dog's life; for as he was new to the work, I had a hundred
opportunities of setting him right and putting him down,
and I was not slow to profit by them.

The night passed, and the next day, after dinner, Redruth
and I were afoot again, and on the road. I said good-bye to
mother and the cove where I had lived since I was born, and
the dear old 'Admiral Benbow' – since he was repainted, no
longer quite so dear. One of my last thoughts was of the
captain, who had so often strode along the beach with his
cocked hat, his sabre-cut cheek, and his old brass telescope.
Next moment we had turned the corner and my home was
out of sight.

The mail picked us up about dusk at the 'Royal George' on the heath. I was wedged in between Redruth and a stout old gentleman, and in spite of the swift motion and the cold night air, I must have dozed a great deal from the very first, and then slept like a log up hill and down dale through stage after stage; for when I was awakened, at last, it was by a punch in the ribs, and I opened my eyes to find that we were standing still before a large building in a city street, and that the day had already broken a long time.

'Where are we?' I asked.

'Bristol,' said Tom. 'Get down.'

Mr Trelawney had taken up his residence at an inn far down the docks, to superintend the work upon the schooner. Thither we had now to walk, and our way, to my great delight, lay along the quays and beside the great multitude of ships of all sizes and rigs and nations. In one, sailors were singing at their work; in another, there were men aloft, high over my head, hanging to threads that seemed no thicker than a spider's. Though I had lived by the shore all my life, I seemed never to have been near the sea till then. The smell of tar and salt was something new. I saw the most wonderful figureheads, that had all been far over the ocean. I saw, besides, many old sailors, with rings in their ears, and whiskers curled in ringlets, and tarry pigtails, and their swaggering, clumsy sea-walk; and if I had seen as many kings or archbishops I could not have been more delighted.

And I was going to sea myself; to sea in a schooner, with a piping boatswain, and pig-tailed singing seamen; to sea, bound for an unknown island, and to seek for buried treasures!

While I was still in this delightful dream, we came suddenly in front of a large inn, and met Squire Trelawney, all dressed out like a sea-officer, in stout blue cloth, coming out of the door with a smile on his face, and a capital imitation of a sailor's walk.

'Here you are,' he cried, 'and the doctor came last night from London. Bravo! the ship's company complete!'

'Oh, sir,' cried I, 'when do we sail?'

'Sail!' says he. 'We sail to-morrow!'

At the Sign of the 'Spy-glass'

WHEN I had done breakfasting the squire gave me a note addressed to John Silver, at the sign of the 'Spy-glass,' and told me I should easily find the place by following the line of the docks, and keeping a bright look-out for a little tavern with a large brass telescope for a sign. I set off, overjoyed at this opportunity to see some more of the ships and seamen, and picked my way among a great crowd of people and carts and bales, for the dock was now at its busiest, until I found the tavern in question.

It was a bright enough little place of entertainment. The sign was newly painted; the windows had neat red curtains; the floor was cleanly sanded. There was a street on each side, and an open door on both, which made the large, low room pretty clear to see in, in spite of clouds of tobacco smoke.

The customers were mostly seafaring men; and they talked so loudly that I hung at the door, almost afraid to enter.

As I was waiting, a man came out of a side room, and, at a glance, I was sure he must be Long John. His left leg was cut off close by the hip, and under the left shoulder he carried a crutch, which he managed with wonderful dexterity, hopping about upon it like a bird. He was very tall and strong, with a face as big as a ham – plain and pale, but intelligent and smiling. Indeed, he seemed in the most cheerful spirits, whistling as he moved about among the tables, with a merry word or a slap on the shoulder for the more favoured of his guests.

Now, to tell you the truth, from the very first mention of Long John in Squire Trelawney's letter, I had taken a fear in my mind that he might prove to be the very one-legged sailor whom I had watched for so long at the old 'Benbow.' But one look at the man before me was enough. I had seen the captain, and Black Dog, and the blind man Pew, and I thought I knew what a buccaneer was like – a very different creature, according to me, from this clean and pleasant-tempered landlord.

I plucked up courage at once, crossed the threshold, and walked right up to the man where he stood, propped on his crutch, talking to a customer.

'Mr Silver, sir?' I asked, holding out the note.

'Yes, my lad,' said he; 'such is my name, to be sure. And who may you be?' And then as he saw the squire's letter, he seemed to me to give something almost like a start.

'Oh!' said he, quite loud, and offering his hand, 'I see. You are our new cabin-boy; pleased I am to see you.'

And he took my hand in his large firm grasp.

Just then one of the customers at the far side rose suddenly and made for the door. It was close by him, and he was out in the street in a moment. But his hurry had attracted my notice, and I recognised him at a glance. It was the tallow-faced man, wanting two fingers, who had come first to the 'Admiral Benbow.'

'Oh,' I cried, 'stop him! it's Black Dog!'

'I don't care two coppers who he is,' cried Silver. 'But he hasn't paid his score. Harry, run and catch him.'

One of the others who was nearest the door leaped up, and started in pursuit.

'If he were Admiral Hawke he shall pay his score,' cried Silver; and then, relinquishing my hand – 'Who did you say he was?' he asked. 'Black what?'

'Dog, sir,' said I. 'Has Mr Trelawney not told you of the buccaneers? He was one of them.'

'So?' cried Silver. 'In my house! Ben, run and help Harry. One of those swabs, was he? Was that you drinking with him, Morgan? Step up here.'

The man whom he called Morgan – an old, grey-haired, mahogany-faced sailor – came forward pretty sheepishly, rolling his quid.

'Now, Morgan,' said Long John, very sternly; 'you never

clapped your eyes on that Black – Black Dog before, did you, now?'

'Not I, sir,' said Morgan, with a salute.

'You didn't know his name, did you?'

'No, sir.'

'By the powers, Tom Morgan, it's as good for you!' exclaimed the landlord. 'If you had been mixed up with the like of that, you would never have put another foot in my house, you may lay to that. And what was he saying to you?'

'I don't rightly know, sir,' answered Morgan.

'Do you call that a head on your shoulders, or a blessed dead-eye?' cried Long John. 'Don't rightly know, don't you! Perhaps you don't happen to rightly know who you was speaking to, perhaps? Come, now, what was he jawing – v'yages, cap'ns, ships? Pipe up! What was it?'

'We was a-talkin' of keel-hauling,' answered Morgan.

'Keel-hauling, was you? and a mighty suitable thing, too, and you may lay to that. Get back to your place for a lubber, Tom.'

And then, as Morgan rolled back to his seat, Silver added to me in a confidential whisper, that was very flattering, as I thought:—

'He's quite an honest man, Tom Morgan, on'y stupid. And now,' he ran on again, aloud, 'let's see – Black Dog? No, I don't know the name, not I. Yet I kind of think I've – yes, I've seen the swab. He used to come here with a blind beggar, he used.'

'That he did, you may be sure,' said I. 'I knew that blind man, too. His name was Pew.'

'It was!' cried Silver, now quite excited. 'Pew! That were his name for certain. Ah, he looked a shark, he did! If we run down this Black Dog, now, there'll be news for Cap'n Trelawney! Ben's a good runner; few seamen run better than Ben. He should run him down, hand over hand, by the powers! He talked o' keel-hauling, did he? *I'll* keel-haul him!'

All the time he was jerking out these phrases he was stumping up and down the tavern on his crutch, slapping tables with his hand, and giving such a show of excitement as would have convinced an Old Bailey judge or a Bow Street runner. My suspicions had been thoroughly re-awakened on finding Black Dog at the 'Spy-glass,' and I watched the cook narrowly. But he was too deep, and too ready, and too clever for me, and by the time the two men had come back out of breath, and confessed that they had lost the track in a crowd, and been scolded like thieves, I would have gone bail for the innocence of Long John Silver.

'See here, now, Hawkins,' said he, 'here's a blessed hard thing on a man like me, now, ain't it? There's Cap'n Trelawney – what's he to think? Here I have this confounded son of a Dutchman sitting in my own house, drinking of my own rum! Here you comes and tells me of it plain; and here I let him give us all the slip before my blessed dead-lights! Now, Hawkins, you do me justice with the cap'n. You're a lad, you are, but you're as smart as paint. I see that when you first came in. Now, here it is: What could I do, with this old timber I hobble on? When I was an A B master mariner I'd have come up alongside of him, hand over hand, and broached him to in a brace of old shakes, I would; but now—'

And then, all of a sudden, he stopped, and his jaw dropped as though he had remembered something.

'The score!' he burst out. 'Three goes o' rum! Why, shiver my timbers, if I hadn't forgotten my score!'

And, falling on a bench, he laughed until the tears ran down his cheeks. I could not help joining; and we laughed together, peal after peal, until the tavern rang again.

'Why, what a precious old sea-calf I am!' he said, at last, wiping his cheeks. 'You and me should get on well, Hawkins, for I'll take my davy I should be rated ship's boy. But, come, now, stand by to go about. This won't do. Dooty is dooty, messmates. I'll put on my old cocked hat, and step along of you to Cap'n Trelawney, and report this here affair. For, mind you, it's serious, young Hawkins; and neither you nor me's come out of it with what I should make so bold as to call credit. Nor you neither, says you; not smart – none of the pair of us smart. But dash my buttons! that was a good 'un about my score.'

And he began to laugh again, and that so heartily, that

though I did not see the joke as he did, I was again obliged to join him in his mirth.

On our little walk along the quays, he made himself the most interesting companion, telling me about the different ships that we passed by, their rig, tonnage, and nationality, explaining the work that was going forward – how one was discharging, another taking in cargo, and a third making ready for sea; and every now and then telling me some little anecdote of ships or seamen, or repeating a nautical phrase till I had learned it perfectly. I began to see that here was one of the best of possible shipmates.

When we got to the inn, the squire and Dr Livesey were seated together, finishing a quart of ale with a toast in it, before they should go aboard the schooner on a visit of inspection.

Long John told the story from first to last, with a great deal of spirit and the most perfect truth. 'That was how it were, now, weren't it, Hawkins?' he would say, now and again, and I could always bear him entirely out.

The two gentlemen regretted that Black Dog had got away; but we all agreed there was nothing to be done, and after he had been complimented, Long John took up his crutch and departed.

'All hands aboard by four this afternoon,' shouted the squire, after him.

'Ay, ay, sir,' cried the cook, in the passage.

'Well, squire,' said Dr Livesey, 'I don't put much faith in your discoveries, as a general thing; but I will say this, John Silver suits me.'

'The man's a perfect trump,' declared the squire.

'And now,' added the doctor, 'Jim may come on board with us, may he not?'

'To be sure he may,' says squire. 'Take your hat, Hawkins, and we'll see the ship.'

Powder and Arms

THE *Hispaniola* lay some way out, and we went under the figureheads and round the sterns of many other ships, and their cables sometimes grated underneath our keel, and sometimes swung above us. At last, however, we got alongside, and were met and saluted as we stepped aboard by the mate, Mr Arrow, a brown old sailor, with earrings in his ears and a squint. He and the squire were very thick and friendly, but I soon observed that things were not the same between Mr Trelawney and the captain.

This last was a sharp-looking man, who seemed angry with everything on board, and was soon to tell us why, for we had hardly got down into the cabin when a sailor followed us.

'Captain Smollett, sir, axing to speak with you,' said he.

'I am always at the captain's order. Show him in,' said the squire.

The captain, who was close behind his messenger, entered at once, and shut the door behind him.

'Well, Captain Smollett, what have you to say? All well, I hope; all shipshape and seaworthy?'

'Well, sir,' said the captain, 'better speak plain, I believe, even at the risk of offence. I don't like this cruise; I don't like the men; and I don't like my officer. That's short and sweet.'

'Perhaps, sir, you don't like the ship?' inquired the squire, very angry, as I could see.

'I can't speak as to that, sir, not having seen her tried,' said the captain. 'She seems a clever craft; more I can't say.'

'Possibly, sir, you may not like your employer, either?' says the squire.

But here Dr Livesey cut in.

'Stay a bit,' said he, 'stay a bit. No use of such questions as that but to produce ill-feeling. The captain has said too much or he has said too little, and I'm bound to say that I require an explanation of his words. You don't, you say, like this cruise. Now, why?'

'I was engaged, sir, on what we call sealed orders, to sail this ship for that gentleman where he should bid me,' said the captain. 'So far so good. But now I find that every man before the mast knows more than I do. I don't call that fair, now, do you?'

'No,' said Dr Livesey, 'I don't.'

'Next,' said the captain, 'I learn we are going after treasure – hear it from my own hands, mind you. Now, treasure is ticklish work; I don't like treasure voyages on any account; and I don't like them, above all, when they are secret, and when (begging your pardon, Mr Trelawney) the secret has been told to the parrot.'

'Silver's parrot?' asked the squire.

'It's a way of speaking,' said the captain. 'Blabbed, I mean. It's my belief neither of you gentlemen know what you are about; but I'll tell you my way of it – life or death, and a close run.'

'That is all clear, and, I daresay, true enough,' replied Dr Livesey. 'We take the risk; but we are not so ignorant as you believe us. Next, you say you don't like the crew. Are they not good seamen?'

'I don't like them, sir,' returned Captain Smollett. 'And I think I should have had the choosing of my own hands, if you go to that.'

'Perhaps you should,' replied the doctor. 'My friend should, perhaps, have taken you along with him; but the slight, if there be one, was unintentional. And you don't like Mr Arrow?'

'I don't, sir. I believe he's a good seaman; but he's too free with the crew to be a good officer. A mate should keep himself to himself – shouldn't drink with the men before the mast!'

'Do you mean he drinks?' cried the squire.

'No, sir,' replied the captain; 'only that he's too familiar.'

'Well, now, and the short and long of it, captain?' asked the doctor. 'Tell us what you want.'

'Well, gentlemen, are you determined to go on this cruise?'

'Like iron,' answered the squire.

'Very good,' said the captain. 'Then, as you've heard me very patiently, saying things that I could not prove, hear me a few words more. They are putting the powder and the arms in the fore hold. Now, you have a good place under the cabin; why not put them there? – first point. Then you are bringing four of your own people with you, and they tell me some of them are to be berthed forward. Why not give them the berths here beside the cabin? – second point.'

'Any more?' asked Mr Trelawney.

'One more,' said the captain. 'There's been too much blabbing already.'

'Far too much,' agreed the doctor.

'I'll tell you what I've heard myself,' continued Captain Smollett: 'that you have a map of an island; that there's crosses on the map to show where treasure is; and that the island lies—' And then he named the latitude and longitude exactly.

'I never told that,' cried the squire, 'to a soul!'

'The hands know it, sir,' returned the captain.

'Livesey, that must have been you or Hawkins,' cried the squire.

'It doesn't much matter who it was,' replied the doctor. And I could see that neither he nor the captain paid much regard to Mr Trelawney's protestations. Neither did I, to be sure, he was so loose a talker; yet in this case I believe he was really right, and that nobody had told the situation of the island.

'Well, gentlemen,' continued the captain, 'I don't know who has this map; but I make it a point, it shall be kept secret even from me and Mr Arrow. Otherwise I would ask you to let me resign.'

'I see,' said the doctor. 'You wish us to keep this matter dark, and to make a garrison of the stern part of the ship, manned with my friend's own people, and provided with all the arms and powder on board. In other words, you fear a mutiny.'

'Sir,' said Captain Smollett, 'with no intention to take offence, I deny your right to put words into my mouth. No captain, sir, would be justified in going to sea at all if he had ground enough to say that. As for Mr Arrow, I believe him thoroughly honest; some of the men are the same; all may be for what I know. But I am responsible for the ship's safety and the life of every man Jack aboard of her. I see things going, as I think, not quite right. And I ask you to take certain precautions, or let me resign my berth. And that's all.'

'Captain Smollett,' began the doctor, with a smile, 'did ever you hear the fable of the mountain and the mouse? You'll excuse me, I daresay, but you remind me of that fable. When you came in here I'll stake my wig you meant more than this.'

'Doctor,' said the captain, 'you are smart. When I came in here I meant to get discharged. I had no thought that Mr Trelawney would hear a word.'

'No more I would,' cried the squire. 'Had Livesey not been here I should have seen you to the deuce. As it is, I have heard you. I will do as you desire; but I think the worse of you.'

'That's as you please, sir,' said the captain. 'You'll find I do my duty.'

And with that he took his leave.

'Trelawney,' said the doctor, 'contrary to all my notions, I believe you have managed to get two honest men on board with you – that man and John Silver.'

'Silver, if you like,' cried the squire; 'but as for that intolerable humbug, I declare I think his conduct unmanly, unsailorly, and downright un-English.'

'Well,' says the doctor, 'we shall see.'

When we came on deck, the men had begun already to take our the arms and powder, yo-ho-ing at their work, while the captain and Mr Arrow stood by superintending.

The new arrangement was quite to my liking. The whole schooner had been overhauled; six berths had been made astern, out of what had been the after-part of the main hold; and this set of cabins was only joined to the galley and forecastle by a sparred passage on the port side. It had been originally meant that the captain, Mr Arrow, Hunter, Joyce, the doctor, and the squire, were to occupy these six berths. Now, Redruth and I were to get two of them, and Mr Arrow and the captain were to sleep on deck in the companion, which had been enlarged on each side till you might almost have called it a round-house. Very low it was still, of course; but there was room to swing two hammocks, and even the mate seemed pleased with the arrangement. Even he, perhaps, had been doubtful as to the crew, but that is only guess; for, as you shall hear, we had not long the benefit of his opinion.

We were all hard at work, changing the powder and the berths, when the last man or two, and Long John along with them, came off in a shore-boat.

The cook came up the side like a monkey for cleverness, and, as soon as he saw what was doing, 'So ho, mates!' says he, 'what's this?'

'We're a-changing of the powder, Jack,' answers one.

'Why, by the powers,' cried Long John, 'if we do, we'll miss the morning tide!'

'My orders!' said the captain shortly. 'You may go below, my man. Hands will want supper.'

'Ay, ay, sir,' answered the cook; and, touching his forelock, he disappeared at once in the direction of his galley.

'That's a good man, captain,' said the doctor.

'Very likely sir,' replied Captain Smollett. 'Easy with that, men – easy,' he ran on, to the fellows who were shifting the powder; and then suddenly observing me examining the swivel we carried amidships, a long brass nine – 'Here, you ship's boy,' he cried, 'out o' that! Off with you to the cook and get some work.'

And then as I was hurrying off I heard him say, quite loudly, to the doctor:—

'I'll have no favourites on my ship.'

I assure you I was quite of the squire's way of thinking, and hated the captain deeply.

The Voyage

ALL that night we were in a great bustle getting things stowed in their place, and boatfuls of the squire's friends, Mr Blandly and the like, coming off to wish him a good voyage and a safe return. We never had a night at the 'Admiral Benbow' when I had half the work; and I was dog-tired when, a little before dawn, the boatswain sounded his pipe, and the crew began to man the capstan-bars. I might have been twice as weary, yet I would not have left the deck; all was so new and interesting to me – the brief commands, the shrill note of the whistle, the men bustling to their places in the glimmer of the ship's lanterns.

'Now, Barbecue, tip us a stave,' cried one voice.

'The old one,' cried another.

'Ay, ay, mates,' said Long John, who was standing by, with his crutch under his arm, and at once broke out in the air and words I knew so well—

Fifteen men on the dead man's chest—

And then the whole crew bore chorus:—

Yo-ho-ho, and a bottle of rum!

And at the third 'ho!' drove the bars before them with a will.

Even at that exciting moment it carried me back to the old 'Admiral Benbow' in a second; and I seemed to hear the voice of the captain piping in the chorus. But soon the anchor was short up; soon it was hanging dripping at the bows; soon the sails began to draw, and the land and shipping to flit by on either side; and before I could lie down to snatch an hour of slumber the *Hispaniola* had begun her voyage to the Isle of Treasure.

I am not going to relate that voyage in detail. It was fairly prosperous. The ship proved to be a good ship, the crew were capable seamen, and the captain thoroughly understood his business. But before we came the length of Treasure Island, two or three things had happened which require to be known.

Mr Arrow, first of all, turned out even worse than the captain had feared. He had no command among the men, and people did what they pleased with him. But that was by no means the worst of it; for after a day or two at sea he began to appear on deck with hazy eye, red cheeks, stuttering tongue, and other marks of drunkenness. Time after time he was ordered below in disgrace. Sometimes he fell and cut himself; sometimes he lay all day long in his little bunk at one side of the companion; sometimes for a day or two he would be almost sober and attend to his work at least passably.

In the meantime, we could never make out where he got the drink. That was the ship's mystery. Watch him as we pleased, we could do nothing to solve it; and when we asked him to his face, he would only laugh, if he were drunk, and if he were sober, deny solemnly that he ever tasted anything but water.

He was not only useless as an officer, and a bad influence amongst the men, but it was plain that at this rate he must soon kill himself outright; so nobody was much surprised, nor very sorry, when one dark night, with a head sea, he disappeared entirely and was seen no more.

'Overboard!' said the captain. 'Well, gentlemen, that saves the trouble of putting him in irons.'

But there we were, without a mate; and it was necessary, of course, to advance one of the men. The boatswain, Job Anderson, was the likeliest man aboard, and, though he kept his old title, he served in a way as mate. Mr Trelawney had followed the sea, and his knowledge made him very useful, for he often took a watch himself in easy weather. And the coxswain, Israel Hands, was a careful, wily, old, experienced seaman, who could be trusted at a pinch with almost anything.

He was a great confidant of Long John Silver, and so

the mention of his name leads me on to speak of our ship's cook, Barbecue, as the men called him.

Aboard ship he carried his crutch by a lanyard round his neck, to have both hands as free as possible. It was something to see him wedge the foot of the crutch against a bulkhead, and, propped against it, yielding to every movement of the ship, get on with his cooking like someone safe ashore. Still more strange was it to see him in the heaviest of weather cross the deck. He had a line or two rigged up to help him across the widest spaces – Long John's earrings, they were called; and he would hand himself from one place to another, now using the crutch, now trailing it alongside by the lanyard, as quickly as another man could walk. Yet some of the men who had sailed with him before expressed their pity to see him so reduced.

'He's no common man, Barbecue,' said the coxswain to me. 'He had good schooling in his young days, and can speak like a book when so minded; and brave – a lion's nothing alongside of Long John! I seen him grapple four, and knock their heads together – him unarmed.'

All the crew respected and even obeyed him. He had a way of talking to each, and doing everybody some particular service. To me he was unweariedly kind; and always glad to see me in the galley, which he kept as clean as a new pin; the dishes hanging up burnished, and his parrot in a cage in one corner.

'Come away, Hawkins,' he would say; 'come and have a yarn with John. Nobody more welcome than yourself, my son. Sit you down and hear the news. Here's Cap'n Flint – I calls my parrot Cap'n Flint, after the famous buccaneer – here's Cap'n Flint predicting success to our v'yage. Wasn't you, cap'n?'

And the parrot would say, with great rapidity, 'Pieces of eight! pieces of eight! pieces of eight!' till you wondered that it was not out of breath, or till John threw his handkerchief over the cage.

'Now, that bird,' he would say, 'is, may be, two hundred years old, Hawkins – they lives for ever mostly; and if any-body's seen more wickedness, it must be the devil himself.

She's sailed with England, the great Cap'n England, the pirate. She's been at Madagascar, and at Malabar, and Surinam, and Providence, and Portobello. She was at the fishing up of the wrecked plate ships. It's there she learned "Pieces of eight," and little wonder; three hundred and fifty thousand of 'em, Hawkins! She was at the boarding of the Viceroy of the Indies out of Goa, she was; and to look at her you would think she was a babby. But you smelt powder – didn't you, cap'n?'

'Stand by to go about,' the parrot would scream.

'Ah, she's a handsome craft, she is,' the cook would say, and give her sugar from his pocket, and then the bird would peck at the bars and swear straight on, passing belief for wickedness. 'There,' John would add, 'you can't touch pitch and not be mucked, lad. Here's this poor old innocent bird o' mine swearing blue fire, and none the wiser, you may lay to that. She would swear the same, in a manner of speaking, before chaplain.' And John would touch his forelock with a solemn way he had, that made me think he was the best of men.

In the meantime, the squire and Captain Smollett were still on pretty distant terms with one another. The squire made no bones about the matter; he despised the captain. The captain, on his part, never spoke but when he was spoken to, and then sharp and short and dry, and not a word wasted. He owned, when driven into a corner, that he seemed to have been wrong about the crew, that some of them were as brisk as he wanted to see, and all had behaved fairly well. As for the ship, he had taken a downright fancy to her. 'She'll lie a point nearer the wind than a man has a right to expect of his own married wife, sir. But,' he would add, 'all I say is we're not home again, and I don't like the cruise.'

The squire, at this, would turn away and march up and down the deck, chin in air.

'A trifle more of that man,' he would say, 'and I shall explode.'

We had some heavy weather, which only proved the qualities of the *Hispaniola*. Every man on board seemed well content, and they must have been hard to please if they had been otherwise; for it is my belief there was never a ship's company so spoiled since Noah put to sea. Double grog was going on the least excuse; there was duff on odd days, as, for instance, if the squire heard it was any man's birthday; and always a barrel of apples standing broached in the waist, for anyone to help himself that had a fancy.

'Never knew good come of it yet,' the captain said to Dr Livesey. 'Spoil foc's'le hands, make devils. That's my belief.'

But good did come of the apple barrel, as you shall hear; for if it had not been for that, we should have had no note of warning, and might all have perished by the hand of treachery.

This was how it came about.

We had run up the trades to get the wind of the island we were after – I am not allowed to be more plain – and now we were running down for it with a bright look-out day and night. It was about the last day of our outward voyage, by the largest computation; some time that night, or, at latest, before noon of the morrow, we should sight the Treasure Island. We were heading S.S.W., and had a steady breeze abeam and a quiet sea. The *Hispaniola* rolled steadily, dipping her bowsprit now and then with a whiff of spray. All was drawing alow and aloft; everyone was in the bravest spirits, because we were now so near an end of the first part of our adventure.

Now, just after sundown, when all my work was over, and I was on my way to my berth, it occurred to me that I should like an apple. I ran on deck. The watch was all forward looking out for the island. The man at the helm was watching the luff of the sail, and whistling away gently to himself; and that was the only sound excepting the swish of the sea against the bows and around the sides of the ship.

In I got bodily into the apple barrel, and found there was scarce an apple left; but, sitting down there in the dark, what with the sound of the waters and the rocking movement of the ship, I had either fallen asleep, or was on the point of doing so, when a heavy man sat down with rather a clash close by. The barrel shook as he leaned his shoulders against it, and I was just about to jump up when the man began to speak. It was Silver's voice, and, before I had heard a dozen words, I would not have shown myself for all the world, but lay there, trembling and listening, in the extreme of fear and curiosity; for from these dozen words I understood that the lives of all the honest men aboard depended upon me alone.

What I Heard in the Apple Barrel

'NO, not I,' said Silver. 'Flint was cap'n; I was quarter-master, along of my timber leg. The same broadside I lost my leg, old Pew lost his deadlights. It was a master surgeon, him that ampytated me – out of college and all – Latin by the bucket, and what not; but he was hanged like a dog, and sun-dried like the rest, at Corso Castle. That was Roberts' men, that was, and comed of changing names to their ships – *Royal Fortune* and so on. Now, what a ship was christened, so let her stay, I says. So it was with the *Cassandra*, as brought us all safe home from Malabar, after England took the Viceroy of the Indies; so it was with the old *Walrus*, Flint's old ship, as I've seen a-muck with the red blood and fit to sink with gold.'

'Ah!' cried another voice, that of the youngest hand on board, and evidently full of admiration, 'he was the flower of the flock, was Flint!'

'Davis was a man, too, by all accounts,' said Silver. 'I never sailed along of him; first with England, then with Flint, that's my story; and now here on my own account, in a manner of speaking. I laid by nine hundred safe, from England, and two thousand after Flint. That ain't bad for a man before the mast – all safe in bank. 'Tain't earning now, it's saving does it, you may lay to that. Where's all England's men now? I dunno. Where's Flint's? Why, most on 'em aboard here, and glad to get the duff – been begging before that, some on 'em. Old Pew, as had lost his sight, and might have thought shame, spends twelve hundred pound in a year, like a lord in Parliament. Where is he now? Well, he's dead now and under hatches; but for two year before that, shiver my timbers! the man was starving.

He begged, and he stole, and he cut throats, and starved at that, by the powers!'

'Well, it ain't much use, after all,' said the young seaman.

''Tain't much use for fools, you may lay to it – that, nor nothing,' cried Silver. 'But now, you look here: you're young, you are, but you're as smart as paint. I see that when I set my eyes on you, and I'll talk to you like a man.'

You may imagine how I felt when I heard this abominable old rogue addressing another in the very same words of flattery as he had used to myself. I think, if I had been able, that I would have killed him through the barrel. Meantime, he ran on, little supposing he was overheard.

'Here it is about gentlemen of fortune. They lives rough, and they risk swinging, but they eat and drink like fighting-cocks, and when a cruise is done, why, it's hundreds of pounds instead of hundreds of farthings in their pockets. Now, the most goes for rum and a good fling, and to sea again in their shirts. But that's not the course I lay. I puts it all away, some here, some there, and none too much anywheres, by reason of suspicion. I'm fifty, mark you; once back from this cruise, I set up gentleman in earnest. Time enough, too, says you. Ah, but I've lived easy in the meantime; never denied myself o' nothing heart desires, and slep' soft and ate dainty all my days, but when at sea. And how did I begin? Before the mast, like you!'

'Well,' said the other, 'but all the other money's gone now, ain't it? You daren't show face in Bristol after this.'

'Why, where might you suppose it was?' asked Silver, derisively.

'At Bristol, in banks and places,' answered his companion.

'It were,' said the cook; 'it were when we weighed anchor. But my old missis has it all by now. And the "Spy-glass" is sold, lease and good-will and rigging; and the old girl's off to meet me. I would tell you where, for I trust you; but it 'ud make jealousy among the mates.'

'And can you trust your missis?' asked the other.

'Gentlemen of fortune,' returned the cook, 'usually trusts

little among themselves, and right they are, you may lay to it.
But I have a way with me, I have. When a mate brings a slip
on his cable – one as knows me, I mean – it won't be in the
same world with old John. There was some that was feared
of Pew, and some that was feared of Flint; but Flint his
own self was feared of me. Feared he was, and proud. They
was the roughest crew afloat, was Flint's; the devil himself
would have been feared to go to sea with them. Well, now,
I tell you, I'm not a boasting man, and you seen yourself
how easy I keep company; but when I was quartermaster,
lambs wasn't the word for Flint's old buccaneers. Ah, you
may be sure of yourself in old John's ship.'

'Well, I tell you now,' replied the lad, 'I didn't half a
quarter like the job till I had this talk with you, John; but
there's my hand on it now.'

'And a brave lad you were, and smart, too,' answered
Silver, shaking hands so heartily that all the barrel shook,
'and a finer figure-head for a gentleman of fortune I never
clapped my eyes on.'

By this time I had begun to understand the meaning
of their terms. By a 'gentleman of fortune' they plainly
meant neither more nor less than a common pirate, and
the little scene that I had overheard was the last act in the
corruption of one of the honest hands – perhaps of the last
one left aboard. But on this point I was soon to be relieved,
for Silver giving a little whistle, a third man strolled up and
sat down by the party.

'Dick's square,' said Silver.

'Oh, I know'd Dick was square,' returned the voice of
the coxswain, Israel Hands. 'He's no fool, is Dick.' And
he turned his quid and spat. 'But, look here,' he went on,
'here's what I want to know, Barbecue: how long are we
a-going to stand off and on like a blessed bumboat? I've
had a'most enough o' Cap'n Smollett; he's hazed me long
enough, by thunder! I want to go into that cabin, I do. I
want their pickles and wines, and that.'

'Israel,' said Silver, 'your head ain't much account, nor
ever was. But you're able to hear, I reckon; leastways, your
ears is big enough. Now, here's what I say: you'll berth
forward, and you'll live hard, and you'll speak soft, and

you'll keep sober, till I give the word; and you may lay to that, my son.'

'Well, I don't say no, do I?' growled the coxswain. 'What I say is, when? That's what I say.'

'When! by the powers!' cried Silver. 'Well, now, if you want to know, I'll tell you when. The last moment I can manage; and that's when. Here's a first-rate seaman, Cap'n Smollett, sails the blessed ship for us. Here's this squire and doctor with a map and such – I don't know where it is, do I? No more do you, says you. Well, then, I mean this squire and doctor shall find the stuff, and help us to get it aboard, by the powers. Then we'll see. If I was sure of you all, sons of double Dutchmen, I'd have Cap'n Smollett navigate us half-way back again before I struck.'

'Why, we're all seamen aboard here, I should think,' said the lad Dick.

'We're all foc's'le hands, you mean,' snapped Silver. 'We can steer a course, but who's to set one? That's what all you gentlemen split on, first and last. If I had my way, I'd have Cap'n Smollett work us back into the trades at least; then we'd have no blessed miscalculations and a spoonful of water a day. But I know the sort you are. I'll finish with 'em at the island, as soon's the blunt's on board, and a pity it is. But you're never happy till you're drunk. Split my sides, I've a sick heart to sail with the likes of you!'

'Easy all, Long John,' cried Israel. 'Who's a-crossin' of you?'

'Why, how many tall ships, think ye, now, have I seen laid aboard? and how many brisk lads drying in the sun at Execution Dock?' cried Silver, 'and all for this same hurry and hurry and hurry. You hear me? I seen a thing or two at sea, I have. If you would on'y lay your course, and a p'int to windward, you would ride in carriages, you would. But not you! I know you. You'll have your mouthful of rum to-morrow, and go hang.'

'Everybody know'd you was a kind of a chapling, John; but there's others as could hand and steer as well as you,' said Israel. 'They liked a bit o' fun, they did. They wasn't so high and dry, nohow, but took their fling, like jolly companions every one.'

'So?' says Silver. 'Well, and where are they now? Pew was that sort, and he died a beggar-man. Flint was, and he died of rum at Savannah. Ah, they was a sweet crew, they was! on'y, where are they?'

'But,' asked Dick, 'when we do lay 'em athwart, what are we to do with 'em, anyhow?'

'There's the man for me!' cried the cook, admiringly. 'That's what I call business. Well, what would you think? Put 'em ashore like maroons? That would have been England's way. Or cut 'em down like that much pork? That would have been Flint's or Billy Bones's.'

'Billy was the man for that,' said Israel. ' "Dead men don't bite," says he. Well, he's dead now hisself; he knows the long and short on it now; and if ever a rough hand come to port, it was Billy.'

'Right you are,' said Silver, 'rough and ready. But mark you here: I'm an easy man – I'm quite the gentleman, says you; but this time it's serious. Dooty is dooty, mates. I give my vote – death. When I'm in Parlyment, and riding in my coach, I don't want none of these sea-lawyers in the cabin a-coming home, unlooked for, like the devil at prayers. Wait is what I say; but when the time comes, why let her rip!'

'John,' cries the coxswain, 'you're a man!'

'You'll say so, Israel, when you see,' said Silver. 'Only one thing I claim – I claim Trelawney. I'll wring his calf's head off his body with these hands. Dick!' he added, breaking off, 'you just jump up, like a sweet lad, and get me an apple, to wet my pipe like.'

You may fancy the terror I was in! I should have leaped out and run for it, if I had found the strength; but my limbs and heart alike misgave me. I heard Dick begin to rise, and then someone seemingly stopped him, and the voice of Hands exclaimed:—

'Oh, stow that! Don't you get sucking of that bilge, John. Let's have a go of the rum.'

'Dick,' said Silver, 'I trust you. I've a gauge on the keg, mind. There's the key; you fill a pannikin and bring it up.'

Terrified as I was, I could not help thinking to myself

that this must have been how Mr Arrow got the strong waters that destroyed him.

Dick was gone but a little while, and during his absence Israel spoke straight on in the cook's ear. It was but a word or two that I could catch, and yet I gathered some important news; for, besides other scraps that tended to the same purpose, this whole clause was audible: 'Not another man of them 'll jine.' Hence there were still faithful men on board.

When Dick returned, one after another of the trio took the pannikin and drank – one 'To luck'; another with a 'Here's to old Flint'; and Silver himself saying, in a kind of song, 'Here's to ourselves, and hold your luff, plenty of prizes and plenty of duff.'

Just then a sort of brightness fell upon me in the barrel, and looking up, I found the moon had risen, and was silvering the mizzen-top and shining white on the luff of the fore-sail; and almost at the same time the voice of the look-out shouted, 'Land ho!'

Council of War

THERE WAS a great rush of feet across the deck. I could hear people tumbling up from the cabin and the foc's'le; and, slipping in an instant outside my barrel, I dived behind the fore-sail, made a double towards the stern, and came out upon the open deck in time to join Hunter and Dr Livesey in the rush for the weather bow.

There all hands were already congregated. A belt of fog had lifted almost simultaneously with the appearance of the moon. Away to the south-west of us we saw two low hills, about a couple of miles apart, and rising behind one of them a third and higher hill, whose peak was still buried in the fog. All three seemed sharp and conical in figure.

So much I saw, almost in a dream, for I had not yet recovered from my horrid fear of a minute or two before. And then I heard the voice of Captain Smollett issuing orders. The *Hispaniola* was laid a couple of points nearer the wind, and now sailed a course that would just clear the island on the east.

'And now, men,' said the captain, when all was sheeted home, 'has any one of you ever seen that land ahead?'

'I have, sir,' said Silver. 'I've watered there with a trader I was cook in.'

'The anchorage is on the south, behind an islet, I fancy?' asked the captain.

'Yes, sir; Skeleton Island they calls it. It were a main place for pirates once, and a hand we had on board knowed all their names for it. That hill to the nor'ard they calls the Fore-mast Hill; there are three hills in a row running south'ard – fore, main, and mizzen, sir. But the main – that's the big 'un, with the cloud on it – they usually calls the Spy-glass, by reason of a look-out they kept when they was in the anchorage cleaning; for it's there they cleaned their ships, sir, asking your pardon.'

'I have a chart here,' says Captain Smollett. 'See if that's the place.'

Long John's eyes burned in his head as he took the chart; but, by the fresh look of the paper, I knew he was doomed to disappointment. This was not the map we found in Billy Bones's chest, but an accurate copy, complete in all things – names and heights and soundings – with the single exception of the red crosses and the written notes. Sharp as must have been his annoyance, Silver had the strength of mind to hide it.

'Yes, sir,' said he, 'this is the spot to be sure; and very prettily drawed out. Who might have done that, I wonder? The pirates were too ignorant, I reckon. Ay, here it is: "Capt. Kidd's Anchorage" – just the name my shipmate called it. There's a strong current runs along the south, and then away nor'ard up the west coast. Right you was, sir,' says he, 'to haul your wind and keep the weather of the island. Leastways, if such was your intention as to enter and careen, and there ain't no better place for that in these waters.'

'Thank you, my man,' says Captain Smollett. 'I'll ask you, later on, to give us a help. You may go.'

I was surprised at the coolness with which John avowed his knowledge of the island; and I own I was half-frightened when I saw him drawing nearer to myself. He did not know, to be sure, that I had overheard his counsel from the apple barrel, and yet I had, by this time, taken such a horror of his cruelty, duplicity, and power, that I could scarce conceal a shudder when he laid his hand upon my arm.

'Ah,' says he, 'this here is a sweet spot, this island – a sweet spot for a lad to get ashore on. You'll bathe, and you'll climb trees, and you'll hunt goats, you will; and you'll get aloft on them hills like a goat yourself. Why, it makes me young again. I was going to forget my timber leg, I was. It's a pleasant thing to be young, and have ten toes, and you may lay to that. When you want to go a bit of exploring, you just ask old John, and he'll put up a snack for you to take along.'

And clapping me in the friendliest way upon the shoulder, he hobbled off forward and went below.

Captain Smollett, the squire, and Dr Livesey were talking together on the quarterdeck, and, anxious as I was to tell them my story, I durst not interrupt them openly. While I was still casting about in my thoughts to find some probable excuse, Dr Livesey called me to his side. He had left his pipe below, and being a slave to tobacco, had meant that I should fetch it; but as soon as I was near enough to speak and not to be overheard, I broke out immediately: 'Doctor, let me speak. Get the captain and squire down to the cabin, and then make some pretence to send for me. I have terrible news.'

The doctor changed countenance a little, but next moment he was master of himself.

'Thank you, Jim,' said he, quite loudly, 'that was all I wanted to know,' as if he had asked me a question.

And with that he turned on his heel and rejoined the other two. They spoke together for a little, and though none of them started, or raised his voice, or so much as whistled, it was plain enough that Dr Livesey had communicated my request; for the next thing that I heard was the captain giving an order to Job Anderson, and all hands were piped on deck.

'My lads,' said Captain Smollett, 'I've a word to say to you. This land that we have sighted is the place we have been sailing for. Mr Trelawney, being a very open-handed gentleman, as we all know, has just asked me a word or two, and as I was able to tell him that every man on board had done his duty, alow and aloft, as I never ask to see it done better, why, he and I and the doctor are going below to the cabin to drink *your* health and luck, and you'll have grog served out for you to drink *our* health and luck. I'll tell you what I think of this: I think it handsome. And if you think as I do, you'll give a good sea cheer for the gentleman that does it.'

The cheer followed – that was a matter of course; but it rang out so full and hearty, that I confess I could hardly believe these same men were plotting for our blood.

'One more cheer for Cap'n Smollett,' cried Long John, when the first had subsided.

And this also was given with a will.

On the top of that the three gentleman went below, and not long after, word was sent forward that Jim Hawkins was wanted in the cabin.

I found them all three seated round the table, a bottle of Spanish wine and some raisins before them, and the doctor smoking away, with his wig on his lap, and that, I knew, was a sign that he was agitated. The stern window was open, for it was a warm night, and you could see the moon shining behind on the ship's wake.

'Now, Hawkins,' said the squire, 'you have something to say. Speak up.'

I did as I was bid, and as short as I could make it, told the whole details of Silver's conversation. Nobody interrupted me till I was done, nor did any one of the three of them make so much as a movement, but they kept their eyes upon my face from first to last.

'Jim,' said Dr Livesey, 'take a seat.'

And they made me sit down at table beside them, poured me out a glass of wine, filled my hands with raisins, and all three, one after the other, and each with a bow, drank my good health, and their service to me, for my luck and courage.

'Now, captain,' said the squire, 'you were right, and I was wrong. I own myself an ass, and I await your orders.'

'No more an ass than I, sir,' returned the captain. 'I never heard of a crew that meant to mutiny but what showed signs before, for any man that had an eye in his head to see the mischief and take steps according. But this crew,' he added, 'beats me.'

'Captain,' said the doctor, 'with your permission, that's Silver. A very remarkable man.'

'He'd look remarkably well from a yard-arm, sir,' returned the captain. 'But this is talk; this don't lead to anything. I see three or four points, and with Mr Trelawney's permission, I'll name them.'

'You, sir, are the captain. It is for you to speak,' says Mr Trelawney, grandly.

'First point,' began Mr Smollett. 'We must go on, because we can't turn back. If I gave the word to go about, they would rise at once. Second point, we have time before us – at least, until this treasure's found. Third point, there are faithful hands. Now, sir, it's got to come to blows sooner or later; and what I propose is, to take time by the forelock, as the saying is, and come to blows some fine day when they least expect it. We can count, I take it, on your own home servants, Mr Trelawney?'

'As upon myself,' declared the squire.

'Three,' reckoned the captain, 'ourselves make seven, counting Hawkins, here. Now, about the honest hands?'

'Most likely Trelawney's own men,' said the doctor; 'those he had picked up for himself, before he lit on Silver.'

'Nay,' replied the squire, 'Hands was one of mine.'

'I did think I could have trusted Hands,' added the captain.

'And to think that they're all Englishmen!' broke out the squire. 'Sir, I could find it in my heart to blow the ship up.'

'Well, gentlemen,' said the captain, 'the best that I can say is not much. We must lay to, if you please, and keep a bright look-out. It's trying on a man, I know. It would be pleasanter to come to blows. But there's no help for it till we know our men. Lay to, and whistle for a wind, that's my view.'

'Jim here,' said the doctor, 'can help us more than anyone. The men are not shy with him, and Jim is a noticing lad.'

'Hawkins, I put prodigious faith in you,' added the squire.

I began to feel pretty desperate at this, for I felt altogether helpless; and yet, by an odd train of circumstances, it was indeed through me that safety came. In the meantime, talk as we pleased, there were only seven out of the twenty-six on whom we knew we could rely; and out of these seven one was a boy, so that the grown men on our side were six to their nineteen.

PART III
MY SHORE ADVENTURE

How My Shore Adventure Began

THE appearance of the island when I came on deck next morning was altogether changed. Although the breeze had now utterly ceased, we had made a great deal of way during the night, and were now lying becalmed about half a mile to the south-east of the low eastern coast. Grey-coloured woods covered a large part of the surface. This even tint was indeed broken up by streaks of yellow sandbreak in the lower lands, and by many tall trees of the pine family, out-topping the others – some singly, some in clumps; but the general colouring was uniform and sad. The hills ran up clear above the vegetation in spires of naked rock. All were strangely shaped, and the Spy-glass, which was by three or four hundred feet the tallest on the island, was likewise the strangest in configuration, running up sheer from almost every side, then suddenly cut off at the top like a pedestal to put a statue on.

The *Hispaniola* was rolling scuppers under in the ocean swell. The booms were tearing at the blocks, the rudder was banging to and fro, and the whole ship creaking, groaning, and jumping like a manufactory. I had to cling light to the backstay, and the world turned giddily before my eyes; for though I was a good enough sailor when there was way on, this standing still and being rolled about like a bottle was a thing I never learned to stand without a qualm or so, above all in the morning, on an empty stomach.

Perhaps it was this – perhaps it was the look of the island, with its grey, melancholy woods, and wild stone spires, and the surf that we could both see and hear foaming and thundering on the steep beach – at least, although the sun shone bright and hot, and the shore birds were fishing and crying all around us, and you would have thought anyone would have been glad to get to land after being so long at sea, my heart sank, as the saying is, into my boots; and from that first look onward, I hated the very thought of Treasure Island.

We had a dreary morning's work before us, for there was no sign of any wind, and the boats had to be got out and manned, and the ship warped three or four miles round the corner of the island, and up the narrow passage to the haven behind Skeleton Island. I volunteered for one of the boats, where I had, of course, no business. The heat was sweltering, and the men grumbled fiercely over their work. Anderson was in command of my boat, and instead of keeping the crew in order, he grumbled as loud as the worst.

'Well,' he said, with an oath, 'it's not for ever.'

I thought this was a very bad sign; for, up to that day, the men had gone briskly and willingly about their business; but the very sight of the island had relaxed the cords of discipline.

All the way in, Long John stood by the steersman and conned the ship. He knew the passage like the palm of his hand; and though the man in the chains got everywhere more water than was down in the chart, John never hesitated once.

'There's a strong scour with the ebb,' he said, 'and this here passage has been dug out, in a manner of speaking, with a spade.'

We brought up just while the anchor was in the chart, about a third of a mile from each shore, the mainland on one side, and Skeleton Island on the other. The bottom was clean sand. The plunge of our anchor sent up clouds of birds wheeling and crying over the woods; but in less than a minute they were down again, and all was once more silent.

The place was entirely land-locked, buried in woods, the trees coming right down to high-water mark, the shores mostly flat, and the hill-tops standing round at a distance in a sort of amphitheatre, one here, one there. Two little rivers, or, rather, two swamps, emptied out into this pond, as you might call it; and the foliage round that part of the shore had a kind of poisonous brightness. From the ship, we could see nothing of the house or stockade, for they were quite buried among trees; and if it had not been for the chart on the companion, we might have been the first that had ever anchored there since the island arose out of the seas.

There was not a breath of air moving, nor a sound but that of the surf booming half a mile away along the beaches and against the rocks outside. A peculiar stagnant smell hung over the anchorage – a smell of sodden leaves and rotting tree trunks. I observed the doctor sniffing and sniffing, like someone tasting a bad egg.

'I don't know about treasure,' he said, 'but I'll stake my wig there's fever here.'

If the conduct of the men had been alarming in the boat, it became truly threatening when they had come aboard. They lay about the deck growling together in talk. The slightest order was received with a black look, and grudgingly and carelessly obeyed. Even the honest hands must have caught the infection, for there was not one man aboard to mend another. Mutiny, it was plain, hung over us like a thunder-cloud.

And it was not only we of the cabin party who perceived the danger. Long John was hard at work going from group to group, spending himself in good advice, and as for example no man could have shown a better. He fairly outstripped himself in willingness and civility; he was all smiles to everyone. If an order were given, John would be on his crutch in an instant, with the cheeriest 'Ay, ay, sir!' in the world; and when there was nothing else to do, he kept up one song after another, as if to conceal the discontent of the rest.

Of all the gloomy features of that gloomy afternoon, this obvious anxiety on the part of Long John appeared the worst.

We held a council in the cabin.

'Sir,' said the captain, 'if I risk another order, the whole ship'll come about our ears by the run. You see, sir, here it is. I get a rough answer, do I not? Well, if I speak back, pikes will be going in two shakes; if I don't, Silver will see there's something under that, and the game's up. Now, we've only one man to rely on.'

'And who is that?' asked the squire.

'Silver, sir,' returned the captain; 'he's as anxious as you and I to smother things up. This is a tiff; he'd soon talk 'em out of it if he had the chance, and what I propose to do is to give him the chance. Let's allow the men an afternoon ashore. If they all go, why, we'll fight the ship. If they none of them go, well, then, we hold the cabin, and God defend the right. If some go, you mark my words, sir, Silver'll bring 'em aboard again as mild as lambs.'

It was so decided; loaded pistols were served out to all the sure men; Hunter, Joyce, and Redruth were taken into our confidence, and received the news with less surprise and a better spirit than we had looked for, and then the captain went on deck and addressed the crew.

'My lads,' said he, 'we've had a hot day, and are all tired and out of sorts. A turn ashore'll hurt nobody – the boats are still in the water; you can take the gigs, and as many as please may go ashore for the afternoon. I'll fire a gun half an hour before sundown.'

I believe the silly fellows must have thought they would break their shins over treasure as soon as they were landed; for they all came out of their sulks in a moment, and gave a cheer that started the echo in a far-away hill, and sent the birds once more flying and squalling round the anchorage.

The captain was too bright to be in the way. He whipped out of sight in a moment, leaving Silver to arrange the party; and I fancy it was as well he did so. Had he been on deck, he could no longer so much as have pretended not to understand the situation. It was as plain as day. Silver was the captain, and a mighty rebellious crew he had of it. The honest hands – and I was soon to see it proved that there were such on board – must have been stupid fellows. Or, rather, I suppose the truth was this, that all hands were disaffected by the example of the ringleaders – only some more, some less: and a few, being good fellows in the main, could neither be led nor driven any further.

It is one thing to be idle and skulk, and quite another to take a ship and murder a number of innocent men.

At last, however, the party was made up. Six fellows were to stay on board, and the remaining thirteen, including Silver, began to embark.

Then it was that there came into my head the first of the mad notions that contributed so much to save our lives. If six men were left by Silver, it was plain our party could not take and fight the ship; and since only six were left, it was equally plain that the cabin party had no present need of my assistance. It occurred to me at once to go ashore. In a jiffy I had slipped over the side, and curled up in the fore-sheets of the nearest boat, and almost at the same moment she shoved off.

No one took notice of me, only the bow oar saying, 'Is that you, Jim? Keep your head down.' But Silver, from the other boat, looked sharply over and called out to know if that were me; and from that moment I began to regret what I had done.

The crews raced for the beach; but the boat I was in, having some start, and being at once the lighter and the better manned, shot far ahead of her consort, and the bow had struck among the shoreside trees, and I had caught a branch and swung myself out, and plunged into the nearest thicket, while Silver and the rest were still a hundred yards behind.

'Jim, Jim!' I heard him shouting.

But you may suppose I paid no heed; jumping, ducking, and breaking through, I ran straight before my nose, till I could run no longer.

The First Blow

I WAS so pleased at having given the slip to Long John, that I began to enjoy myself and look around me with some interest on the strange land that I was in.

I had crossed a marshy tract full of willows, bulrushes, and odd, outlandish, swampy trees; and I had now come out upon the skirts of an open piece of undulating, sandy country, about a mile long, dotted with a few pines, and a great number of contorted trees, not unlike the oak in growth, but pale in the foliage, like willows. On the far side of the open stood one of the hills, with two quaint, craggy peaks, shining vividly in the sun.

I now felt for the first time the joy of exploration. The isle was uninhabited; my shipmates I had left behind, and nothing lived in front of me but dumb brutes and fowls. I turned hither and thither among the trees. Here and there were flowering plants, unknown to me; here and there I saw snakes, and one raised his head from a ledge of rock and hissed at me with a noise not unlike the spinning of a top. Little did I suppose that he was a deadly enemy, and that the noise was the famous rattle.

Then I came to a long thicket of these oak-like trees – live, or evergreen, oaks, I heard afterwards they should be called – which grew low along the sand like brambles, the boughs curiously twisted, the foliage compact, like thatch. The thicket stretched down from the top of one of the sandy knolls, spreading and growing taller as it went, until it reached the margin of the broad, reedy fen, through which the nearest of the little rivers soaked its way into the anchorage. The marsh was steaming in the strong sun, and the outline of the Spy-glass trembled through the haze.

All at once there began to go a sort of bustle among

the bulrushes; a wild duck flew up with a quack, another followed, and soon over the whole surface of the marsh a great cloud of birds hung screaming and circling in the air. I judged at once that some of my shipmates must be drawing near along the borders of the fen. Nor was I deceived; for soon I heard the very distant and low tones of a human voice, which, as I continued to give ear, grew steadily louder and nearer.

This put me in a great fear, and I crawled under cover of the nearest live-oak, and squatted there, hearkening, as silent as a mouse.

Another voice answered; and then the first voice, which I now recognised to be Silver's, once more took up the story, and ran on for a long while in a stream, only now and again interrupted by the other. By the sound they must have been talking earnestly, and almost fiercely; but no distinct word came to my hearing.

At last the speakers seemed to have paused, and perhaps to have sat down; for not only did they cease to draw any nearer, but the birds themselves began to grow more quiet, and to settle again to their places in the swamp.

And now I began to feel that I was neglecting my business; that since I had been so foolhardy as to come ashore with these desperadoes, the least I could do was to overhear them at their councils; and that my plain and obvious duty was to draw as close as I could manage, under the favourable ambush of the crouching trees.

I could tell the direction of the speakers pretty exactly, not only by the sound of their voices, but by the behaviour of the few birds that still hung in alarm above the heads of the intruders.

Crawling on all-fours, I made steadily but slowly towards them; till at last, raising my head to an aperture among the leaves, I could see clear down into a little green dell beside the marsh, and closely set about with trees, where Long John Silver and another of the crew stood face to face in conversation.

The sun beat full upon them. Silver had thrown his hat beside him on the ground, and his great, smooth, blond face, all shining with heat, was lifted to the other man's in a kind of appeal.

'Mate,' he was saying, 'it's because I thinks gold dust of you – gold dust, and you may lay to that! If I hadn't took to you like pitch, do you think I'd have been here a-warning of you? All's up – you can't make nor mend; it's to save your neck that I'm a-speaking, and if one of the wild 'uns knew it, where 'ud I be, Tom – now, tell me, where 'ud I be?'

'Silver,' said the other man – and I observed he was not only red in the face, but spoke as hoarse as a crow, and his voice shook, too, like a taut rope – 'Silver,' says he, 'you're old, and you're honest, or has the name for it; and you've money, too, which lots of poor sailors hasn't; and you're brave, or I'm mistook. And will you tell me you'll let yourself be led away with that kind of a mess of swabs? not you! As sure as God sees me, I'd sooner lose my hand. If I turn agin my dooty—'

And then all of a sudden he was interrupted by a noise. I had found one of the honest hands – well, here, at that same moment, came news of another. Far away out in the marsh there arose, all of a sudden, a sound like the cry of anger, then another on the back of it; and then one horrid, long-drawn scream. The rocks of the Spy-glass re-echoed it a score of times; the whole troop of marsh-birds rose again, darkening heaven, with a simultaneous whirr; and long after that death yell was still ringing in my brain, silence had re-established its empire, and only the rustle of the redescending birds and the boom of the distant surges disturbed the languor of the afternoon.

Tom had leaped at the sound, like a horse at the spur; but Silver had not winked an eye. He stood where he was, resting lightly on his crutch, watching his companion like a snake about to spring.

'John!' said the sailor, stretching out his hand.

'Hands off!' cried Silver, leaping back a yard, as it seemed to me, with the speed and security of a trained gymnast.

'Hands off, if you like, John Silver,' said the other. 'It's a black conscience that can make you feared of me. But, in heaven's name, tell me what was that?'

'That?' returned Silver, smiling away, but warier than ever, his eye a mere pin-point in his big face, but gleaming like a crumb of glass. 'That? Oh, I reckon that'll be Alan.'

And at this poor Tom flashed out like a hero.

'Alan!' he cried. 'Then rest his soul for a true seaman! And as for you, John Silver, long you've been a mate of mine, but you're mate of mine no more. If I die like a dog, I'll die in my dooty. You've killed Alan, have you? Kill me, too, if you can. But I defies you.'

And with that, this brave fellow turned his back directly on the cook, and set off walking for the beach. But he was not destined to go far. With a cry, John seized the branch of a tree, whipped the crutch out of his armpit, and sent that uncouth missile hurtling through the air. It struck poor Tom, point foremost, and with stunning violence, right between the shoulders in the middle of his back. His hands flew up, he gave a sort of gasp, and fell.

Whether he were injured much or little, none could ever tell. Like enough, to judge from the sound, his back was broken on the spot. But he had no time given him to recover. Silver, agile as a monkey, even without leg or crutch, was on the top of him next moment, and had twice buried his knife up to the hilt in that defenceless body. From my place of ambush, I could hear him pant aloud as he struck the blows.

I do not know what it rightly is to faint, but I do know that for the next little while the whole world swam away from before me in a whirling mist; Silver and the birds, and the tall Spy-glass hill-top, going round and round and topsy-turvy before my eyes, and all manner of bells ringing and distant voices shouting in my ear.

When I came again to myself, the monster had pulled himself together, his crutch under his arm, his hat upon his head. Just before him Tom lay motionless upon the sward; but the murderer minded him not a whit, cleansing his bloodstained knife the while upon a wisp of grass. Everything else was unchanged, the sun still shining mercilessly on the steaming marsh and the tall pinnacle of the mountain, and I could scarce persuade myself that murder had been actually done, and a human life cruelly cut short a moment since, before my eyes.

But now John put his hand into his pocket, brought out a whistle, and blew upon it several modulated blasts, that rang far across the heated air. I could not tell, of course, the meaning of the signal; but it instantly awoke my fears. More men would be coming. I might be discovered. They had already slain two of the honest people; after Tom and Alan, might not I come next?

Instantly I began to extricate myself and crawl back again, with what speed and silence I could manage, to the more open portion of the wood. As I did so, I could hear hails coming and going between the old buccaneer and his comrades, and this sound of danger lent me wings. As soon as I was clear of the thicket, I ran as I never ran before, scarce minding the direction of my flight, so long as it led me from the murderers; and as I ran, fear grew and grew upon me, until it turned into a kind of frenzy.

Indeed, could anyone be more entirely lost than I? When the gun fired, how should I dare to go down to the boats among those fiends, still smoking from their crime? Would not the first of them who saw me wring my neck like a snipe's? Would not my absence itself be an evidence to them of my alarm, and therefore of my fatal knowledge? It was all over, I thought. Good-bye to the *Hispaniola*; good-bye to the squire, the doctor, and the captain! There was nothing left for me but death by starvation, or death by the hands of the mutineers.

All this while, as I say, I was still running, and, without taking any notice, I had drawn near to the foot of the little hill with the two peaks, and had got into a part of the island where the live-oaks grew more widely apart, and seemed more like forest trees in their bearing and dimensions. Mingled with these were a few scattered pines, some fifty, some nearer seventy, feet high. The air, too, smelt more freshly than down beside the marsh.

And here a fresh alarm brought me to a standstill with a thumping heart.

The Man of the Island

FROM THE side of the hill, which was here steep and stony, a spout of gravel was dislodged, and fell rattling and bounding through the trees. My eyes turned instinctively in that direction, and I saw a figure leap with great rapidity behind the trunk of a pine. What it was, whether bear or man or monkey, I could in no wise tell. It seemed dark and shaggy; more I knew not. But the terror of this new apparition brought me to a stand.

I was now, it seemed, cut off upon both sides; behind me the murderers, before me this lurking nondescript. And immediately I began to prefer the dangers that I knew to those I knew not. Silver himself appeared less terrible in contrast with this creature of the woods, and I turned on my heel, and, looking sharply behind me over my shoulder, began to retrace my steps in the direction of the boats.

Instantly the figure reappeared, and, making a wide circuit, began to head me off. I was tired, at any rate; but had I been as fresh as when I rose, I could see it was in vain for me to contend in speed with such an adversary. From trunk to trunk the creature flitted like a deer, running manlike on two legs, but unlike any man that I had ever seen, stooping almost double as it ran. Yet a man it was, I could no longer be in doubt about that.

I began to recall what I had heard of cannibals. I was within an ace of calling for help. But the mere fact that he was a man, however wild, had somewhat reassured me, and my fear of Silver began to revive in proportion. I stood still, therefore, and cast about for some method of escape; and as I was so thinking, the recollection of my pistol flashed into my mind. As soon as I remembered I was not defenceless, courage glowed again in my heart;

and I set my face resolutely for this man of the island, and walked briskly towards him.

He was concealed by this time, behind another tree trunk; but he must have been watching me closely, for as soon as I began to move in his direction he reappeared and took a step to meet me. Then he hesitated, drew back, came forward again, and at last, to my wonder and confusion, threw himself on his knees and held out his clasped hands in supplication.

At that I once more stopped.

'Who are you?' I asked.

'Ben Gunn,' he answered, and his voice sounded hoarse and awkward, like a rusty lock. 'I'm poor Ben Gunn, I am; and I haven't spoke with a Christian these three years.'

I could now see that he was a white man like myself, and that his features were even pleasing. His skin, wherever it was exposed, was burnt by the sun; even his lips were black; and his fair eyes looked quite startling in so dark a face. Of all the beggar-men that I had seen or fancied, he was the chief for raggedness. He was clothed with tatters of old ship's canvas and old sea cloth; and this extraordinary patchwork was all held together by a system of the most various and incongruous fastenings, brass buttons, bits of stick, and loops of tarry gaskin. About his waist he wore an old brass-buckled leather belt, which was the one thing solid in his whole accoutrement.

'Three years!' I cried. 'Were you shipwrecked?'

'Nay, mate,' said he – 'marooned.'

I had heard the word, and I knew it stood for a horrible kind of punishment common enough among the buccaneers, in which the offender is put ashore with a little powder and shot, and left behind on some desolate and distant island.

'Marooned three years agone,' he continued, 'and lived on goats since then, and berries, and oysters. Wherever a man is, says I, a man can do for himself. But, mate, my heart is sore for Christian diet. You mightn't happen to have a piece of cheese about you, now? No? Well, many's the long night I've dreamed of cheese – toasted, mostly – and woke up again, and here I were.'

'If ever I can get aboard again,' said I, 'you shall have cheese by the stone.'

All this time he had been feeling the stuff of my jacket, smoothing my hands, looking at my boots, and generally, in the intervals of his speech, showing a childish pleasure in the presence of a fellow-creature. But at my last words he perked up into a kind of startled slyness.

'If ever you can get aboard again, says you?' he repeated. 'Why, now, who's to hinder you?'

'Not you, I know,' was my reply.

'And right you was,' he cried. 'Now you – what do you call yourself, mate?'

'Jim,' I told him.

'Jim, Jim,' says he, quite pleased apparently. 'Well, now, Jim, I've lived that rough as you'd be ashamed to hear of. Now, for instance, you wouldn't think I had had a pious mother – to look at me?' he asked.

'Why, no, not in particular,' I answered.

'Ah, well,' said he, 'but I had – remarkable pious. And I was a civil, pious boy, and could rattle off my catechism that fast, as you couldn't tell one word from another. And here's what it come to, Jim, and it begun with chuck-farthen on the blessed grave-stones! That's what it begun with, but it went further'n that; and so my mother told me, and predicked the whole, she did, the pious woman! But it were Providence that put me here. I've thought it all out in this here lonely island, and I'm back on piety. You don't catch me tasting rum so much; but just a thimbleful for luck, of course, the first chance I have. I'm bound I'll be good, and I see the way to. And, Jim' – looking all round him, and lowering his voice to a whisper – 'I'm rich.'

I now felt sure that the poor fellow had gone crazy in his solitude, and I suppose I must have shown the feeling in my face, for he repeated the statement hotly:—

'Rich! rich! I says. And I'll tell you what: I'll make a man of you, Jim. Ah, Jim, you'll bless your stars, you will, you was the first that found me!'

And at this there came suddenly a lowering shadow over his face; and he tightened his grasp upon my hand, and raised a forefinger threateningly before my eyes.

'Now, Jim, you tell me true: that ain't Flint's ship?' he asked.

At this I had a happy inspiration. I began to believe that I had found an ally, and I answered him at once.

'It's not Flint's ship, and Flint is dead; but I'll tell you true, as you ask me – there are some of Flint's hands aboard; worse luck for the rest of us.'

'Not a man – with one – leg?' he gasped.

'Silver?' I asked.

'Ah, Silver!' says he; 'that were his name.'

'He's the cook; and the ringleader, too.'

He was still holding me by the wrist, and at that he gave it quite a wring.

'If you was sent by Long John,' he said, 'I'm as good as pork, and I know it. But where was you, do you suppose?'

I had made my mind up in a moment, and by way of answer told him the whole story of our voyage, and the predicament in which we found ourselves. He heard me with the keenest interest, and when I had done he patted me on the head.

'You're a good lad, Jim,' he said; 'and you're all in a clove hitch, ain't you? Well, you just put your trust in Ben Gunn – Ben Gunn's the man to do it. Would you think it likely, now, that your squire would prove a liberal-minded one in case of help – him being in a clove hitch, as you remark?'

I told him the squire was the most liberal of men.

'Ay, but you see,' returned Ben Gunn, 'I didn't mean giving me a gate to keep, and a shuit of livery clothes, and such; that's not my mark, Jim. What I mean is, would he be likely to come down to the toon of, say one thousand pounds out of money that's as good as a man's own already?'

'I am sure he would,' said I. 'As it was, all hands were to share.'

'*And* a passage home?' he added, with a look of great shrewdness.

'Why,' I cried, 'the squire's a gentleman. And, besides, if we got rid of the others, we should want you to help work the vessel home.'

'Ah,' said he, 'so you would.' And he seemed very much relieved.

'Now, I'll tell you what,' he went on. 'So much I'll tell you, and no more. I were in Flint's ship when he buried the treasure; he and six along – six strong seamen. They were ashore nigh on a week, and us standing off and on in the old *Walrus*. One fine day up went the signal, and here come Flint by himself in a little boat, and his head done up in a blue scarf. The sun was getting up, and mortal white he looked about the cut-water. But, there he was, you mind, and the six all dead – dead and buried. How he done it, not a man aboard us could make out. It was battle, murder, and sudden death, leastways – him against six. Billy Bones was the mate; Long John, he was quartermaster; and they asked him where the treasure was. "Ah," says he, "you can go ashore, if you like, and stay," he says; "but as for the ship, she'll beat up for more, by thunder!" That's what he said.

'Well, I was in another ship three years back, and we sighted this island. "Boys," said I, "here's Flint's treasure; let's land and find it." The cap'n was displeased at that; but my messmates were all of a mind, and landed. Twelve days they looked for it, and every day they had the worse word for me, until one fine morning all hands went aboard. "As for you, Benjamin Gunn," says they, "here's a musket," they says, "and a spade, and pick-axe. You can stay here, and find Flint's money for yourself," they says.

'Well, Jim, three years have I been here, and not a bite of Christian diet from that day to this. But now, you look here; look at me. Do I look like a man before the mast? No, says you. Nor I weren't, neither, I says.'

And with that he winked and pinched me hard.

'Just you mention them words to your squire, Jim' – he went on: 'Nor he weren't, neither – that's the words. Three years he were the man of this island, light and dark, fair and rain; and sometimes he would, maybe, think upon a prayer (says you), and sometimes he would, maybe, think of his old mother, so be as she's alive (you'll say); but the most part of Gunn's time (this is what you'll say) – the most part of his time was took up with another matter. And then you'll give him a nip, like I do.'

And he pinched me again in the most confidential manner.

'Then,' he continued – 'then you'll up, and you'll say this:— Gunn is a good man (you'll say), and he puts a precious sight more confidence – a precious sight, mind that – in a gen'leman born than in these gen'lemen of fortune, having been one hisself.'

'Well,' I said, 'I don't understand one word that you've been saying. But that's neither here nor there; for how am I to get on board?'

'Ah,' said he, 'that's the hitch, for sure. Well, there's my boat, that I made with my two hands. I keep her under the white rock. If the worst come to the worst, we might try that after dark. Hi!' he broke out, 'what's that?'

For just then, although the sun had still an hour or two to run, all the echoes of the island awoke and bellowed to the thunder of a cannon.

'They have begun to fight!' I cried. 'Follow me.'

And I began to run towards the anchorage, my terrors all forgotten; while, close at my side, the marooned man in his goatskins trotted easily and lightly.

'Left, left,' says he; 'keep to your left hand, mate Jim! Under the trees with you! Theer's where I killed my first goat. They don't come down here now; they're all mast-headed on them mountings for the fear of Benjamin Gunn. Ah! and there's the cetemery' – cemetery, he must have meant. 'You see the mounds? I come here and prayed, nows and thens, when I thought maybe a Sunday would be about doo. It weren't quite a chapel, but it seemed more solemn like; and then, says you, Ben Gunn was short-handed – no chapling, nor so much as a Bible and a flag, you says.'

So he kept talking as I ran, neither expecting nor receiving any answer.

The cannon-shot was followed, after a considerable interval, by a volley of small arms.

Another pause, and then, not a quarter of a mile in front of me, I beheld the Union Jack flutter in the air above a wood.

PART IV
THE STOCKADE

Narrative Continued by the Doctor: How the Ship was Abandoned

IT was about half-past one – three bells in the sea phrase – that the two boats went ashore from the *Hispaniola*. The captain, the squire, and I were talking matters over in the cabin. Had there been a breath of wind we should have fallen on the six mutineers who were left aboard with us, slipped our cable, and away to sea. But the wind was wanting; and, to complete our helplessness, down came Hunter with the news that Jim Hawkins had slipped into a boat and gone ashore with the rest.

It never occurred to us to doubt Jim Hawkins; but we were alarmed for his safety. With the men in the temper they were in, it seemed an even chance if we should see the lad again. We ran on deck. The pitch was bubbling in the seams; the nasty stench of the place turned me sick; if ever a man smelt fever and dysentery, it was in that abominable anchorage. The six scoundrels were sitting grumbling under a sail in the forecastle; ashore we could see the gigs made fast, and a man sitting in each, hard by where the river runs in. One of them was whistling 'Lillibullero.'

Waiting was a strain; and it was decided that Hunter and I should go ashore with the jolly-boat, in quest of information. The gigs had leaned to their right; but Hunter and I pulled straight in, in the direction of the stockade upon the chart. The two who were left guarding their boats seemed in a bustle at our appearance; 'Lillibullero' stopped off, and I could see the pair discussing what they ought to do. Had they gone and told Silver, all might have turned out differently; but they had their orders, I suppose, and decided to sit quietly where they were and hark back again to 'Lillibullero.'

There was a slight bend in the coast, and I steered so as to put it between us; even before we landed we had thus lost sight of the gigs. I jumped out, and came as near running as I durst, with a big silk handkerchief under my hat for coolness' sake, and a brace of pistols ready primed for safety.

I had not gone a hundred yards when I reached the stockade.

This was how it was: a spring of clear water rose almost at the top of a knoll. Well, on the knoll, and enclosing the spring, they had clapped a stout log-house, fit to hold two score of people on a pinch, and loop-holed for musketry on every side. All round this they had cleared a wide space, and then the thing was completed by a paling six feet high, without door or opening, too strong to pull down without time and labour, and too open to shelter the besiegers. The people in the log-house had them in every way; they stood quiet in shelter and shot the others like partridges. All they wanted was a good watch and food; for, short of a complete surprise, they might have held the place against a regiment.

What particularly took my fancy was the spring. For, though we had a good enough place of it in the cabin of the *Hispaniola*, with plenty of arms and ammunition, and things to eat, and excellent wines, there had been one thing overlooked – we had no water. I was thinking this over, when there came ringing over the island the cry of a man at the point of death. I was not new to violent death – I have served his Royal Highness the Duke of Cumberland, and got a wound myself at Fontenoy – but I know my pulse went dot and carry one. 'Jim Hawkins is gone' was my first thought.

It is something to have been an old soldier, but more still to have been a doctor. There is no time to dilly-dally in our work. And so now I made up my mind instantly, and with no time lost returned to the shore, and jumped on board the jolly-boat.

By good fortune Hunter pulled a good oar. We made the water fly; and the boat was soon alongside, and I aboard the schooner.

I found them all shaken, as was natural. The squire was sitting down, as white as a sheet, thinking of the harm he had led us to, the good soul! and one of the six forecastle hands was little better.

'There's a man,' says Captain Smollett, nodding towards him, 'new to this work. He came nigh-hand fainting, doctor, when he heard the cry. Another touch of the rudder and that man would join us.'

I told my plan to the captain, and between us we settled on the details of its accomplishment.

We put old Redruth in the gallery between the cabin and the forecastle, with three or four loaded muskets and a mattress for protection. Hunter brought the boat round under the stern-port, and Joyce and I set to work loading her with powder tins, muskets, bags of biscuits, kegs of pork, a cask of cognac, and my invaluable medicine chest.

In the meantime, the squire and the captain stayed on deck, and the latter hailed the coxswain, who was the principal man aboard.

'Mr Hands,' he said, 'here are two of us with a brace of pistols each. If any one of you six make a signal of any description, that man's dead.'

They were a good deal taken aback; and, after a little consultation, one and all tumbled down the fore companion, thinking, no doubt, to take us on the rear. But when they saw Redruth waiting for them in the sparred gallery, they went about ship at once, and a head popped out again on deck.

'Down, dog!' cries the captain.

And the head popped back again; and we heard no more, for the time, of these six very faint-hearted seamen.

By this time, tumbling things in as they came, we had the jolly-boat loaded as much as we dared. Joyce and I got out through the stern-port, and we made for shore again, as fast as oars could take us.

This second trip fairly aroused the watchers along shore. 'Lillibullero' was dropped again; and just before we lost sight of them behind the little point, one of them whipped ashore and disappeared. I had half a mind to change my plan and destroy their boats, but I feared that Silver and

the others might be close at hand, and all might very well
be lost by trying for too much.

We had soon touched land in the same place as before,
and set to provision the block house. All three made the
first journey, heavily laden, and tossed our stores over the
palisade. Then, leaving Joyce to guard them – one man,
to be sure, but with half a dozen muskets – Hunter and
I returned to the jolly-boat, and loaded ourselves once
more. So we proceeded without pausing to take breath,
till the whole cargo was bestowed, when the two servants
took up their position in the block house, and I, with all
my power, sculled back to the *Hispaniola*.

That we should have risked a second boat load seems
more daring than it really was. They had the advantage of
numbers, of course, but we had the advantage of arms. Not
one of the men ashore had a musket, and before they could
get within range for pistol shooting, we flattered ourselves
we should be able to give a good account of a half-dozen
at least.

The squire was waiting for me at the stern window, all
his faintness gone from him. He caught the painter and
made it fast, and we fell to loading the boat for our very
lives. Pork, powder, and biscuit was the cargo, with only
a musket and a cutlass apiece for the squire and me and
Redruth and the captain. The rest of the arms and powder
we dropped overboard in two fathoms and a half of water,
so that we could see the bright steel shining far below us
in the sun, on the clean, sandy bottom.

By this time the tide was beginning to ebb, and the ship
was swinging round to her anchor. Voices were heard faintly
halloaing in the direction of the two gigs; and though this
reassured us for Joyce and Hunter, who were well to the
eastward, it warned our party to be off.

Redruth retreated from his place in the gallery, and
dropped into the boat, which we then brought round to
the ship's counter, to be handier for Captain Smollett.

'Now men,' said he, 'do you hear me?'

There was no answer from the forecastle.

'It's to you, Abraham Gray – it's to you, I am speaking.'

Still no reply.

'Gray,' resumed Mr Smollett, a little louder, 'I am leaving this ship, and I order you to follow your captain. I know you are a good man at bottom, and I daresay not one of the lot of you's as bad as he makes out. I have my watch here in my hand; I give you thirty seconds to join me in.'

There was a pause.

'Come, my fine fellow,' continued the captain, 'don't hang so long in stays. I'm risking my life, and the lives of these good gentlemen every second.'

There was a sudden scuffle, a sound of blows, and out burst Abraham Gray with a knife-cut on the side of the cheek, and came running to the captain, like a dog to the whistle.

'I'm with you, sir,' said he.

And the next moment he and the captain had dropped aboard of us, and we had showed off and given way.

We were clear out of the ship; but not yet ashore in our stockade.

Narrative Continued by the Doctor: the Jolly-boat's Last Trip

THIS FIFTH trip was quite different from any of the others. In the first place, the little gallipot of a boat that we were in was gravely overloaded. Five grown men, and three of them – Trelawney, Redruth, and the captain – over six feet high, was already more than she was meant to carry. Add to that the powder, pork, and bread-bags. The gunwale was lipping astern. Several times we shipped a little water, and my breeches and the tails of my coat were all soaking wet before we had gone a hundred yards.

The captain made us trim the boat, and we got her to lie a little more evenly. All the same, we were afraid to breathe.

In the second place, the ebb was now making – a strong rippling current running westward through the basin, and then south'ard and seaward down the straits by which we had entered in the morning. Even the ripples were a danger to our overloaded craft; but the worst of it was that we were swept out of our true course, and away from our proper landing-place behind the point. If we let the current have its way we should come ashore beside the gigs, where the pirates might appear at any moment.

'I cannot keep her head for the stockade, sir,' said I to the captain. I was steering, while he and Redruth, two fresh men, were at the oars. 'The tide keeps washing her down. Could you pull a little stronger?'

'Not without swamping the boat,' said he. 'You must bear up, sir, if you please – bear up until you see you're gaining.'

I tried, and found by experiment that the tide kept sweeping us westward until I had laid her head due east, or just about right angles to the way we ought to go.

'We'll never get ashore at this rate,' said I.

'If it's the only course that we can lie, sir, we must even lie it,' returned the captain. 'We must keep up-stream. You see, sir,' he went on, 'if once we dropped to leeward of the landing-place, it's hard to say where we should get ashore, besides the chance of being boarded by the gigs; whereas, the way we go the current must slacken, and then we can dodge back along the shore.'

'The current's less a'ready, sir,' said the man Gray, who was sitting in the fore-sheets; 'you can ease her off a bit.'

'Thank you, my man,' said I, quite as if nothing had happened; for we had all quietly made up our minds to treat him like one of ourselves.

Suddenly the captain spoke up again, and I thought his voice was a little changed.

'The gun!' said he.

'I have thought of that,' said I, for I made sure he was thinking of a bombardment of the fort. 'They could never get the gun ashore, and if they did, they could never haul it through the woods.'

'Look astern, doctor,' replied the captain.

We had entirely forgotten the long nine; and there, to our horror, were the five rogues busy about her, getting off her jacket, as they called the stout tarpaulin cover under which she sailed. Not only that, but it flashed into my mind at the same moment that the round-shot and the powder for the gun had been left behind, and a stroke with an axe would put it all into the possession of the evil ones aboard.

'Israel was Flint's gunner,' said Gray, hoarsely.

At any risk, we put the boat's head direct for the landing-place. By this time we had got so far out of the run of the current that we kept steerage way even at our necessarily gentle rate of rowing, and I could keep her steady for the goal. But the worst of it was, that with the course I now held, we turned our broadside instead of our stern to the *Hispaniola*, and offered a target like a barn door.

I could hear, as well as see, that brandy-faced rascal, Israel Hands, plumping down a round-shot on the deck.

'Who's the best shot?' asked the captain.

'Mr Trelawney, out and away,' said I.

'Mr Trelawney, will you please pick me off one of these men, sir? Hands, if possible,' said the captain.

Trelawney was as cool as steel. He looked to the priming of his gun.

'Now,' cried the captain, 'easy with that gun, sir, or you'll swamp the boat. All hands stand by to trim her when he aims.'

The squire raised his gun, the rowing ceased, and we leaned over to the other side to keep the balance, and all was so nicely contrived that we did not ship a drop.

They had the gun, by this time, slewed round upon the swivel, and Hands, who was at the muzzle with the rammer, was, in consequence, the most exposed. However, we had no luck; for just as Trelawney fired, down he stooped, the ball whistled over him, and it was one of the other four who fell.

The cry he gave was echoed, not only by his companions on board, but by a great number of voices from the shore, and looking in that direction I saw the other pirates trooping out from among the trees and tumbling into their places in the boats.

'Here come the gigs, sir,' said I.

'Give way then,' cried the captain. 'We mustn't mind if we swamp her now. If we can't get ashore, all's up.'

'Only one of the gigs is being manned, sir,' I added, 'the crew of the other most likely going round by shore to cut us off.'

'They'll have a hot run, sir,' returned the captain. 'Jack ashore, you know. It's not them I mind; it's the round-shot. Carpet-bowls! My lady's maid couldn't miss. Tell us, squire, when you see the match, and we'll hold water.'

In the meanwhile we had been making headway at a good pace for a boat so overloaded, and we had shipped but little water in the process. We were now close in; thirty or forty strokes and we should beach her; for the ebb had already disclosed a narrow belt of sand below the clustering trees. The gig was no longer to be feared; the little point had already concealed it from our eyes. The ebb-tide, which had so cruelly delayed us, was now making reparation, and delaying our assailants. The one source of danger was the gun.

'If I durst,' said the captain, 'I'd stop and pick off another man.'

But it was plain that they meant nothing should delay their shot. They had never so much as looked at their fallen comrade, though he was not dead, and I could see him trying to crawl away.

'Ready!' cried the squire.

'Hold!' cried the captain, quick as an echo.

And he and Redruth backed with a great heave that sent her stern bodily under water. The report fell in at the same instant of time. This was the first that Jim heard, the sound of the squire's shot not having reached him. Where the ball passed, not one of us precisely knew; but I fancy it must have been over our heads, and that the wind of it may have contributed to our disaster.

At any rate, the boat sank by the stern, quite gently, in three feet of water, leaving the captain and myself, facing each other, on our feet. The other three took complete headers, and came up again, drenched and bubbling.

So far there was no great harm. No lives were lost, and we could wade ashore in safety. But there were all our stores at the bottom, and, to make things worse, only two guns out of five remained in a state for service. Mine I had snatched from my knees and held over my head, by a sort of instinct. As for the captain, he had carried his over his shoulder by a bandoleer, and, like a wise man, lock uppermost. The other three had gone down with the boat.

To add to our concern, we heard voices already drawing near us in the woods along shore; and we had not only the danger of being cut off from the stockade in our half-crippled state, but the fear before us whether, if Hunter and Joyce were attacked by half a dozen, they would have the sense and conduct to stand firm. Hunter was steady, that we knew; Joyce was a doubtful case – a pleasant, polite man for a valet, and to brush one's clothes, but not entirely fitted for a man of war.

With all this in our minds, we waded ashore as fast as we could, leaving behind us the poor jolly-boat, and a good half of all our powder and provisions.

Narrative Continued by the Doctor: End of the First Day's Fighting

WE made our best speed across the strip of wood that now divided us from the stockade; and at every step we took the voices of the buccaneers rang nearer. Soon we could hear their footfalls as they ran, and the cracking of the branches as they breasted across a bit of thicket.

I began to see we should have a brush for it in earnest, and looked to my priming.

'Captain,' said I, 'Trelawney is the dead shot. Give him your gun; his own is useless.'

They exchanged guns, and Trelawney, silent and cool as he had been since the beginning of the bustle, hung a moment on his heel to see that all was fit for service. At the same time, observing Gray to be unarmed, I handed him my cutlass. It did all our hearts good to see him spit in his hand, knit his brows, and make the blade sing through the air. It was plain from every line of his body that our new hand was worth his salt.

Forty paces farther we came to the edge of the wood and saw the stockade in front of us. We struck the enclosure about the middle of the south side, and, almost at the same time, seven mutineers – Job Anderson, the boatswain, at their head – appeared in full cry at the south-western corner.

They paused, as if taken aback; and before they recovered, not only the squire and I, but Hunter and Joyce from the block house, had time to fire. The four shots came in rather a scattering volley; but they did the business: one of the enemy actually fell, and the rest, without hesitation, turned and plunged into the trees.

After reloading, we walked down the outside of the

palisade to see the fallen enemy. He was stone dead –
shot through the heart.

We began to rejoice over our good success, when just at
that moment a pistol cracked in the bush, a ball whistled
close past my ear, and poor Tom Redruth stumbled and
fell his length on the ground. Both the squire and I returned
the shot; but as we had nothing to aim at, it is probable we
only wasted powder. Then we reloaded, and turned our
attention to poor Tom.

The captain and Gray were already examining him; and
I saw with half an eye that all was over.

I believe the readiness of our return volley had scattered
the mutineers once more, for we were suffered without
further molestation to get the poor old gamekeeper hoisted
over the stockade, and carried, groaning and bleeding, into
the log-house.

Poor old fellow, he had not uttered one word of surprise,
complaint, fear, or even acquiescence, from the very beginning of our troubles till now, when we had laid him down in
the log-house to die. He had lain like a Trojan behind his
mattress in the gallery; he had followed every order silently,
doggedly, and well; he was the oldest of our party by a score
of years; and now, sullen, old, serviceable servant, it was he
that was to die.

The squire dropped down beside him on his knees and
kissed his hand, crying like a child.

'Be I going, doctor?' he asked.

'Tom, my man,' said I, 'you're going home.'

'I wish I had had a lick at them with the gun first,' he
replied.

'Tom,' said the squire, 'say you forgive me, won't
you?'

'Would that be respectful like, from me to you, squire?'
was the answer. 'Howsoever, so be it, amen!'

After a little while of silence, he said he thought somebody
might read a prayer. 'It's the custom, sir,' he added,
apologetically. And not long after, without another word,
he passed away.

In the meantime the captain, whom I had observed to
be wonderfully swollen about the chest and pockets, had

turned out a great many various stores – the British colours, a Bible, a coil of stoutish rope, pen, ink, the log-book, and pounds of tobacco. He had found a longish fir-tree lying felled and trimmed in the enclosure, and, with the help of Hunter, he had set it up at the corner of the log-house where the trunks crossed and made an angle. Then, climbing on the roof, he had with his own hand bent and run up the colours.

This seemed mightily to relieve him. He re-entered the log-house, and set about counting up the stores, as if nothing else existed. But he had an eye on Tom's passage for all that; and as soon as all was over, came forward with another flag, and reverently spread it on the body.

'Don't you take on, sir,' he said, shaking the squire's hand. 'All's well with him; no fear for a hand that's been shot down in his duty to captain and owner. It mayn't be good divinity, but it's a fact.'

Then he pulled me aside.

'Dr Livesey,' he said, 'in how many weeks do you and squire expect the consort?'

I told him it was a question, not of weeks, but of months; that if we were not back by the end of August, Blandly was to send to find us; but neither sooner nor later. 'You can calculate for yourself,' I said.

'Why, yes,' returned the captain, scratching his head, 'and making a large allowance, sir, for all the gifts of Providence, I should say we were pretty close hauled.'

'How do you mean?' I asked.

'It's a pity, sir, we lost that second load. That's what I mean,' replied the captain. 'As for powder and shot, we'll do. But the rations are short, very short – so short, Dr Livesey, that we're, perhaps, as well without that extra mouth.'

And he pointed to the dead body under the flag.

Just then, with a roar and a whistle, a round-shot passed high above the roof of the log-house and plumped far beyond us in the wood.

'Oho!' said the captain. 'Blaze away! You've little enough powder already, my lads.'

At the second trial, the aim was better, and the ball

descended inside the stockade, scattering a cloud of sand, but doing no further damage.

'Captain,' said the squire, 'the house is quite invisible from the ship. It must be the flag they are aiming at. Would it not be wiser to take it in?'

'Strike my colours!' cried the captain. 'No, sir, not I;' and, as soon as he had said the words, I think we all agreed with him. For it was not only a piece of stout, seamanly, good feeling; it was good policy besides, and showed our enemies that we despised their cannonade.

All through the evening they kept thundering away. Ball after ball flew over or fell short, or kicked up the sand in the enclosure; but they had to fire so high that the shot fell dead and buried itself in the soft sand. We had no ricochet to fear; and though one popped in through the roof of the log-house and out again through the floor, we soon got used to that sort of horse-play, and minded it no more than cricket.

'There is one thing good about all this,' observed the captain; 'the wood in front of us is likely clear. The ebb has made a good while; our stores should be uncovered. Volunteers to go and bring in pork.'

Gray and Hunter were the first to come forward. Well armed, they stole out of the stockade; but it proved a useless mission. The mutineers were bolder than we fancied, or they put more trust in Israel's gunnery. For four or five of them were busy carrying off our stores, and wading out with them to one of the gigs that lay close by, pulling an oar or so to hold her steady against the current. Silver was in the stern-sheets in command; and every man of them was now provided with a musket from some secret magazine of their own.

The captain sat down to his log, and here is the beginning of the entry:—

'Alexander Smollett, master; David Livesey, ship's doctor; Abraham Gray, carpenter's mate; John Trelawney, owner; John Hunter and Richard Joyce, owner's servants, landsmen – being all that is left faithful of the ship's company – with stores for ten days at short rations, came ashore this day, and flew British colours on the log-house in Treasure Island. Thomas Redruth, owner's servant, landsman, shot by the mutineers; James Hawkins, cabin-boy—'

And at the same time I was wondering over poor Jim Hawkins's fate.

A hail on the land side.

'Somebody hailing us,' said Hunter, who was on guard.

'Doctor! squire! captain! Hullo, Hunter, is that you?' came the cries.

And I ran to the door in time to see Jim Hawkins, safe and sound, come climbing over the stockade.

Narrative Resumed by Jim Hawkins: The Garrison in the Stockade

AS soon as Benn Gunn saw the colours he came to a halt, stopped me by the arm, and sat down.

'Now,' said he 'there's your friends, sure enough.'

'Far more likely it's the mutineers,' I answered.

'That!' he cried. 'Why, in a place like this, where nobody puts in but gen'lemen of fortune, Silver would fly the Jolly Roger, you don't make no doubt of that. No; that's your friends. There's been blows, too, and I reckon your friends has had the best of it; and here they are ashore in the old stockade, as was made years and years ago by Flint. Ah, he was the man to have a headpiece, was Flint! Barring rum, his match were never seen. He were afraid of none, not he; on'y Silver – Silver was that genteel.'

'Well,' said I, 'that may be so, and so be it; all the more reason that I should hurry on and join my friends.'

'Nay, mate,' returned Ben, 'not you. You're a good boy, or I'm mistook; but you're on'y a boy, all told. Now, Ben Gunn is fly. Rum wouldn't bring me there, where you're going – not rum wouldn't, till I see your born gen'leman, and gets it on his word of honour. And you won't forget my words: "A precious sight (that's what you'll say), a precious sight more confidence" – and then nips him.'

And he pinched me the third time with the same air of cleverness.

'And when Ben Gunn is wanted, you know where to find him, Jim. Just wheer you found him to-day. And him that comes is to have a white thing in his hand: and he's to come alone. Oh! and you'll say this: "Ben Gunn," says you, "has reasons of his own."'

'Well,' said I, 'I believe I understand. You have something

to propose, and you wish to see the squire or the doctor; and you're to be found where I found you: Is that all?'

'And when? says you,' he added. 'Why, from about noon observation to about six bells.'

'Good,' said I, 'and now may I go?'

'You won't forget?' he inquired, anxiously. 'Precious sight, and reasons of his own, says you. Reasons of his own; that's the mainstay; as between man and man. Well, then' – still holding me – 'I reckon you can go, Jim. And, Jim, if you was to see Silver, you wouldn't go for to sell Ben Gunn? wild horses wouldn't draw it from you? No, says you. And if them pirates camp ashore, Jim, what would you say but there'd be widders in the morning?'

Here he was interrupted by a loud report, and a cannonball came tearing through the trees and pitched in the sand, not a hundred yards from where we two were talking. The next moment each of us had taken to his heels in a different direction.

For a good hour to come frequent reports shook the island, and balls kept crashing through the woods. I moved from hiding-place to hiding-place, always pursued, or so it seemed to me, by these terrifying missiles. But towards the end of the bombardment, though still I durst not venture in the direction of the stockade, where the balls fell oftenest, I had begun, in a manner, to pluck up my heart again; and after a long detour to the east, crept down among the shore-side trees.

The sun had just set, the sea breeze was rustling and tumbling in the woods, and ruffling the grey surface of the anchorage; the tide, too, was far out, and great tracts of sand lay uncovered; the air, after the heat of the day, chilled me through my jacket.

The *Hispaniola* still lay where she had anchored; but, sure enough, there was the Jolly Roger – the black flag of piracy – flying from her peak. Even as I looked, there came another red flash and another report, that sent the echoes clattering, and one more round-shot whistled through the air. It was the last of the cannonade.

I lay for some time, watching the bustle which succeeded the attack. Men were demolishing something with axes on the beach near the stockade; the poor jolly-boat, I afterwards discovered. Away, near the mouth of the river, a great fire was glowing among the trees, and between that point and the ship one of the gigs kept coming and going, the men, whom I had seen so gloomy, shouting at the oars like children. But there was a sound in their voices which suggested rum.

At length I thought I might return towards the stockade. I was pretty far down on the low, sandy spit that encloses the anchorage to the east, and is joined at half-water to Skeleton Island; and now, as I rose to my feet, I saw, some distance further down the spit, and rising from among low bushes, an isolated rock, pretty high, and peculiarly white in colour. It occurred to me that this might be the white rock of which Ben Gunn had spoken, and that some day or other a boat might be wanted, and I should know where to look for one.

Then I skirted among the woods until I had regained the rear, or shoreward side, of the stockade, and was soon warmly welcomed by the faithful party.

I had soon told my story, and began to look about me. The log-house was made of unsquared trunks of pine – roof, walls, and floor. The latter stood in several places as much as a foot or a foot and a half above the surface of the sand. There was a porch at the door, and under this porch the little spring welled up into an artificial basin of a rather odd kind – no other than a great ship's kettle of iron, with the bottom knocked out, and sunk 'to her bearings,' as the captain said, among the sand.

Little had been left beside the framework of the house; but in one corner there was a stone slab laid down by way of hearth, and an old rusty iron basket to contain the fire.

The slopes of the knoll and all the inside of the stockade had been cleared of timber to build the house, and we could see by the stumps what a fine and lofty grove had been destroyed. Most of the soil had been washed away or buried in drift after the removal of the trees; only where the streamlet ran down from the kettle a thick bed of moss and some ferns and little creeping bushes were still green among the sand. Very close around the stockade – too close for defence, they said – the wood still flourished high and dense, all of fir on the land side, but towards the sea with a large admixture of live-oaks.

The cold evening breeze, of which I have spoken, whistled through every chink of the rude building, and sprinkled the floor with a continual rain of fine sand. There was sand in our eyes, sand in our teeth, sand in our suppers, sand dancing in the spring at the bottom of the kettle, for all the world like porridge beginning to boil. Our chimney was a square hole in the roof; it was but a little part of the smoke that found its way out, and the rest eddied about the house, and kept us coughing and piping the eye.

Add to this that Gray, the new man, had his face tied up in a bandage for a cut he had got in breaking away from the mutineers; and that poor old Tom Redruth, still unburied, lay along the wall, stiff and stark, under the Union Jack.

If we had been allowed to sit idle, we should all have fallen in the blues but Captain Smollett was never the man for that. All hands were called up before him, and he divided us into watches. The doctor, and Gray, and I, for one; the squire, Hunter, and Joyce, upon the other. Tired though we all were, two were sent out for firewood; two more were set to dig a grave for Redruth; the doctor was named cook; I was put sentry at the door; and the captain himself went from one to another, keeping up our spirits and lending a hand wherever it was wanted.

From time to time the doctor came to the door for a little air and to rest his eyes, which were almost smoked out of his head; and whenever he did so, he had a word for me.

'That man Smollett,' he said once, 'is a better man than I am. And when I say that it means a deal, Jim.'

Another time he came and was silent for a while. Then he put his head on one side, and looked at me.

'Is this Ben Gunn a man?' he asked.

'I do not know, sir,' said I. 'I am not very sure whether he's sane.'

'If there's any doubt about the matter, he is,' returned the doctor. 'A man who has been three years biting his nails on a desert island, Jim, can't expect to appear as

sane as you or me. It doesn't lie in human nature. Was
it cheese you said he had a fancy for?'

'Yes, sir, cheese,' I answered.

'Well, Jim,' says he, 'just see the good that comes of being
dainty in your food. You've seen my snuff-box, haven't
you? And you never saw me take snuff; the reason being
that in my snuff-box I carry a piece of Parmesan cheese
– a cheese made in Italy, very nutritious. Well, that's for
Ben Gunn!'

Before supper was eaten we buried old Tom in the sand,
and stood round him for a while bareheaded in the breeze.
A good deal of firewood had been got in, but not enough
for the captain's fancy; and he shook his head over it, and
told us we 'must get back to this to-morrow rather livelier.'
Then, when we had eaten our pork, and each had a good
stiff glass of brandy grog, the three chiefs got together in
a corner to discuss our prospects.

It appears they were at their wits' end what to do, the
stores being so low that we must have been starved into
surrender long before help came. But our best hope, it
was decided, was to kill off the buccaneers until they either
hauled down their flag or ran away with the *Hispaniola*.
From nineteen they were already reduced to fifteen, two
others were wounded, and one, at least – the man shot
beside the gun – severely wounded, if he were not dead.
Every time we had a crack at them, we were to take it,
saving our own lives, with the extremest care. And, besides
that, we had two able allies – rum and the climate.

As for the first, though we were about half a mile away,
we could hear them roaring and singing late into the night;
and as for the second, the doctor staked his wig that,
camped where they were in the marsh, and unprovided
with remedies, the half of them would be on their backs
before a week.

'So,' he added, 'if we are not all shot down first they'll
be glad to be packing in the schooner. It's always a
ship, and they can get to buccaneering again, I suppose.'

'First ship that ever I lost,' said Captain Smollett.

I was dead tired, as you may fancy; and when I got to

sleep, which was not till after a great deal of tossing, I slept like a log of wood.

The rest had long been up, and had already breakfasted and increased the pile of firewood by about half as much again, when I was wakened by a bustle and the sound of voices.

'Flag of truce!' I heard someone say; and then, immediately after, with a cry of surprise, 'Silver himself!'

And, at that, up I jumped, and, rubbing my eyes, ran to a loophole in the wall.

Silver's Embassy

SURE ENOUGH, there were two men just outside the stockade, one of them waving a white cloth; the other, no less a person than Silver himself, standing placidly by.

It was still quite early, and the coldest morning that I think I ever was abroad in; a chill that pierced into the marrow. The sky was bright and cloudless overhead, and the tops of the trees shone rosily in the sun. But where Silver stood with his lieutenant all was still in shadow, and they waded knee deep in a low, white vapour, that had crawled during the night out of the morass. The chill and the vapour taken together told a poor tale of the island. It was plainly a damp, feverish, unhealthy spot.

'Keep indoors, men,' said the captain. 'Ten to one this is a trick.'

Then he hailed the buccaneer.

'Who goes? Stand, or we fire.'

'Flag of truce,' cried Silver.

The captain was in the porch, keeping himself carefully out of the way of a treacherous shot should any be intended. He turned and spoke to us:—

'Doctor's watch on the look-out. Dr Livesey take the north side, if you please; Jim, the east; Gray, west. The watch below, all hands to load muskets. Lively, men, and careful.'

And then he turned again to the mutineers.

'And what do you want with your flag of truce?' he cried.

This time it was the other man who replied.

'Cap'n Silver, sir, to come on board and make terms,' he shouted.

'Cap'n Silver! Don't know him. Who's he?' cried the captain. And we could hear him adding to himself: 'Cap'n, is it? My heart, and here's promotion!'

Long John answered for himself.

'Me, sir. These poor lads have chosen me cap'n, after your desertion, sir' – laying a particular emphasis upon the word 'desertion.' 'We're willing to submit, if we can come to terms, and no bones about it. All I ask is your word, Cap'n Smollett, to let me safe and sound out of this here stockade, and one minute to get out o' shot before a gun is fired.'

'My man,' said Captain Smollett, 'I have not the slightest desire to talk to you. If you wish to talk to me, you can come, that's all. If there's any treachery, it'll be on your side, and the Lord help you.'

'That's enough, cap'n,' shouted Long John, cheerily. 'A word from you's enough. I know a gentleman, and you may lay to that.'

We could see the man who carried the flag of truce attempting to hold Silver back. Nor was that wonderful, seeing how cavalier had been the captain's answer. But Silver laughed at him aloud, and slapped him on the back, as if the idea of alarm had been absurd. Then he advanced to the stockade, threw over his crutch, got a leg up, and with great vigour and skill succeeded in surmounting the fence and dropping safely to the other side.

I will confess that I was far too much taken up with what was going on to be of the slightest use as sentry; indeed, I had already deserted my eastern loophole, and crept up behind the captain, who had now seated himself on the threshold, with his elbows on his knees, his head in his hands, and his eyes fixed on the water, as it bubbled out of the old iron kettle in the sand. He was whistling to himself, 'Come, Lasses and Lads.'

Silver had terrible hard work getting up the knoll. What with the steepness of the incline, the thick tree stumps, and the soft sand, he and his crutch were as helpless as a ship in stays. But he stuck to it like a man in silence, and at last arrived before the captain, whom he saluted in the handsomest style. He was tricked out in his best; an immense blue coat, thick with brass buttons, hung as low as to his knees, and a fine laced hat was set on the back of his head.

'Here you are, my man,' said the captain, raising his head. 'You had better sit down.'

'You aint a-going to let me inside, cap'n?' complained Long John. 'It's a main cold morning, to be sure, sir, to sit outside upon the sand.'

'Why, Silver,' said the captain, 'if you had pleased to be an honest man, you might have been sitting in your galley. It's your own doing. You're either my ship's cook – and then you were treated handsome – or Cap'n Silver, a common mutineer and pirate, and then you can go hang!'

'Well, well, cap'n,' returned the sea-cook, sitting down as he was bidden on the sand, 'you'll have to give me a hand up again, that's all. A sweet pretty place you have of it here. Ah, there's Jim! The top of the morning to you, Jim. Doctor, here's my service. Why, there you all are together like a happy family, in a manner of speaking.'

'If you have anything to say, my man, better say it,' said the captain.

'Right you were, Cap'n Smollett,' replied Silver. 'Dooty is dooty, to be sure. Well, now, you look here, that was a good lay of yours last night. I don't deny it was a good lay. Some of you pretty handy with a handspike-end. And I'll not deny neither but what some of my people was shook – maybe all was shook; maybe I was shook myself; maybe that's why I'm here for terms. But you mark me, cap'n, it won't do twice, by thunder! We'll have to do sentry-go, and ease off a point or so on the rum. Maybe you think we were all a sheet in the wind's eye. But I'll tell you I was sober; I was on'y dog tired; and if I'd awoke a second sooner I'd a' caught you at the act, I would. He wasn't dead when I got round to him, not he.'

'Well?' says Captain Smollett, as cool as can be.

All that Silver said was a riddle to him, but you would never have guessed it from his tone. As for me, I began to have an inkling. Ben Gunn's last words came back to my mind. I began to suppose that he had paid the buccaneers a visit while they all lay drunk together round their fire, and I reckoned up with glee that we had only fourteen enemies to deal with.

'Well, here it is,' said Silver. 'We want that treasure, and we'll have it – that's our point! You would just as soon save your lives, I reckon; and that's yours. You have a chart, haven't you?'

'That's as may be,' replied the captain.

'Oh, well, you have, I know that,' returned Long John. 'You needn't be so husky with a man; there ain't a particle of service in that, and you may lay to it. What I mean is, we want your chart. Now, I never meant you no harm, myself.'

'That won't do with me, my man,' interrupted the captain. 'We know exactly what you meant to do, and we don't care; for now, you see, you can't do it.'

And the captain looked at him calmly, and proceeded to fill a pipe.

'If Abe Gray—' Silver broke out.

'Avast there!' cried Mr Smollett. 'Gray told me nothing, and I asked him nothing; and what's more I would see you and him and this whole island blown clean out of the water into blazes first. So there's my mind for you, my man, on that.'

This little whiff of temper seemed to cool Silver down. He had been growing nettled before, but now he pulled himself together.

'Like enough,' said he. 'I would set no limits to what gentlemen might consider shipshape, or might not, as the case were. And, seein' as how you are about to take a pipe, cap'n, I'll make so free as do likewise.'

And he filled a pipe and lighted it; and the two men sat silently smoking for quite a while, now looking each other in the face, now stopping their tobacco, now leaning forward to spit. It was as good as the play to see them.

'Now,' resumed Silver, 'here it is. You give us the chart to get the treasure by, and drop shooting poor seamen, and stoving of their heads in while asleep. You do that, and we'll offer you a choice. Either you come aboard along of us, once the treasure shipped, and then I'll give you my affy-davy, upon my word of honour, to clap you somewhere safe ashore. Or, if that ain't to your fancy, some of my hands being rough, and having old scores, on account of hazing, then you can stay here, you can. We'll divide stores with you, man for man; and I'll give my affy-davy, as before, to speak the first ship I sight, and send 'em here to pick you up. Now you'll own that's talking. Handsomer you couldn't look to get, not you. And I hope' – raising his voice – 'that all hands in this here block-house will overhaul my words, for what is spoke to one is spoke to all.'

Captain Smollett rose from his seat, and knocked out the ashes of his pipe in the palm of his left hand.

'Is that all?' he asked.

'Every last word, by thunder!' answered John. 'Refuse that, and you've seen the last of me but musket-balls.'

'Very good,' said the captain. 'Now you'll hear me. If you'll come up one by one, unarmed, I'll engage to clap you all in irons, and take you home to a fair trial in England. If you won't, my name is Alexander Smollett, I've flown my sovereign's colours, and I'll see you all to Davy Jones. You can't find the treasure. You can't sail the ship – there's not a man among you fit to sail the ship. You can't fight us – Gray, there, got away from five of you. Your ship's in irons, Master Silver; you're on a lee shore, and so you'll find. I stand here and tell you so; and they're the last good words you'll get from me; for, in the name of heaven, I'll put a bullet in your back when next I meet you. Tramp, my lad. Bundle out of this, please, hand over hand, and double quick.'

Silver's face was a picture; his eyes started in his head with wrath. He shook the fire out of his pipe.

'Give me a hand up!' he cried.

'Not I,' returned the captain.

'Who'll give me a hand up?' he roared.

Not a man among us moved. Growling the foulest imprecations, he crawled along the sand till he got hold of the porch and could hoist himself again upon his crutch. Then he spat into the spring.

'There!' he cried, 'that's what I think of ye. Before an hour's out, I'll stove in your old block-house like a rum puncheon. Laugh, by thunder, laugh! Before an hour's out, ye'll laugh upon the other side. Them that die'll be the lucky ones.'

And with a dreadful oath he stumbled off, ploughed down the sand, was helped across the stockade, after four or five failures, by the man with the flag of truce, and disappeared in an instant afterwards among the trees.

The Attack

AS soon as Silver disappeared, the captain, who had been closely watching him, turned towards the interior of the house, and found not a man of us at his post but Gray. It was the first time we had ever seen him angry.

'Quarters!' he roared. And then, as we all slunk back to our places, 'Gray,' he said, 'I'll put your name in the log; you've stood by your duty like a seaman. Mr Trelawney, I'm surprised at you, sir. Doctor, I thought you had worn the king's coat! If that was how you served at Fontenoy, sir, you'd have been better in your berth.'

The doctor's watch were all back at their loopholes, the rest were busy loading the spare muskets, and every one with a red face, you may be certain, and a flea in his ear, as the saying is.

The captain looked on for a while in silence. Then he spoke.

'My lads,' said he, 'I've given Silver a broadside. I pitched it in red-hot on purpose; and before the hour's out, as he said, we shall be boarded. We're outnumbered, I needn't tell you that, but we fight in shelter; and, a minute ago, I should have said we fought with discipline. I've no manner of doubt that we can drub them, if you choose.'

Then he went the rounds, and saw, as he said, that all was clear.

On the two short sides of the house, east and west, there were two loopholes; on the south side where the porch was, two again, and on the north side, five. There was a round score of muskets for the seven of us; the firewood had been built into four piles – tables, you might say – one about the middle of each side, and on each of these tables some ammunition and four loaded muskets were laid ready to the hand of the defenders. In the middle, the cutlasses lay ranged.

'Toss out the fire,' said the captain; 'the chill is past, and we mustn't have smoke in our eyes.'

The iron fire-basket was carried bodily out by Mr Trelawney, and the embers smothered among sand.

'Hawkins hasn't had his breakfast. Hawkins, help yourself, and back to your post to eat it,' continued Captain Smollett. 'Lively, now, my lad; you'll want it before you've done. Hunter, serve out a round of brandy to all hands.'

And while this was going on, the captain completed, in his own mind, the plan of the defence.

'Doctor, you will take the door,' he resumed. 'See, and don't expose yourself; keep within, and fire through the porch. Hunter, take the east side, there. Joyce, you stand by the west, my man. Mr Trelawney, you are the best shot – you and Gray will take this long north side, with the five loopholes; it's there the danger is. If they can get up to it, and fire in upon us through our own ports, things would begin to look dirty. Hawkins, neither you nor I are much account at the shooting; we'll stand by to load and bear a hand.'

As the captain had said, the chill was past. As soon as the sun had climbed above our girdle of trees, it fell with all its force upon the clearing, and drank up the vapours at a draught. Soon the sand was baking, and the resin melting in the logs of the block-house. Jackets and coats were flung aside; shirts thrown open at the neck, and rolled up to the shoulders; and we stood there, each at his post, in a fever of heat and anxiety.

An hour passed away.

'Hang them!' said the captain. 'This is as dull as the doldrums. Gray, whistle for a wind.'

And just at that moment came the first news of the attack.

'If you please, sir,' said Joyce, 'if I see anyone am I to fire?'

'I told you so!' cried the captain.

'Thank you, sir,' returned Joyce, with the same quiet civility.

Nothing followed for a time; but the remark had set us all on the alert, straining ears and eyes – the musketeers with their pieces balanced in their hands, the captain out in the middle of the block-house, with his mouth very tight and a frown on his face.

So some seconds passed, till suddenly Joyce whipped up his musket and fired. The report had scarcely died away ere it was repeated and repeated from without in a scattering volley, shot behind shot, like a string of geese, from every side of the enclosure. Several bullets struck the log-house, but not one entered; and, as the smoke cleared away and vanished, the stockade and the woods around it looked as quiet and empty as before. Not a bough waved, not the gleam of a musket-barrel betrayed the presence of our foes.

'Did you hit your man?' asked the captain.

'No, sir,' replied Joyce. 'I believe not, sir.'

'Next best thing to tell the truth,' muttered Captain Smollett. 'Load his gun, Hawkins. How many should you say there were on your side, doctor?'

'I know precisely,' said Dr Livesey. 'Three shots were fired on this side. I saw the three flashes – two close together – one farther to the west.'

'Three!' repeated the captain. 'And how many on yours, Mr Trelawney?'

But this was not so easily answered. There had come many from the north – seven, by the squire's computation; eight or nine, according to Gray. From the east and west only a single shot had been fired. It was plain, therefore, that the attack would be developed from the north, and that on the other three sides we were only to be annoyed by a show of hostilities. But Captain Smollett made no change in his arrangements. If the mutineers succeeded in crossing the stockade, he argued, they would take possession of any unprotected loophole, and shoot us down like rats in our own stronghold.

Nor had we much time left to us for thought. Suddenly, with a loud huzza, a little cloud of pirates leaped from the woods on the north side, and ran straight on the stockade. At the same moment, the fire was once more opened from the woods, and a rifle-ball sang through the doorway, and knocked the doctor's musket into bits.

The boarders swarmed over the fence like monkeys. Squire and Gray fired again and yet again; three men fell, one forwards into the enclosure, two back on the outside. But of these, one was evidently more frightened than hurt, for he was on his feet again in a crack, and instantly disappeared among the trees.

Two had bit the dust, one had fled, four had made good their footing inside our defences; while from the shelter of the woods seven or eight men, each evidently supplied with several muskets, kept up a hot though useless fire on the log-house.

The four who had boarded made straight before them for the building, shouting as they ran, and the men among the trees shouted back to encourage them. Several shots were fired; but, such was the hurry of the marksmen, that not one appeared to have taken effect. In a moment, the four pirates had swarmed up the mound and were upon us.

The head of Job Anderson, the boatswain, appeared at the middle loophole.

'At 'em, all hands – all hands!' he roared, in a voice of thunder.

At the same moment, another pirate grasped Hunter's musket by the muzzle, wrenched it from his hands, plucked it through the loophole, and, with one stunning blow, laid the poor fellow senseless on the floor. Meanwhile a third, running unharmed all round the house, appeared suddenly in the doorway, and fell with his cutlass on the doctor.

Our position was utterly reversed. A moment since we were firing, under cover, at an exposed enemy; now it was we who lay uncovered, and could not return a blow.

The log-house was full of smoke, to which we owed our comparative safety. Cries and confusion, the flashes and reports of pistol-shots, and one loud groan, rang in my ears.

'Out, lads, out, and fight 'em in the open! Cutlasses!' cried the captain.

I snatched a cutlass from the pile, and someone, at the same time snatching another, gave me a cut across the knuckles which I hardly felt. I dashed out of the door into the clear sunlight. Someone was close behind, I knew not whom. Right in front, the doctor was pursuing his assailant down the hill, and, just as my eyes fell upon him, beat down his guard, and sent him sprawling on his back, with a great slash across the face.

'Round the house, lads! round the house!' cried the captain; and even in the hurly-burly I perceived a change in his voice.

Mechanically I obeyed, turned eastwards, and with my cutlass raised, ran round the corner of the house. Next moment I was face to face with Anderson. He roared aloud, and his hanger went up above his head, flashing in the sunlight. I had not time to be afraid, but, as the blow still hung impending, leaped in a trice upon one side, and missing my foot in the soft sand, rolled headlong down the slope.

When I had first sallied from the door, the other mutineers had been already swarming up the palisade to make an end of us. One man, in a red night-cap, with his cutlass in his mouth, had even got upon the top and thrown a leg across. Well, so short had been the interval, that when I found my feet again all was in the same posture, the fellow with the red night-cap still half-way over, another still just showing his head above the top of the stockade. And yet, in this breath of time, the fight was over, and the victory was ours.

Gray, following close behind me, had cut down the big boatswain ere he had time to recover from his lost blow. Another had been shot at a loophole in the very act of firing into the house, and now lay in agony, the pistol still smoking in his hand. A third, as I had seen, the doctor had disposed of at a blow. Of the four who had scaled the palisade, one only remained unaccounted for, and he, having left his cutlass on the field, was now clambering out again with the fear of death upon him.

'Fire – fire from the house!' cried the doctor. 'And you, lads, back into cover.'

But his words were unheeded, no shot was fired, and the last boarder made good his escape, and disappeared with the rest into the wood. In three seconds nothing remained of the attacking party but the five who had fallen, four on the inside, and one on the outside, of the palisade.

The doctor and Gray and I ran full speed for shelter. The survivors would soon be back where they had left their muskets, and at any moment the fire might recommence.

The house was by this time somewhat cleared of smoke, and we saw at a glance the price we had paid for victory. Hunter lay beside his loophole, stunned; Joyce by his, shot through the head, never to move again; while right in the centre, the squire was supporting the captain, one as pale as the other.

'The captain's wounded,' said Mr Trelawney.

'Have they run?' asked Mr Smollett.

'All that could, you may be bound,' returned the doctor; 'but there's five of them will never run again.'

'Five!' cried the captain. 'Come, that's better. Five against three leaves us four to nine. That's better odds than we had at starting. We were seven to nineteen then, or thought we were, and that's as bad to bear.'†

† The mutineers were soon only eight in number, for the man shot by Mr Trelawney on board the schooner died that same evening of his wound. But this was, of course, not known till after by the faithful party.

PART V
MY SEA ADVENTURE

How My Sea Adventure Began

THERE WAS no return of the mutineers – not so much as another shot out of the woods. They had 'got their rations for that day,' as the captain put it, and we had the place to ourselves and a quiet time to overhaul the wounded and get dinner. Squire and I cooked outside in spite of the danger, and even outside we could hardly tell what we were at for horror of the loud groans that reached us from the doctor's patients.

Out of the eight men who had fallen in the action, only three still breathed – that one of the pirates who had been shot at the loophole, Hunter, and Captain Smollett; and of these the first two were as good as dead; the mutineer, indeed, died under the doctor's knife, and Hunter, do what we could, never recovered consciousness in this world. He lingered all day, breathing loudly like the old buccaneer at home in his apoplectic fit; but the bones of his chest had been crushed by the blow and his skull fractured in falling, and some time in the following night, without sign or sound, he went to his Maker.

As for the captain, his wounds were grievous indeed, but not dangerous. No organ was fatally injured. Anderson's ball – for it was Job that shot him first – had broken his shoulder-blade and touched the lung, not badly; the second had only torn and displaced some muscles in the calf. He was sure to recover, the doctor said, but, in the meantime and for weeks to come, he must not walk nor move his arm, nor so much as speak when he could help it.

My own accidental cut across the knuckles was a flea-bite. Dr Livesey patched it up with plaster, and pulled my ears for me into the bargain.

After dinner the squire and the doctor sat by the captain's

side a while in consultation; and when they had talked to their heart's content, it being then a little past noon, the doctor took up his hat and pistols, girt on a cutlass, put the chart in his pocket, and with a musket over his shoulder, crossed the palisade on the north side, and set off briskly through the trees.

Gray and I were sitting together at the far end of the block-house, to be out of earshot of our officers consulting; and Gray took his pipe out of his mouth and fairly forgot to put it back again, so thunderstruck he was at this occurrence.

'Why, in the name of Davy Jones,' said he, 'is Dr Livesey mad?'

'Why, no,' says I. 'He's about the last of this crew for that, I take it.'

'Well, shipmate,' said Gray, 'mad he may not be; but if *he's* not, you mark my words, *I* am.'

'I take it,' replied I, 'the doctor has his idea; and if I am right, he's going now to see Ben Gunn.'

I was right, as appeared later; but, in the meantime, the house being stifling hot, and the little patch of sand inside the palisade ablaze with midday sun, I began to get another thought into my head, which was not by any means so right. What I began to do was to envy the doctor, walking in the cool shadow of the woods, with the birds about him, and the pleasant smell of the pines, while I sat grilling, with my clothes stuck to the hot resin, and so much blood about me, and so many poor dead bodies lying all around, that I took a disgust of the place that was almost as strong as fear.

All the time I was washing out the block-house, and then washing up the things from dinner, this disgust and envy kept growing stronger and stronger, till at last, being near a bread-bag, and no one then observing me, I took the first step towards my escapade, and filled both pockets of my coat with biscuit.

I was a fool, if you like, and certainly I was going to do a foolish, over-bold act; but I was determined to do it with all the precautions in my power. These biscuits, should anything befall me, would keep me, at least, from starving till far on in the next day.

The next thing I laid hold of was a brace of pistols, and as I already had a powder-horn and bullets, I felt myself well supplied with arms.

As for the scheme I had in my head, it was not a bad one in itself. I was to go down the sandy spit that divides the anchorage on the east from the open sea, find the white rock I had observed last evening, and ascertain whether it was there or not that Ben Gunn had hidden his boat; a thing quite worth doing, as I still believe. But as I was certain I should not be allowed to leave the enclosure, my only plan was to take French leave, and slip out when nobody was watching; and that was so bad a way of doing it as made the thing itself wrong. But I was only a boy, and I had made my mind up.

Well, as things at last fell out, I found an admirable opportunity. The squire and Gray were busy helping the captain with his bandages; the coast was clear; I made a bolt for it over the stockade and into the thickest of the trees, and before my absence was observed I was out of cry of my companions.

This was my second folly, far worse than the first, as I left but two sound men to guard the house; but like the first, it was a help towards saving all of us.

I took my way straight for the east coast of the island, for I was determined to go down the sea side of the spit to avoid all chance of observation from the anchorage. It was already late in the afternoon, although still warm and sunny. As I continued to thread the tall woods I could hear from far before me not only the continuous thunder of the surf, but a certain tossing of foliage and grinding of boughs which showed me the sea breeze had set in higher than usual. Soon cool draughts of air began to reach me; and a few steps farther I came forth into the open borders of the grove, and saw the sea lying blue and sunny to the horizon, and the surf tumbling and tossing its foam along the beach.

I have never seen the sea quiet round Treasure Island. The sun might blaze overhead, the air be without a breath, the surface smooth and blue, but still these great rollers would be running along all the external coast, thundering and thundering by day and night; and I scarce believe there is one spot in the island where a man would be out of earshot of their noise.

I walked along beside the surf with great enjoyment, till, thinking I was now got far enough to the south, I took the cover of some thick bushes, and crept warily up to the ridge of the spit.

Behind me was the sea, in front the anchorage. The sea breeze, as though it had the sooner blown itself out by its unusual violence, was already at an end; it had been succeeded by light, variable airs from the south and south-east, carrying great banks of fog; and the anchorage, under lee of Skeleton Island, lay still and leaden as when first we entered it. The *Hispaniola*, in that unbroken mirror, was exactly portrayed from the truck to the water line, the Jolly Roger hanging from her peak.

Alongside lay one of the gigs, Silver in the stern-sheets – him I could always recognise – while a couple of men were leaning over the stern bulwarks, one of them with a red cap – the very rogue that I had seen some hours before stride-legs upon the palisade. Apparently they were talking and laughing, though at that distance – upwards of a mile – I could, of course, hear no word of what was said. All at once, there began the most horrid, unearthly screaming, which at first startled me badly, though I had soon remembered the voice of Captain Flint, and even thought I could make out the bird by her bright plumage as she sat perched upon her master's wrist.

Soon after the jolly-boat shoved off and pulled for shore, and the man with the red cap and his comrade went below by the cabin companion.

Just about the same time the sun had gone down behind the Spy-glass, and as the fog was collecting rapidly, it began to grow dark in earnest. I saw I must lose no time if I were to find the boat that evening.

The white rock, visible enough above the brush, was still some eighth of a mile further down the spit, and it took me a goodish while to get up with it, crawling, often on all-fours, among the scrub. Night had almost come when I laid my hand on its rough sides. Right below it there was an exceedingly small hollow of green turf, hidden by banks and a thick underwood about knee-deep, that grew there very plentifully; and in the centre of the dell, sure enough, a little tent of goatskins, like what the gipsies carry about with them in England.

I dropped into the hollow, lifted the side of the tent, and there was Ben Gunn's boat – home-made if ever anything was home-made: a rude, lop-sided framework of tough wood, and stretched upon that a covering of goatskin, with the hair inside. The thing was extremely small, even for me, and I can hardly imagine that it could have floated with a full-sized man. There was one thwart set as low as possible, a kind of stretcher in the bows, and a double paddle for propulsion.

I had not then seen a coracle, such as the ancient Britons made, but I have seen one since, and I can give you no fairer idea of Ben Gunn's boat than by saying it was like the first and the worst coracle ever made by man. But the great advantage of the coracle it certainly possessed, for it was exceedingly light and portable.

Well, now that I had found the boat, you would have thought I had had enough of truantry for once; but, in the meantime, I had taken another notion, and became so obstinately fond of it, that I would have carried it out, I believe, in the teeth of Captain Smollett himself. This was to slip out under cover of the night, cut the *Hispaniola* adrift, and let her go ashore where she fancied. I had quite made up my mind that the mutineers, after their repulse of the morning, had nothing nearer their hearts than to up anchor and away to sea; this, I thought, it would be a fine thing to prevent, and now that I had seen how they left their watchmen unprovided with a boat, I thought it might be done with little risk.

Down I sat to wait for darkness, and made a hearty meal of biscuit. It was a night out of ten thousand for my purpose. The fog had now buried all heaven. As the last rays of daylight dwindled and disappeared, absolute blackness settled down on Treasure Island. And when, at last, I shouldered the coracle, and groped my way stumblingly out of the hollow where I had supped, there were but two points visible on the whole anchorage.

One was the great fire on shore, by which the defeated pirates lay carousing in the swamp. The other, a mere blur of light upon the darkness, indicated the position of the anchored ship. She had swung round to the ebb – her bow was now towards me – the only lights on board were in the cabin; and what I saw was merely a reflection on the fog of the strong rays that flowed from the stern window.

The ebb had already run some time, and I had to wade through a long belt of swampy sand, where I sank several times above the ankle, before I came to the edge of the retreating water, and wading a little way in, with some strength and dexterity, set my coracle, keel downwards, on the surface.

The Ebb-tide Runs

THE coracle – as I had ample reason to know before I was done with her – was a very safe boat for a person of my height and weight, both buoyant and clever in a seaway; but she was the most cross-grained lop-sided craft to manage. Do as you please, she always made more leeway than anything else, and turning round and round was the manoeuvre she was best at. Even Ben Gunn himself has admitted that she was 'queer to handle till you knew her way.'

Certainly I did not know her way. She turned in every direction but the one I was bound to go; the most part of the time we were broadside on, and I am very sure I never should have made the ship at all but for the tide. By good fortune, paddle as I pleased, the tide was still sweeping me down; and there lay the *Hispaniola* right in the fairway, hardly to be missed.

First she loomed before me like a blot of something yet blacker than darkness, then her spars and hull began to take shape, and the next moment, as it seemed (for, the further I went, the brisker grew the current of the ebb), I was alongside of her hawser, and had laid hold.

The hawser was as taut as a bowstring, and the current so strong she pulled upon her anchor. All round the hull, in the blackness, the rippling current bubbled and chattered like a little mountain stream. One cut with my sea-gully, and the *Hispaniola* would go humming down the tide.

So far so good; but it next occurred to my recollection that a taut hawser, suddenly cut, is a thing as dangerous as a kicking horse. Ten to one, if I were so foolhardy as to cut the *Hispaniola* from her anchor, I and the coracle would be knocked clean out of the water.

This brought me to a full stop, and if fortune had not again particularly favoured me, I should have had to abandon my design. But the light airs which had begun blowing from the south-east and south had hauled round after nightfall into the south-west. Just while I was meditating, a puff came, caught the *Hispaniola*, and forced her up into the current; and to my great joy, I felt the hawser slacken in my grasp, and the hand by which I held it dip for a second under water.

With that I made my mind up, took out my gully, opened it with my teeth, and cut one strand after another, till the vessel swung only by two. Then I lay quiet, waiting to sever these last when the strain should be once more lightened by a breath of wind.

All this time I had heard the sound of loud voices from the cabin; but, to say truth, my mind had been so entirely taken up with other thoughts that I had scarcely given ear. Now, however, when I had nothing else to do, I began to pay more heed.

One I recognised for the coxswain's, Israel Hands, that had been Flint's gunner in former days. The other was, of course, my friend of the red night-cap. Both men were plainly the worse of drink, and they were still drinking; for, even while I was listening, one of them, with a drunken cry, opened the stern window and threw out something, which I divined to be an empty bottle. But they were not only tipsy; it was plain that they were furiously angry. Oaths flew like hailstones, and every now and then there came forth such an explosion as I thought was sure to end in blows. But each time the quarrel passed off, and the voices grumbled lower for a while, until the next crisis came, and, in its turn, passed away without result.

On shore, I could see the glow of the great camp fire burning warmly through the shore-side trees. Someone was singing, a dull, old, droning sailor's song, with a droop and a quaver at the end of every verse, and seemingly no end to it at all but the patience of the singer. I had heard it on the voyage more than once, and remembered these words:—

> But one man of her crew alive,
> What put to sea with seventy-five.

And I thought it was a ditty rather too dolefully appropriate for a company that had met such cruel losses in the morning. But, indeed, from what I saw, all these buccaneers were as callous as the sea they sailed on.

At last the breeze came; the schooner sidled and drew nearer in the dark; I felt the hawser slacken once more, and with a good, tough effort, cut the last fibres through.

The breeze had but little action on the coracle, and I was almost instantly swept against the bows of the *Hispaniola*. At the same time the schooner began to turn upon her heel, spinning slowly, end for end, across the current.

I wrought like a fiend, for I expected every moment to be swamped; and since I found I could not push the coracle directly off, I now shoved straight astern. At length I was clear of my dangerous neighbour; and just as I gave the last impulsion, my hands came across a light cord that was trailing overboard across the stern bulwarks. Instantly I grasped it.

Why I should have done so I can hardly say. It was at first mere instinct; but once I had it in my hands and found it fast, curiosity began to get the upper hand, and I determined I should have one look through the cabin window.

I pulled in hand over hand on the cord, and, when I judged myself near enough, rose at infinite risk to about half my height, and thus commanded the roof and a slice of the interior of the cabin.

By this time the schooner and her little consort were gliding pretty swiftly through the water; indeed, we had already fetched up level with the camp fire. The ship was talking, as sailors say, loudly, treading the innumerable ripples with an incessant weltering splash; and until I got my eye above the window-sill I could not comprehend why the watchmen had taken no alarm. One glance, however, was sufficient; and it was only one glance that I durst take from that unsteady skiff. It showed me Hands and his companion locked together in deadly wrestle, each with a hand upon the other's throat.

I dropped upon the thwart again, none too soon, for I was near overboard. I could see nothing for the moment but these two furious, encrimsoned faces, swaying together under the smoky lamp; and I shut my eyes to let them grow once more familiar with the darkness.

The endless ballad had come to an end at last, and the whole diminished company about the camp fire had broken into the chorus I had heard so often:—

> Fifteen men on the dead man's chest—
>   Yo-ho-ho, and a bottle of rum!
> Drink and the devil had done for the rest—
>   Yo-ho-ho, and a bottle of rum!

I was just thinking how busy drink and the devil were at that very moment in the cabin of the *Hispaniola*, when I was surprised by a sudden lurch of the coracle. At the same moment she yawed sharply and seemed to change her course. The speed in the meantime had strangely increased.

I opened my eyes at once. All round me were little ripples, combing over with a sharp, bristling sound and slightly phosphorescent. The *Hispaniola* herself, a few yards in whose wake I was still being whirled along, seemed to stagger in her course, and I saw her spars toss a little against the blackness of the night; nay, as I looked longer, I made sure she also was wheeling to the southward.

I glanced over my shoulder, and my heart jumped against my ribs. There, right behind me, was the glow of the camp fire. The current had turned at right angles, sweeping round along with it the tall schooner and the little dancing coracle; ever quickening, ever bubbling higher, ever muttering louder, it went spinning through the narrows for the open sea.

Suddenly the schooner in front of me gave a violent yaw, turning, perhaps, through twenty degrees; and almost at the same moment one shout followed another from on board; I could hear feet pounding on the companion ladder; and I knew that the two drunkards had at last been interrupted in their quarrel and awakened to a sense of their disaster.

I lay down flat in the bottom of that wretched skiff, and devoutly recommended my spirit to its Maker. At the end of

the straits, I made sure we must fall into some bar of raging
breakers, where all my troubles would be ended speedily;
and though I could, perhaps, bear to die, I could not bear
to look upon my fate as it approached.

So I must have lain for hours, continually beaten to and
fro upon the billows, now and again wetted with flying
sprays, and never ceasing to expect death at the next
plunge. Gradually weariness grew upon me; a numbness,
an occasional stupor, fell upon my mind even in the midst
of my terrors; until sleep at last supervened, and in my
sea-tossed coracle I lay and dreamed of home and the old
'Admiral Benbow.'

The Cruise of the Coracle

IT was broad day when I awoke, and found myself tossing at the south-west end of Treasure Island. The sun was up, but was still hid from me behind the great bulk of the Spy-glass, which on this side descended almost to the sea in formidable cliffs.

Haulbowline Head and Mizzen-mast Hill were at my elbow; the hill bare and dark, the head bound with cliffs forty or fifty feet high, and fringed with great masses of fallen rock. I was scarce a quarter of a mile to seaward, and it was my first thought to paddle in and land.

That notion was soon given over. Among the fallen rocks the breakers spouted and bellowed; loud reverberations, heavy sprays flying and falling, succeeded one another from second to second; and I saw myself, if I ventured nearer, dashed to death upon the rough shore, or spending my strength in vain to scale the beetling crags.

Nor was that all; for crawling together on flat tables of rock, or letting themselves drop into the sea with loud reports, I beheld huge slimy monsters – soft snails as it were, of incredible bigness – two or three score of them together, making the rocks to echo with their barkings.

I have understood since that they were sea lions, and entirely harmless. But the look of them, added to the difficulty of the shore and the high running of the surf, was more than enough to disgust me of that landing-place. I felt willing rather to starve at sea than to confront such perils.

In the meantime I had a better chance, as I supposed, before me. North of Haulbowline Head, the land runs in a long way, leaving, at low tide, a long stretch of yellow sand. To the north of that, again, there comes another cape – Cape of the Woods, as it was marked upon the chart – buried in tall green pines, which descended to the margin of the sea.

I remembered what Silver had said about the current that sets northward along the whole west coast of Treasure Island; and seeing from my position that I was already under its influence, I preferred to leave Haulbowline Head behind me, and reserve my strength for an attempt to land upon the kindlier-looking Cape of the Woods.

There was a great, smooth swell upon the sea. The wind blowing steady and gentle from the south, there was no contrariety between that and the current, and the billows rose and fell unbroken.

Had it been otherwise, I must long ago have perished; but as it was, it is surprising how easily and securely my little and light boat could ride. Often, as I still lay at the bottom, and kept no more than an eye above the gunwale, I would see a big blue summit heaving close above me; yet the coracle would but bounce a little, dance as if on springs, and subside on the other side into the trough as lightly as a bird.

I began after a little to grow very bold, and sat up to try my skill at paddling. But even a small change in the disposition of the weight will produce violent changes in the behaviour of a coracle. And I had hardly moved before the boat, giving up at once her gentle dancing movement, ran straight down a slope of water so steep that it made me giddy, and struck her nose, with a spout of spray, deep into the side of the next wave.

I was drenched and terrified, and fell instantly back into my old position, whereupon the coracle seemed to find her head again, and led me as softly as before among the billows. It was plain she was not to be interfered with, and at that rate, since I could in no way influence her course, what hope had I left of reaching land?

I began to be horribly frightened, but I kept my head, for all that. First, moving with all care, I gradually baled out the coracle with my sea-cap; then getting my eye once more above the gunwale, I set myself to study how it was she managed to slip so quietly through the rollers.

I found each wave, instead of the big, smooth glossy mountain it looks from shore, or from a vessel's deck, was for all the world like any range of hills on the dry land, full of peaks and smooth places and valleys. The coracle, left to herself, turning from side to side, threaded, so to speak, her way through these lower parts, and avoided the steep slopes and higher, toppling summits of the wave.

'Well, now,' thought I to myself, 'it is plain I must lie where I am, and not disturb the balance; but it is plain, also, that I can put the paddle over the side, and from time to time, in smooth places, give her a shove or two towards land.' No sooner thought upon than done. There I lay on my elbows, in the most trying attitude, and every now and again gave a weak stroke or two to turn her head to shore.

It was very tiring, and slow work, yet I did visibly gain ground; and, as we drew near the Cape of the Woods, though I saw I must infallibly miss that point, I had still made some hundred yards of easting. I was, indeed, close in. I could see the cool, green tree-tops swaying together in the breeze, and I felt sure I should make the next promontory without fail.

It was high time, for I now began to be tortured with thirst. The glow of the sun from above, its thousandfold reflection from the waves, the sea-water that fell and dried upon me, caking my very lips with salt, combined to make my throat burn and my brain ache. The sight of the trees so near at hand had almost made me sick with longing; but the current had soon carried me past the point; and, as the next reach of sea opened out, I beheld a sight that changed the nature of my thoughts.

Right in front of me, not half a mile away, I beheld the *Hispaniola* under sail. I made sure, of course, that I should be taken; but I was so distressed for want of water, that I scarce knew whether to be glad or sorry at the thought; and, long before I had come to a conclusion, surprise had taken entire possession of my mind, and I could do nothing but stare and wonder.

The *Hispaniola* was under her main-sail and two jibs, and the beautiful white canvas shone in the sun like snow or silver. When I first sighted her, all her sails were drawing; she was lying a course about north-west; and I presumed the men on board were going round the island on their way back to the anchorage. Presently she began to fetch more and more to the westward, so that I thought they had sighted me and were going about in chase. At last, however, she fell right into the wind's eye, was taken dead aback, and stood there a while helpless, with her sails shivering.

'Clumsy fellows,' said I; 'they must still be drunk as owls.' And I thought how Captain Smollett would have set them skipping.

Meanwhile, the schooner gradually fell off, and filled again upon another tack, sailed swiftly for a minute or so, and brought up once more dead in the wind's eye. Again and again was this repeated. To and fro, up and down, north, south, east, and west, the *Hispaniola* sailed by swoops and dashes, and at each repetition ended as she had begun, with idly-flapping canvas. It became plain to me that nobody was steering. And, if so, where were the men? Either they were dead drunk, or had deserted her, I thought, and perhaps if I could get on board, I might return the vessel to her captain.

The current was bearing coracle and schooner southward at an equal rate. As for the latter's sailing, it was so wild and intermittent, and she hung each time so long in irons, that she certainly gained nothing, if she did not even lose. If only I dared to sit up and paddle, I made sure that I could overhaul her. The scheme had an air of adventure that inspired me, and the thought of the water-breaker beside the fore companion doubled my growing courage.

Up I got, was welcomed almost instantly by another cloud of spray, but this time stuck to my purpose; and set myself, with all my strength and caution, to paddle after the unsteered *Hispaniola*. Once I shipped a sea so heavy that I had to stop and bale, with my heart fluttering like a bird; but gradually I got into the way of the thing, and guided my coracle among the waves, with only now and then a blow upon her bows and a dash of foam in my face.

I was now gaining rapidly on the schooner; I could see the brass glisten on the tiller as it banged about; and still no soul appeared upon her decks. I could not choose but suppose she was deserted. If not, the men were lying drunk below, where I might batten them down, perhaps, and do what I chose with the ship.

For some time she had been doing the worst thing possible for me – standing still. She headed nearly due south, yawing, of course, all the time. Each time she fell off her sails partly filled, and these brought her, in a moment, right to the wind again. I have said this was the worst thing possible for me; for helpless as she looked in this situation, with the canvas cracking like cannon, and the blocks trundling and banging on the deck, she still continued to run away from me, not only with the speed of the current, but by the whole amount of her leeway, which was naturally great.

But now, at last, I had my chance. The breeze fell, for some seconds, very low, and the current gradually turning her, the *Hispaniola* revolved slowly round her centre, and at last presented me her stern, with the cabin window still gaping open, and the lamp over the table still burning on into the day. The main-sail hung drooped like a banner. She was stock-still, but for the current.

For the last little while I had even lost; but now, redoubling my efforts, I began once more to overhaul the chase.

I was not a hundred yards from her when the wind came again in a clap; she filled on the port tack, and was off again, stooping and skimming like a swallow.

My first impulse was one of despair, but my second was towards joy. Round she came, till she was broadside on to me – round still till she had covered a half, and then two-thirds, and then three-quarters of the distance that separated us. I could see the waves boiling white under her forefoot. Immensely tall she looked to me from my low station in the coracle.

And then, of a sudden, I began to comprehend. I had scarce time to think – scarce time to act and save myself. I was on the summit of one swell when the schooner came stooping over the next. The bowsprit was over my head. I sprang to my feet, and leaped, stamping the coracle under water. With one hand I caught the jib-boom, while my foot was lodged between the stay and the brace; and as I still clung there panting, a dull blow told me that the schooner had charged down upon and struck the coracle, and that I was left without retreat on the *Hispaniola*.

I Strike the Jolly Roger

I HAD scarce gained a position on the bowsprit, when the flying jib flapped and filled upon the other tack, with a report like a gun. The schooner trembled to her keel under the reverse; but next moment, the other sails still drawing, the jib flapped back again, and hung idle.

This had nearly tossed me off into the sea; and now I lost no time, crawled back along the bowsprit, and tumbled head foremost on the deck.

I was on the lee-side of the forecastle, and the main-sail, which was still drawing, concealed from me a certain portion of the after-deck. Not a soul was to be seen. The planks, which had not been swabbed since the mutiny, bore the print of many feet; and an empty bottle, broken by the neck, tumbled to and fro like a live thing in the scuppers.

Suddenly the *Hispaniola* came right into the wind. The jibs behind me cracked aloud; the rudder slammed to; the whole ship gave a sickening heave and shudder, and at the same moment the main-boom swung inboard, the sheet groaning in the blocks, and showed me the lee after-deck.

There were the two watchmen, sure enough: red-cap on his back, as stiff as a handspike, with his arms stretched out like those of a crucifix, and his teeth showing through his open lips; Israel Hands propped against the bulwarks, his chin on his chest, his hands lying open before him on the deck, his face as white, under its tan, as a tallow candle.

For a while the ship kept bucking and sidling like a vicious horse, the sails filling, now on one tack, now on another, and the boom swinging to and fro till the mast groaned aloud under the strain. Now and again, too, there would come a cloud of light spray over the bulwark, and a heavy blow of the ship's bows against the swell: so much heavier weather was made of it by this great rigged ship than by my homemade, lop-sided coracle, now gone to the bottom of the sea.

At every jump of the schooner, red-cap slipped to and fro; but – what was ghastly to behold – neither his attitude nor his fixed teeth-disclosing grin was anyway disturbed by this rough usage. At every jump, too, Hands appeared still more to sink into himself and settle down upon the desk, his feet sliding ever the farther out, and the whole body canting towards the stern, so that his face became, little by little, hid from me; and at last I could see nothing beyond his ear and the frayed ringlet of one whisker.

At the same time, I observed around both of them, splashes of dark blood upon the planks, and began to feel sure that they had killed each other in their drunken wrath.

While I was thus looking and wondering, in a calm moment, when the ship was still, Israel Hands turned partly round, and, with a low moan, writhed himself back to the position in which I had seen him first. The moan, which told of pain and deadly weakness, and the way in which his jaw hung open, went right to my heart. But when I remembered the talk I had overheard from the apple barrel, all pity left me.

I walked aft until I reached the mainmast.

'Come aboard, Mr Hands,' I said ironically.

He rolled his eyes round heavily; but he was too far gone to express surprise. All he could do was to utter one word, 'Brandy.'

It occurred to me there was no time to lose; and, dodging the boom as it once more lurched across the deck, I slipped aft, and down the companion-stairs into the cabin.

It was such a scene of confusion as you can hardly fancy. All the lock-fast places had been broken open in quest of the chart. The floor was thick with mud, where ruffians had sat down to drink or consult after wading in the marshes round their camp. The bulkheads, all painted in clear white, and beaded round with gilt, bore a pattern of dirty hands. Dozens of empty bottles clinked together in corners to the rolling of the ship. One of the doctor's medical books lay open on the table, half of the leaves gutted out, I suppose, for pipelights. In the midst of all this the lamp still cast a smoky glow, obscure and brown as umber.

I went into the cellar; all the barrels were gone, and of the bottles a most surprising number had been drunk out and thrown away. Certainly, since the mutiny began, not a man of them could ever have been sober.

Foraging about, I found a bottle with some brandy left, for Hands; and for myself I routed out some biscuits, some pickled fruits, a great bunch of raisins, and a piece of cheese. With these I came on deck, put down my own stock behind the rudder-head, and well out of the coxswain's reach, went forward to the water-breaker, and had a good, deep drink of water, and then, and not till then, gave Hands the brandy.

He must have drunk a gill before he took the bottle from his mouth.

'Aye,' said he, 'by thunder, but I wanted some o' that!'

I had sat down already in my own corner and begun to eat.

'Much hurt?' I asked him.

He grunted, or, rather I might say, he barked.

'If that doctor was aboard,' he said, 'I'd be right enough in a couple of turns; but I don't have no manner of luck, you see, and that's what's the matter with me. As for that swab, he's good and dead, he is,' he added, indicating the man with the red cap. 'He warn't no seaman, anyhow. And where mought you have come from?'

'Well,' said I, 'I've come aboard to take possession of this ship, Mr Hands; and you'll please regard me as your captain until further notice.'

He looked at me sourly enough, but said nothing. Some of the colour had come back into his cheeks, though he still looked very sick, and still continued to slip out and settle down as the ship banged about.

'By-the-bye,' I continued, 'I can't have these colours, Mr Hands; and, by your leave, I'll strike 'em. Better none than these.'

And, again dodging the boom, I ran to the colour

lines, handed down their cursed black flag, and chucked it overboard.

'God save the king!' said I, waving my cap; 'and there's an end to Captain Silver!'

He watched me keenly and slyly, his chin all the while on his breast.

'I reckon,' he said at last – 'I reckon, Cap'n Hawkins, you'll kind of want to get ashore, now. S'pose we talks.'

'Why, yes,' says I, 'with all my heart, Mr Hands. Say on.' And I went back to my meal with a good appetite.

'This man,' he began, nodding feebly at the corpse – 'O'Brien were his name – a rank Irelander – this man and me got the canvas on her, meaning for to sail her back. Well, *he's* dead now, he is – as dead as bilge; and who's to sail this ship, I don't see. Without I gives you a hint, you ain't that man, as far's I can tell. Now, look here, you gives me food and drink, and a old scarf or ankecher to tie my wound up, you do; and I'll tell you how to sail her; and that's about square all round, I take it.'

'I'll tell you one thing,' says I: 'I'm not going back to Captain Kidd's anchorage. I mean to get into North Inlet, and beach her quietly there.'

'To be sure you did,' he cried. 'Why, I ain't sich an infernal lubber, after all. I can see, can't I? I've tried my fling, I have, and I've lost, and it's you has the wind of me. North Inlet? Why, I haven't no ch'ice, not I! I'd help you sail her up to Execution Dock, by thunder! so I would.'

Well, as it seemed to me, there was some sense in this. We struck our bargain on the spot. In three minutes I had the *Hispaniola* sailing easily before the wind along the coast of Treasure Island, with good hopes of turning the northern point ere noon, and beating down again as far as North Inlet before high water, when we might beach her safely, and wait till the subsiding tide permitted us to land.

Then I lashed the tiller and went below to my own chest, where I got a soft silk handkerchief of my mother's. With this, and with my aid, Hands bound up the great bleeding stab he had received in the thigh, and after he had eaten a little and had a swallow or two more of the brandy, he began to pick up visibly, sat straighter up, spoke louder and clearer, and looked in every way another man.

The breeze served us admirably. We skimmed before it like a bird, the coast of the island flashing by, and the view changing every minute. Soon we were past the high lands and bowling beside low, sandy country, sparsely dotted with dwarf pines, and soon we were beyond that again, and had turned the corner of the rocky hill that ends the island on the north.

I was greatly elated with my new command, and pleased with the bright, sunshiny weather and these different prospects of the coast. I had now plenty of water and good things to eat, and my conscience, which had smitten me hard for my desertion, was quieted by the great conquest I had made. I should, I think, have had nothing left me to desire but for the eyes of the coxswain as they followed me derisively about the deck, and the odd smile that appeared continually on his face. It was a smile that had in it something both of pain and weakness – a haggard, old man's smile; but there was, besides that, a grain of derision, a shadow of treachery, in his expression as he craftily watched, and watched, and watched me at my work.

Israel Hands

THE wind, serving us to a desire, now hauled into the west. We could run so much the easier from the north-east corner of the island to the mouth of the North Inlet. Only, as we had no power to anchor, and dared not beach her till the tide had flowed a good deal farther, time hung on our hands. The coxswain told me how to lay the ship to; after a good many trials I succeeded, and we both sat in silence, over another meal.

'Cap'n,' said he, at length, with that same uncomfortable smile, 'here's my old shipmate, O'Brien; s'pose you was to heave him overboard. I ain't partic'lar as a rule, and I don't take no blame for settling his hash; but I don't reckon him ornamental, now, do you?'

'I'm not strong enough, and I don't like the job; and there he lies, for me,' said I.

'This here's an unlucky ship – this *Hispaniola*, Jim,' he went on, blinking. 'There's a power of men been killed in this *Hispaniola* – a sight o' poor seamen dead and gone since you and me took ship to Bristol. I never seen sich dirty luck, not I. There was this here O'Brien, now – he's dead, ain't he? Well, now, I'm no scholar, and you're a lad as can read and figure; and, to put it straight, do you take it as a dead man is dead for good, or do he come alive again?'

'You can kill the body, Mr Hands, but not the spirit; you must know that already,' I replied. 'O'Brien there is in another world, and maybe watching us.'

'Ah!' says he. 'Well, that's unfort'nate – appears as if killing parties was a waste of time. Howsomever, sperrits don't reckon for much, by what I've seen. I'll chance it with the sperrits, Jim. And now, you've spoke up free, and

I'll take it kind if you'd step down into that there cabin and get me a – well, a – shiver my timbers! I can't hit the name on't; well, you get me a bottle of wine, Jim – this here brandy's too strong for my head.'

Now, the coxswain's hesitation seemed to be unnatural; and as for the notion of his preferring wine to brandy, I entirely disbelieved it. The whole story was a pretext. He wanted me to leave the deck – so much was plain; but with what purpose I could in no way imagine. His eyes never met mine; they kept wandering to and fro, up and down, now with a look to the sky, now with a flitting glance upon the dead O'Brien. All the time he kept smiling, and putting his tongue out in the most guilty, embarrassed manner, so that a child could have told that he was bent on some deception. I was prompt with my answer, however, for I saw where my advantage lay; and that with a fellow so densely stupid I could easily conceal my suspicions to the end.

'Some wine?' I said. 'Far better. Will you have white or red?'

'Well, I reckon it's about the blessed same to me, shipmate,' he replied; 'so it's strong, and plenty of it, what's the odds?'

'All right,' I answered. 'I'll bring you port, Mr Hands. But I'll have to dig for it.'

With that I scuttled down the companion with all the noise I could, slipped off my shoes, ran quietly along the sparred gallery, mounted the forecastle ladder, and popped my head out of the fore companion. I knew he would not expect to see me there; yet I took every precaution possible; and certainly the worst of my suspicions proved too true.

He had risen from his position to his hands and knees; and, though his leg obviously hurt him pretty sharply when he moved – for I could hear him stifle a groan – yet it was at a good, rattling rate that he trailed himself across the deck. In half a minute he had reached the port scuppers, and picked, out of a coil of rope, a long knife, or rather a short dirk, discoloured to the hilt with blood. He looked upon it for a moment, thrusting forth his under jaw, tried the point upon his hand, and then, hastily concealing it in the bosom of his jacket, trundled back again into his old place against the bulwark.

This was all that I required to know. Israel could move about; he was now armed; and if he had been at so much trouble to get rid of me, it was plain that I was meant to be the victim. What he would do afterwards – whether he would try to crawl right across the island from North Inlet to the camp among the swamps, or whether he would fire Long Tom, trusting that his own comrades might come first to help him, was, of course, more than I could say.

Yet I felt sure that I could trust him in one point, since in that our interests jumped together, and that was in the disposition of the schooner. We both desired to have her stranded safe enough, in a sheltered place, and so that, when the time came, she could be got off again with as little labour and danger as might be; and until that was done I considered that my life would certainly be spared.

While I was thus turning the business over in my mind, I had not been idle with my body. I had stolen back to the cabin, slipped once more into my shoes, and laid my hand at random on a bottle of wine, and now, with this for an excuse, I made my reappearance on the deck.

Hands lay as I had left him, all fallen together in a bundle, and with his eyelids lowered, as though he were too weak to bear the light. He looked up, however, at my coming, knocked the neck off the bottle, like a man who had done the same thing often, and took a good swig, with his favourite toast of 'Here's luck!' Then he lay quiet for a little, and then, pulling out a stick of tobacco, begged me to cut him a quid.

'Cut me a hunk o' that,' says he, 'for I haven't no knife, and hardly strength enough, so be as I had. Ah, Jim, Jim, I reckon I've missed stays! Cut me a quid, as 'll likely be the last, lad; for I'm for my long home, and no mistake.'

'Well,' said I, 'I'll cut you some tobacco; but if I was you and thought myself so badly, I would go to my prayers, like a Christian man.'

'Why?' said he. 'Now, you tell me why.'

'Why?' I cried. 'You were asking me just now about the dead. You've broken your trust; you've lived in sin and lies and blood; there's a man you killed lying at your feet this moment; and you ask me why! For God's mercy, Mr Hands, that's why.'

I spoke with a little heat, thinking of the bloody dirk he had hidden in his pocket, and designed, in his ill thoughts, to end me with. He, for his part, took a great draught of the wine, and spoke with the most unusual solemnity.

'For thirty years,' he said, 'I've sailed the seas, and seen good and bad, better and worse, fair weather and foul, provisions running out, knives going, and what not. Well, now I tell you, I never seen good come o' goodness yet. Him as strikes first is my fancy; dead men don't bite; them's my views – amen, so be it. And now, you look here,' he added, suddenly changing his tone, 'we've had about enough of this foolery. The tide's made good enough by now. You just take my orders, Cap'n Hawkins, and we'll sail slap in and be done with it.'

All told, we had scarce two miles to run; but the navigation was delicate, the entrance to this northern anchorage was not only narrow and shoal, but lay east and west, so that the schooner must be nicely handled to be got in. I think I was a good, prompt subaltern, and I am very sure that Hands was an excellent pilot; for we went about and about, and dodged in, shaving the banks, with a certainty and a neatness that were a pleasure to behold.

Scarcely had we passed the heads before the land closed around us. The shores of North Inlet were as thickly wooded as those of the southern anchorage; but the space was longer and narrower, and more like, what in truth it was, the estuary of a river. Right before us, at the southern end, we saw the wreck of a ship in the last stages of dilapidation. It had been a great vessel of three masts, but had lain so long exposed to the injuries of the weather, that it was hung about with great webs of dripping seaweed, and on the deck of it shore bushes had taken root, and now flourished thick with flowers. It was a sad sight, but it showed us that the anchorage was calm.

'Now,' said Hands, 'look there; there's a pet bit for to beach a ship in. Fine flat sand, never a catspaw, trees all around of it, and flowers a-blowing like a garding on that old ship.'

'And once beached,' I inquired, 'how shall we get her off again?'

'Why, so,' he replied: 'you take a line ashore there on the other side at low water: take a turn about one o' them big pines; bring it back, take a turn round the capstan, and lie-to for the tide. Come high water, all hands take a pull upon the line, and off she comes as sweet as natur'. And now, boy, you stand by. We're near the bit now, and she's too much way on her. Starboard a little – so – steady – starboard – larboard a little – steady – steady!'

So he issued his commands, which I breathlessly obeyed; till, all of a sudden, he cried, 'Now, my hearty, luff!' And I put the helm hard up, and the *Hispaniola* swung round rapidly, and ran stem on for the low wooded shore.

The excitement of these last manoeuvres had somewhat interfered with the watch I had kept hitherto, sharply enough, upon the coxswain. Even then I was still so much interested, waiting for the ship to touch, that I had quite forgot the peril that hung over my head, and stood craning over the starboard bulwarks and watching the ripples spreading wide before the bows. I might have fallen without a struggle for my life, had not a sudden disquietude seized upon me, and made me turn my head. Perhaps I had heard a creak, or seen his shadow moving with the tail of my eye; perhaps it was an instinct like a cat's; but, sure enough, when I looked round, there was Hands, already half-way towards me, with the dirk in his right hand.

We must both have cried out aloud when our eyes met; but while mine was the shrill cry of terror, his was a roar of fury like a charging bull's. At the same instant he threw himself forward, and I leapt sideways towards the bows. As I did so, I let go of the tiller, which sprang sharp to leeward; and I think this saved my life, for it struck Hands across the chest, and stopped him, for the moment, dead.

Before he could recover, I was safe out of the corner where he had me trapped, with all the deck to dodge about. Just forward of the mainmast I stopped, drew a pistol from my

pocket, took a cool aim, though he had already turned
and was once more coming directly after me, and drew
the trigger. The hammer fell, but there followed neither
flash nor sound; the priming was useless with sea-water. I
cursed myself for my neglect. Why had not I, long before,
reprimed and reloaded my only weapons? Then I should
not have been as now, a mere fleeing sheep before this
butcher.

Wounded as he was, it was wonderful how fast he could
move, his grizzled hair tumbling over his face, and his face
itself as red as a red ensign with his haste and fury. I had no
time to try my other pistol, nor, indeed, much inclination,
for I was sure it would be useless. One thing I saw plainly:
I must not simply retreat before him, or he would speedily
hold me boxed into the bows, as a moment since he had
so nearly boxed me in the stern. Once so caught, and nine
or ten inches of the bloodstained dirk would be my last
experience on this side of eternity. I placed my palms
against the mainmast, which was of a goodish bigness,
and waited, every nerve upon the stretch.

Seeing that I meant to dodge, he also paused; and
a moment or two passed in feints on his part, and
corresponding movements upon mine. It was such a
game as I had often played at home about the rocks of
Black Hill Cove; but never before, you may be sure, with
such a wildly beating heart as now. Still, as I say, it was
a boy's game, and I thought I could hold my own at it,
against an elderly seaman with a wounded thigh. Indeed,
my courage had begun to rise so high, that I allowed myself
a few darting thoughts on what would be the end of the
affair; and while I saw certainly that I could spin it out for
long, I saw no hope of any ultimate escape.

Well, while things stood thus, suddenly the *Hispaniola*
struck, staggered, ground for an instant in the sand, and
then, swift as a blow, canted over to the port side, till the
deck stood at an angle of forty-five degrees, and about a
puncheon of water splashed into the scupper holes, and
lay, in a pool, between the deck and bulwark.

We were both of us capsized in a second, and both of
us rolled, almost together, into the scuppers; the dead

red-cap, with his arms still spread out, tumbling stiffly after us. So near were we, indeed, that my head came against the coxswain's foot with a crack that made my teeth rattle. Blow and all, I was the first afoot again; for Hands had got involved with the dead body. The sudden canting of the ship had made the deck no place for running on; I had to find some new way of escape, and that upon the instant, for my foe was almost touching me. Quick as thought, I sprang into the mizzen shrouds, rattled up hand over hand, and did not draw a breath till I was seated on the cross-trees.

I had been saved by being prompt; the dirk had struck not half a foot below me, as I pursued my upward flight; and there stood Israel Hands with his mouth open and his face upturned to mine, a perfect statue of surprise and disappointment.

Now that I had a moment to myself, I lost no time in changing the priming of my pistol, and then, having one ready for service, and to make assurance doubly sure, I proceeded to draw the load of the other, and recharge it afresh from the beginning.

My new employment struck Hands all of a heap; he began to see the dice going against him; and after an obvious hesitation, he also hauled himself heavily into the shrouds, and, with the dirk in his teeth, began slowly and painfully to mount. It cost him no end of time and groans to haul his wounded leg behind him; and I had quietly finished my arrangements before he was much more than a third of the way up. Then, with a pistol in either hand, I addressed him.

'One more step, Mr Hands,' said I, 'and I'll blow your brains out! Dead men don't bite, you know,' I added, with a chuckle.

He stopped instantly. I could see by the working of his face that he was trying to think, and the process was so slow and laborious that, in my new-found security, I laughed aloud. At last, with a swallow or two, he spoke, his face still wearing the same expression of extreme perplexity. In order to speak he had to take the dagger from his mouth, but, in all else, he remained unmoved.

'Jim,' says he, 'I reckon we're fouled, you and me, and we'll have to sign articles. I'd have had you but for that there lurch: but I don't have no luck, not I; and I reckon I'll have to strike, which comes hard, you see, for a master mariner to a ship's younker like you, Jim.'

I was drinking in his words and smiling away, as conceited as a cock upon a wall, when, all in a breath, back went his right hand over his shoulder. Something sang like an arrow through the air; I felt a blow and then a sharp pang, and there I was pinned by the shoulder to the mast. In the horrid pain and surprise of the moment – I scarce can say it was by my own volition, and I am sure it was without a conscious aim – both my pistols went off, and both escaped out of my hands. They did not fall alone; with a choked cry, the coxswain loosed his grasp upon the shrouds, and plunged head first into the water.

'Pieces of Eight'

OWING TO the cant of the vessel, the masts hung far out over the water, and from my perch on the cross-trees I had nothing below me but the surface of the bay. Hands, who was not so far up, was, in consequence, nearer to the ship, and fell between me and the bulwarks. He rose once to the surface in a lather of foam and blood, and then sank again for good. As the water settled, I could see him lying huddled together on the clean, bright sand in the shadow of the vessel's sides. A fish or two whipped past his body. Sometimes, by the quivering of the water, he appeared to move a little, as if he were trying to rise. But he was dead enough, for all that, being both shot and drowned, and was food for fish in the very place where he had designed my slaughter.

I was no sooner certain of this than I began to feel sick, faint, and terrified. The hot blood was running over my back and chest. The dirk, where it had pinned my shoulder to the mast, seemed to burn like a hot iron; yet it was not so much these real sufferings that distressed me, for these, it seemed to me, I could bear without a murmur; it was the horror I had upon my mind of falling from the cross-trees into that still green water, beside the body of the coxswain.

I clung with both hands till my nails ached, and I shut my eyes as if to cover up the peril. Gradually my mind came back again, my pulses quieted down to a more natural time, and I was once more in possession of myself.

It was my first thought to pluck forth the dirk; but either it stuck too hard or my nerve failed me; and I desisted with a violent shudder. Oddly enough, that very shudder did the business. The knife, in fact, had come the nearest in the world to missing me altogether; it held me by a mere pinch of skin, and this the shudder tore away. The blood ran down the faster, to be sure; but I was my own master again, and only tacked to the mast by my coat and shirt.

These last I broke through with a sudden jerk, and then regained the deck by the starboard shrouds. For nothing in the world would I have again ventured, shaken as I was, upon the overhanging port shrouds, from which Israel had so lately fallen.

I went below, and did what I could for my wound; it pained me a good deal, and still bled freely; but it was neither deep nor dangerous, nor did it greatly gall me when I used my arm. Then I looked around me, and as the ship was now, in a sense, my own, I began to think of clearing it from its last passenger – the dead man, O'Brien.

He had pitched, as I have said, against the bulwarks, where he lay like some horrible, ungainly sort of puppet; life-sized, indeed, but how different from life's colour or life's comeliness! In that position, I could easily have my way with him; and as the habit of tragical adventures had worn off almost all my terror for the dead, I took him by the waist as if he had been a sack of bran, and, with one good heave, tumbled him overboard. He went in with a sounding plunge; the red cap came off, and remained floating on the surface; and as soon as the splash subsided, I could see him and Israel lying side by side, both wavering with the tremulous movement of the water. O'Brien, though still quite a young man, was very bald. There he lay, with that bald head across the knees of the man who had killed him, and the quick fishes steering to and fro over both.

I was now alone upon the ship; the tide had just turned. The sun was within so few degrees of setting that already the shadow of the pines upon the western shore began to reach right across the anchorage, and fall in patterns on the deck. The evening breeze had sprung up, and though it was well warded off by the hill with the two peaks upon the east, the cordage had begun to sing a little softly to itself and the idle sails to rattle to and fro.

I began to see a danger to the ship. The jibs I speedily doused and brought tumbling to the deck; but the mainsail was a harder matter. Of course, when the schooner canted over, the boom had swung out-board, and the cap of it and a foot or two of sail hung even under water. I thought this made it still more dangerous; yet the strain was so heavy that I half feared to meddle. At last, I got my knife and cut the halyards. The peak dropped instantly, a great belly of loose canvas floated broad upon the water; and since, pull as I liked, I could not budge the downhaul; that was the extent of what I could accomplish. For the rest, the *Hispaniola* must trust to luck, like myself.

By this time the whole anchorage had fallen into shadow – the last rays, I remember, falling through a glade of the wood, and shining bright as jewels, on the flowery mantle of the wreck. It began to be chill; the tide was rapidly fleeting seaward, the schooner settling more and more on her beam-ends.

I scrambled forward and looked over. It seemed shallow enough, and holding the cut hawser in both hands for a last security, I let myself drop softly overboard. The water scarcely reached my waist; the sand was firm and covered with ripple marks, and I waded ashore in great spirits, leaving the *Hispaniola* on her side, with her mainsail trailing wide upon the surface of the bay. About the same time the sun went fairly down, and the breeze whistled low in the dusk among the tossing pines.

At least, and at last, I was off the sea, nor had I returned thence empty-handed. There lay the schooner, clear at last from buccaneers and ready for our own men to board and get to sea again. I had nothing nearer my fancy than to get home to the stockade and boast of my achievements. Possibly I might be blamed a bit for my truantry, but the recapture of the *Hispaniola* was a clenching answer, and I hoped that even Captain Smollett would confess I had not lost my time.

So thinking, and in famous spirits, I began to set my face homeward for the block-house and my companions. I remembered that the most easterly of the rivers which drain into Captain Kidd's anchorage ran from the two-peaked hill upon my left; and I bent my course in that direction that I might pass the stream while it was small. The wood was pretty open, and keeping along the lower spurs, I had soon turned the corner of that hill, and not long after waded to the midcalf across the water-course.

This brought me near to where I had encountered Ben Gunn, the maroon; and I walked more circumspectly, keeping an eye on every side. The dusk had come nigh hand completely, and, as I opened out the cleft between the two peaks, I became aware of a wavering glow against the sky, where, as I judged, the man of the island was cooking his supper before a roaring fire. And yet I wondered, in my heart, that he should show himself so careless. For if I could see this radiance, might it not reach the eyes of Silver himself where he camped upon the shore among the marshes?

Gradually the night fell blacker; it was all I could do to guide myself even roughly towards my destination; the double hill behind me and the Spy-glass on my right hand loomed faint and fainter; the stars were few and pale; and in the low ground where I wandered I kept tripping among bushes and rolling into sandy pits.

Suddenly a kind of brightness fell about me. I looked up; a pale glimmer of moonbeams had alighted on the summit of the Spy-glass, and soon after I saw something broad and silvery moving low down behind the trees, and knew the moon had risen.

With this to help me, I passed rapidly over what remained to me of my journey; and, sometimes walking, sometimes running, impatiently drew near to the stockade. Yet, as I began to thread the grove that lies before it, I was not so thoughtless but that I slacked my pace and went a trifle warily. It would have been a poor end of my adventures to get shot down by my own party in mistake.

The moon was climbing higher and higher; its light began to fall here and there in masses through the more open districts of the wood; and right in front of me a glow of a different colour appeared among the trees. It was red and hot, and now and again it was a little darkened – as it were the embers of a bonfire smouldering.

For the life of me, I could not think what it might be.

At last I came right down upon the borders of the clearing. The western end was already steeped in moonshine; the rest, and the block-house itself, still lay in a black shadow, chequered with long, silvery streaks of light. On the other side of the house an immense fire had burned itself into clear embers and shed a steady, red reverberation, contrasted strongly with the mellow paleness of the moon. There was not a soul stirring, nor a sound beside the noises of the breeze.

I stopped, with much wonder in my heart, and perhaps a little terror also. It had not been our way to build great fires; we were, indeed, by the captain's orders, somewhat niggardly of firewood; and I began to fear that something had gone wrong while I was absent.

I stole round by the eastern end, keeping close in shadow, and at a convenient place, where the darkness was thickest, crossed the palisade.

To make assurance surer, I got upon my hands and knees, and crawled, without a sound, towards the corner of the house. As I drew nearer, my heart was suddenly and greatly lightened. It is not a pleasant noise in itself, and I have often complained of it at other times; but just then it was like music to hear my friends snoring together so loud and peaceful in their sleep. The sea cry of the watch, that beautiful 'All's well,' never fell more reassuringly on my ear.

In the meantime, there was no doubt of one thing; they kept an infamous bad watch. If it had been Silver and his lads that were now creeping in on them, not a soul would have seen daybreak. That was what it was, thought I, to have the captain wounded; and again I blamed myself sharply for leaving them in that danger with so few to mount guard.

By this time I had got to the door and stood up. All was dark within, so that I could distinguish nothing by the eye. As for sounds, there was the steady drone of the snorers, and a small occasional noise, a flickering or pecking that I could in no way account for.

With my arms before me I walked steadily in. I should lie down in my own place (I thought, with a silent chuckle) and enjoy their faces when they found me in the morning.

My foot struck something yielding – it was a sleeper's leg; and he turned and groaned, but without awaking.

And then, all of a sudden, a shrill voice broke forth out of the darkness:—

'Pieces of eight! pieces of eight! pieces of eight! pieces of eight! pieces of eight!' and so forth, without pause or change, like the clacking of a tiny mill.

Silver's green parrot, Captain Flint! It was she whom I had heard pecking at a piece of bark; it was she, keeping better watch than any human being, who thus announced my arrival with her wearisome refrain.

I had no time left me to recover. At the sharp, clipping tone of the parrot, the sleepers awoke and sprang up; and with a mighty oath, the voice of Silver cried:—

'Who goes?'

I turned to run, struck violently against one person, recoiled, and ran full into the arms of a second, who, for his part, closed upon and held me tight.

'Bring a torch, Dick,' said Silver, when my capture was thus assured.

And one of the men left the log-house, and presently returned with a lighted brand.

PART VI
CAPTAIN SILVER

In the Enemy's Camp

THE red glare of the torch, lighting up the interior of the block-house, showed me the worst of my apprehensions realised. The pirates were in possession of the house and stores: there was the cask of cognac, there were the pork and bread, as before; and, what tenfold increased my horror, not a sign of any prisoner. I could only judge that all had perished, and my heart smote me sorely that I had not been there to perish with them.

There were six of the buccaneers, all told; not another man was left alive. Five of them were on their feet, flushed and swollen, suddenly called out of the first sleep of drunkenness. The sixth had only risen upon his elbow: he was deadly pale, and the bloodstained bandage round his head told that he had recently been wounded, and still more recently dressed. I remembered the man who had been shot and had run back among the woods in the great attack, and doubted not that this was he.

The parrot sat, preening her plumage, on Long John's shoulder. He himself, I thought, looked somewhat paler and more stern than I was used to. He still wore the fine broadcloth suit in which he had fulfilled his mission, but it was bitterly the worse for wear, daubed with clay and torn with the sharp briers of the wood.

'So,' said he, 'here's Jim Hawkins, shiver my timbers! dropped in, like, eh? Well, come, I take that friendly.'

And thereupon he sat down across the brandy cask, and began to fill a pipe.

'Give me a loan of the link, Dick,' said he; and then, when he had a good light, 'that'll do, lad,' he added; 'stick the glim in the wood heap; and you, gentlemen, bring yourselves to! – you needn't stand up for Mr Hawkins; *he'll* excuse you,

you may lay to that. And so, Jim' – stopping the tobacco – 'here you were, and quite a pleasant surprise for poor old John. I see you were smart when first I set my eyes on you; but this here gets away from me clean, it do.'

To all this, as may be well supposed, I made no answer. They had set me with my back against the wall; and I stood there, looking Silver in the face, pluckily enough, I hope, to all outward appearance, but with black despair in my heart.

Silver took a whiff or two of his pipe with great composure, and then ran on again.

'Now, you see, Jim, so be as you *are* here,' says he, 'I'll give you a piece of my mind. I've always liked you, I have, for a lad of spirit, and the picter of my own self when I was young and handsome. I always wanted you to jine and take your share, and die a gentleman, and now, my cock, you've got to. Cap'n Smollett's a fine seaman, as I'll own up to any day, but stiff on discipline. "Dooty is dooty," says he, and right he is. Just you keep clear of the cap'n. The doctor himself is gone dead again you – "ungrateful scamp" was what he said; and the short and the long of the whole story is about here: you can't go back to your own lot, for they won't have you; and, without you start a third ship's company all by yourself, which might be lonely, you'll have to jine with Cap'n Silver.'

So far so good. My friends, then, were still alive, and though I partly believed the truth of Silver's statement, that the cabin party were incensed at me for my desertion, I was more relieved than distressed by what I heard.

'I don't say nothing as to your being in our hands,' continued Silver, 'though there you are, and you may lay to it. I'm all for argyment; I never seen good come out o' threatening. If you like the service, well, you'll jine; and if you don't, Jim, why, you're free to answer no – free and welcome, shipmate; and if fairer can be said by mortal seaman, shiver my sides!'

'Am I to answer, then?' I asked, with a very tremulous voice. Through all this sneering talk, I was made to feel the threat of death that overhung me, and my cheeks burned and my heart beat painfully in my breast.

'Lad,' said Silver, 'no one's a-pressing of you. Take your bearings. None of us won't hurry you, mate; time goes so pleasant in your company, you see.'

'Well,' says I, growing a bit bolder, 'if I'm to choose, I declare I have a right to know what's what, and why you're here, and where my friends are.'

'Wot's wot?' repeated one of the buccaneers, in a deep growl. 'Ah, he'd be a lucky one as knowed that!'

'You'll, perhaps, batten down your hatches till you're spoke to, my friend,' cried Silver truculently to this speaker. And then, in his first gracious tones, he replied to me: 'Yesterday morning, Mr Hawkins,' said he, 'in the dogwatch, down came Doctor Livesey with a flag of truce. Says he, "Cap'n Silver, you're sold out. Ship's gone." Well, maybe we'd been taking a glass, and a song to help it round. I won't say no. Leastways, none of us had looked out. We looked out, and, by thunder! the old ship was gone. I never seen a pack o' fools look fishier; and you may lay to that, if I tells you that looked the fishiest. "Well," says the doctor, "let's bargain." We bargained, him and I, and here we are: stores, brandy, block-house, the firewood you was thoughtful enough to cut, and, in a manner of speaking, the whole blessed boat, from cross-trees to kelson. As for them, they've tramped; I don't know where's they are.'

He drew again quietly at his pipe

'And lest you should take it into that head of yours,' he went on, 'that you was included in the treaty, here's the last word that was said: "How many are you," says I, "to leave?" "Four," says he – "four, and one of us wounded. As for that boy, I don't know where he is, confound him," says he, "nor I don't much care. We're about sick of him." These was his words.'

'Is that all?' I asked.

'Well, it's all that you're to hear, my son,' returned Silver.

'And now I am to choose?'

'And now you are to choose, and you may lay to that,' said Silver.

'Well,' said I, 'I am not such a fool but I know pretty well what I have to look for. Let the worst come to the worst, it's little I care. I've seen too many die since I fell in with you. But there's a thing or two I have to tell you,' I said, and by this time I was quite excited; 'and the first is this: here you are, in a bad way: ship lost, treasure lost, men lost; your whole business gone to wreck; and if you want to know who did it – it was I! I was in the apple barrel the night we sighted land, and I heard you, John, and you, Dick Johnson, and Hands, who is now at the bottom of the sea, and told every word you said before the hour was out. And as for the schooner, it was I who cut her cable, and it was I that killed the men you had aboard of her, and it was I who brought her where you'll never see her more, not one of you. The laugh's on my side; I've had the top of this business from the first; I no more fear you than I fear a fly. Kill me, if you please, or spare me. But one thing I'll say, and no more; if you spare me, bygones are bygones, and when you fellows are in court for piracy, I'll save you all I can. It is for you to choose. Kill another and do yourselves no good, or spare me and keep a witness to save you from the gallows.'

I stopped, for, I tell you, I was out of breath, and, to my wonder, not a man of them moved, but all sat staring at me like as many sheep. And while they were still staring, I broke out again:—

'And now, Mr Silver,' I said, 'I believe you're the best man here, and if things go to the worst, I'll take it kind of you to let the doctor know the way I took it.'

'I'll bear it in mind,' said Silver, with an accent so curious that I could not, for the life of me, decide whether he were laughing at my request, or had been favourably affected by my courage.

'I'll put one to that,' cried the old mahogany-faced seaman – Morgan by name – whom I had seen in Long John's public house upon the quays of Bristol. 'It was him that knowed Black Dog.'

'Well, and see here,' added the sea-cook. 'I'll put another again to that, by thunder! for it was this same boy that faked the chart from Billy Bones. First and last, we've split upon Jim Hawkins!'

'Then here goes!' said Morgan, with an oath.

And he sprang up, drawing his knife as if he had been twenty.

'Avast, there!' cried Silver. 'Who are you, Tom Morgan? Maybe you thought you was cap'n here, perhaps. By the powers, but I'll teach you better! Cross me, and you'll go where many a good man's gone before you, first and last, these thirty year back – some to the yard-arm, shiver my timbers! and some by the board, and all to feed the fishes. There's never a man looked me between the eyes and seen a good day a'terwards, Tom Morgan, you may lay to that.'

Morgan paused; but a hoarse murmur rose from the others.

'Tom's right,' said one.

'I stood hazing long enough from one,' added another. 'I'll be hanged if I'll be hazed by you, John Silver.'

'Did any of you gentlemen want to have it out with *me*?' roared Silver, bending far forward from his position on the keg, with his pipe still glowing in his right hand. 'Put a name on what you're at; you ain't dumb, I reckon. Him that wants shall get it. Have I lived this many years, and a son of a rum puncheon cock his hat athwart my hawse at the latter end of it? You know the way; you're all gentlemen o' fortune, by your account. Well, I'm ready. Take a cutlass, him that dares, and I'll see the colour of his inside, crutch and all, before that pipe's empty.'

Not a man stirred; not a man answered.

'That's your sort, is it?' he added, returning his pipe to his mouth. 'Well, you're a gay lot to look at, anyway. Not much worth to fight, you ain't. P'r'aps you can understand King George's English. I'm cap'n here by 'lection. I'm cap'n here because I'm the best man by a long sea-mile. You won't fight, as gentlemen o' fortune should; then, by thunder, you'll obey, and you may lay to it! I like that boy, now; I never seen a better boy than that. He's more a man than any pair of rats of you in this here house, and what I say is this: let me see him that'll lay a hand on him – that's what I say, and you may lay to it.'

There was a long pause after this. I stood straight up against the wall, my heart still going like a sledge-hammer, but with a ray of hope now shining in my bosom. Silver leant back against the wall, his arms crossed, his pipe in the corner of his mouth, as calm as though he had been in church; yet his eye kept wandering furtively, and he kept the tail of it on his unruly followers. They, on their part, drew gradually together towards the far end of the block-house, and the low hiss of their whispering sounded in my ear continuously, like a stream. One after another, they would look up, and the red light of the torch would fall for a second on their nervous faces; but it was not towards me, it was towards Silver that they turned their eyes.

'You seem to have a lot to say,' remarked Silver, spitting far into the air. 'Pipe up and let me hear it, or lay to.'

'Ax your pardon, sir,' returned one of the men, 'you're pretty free with some of the rules; maybe you'll kindly keep an eye upon the rest. This crew's dissatisfied; this crew don't vally bullying a marlin-spike; this crew has its rights like other crews, I'll make so free as that; and by your own rules, I take it we can talk together. I ax your pardon, sir, acknowledging you for to be capting at this present; but I claim my right, and steps outside for a council.'

And with an elaborate sea-salute, this fellow, a long, ill-looking, yellow-eyed man of five-and-thirty, stepped coolly towards the door and disappeared out of the house. One after another, the rest followed his example; each making a salute as he passed; each adding some apology. 'According to rules,' said one. 'Fo'c's'le council,' said Morgan. And so with one remark or another, all marched out, and left Silver and me alone with the torch.

The sea-cook instantly removed his pipe.

'Now, look you here, Jim Hawkins,' he said, in a steady whisper, that was no more than audible, 'you're within half a plank of death, and, what's a long sight worse, of torture. They're going to throw me off. But, you mark, I stand by you through thick and thin. I didn't mean to; no, not till you spoke up. I was about desperate to lose that much blunt, and be hanged into the bargain. But I see you was the right sort. I says to myself: You stand by Hawkins, John, and Hawkins 'll stand by you. You're his last card, and, by the living thunder, John, he's yours! Back to back, says I. You save your witness, and he'll save your neck!'

I began dimly to understand.

'You mean all's lost?' I asked.

'Ay, by gum, I do!' he answered. 'Ship gone, neck gone – that's the size of it. Once I looked into that bay, Jim Hawkins, and seen no schooner – well, I'm tough, but I gave out. As for that lot and their council, mark me, they're outright fools and cowards. I'll save your life – if so be as I can – from them. But, see here, Jim – tit for tat – you save Long John from swinging.'

I was bewildered; it seemed a thing so hopeless he was asking – he, the old buccaneer, the ringleader throughout.

'What I can do, that I'll do,' I said.

'It's a bargain!' cried Long John. 'You speak up plucky, and, by thunder! I've a chance.'

He hobbled to the torch, where it stood propped among the firewood, and took a fresh light to his pipe.

'Understand me, Jim,' he said, returning. 'I've a head on my shoulders, I have. I'm on squire's side now. I know you've got that ship safe somewheres. How you done it, I don't know, but safe it is. I guess Hands and O'Brien turned soft. I never much believed in neither of *them*. Now you mark me. I ask no questions, nor I won't let others. I know when a game's up, I do; and I know a lad that's staunch. Ah, you that's young – you and me might have done a power of good together!'

He drew some cognac from the cask into a tin cannikin.

'Will you taste, messmate?' he asked; and when I had refused: 'Well, I'll take a drain myself, Jim,' said he. 'I need a caulker, for there's trouble on hand. And, talking o' trouble, why did that doctor give me the chart, Jim?'

My face expressed a wonder so unaffected that he saw the needlessness of further questions.

'Ah, well, he did, though,' said he. 'And there's something under that, no doubt – something, surely, under that, Jim – bad or good.'

And he took another swallow of the brandy, shaking his great fair head like a man who looks forward to the worst.

The Black Spot Again

THE council of the buccaneers had lasted some time, when one of them re-entered the house, and with a repetition of the same salute, which had in my eyes an ironical air, begged for a moment's loan of the torch. Silver briefly agreed; and this emissary retired again, leaving us together in the dark.

'There's a breeze coming, Jim,' said Silver, who had, by this time, adopted quite a friendly and familiar tone.

I turned to the loophole nearest me and looked out. The embers of the great fire had so far burned themselves out, and now glowed so low and duskily, that I understood why these conspirators desired a torch. About half way down the slope to the stockade, they were collected in a group; one held the light; another was on his knees in their midst, and I saw the blade of an open knife shine in his hand with varying colours, in the moon and torchlight. The rest were all somewhat stooping, as though watching the manoeuvres of this last. I could just make out that he had a book as well as a knife in his hand; and was still wondering how anything so incongruous had come in their possession, when the kneeling figure rose once more to his feet, and the whole party began to move together towards the house.

'Here they come,' said I; and I returned to my former position, for it seemed beneath my dignity that they should find me watching them.

'Well, let 'em come, lad – let 'em come,' said Silver, cheerily. 'I've still a shot in my locker.'

The door opened, and the five men, standing huddled together just inside, pushed one of their number forward. In any other circumstances it would have been comical to see his slow advance, hesitating as he set down each foot, but holding his closed right hand in front of him.

'Step up, lad,' cried Silver. 'I won't eat you. Hand it over, lubber. I know the rules, I do; I won't hurt a depytation.'

Thus encouraged, the buccaneer stepped forth more briskly, and having passed something to Silver, from hand to hand, slipped yet more smartly back again to his companions.

The sea-cook looked at what had been given him.

'The black spot! I thought so,' he observed. 'Where might you have got the paper? Why, hillo! look here, now: this ain't lucky! You've gone and cut this out of a Bible. What fool's cut a Bible?'

'Ah, there!' said Morgan – 'there! Wot did I say? No good'll come o' that, I said.'

'Well, you've about fixed it now, among you,' continued Silver. 'You'll all swing now, I reckon. What soft-headed lubber had a Bible?'

'It was Dick,' said one.

'Dick, was it? Then Dick can get to prayers,' said Silver. 'He's seen his slice of luck, has Dick, and you may lay to that.'

But here the long man with the yellow eyes struck in.

'Belay that talk, John Silver,' he said. 'This crew has tipped you the black spot in full council, as in dooty bound; just you turn it over, as in dooty bound, and see what's wrote there. Then you can talk.'

'Thanky, George,' replied the sea-cook. 'You always was brisk for business, and has the rules by heart, George, as I'm pleased to see. Well, what is it, anyway? Ah! "Deposed" – that's it, is it? Very pretty wrote, to be sure; like print, I swear. Your hand o' write, George? Why, you was gettin' quite a leadin' man in this here crew. You'll be cap'n next, I shouldn't wonder. Just oblige me with that torch again, will you? this pipe don't draw.'

'Come, now,' said George, 'you don't fool this crew no more. You're a funny man, by your account; but you're over now, and you'll maybe step down off that barrel, and help vote.'

'I thought you said you knowed the rules,' returned Silver,

contemptuously. 'Leastways, if you don't, I do; and I wait here – and I'm still your cap'n, mind – till you outs with your grievances, and I reply, in the meantime, your black spot ain't worth a biscuit. After that, we'll see.'

'Oh,' replied George, 'you don't be under no kind of apprehension; *we're* all square, we are. First, you've made a hash of this cruise – you'll be a bold man to say no to that. Second, you let the enemy out o' this here trap for nothing. Why did they want out? I dunno; but it's pretty plain they wanted it. Third, you wouldn't let us go at them upon the march. Oh, we see through you, John Silver; you want to play booty, that's what's wrong with you. And then, fourth, there's this here boy.'

'Is that all?' asked Silver quietly.

'Enough, too,' retorted George. 'We'll all swing and sundry for your bungling.'

'Well, now, look here, I'll answer these four p'ints; one after another I'll answer 'em. I made a hash o' this cruise, did I? Well, now, you all know what I wanted; and you all know, if that had been done, that we'd 'a' been aboard the *Hispaniola* this night as ever was, every man of us alive, and fit, and full of good plum-duff, and the treasure in the hold of her, by thunder! Well, who crossed me? Who forced my hand, as was the lawful cap'n? Who tipped me the black spot the day we landed, and began this dance? Ah, it's a fine dance – I'm with you there – and looks mighty like a hornpipe in a rope's end at Execution Dock by London town, it does. But who done it? Why, it was Anderson, and Hands, and you, George Merry! And you're the last above board of that same meddling crew; and you have the Davy Jones's insolence to up and stand for cap'n over me – you, that sank the lot of us! By the powers! but this tops the stiffest yarn to nothing.'

Silver paused, and I could see by the faces of George and his late comrades that these words had not been said in vain.

'That's for number one,' cried the accused, wiping the sweat from his brow, for he had been talking with a vehemence that shook the house. 'Why, I give you my word, I'm sick to speak to you. You've neither sense nor memory, and I leave it to fancy where your mothers was that let you come to sea. Sea! Gentlemen o' fortune! I reckon tailors is your trade.'

'Go on, John,' said Morgan. 'Speak up to the others.'

'Ah, the others!' returned John. 'They're a nice lot, ain't they? You say this cruise is bungled. Ah! by gum, if you could understand how bad it's bungled, you would see! We're that near the gibbet that my neck's stiff with thinking on it. You've seen 'em, maybe, hanged in chains, birds about 'em, seamen p'inting 'em out as they go down with the tide. "Who's that?" says one. "That! Why, that's John Silver. I knowed him well," says another. And you can hear the chains a-jangle as you go about and reach for the other buoy. Now, that's about where we are, every mother's son of us, thanks to him, and Hands, and Anderson, and other ruination fools of you. And if you want to know about number four, and that boy, why, shiver my timbers! isn't he a hostage? Are we a-going to waste a hostage? No, not us; he might be our last chance, and I shouldn't wonder. Kill that boy? not me, mates! And number three? Ah, well, there's a deal to say to number three. Maybe you don't count it nothing to have a real college doctor come to see you every day – you, John, with your head broke – or you, George Merry, that had the ague shakes upon you not six hours agone, and has your eyes the colour of lemon peel to this same moment on the clock? And maybe, perhaps, you didn't know there was a consort coming, either? But there is; and not so long till then; and we'll see who'll be glad to have a hostage when it comes to that. And as for number two, and why I made a bargain – well, you came crawling on your knees to me to make it – on your knees you came, you was that downhearted – and you'd have starved, too, if I hadn't – but that's a trifle! you look there – that's why!'

And he cast down upon the floor a paper that I instantly recognised – none other than the chart on yellow paper, with the three red crosses, that I had found in the oilcloth at the bottom of the captain's chest. Why the doctor had given it to him was more than I could fancy.

But if it were inexplicable to me, the appearance of the chart was incredible to the surviving mutineers. They

leaped upon it like cats upon a mouse. It went from hand
to hand, one tearing it from another; and by the oaths
and the cries and the childish laughter with which they
accompanied their examination, you would have thought,
not only they were fingering the very gold, but were at sea
with it, besides, in safety.

'Yes,' said one, 'that's Flint, sure enough. J.F., and a
score below, with a clove hitch to it; so he done ever.'

'Mighty pretty,' said George. 'But how are we to get
away with it, and us no ship?'

Silver suddenly sprang up, and supporting himself with a
hand against the wall: 'Now I give you warning, George,' he
cried. 'One more word of your sauce, and I'll call you down
and fight you. How? Why, how do I know? You had ought
to tell me that – you and the rest, that lost me my schooner,
with your interference, burn you! But not you, you can't;
you hain't got the invention of a cockroach. But civil you can
speak, and shall, George Merry, you may lay to that.'

'That's fair enow,' said the old man Morgan.

'Fair! I reckon so,' said the sea-cook. 'You lost the ship;
I found the treasure. Who's the better man at that? And
now I resign, by thunder! Elect whom you please to be
your cap'n now; I'm done with it.'

'Silver!' they cried. 'Barbecue for ever! Barbecue for
cap'n!'

'So that's the toon, is it?' cried the cook. 'George, I reckon
you'll have to wait another turn, friend; and lucky for you
as I'm not a revengeful man. But that was never my way.
And now, shipmates, this black spot? 'Tain't much good
now, is it? Dick's crossed his luck and spoiled his Bible,
and that's about all.'

'It'll do to kiss the book on still, won't it?' growled Dick,
who was evidently uneasy at the curse he had brought upon
himself.

'A Bible with a bit cut out!' returned Silver, derisively.
'Not it. It don't bind no more'n a ballad-book.'

'Don't it, though?' cried Dick, with a sort of joy. 'Well,
I reckon that's worth having, too.'

'Here, Jim – here's a cur'osity for you,' said Silver; and
he tossed me the paper.

It was a round about the size of a crown piece. One side was blank, for it had been the last leaf; the other contained a verse or two of Revelation – these words among the rest, which struck sharply home upon my mind: 'Without are dogs and murderers.' The printed side had been blackened with wood ash, which already began to come off and soil my fingers; on the blank side had been written with the same material the one word 'Depposed.' I have that curiosity beside me at this moment; but not a trace of writing now remains beyond a single scratch, such as a man might make with his thumb-nail.

That was the end of the night's business. Soon after, with a drink all round, we lay down to sleep, and the outside of Silver's vengeance was to put George Merry up for sentinel, and threaten him with death if he should prove unfaithful.

It was long ere I could close an eye, and Heaven knows I had matter enough for thought in the man whom I had slain that afternoon, in my own most perilous position, and, above all, in the remarkable game that I saw Silver now engaged upon – keeping the mutineers together with one hand, and grasping, with the other, after every means, possible and impossible, to make his peace and save his miserable life. He himself slept peacefully, and snored aloud; yet my heart was sore for him, wicked as he was, to think on the dark perils that environed, and the shameful gibbet that awaited him.

On Parole

I WAS wakened – indeed, we were all wakened, for I could see even the sentinel shake himself together from where he had fallen against the door-post – by a clear, hearty voice hailing us from the margin of the wood:—

'Block-house, ahoy!' it cried. 'Here's the doctor.'

And the doctor it was. Although I was glad to hear the sound, yet my gladness was not without admixture. I remembered with confusion my insubordinate and stealthy conduct; and when I saw where it had brought me – among what companions and surrounded by what dangers – I felt ashamed to look him in the face.

He must have risen in the dark, for the day had hardly come; and when I ran to a loophole and looked out, I saw him standing, like Silver once before, up to the mid-leg in creeping vapour.

'You, doctor! Top o' the morning to you, sir!' cried Silver, broad awake and beaming with good-nature in a moment. 'Bright and early, to be sure; and it's the early bird, as the saying goes, that gets the rations. George, shake up your timbers, son, and help Dr Livesey over the ship's side. All a-doin' well, your patients was – all well and merry.'

So he pattered on, standing on the hill-top, with his crutch under his elbow, and one hand upon the side of the log-house – quite the old John in voice, manner, and expression.

'We've quite a surprise for you, too, sir,' he continued. 'We've a little stranger here – he! he! A noo boarder and lodger, sir, and looking fit and taut as a fiddle; slep' like a supercargo, he did, right alongside of John – stem to stem we was, all night.'

Dr Livesey was by this time across the stockade and

pretty near the cook; and I could hear the alteration in his voice as he said:—

'Not Jim?'

'The very same Jim as ever was,' says Silver.

The doctor stopped outright, although he did not speak, and it was some seconds before he seemed able to move on.

'Well, well,' he said, at last, 'duty first and pleasure afterwards, as you might have said yourself, Silver. Let us overhaul these patients of yours.'

A moment afterwards he had entered the block-house, and, with one grim nod to me, proceeded with his work among the sick. He seemed under no apprehension, though he must have known that his life, among these treacherous demons, depended on a hair; and he rattled on to his patients as if he were paying an ordinary professional visit in a quiet English family. His manner, I suppose, reacted on the men; for they behaved to him as if nothing had occurred – as if he were still ship's doctor, and they still faithful hands before the mast.

'You're doing well, my friend,' he said to the fellow with the bandaged head, 'and if ever any person had a close shave, it was you; your head must be as hard as iron. Well, George, how goes it? You're a pretty colour, certainly; why, your liver, man, is upside down. Did you take that medicine? Did he take that medicine, men?'

'Ay, ay, sir, he took it, sure enough,' returned Morgan.

'Because, you see, since I am mutineers' doctor, or prison doctor, as I prefer to call it,' says Dr Livesey, in his pleasantest way, 'I make it a point of honour not to lose a man for King George (God bless him!) and the gallows.'

The rogues looked at each other, but swallowed the home-thrust in silence.

'Dick don't feel well, sir,' said one.

'Don't he?' replied the doctor. 'Well, step up here, Dick, and let me see your tongue. No, I should be surprised if he did! the man's tongue is fit to frighten the French. Another fever.'

'Ah, there,' said Morgan, 'that comed of sp'iling Bibles.'

'That comed – as you call it – of being arrant asses,'

retorted the doctor, 'and not having sense enough to
know honest air from poison, and the dry land from a
vile, pestiferous slough. I think it most probable – though,
of course, it's only an opinion – that you'll all have the deuce
to pay before you get that malaria out of your systems. Camp
in a bog, would you? Silver, I'm surprised at you. You're
less of a fool than many, take you all round; but you don't
appear to me to have the rudiments of a notion of the rules
of health.'

'Well,' he added, after he had dosed them round, and they
had taken his prescriptions, with really laughable humility,
more like charity school-children than blood-guilty mutineers and pirates – 'well, that's done for to-day. And now
I should wish to have a talk with that boy, please.'

And he nodded his head in my direction carelessly.

George Merry was at the door, spitting and spluttering
over some bad-tasted medicine; but at the first word of
the doctor's proposal he swung round with a deep flush,
and cried 'No!' and swore.

Silver struck the barrel with his open hand.

'Si-lence!' he roared, and looked about him positively
like a lion. 'Doctor,' he went on, in his usual tones, 'I was
a-thinking of that, knowing as how you had a fancy for the
boy. We're all humbly grateful for your kindness, and, as
you see, puts faith in you, and takes the drugs down like
that much grog. And I take it I've found a way as'll suit all.
Hawkins, will you give me your word of honour as a young
gentleman – for a young gentleman you are, although poor
born – your word of honour not to slip your cable?'

I readily gave the pledge required.

'Then, doctor,' said Silver, 'you just step outside o' that
stockade, and once you're there, I'll bring the boy down
on the inside, and I reckon you can yarn through the spars.
Good-day to you, sir, and all our dooties to the squire and
Cap'n Smollett.'

The explosion of disapproval, which nothing but Silver's
black looks had restrained, broke out immediately the
doctor had left the house. Silver was roundly accused of
playing double – of trying to make a separate peace for
himself – of sacrificing the interests of his accomplices and

victims; and, in one word, of the identical, exact thing that he was doing. It seemed to me so obvious, in this case, that I could not imagine how he was to turn their anger. But he was twice the man the rest were; and his last night's victory had given him a huge preponderance on their minds. He called them all the fools and dolts you can imagine, said it was necessary I should talk to the doctor, fluttered the chart in their faces, asked them if they could afford to break the treaty the very day they were bound a-treasure-hunting.

'No, by thunder!' he cried, 'it's us must break the treaty when the time comes; and till then I'll gammon that doctor, if I have to ile his boots with brandy.'

And then he bade them get the fire lit, and stalked out upon his crutch, with his hand on my shoulder, leaving them in a disarray, and silenced by his volubility rather than convinced.

'Slow, lad, slow,' he said. 'They might round upon us in a twinkle of an eye, if we was seen to hurry.'

Very deliberately, then, did we advance across the sand to where the doctor awaited us on the other side of the stockade, and as soon as we were within easy speaking distance, Silver stopped.

'You'll make a note of this here also, doctor,' says he, 'and the boy'll tell you how I saved his life, and were deposed for it, too, and you may lay to that. Doctor, when a man's steering as near the wind as me – playing chuck-farthing with the last breath in his body, like – you wouldn't think it too much, mayhap, to give him one good word? You'll please bear in mind it's not my life only now – it's that boy's into the bargain; and you'll speak me fair, doctor, and give me a bit o' hope to go on, for the sake of mercy.'

Silver was a changed man, once he was out there and had his back to his friends and the block-house; his cheeks seemed to have fallen in, his voice trembled; never was a soul more dead in earnest.

'Why, John, you're not afraid?' asked Dr Livesey.

'Doctor, I'm no coward; no, not I – not *so* much!' and he snapped his fingers. 'If I was I wouldn't say it. But I'll own up fairly, I've the shakes upon me for the gallows.

You're a good man and a true; I never seen a better man! And you'll not forget what I done good, not any more than you'll forget the bad, I know. And I step aside – see here – and leave you and Jim alone. And you'll put that down for me, too, for it's a long stretch, is that!'

So saying, he stepped back a little way, till he was out of earshot, and there sat down upon a tree-stump and began to whistle; spinning round now and again upon his seat so as to command a sight, sometimes of me and the doctor, and sometimes of his unruly ruffians as they went to and fro in the sand, between the fire – which they were busy rekindling – and the house, from which they brought forth pork and bread to make the breakfast.

'So, Jim,' said the doctor, sadly, 'here you are. As you have brewed, so shall you drink, my boy. Heaven knows, I cannot find it in my heart to blame you; but this much I will say, be it kind or unkind: when Captain Smollett was well, you dared not have gone off; and when he was ill, and couldn't help it, by George, it was downright cowardly!'

I will own that I here began to weep. 'Doctor,' I said, 'you might spare me. I have blamed myself enough; my life's forfeit anyway, and I should have been dead by now, if Silver hadn't stood for me; and doctor, believe this, I can die – and I daresay I deserve it – but what I fear is torture. If they come to torture me—'

'Jim,' the doctor interrupted, and his voice was quite changed, 'Jim, I can't have this. Whip over, and we'll run for it.'

'Doctor,' said I, 'I passed my word.'

'I know, I know,' he cried. 'We can't help that, Jim, now. I'll take it on my shoulders, holus bolus, blame and shame, my boy; but stay here, I cannot let you. Jump! One jump, and you're out, and we'll run for it like antelopes.'

'No,' I replied, 'you know right well you wouldn't do the thing yourself; neither you, nor squire, nor captain; and no more will I. Silver trusted me; I passed my word, and back I go. But, doctor, you did not let me finish. If they come to torture me, I might let slip a word of where the ship is; for I got the ship, part by luck and part by risking, and she lies in North Inlet, on the southern beach, and just below high water. At half-tide she must be high and dry.'

'The ship!' exclaimed the doctor.

Rapidly I described to him my adventures, and he heard me out in silence.

'There is a kind of fate in this,' he observed, when I had done. 'Every step, it's you that saves our lives; and do you suppose by any chance that we are going to let you lose yours? That would be a poor return, my boy. You found out the plot; you found Ben Gunn – the best deed that ever you did, or will do, though you live to ninety. Oh, by Jupiter, and talking of Ben Gunn! why, this is the mischief in person. Silver!' he cried, 'Silver! – I'll give you a piece of advice,' he continued, as the cook drew near again; 'don't you be in any great hurry after that treasure.'

'Why, sir, I do my possible, which that ain't,' said Silver. 'I can only, asking your pardon, save my life and the boy's by seeking for that treasure; and you may lay to that.'

'Well, Silver,' replied the doctor, 'if that is so, I'll go one step further: look out for squalls when you find it.'

'Sir,' said Silver, 'as between man and man, that's too much and too little. What you're after, why you left the block-house, why you given me that there chart, I don't know, now, do I? and yet I done your bidding with my eyes shut and never a word of hope! But no, this here's too much. If you won't tell me what you mean plain out, just say so, and I'll leave the helm.'

'No,' said the doctor, musingly, 'I've no right to say more; it's not my secret, you see, Silver, or, I give you my word, I'd tell it you. But I'll go as far with you as I dare go, and a step beyond; for I'll have my wig sorted by the captain or I'm mistaken! And, first, I'll give you a bit of hope: Silver, if we both get alive out of this wolf-trap, I'll do my best to save you, short of perjury.'

Silver's face was radiant. 'You couldn't say more, I'm sure, sir, not if you was my mother,' he cried.

'Well, that's my first concession,' added the doctor. 'My second is a piece of advice: Keep the boy close beside you, and when you need help, halloo. I'm off to seek it for you, and that itself will show you if I speak at random. Good-bye, Jim.'

And Dr Livesey shook hands with me through the stockade, nodded to Silver, and set off at a brisk pace into the wood.

The Treasure Hunt – Flint's Pointer

'JIM,' said Silver, when we were alone, 'if I saved your life, you saved mine; and I'll not forget it. I seen the doctor waving you to run for it – with the tail of my eye, I did; and I seen you say no, as plain as hearing. Jim, that's one to you. This is the first glint of hope I had since the attack failed, and I owe it you. And now, Jim, we're to go in for this here treasure hunting, with sealed orders, too, and I don't like it; and you and me must stick close, back to back like, and we'll save our necks in spite o' fate and fortune.'

Just then a man hailed us from the fire that breakfast was ready, and we were soon seated here and there about the sand over biscuit and fried junk. They had lit a fire fit to roast an ox; and it was now grown so hot that they could only approach it from the windward, and even there not without precaution. In the same wasteful spirit, they had cooked, I suppose, three times more than we could eat; and one of them, with an empty laugh, threw what was left into the fire, which blazed and roared again over this unusual fuel. I never in my life saw men so careless of the morrow; hand to mouth is the only word that can describe their way of doing; and what with wasted food and sleeping sentries, though they were bold enough for a brush and be done with it, I could see their entire unfitness for anything like a prolonged campaign.

Even Silver, eating away, with Captain Flint upon his shoulder, had not a word of blame for their recklessness. And this the more surprised me, for I thought he had never shown himself so cunning as he did then.

'Ay, mates,' said he, 'it's lucky you have Barbecue to think for you with this here head. I got what I wanted, I did. Sure enough, they have the ship. Where they have it,

I don't know yet; but once we hit the treasure, we'll have to jump about and find out. And then, mates, us that has the boats, I reckon, has the upper hand.'

Thus he kept running on, with his mouth full of the hot bacon: thus he restored their hope and confidence, and, I more than suspect, repaired his own at the same time.

'As for hostage,' he continued, 'that's his last talk, I guess, with them he loves so dear. I've got my piece o' news, and thanky to him for that; but it's over and done. I'll take him in a line when we go treasure-hunting, for we'll keep him like so much gold, in case of accidents, you mark, and in the meantime. Once we got the ship and treasure both, and off to sea like jolly companions, why, then, we'll talk Mr Hawkins over, we will, and we'll give him his share, to be sure, for all his kindness.'

It was no wonder the men were in a good humour now. For my part, I was horribly cast down. Should the scheme he had now sketched prove feasible, Silver, already doubly a traitor, would not hesitate to adopt it. He had still a foot in either camp, and there was no doubt he would prefer wealth and freedom with the pirates to a bare escape from hanging, which was the best he had to hope on our side.

Nay, and even if things so fell out that he was forced to keep his faith with Dr Livesey, even then what danger lay before us! What a moment that would be when the suspicions of his followers turned to certainty, and he and I should have to fight for dear life – he, a cripple, and I, a boy – against five strong and active seamen!

Add to this double apprehension the mystery that still hung over the behaviour of my friends; their unexplained desertion of the stockade; their inexplicable cession of the chart; or, harder still to understand, the doctor's last warning to Silver, 'Look out for squalls when you find it;' and you will readily believe how little taste I found in my breakfast, and with how uneasy a heart I set forth behind my captors on the quest for treasure.

We made a curious figure, had anyone been there to see us; all in soiled sailor clothes, and all but me armed to the teeth. Silver had two guns slung about him – one before and one behind – besides the great cutlass at his waist, and a pistol in each pocket of his square-tailed coat. To complete his strange appearance, Captain Flint sat perched upon his shoulder and gabbling odds and ends of purposeless sea-talk. I had a line about my waist, and followed obediently after the sea-cook, who held the loose end of the rope, now in his free hand, now between his powerful teeth. For all the world, I was led like a dancing bear.

The other men were variously burthened; some carrying picks and shovels – for that had been the very first necessary they brought ashore from the *Hispaniola* – others laden with pork, bread, and brandy for the midday meal. All the stores, I observed, came from our stock; and I could see the truth of Silver's words the night before. Had he not struck a bargain with the doctor, he and his mutineers, deserted by the ship, must have been driven to subsist on clear water and the proceeds of their hunting. Water would have been little to their taste; a sailor is not usually a good shot; and, besides all that, when they were so short of eatables, it was not likely they would be very flush of powder.

Well, thus equipped, we all set out – even the fellow with the broken head, who should certainly have kept in shadow – and straggled, one after another, to the beach, where the two gigs awaited us. Even these bore trace of the drunken folly of the pirates, one in a broken thwart, and both in their muddy and unbailed condition. Both were to be carried along with us, for the sake of safety; and so, with our numbers divided between them, we set forth upon the bosom of the anchorage.

As we pulled over, there was some discussion on the chart. The red cross was, of course, far too large to be a guide; and the terms of the note on the back, as you will hear, admitted of some ambiguity. They ran, the reader may remember, thus:—

Tall tree, Spy-glass shoulder, bearing a point to the N. of N.N.E.
Skeleton Island E.S.E. and by E.
Ten feet.

A tall tree was thus the principal mark. Now, right before us, the anchorage was bounded by a plateau from

two to three hundred feet high, adjoining on the north the
sloping southern shoulder of the Spy-glass, and rising again
towards the south into the rough, cliffy eminence called the
Mizzen-mast Hill. The top of the plateau was dotted thickly
with pine trees of varying height. Every here and there, one
of a different species rose forty or fifty feet clear above its
neighbours, and which of these was the particular 'tall tree'
of Captain Flint could only be decided on the spot, and by
the readings of the compass.

Yet, although that was the case, every man on board the
boats had picked a favourite of his own ere we were half
way over, Long John alone shrugging his shoulders and
bidding them wait till they were there.

We pulled easily, by Silver's directions, not to weary the
hands prematurely; and, after quite a long passage, landed
at the mouth of the second river – that which runs down a
woody cleft of the Spy-glass. Thence, bending to our left,
we began to ascend the slope towards the plateau.

At the first outset, heavy, miry ground and a matted,
marish vegetation, greatly delayed our progress; but by
little and little the hill began to steepen and become
stony under foot, and the wood to change its character
and to grow in a more open order. It was, indeed, a
most pleasant portion of the island that we were now
approaching. A heavy-scented broom and many flowering
shrubs had almost taken the place of grass. Thickets of
green nutmeg trees were dotted here and there with the
red columns and the broad shadow of the pines; and the
first mingled their spice with the aroma of the others. The
air, besides, was fresh and stirring, and this, under the sheer
sunbeams, was a wonderful refreshment to our senses.

The party spread itself abroad, in a fan shape, shouting
and leaping to and fro. About the centre, and a good way
behind the rest, Silver and I followed – I tethered by my
rope, he ploughing, with deep pants, among the sliding
gravel. From time to time, indeed, I had to lend him
a hand, or he must have missed his footing and fallen
backward down the hill.

We had thus proceeded for about half a mile, and were
approaching the brow of the plateau, when the man upon

the farthest left began to cry aloud, as if in terror. Shout after shout came from him, and the others began to run in his direction.

'He can't 'a' found the treasure,' said old Morgan, hurrying past us from the right, 'for that's clean a-top.'

Indeed, as we found when we also reached the spot, it was something very different. At the foot of a pretty big pine, and involved in a green creeper, which had even partly lifted some of the smaller bones, a human skeleton lay, with a few shreds of clothing, on the ground. I believe a chill struck for a moment to every heart.

'He was a seaman,' said George Merry, who, bolder than the rest, had gone up close, and was examining the rags of clothing. 'Leastways, this is good sea-cloth.'

'Ay, ay,' said Silver, 'like enough; you wouldn't look to find a bishop here, I reckon. But what sort of a way is that for bones to lie? 'Tain't in natur'.'

Indeed, on a second glance, it seemed impossible to fancy that the body was in a natural position. But for some disarray (the work, perhaps, of the birds that had fed upon him, or of the slow-growing creeper that had gradually enveloped his remains) the man lay perfectly straight – his feet pointing in one direction, his hands, raised above his head like a diver's, pointing directly in the opposite.

'I've taken a notion into my old numskull,' observed Silver. 'Here's the compass; there's the tip-top p'int o' Skeleton Island, stickin' out like a tooth. Just take a bearing, will you, along the line of them bones.'

It was done. The body pointed straight in the direction of the island, and the compass read duly E.S.E. and by E.

'I thought so,' cried the cook; 'this here is a p'inter. Right up there is our line for the Pole Star and the jolly dollars. But, by thunder! if it don't make me cold inside to think of Flint. This is one of *his* jokes, and no mistake. Him and these six was alone here; he killed 'em, every man; and this one he hauled here and laid down by compass, shiver my timbers! They're long bones, and the hair's been yellow. Ay, that would be Allardyce. You mind Allardyce, Tom Morgan?'

'Ay, ay,' returned Morgan, 'I mind him; he owed me money, he did, and took my knife ashore with him.'

'Speaking of knives,' said another, 'why don't we find his'n lying round? Flint warn't the man to pick a seaman's pocket; and the birds, I guess, would leave it be.'

'By the powers, and that's true!' cried Silver.

'There ain't a thing left here,' said Merry, still feeling round among the bones, 'not a copper doit nor a baccy box. It don't look nat'ral to me.'

'No, by gum, it don't,' agreed Silver; 'not nat'ral, nor not nice, says you. Great guns! messmates, but if Flint was living, this would be a hot spot for you and me. Six they were, and six are we; and bones is what they are now.'

'I saw him dead with these here dead-lights,' said Morgan. 'Billy took me in. There he laid, with penny-pieces on his eyes.'

'Dead – ay, sure enough he's dead and gone below,' said the fellow with the bandage; 'but if ever sperrit walked, it would be Flint's. Dear heart, but he died bad, did Flint!'

'Ay, that he did,' observed another; 'now he raged, and now he hollered for the rum, and now he sang. "Fifteen Men" were his only song, mates; and I tell you true, I never rightly liked to hear it since. It was main hot, and the windy was open, and I hear that old song comin' out as clear as clear – and the death-haul on the man already.'

'Come, come,' said Silver, 'stow this talk. He's dead, and he don't walk, that I know; leastways, he won't walk by day, and you may lay to that. Care killed a cat. Fetch ahead for the doubloons.'

We started, certainly; but in spite of the hot sun and the staring daylight, the pirates no longer ran separate and shouting through the wood, but kept side by side and spoke with bated breath. The terror of the dead buccaneer had fallen on their spirits.

The Treasure Hunt –
The Voice Among the Trees

PARTLY FROM the damping influence of this alarm, partly to rest Silver and the sick folk, the whole party sat down as soon as they had gained the brow of the ascent.

The plateau being somewhat tilted towards the west, this spot on which we had paused commanded a wide prospect on either hand. Before us, over the tree-tops, we beheld the Cape of the Woods fringed with surf; behind, we not only looked down upon the anchorage and Skeleton Island, but saw – clear across the spit and the eastern lowlands – a great field of open sea upon the east. Sheer above us rose the Spy-glass, here dotted with single pines, there black with precipices. There was no sound but that of the distant breakers, mounting from all round, and the chirp of countless insects in the brush. Not a man, not a sail upon the sea; the very largeness of the view increased the sense of solitude.

Silver, as he sat, took certain bearings with his compass.

'There are three "tall trees",' said he, 'about in the right line from Skeleton Island. "Spy-glass Shoulder," I take it, means that lower p'int there. It's child's play to find the stuff now. I've half a mind to dine first.'

'I don't feel sharp,' growled Morgan. 'Thinkin' o' Flint – I think it were – 'as done me.'

'Ah, well, my son, you praise your stars he's dead,' said Silver.

'He were an ugly devil,' cried a third pirate, with a shudder; 'that blue in the face, too!'

'That was how the rum took him,' added Merry. 'Blue! well, I reckon he was blue. That's a true word.'

Ever since they had found the skeleton and got upon this

train of thought, they had spoken lower and lower, and they had almost got to whispering by now, so that the sound of their talk hardly interrupted the silence of the wood. All of a sudden, out of the middle of the trees in front of us, a thin, high, trembling voice struck up the well-known air and words:—

> Fifteen men on the dead man's chest—
> Yo-ho-ho, and a bottle of rum!

I never have seen men more dreadfully affected than the pirates. The colour went from their six faces like enchantment; some leaped to their feet, some clawed hold of others; Morgan grovelled on the ground.

'It's Flint, by—!' cried Merry.

The song had stopped as suddenly as it began – broken off, you would have said, in the middle of a note, as though someone had laid his hand upon the singer's mouth. Coming so far through the clear, sunny atmosphere among the green tree-tops, I thought it had sounded airily and sweetly; and the effect on my companions was the stranger.

'Come,' said Silver, struggling with his ashen lips to get the word out, 'this won't do. Stand by to go about. This is a rum start, and I can't name the voice: but it's someone skylarking – someone that's flesh and blood, and you may lay to that.'

His courage had come back as he spoke, and some of the colour to his face along with it. Already the others had begun to lend an ear to this encouragement, and were coming a little to themselves, when the same voice broke out again – not this time singing, but in a faint distant hail, that echoed yet fainter among the clefts of the Spy-glass.

'Darby M'Graw,' it wailed – for that is the word that best describes the sound – 'Darby M'Graw! Darby M'Graw!' again and again and again; and then rising a little higher, and with an oath that I leave out, 'Fetch aft the rum, Darby!'

The buccaneers remained rooted to the ground, their eyes starting from their heads. Long after the voice had died away they still stared in silence, dreadfully, before them.

'That fixes it!' gasped one. 'Let's go.'

'They was his last words,' moaned Morgan, 'his last words above board.'

Dick had his Bible out, and was praying volubly. He had been well brought up, had Dick, before he came to sea and fell among bad companions.

Still, Silver was unconquered. I could hear his teeth rattle in his head; but he had not yet surrendered.

'Nobody in this here island ever heard of Darby,' he muttered; 'not one but us that's here.' And then, making a great effort, 'Shipmates,' he cried, 'I'm here to get that stuff, and I'll not be beat by man nor devil. I never was feared of Flint in his life, and, by the powers, I'll face him dead. There's seven hundred thousand pound not a quarter of a mile from here. When did ever a gentleman o' fortune show his stern to that much dollars, for a boozy old seaman with a blue mug – and him dead, too?'

But there was no sign of re-awakening courage in his followers; rather, indeed, of growing terror at the irreverence of his words.

'Belay there, John!' said Merry. 'Don't you cross a sperrit.'

And the rest were all too terrified to reply. They would have run away severally had they dared; but fear kept them together, and kept them close by John, as if his daring helped them. He, on this part, had pretty well fought his weakness down.

'Sperrit? Well, maybe,' he said. 'But there's one thing not clear to me. There was an echo. Now, no man ever seen a sperrit with a shadow; well, then, what's he doing with an echo to him, I should like to know? That ain't in natur', surely?'

This argument seemed weak enough to me. But you can never tell what will affect the superstitious, and, to my wonder, George Merry was greatly relieved.

'Well, that's so,' he said. 'You've a head upon your shoulders, John, and no mistake. 'Bout ship, mates! This here crew is on a wrong tack, I do believe. And come to think on it, it was like Flint's voice, I grant you, but not just so clear-away like it, after all. It was liker somebody else's voice now – it was liker—'

'By the powers, Ben Gunn!' roared Silver.

'Ay, and so it were,' cried Morgan, springing on his knees 'Ben Gunn it were!'

'It don't make much odds, do it, now?' asked Dick. 'Ben Gunn's not here in the body, any more'n Flint.'

But the older hands greeted this remark with scorn.

'Why nobody minds Ben Gunn,' cried Merry; 'dead or alive, nobody minds him.'

It was extraordinary how their spirits had returned, and how the natural colour had revived in their faces. Soon they were chatting together, with intervals of listening; and not long after, hearing no further sound, they shouldered the tools and set forth again, Merry walking first with Silver's compass to keep them on the right line with Skeleton Island. He had said the truth: dead or alive, nobody minded Ben Gunn.

Dick alone still held his Bible, and looked around him as he went, with fearful glances; but he found no sympathy, and Silver even joked him on his precautions.

'I told you,' said he – 'I told you, you had sp'iled your Bible. If it ain't no good to swear by, what do you suppose a sperrit would give for it? Not that!' and he snapped his big fingers, halting a moment on his crutch.

But Dick was not to be comforted; indeed, it was soon plain to me that the lad was falling sick; hastened by heat, exhaustion, and the shock of his alarm, the fever, predicted by Doctor Livesey, was evidently growing swiftly higher.

It was fine open walking here, upon the summit; our way lay a little downhill, for, as I have said, the plateau tilted towards the west. The pines, great and small, grew wide apart; and even between the clumps of nutmeg and azalea, wide open spaces baked in the hot sunshine. Striking, as we did, pretty near north-west across the island, we drew, on the one hand ever nearer under the shoulders of the Spy-glass, and on the other, looked ever wider over that western bay where I had once tossed and trembled in the coracle.

The first of the tall trees was reached, and by the bearing, proved the wrong one. So with the second. The third rose nearly two hundred feet into the air above a clump of underwood; a giant of a vegetable, with a red column as big as a cottage, and a wide shadow around in which a company could have manœuvred. It was conspicuous far to sea both on the east and west, and might have been entered as a sailing mark upon the chart.

But it was not its size that now impressed my companions; it was the knowledge that seven hundred thousand pounds in gold lay somewhere buried below its spreading shadow. The thought of the money, as they drew nearer, swallowed up their previous terrors. Their eyes burned in their heads; their feet grew speedier and lighter; their whole soul was bound up in that fortune, that whole lifetime of extravagance and pleasure, that lay waiting there for each of them.

Silver hobbled, grunting, on his crutch; his nostrils stood out and quivered; he cursed like a madman when the flies settled on his hot and shiny countenance; he plucked furiously at the line that held me to him, and, from time to time, turned his eyes upon me with a deadly look. Certainly he took no pains to hide his thoughts; and certainly I read them like print. In the immediate nearness of the gold, all else had been forgotten; his promise and the doctor's warning were both things of the past; and I could not doubt that he hoped to seize upon the treasure, find and board the *Hispaniola* under cover of night, cut every honest throat about that island, and sail away as he had at first intended, laden with crimes and riches.

Shaken as I was with these alarms, it was hard for me to keep up with the rapid pace of the treasure-hunters. Now and again I stumbled; and it was then that Silver plucked so roughly at the rope and launched at me his murderous glances. Dick, who had dropped behind us, and now brought up the rear, was babbling to himself both prayers and curses, as his fever kept rising. This also added to my wretchedness, and, to crown all, I was haunted by the thought of the tragedy that had once been acted on that plateau, when that ungodly buccaneer with the blue face – he who died at Savannah, singing and shouting for drink – had there, with his own hand, cut down his six accomplices. This grove, that was now so peaceful, must then have rung with cries, I thought; and even with the thought I could believe I heard it ringing still.

We were now at the margin of the thicket.

'Huzza, mates, altogether!' shouted Merry; and the foremost broke into a run.

And suddenly, not ten yards further, we beheld them stop. A low cry arose. Silver doubled his pace, digging away with the foot of his crutch like one possessed; and the next moment he and I had come also to a dead halt.

Before us was a great excavation, not very recent, for the sides had fallen in and grass had sprouted on the bottom. In this were the shaft of a pick broken in two and the boards of several packing-cases strewn around. On one of these boards I saw, branded with a hot iron, the name *Walrus* – the name of Flint's ship.

All was clear to probation. The *cache* had been found and rifled: the seven hundred thousand pounds were gone!

The Fall of a Chieftain

THERE NEVER was such an overturn in this world. Each of these six men was as though he had been struck. But with Silver the blow passed almost instantly. Every thought of his soul had been set full-stretch, like a racer, on that money; well, he was brought up in a single second, dead; and he kept his head, found his temper, and changed his plan before the others had had time to realise the disappointment.

'Jim,' he whispered, 'take that, and stand by for trouble.' And he passed me a double-barrelled pistol.

At the same time he began quietly moving northward, and in a few steps had put the hollow between us two and the other five. Then he looked at me and nodded, as much as to say, 'Here is a narrow corner,' as, indeed, I thought it was. His looks were now quite friendly; and I was so revolted at these constant changes, that I could not forbear whispering, 'So you've changed sides again.'

There was no time left for him to answer in. The buccaneers, with oaths and cries, began to leap, one after another, into the pit, and to dig with their fingers, throwing the boards aside as they did so. Morgan found a piece of gold. He held it up with a perfect spout of oaths. It was a two-guinea piece, and it went from hand to hand among them for a quarter of a minute.

'Two guineas!' roared Merry, shaking it at Silver. 'That's your seven hundred thousand pounds, is it? You're the man for bargains, ain't you? You're him that never bungled nothing, you wooden-headed lubber!'

'Dig away, boys,' said Silver, with the coolest insolence; 'you'll find some pig-nuts and I shouldn't wonder.'

'Pig-nuts!' repeated Merry, in a scream. 'Mates, do you

hear that? I tell you, now, that man there knew it all along. Look in the face of him, and you'll see it wrote there.'

'Ah, Merry,' remarked Silver, 'standing for cap'n again? You're a pushing lad, to be sure.'

But this time everyone was entirely in Merry's favour. They began to scramble out of the excavation, darting furious glances behind them. One thing I observed, which looked well for us: they all got out upon the opposite side from Silver.

Well, there we stood, two on one side, five on the other, the pit between us, and nobody screwed up high enough to offer the first blow. Silver never moved; he watched them, very upright on his crutch, and looked as cool as ever I saw him. He was brave, and no mistake.

At last, Merry seemed to think a speech might help matters.

'Mates,' says he, 'there's two of them alone there; one's the old cripple that brought us all here and blundered us down to this; the other's that cub that I mean to have the heart of. Now, mates—'

He was raising his arm and his voice, and plainly meant to lead a charge. But just then – crack! crack! crack! – three musket-shots flashed out of the thicket. Merry tumbled head foremost into the excavation; the man with the bandage spun round like a teetotum, and fell all his length upon his side, where he lay dead, but still twitching; and the other three turned and ran for it with all their might.

Before you could wink, Long John had fired two barrels of a pistol into the struggling Merry; and as the man rolled up his eyes at him in the last agony, 'George,' said he, 'I reckon I settled you.'

At the same moment the doctor, Gray, and Ben Gunn joined us, with smoking muskets, from among the nut-meg trees.

'Forward!' cried the doctor. 'Double quick, my lads. We must head 'em off the boats.'

And we set off at a great pace, sometimes plunging through the bushes to the chest.

I tell you, but Silver was anxious to keep up with us. The

work that man went through, leaping on his crutch till the muscles of his chest were fit to burst, was work no sound man ever equalled; and so thinks the doctor. As it was, he was already thirty yards behind us, and on the verge of strangling, when we reached the brow of the slope.

'Doctor,' he hailed, 'see there! no hurry!'

Sure enough there was no hurry. In a more open part of the plateau, we could see the three survivors still running in the same direction as they had started, right for Mizzen-mast Hill. We were already between them and the boats; and so we four sat down to breathe, while Long John, mopping his face, came slowly up with us.

'Thank ye kindly, doctor,' says he. 'You came in in about the nick, I guess, for me and Hawkins. And so it's you, Ben Gunn!' he added. 'Well, you're a nice one to be sure.'

'I'm Ben Gunn, I am,' replied the maroon, wriggling like an eel in his embarrassment. 'And,' he added, after a long pause, 'how do, Mr Silver? Pretty well, I thank ye, says you.'

'Ben, Ben,' murmured Silver, 'to think as you've done me!'

The doctor sent back Gray for one of the pickaxes, deserted, in their flight, by the mutineers; and then as we proceeded leisurely down hill to where the boats were lying, related, in a few words, what had taken place. It was a story that profoundly interested Silver; and Ben Gunn, the half-idiot maroon, was the hero from beginning to end.

Ben, in his long, lonely wanderings about the island, had found the skeleton – it was he that had rifled it; he had found the treasure; he had dug it up (it was the haft of his pickaxe that lay broken in the excavation); he had carried it on his back, in many weary journeys, from the foot of the tall pine to a cave he had on the two-pointed hill at the north-east angle of the island, and there it had lain stored in safety since two months before the arrival of the *Hispaniola*.

When the doctor had wormed this secret from him, on the afternoon of the attack, and when, next morning he saw the anchorage deserted, he had gone to Silver, given him the chart, which was now useless – given him the stores, for

Ben Gunn's cave was well supplied with goat's meat salted by himself – given anything and everything to get a chance of moving in safety from the stockade to the two-pointed hill, there to be clear of malaria and keep a guard upon the money.

'As for you, Jim,' he said, 'it went against my heart, but I did what I thought best for those who had stood by their duty; and if you were not one of these, whose fault was it?'

That morning, finding that I was to be involved in the horrid disappointment he had prepared for the mutineers, he had run all the way to the cave, and, leaving the squire to guard the captain, had taken Gray and the maroon, and started, making the diagonal across the island, to be at hand beside the pine. Soon, however, he saw that our party had the start of him; and Ben Gunn, being fleet of foot, had been despatched in front to do his best alone. Then it had occurred to him to work upon the superstitions of his former shipmates; and he was so far successful that Gray and the doctor had come up and were already ambushed before the arrival of the treasure-hunters.

'Ah,' said Silver, 'it were fortunate for me that I had Hawkins here. You would have let old John be cut to bits, and never given it a thought, doctor.'

'Not a thought,' replied Doctor Livesey, cheerily.

And by this time we had reached the gigs. The doctor, with the pick-axe, demolished one of them, and then we all got aboard the other, and set out to go round by sea for North Inlet.

This was a run of eight or nine miles. Silver, though he was almost killed already with fatigue, was set to an oar, like the rest of us, and we were soon skimming swiftly over a smooth sea. Soon we passed out of the straits and doubled the south-east corner of the island, round which, four days ago, we had towed the *Hispaniola*.

As we passed the two-pointed hill, we could see the black mouth of Ben Gunn's cave, and a figure standing by it, leaning on a musket. It was the squire; and we waved a handkerchief and gave him three cheers, in which the voice of Silver joined as heartily as any.

Three miles farther, just inside the mouth of North Inlet, what should we meet but the *Hispaniola*, cruising by herself? The last flood had lifted her; and had there been much wind, or a strong tide current, as in the southern anchorage, we should never have found her more, or found her stranded beyond help. As it was, there was little amiss, beyond the wreck of the mainsail. Another anchor was got ready, and dropped in a fathom and a half of water. We all pulled round again to Rum Cove, the nearest point for Ben Gunn's treasure-house; and then Gray, single-handed, returned with the gig to the *Hispaniola*, where he was to pass the night on guard.

A gentle slope ran up from the beach to the entrance of the cave. At the top, the squire met us. To me he was cordial and kind, saying nothing of my escapade, either in the way of blame or praise. At Silver's polite salute he somewhat flushed.

'John Silver,' he said, 'you're a prodigious villain and impostor – a monstrous impostor, sir. I am told I am not to prosecute you. Well, then, I will not. But the dead men, sir, hang about your neck like millstones.'

'Thank you kindly, sir,' replied Long John, again saluting.

'I dare you to thank me!' cried the squire. 'It is a gross dereliction of my duty. Stand back.'

And thereupon we all entered the cave. It was a large, airy place, with a little spring and a pool of clear water, overhung with ferns. The floor was sand. Before a big fire lay Captain Smollett; and in a far corner, only duskily flickered over by the blaze, I beheld great heaps of coin and quadrilaterals built of bars of gold. That was Flint's treasure that we had come so far to seek, and that had cost already the lives of seventeen men from the *Hispaniola*. How many it had cost in the amassing, what blood and sorrow, what good ships scuttled on the deep, what brave men walking the plank blindfold, what shot of cannon, what shame and lies and cruelty, perhaps no man alive could tell. Yet there were still three upon that island – Silver, and old Morgan, and Ben Gunn – who had each taken his share in these crimes, as each had hoped in vain to share in the reward.

'Come in, Jim,' said the captain. 'You're a good boy in your line, Jim; but I don't think you and me'll go to sea again. You're too much of the born favourite for me. Is that you, John Silver? What brings you here, man?'

'Come back to my dooty, sir,' returned Silver.

'Ah!' said the captain; and that was all he said.

What a supper I had of it that night, with all my friends around me; and what a meal it was, with Ben Gunn's salted goat, and some delicacies and a bottle of old wine from the *Hispaniola*. Never, I am sure, were people gayer or happier. And there was Silver, sitting back almost out of the firelight, but eating heartily, prompt to spring forward when anything was wanted, even joining quietly in our laughter – the same bland, polite, obsequious seaman of the voyage out.

And Last

THE next morning we fell early to work, for the transportation of this great mass of gold near a mile by land to the beach, and thence three miles by boat to the *Hispaniola*, was a considerable task for so small a number of workmen. The three fellows still abroad upon the island did not greatly trouble us; a single sentry on the shoulder of the hill was sufficient to insure us against any sudden onslaught, and we thought, besides, they had had more than enough of fighting.

Therefore the work was pushed on briskly. Gray and Ben Gunn came and went with the boat, while the rest during their absences, piled treasure on the beach. Two of the bars, slung in a rope's-end, made a good load for a grown man – one that he was glad to walk slowly with. For my part, as I was not much use at carrying, I was kept busy all day in the cave, packing the minted money into bread-bags.

It was a strange collection, like Billy Bones's hoard for the diversity of coinage, but so much larger and so much more varied that I think I never had more pleasure than in sorting them. English, French, Spanish, Portuguese, Georges, and Louises, doubloons and double guineas and moidores and sequins, the pictures of all the kings of Europe for the last hundred years, strange Oriental pieces stamped with what looked like wisps of string or bits of spider's web, round pieces and square pieces, and pieces bored through the middle, as if to wear them round your neck – nearly every variety of money in the world must, I think, have found a place in that collection; and for number, I am sure they were like autumn leaves, so that my back ached with stooping and my fingers with sorting them out.

Day after day this work went on; by every evening a fortune had been stowed aboard, but there was another fortune waiting for the morrow; and all this time we heard nothing of the three surviving mutineers.

At last – I think it was on the third night – the doctor and I were strolling on the shoulder of the hill where it overlooks the lowlands of the isle, when, from out the thick darkness below, the wind brought us a noise between shrieking and singing. It was only a snatch that reached our ears, followed by the former silence.

'Heaven forgive them,' said the doctor; ''tis the mutineers!'

'All drunk, sir,' struck in the voice of Silver from behind us.

Silver, I should say, was allowed his entire liberty, and, in spite of daily rebuffs, seemed to regard himself once more as quite a privileged and friendly dependant. Indeed, it was remarkable how well he bore these slights, and with what unwearying politeness he kept on trying to ingratiate himself with all. Yet, I think, none treated him better than a dog; unless it was Ben Gunn, who was still terribly afraid of his old quartermaster, or myself, who had really something to thank him for; although for that matter, I suppose, I had reason to think even worse of him than anybody else, for I had seen him meditating a fresh treachery upon the plateau. Accordingly, it was pretty gruffly that the doctor answered him.

'Drunk or raving,' said he.

'Right you were, sir,' replied Silver; 'and precious little odds which, to you and me.'

'I suppose you would hardly ask me to call you a humane man,' returned the doctor, with a sneer, 'and so my feelings may surprise you, Master Silver. But if I were sure they were raving – as I am morally certain one, at least, of them is down with fever – I should leave this camp, and, at whatever risk to my own carcase, take them the assistance of my skill.'

'Ask your pardon, sir, you would be very wrong,' quoth Silver. 'You would lose your precious life, and you may lay to that. I'm on your side now, hand and glove; and I shouldn't wish for to see the party weakened, let alone yourself, seeing as I know what I owes you. But these men down there, they couldn't keep their word – no, not supposing they wished to; and what's more, they couldn't believe as you could.'

'No,' said the doctor. 'You're the man to keep your word, we know that.'

Well, that was about the last news we had of the three pirates. Only once we heard a gunshot a great way off, and supposed them to be hunting. A council was held, and it was decided that we must desert them on the island – to the huge glee, I must say, of Ben Gunn, and with the strong approval of Gray. We left a good stock of powder and shot, the bulk of the salt goat, a few medicines, and some other necessaries, tools, clothing, a spare sail, a fathom or two of rope, and, by the particular desire of the doctor, a handsome present of tobacco.

That was about our last doing on the island. Before that, we had got the treasure stowed, and had shipped enough water and the remainder of the goat meat, in case of any distress; and at last, one fine morning, we weighed anchor, which was about all that we could manage, and stood out of North Inlet, the same colours flying that the captain had flown and fought under at the palisade.

The three fellows must have been watching us closer than we thought for, as we soon had proved. For, coming through the narrows, we had to lie very near the southern point, and there we saw all three of them kneeling together on a spit of sand, with their arms raised in supplication. It went to all our hearts, I think, to leave them in that wretched state; but we could not risk another mutiny; and to take them home for the gibbet would have been a cruel sort of kindness. The doctor hailed them and told them of the stores we had left, and where they were to find them. But they continued to call us by name, and appeal to us, for God's sake, to be merciful, and not leave them to die in such a place.

At last, seeing the ship still bore on her course, and was now swiftly drawing out of earshot, one of them – I know not which it was – leapt to his feet with a hoarse cry, whipped his musket to his shoulder, and sent a shot whistling over Silver's head and through the mainsail.

After that, we kept under cover of the bulwarks, and when next I looked out they had disappeared from the spit, and the spit itself had almost melted out of sight in the growing distance. That was, at least, the end of that; and before noon, to my inexpressible joy, the highest rock of Treasure Island had sunk into the blue round of sea.

We were so short of men, that everyone on board had to bear a hand – only the captain lying on a mattress in the stern and giving his orders; for, though greatly recovered he was still in want of quiet. We laid her head for the nearest port in Spanish America, for we could not risk the voyage home without fresh hands; and as it was, what with baffling winds and a couple of fresh gales, we were all worn out before we reached it.

It was just at sundown when we cast anchor in a most beautiful land-locked gulf, and were immediately surrounded by shore boats full of negroes, and Mexican Indians, and half-bloods, selling fruits and vegetables, and offering to dive for bits of money. The sight of so many good-humoured faces (especially the blacks), the taste of the tropical fruits, and above all, the lights that began to shine in the town, made a most charming contrast to our dark and bloody sojourn on the island; and the doctor and the squire, taking me along with them, went ashore to pass the early part of the night. Here they met the captain of an English man-of-war, fell in talk with him, went on board his ship, and, in short, had so agreeable a time, that day was breaking when we came alongside the *Hispaniola*.

Ben Gunn was on deck alone, and, as soon as we came on board, he began, with wonderful contortions, to make us a confession. Silver was gone. The maroon had connived at his escape in a shore boat some hours ago, and he now assured us he had only done so to preserve our lives, which would certainly have been forfeit if 'that man with the one leg had stayed aboard.' But this was not all. The sea-cook had not gone empty handed. He had cut through a bulkhead unobserved, and had removed one of the sacks of coin, worth, perhaps, three or four hundred guineas, to help him on his further wanderings.

I think we were all pleased to be so cheaply quit of him.

Well, to make a long story short, we got a few hands on board, made a good cruise home, and the *Hispaniola* reached Bristol just as Mr Blandly was beginning to think of fitting out her consort. Five men only of those who had sailed returned with her. 'Drink and the devil had done for the rest,' with a vengeance; although, to be sure, we were not quite in so bad a case as that other ship they sang about:

> With one man of her crew alive,
> What put to sea with seventy-five.

All of us had an ample share of the treasure, and used it wisely or foolishly, according to our natures. Captain Smollett is now retired from the sea. Gray not only saved his money, but, being suddenly smit with the desire to rise, also studied his profession; and he is now mate and part owner of a fine full-rigged ship; married besides, and the father of a family. As for Ben Gunn, he got a thousand pounds, which he spent or lost in three weeks, or, to be more exact, in nineteen days, for he was back begging on the twentieth. Then he was given a lodge to keep, exactly as he had feared upon the island; and he still lives, a great favourite, though something of a butt, with the country boys, and a notable singer in church on Sundays and saints' days.

Of Silver we have heard no more. That formidable seafaring man with one leg has at last gone clean out of my life; but I daresay he met his old negress, and perhaps still lives in comfort with her and Captain Flint. It is to be hoped so, I suppose, for his chances of comfort in another world are very small.

The bar silver and the arms still lie, for all that I know, where Flint buried them; and certainly they shall lie there for me. Oxen and wain-ropes would not bring me back again to that accursed island; and the worst dreams that ever I have are when I hear the surf booming about its coasts, or start upright in bed, with the sharp voice of Captain Flint still ringing in my ears: 'Pieces of eight! pieces of eight!'

The Treasure of Franchard

CHAPTER ONE

By the Dying Mountebank

THEY had sent for the doctor from Bourron before six. About eight some villagers came round for the performance, and were told how matters stood. It seemed a liberty for a mountebank to fall ill like real people, and they made off again in dudgeon. By ten Madame Tentaillon was gravely alarmed, and had sent down the street for Doctor Desprez.

The Doctor was at work over his manuscripts in one corner of the little dining-room, and his wife was asleep over the fire in another, when the messenger arrived.

'*Sapristi!*' said the Doctor, 'you should have sent for me before. It was a case for hurry.' And he followed the messenger as he was, in his slippers and skull-cap.

The inn was not thirty yards away, but the messenger did not stop there; he went in at one door and out by another into the court, and then led the way by a flight of steps beside the stable, to the loft where the mountebank lay sick. If Doctor Desprez were to live a thousand years, he would never forget his arrival in that room; for not only was the scene picturesque, but the moment made a date in his existence. We reckon our lives, I hardly know why, from the date of our first sorry appearance in society, as if from a first humiliation; for no actor can come upon the stage with a worse grace. Not to go further back, which would be judged too curious, there are subsequently many moving and decisive accidents in the lives of all, which would make as logical a period as this of birth. And here, for instance, Doctor Desprez, a man past forty, who had made what is called a failure in life, and was moreover married, found himself at a new point of departure when he opened the door of the loft above Tentaillon's stable.

It was a large place, lighted only by a single candle set upon the floor. The mountebank lay on his back upon a pallet; a large man, with a Quixotic nose inflamed with drinking. Madame Tentaillon stooped over him, applying a hot-water and mustard embrocation to his feet; and on a chair close by sat a little fellow of eleven or twelve, with his feet dangling. These three were the only occupants, except the shadows. But the shadows were a company in themselves; the extent of the room exaggerated them to a gigantic size, and from the low position of the candle the light struck upwards and produced deformed foreshortenings. The mountebank's profile was enlarged upon the wall in caricature, and it was strange to see his nose shorten and lengthen as the flame was blown about by draughts. As for Madame Tentaillon, her shadow was no more than a gross hump of shoulders, with now and again a hemisphere of head. The chair legs were spindled out as long as stilts, and the boy sat perched atop of them, like a cloud, in the corner of the room.

It was the boy who took the Doctor's fancy. He had a great arched skull, the forehead and the hands of a musician, and a pair of haunting eyes. It was not merely that these eyes were large, or steady, or the softest ruddy brown. There was a look in them, besides, which thrilled the Doctor, and made him half uneasy. He was sure he had seen such a look before, and yet he could not remember how or where. It was as if this boy, who was quite a stranger to him, had the eyes of an old friend or an old enemy. And the boy would give him no peace; he seemed profoundly indifferent to what was going on, or rather abstracted from it in a superior contemplation, beating gently with his feet against the bars of the chair, and holding his hands folded on his lap. But, for all that, his eyes kept following the Doctor about the room with a thoughtful fixity of gaze. Desprez could not tell whether he was fascinating the boy, or the boy was fascinating him. He busied himself over the sick man: he put questions, he felt the pulse, he jested, he grew a little hot and swore: and still, whenever he looked round, there were the brown eyes waiting for his with the same inquiring, melancholy gaze.

At last the Doctor hit on the solution at a leap. He remembered the look now. The little fellow, although he was as straight as a dart, had the eyes that go usually with a crooked back; he was not at all deformed, and yet a deformed person seemed to be looking at you from below his brows. The Doctor drew a long breath, he was so much relieved to find a theory (for he loved theories) and to explain away his interest.

For all that, he despatched the invalid with unusual haste, and, still kneeling with one knee on the floor, turned a little round and looked the boy over at his leisure. The boy was not in the least put out, but looked placidly back at the Doctor.

'Is this your father?' asked Desprez.

'Oh, no,' returned the boy; 'my master.'

'Are you fond of him?' continued the Doctor.

'No, sir,' said the boy.

Madame Tentaillon and Desprez exchanged expressive glances.

'That is bad, my man,' resumed the latter, with a shade of sternness. 'Every one should be fond of the dying, or conceal their sentiments; and your master here is dying. If I have watched a bird a little while stealing my cherries, I have a thought of disappointment when he flies away over my garden wall, and I see him steer for the forest and vanish. How much more a creature such as this, so strong, so astute, so richly endowed with faculties! When I think that, in a few hours the speech will be silenced, the breath extinct, and even the shadow vanished from the wall, I who never saw him, this lady who knew him only as a guest, are touched with some affection.'

The boy was silent for a little, and appeared to be reflecting.

'You did not know him,' he replied at last. 'He was a bad man.'

'He is a little pagan,' said the landlady. 'For that matter, they are all the same, these mountebanks, tumblers, artists, and what not. They have no interior.'

But the Doctor was still scrutinising the little pagan, his eyebrows knotted and uplifted.

'What is your name?' he asked.

'Jean-Marie,' said the lad.

Desprez leaped upon him with one of his sudden flashes of excitement, and felt his head all over from an ethnological point of view.

'Celtic, Celtic!' he said.

'Celtic!' cried Madame Tentaillon, who had perhaps confounded the word with hydrocephalous. 'Poor lad! is it dangerous?'

'That depends,' returned the Doctor, grimly. And then once more addressing the boy: 'And what do you do for your living, Jean-Marie?' he inquired.

'I tumble,' was the answer.

'So! Tumble?' repeated Desprez. 'Probably healthful. I hazard the guess, Madame Tentaillon, that tumbling is a healthful way of life. And have you never done anything else but tumble?'

'Before I learned that, I used to steal,' answered Jean-Marie gravely.

'Upon my word!' cried the Doctor. 'You are a nice little man for your age. Madame, when my *confrère* comes from Bourron, you will communicate my unfavourable opinion. I leave the case in his hands; but of course, on any alarming symptom, above all if there should be a sign of rally, do not hesitate to knock me up. I am a doctor no longer, I thank God; but I have been one. Good-night, madame. – Good sleep to you, Jean-Marie.'

CHAPTER TWO

Morning Talk

DOCTOR DESPREZ always rose early. Before the smoke arose, before the first cart rattled over the bridge to the day's labour in the fields, he was to be found wandering in his garden. Now he would pick a bunch of grapes; now he would eat a big pear under the trellis; now he would draw all sorts of fancies on the path with the end of his cane; now he would go down and watch the river running endlessly past the timber landing-place at which he moored his boat. There was no time, he used to say, for making theories like the early morning. 'I rise earlier than any one else in the village,' he once boasted. 'It is a fair consequence that I know more and wish to do less with my knowledge.'

The Doctor was a connoisseur of sunrises, and loved a good theatrical effect to usher in the day. He had a theory of dew, by which he could predict the weather. Indeed, most things served him to that end: the sound of the bells from all the neighbouring villages, the smell of the forest, the visits and the behaviour of both birds and fishes, the look of the plants in his garden, the disposition of cloud, the colour of the light, and last, although not least, the arsenal of meteorological instruments in a louvre-boarded hutch upon the lawn. Ever since he had settled at Gretz, he had been growing more and more into the local meteorologist, the unpaid champion of the local climate. He thought at first there was no place so healthful in the arrondissement. By the end of the second year, he protested there was none so wholesome in the whole department. And for some time before he met Jean-Marie, he had been prepared to challenge all France and the better part of Europe for a rival to his chosen spot.

'Doctor,' he would say – 'doctor is a foul word. It should

not be used to ladies. It implies disease. I remark it, as a flaw in our civilisation, that we have not the proper horror of disease. Now I, for my part, have washed my hands of it; I have renounced my laureation; I am no doctor; I am only a worshipper of the true goddess Hygieia. Ah, believe me, it is she who has the cestus! And here, in this exiguous hamlet, has she placed her shrine: here she dwells and lavishes her gifts; here I walk with her in the early morning, and she shows me how strong she has made the peasants, how fruitful she has made the fields, how the trees grow up tall and comely under her eyes, and the fishes in the river become clean and agile at her presence. – Rheumatism!' he would cry, on some malapert interruption, 'oh, yes, I believe we do have a little rheumatism. That could hardly be avoided, you know, on a river. And of course the place stands a little low; and the meadows are marshy, there's no doubt. But, my dear sir, look at Bourron! Bourron stands high, Bourron is close to the forest; plenty of ozone there, you would say. Well, compared with Gretz, Bourron is a perfect shambles.'

The morning after he had been summoned to the dying mountebank, the Doctor visited the wharf at the tail of his garden, and had a long look at the running water. This he called prayer; but whether his adorations were addressed to the goddess Hygieia or some more orthodox deity, never plainly appeared. For he had uttered doubtful oracles, sometimes declaring that a river was the type of bodily health, sometimes extolling it as the great moral preacher, continually preaching peace, continuity, and diligence to man's tormented spirits. After he had watched a mile or so of the clear water running by before his eyes, seen a fish or two come to the surface with a gleam of silver, and sufficiently admired the long shadows of the trees falling half across the river from the opposite bank, with patches of moving sunlight in between, he strolled once more up the garden and through his house into the street, feeling cool and renovated.

The sound of his feet upon the causeway began the business of the day; for the village was still sound asleep. The church tower looked very airy in the sunlight; a few birds that turned about it, seemed to swim in an atmosphere of more than usual rarity; and the Doctor, walking in long transparent shadows, filled his lungs amply, and proclaimed himself well contented with the morning.

On one of the posts before Tentaillon's carriage entry he espied a little dark figure perched in a meditative attitude, and immediately recognised Jean-Marie.

'Aha!' he said, stopping before him humorously, with a hand on either knee. 'So we rise early in the morning, do we? It appears to me that we have all the vices of a philosopher.'

The boy got to his feet and made a grave salutation.

'And how is our patient?' asked Desprez.

It appeared the patient was about the same.

'And why do you rise early in the morning?' he pursued.

Jean-Marie, after a long silence, professed that he hardly knew.

'You hardly know?' repeated Desprez. 'We hardly know anything, my man, until we try to learn. Interrogate your consciousness. Come, push me this inquiry home. Do you like it?'

'Yes,' said the boy slowly; 'yes, I like it.'

'And why do you like it?' continued the Doctor. '(We are now pursuing the Socratic method.) Why do you like it?'

'It is quiet,' answered Jean-Marie; 'and I have nothing to do; and then I feel as if I were good.'

Doctor Desprez took a seat on the post at the opposite side. He was beginning to take an interest in the talk, for the boy plainly thought before he spoke, and tried to answer truly. 'It appears you have a taste for feeling good,' said the Doctor. 'Now, there you puzzle me extremely; for I thought you said you were a thief; and the two are incompatible.'

'Is it very bad to steal?' asked Jean-Marie.

'Such is the general opinion, little boy,' replied the Doctor.

'No; but I mean as I stole,' exclaimed the other. 'For I had no choice. I think it is surely right to have bread; it must be right to have bread, there comes so plain a want of it. And then they beat me cruelly if I returned with nothing,' he added. 'I was not ignorant of right and wrong; for before that I had been well taught by a priest, who was very kind to me.' (The Doctor made a horrible grimace at the word 'priest.') 'But it seemed to me, when one had nothing to eat and was beaten, it was a different affair. I would not have stolen for tartlets, I believe; but any one would steal for baker's bread.'

'And so I suppose,' said the Doctor, with a rising sneer, 'you prayed God to forgive you, and explained the case to Him at length.'

'Why, sir?' asked Jean-Marie. 'I do not see.'

'Your priest would see, however,' retorted Desprez.

'Would he?' asked the boy, troubled for the first time. 'I should have thought God would have known.'

'Eh?' snarled the Doctor.

'I should have thought God would have understood me,' replied the other. 'You do not, I see; but then it was God that made me think so, was it not?'

'Little boy, little boy,' said Doctor Desprez, 'I told you already you had the vices of philosophy; if you display the virtues also, I must go. I am a student of the blessed laws of health, an observer of plain and temperate nature in her common walks; and I cannot preserve my equanimity in presence of a monster. Do you understand?'

'No, sir,' said the boy.

'I will make my meaning clear to you,' replied the Doctor. 'Look there at the sky – behind the belfry first, where it is so light, and then up and up, turning your chin back, right to the top of the dome, where it is already as blue as at noon. Is not that a beautiful colour? Does it not please the heart? We have seen it all our lives, until it has grown in with our familiar thoughts. Now,' changing his tone, 'suppose that sky to become suddenly of a live and fiery amber, like the colour of clear coals, and growing scarlet towards the top – I do not say it would be any the less beautiful; but would you like it as well?'

'I suppose not,' answered Jean-Marie.

'Neither do I like you,' returned the Doctor, roughly. 'I hate all odd people, and you are the most curious little boy in all the world.'

Jean-Marie seemed to ponder for a while, and then he raised his head again and looked over at the Doctor with an air of candid inquiry. 'But are not you a very curious gentleman?' he asked.

The Doctor threw away his stick, bounded on the boy, clasped him to his bosom, and kissed him on both cheeks. 'Admirable, admirable imp!' he cried. 'What a morning, what an hour for a theorist of forty-two! No,' he continued, apostrophising heaven, 'I did not know that such boys existed; I was ignorant they made them so; I had doubted of my race; and now! It is like,' he added, picking up his stick, 'like a lovers' meeting. I have bruised my favourite staff in that moment of enthusiasm. The injury, however, is not grave.' He caught the boy looking at him in obvious wonder, embarrassment, and alarm. 'Hullo!' said he, 'why do you look at me like that? Egad, I believe the boy despises me. Do you despise me, boy?'

'Oh, no,' replied Jean-Marie, seriously; 'only I do not understand.'

'You must excuse me, sir,' returned the Doctor, with gravity; 'I am still so young. Oh, hang him!' he added to himself. And he took his seat again and observed the boy sardonically. 'He has spoiled the quiet of my morning,' thought he. 'I shall be nervous all day, and have a febricule when I digest. Let me compose myself.' And so he dismissed his preoccupations by an effort of the will which he had long practised, and let his soul roam abroad in the contemplation of the morning. He inhaled the air, tasting it critically as a connoisseur tastes a vintage, and prolonging the expiration with hygienic gusto. He counted the little flecks of cloud along the sky. He followed the movements of the birds round the church tower – making long sweeps, hanging poised, or turning airy somersaults in fancy, and beating the wind with imaginary pinions. And in this way he regained peace of mind and animal composure, conscious of his limbs, conscious of the sight of his eyes, conscious that the air had a cool taste, like a fruit, at the top of his throat; and at last, in complete abstraction, he began to sing. The Doctor had but one air – 'Malbrouck s'en va-t-en guerre'; even with that he was on terms of mere politeness; and his musical exploits were always reserved for moments when he was alone and entirely happy.

He was recalled to earth rudely by a pained expression on the boy's face. 'What do you think of my singing?' he inquired, stopping in the middle of a note; and then, after he had waited some little while and received no answer, 'What do you think of my singing?' he repeated, imperiously.

'I do not like it,' faltered Jean-Marie.

'Oh, come!' cried the Doctor. 'Possibly you are a performer yourself?'

'I sing better than that,' replied the boy.

The Doctor eyed him for some seconds in stupefaction. He was aware that he was angry, and blushed for himself in consequence, which made him angrier. 'If this is how you address your master!' he said at last, with a shrug and a flourish of his arms.

'I do not speak to him at all,' returned the boy. 'I do not like him.'

'Then you like me?' snapped Doctor Desprez, with unusual eagerness.

'I do not know,' answered Jean-Marie.

The Doctor rose. 'I shall wish you a good-morning,' he said. 'You are too much for me. Perhaps you have blood in your veins, perhaps celestial ichor, or perhaps you circulate nothing more gross than respirable air; but of one thing I am inexpugnably assured: – that you are no human being. No, boy' – shaking his stick at him – 'you are not a human being. Write, write it in your memory – "I am not a human being – I have no pretension to be a human being – I am a dive, a dream, an angel, an acrostic, an illusion – what you please, but not a human being." And so accept my humble salutations and farewell!'

And with that the Doctor made off along the street in some emotion, and the boy stood, mentally gaping, where he left him.

CHAPTER THREE

The Adoption

MADAME DESPREZ, who answered to the Christian name of Anastasie, presented an agreeable type of her sex; exceedingly wholesome to look upon, a stout *brune*, with cool smooth cheeks, steady, dark eyes, and hands that neither art nor nature could improve. She was the sort of person over whom adversity passes like a summer cloud; she might, in the worst of conjunctions, knit her brows into one vertical furrow for a moment, but the next it would be gone. She had much of the placidity of a contented nun; with little of her piety, however; for Anastasie was of a very mundane nature, fond of oysters and old wine, and somewhat bold pleasantries, and devoted to her husband for her own sake rather than for his. She was imperturbably good-natured, but had no idea of self-sacrifice. To live in that pleasant old house, with a green garden behind and bright flowers about the window, to eat and drink of the best, to gossip with a neighbour for a quarter of an hour, never to wear stays or a dress except when she went to Fontainebleau shopping, to be kept in a continual supply of racy novels, and to be married to Doctor Desprez and have no ground of jealousy, filled the cup of her nature to the brim. Those who had known the Doctor in bachelor days, when he had aired quite as many theories, but of a different order, attributed his present philosophy to the study of Anastasie. It was her brute enjoyment that he rationalised and perhaps vainly imitated.

Madame Desprez was an artist in the kitchen, and made coffee to a nicety. She had a knack of tidiness, with which she had infected the Doctor; everything was in its place; everything capable of polish shone gloriously; and dust was a thing banished from her empire. Aline, their single servant, had no other business in the world but to scour and burnish. So Doctor Desprez lived in his house like a fatted calf, warmed and cosseted to his heart's content.

The midday meal was excellent. There was a ripe melon, a fish from the river in a memorable Béarnaise sauce, a fat fowl in a fricassée, and a dish of asparagus, followed by some fruit. The Doctor drank half a bottle *plus* one glass, the wife half a bottle *minus* the same quantity, which was a marital privilege, of an excellent Côte-Rôtie, seven years old. Then the coffee was brought, and a flask of Chartreuse for madame, for the Doctor despised and distrusted such decoctions; and then Aline left the wedded pair to the pleasures of memory and digestion.

'It is a very fortunate circumstance, my cherished one,' observed the Doctor – 'this coffee is adorable – a very fortunate circumstance upon the whole – Anastasie, I beseech you, go without that poison for to-day; only one day, and you will feel the benefit, I pledge my reputation.'

'What is this fortunate circumstance, my friend?' inquired Anastasie, not heeding his protest, which was of daily recurrence.

'That we have no children, my beautiful,' replied the Doctor. 'I think of it more and more as the years go on, and with more and more gratitude towards the Power that dispenses such afflictions. Your health, my darling, my studious quiet, our little kitchen delicacies, how they would all have suffered, how they would all have been sacrificed! And for what? Children are the last word of human imperfection. Health flees before their face. They cry, my dear; they put vexatious questions; they demand to be fed, to be washed, to be educated, to have their noses blown; and then, when the time comes, they break our hearts, as I break this piece of sugar. A pair of professed egoists, like you and me, should avoid offspring, like an infidelity.'

'Indeed!' said she; and she laughed. 'Now, that is like you – to take credit for the thing you could not help.'

'My dear,' returned the Doctor, solemnly, 'we might have adopted.'

'Never!' cried madame. 'Never, Doctor, with my consent. If the child were my own flesh and blood, I would not say so. But to take another person's indiscretion on my shoulders, my dear friend, I have too much sense.'

'Precisely,' replied the Doctor. 'We both had. And I am all the better pleased with our wisdom, because – because—' He looked at her sharply.

'Because what?' she asked, with a faint premonition of danger.

'Because I have found the right person,' said the Doctor firmly, 'and shall adopt him this afternoon.'

Anastasie looked at him out of a mist. 'You have lost your reason,' she said; and there was a clang in her voice that seemed to threaten trouble.

'Not so, my dear,' he replied; 'I retain its complete exercise. To the proof: instead of attempting to cloak my inconsistency, I have, by way of preparing you, thrown it into strong relief. You will there, I think, recognise the philosopher who has the ecstasy to call you wife. The fact is, I have been reckoning all this while without an accident. I never thought to find a son of my own. Now, last night I found one. Do not unnecessarily alarm yourself, my dear; he is not a drop of blood to me that I know. It is his mind, darling, his mind that calls me father.'

'His mind!' she repeated with a titter between scorn and hysterics. 'His mind, indeed! Henri, is this an idiotic pleasantry or are you mad? His mind! And what of my mind?'

'Truly,' replied the Doctor with a shrug, 'you have your finger on the hitch. He will be strikingly antipathetic to my beautiful Anastasie. She will never understand him; he will never understand her. You married the animal side of my nature, dear; and it is on the spiritual side that I find my affinity for Jean-Marie. So much so, that, to be perfectly frank, I stand in some awe of him myself. You will easily perceive that I am announcing a calamity for you. Do not,' he broke out in tones of real solicitude – 'do not give way to tears after a meal, Anastasie. You will certainly give yourself a false digestion.'

Anastasie controlled herself. 'You know how willing I

am to humour you,' she said, 'in all reasonable matters. But on this point—'

'My dear love,' interrupted the Doctor, eager to prevent a refusal, 'who wished to leave Paris? Who made me give up cards, and the opera, and the boulevard, and my social relations, and all that was my life before I knew you? Have I been faithful? Have I been obedient? Have I not borne my doom with cheerfulness? In all honesty, Anastasie, have I not a right to a stipulation on my side? I have, and you know it. I stipulate my son.'

Anastasie was aware of defeat; she struck her colours instantly. 'You will break my heart,' she sighed.

'Not in the least,' said he. 'You will feel a trifling inconvenience for a month, just as I did when I was first brought to this vile hamlet; then your admirable sense and temper will prevail, and I see you already as content as ever, and making your husband the happiest of men.'

'You know I can refuse you nothing,' she said, with a last flicker of resistance; 'nothing that will make you truly happier. But will this? Are you sure, my husband? Last night, you say, you found him! He may be the worst of humbugs.'

'I think not,' replied the Doctor. 'But do not suppose me so unwary as to adopt him out of hand. I am, I flatter myself, a finished man of the world; I have had all possibilities in view; my plan is contrived to meet them all. I take the lad as stable-boy. If he pilfer, if he grumble, if he desire to change, I shall see I was mistaken; I shall recognise him for no son of mine, and send him tramping.'

'You will never do so when the time comes,' said his wife; 'I know your good heart.'

She reached out her hand to him, with a sigh; the Doctor smiled as he took it and carried it to his lips; he had gained his point with greater ease than he had dared to hope; for perhaps the twentieth time he had proved the efficacy of his trusty argument, his Excalibur, the hint of a return to Paris. Six months in the capital, for a man of the Doctor's antecedents and relations, implied no less a calamity than total ruin. Anastasie had saved the remainder of his fortune by keeping him strictly in the country. The very name of

Paris put her in a blue fear; and she would have allowed her husband to keep a menagerie in the back-garden, let alone adopting a stable-boy, rather than permit the question of return to be discussed.

About four of the afternoon, the mountebank rendered up his ghost; he had never been conscious since his seizure. Doctor Desprez was present at his last passage, and declared the farce over. Then he took Jean-Marie by the shoulder and led him out into the inn garden where there was a convenient bench beside the river. Here he sat him down and made the boy place himself on his left.

'Jean-Marie,' he said very gravely, 'this world is exceedingly vast; and even France, which is only a small corner of it, is a great place for a little lad like you. Unfortunately it is full of eager, shouldering people moving on; and there are very few bakers' shops for so many eaters. Your master is dead; you are not fit to gain a living by yourself; you do not wish to steal? No. Your situation then is undesirable; it is, for the moment, critical. On the other hand, you behold in me a man not old, though elderly, still enjoying the youth of the heart and the intelligence; a man of instruction; easily situated in this world's affairs; keeping a good table: – a man, neither as friend nor host, to be despised. I offer you your food and clothes, and to teach you lessons in the evening, which will be infinitely more to the purpose for a lad of your stamp than those of all the priests in Europe. I propose no wages, but if ever you take a thought to leave me, the door shall be open, and I will give you a hundred francs to start the world upon. In return, I have an old horse and chaise, which you would very speedily learn to clean and keep in order. Do not hurry yourself to answer, and take it or leave it as you judge aright. Only remember this, that I am no sentimentalist or charitable person, but a man who lives rigorously to himself; and that if I make the proposal, it is for my own ends – it is because I perceive clearly an advantage to myself. And now, reflect.'

'I shall be very glad. I do not see what else I can do. I thank you, sir, most kindly, and I will try to be useful,' said the boy.

'Thank you,' said the Doctor warmly, rising at the same

time and wiping his brow, for he had suffered agonies while the thing hung in the wind. A refusal, after the scene at noon, would have placed him in a ridiculous light before Anastasie. 'How hot and heavy is the evening, to be sure! I have always had a fancy to be a fish in summer, Jean-Marie, here in the Loing beside Gretz. I should lie under a water-lily and listen to the bells, which must sound most delicately down below. That would be a life – do you not think so too?'

'Yes,' said Jean-Marie.

'Thank God you have imagination!' cried the Doctor, embracing the boy with his usual effusive warmth, though it was a proceeding that seemed to disconcert the sufferer almost as much as if he had been an English schoolboy of the same age. 'And now,' he added, 'I will take you to my wife.'

Madame Desprez sat in the dining-room in a cool wrapper. All the blinds were down, and the tile floor had been recently sprinkled with water; her eyes were half shut, but she affected to be reading a novel as they entered. Though she was a bustling woman, she enjoyed repose between whiles and had a remarkable appetite for sleep.

The Doctor went through a solemn form of introduction, adding, for the benefit of both parties, 'You must try to like each other for my sake.'

'He is very pretty,' said Anastasie. – 'Will you kiss me, my pretty little fellow?'

The Doctor was furious, and dragged her into the passage. 'Are you a fool, Anastasie?' he said. 'What is all this I hear about the tact of women? Heaven knows I have not met with it in my experience. You address my little philosopher as if he were an infant. He must be spoken to with more respect, I tell you; he must not be kissed and Georgy-porgy'd like an ordinary child.'

'I only did it to please you, I am sure,' replied Anastasie; 'but I will try to do better.'

The Doctor apologised for his warmth. 'But I do wish him,' he continued, 'to feel at home among us. And really your conduct was so idiotic, my cherished one, and so utterly and distantly out of place, that a saint might have been pardoned a little vehemence in disapproval. Do, do try – if it is possible for a woman to understand young people – but of course it is not, and I waste my breath. Hold your tongue as much as possible at least, and observe my conduct narrowly; it will serve you for a model.'

Anastasie did as she was bidden, and considered the Doctor's behaviour. She observed that he embraced the boy three times in the course of the evening, and managed generally to confound and abash the little fellow out of speech and appetite. But she had the true womanly heroism in little affairs. Not only did she refrain from the cheap revenge of exposing the Doctor's errors to himself, but she did her best to remove their ill-effect on Jean-Marie. When Desprez went out for his last breath of air before retiring for the night, she came over to the boy's side and took his hand.

'You must not be surprised nor frightened by my husband's manners,' she said. 'He is the kindest of men, but so clever that he is sometimes difficult to understand. You will soon grow used to him, and then you will love him, for that nobody can help. As for me, you may be sure, I shall try to make you happy, and will not bother you at all. I think we should be excellent friends, you and I. I am not clever, but I am very good-natured. Will you give me a kiss?'

He held up his face, and she took him in her arms and then began to cry. The woman had spoken in complaisance; but she had warmed to her own words, and tenderness followed. The Doctor, entering, found them enlaced: he concluded that his wife was in fault; and he was just beginning, in an awful voice, 'Anastasie—,' when she looked up at him, smiling, with an upraised finger; and he held his peace, wondering, while she led the boy to his attic.

CHAPTER FOUR

The Education of a Philosopher

THE installation of the adopted stable-boy was thus happily effected, and the wheels of life continued to run smoothly in the Doctor's house. Jean-Marie did his horse and carriage duty in the morning; sometimes helped in the housework; sometimes walked abroad with the Doctor, to drink wisdom from the fountain-head; and was introduced at night to the sciences and the dead tongues. He retained his singular placidity of mind and manner; he was rarely in fault; but he made only a very partial progress in his studies, and remained much of a stranger in the family.

The Doctor was a pattern of regularity. All forenoon he worked on his great book, the *Comparative Pharmacopœia, or Historical Dictionary of all Medicines*, which as yet consisted principally of slips of paper and pins. When finished, it was to fill many personable volumes and to combine antiquarian interest with professional utility. But the Doctor was studious of literary graces and the picturesque; an anecdote, a touch of manners, a moral qualification, or a sounding epithet was sure to be preferred before a piece of science; a little more, and he would have written the *Comparative Pharmacopœia* in verse! The article 'Mummia,' for instance, was already complete, though the remainder of the work had not progressed beyond the letter A. It was exceedingly copious and entertaining, written with quaintness and colour, exact, erudite, a literary article; but it would hardly have afforded guidance to a practising physician of to-day. The feminine good-sense of his wife had led her to point this out with uncompromising sincerity; for the Dictionary was duly read aloud to her, betwixt sleep and waking, as it proceeded towards an infinitely distant completion; and the doctor was a little sore on the subject of mummies, and sometimes resented an allusion with asperity.

After the midday meal and a proper period of digestion, he walked, sometimes alone, sometimes accompanied by Jean-Marie; for madame would have preferred any hardship rather than walk.

She was, as I have said, a very busy person, continually occupied about material comforts, and ready to drop asleep over a novel the instant she was disengaged. This was the less objectionable, as she never snored or grew distempered in complexion when she slept. On the contrary, she looked the very picture of luxurious and appetising ease, and woke without a start to the perfect possession of her faculties. I am afraid she was greatly an animal, but she was a very nice animal to have about. In this way, she had little to do with Jean-Marie; but the sympathy which had been established between them on the first night remained unbroken; they held occasional conversations, mostly on household matters; to the extreme disappointment of the Doctor, they occasionally sallied off together to that temple of debasing superstition, the village church; madame and he, both in their Sunday's best, drove twice a month to Fontainebleau and returned laden with purchases; and in short, although the Doctor still continued to regard them as irreconcilably antipathetic, their relation was as intimate, friendly, and confidential as their natures suffered.

I fear, however, that in her heart of hearts, madame kindly despised and pitied the boy. She had no admiration for his class of virtues; she liked a smart, polite, forward, roguish sort of boy, cap in hand, light of foot, meeting the eye; she liked volubility, charm, a little vice – the promise of a second Doctor Desprez. And it was her indefeasible belief that Jean-Marie was dull. 'Poor dear boy,' she had said once, 'how sad it is that he should be so stupid!' She had never repeated that remark, for the Doctor had raged like a wild bull, denouncing the brutal bluntness of her mind, bemoaning his own fate to be so unequally mated with an ass, and, what touched Anastasie more nearly, menacing the table china by the fury of his gesticulations. But she adhered silently to her opinion; and when Jean-Marie was sitting, stolid, blank, but not unhappy, over his unfinished tasks, she would snatch her opportunity in the Doctor's absence, go over to him, put her arms about his neck, lay her cheek to his, and communicate her sympathy with his distress. 'Do not mind,' she would say; 'I, too, am not at all clever, and I can assure you that it makes no difference in life.'

The Doctor's view was naturally different. That gentleman never wearied of the sound of his own voice, which was, to say the truth, agreeable enough to hear. He now had a listener, who was not so cynically indifferent as Anastasie, and who sometimes put him on his mettle by the most relevant objections. Besides, was he not educating the boy? And education, philosophers are agreed, is the most philosophical of duties. What can be more heavenly to poor mankind than to have one's hobby grow into a duty to the State? Then, indeed, do the ways of life become ways of pleasantness. Never had the Doctor seen reason to be more content with his endowments. Philosophy flowed smoothly from his lips. He was so agile a dialectician that he could trace his nonsense, when challenged, back to some root in sense, and prove it to be a sort of flower upon his system. He slipped out of antinomies like a fish, and left his disciple marvelling at the rabbi's depth.

Moreover, deep down in his heart the Doctor was disappointed with the ill-success of his more formal education. A boy, chosen by so acute an observer for his aptitude, and guided along the path of learning by so philosophic an instructor, was bound, by the nature of the universe, to make a more obvious and lasting advance. Now Jean-Marie was slow in all things, impenetrable in others; and his power of forgetting was fully on a level with his power to learn. Therefore the Doctor cherished his peripatetic lectures, to which the boy attended, which he generally appeared to enjoy, and by which he often profited.

Many and many were the talks they had together; and health and moderation proved the subject of the Doctor's divagations. To these he lovingly returned.

'I lead you,' he would say, 'by the green pastures. My system, my beliefs, my medicines, are resumed in one phrase

– to avoid excess. Blessed nature, healthy, temperate nature, abhors and exterminates excess. Human law, in this matter, imitates at a great distance her provisions; and we must strive to supplement the efforts of the law. Yes, boy, we must be a law to ourselves and for our neighbours – *lex armata* – armed, emphatic, tyrannous law. If you see a crapulous human ruin snuffing, dash him from his box! The judge, though in a way an admission of disease, is less offensive to me than either the doctor or the priest. Above all the doctor – the doctor and the purulent trash and garbage of his pharmacopœia! Pure air – from the neighbourhood of a pinetum for the sake of the turpentine – unadulterated wine, and the reflections of an unsophisticated spirit in the presence of the works of nature – these, my boy, are the best medical appliances and the best religious comforts. Devote yourself to these. Hark! there are the bells of Bourron (the wind is in the north, it will be fair). How clear and airy is the sound! The nerves are harmonised and quieted; the mind attuned to silence; and observe how easily and regularly beats the heart! Your unenlightened doctor would see nothing in these sensations; and yet you yourself perceive they are a part of health. – Did you remember your cinchona this morning? Good. Cinchona also is a work of nature: it is, after all, only the bark of a tree which we might gather for ourselves if we lived in the locality. – What a world is this! Though a professed atheist, I delight to bear my testimony to the world. Look at the gratuitous remedies and pleasures that surround our path! The river runs by the garden end, our bath, our fish-pond, our natural system of drainage. There is a well in the court which sends up sparkling water from the earth's very heart, clean, cool, and, with a little wine, most wholesome. The district is notorious for its salubrity; rheumatism is the only prevalent complaint, and I myself have never had a touch of it. I tell you – and my opinion is based upon the coldest, clearest processes of reason – if I, if you, desired to leave this home of pleasures, it would be the duty, it would be the privilege, of our best friend to prevent us with a pistol bullet.'

One beautiful June day they sat upon the hill outside the village. The river, as blue as heaven, shone here and

there among the foliage. The indefatigable birds turned
and flickered about Gretz church-tower. A healthy wind
blew from over the forest, and the sound of innumerable
thousands of tree-tops and innumerable millions on millions of green leaves was abroad in the air, and filled the ear
with something between whispered speech and singing. It
seemed as if every blade of grass must hide a cigale; and the
fields rang merrily with their music, jingling far and near as
with the sleigh-bells of the fairy queen. From their station
on the slope the eye embraced a large space of poplar'd
plain upon the one hand, the waving hill-tops of the forest
on the other, and Gretz itself in the middle, a handful of
roofs. Under the bestriding arch of the blue heavens, the
place seemed dwindled to a toy. It seemed incredible that
people dwelt, and could find room to turn or air to breathe,
in such a corner of the world. The thought came home to
the boy, perhaps for the first time, and he gave it words.

'How small it looks!' he sighed.

'Ay,' replied the Doctor, 'small enough now. Yet it was
once a walled city; thriving, full of furred burgesses and
men in armour, humming with affairs; – with tall spires, for
aught that I know, and portly towers along the battlements.
A thousand chimneys ceased smoking at the curfew bell.
There were gibbets at the gate as thick as scarecrows. In
time of war, the assault swarmed against it with ladders,
the arrows fell like leaves, the defenders sallied hotly over
the drawbridge, each side uttered its cry as they plied their
weapons. Do you know that the walls extended as far as the
Commanderie? Tradition so reports. Alas, what a long way
off is all this confusion – nothing left of it but my quiet words
spoken in your ear – and the town itself shrunk to the hamlet
underneath us! By and by came the English wars – you shall
hear more of the English, a stupid people, who sometimes
blundered into good – and Gretz was taken, sacked, and
burned. It is the history of many towns; but Gretz never
rose again; it was never rebuilt; its ruins were a quarry to
serve the growth of rivals; and the stones of Gretz are now
erect along the streets of Nemours. It gratifies me that our
old house was the first to rise after the calamity; when the
town had come to an end, it inaugurated the hamlet.'

'I, too, am glad of that,' said Jean-Marie.

'It should be the temple of the humbler virtues,' responded the Doctor with a savoury gusto. 'Perhaps one of the reasons why I love my little hamlet as I do, is that we have a similar history, she and I. Have I told you that I was once rich?'

'I do not think so,' answered Jean-Marie. 'I do not think I should have forgotten. I am sorry you should have lost your fortune.'

'Sorry?' cried the Doctor. 'Why, I find I have scarce begun your education after all. Listen to me! Would you rather live in the old Gretz or in the new, free from the alarms of war, with the green country at the door, without noise, passports, the exactions of the soldiery, or the jangle of the curfew bell to send us off to bed by sundown?'

'I suppose I should prefer the new,' replied the boy.

'Precisely,' returned the Doctor; 'so do I. And, in the same way, I prefer my present moderate fortune to my former wealth. Golden mediocrity! cried the adorable ancients; and I subscribe to their enthusiasm. Have I not good wine, good food, good air, the fields and the forest for my walk, a house, an admirable wife, a boy whom I protest I cherish like a son? Now, if I were still rich, I should indubitably make my residence in Paris – you know Paris – Paris and Paradise are not convertible terms. This pleasant noise of the wind streaming among leaves changed into the grinding Babel of the street, the stupid glare of plaster substituted for this quiet pattern of greens and greys, the nerves shattered, the digestion falsified – picture the fall! Already you perceive the consequences; the mind is stimulated, the heart steps to a different measure, and the man is himself no longer. I have passionately studied myself – the true business of philosophy. I know my character as the musician knows the ventages of his flute. Should I return to Paris, I should ruin myself gambling; nay, I go further – I should break the heart of my Anastasie with infidelities.'

This was too much for Jean-Marie. That a place should so transform the most excellent of men transcended his belief. Paris, he protested, was even an agreeable place of residence. 'Nor when I lived in that city did I feel much difference,' he pleaded.

'What!' cried the Doctor. 'Did you not steal when you were there?'

But the boy could never be brought to see that he had done anything wrong when he stole. Nor, indeed, did the Doctor think he had; but that gentleman was never very scrupulous when in want of a retort.

'And now,' he concluded, 'do you begin to understand? My only friends were those who ruined me. Gretz has been my academy, my sanatorium, my heaven of innocent pleasure. If millions are offered me, I wave them back: *Retro, Sathanas!* – evil one, begone! Fix your mind on my example; despise riches, avoid the debasing influence of cities. Hygiene – hygiene and mediocrity of fortune – these be your watchwords during life!'

The Doctor's system of hygiene strikingly coincided with his tastes; and his picture of the perfect life was a faithful description of the one he was leading at the time. But it is easy to convince a boy, whom you supply with all the facts for the discussion. And besides, there was one thing admirable in the philosophy, and that was the enthusiasm of the philosopher. There was never any one more vigorously determined to be pleased; and if he was not a great logician, and so had no right to convince the intellect, he was certainly something of a poet, and had a fascination to seduce the heart. What he could not achieve in his customary humour of a radiant admiration of himself and his circumstances, he sometimes effected in his fits of gloom.

'Boy,' he would say, 'avoid me to-day. If I were superstitious, I should even beg for an interest in your prayers. I am in the black fit; the evil spirit of King Saul, the hag of the merchant Abudah, the personal devil of the mediæval monk, is with me – is in me,' tapping on his breast. 'The vices of my nature are now uppermost; innocent pleasures woo me in vain; I long for Paris, for my wallowing in the mire. See,' he would continue, producing a handful of silver, 'I denude myself, I am not to be trusted with the price of a fare. Take it, keep it for me, squander it on deleterious candy, throw it in the deepest of the river – I will homologate your action.

Save me from that part of myself which I disown. If you see me falter, do not hesitate; if necessary, wreck the train! I speak, of course, by a parable. Any extremity were better than for me to reach Paris alive.'

Doubtless the Doctor enjoyed these little scenes, as a variation in his part; they represented the Byronic element in the somewhat artificial poetry of his existence; but to the boy, though he was dimly aware of their theatricality, they represented more. The Doctor made perhaps too little, the boy possibly too much, of the reality and gravity of these temptations.

One day a great light shone for Jean-Marie. 'Could not riches be used well?' he asked.

'In theory, yes,' replied the Doctor. 'But it is found in experience that no one does so. All the world imagine they will be exceptional when they grow wealthy; but possession is debasing, new desires spring up; and the silly taste for ostentation eats out the heart of pleasure.'

'Then you might be better if you had less,' said the boy.

'Certainly not,' replied the Doctor; but his voice quavered as he spoke.

'Why?' demanded pitiless innocence.

Doctor Desprez saw all the colours of the rainbow in a moment; the stable universe appeared to be about capsizing with him. 'Because,' said he – affecting deliberation after an obvious pause – 'because I have formed my life for my present income. It is not good for men of my years to be violently dissevered from their habits.'

That was a sharp brush. The Doctor breathed hard, and fell into taciturnity for the afternoon. As for the boy, he was delighted with the resolution of his doubts; even wondered that he had not foreseen the obvious and conclusive answer. His faith in the Doctor was a stout piece of goods. Desprez was inclined to be a sheet in the wind's eye after dinner, especially after Rhone wine, his favourite weakness. He would then remark on the warmth of his feeling for Anastasie, and with inflamed cheeks and a loose, flustered smile, debate upon all sorts of topics, and be feebly and indiscreetly witty. But the adopted stable-boy would not permit himself to entertain a doubt that savoured of ingratitude. It is quite true that a man may be a second father to you, and yet take too much to drink; but the best natures are ever slow to accept such truths.

The Doctor thoroughly possessed his heart, but perhaps he exaggerated his influence over his mind. Certainly Jean-Marie adopted some of his master's opinions, but I have yet to learn that he ever surrendered one of his own. Convictions existed in him by divine right; they were virgin, unwrought, the brute metal of decision. He could add others indeed, but he could not put away; neither did he care if they were perfectly agreed among themselves; and his spiritual pleasures had nothing to do with turning them over or justifying them in words. Words were with him a mere accomplishment, like dancing. When he was by himself, his pleasures were almost vegetable. He would slip into the woods towards Achères, and sit in the mouth of a cave among grey birches. His soul stared straight out of his eyes; he did not move or think; sunlight, thin shadows moving in the wind, the edge of firs against the sky, occupied and bound his faculties. He was pure unity, a spirit wholly abstracted. A single mood filled him, to which all the objects of sense contributed, as the colours of the spectrum merge and disappear in white light.

So while the Doctor made himself drunk with words, the adopted stable-boy bemused himself with silence.

CHAPTER FIVE

Treasure Trove

THE Doctor's carriage was a two-wheeled gig with a hood; a kind of vehicle in much favour among country doctors. On how many roads has one not seen it, a great way off between the poplars! – in how many village streets, tied to a gate-post! This sort of chariot is affected – particularly at the trot – by a kind of pitching movement to and fro across the axle, which well entitles it to the style of a noddy. The hood describes a considerable arc against the landscape, with a solemnly absurd effect on the contemplative pedestrian. To ride in such a carriage cannot be numbered among the things that appertain to glory; but I have no doubt it may be useful in liver complaint. Thence, perhaps, its wide popularity among physicians.

One morning early, Jean-Marie led forth the Doctor's noddy, opened the gate, and mounted to the driving-seat. The Doctor followed, arrayed from top to toe in spotless linen, armed with an immense flesh-coloured umbrella, and girt with a botanical case on a baldric; and the equipage drove off smartly in a breeze of its own provocation. They were bound for Franchard, to collect plants, with an eye to the *Comparative Pharmacopœiae.*

A little rattling on the open roads, and they came to the borders of the forest and struck into an unfrequented track; the noddy yawed softly over the sand, with an accompaniment of snapping twigs. There was a great, green, softly murmuring cloud of congregated foliage overhead. In the arcades of the forest the air retained the freshness of the night. The athletic bearing of the trees, each bearing its leafy mountain, pleased the mind like so many statues, and the lines of the trunk led the eye admiringly upward to where the extreme leaves sparkled in a patch of azure. Squirrels leaped in mid-air. It was a proper spot for a devotee of the goddess Hygieia.

'Have you been to Franchard, Jean-Marie?' inquired the Doctor. 'I fancy not.'

'Never,' replied the boy.

'It is a ruin in a gorge,' continued Desprez, adopting his expository voice; 'the ruin of a hermitage and chapel. History tells us much of Franchard; how the recluse was often slain by robbers; how he lived on a most insufficient diet; how he was expected to pass his days in prayer. A letter is preserved, addressed to one of these solitaries by the superior of his order, full of admirable hygienic advice; bidding him go from his book to praying, and so back again, for variety's sake, and when he was weary of both to stroll about his garden and observe the honey bees. It is to this day my own system. You must have often remarked me leaving the *Pharmacopœia* – often even in the middle of a phrase – to come forth into the sun and air. I admire the writer of that letter from my heart; he was a man of thought on the most important subjects. But, indeed, had I lived in the Middle Ages (I am heartily glad that I did not) I should have been an eremite myself – if I had not been a professed buffoon, that is. These were the only philosophical lives yet open: laughter or prayer; sneers, we might say, and tears. Until the sun of the Positive arose, the wise man had to make his choice between these two.'

'I have been a buffoon, of course,' observed Jean-Marie.

'I cannot imagine you to have excelled in your profession,' said the Doctor, admiring the boy's gravity. 'Do you ever laugh?'

'Oh, yes,' replied the other. 'I laugh often. I am very fond of jokes.'

'Singular being!' said Desprez. 'But I divagate (I perceive in a thousand ways that I grow old). Franchard was at length destroyed in the English wars, the same that levelled Gretz. But – here is the point – the hermits (for there were already more than one) had foreseen the danger and carefully concealed the sacrificial vessels. These vessels were of monstrous value, Jean-Marie – monstrous value – priceless, we may say; exquisitely worked, of exquisite material. And now, mark me, they have never been found. In the reign of Louis Quatorze some fellows were digging hard by the ruins. Suddenly – tock! – the spade hit upon an obstacle. Imagine the men looking one to another; imagine how their hearts bounded, how their colour came and went. It was a coffer, and in Franchard, the place of buried treasure! They tore it open like famished beasts. Alas! it was not the treasure; only some priestly robes, which, at the touch of the eating air, fell upon themselves and instantly wasted into dust. The perspiration of these good fellows turned cold upon them, Jean-Marie. I will pledge my reputation, if there was anything like a cutting wind, one or other had a pneumonia for his trouble.'

'I should like to have seen them turning into dust,' said Jean-Marie. 'Otherwise, I should not have cared so greatly.'

'You have no imagination,' cried the Doctor. 'Picture to yourself the scene. Dwell on the idea – a great treasure lying in the earth for centuries: the material for a giddy, copious, opulent existence not employed; dresses and exquisite pictures unseen; the swiftest galloping horses not stirring a hoof, arrested by a spell; women with the beautiful faculty of smiles, not smiling; cards, dice, opera singing, orchestras, castles, beautiful parks and gardens, big ships with a tower of sailcloth, all lying unborn in a coffin – and the stupid trees growing overhead in the sunlight, year after year. The thought drives one frantic.'

'It is only money,' replied Jean-Marie. 'It would do harm.'

'Oh, come!' cried Desprez, 'that is philosophy; it is all very fine, but not to the point just now. And besides, it is not "only money," as you call it; there are works of art in the question; the vessels were carved. You speak like a child. You weary me exceedingly, quoting my words out of all logical connection, like a parroquet.'

'And at any rate, we have nothing to do with it,' returned the boy submissively.

They struck the Route Ronde at that moment; and the sudden change to the rattling causeway combined, with the doctor's irritation, to keep him silent. The noddy jigged along; the trees went by, looking on silently, as if they had something on their minds. The Quadrilateral was passed; then came Franchard. They put up the horse at the little solitary inn, and went forth strolling; the gorge was dyed deeply with heather; the rocks and birches standing luminous in the sun. A great humming of bees about the flowers disposed Jean-Marie to sleep, and he sat down against a clump of heather, while the doctor went briskly to and fro, with quick turns, culling his simples.

The boy's head had fallen a little forward, his eyes were closed, his fingers had fallen lax about his knees, when a sudden cry called him to his feet. It was a strange sound, thin and brief; it fell dead, and silence returned as though it had never been interrupted. He had not recognised the Doctor's voice; but, as there was no one else in all the valley, it was plainly the Doctor who had given utterance to the sound. He looked right and left, and there was Desprez, standing in a niche between two boulders, and looking round on his adopted son with a countenance as white as paper.

'A viper!' cried Jean-Marie, running towards him. 'A viper! You are bitten!'

The Doctor came down heavily out of the cleft, and advanced in silence to meet the boy, whom he took roughly by the shoulder.

'I have found it,' he said, with a gasp.

'A plant?' asked Jean-Marie.

Desprez had a fit of unnatural gaiety, which the rocks took up and mimicked. 'A plant!' he repeated scornfully. 'Well – yes – a plant. And here,' he added suddenly, showing his right hand, which he had hitherto concealed behind his back – 'here is one of the bulbs.'

Jean-Marie saw a dirty platter, coated with earth.

'That?' said he. 'It is a plate!'

'It is a coach and horses,' cried the Doctor. 'Boy,' he continued, growing warmer, 'I plucked away a great pad of moss from between these boulders, and disclosed a crevice; and when I looked in, what do you suppose I saw? I saw a house in Paris with a court and garden, I saw my wife

shining with diamonds, I saw myself a deputy, I saw you
– well, I – I saw your future,' he concluded, rather feebly.
'I have just discovered America,' he added.

'But what is it?' asked the boy.

'The Treasure of Franchard,' cried the Doctor; and,
throwing his brown straw hat upon the ground, he whooped
like an Indian and sprang upon Jean-Marie, whom he
suffocated with embraces and bedewed with tears. Then
he flung himself down among the heather and once more
laughed until the valley rang.

But the boy had now an interest of his own, a boy's
interest. No sooner was he released from the Doctor's
accolade than he ran to the boulders, sprang into the niche,
and, thrusting his hand into the crevice, drew forth one
after another, encrusted with the earth of ages, the flagons,
candlesticks and patens of the hermitage of Franchard. A
casket came last, tightly shut and very heavy.

'Oh what fun, what fun!' he cried.

But when he looked back at the Doctor, who had
followed close behind and was silently observing, the
words died from his lips. Desprez was once more the
colour of ashes; his lip worked and trembled; a sort of
bestial greed possessed him.

'This is childish,' he said. 'We lose precious time. Back
to the inn, harness the trap, and bring it to yon bank. Run
for your life, and remember – not one whisper. I stay here
to watch.'

Jean-Marie did as he was bid, though not without surprise. The noddy was brought round to the spot indicated;
and the two gradually transported the treasure from its place
of concealment to the boot below the driving-seat. Once it
was all stored the Doctor recovered his gaiety.

'I pay my grateful duties to the genius of this dell,' he
said. 'Oh, for a live coal, a heifer, and a jar of country wine!
I am in the vein for sacrifice, for a superb libation. Well,
and why not? We are at Franchard? English pale ale is to
be had – not classical, indeed, but excellent. Boy, we shall
drink ale.'

'But I thought it was so unwholesome,' said Jean-Marie,
'and very dear besides.'

'Fiddle-de-dee!' exclaimed the Doctor gaily. 'To the inn!'

And he stepped into the noddy, tossing his head, with an elastic, youthful air. The horse was turned, and in a few seconds they drew up beside the palings of the inn garden.

'Here,' said Desprez – 'here, near the stable, so that we may keep an eye upon things.'

They tied the horse, and entered the garden, the Doctor singing, now in fantastic high notes, now producing deep reverberations from his chest. He took a seat, rapped loudly on the table, assailed the waiter with witticisms; and when the bottle of Bass was at length produced, far more charged with gas than the most delirious champagne, he filled out a long glassful of froth and pushed it over to Jean-Marie. 'Drink,' he said; 'drink deep.'

'I would rather not,' faltered the boy, true to his training.

'What?' thundered Desprez.

'I am afraid of it,' said Jean-Marie; 'my stomach—'

'Take it or leave it,' interrupted Desprez fiercely; 'but understand it once for all – there is nothing so contemptible as a precisian.'

Here was a new lesson! The boy sat bemused, looking at the glass but not tasting it, while the Doctor emptied and refilled his own, at first with clouded brow, but gradually yielding to the sun, the heady, prickling beverage, and his own predisposition to be happy.

'Once in a way,' he said at last, by way of a concession to the boy's more rigorous attitude, 'once in a way, and at so critical a moment, this ale is a nectar for the gods. The habit, indeed, is debasing; wine, the juice of the grape, is the true drink of the Frenchman, as I have often had occasion to point out; and I do not know that I can blame you for refusing this outlandish stimulant. You can have some wine and cakes. Is the bottle empty? Well, we will not be proud; we will have pity on your glass.'

The beer being done, the Doctor chafed bitterly while Jean-Marie finished his cakes. 'I burn to be gone,' he said, looking at his watch. 'Good God, how slow you eat!' And yet to eat slowly was his own particular prescription, the main secret of longevity!

His martyrdom, however, reached an end at last; the pair resumed their places in the buggy, and Desprez, leaning luxuriously back, announced his intention of proceeding to Fontainebleau.

'To Fontainebleau?' repeated Jean-Marie.

'My words are always measured,' said the Doctor. 'On!'

The Doctor was driven through the glades of paradise; the air, the light, the shining leaves, the very movements of the vehicle, seemed to fall in tune with his golden meditations; with his head thrown back, he dreamed a series of sunny visions, ale and pleasure dancing in his veins. At last he spoke.

'I shall telegraph for Casimir,' he said. 'Good Casimir! a fellow of the lower order of intelligence, Jean-Marie, distinctly not creative, not poetic; and yet he will repay your study; his fortune is vast, and is entirely due to his own exertions. He is the very fellow to help us to dispose of our trinkets, find us a suitable house in Paris, and manage the details of our installation. Admirable Casimir, one of my oldest comrades! It was on his advice, I may add, that I invested my little fortune in Turkish bonds; when we have added these spoils of the mediæval church to our stake in the Mahometan empire, little boy, we shall positively roll among doubloons, positively roll! Beautiful forest,' he cried, 'farewell! Though called to other scenes, I will not forget thee. Thy name is graven in my heart. Under the influence of prosperity I become dithyrambic, Jean-Marie. Such is the impulse of the natural soul; such was the constitution of primæval man. And I – well, I will not refuse the credit – I have preserved my youth like a virginity; another, who should have led the same snoozing, countrified existence for these years, another had become rusted, become stereotyped; but I, I praise my happy constitution, retain the spring unbroken. Fresh opulence and a new sphere of duties find me unabated in ardour and only more mature by knowledge. For this prospective change, Jean-Marie – it may probably have shocked you.

Tell me now, did it not strike you as an inconsistency? Confess – it is useless to dissemble – it pained you?'

'Yes,' said the boy.

'You see,' returned the Doctor, with sublime fatuity, 'I read your thoughts! Nor am I surprised – your education is not yet complete; the higher duties of men have not been yet presented to you fully. A hint – till we have leisure – must suffice. Now that I am once more in possession of a modest competence; now that I have so long prepared myself in silent meditation, it becomes my superior duty to proceed to Paris. My scientific training, my undoubted command of language, mark me out for the service of my country. Modesty in such a case would be a snare. If sin were a philosophical expression, I should call it sinful. A man must not deny his manifest abilities, for that is to evade his obligations. I must be up and doing; I must be no skulker in life's battle.'

So he rattled on, copiously greasing the joint of his inconsistency with words; while the boy listened silently, his eyes fixed on the horse, his mind seething. It was all lost eloquence; no array of words could unsettle a belief of Jean-Marie's; and he drove into Fontainebleau filled with pity, horror, indignation, and despair.

In the town Jean-Marie was kept a fixture on the driving-seat to guard the treasure; while the Doctor, with a singular, slightly tipsy airiness of manner, fluttered in and out of cafés, where he shook hands with garrison officers, and mixed an absinthe with the nicety of old experience; in and out of shops, from which he returned laden with costly fruits, real turtle, a magnificent piece of silk for his wife, a preposterous cane for himself, and a képi of the newest fashion for the boy; in and out of the telegraph office, whence he despatched his telegram, and where three hours later he received an answer promising a visit on the morrow; and generally pervaded Fontainebleau with the first fine aroma of his divine good-humour.

The sun was very low when they set forth again; the shadows of the forest trees extended across the broad white road that led them home; the penetrating odour of the evening wood had already arisen, like a cloud of incense, from that broad field of tree-tops; and even in the streets of the town, where the air had been baked all day between white walls, it came in whiffs and pulses, like a distant music. Half-way home, the last gold flicker vanished from a great oak upon the left; and when they came forth beyond the borders of the wood, the plain was already sunken in pearly greyness, and a great, pale moon came swinging skyward through the filmy poplars.

The Doctor sang, the Doctor whistled, the Doctor talked. He spoke of the woods, and the wars, and the deposition of dew; he brightened and babbled of Paris; he soared into cloudy bombast on the glories of the political arena. All was to be changed; as the day departed, it took with it the vestiges of an outworn existence, and tomorrow's sun was to inaugurate the new. 'Enough,' he cried, 'of this life of maceration!' His wife (still beautiful, or he was sadly partial) was to be no longer buried; she should now shine before society. Jean-Marie would find the world at his feet; the roads open to success, wealth, honour, and posthumous renown. 'And oh, by the way,' said he, 'for God's sake keep your tongue quiet! You are, of course, a very silent fellow; it is a quality I gladly recognise in you – silence, golden silence! But this is a matter of gravity. No word must get abroad; none but the good Casimir is to be trusted; we shall probably dispose of the vessels in England.'

'But are they not even ours?' the boy said, almost with a sob – it was the only time he had spoken.

'Ours in this sense, that they are nobody else's,' replied the Doctor. 'But the State would have some claim. If they were stolen, for instance, we should be unable to demand their restitution; we should have no title; we should be unable even to communicate with the police. Such is the monstrous condition of the law.[1] It is a mere instance of what remains to be done, of the injustices that may yet be righted by an ardent, active, and philosophical deputy.'

Jean-Marie put his faith in Madame Desprez; and as they drove forward down the road from Bourron, between

1. Let it be so, for my tale!

the rustling poplars, he prayed in his teeth, and whipped up the horse to an unusual speed. Surely, as soon as they arrived, madame would assert her character, and bring this waking nightmare to an end.

Their entrance into Gretz was heralded and accompanied by a most furious barking; all the dogs in the village seemed to smell the treasure in the noddy. But there was no one in the street, save three lounging landscape-painters at Tentaillon's door. Jean-Marie opened the green gate and led in the horse and carriage; and almost at the same moment Madame Desprez came to the kitchen threshold with a lighted lantern; for the moon was not yet high enough to clear the garden walls.

'Close the gates, Jean-Marie!' cried the Doctor, somewhat unsteadily alighting. – 'Anastasie, where is Aline?'

'She has gone to Montereau to see her parents,' said madame.

'All is for the best!' exclaimed the Doctor fervently. 'Here, quick, come near to me; I do not wish to speak too loud,' he continued. 'Darling, we are wealthy!'

'Wealthy!' repeated the wife.

'I have found the treasure of Franchard,' replied her husband. 'See, here are the first-fruits; a pineapple, a dress for my ever-beautiful – it will suit her – trust a husband's, trust a lover's, taste! Embrace me, darling! This grimy episode is over; the butterfly unfolds its painted wings. To-morrow Casimir will come; in a week we may be in Paris – happy at last! You shall have diamonds. Jean-Marie, take it out of the boot, with religious care, and bring it piece by piece into the dining-room. We shall have plate at table! Darling, hasten and prepare this turtle; it will be a whet – it will be an addition to our meagre ordinary. I myself will proceed to the cellar. We shall have a bottle of that little Beaujolais you like, and finish with the Hermitage; there are still three bottles left. Worthy wine for a worthy occasion.'

'But, my husband; you put me in a whirl,' she cried. 'I do not comprehend.'

'The turtle, my adored, the turtle!' cried the Doctor; and he pushed her towards the kitchen, lantern and all.

Jean-Marie stood dumbfounded. He had pictured to himself a different scene – a more immediate protest, and his hope began to dwindle on the spot.

The Doctor was everywhere, a little doubtful on his legs, perhaps, and now and then taking the wall with his shoulder; for it was long since he had tasted absinthe, and he was even then reflecting that the absinthe had been a misconception. Not that he regretted excess on such a glorious day, but he made a mental memorandum to beware; he must not, a second time, become the victim of a deleterious habit. He had his wine out of the cellar in a twinkling; he arranged the sacrificial vessels, some on the white table-cloth, some on the sideboard, still crusted with historic earth. He was in and out of the kitchen, plying Anastasie with vermouth, heating her with glimpses of the future, estimating their new wealth at ever larger figures; and before they sat down to supper, the lady's virtue had melted in the fire of his enthusiasm, her timidity had disappeared; she, too, had begun to speak disparagingly of the life at Gretz; and as she took her place and helped the soup, her eyes shone with the glitter of prospective diamonds.

All through the meal, she and the Doctor made and unmade fairy plans. They bobbed and bowed and pledged each other. Their faces ran over with smiles; their eyes scattered sparkles, as they projected the Doctor's political honours and the lady's drawing-room ovations.

'But you will not be a Red!' cried Anastasie.

'I am Left Centre to the core,' replied the Doctor.

'Madame Gastein will present us – we shall find ourselves forgotten,' said the lady.

'Never,' protested the Doctor. 'Beauty and talent leave a mark.'

'I have positively forgotten how to dress,' she sighed.

'Darling, you make me blush,' cried he. 'Yours has been a tragic marriage!'

'But your success – to see you appreciated, honoured, your name in all the papers, that will be more than pleasure – it will be heaven!' she cried.

'And once a week,' said the Doctor, archly scanning the syllables, 'once a week – one good little game of baccarat?'

'Only once a week?' she questioned, threatening him with a finger.

'I swear it by my political honour,' cried he.

'I spoil you,' she said, and gave him her hand. He covered it with kisses.

Jean-Marie escaped into the night. The moon swung high over Gretz. He went down to the garden end and sat on the jetty. The river ran by with eddies of oily silver, and a low, monotonous song. Faint veils of mist moved among the poplars on the farther side. The reeds were quietly nodding. A hundred times already had the boy sat, on such a night, and watched the streaming river with untroubled fancy. And this perhaps was to be the last. He was to leave this familiar hamlet, this green, rustling country, this bright and quiet stream; he was to pass into the great city; his dear lady mistress was to move bedizened into saloons; his good, garrulous, kind-hearted master to become a brawling deputy; and both be lost for ever to Jean-Marie and their better selves. He knew his own defects; he knew he must sink into less and less consideration in the turmoil of a city life; sink more and more from the child into the servant. And he began dimly to believe the Doctor's prophecies of evil. He could see a change in both. His generous incredulity failed him for this once; a child must have perceived that the Hermitage had completed what the absinthe had begun. If this were the first day, what would be the last? 'If necessary, wreck the train,' thought he, remembering the Doctor's parable. He looked round on the delightful scene; he drank deep of the charmed night air, laden with the scent of hay. 'If necessary, wreck the train,' he repeated. And he rose and returned to the house.

CHAPTER SIX

A Criminal Investigation in Two Parts

THE next morning there was a most unusual outcry in the Doctor's house. The last thing before going to bed, the Doctor had locked up some valuables in the dining-room cupboard; and behold, when he rose again, as he did about four o'clock, the cupboard had been broken open, and the valuables in question had disappeared. Madame and Jean-Marie were summoned from their rooms, and appeared in hasty toilettes; they found the Doctor raving, calling the heavens to witness and avenge his injury, pacing the room barefooted, with the tails of his night-shirt flirting as he turned.

'Gone!' he said: 'the things are gone, the fortune gone! We are paupers once more. Boy! what do you know of this? Speak up, sir, speak up. Do you know of it? Where are they?' He had him by the arm, shaking him like a bag, and the boy's words, if he had any, were jolted forth in inarticulate murmurs. The Doctor, with a revulsion from his own violence, set him down again. He observed Anastasie in tears. 'Anastasie,' he said, in quite an altered voice, 'compose yourself, command your feelings. I would not have you give way to passion like the vulgar. This – this trifling accident must be lived down. Jean-Marie, bring me my smaller medicine chest. A gentle laxative is indicated.'

And he dosed the family all round, leading the way himself with a double quantity. The wretched Anastasie, who had never been ill in the whole course of her existence, and whose soul recoiled from remedies, wept floods of tears as she sipped, and shuddered, and protested, and then was bullied and shouted at until she sipped again. As for Jean-Marie, he took his portion down with stoicism.

'I have given him a less amount,' observed the Doctor, 'his youth protecting him against emotion. And now that we have thus parried any morbid consequences, let us reason.'

'I am so cold,' wailed Anastasie.

'Cold!' cried the Doctor. 'I give thanks to God that I am made of fierier material. Why, madame, a blow like this would set a frog into a transpiration. If you're cold, you can retire; and, by the way, you might throw me down my trousers. It is chilly for the legs.'

'Oh, no!' protested Anastasie; 'I will stay with you.'

'Nay, madame, you shall not suffer for your devotion,' said the Doctor. 'I will myself fetch you a shawl.' And he went upstairs and returned more fully clad and with an armful of wraps for the shivering Anastasie. 'And now,' he resumed, 'to investigate this crime. Let us proceed by induction. Anastasie, do you know anything that can help us?' Anastasie knew nothing. 'Or you, Jean-Marie?'

'Not I,' replied the boy steadily.

'Good,' returned the Doctor. 'We shall now turn our attention to the material evidences. (I was born to be a detective; I have the eye and the systematic spirit.) First, violence has been employed. The door was broken open; and it may be observed, in passing, that the lock was dear indeed at what I paid for it: a crow to pluck with Master Goguelat. Second, here is the instrument employed, one of our own table-knives, one of our best, my dear; which seems to indicate no preparation on the part of the gang – if gang it was. Thirdly, I observe that nothing has been removed except the Franchard dishes and the casket; our own silver has been minutely respected. This is why; it shows intelligence, a knowledge of the code, a desire to avoid legal consequences. I argue from this fact that the gang numbers persons of respectability – outward, of course, and merely outward, as the robbery proves. But I argue, second, that we must have been observed at Franchard itself by some occult observer, and dogged throughout the day with a skill and patience that I venture to qualify as consummate. No ordinary man, no occasional criminal, would have shown himself capable of this combination.

We have in our neighbourhood, it is far from improbable, a retired bandit of the highest order of intelligence.'

'Good heaven!' cried the horrified Anastasie. 'Henri, how can you!'

'My cherished one, this is a process of induction,' said the Doctor. 'If any of my steps are unsound, correct me. You are silent? Then do not, I beseech you, be so vulgarly illogical as to revolt from my conclusion. We have now arrived,' he resumed, 'at some idea of the composition of the gang – for I incline to the hypothesis of more than one – and we now leave this room, which can disclose no more, and turn our attention to the court and garden. (Jean-Marie, I trust you are observantly following my various steps; this is an excellent piece of education for you.) Come with me to the door. No steps on the court; it is unfortunate our court should be paved. On what small matters hangs the destiny of these delicate investigations! Hey! What have we here? I have led you to the very spot,' he said, standing grandly backward and indicating the green gate. 'An escalade, as you can now see for yourselves, has taken place.'

Sure enough, the green paint was in several places scratched and broken; and one of the panels preserved the print of a nailed shoe. The foot had slipped, however, and it was difficult to estimate the size of the shoe, and impossible to distinguish the pattern of the nails.

'The whole robbery,' concluded the Doctor, 'step by step, has been reconstituted. Inductive science can no further go.'

'It is wonderful,' said his wife. 'You should indeed have been a detective, Henri. I had no idea of your talents.'

'My dear,' replied Desprez, condescendingly, 'a man of scientific imagination combines the lesser faculties; he is a detective just as he is a publicist or a general; these are but local applications of his special talent. But now,' he continued, 'would you have me go further? Would you have me lay my finger on the culprits – or rather, for I cannot promise quite so much, point out to you the very house where they consort? It may be a satisfaction, at least it is all we are likely to get, since we are denied the remedy of law. I reach the further stage in this way. In order to fill my outline of the robbery, I require a man of education, I require a man superior to considerations of morality. The three requisites all centre in Tentaillon's boarders. They are painters, therefore they are continually lounging in the forest. They are painters, therefore they are not unlikely to have some smattering of education. Lastly, because they are painters, they are probably immoral. And this I prove in two ways. First, painting is an art which merely addresses the eye; it does not in any particular exercise the moral sense. And second, painting, in common with all the other arts, implies the dangerous quality of imagination. A man of imagination is never moral; he outsoars literal demarcations and reviews life under too many shifting lights to rest content with the invidious distinctions of the law!'

'But you always say – at least, so I understood you' – said madame, 'that these lads display no imagination whatever.'

'My dear, they displayed imagination, and of a very fantastic order, too,' returned the Doctor, 'when they embraced their beggarly profession. Besides – and this is an argument exactly suited to your intellectual level – many of them are English and American. Where else should we expect to find a thief? – And now you had better get your coffee. Because we have lost a treasure, there is no reason for starving. For my part, I shall break my fast with white wine. I feel unaccountably heated and thirsty to-day. I can only attribute it to the shock of the discovery. And yet, you will bear me out, I supported the emotion nobly.'

The Doctor had now talked himself back into an admirable humour; and as he sat in the arbour and slowly imbibed a large allowance of white wine and picked a little bread and cheese with no very impetuous appetite, if a third of his meditations ran upon the missing treasure, the other two-thirds were more pleasingly busied in the retrospect of his detective skill.

About eleven Casimir arrived; he had caught an early train to Fontainebleau, and driven over to save time; and now his cab was stabled at Tentaillon's, and he remarked, studying his watch, that he could spare an hour and a half.

He was much the man of business, decisively spoken, given to frowning in an intellectual manner. Anastasie's born brother, he did not waste much sentiment on the lady, gave her an English family kiss, and demanded a meal without delay.

'You can tell me your story while we eat,' he observed. 'Anything good to-day, Stasie?'

He was promised something good. The trio sat down to table in the arbour, Jean-Marie waiting as well as eating, and the Doctor recounted what had happened in his richest narrative manner. Casimir heard it with explosions of laughter.

'What a streak of luck for you, my good brother,' he observed, when the tale was over. 'If you had gone to Paris, you would have played dick-duck-drake with the whole consignment in three months. Your own would have followed; and you would have come to me in a procession like the last time. But I give you warning – Stasie may weep and Henri ratiocinate – it will not serve you twice. Your next collapse will be fatal. I thought I had told you so, Stasie? Hey? No sense?'

The Doctor winced and looked furtively at Jean-Marie; but the boy seemed apathetic.

'And then again,' broke out Casimir, 'what children you are – vicious children, my faith! How could you tell the value of this trash? It might have been worth nothing, or next door.'

'Pardon me,' said the Doctor. 'You have your usual flow of spirits, I perceive, but even less than your usual deliberation. I am not entirely ignorant of these matters.'

'Not entirely ignorant of anything ever I heard of,' interrupted Casimir, bowing, and raising his glass with a sort of pert politeness.

'At least,' resumed the Doctor, 'I gave my mind to the subject – that you may be willing to believe – and I estimated that our capital would be doubled.' And he described the nature of the find.

'My word of honour!' said Casimir, 'I half believe you! But much would depend on the quality of the gold.'

'The quality, my dear Casimir, was—' And the Doctor, in default of language, kissed his finger-tips.

'I would not take your word for it, my good friend,' retorted the man of business. 'You are a man of very rosy views. But this robbery,' he continued – 'this robbery is an odd thing. Of course I pass over your nonsense about gangs and landscape painters. For me, that is a dream. Who was in the house last night?'

'None but ourselves,' replied the Doctor.

'And this young gentleman?' asked Casimir, jerking a nod in the direction of Jean-Marie.

'He too' – the Doctor bowed.

'Well; and if it is a fair question, who is he?' pursued the brother-in-law.

'Jean-Marie,' answered the Doctor, 'combines the functions of a son and stable-boy. He began as the latter, but he rose rapidly to the more honourable rank in our affections. He is, I may say, the greatest comfort in our lives.'

'Ha!' said Casimir. 'And previous to becoming one of you?'

'Jean-Marie has lived a remarkable existence; his experience has been eminently formative,' replied Desprez. 'If I had to choose an education for my son, I should have chosen such another. Beginning life with mountebanks and thieves, passing onward to the society and friendship of philosophers, he may be said to have skimmed the volume of human life.'

'Thieves?' repeated the brother-in-law, with a meditative air.

The Doctor could have bitten his tongue out. He foresaw what was coming, and prepared his mind for a vigorous defence.

'Did you ever steal yourself?' asked Casimir, turning suddenly on Jean-Marie, and for the first time employing a single eyeglass which hung round his neck.

'Yes, sir,' replied the boy, with a deep blush.

Casimir turned to the others with pursed lips, and nodded to them meaningly. 'Hey?' said he; 'how is that?'

'Jean-Marie is a teller of the truth,' returned the Doctor, throwing out his bust.

'He has never told a lie,' added madame. 'He is the best of boys.'

'Never told a lie, has he not?' reflected Casimir. 'Strange, very strange. Give me your attention, my young friend,' he continued. 'You knew about this treasure?'

'He helped to bring it home,' interposed the Doctor.

'Desprez, I ask you nothing but to hold your tongue,' returned Casimir. 'I mean to question this stable-boy of yours; and if you are so certain of his innocence, you can afford to let him answer for himself. Now, sir,' he resumed, pointing his eyeglass straight at Jean-Marie. 'You knew it could be stolen with impunity? You knew you could not be prosecuted? Come! Did you, or did you not?'

'I did,' answered Jean-Marie, in a miserable whisper. He sat there changing colour like a revolving pharos, twisting his fingers hysterically, swallowing air, the picture of guilt.

'You knew where it was put?' resumed the inquisitor.

'Yes,' from Jean-Marie.

'You say you have been a thief before,' continued Casimir. 'Now how am I to know that you are not one still? I suppose you could climb the green gate?'

'Yes,' still lower, from the culprit.

'Well, then, it was you who stole these things. You know it, and you dare not deny it. Look me in the face! Raise your sneak's eyes, and answer!'

But in place of anything of that sort Jean-Marie broke into a dismal howl and fled from the arbour. Anastasie, as she pursued to capture and reassure the victim, found time to send one Parthian arrow – 'Casimir, you are a brute!'

'My brother,' said Desprez, with the greatest dignity, 'you take upon yourself a license—'

'Desprez,' interrupted Casimir, 'for Heaven's sake be a man of the world. You telegraph me to leave my business and come down here on yours. I come, I ask the business, you say "Find me this thief!" Well, I find him; I say "There he is!" You need not like it, but you have no manner of right to take offence.'

'Well,' returned the Doctor, 'I grant that; I will even thank you for your mistaken zeal. But your hypothesis was so extravagantly monstrous—'

'Look here,' interrupted Casimir; 'was it you or Stasie?'

'Certainly not,' answered the Doctor.

'Very well; then it was the boy. Say no more about it,' said the brother-in-law, and he produced his cigar-case.

'I will say this much more,' returned Desprez: 'if that boy came and told me so himself, I should not believe him; and if I did believe him, so implicit is my trust, I should conclude that he had acted for the best.'

'Well, well,' said Casimir, indulgently. 'Have you a light? I must be going. And by the way, I wish you would let me sell your Turks for you. I always told you, it meant smash. I tell you so again. Indeed, it was partly that which brought me down. You never acknowledged my letters – a most unpardonable habit.'

'My good brother,' replied the Doctor blandly, 'I have never denied your ability in business; but I can perceive your limitations.'

'Egad, my friend, I can return the compliment,' observed the man of business. 'Your limitation is to be downright irrational.'

'Observe the relative position,' returned the Doctor, with a smile. 'It is your attitude to believe through thick and thin in one man's judgment – your own. I follow the same opinion, but critically and with open eyes. Which is the more irrational? – I leave it to yourself.'

'Oh, my dear fellow!' cried Casimir, 'stick to your Turks, stick to your stable-boy, go to the devil in general in your own way and be done with it. But don't ratiocinate with me – I cannot bear it. And so, ta-ta. I might as well have stayed away for any good I've done. Say goodbye from me to Stasie, and to the sullen hang-dog of a stable-boy, if you insist on it; I'm off.'

And Casimir departed. The Doctor, that night, dissected his character before Anastasie. 'One thing, my beautiful,' he said, 'he has learned one thing from his life-long acquaintance with your husband: the word *ratiocinate*. It shines in his vocabulary, like a jewel in a muck-heap. And, even so, he continually misapplies it. For you must have observed he uses it as a sort of taunt, in the case of *to ergotise*, implying, as it were – the poor, dear fellow! – a vein of sophistry. As for his cruelty to Jean-Marie, it must be forgiven him – it is not his nature, it is the nature of his life. A man who deals with money, my dear, is a man lost.'

With Jean-Marie the process of reconciliation had been somewhat slow. At first he was inconsolable, insisted on leaving the family, went from paroxysm to paroxysm of tears; and it was only after Anastasie had been closeted for an hour with him, alone, that she came forth, sought out the Doctor, and, with tears in her eyes, acquainted that gentleman with what had passed.

'At first, my husband, he would hear of nothing,' she said. 'Imagine! if he had left us! what would the treasure be to that? Horrible treasure, it has brought all this about! At last, after he has sobbed his very heart out, he agrees to stay on a condition – we are not to mention this matter, this infamous suspicion, not even to mention the robbery. On that agreement only, the poor, cruel boy will consent to remain among his friends.'

'But this inhibition,' said the Doctor, 'this embargo – it cannot possibly apply to me?'

'To all of us.' Anastasie assured him.

'My cherished one,' Desprez protested, 'you must have misunderstood. It cannot apply to me. He would naturally come to me.'

'Henri,' she said, 'it does; I swear to you it does.'

'This is a painful, a very painful circumstance,' the Doctor said, looking a little black. 'I cannot affect, Anastasie, to be anything but justly wounded. I feel this, I feel it, my wife, acutely.'

'I knew you would,' she said. 'But if you had seen his distress! We must make allowances, we must sacrifice our feelings.'

'I trust, my dear, you have never found me averse to sacrifices,' returned the Doctor very stiffly.

'And you will let me go and tell him that you have agreed? It will be like your noble nature,' she cried.

So it would, he perceived – it would be like his noble nature! Up jumped his spirits, triumphant at the thought. 'Go, darling,' he said nobly, 'reassure him. The subject is buried; more – I make an effort, I have accustomed my will to these exertions – and it is for-gotten.'

A little after, but still with swollen eyes and looking mortally sheepish, Jean-Marie reappeared and went osten-tatiously about his business. He was the only unhappy member of the party that sat down that night to supper. As for the Doctor, he was radiant. He thus sang the requiem of the treasure:—

'This has been, on the whole, a most amusing episode,' he said. 'We are not a penny the worse – nay, we are immensely gainers. Our philosophy has been exercised; some of the turtle is still left – the most wholesome of delicacies; I have my staff, Anastasie has her new dress, Jean-Marie is the proud possessor of a fashionable képi. Besides, we had a glass of Hermitage last night; the glow still suffuses my memory. I was growing positively niggardly with that Hermitage, positively niggardly. Let me take the hint: we had one bottle to celebrate the appearance of our visionary fortune; let us have a second to console us for its occultation. The third I hereby dedicate to Jean-Marie's wedding breakfast.'

CHAPTER SEVEN

The Fall of the House of Desprez

THE Doctor's house has not yet received the compliment of a description, and it is now high time that the omission were supplied, for the house is itself an actor in the stories, and one whose part is nearly at an end. Two storeys in height, walls of a warm yellow, tiles of an ancient ruddy brown diversified with moss and lichen, it stood with one wall to the street in the angle of the Doctor's property. It was roomy, draughty, and inconvenient. The large rafters were here and there engraven with rude marks and patterns; the hand-rail of the stair was carved in countrified arabesque; a stout timber pillar, which did duty to support the dining-room roof, bore mysterious characters on its darker side, runes, according to the Doctor; nor did he fail, when he ran over the legendary history of the house and its possessors, to dwell upon the Scandinavian scholar who had left them. Floors, doors, and rafters made a great variety of angles; every room had a particular inclination; the gable had tilted towards the garden, after the manner of a leaning tower, and one of the former proprietors had buttressed the building from that side with a great strut of wood, like the derrick of a crane. Altogether, it had many marks of ruin; it was a house for the rats to desert; and nothing but its excellent brightness – the window-glass polished and shining, the paint well scoured, the brasses radiant, the very prop all wreathed about with climbing flowers – nothing but its air of a well-tended, smiling veteran, sitting, crutch and all, in the sunny corner of a garden, marked it as a house for comfortable people to inhabit. In poor or idle management it would soon have hurried into the blackguard stages of decay. As it was, the whole family loved it, and the Doctor was never better inspired than when he narrated its imaginary story and drew the character of its successive masters, from the Hebrew merchant who had re-edified its walls after the sack of the town, and past the mysterious engraver of the runes, down to the long-headed, dirty-handed boor from whom he had himself acquired it at a ruinous expense. As for any alarm about its security, the idea had never presented itself. What had stood four centuries might well endure a little longer.

Indeed, in this particular winter, after the finding and losing of the treasure, the Desprez had an anxiety of a very different order, and one which lay nearer their hearts. Jean-Marie was plainly not himself. He had fits of hectic activity, when he made unusual exertions to please, spoke more and faster, and redoubled in attention to his lessons. But these were interrupted by spells of melancholia and brooding silence, when the boy was little better than unbearable.

'Silence,' the Doctor moralised – 'you see, Anastasie, what comes of silence. Had the boy properly unbosomed himself, the little disappointment about the treasure, the little annoyance about Casimir's incivility, would long ago have been forgotten. As it is, they prey upon him like a disease. He loses flesh, his appetite is variable, and, on the whole, impaired. I keep him on the strictest regimen, I exhibit the most powerful tonics both in vain.'

'Don't you think you drug him too much?' asked madame, with an irrepressible shudder.

'Drug?' cried the Doctor; 'I drug? Anastasie, you are mad!'

Time went on, and the boy's health still slowly declined. The Doctor blamed the weather, which was cold and boisterous. He called in his *confrère* from Bourron, took a fancy for him, magnified his capacity, and was pretty soon under treatment himself – it scarcely appeared for what complaint. He and Jean-Marie had each medicine to take at different periods of the day. The Doctor used to lie in wait for the exact moment, watch in hand. 'There is nothing like regularity,' he would say, fill out the doses, and dilate on the virtues of the draught; and if the boy seemed none the better, the Doctor was not at all the worse.

Gunpowder Day, the boy was particularly low. It was

scowling, squally weather. Huge broken companies of cloud sailed swiftly overhead; raking gleams of sunlight swept the village, and were followed by intervals of darkness and white, flying rain. At times the wind lifted up its voice and bellowed. The trees were all scourging themselves along the meadows, the last leaves flying like dust.

The Doctor, between the boy and the weather, was in his element; he had a theory to prove. He sat with his watch out and a barometer in front of him, waiting for the squalls and noting their effect upon the human pulse. 'For the true philosopher,' he remarked delightedly, 'every fact in nature is a toy.' A letter came to him; but, as its arrival coincided with the approach of another gust, he merely crammed it into his pocket, gave the time to Jean-Marie, and the next moment they were both counting their pulses as if for a wager.

At nightfall the wind rose into a tempest. It besieged the hamlet, apparently from every side, as if with batteries of cannon; the houses shook and groaned; live coals were blown upon the floor. The uproar and terror of the night kept people long awake, sitting with pallid faces giving ear.

It was twelve before the Desprez family retired. By half-past one, when the storm was already somewhat past its height, the Doctor was awakened from a troubled slumber, and sat up. A noise still rang in his ears, but whether of this world or the world of dreams he was not certain. Another clap of wind followed. It was accompanied by a sickening movement of the whole house, and in the subsequent lull Desprez could hear the tiles pouring like a cataract into the loft above his head. He plucked Anastasie bodily out of bed.

'Run!' he cried, thrusting some wearing apparel into her hands; 'the house is falling! To the garden!'

She did not pause to be twice bidden; she was down the stair in an instant. She had never before suspected herself of such activity. The Doctor meanwhile, with the speed of a piece of pantomime business, and undeterred by broken shins, proceeded to rout out Jean-Marie, tore Aline from her virgin slumbers, seized her by the hand, and tumbled downstairs and into the garden, with the girl tumbling behind him, still not half awake.

The fugitives rendezvoused in the arbour by some common instinct. Then came a bull's-eye flash of struggling moonshine, which disclosed their four figures standing huddled from the wind in a raffle of flying drapery, and not without a considerable need for more. At the humiliating spectacle Anastasie clutched her night-dress desperately about her and burst loudly into tears. The Doctor flew to console her; but she elbowed him away. She suspected everybody of being the general public, and thought the darkness was alive with eyes.

Another gleam and another violent gust arrived together; the house was seen to rock on its foundation, and, just as the light was once more eclipsed, a crash which triumphed over the shouting of the wind announced its fall, and for a moment the whole garden was alive with skipping tiles and brickbats. One such missile grazed the Doctor's ear; another descended on the bare foot of Aline, who instantly made night hideous with her shrieks.

By this time the hamlet was alarmed, lights flashed from the windows, hails reached the party, and the Doctor answered, nobly contending against Aline and the tempest. But this prospect of help only awakened Anastasie to a more active stage of terror.

'Henri, people will be coming,' she screamed in her husband's ear.

'I trust so,' he replied.

'They cannot. I would rather die,' she wailed.

'My dear,' said the Doctor reprovingly, 'you are excited. I gave you some clothes. What have you done with them?'

'Oh, I don't know – I must have thrown them away! Where are they?' she sobbed.

Desprez groped about in the darkness. 'Admirable!' he remarked; 'my grey velveteen trousers! This will exactly meet your necessities.'

'Give them to me!' she cried fiercely; but as soon as she had them in her hands her mood appeared to alter – she stood silent for a moment, and then pressed the garment back upon the Doctor. 'Give it to Aline,' she said – 'poor girl.'

'Nonsense!' said the Doctor. 'Aline does not know what she is about. Aline is beside herself with terror; and at any rate, she is a peasant. Now I am really concerned at this exposure for a person of your housekeeping habits; my solicitude and your fantastic modesty both point to the same remedy – the pantaloons.' He held them ready.

'It is impossible. You do not understand,' she said with dignity.

By this time rescue was at hand. It had been found impracticable to enter by the street, for the gate was blocked with masonry, and the nodding ruin still threatened further avalanches. But between the Doctor's garden and the one on the right hand there was that very picturesque contrivance – a common well; the door on the Desprez side had chanced to be unbolted, and now, through the arched aperture a man's bearded face and an arm supporting a lantern were introduced into the world of windy darkness, where Anastasie concealed her woes. The light struck here and there among the tossing apple boughs, it glinted on the grass; but the lantern and the glowing face became the centre of the world. Anastasie crouched back from the intrusion.

'This way!' shouted the man. 'Are you all safe?'

Aline, still screaming, ran to the newcomer, and was presently hauled head-foremost through the wall.

'Now, Anastasie, come on; it is your turn,' said the husband.

'I cannot,' she replied.

'Are we all to die of exposure, madame?' thundered Doctor Desprez.

'You can go!' she cried. 'Oh, go, go away! I can stay here; I am quite warm.'

The Doctor took her by the shoulders with an oath.

'Stop!' she screamed. 'I will put them on.'

She took the detested lendings in her hand once more; but her repulsion was stronger than shame. 'Never!' she cried, shuddering, and flung them far away into the night.

Next moment the Doctor had whirled her to the well.

The man was there and the lantern; Anastasie closed her eyes and appeared to herself to be about to die. How she was transported through the arch she knew not; but once on the other side she was received by the neighbour's wife, and enveloped in a friendly blanket.

Beds were made ready for the two women, clothes of very various sizes for the Doctor and Jean-Marie; and for the remainder of the night, while madame dozed in and out on the borderland of hysterics, her husband sat beside the fire and held forth to the admiring neighbours. He showed them, at length, the causes of the accident; for years, he explained, the fall had been impending; one sign had followed another, the joints had opened, the plaster had cracked, the old walls bowed inward; last, not three weeks ago, the cellar-door had begun to work with difficulty in its grooves. 'The cellar!' he said, gravely shaking his head over a glass of mulled wine. 'That reminds me of my poor vintages. By a manifest providence the Hermitage was nearly at an end. One bottle – I lose but one bottle of that incomparable wine. It had been set apart against Jean-Marie's wedding. Well, I must lay down some more; it will be an interest in life. I am, however, a man somewhat advanced in years. My great work is now buried in the fall of my humble roof; it will never be completed – my name will have been writ in water. And yet you find me calm – I would say cheerful. Can your priest do more?'

By the first glimpse of day the party sallied forth from the fireside into the street. The wind had fallen, but still charioted a world of troubled clouds; the air bit like frost; and the party, as they stood about the ruins in the rainy twilight of the morning, beat upon their breasts and blew into their hands for warmth. The house had entirely fallen, the walls outward, the roof in; it was a mere heap of rubbish, with here and there a forlorn spear of broken rafter. A sentinel was placed over the ruins to protect the property, and the party adjourned to Tentaillon's to break their fast at the Doctor's expense. The bottle circulated somewhat freely; and before they left the table it had begun to snow.

For three days the snow continued to fall, and the ruins,

covered with tarpaulin and watched by sentries, were left undisturbed. The Desprez meanwhile had taken up their abode at Tentaillon's. Madame spent her time in the kitchen, concocting little delicacies, with the admiring aid of Madame Tentaillon, or sitting by the fire in thoughtful abstraction. The fall of the house affected her wonderfully little; that blow had been parried by another; and in her mind she was continually fighting over again the battle of the trousers. Had she done right? Had she done wrong? And now she would applaud her determination; and anon, with a horrid flush of unavailing penitence, she would regret the trousers. No juncture in her life had so much exercised her judgment. In the meantime the Doctor had become vastly pleased with his situation. Two of the summer boarders still lingered behind the rest, prisoners for lack of a remittance; they were both English, but one of them spoke French pretty fluently, and was, besides, a humorous, agile-minded fellow, with whom the Doctor could reason by the hour, secure of comprehension. Many were the glasses they emptied, many the topics they discussed.

'Anastasie,' the Doctor said on the third morning, 'take an example from your husband, from Jean-Marie. The excitement has done more for the boy than all my tonics, he takes his turn as sentry with positive gusto. As for me, you behold me. I have made friends with the Egyptians; and my Pharaoh is, I swear it, a most agreeable companion. You alone are hipped. About a house – a few dresses? What are they in comparison to the *Pharmacopœia* – the labour of years lying buried below stones and sticks in this depressing hamlet? The snow falls; I shake it from my cloak! Imitate me. Our income will be impaired, I grant it, since we must rebuild; but moderation, patience, and philosophy will gather about the hearth. In the meanwhile, the Tentaillons are obliging; the table, with your additions, will pass; only the wine is execrable – well, I shall send for some to-day. My Pharaoh will be gratified to drink a decent glass; aha! and I shall see if he possesses that acme of organisation – a palate. If he has a palate, he is perfect.'

'Henri,' she said, shaking her head, 'you are a man; you

cannot understand my feelings; no woman could shake off the memory of so public a humiliation.'

The Doctor could not restrain a titter. 'Pardon me, darling,' he said; 'but really, to the philosophical intelligence, the incident appears so small a trifle. You looked extremely well—'

'Henri!' she cried.

'Well, well, I will say no more,' he replied. 'Though, to be sure, if you had consented to indue—*À propos*,' he broke off, 'and my trousers! They are lying in the snow – my favourite trousers!' And he dashed in quest of Jean-Marie.

Two hours afterwards the boy returned to the inn with a spade under one arm and a curious sop of clothing under the other.

The Doctor ruefully took it in his hands. 'They have been!' he said. 'Their tense is past. Excellent pantaloons, you are no more! Stay! something in the pocket,' and he produced a piece of paper. 'A letter! ay, now I mind me; it was received on the morning of the gale, when I was absorbed in delicate investigations. It is still legible. From poor, dear Casimir! It is as well,' he chuckled, 'that I have educated him to patience. Poor Casimir and his correspondence – his infinitesimal, timorous, idiotic correspondence!'

He had by this time cautiously unfolded the wet letter; but, as he bent himself to decipher the writing, a cloud descended on his brow.

'*Bigre!*' he cried, with a galvanic start.

And then the letter was whipped into the fire, and the Doctor's cap was on his head in the turn of a hand.

'Ten minutes! I can catch it, if I run,' he cried. 'It is always late. I go to Paris. I shall telegraph.'

'Henri! What is wrong?' cried his wife.

'Ottoman Bonds!' came from the disappearing Doctor; and Anastasie and Jean-Marie were left face to face with the wet trousers. Desprez had gone to Paris, for the second time in seven years; he had gone to Paris with a pair of wooden shoes, a knitted spencer, a black blouse, a country nightcap, and twenty francs in his pocket. The fall of the house was but a secondary marvel; the whole world might have fallen and scarce left his family more petrified.

CHAPTER EIGHT

The Wages of Philosophy

ON the morning of the next day, the Doctor, a mere spectre of himself, was brought back in the custody of Casimir. They found Anastasie and the boy sitting together by the fire; and Desprez, who had exchanged his toilette for a ready-made rig-out of poor materials, waved his hand as he entered, and sank speechless on the nearest chair. Madame turned direct to Casimir.

'What is wrong?' she cried.

'Well,' replied Casimir, 'what have I told you all along? It has come. It is a clean shave, this time; so you may as well bear up and make the best of it. House down, too, eh? Bad luck, upon my soul.'

'Are we – are we – ruined?' she gasped.

The Doctor stretched out his arms to her. 'Ruined,' he replied, 'you are ruined by your sinister husband.'

Casimir observed the consequent embrace through his eyeglass; then he turned to Jean-Marie. 'You hear?' he said. 'They are ruined; no more pickings, no more house, no more fat cutlets. It strikes me, my friend, that you had best be packing; the present speculation is about worked out.' And he nodded to him meaningly.

'Never!' cried Desprez, springing up. 'Jean-Marie, if you prefer to leave me, now that I am poor, you can go; you shall receive your hundred francs, if so much remains to me. But if you will consent to stay' – the Doctor wept a little – 'Casimir offers me a place – as clerk,' he resumed. 'The emoluments are slender, but they will be enough for three. It is too much already to have lost my fortune; must I lose my son?'

Jean-Marie sobbed bitterly, but without a word.

'I don't like boys who cry,' observed Casimir. 'This one

is always crying. Here! you clear out of this for a little; I have business with your master and mistress, and these domestic feelings may be settled after I am gone. March!' and he held the door open.

Jean-Marie slunk out, like a detected thief.

By twelve they were all at table but Jean-Marie.

'Hey?' said Casimir. 'Gone, you see. Took the hint at once.'

'I do not, I confess,' said Desprez, 'I do not seek to excuse his absence. It speaks a want of heart that disappoints me sorely.'

'Want of manners,' corrected Casimir. 'Heart, he never had. Why, Desprez, for a clever fellow, you are the most gullible mortal in creation. Your ignorance of human nature and human business is beyond belief. You are swindled by heathen Turks, swindled by vagabond children, swindled right and left, upstairs and downstairs. I think it must be your imagination. I thank my stars I have none.'

'Pardon me,' replied Desprez, still humbly, but with a return of spirit at sight of a distinction to be drawn; 'pardon me, Casimir. You possess, even to an eminent degree, the commercial imagination. It was the lack of that in me – it appears it is my weak point – that has led to these repeated shocks. By the commercial imagination the financier forecasts the destiny of his investments, marks the falling house—'

'Egad,' interrupted Casimir: 'our friend the stable-boy appears to have his share of it.'

The Doctor was silenced; and the meal was continued and finished principally to the tune of the brother-in-law's not very consolatory conversation. He entirely ignored the two young English painters, turning a blind eyeglass to their salutations, and continuing his remarks as if he were alone in the bosom of his family; and with every second word he ripped another stitch out of the air-balloon of Desprez's vanity. By the time coffee was over the poor Doctor was as limp as a napkin.

'Let us go and see the ruins,' said Casimir.

They strolled forth into the street. The fall of the house, like the loss of a front tooth, had quite transformed the village. Through the gap the eye commanded a great stretch of open snowy country, and the place shrank in comparison. It was like a room with an open door. The sentinel stood by the green gate, looking very red and cold, but he had a pleasant word for the Doctor and his wealthy kinsman.

Casimir looked at the mound of ruins, he tried the quality of the tarpaulin. 'H'm,' he said, 'I hope the cellar arch has stood. If it has, my good brother, I will give you a good price for the wines.'

'We shall start digging to-morrow,' said the sentry. 'There is no more fear of snow.'

'My friend,' returned Casimir sententiously, 'you had better wait till you get paid.'

The Doctor winced, and began dragging his offensive brother-in-law towards Tentaillon's. In the house there would be fewer auditors, and these already in the secret of his fall.

'Hullo,' cried Casimir, 'there goes the stable-boy with his luggage; no, egad, he is taking it into the inn.'

And sure enough, Jean-Marie was seen to cross the snowy street and enter Tentaillon's, staggering under a large hamper.

The Doctor stopped with a sudden, wild hope.

'What can he have?' he said. 'Let us go and see.' And he hurried on.

'His luggage, to be sure,' answered Casimir. 'He is on the move – thanks to the commercial imagination.'

'I have not seen that hamper for – for ever so long,' remarked the Doctor.

'Nor will you see it much longer,' chuckled Casimir; 'unless, indeed, we interfere. And by the way, I insist on an examination.'

'You will not require,' said Desprez, positively with a sob; and, casting a moist, triumphant glance at Casimir, he began to run.

'What the devil is up with him, I wonder?' Casimir reflected; and then, curiosity taking the upper hand, he followed the Doctor's example and took to his heels.

The hamper was so heavy and large, and Jean-Marie himself so little and so weary, that it had taken him a great while to bundle it upstairs to the Desprez private room; and he had just set it down on the floor in front of Anastasie, when the Doctor arrived, and was closely followed by the man of business. Boy and hamper were both in a most sorry plight; for the one had passed four months underground in a certain cave on the way to Achères, and the other had run about five miles, as hard as his legs would carry him, half that distance under a staggering weight.

'Jean-Marie,' cried the Doctor, in a voice that was only too seraphic to be called hysterical, 'is it—? It is!' he cried. 'Oh, my son, my son!' And he sat down upon the hamper and sobbed like a little child.

'You will not go to Paris now,' said Jean-Marie sheepishly.

'Casimir,' said Desprez, raising his wet face, 'do you see that boy, that angel boy? He is the thief; he took the treasure from a man unfit to be entrusted with its use; he brings it back to me when I am sobered and humbled. These, Casimir, are the Fruits of my Teaching, and this moment is the Reward of my Life.'

'*Tiens!*' said Casimir.

THE BLACK ARROW
A Tale of the Two Roses

Contents

Prefatory Note by Mrs R. L. Stevenson   343
Dedication   347

PROLOGUE
John Amend-All   351

BOOK I – THE TWO LADS
I	At the Sign of the 'Sun' in Kettley	369
II	In the Fen	377
III	The Fen Ferry	383
IV	A Greenwood Company	390
V	'Bloody as the Hunter'	397
VI	To the Day's End	405
VII	The Hooded Face	412

BOOK II – THE MOAT HOUSE
I	Dick Asks Questions	423
II	The Two Oaths	431
III	The Room over the Chapel	438
IV	The Passage	445
V	How Dick Changed Sides	450

BOOK III – MY LORD FOXHAM
I	The House by the Shore	461
II	A Skirmish in the Dark	468
III	St Bride's Cross	474
IV	The 'Good Hope'	477
V	The 'Good Hope' (*continued*)	485
VI	The 'Good Hope' (*concluded*)	491

BOOK IV – THE DISGUISE

I	The Den	499
II	'In Mine Enemies' House'	506
III	The Dead Spy	515
IV	In the Abbey Church	522
V	Earl Risingham	531
VI	Arblaster Again	535

BOOK V – CROOKBACK

I	The Shrill Trumpet	547
II	The Battle of Shoreby	554
III	The Battle of Shoreby (*concluded*)	561
IV	The Sack of Shoreby	565
V	Night in the Woods: Alicia Risingham	574
VI	Night in the woods (*concluded*): Dick and Joan	581
VII	Dick's Revenge	590
VIII	Conclusion	594

Prefatory Note

BY MRS R. L. STEVENSON

THE season for invalids in Hyères, where we had spent the winter of 1883–1884, comes to an end with the spring months. My husband was still so weak after an almost fatal illness that we were in doubt whether he would be strong enough to join in the general exodus; but the increasing epidemic of cholera so near as Toulon forced us to make the attempt. Travelling by easy stages, we first tried Vichy, with ill-success. The climate proved enervating, and the meals at the hotel – at all the hotels so far as we could judge – were apparently meant for persons suffering from a plethoric habit, and hardly a proper diet for visitors with weak lungs.

After a couple of days' trial we shook the dust of Vichy from our feet and moved on to Clermont-Ferrand. This was a shade better, though we had doubts as to its sanitary condition; and the picturesque streets, besides, were close, and likely to become more airless as the summer advanced. However, *The Black Arrow*, begun in the chalet in Hyères, and continued here and there at our various stopping places, was again taken up and another chapter written, while my son and I scoured the neighbourhood in search of a more suitable spot for the ensuing months.

The Black Arrow was conceived and written to fill a serial order from Mr Henderson for his paper, *Young Folks*, where *Treasure Island* first saw the light. No one could accuse my husband of showing a mercenary spirit in the sale of *The Black Arrow*, for which he accepted Mr Henderson's offer of about three dollars a thousand words, just after receiving two hundred and fifty pounds from Mr C. J. Longman for the magazine rights of *Prince Otto*.

Treasure Island did not score the success in *Young Folks* that it did afterwards in book form. The measure of its popularity could be gauged by a space in the paper devoted to questions and answers. The boys and girls used pseudonyms taken from the various stories of the day; we looked in vain for Jim Hawkins or John Silver, while Don Zalva eagerly demanded information on raising chickens for profit, and Gonzales de Bel wished to learn the tonnage of the *Great Eastern*. My husband was seized by a desire to capture this audience, and he had, besides, taken a sincere liking to Mr Henderson, whom he met in Red Lion Court when we passed through London on our way to Switzerland. *The Black Arrow* seemed to meet the requirements of the subscribers of *Young Folks*, for while it was running through the paper at every week's end, numbers of questioners signed themselves John Amend-All, Dick Shelton, or Joanna Sedley.

The first-page artist of *Young Folks* must have been, perhaps at an earlier stage of his career, a political cartoonist of some merit; at least Gladstone, Disraeli, and other national celebrities figured conspicuously in his illustrations. It was an endless amusement to my husband to discover Mr Gladstone in mediæval armour on the poop of a Spanish galleon, or Lord Beaconsfield scaling a wall with a broadsword in his teeth, or John Bright throwing down the gauntlet to the Saracens.

Within a short distance of Clermont my son and I came upon an enchanting little watering-place, then comparatively unknown to the English tourists, called Royat. It lay on high ground, had comfortable hotels, and the surroundings were charming. Behind the town rose the Puy de Dome, and in front stretched the broad plains once covered by Roman armies. Cæsar himself had bathed in the healing water of the Royat springs.

The beginning of the road leading to the Puy de Dome, to us the main attraction of Royat, ran along wooded ravines and cliffs where the sound of waterfalls was almost continuous. In the centre of the old town, a little above the hotels, stood an ancient cathedral, part of it in tolerable preservation, and still used for the services of the Catholic Church. Its walls were loopholed for purposes of defence, there were hooded projections on the towers for sentries, or perhaps archers, and the iron-bound doors were solid enough to withstand a battering-ram.

The baths were more or less arsenical; some so strongly impregnated that they were dangerous, and only given out to drink, in limited quantities, by virtue of the doctor's prescription. One *source* had a flavour that reminded you of weak chicken broth, and another effervesced, when you plunged into it, like champagne.

There were two ways to reach the baths from our hotel; we might choose an exceedingly steep street, or go more directly down an immense flight of precipitous stairs. As it was our stately, though uncomfortable, custom to be carried in sedan chairs, we generally went by way of the street. There had already been accidents on the stairs; should a bearer slip or lose his hold the consequences would be disastrous. It was against the law for chairs to be taken down the stairs; but if the bearers had several fares in view they were very apt to ignore the regulation. When you ordered a chair, unless ordinary directions were given, it was brought into your bedroom. You stepped inside, usually in your dressing-gown; the door was closed and the curtains drawn until you arrived at your destination, where you alighted in front of your bathtub. The privacy was absolute and the discomfort extreme. As you could not see out, you were always nervously uncertain what route your bearer had taken, and you might unexpectedly find yourself in the middle of the forbidden stairs. The air space was limited, and in warm weather the interior of the chair became very stuffy. There were two bearers to each chair, who went at a jogtrot, purposely refraining from keeping step, which would swing their burden from side to side. The uneven movement gave a jolting effect that was the most tiring thing imaginable.

Here amid these romantic, almost theatrical surround-ings, *The Black Arrow* was continued with almost no effort, and chapter after chapter was despatched to Mr Henderson.

The fresh air of the hills, the easy nature of his work, and the pleasant, quiet life had a favourable effect on my husband's health. He was soon able to take long drives on the beautiful Puy de Dome road; and in the evenings he often went down to the grounds of the casino, where an excellent string band played in a little kiosk. The management of the casino printed a daily sheet giving the musical programme of the day and the title of the piece to be played in the casino theatre the same evening. Among the advertisements were, 'English service every Simday ate one o'clock, begirning the first of July.'

Our descriptions of Royat in our letters to my husband's parents induced them to join us. They were so charmed with the place that they remained with us the rest of the summer, which gave my husband the advantage of his father's able criticism on *The Black Arrow*.

Although to all outward appearances my father-in-law was a vigorous man of well-preserved middle age, his health was already beginning to fail. Of this he was acutely conscious. He had a power of transmitting his own tragic gloom to those about him that was overwhelming; but these shadows of a great mind falling into eclipse were instantly dissipated by the presence of his son. In the midst of a wild monologue on religion, death, and eternity, I would see a change pass over his face, the stern features relaxing into a smile, the eyes softening with a pathetic tenderness. 'Here comes Lou,' he would say; 'we will change the subject.' The son would be greeted with a droll witticism, or perhaps a pertinent suggestion for *The Black Arrow*. Even at the very end of my father-in-law's life, which closed in darkness, he was able for short periods to concentrate his mind sufficiently to give intelligent advice on his son's work.

With the end of the summer came the last chapter of *The Black Arrow* and our return to Hyères, where my husband took up other more exacting work.

F.V. DE G.S.

Critic on the Hearth,

No one but myself knows what I have suffered, nor what my books have gained, by your unsleeping watchfulness and admirable pertinacity. And now here is a volume that goes into the world and lacks your *imprimatur:* a strange thing in our joint lives; and the reason of it stranger still! I have watched with interest, with pain, and at length with amusement, your unavailing attempts to peruse 'The Black Arrow'; and I think I should lack humour indeed, if I let the occasion slip and did not place your name in the fly-leaf of the only book of mine that you have never read – and never will read.

That others may display more constancy is still my hope. The tale was written years ago for a particular audience and (I may say) in rivalry with a particular author; I think I should do well to name him – Mr Alfred R. Phillips. It was not without its reward at the time. I could not, indeed, displace Mr Phillips from his well-won priority; but in the eyes of readers who thought less than nothing of 'Treasure Island,' 'The Black Arrow' was supposed to mark a clear advance. Those who read volumes and those who read story papers belong to different worlds. The verdict on 'Treasure Island' was reversed in the other court: I wonder, will it be the same with its successor?

R.L.S.

Saranac Lake,
April 8, 1888.

PROLOGUE
JOHN AMEND-ALL

John Amend-All

ON a certain afternoon, in the late springtime, the bell upon Tunstall Moat House was heard ringing at an unaccustomed hour. Far and near, in the forest and in the fields along the river, people began to desert their labours and hurry towards the sound; and in Tunstall hamlet a group of poor country-folk stood wondering at the summons.

Tunstall hamlet at that period, in the reign of old King Henry VI, wore much the same appearance as it wears to-day. A score or so of houses, heavily framed with oak, stood scattered in a long green valley ascending from the river. At the foot, the road crossed a bridge, and mounting on the other side, disappeared into the fringes of the forest on its way to the Moat House, and further forth to Holywood Abbey. Half-way up the village the church stood among yews. On every side the slopes were crowned and the view bounded by the green elms and greening oak-trees of the forest.

Hard by the bridge, there was a stone cross upon a knoll, and here the group had collected – half a dozen women and one tall fellow in a russet smock – discussing what the bell betided. An express had gone through the hamlet half an hour before, and drunk a pot of ale in the saddle, not daring to dismount for the hurry of his errand; but he had been ignorant himself of what was forward, and only bore sealed letters from Sir Daniel Brackley to Sir Oliver Oates, the parson, who kept the Moat House in the master's absence.

But now there was the noise of a horse; and soon, out of the edge of the wood and over the echoing bridge, there rode up young Master Richard Shelton, Sir Daniel's ward. He,

at the least, would know, and they hailed him and begged
him to explain. He drew bridle willingly enough – a young
fellow not yet eighteen, sun-browned and grey-eyed, in a
jacket of deer's leather, with a black velvet collar, a green
hood upon his head, and a steel crossbow at his back. The
express, it appeared, had brought great news. A battle was
impending. Sir Daniel had sent for every man that could
draw a bow or carry a bill to go post-haste to Kettley,
under pain of his severe displeasure; but for whom they
were to fight, or of where the battle was expected, Dick
knew nothing. Sir Oliver would come shortly himself, and
Bennet Hatch was arming at that moment, for he it was
who should lead the party.

'It is the ruin of this kind land,' a woman said. 'If the
barons live at war, ploughfolk must eat roots.'

'Nay,' said Dick, 'every man that follows shall have
sixpence a day, and archers twelve.'

'If they live,' returned the woman, 'that may very well
be; but how if they die, my master?'

'They cannot better die than for their natural lord,'
said Dick.

'No natural lord of mine,' said the man in the smock.
'I followed the Walsinghams; so we all did down Brierly
way, till two years ago come Candlemas. And now I must
side with Brackley! It was the law that did it; call ye that
natural? But now, what with Sir Daniel and what with Sir
Oliver – that knows more of law than honesty – I have no
natural lord but poor King Harry the Sixt, God bless him!
– the poor innocent that cannot tell his right hand from
his left.'

'Ye speak with an ill tongue, friend,' answered Dick,
'to miscall your good master and my lord the king in
the same libel. But King Harry – praised be the saints!
– has come again into his right mind, and will have all
things peaceably ordained. And as for Sir Daniel, y' are
very brave behind his back. But I will be no tale-bearer;
and let that suffice.'

'I say no harm of you, Master Richard,' returned the
peasant. 'Y' are a lad; but when ye come to a man's inches,
ye will find ye have an empty pocket. I say no more: the

saints help Sir Daniel's neighbours, and the Blessed Maid protect his wards!'

'Clipsby,' said Richard, 'you speak what I cannot hear with honour. Sir Daniel is my good master, and my guardian.'

'Come, now, will ye read me a riddle?' returned Clipsby. 'On whose side is Sir Daniel?'

'I know not,' said Dick, colouring a little; for his guardian had changed sides continually in the troubles of that period, and every change had brought him some increase of fortune.

'Ay,' returned Clipsby, 'you, nor no man. For, indeed, he is one that goes to bed Lancaster and gets up York.'

Just then the bridge rang under horse-shoe iron, and the party turned and saw Bennet Hatch come galloping – a brown-faced, grizzled fellow, heavy of hand and grim of mien, armed with sword and spear, a steel salet on his head, a leather jack upon his body. He was a great man in these parts; Sir Daniel's right hand in peace and war, and at that time, by his master's interest, bailiff of the hundred.

'Clipsby,' he shouted, 'off to the Moat House, and send all other laggards the same gate. Bowyer will give you jack and salet. We must ride before curfew. Look to it: he that is last at the lych-gate Sir Daniel shall reward. Look to it right well! I know you for a man of naught. Nance,' he added, to one of the women, 'is old Appleyard up town?'

'I'll warrant you,' replied the woman. 'In his field, for sure.'

So the group dispersed, and while Clipsby walked leisurely over the bridge, Bennet and young Shelton rode up the road together, through the village and past the church.

'Ye will see the old shrew,' said Bennet. 'He will waste more time grumbling and prating of Harry the Fift than would serve a man to shoe a horse. And all because he has been to the French wars!'

The house to which they were bound was the last in the village, standing alone among lilacs; and beyond it, on three sides, there was open meadow rising towards the borders of the wood.

Hatch dismounted, threw his rein over the fence, and walked down the field, Dick keeping close at his elbow, to where the old soldier was digging, knee-deep in his cabbages, and now and again, in a cracked voice, singing a snatch of song. He was all dressed in leather, only his hood and tippet were of black frieze, and tied with scarlet; his face was like a walnut-shell, both for colour and wrinkles; but his old grey eye was still clear enough, and his sight unabated. Perhaps he was deaf; perhaps he thought it unworthy of an old archer of Agincourt to pay any heed to such disturbances; but neither the surly notes of the alarm-bell, nor the near approach of Bennet and the lad, appeared at all to move him; and he continued obstinately digging, and piped up, very thin and shaky:—

> Now, dear lady, if thy will be,
> I pray you that you will rue on me.

'Nick Appleyard,' said Hatch, 'Sir Oliver commends him to you, and bids that ye shall come within this hour to the Moat House, there to take command.'

The old fellow looked up.

'Save you, my masters!' he said, grinning. 'And where goeth Master Hatch?'

'Master Hatch is off to Kettley, with every man that we can horse,' returned Bennet. 'There is a fight toward, it seems, and my lord stays a reinforcement.'

'Ay, verily,' returned Appleyard. 'And what will ye leave me to garrison withal?'

'I leave you six good men, and Sir Oliver to boot,' answered Hatch.

'It'll not hold the place,' said Appleyard; 'the number sufficeth not. It would take two score to make it good.'

'Why, it's for that we came to you, old shrew!' replied the other. 'Who else is there but you that could do aught in such a house with such a garrison?'

'Ay! when the pinch comes, ye remember the old shoe,' returned Nick. 'There is not a man of you can back a horse or hold a bill; and as for archery – St Michael! if old Harry the Fift were back again, he would stand and let ye shoot at him for a farthing a shoot!'

'Nay, Nick, there's some can draw a good bow yet,' said Bennet.

'Draw a good bow!' cried Appleyard. 'Yes! But who'll shoot me a good shoot? It's there the eye comes in, and the head between your shoulders. Now, what might you call a long shoot, Bennet Hatch?'

'Well,' said Bennet, looking about him, 'it would be a long shoot from here into the forest.'

'Ay, it would be a longish shoot,' said the old fellow, turning to look over his shoulder; and then he put up his hand over his eyes, and stood staring.

'Why, what are you looking at?' asked Bennet, with a chuckle, 'Do you see Harry the Fift?'

The veteran continued looking up the hill in silence. The sun shone broadly over the shelving meadows; a few white sheep wandered browsing; all was still but the distant jangle of the bell.

'What is it, Appleyard?' asked Dick.

'Why, the birds,' said Appleyard.

And, surely enough, over the top of the forest, where it ran down in a tongue among the meadows, and ended in a pair of goodly green elms, about a bowshot from the field where they were standing, a flight of birds was skimming to and fro, in evident disorder.

'What of the birds?' said Bennet.

'Ay!' returned Appleyard, 'y' are a wise man to go to war, Master Bennet. Birds are a good sentry; in forest places they be the first line of battle. Look you, now, if we lay here in camp, there might be archers skulking down to get the wind of us; and here would you be, none the wiser!'

'Why, old shrew,' said Hatch, 'there be no men nearer us than Sir Daniel's, at Kettley; y' are as safe as in London Tower; and ye raise scares upon a man for a few chaffinches and sparrows!'

'Hear him!' grinned Appleyard. 'How many a rogue would give his two crop ears to have a shoot at either of us! Saint Michael, man! they hate us like two polecats!'

'Well, sooth it is, they hate Sir Daniel,' answered Hatch, a little sobered.

'Ay, they hate Sir Daniel, and they hate every man that

serves with him,' said Appleyard; 'and in the first order of hating, they hate Bennet Hatch and old Nicholas the bowman. See ye here: if there was a stout fellow yonder in the wood-edge, and you and I stood fair for him – as, by Saint George, we stand! – which, think ye, would he choose?'

'You, for a good wager,' answered Hatch.

'My surcoat to a leather belt, it would be you!' cried the old archer. 'Ye burned Grimstone, Bennet – they'll ne'er forgive you that, my master. And as for me, I'll soon be in a good place, God grant, and out of bow-shoot – ay, and cannon-shoot – of all their malices. I am an old man, and draw fast to homeward, where the bed is ready. But for you, Bennet, y' are to remain behind here at your own peril, and if ye come to my years unhanged, the old true-blue English spirit will be dead.'

'Y' are the shrewishest old dolt in Tunstall Forest,' returned Hatch, visibly ruffled by these threats. 'Get ye to your arms before Sir Oliver come, and leave prating for one good while. An' ye had talked so much with Harry the Fift, his ears would ha' been richer than his pocket.'

An arrow sang in the air, like a huge hornet; it struck old Appleyard between the shoulder-blades, and pierced him clean through, and he fell forward on his face among the cabbages. Hatch, with a broken cry, leapt into the air; then, stopping double, he ran for the cover of the house. And in the meanwhile Dick Shelton had dropped behind a lilac, and had his cross-bow bent and shouldered, covering the point of the forest.

Not a leaf stirred. The sheep were patiently browsing; the birds had settled. But there lay the old man, with a clothyard arrow standing in his back; and there were Hatch holding to the gable, and Dick crouching and ready behind the lilac bush.

'D'ye see aught?' cried Hatch.

'Not a twig stirs,' said Dick.

'I think shame to leave him lying,' said Bennet, coming forward once more with hesitating steps and a very pale countenance. 'Keep a good eye on the wood, Master

Shelton – keep a clear eye on the wood. The saints assoil us! here was a good shoot!'

Bennet raised the old archer on his knee. He was not yet dead; his face worked, and his eyes shut and opened like machinery, and he had a most horrible, ugly look of one in pain.

'Can ye hear, old Nick?' asked Hatch. 'Have ye a last wish before ye wend, old brother?'

'Pluck out the shaft, and let me pass, a' Mary's name!' gasped Appleyard. 'I be done with Old England. Pluck it out!'

'Master Dick,' said Bennet, 'come hither, and pull me a good pull upon the arrow. He would fain pass, the poor sinner.'

Dick laid down his crossbow, and, pulling hard upon the arrow, drew it forth. A gush of blood followed; the old archer scrambled half upon his feet, called once upon the name of God, and then fell dead. Hatch, upon his knees among the cabbages, prayed fervently for the welfare of the passing spirit. But even as he prayed, it was plain that his mind was still divided, and he kept ever an eye upon the corner of the wood from which the shot had come. When he had done, he got to his feet again, drew off one of his mailed gauntlets, and wiped his pale face, which was all wet with terror.

'Ay,' he said, 'it'll be my turn next.'

'Who hath done this, Bennet?' Richard asked, still holding the arrow in his hand.

'Nay, the saints know,' said Hatch. 'Here are a good two score Christian souls that we have hunted out of house and holding, he and I. He has paid his shot, poor shrew, nor will it be long, mayhap, ere I pay mine. Sir Daniel driveth over-hard.'

'This is a strange shaft,' said the lad, looking at the arrow in his hand.

'Ay, by my faith!' cried Bennet. 'Black, and black-feathered. Here is an ill-favoured shaft, by my sooth! for black, they say, bodes burial. And here be words written. Wipe the blood away. What read ye?'

'"*Appulyaird fro Jon Amend-All*,"' read Shelton.

'What should this betoken?'

'Nay, I like it not,' returned the retainer, shaking his head. 'John Amend-All! Here is a rogue's name for those that be up in the world! But why stand we here to make a mark? Take him by the knees, good Master Shelton, while I lift him by the shoulders, and let us lay him in his house. This will be a rare shog to poor Sir Oliver; he will turn paper-colour; he will pray like a windmill.'

They took up the old archer, and carried him between them into his house, where he had dwelt alone. And there they laid him on the floor, out of regard for the mattress, and sought, as best they might, to straighten and compose his limbs.

Appleyard's house was clean and bare. There was a bed, with a blue cover, a cupboard, a great chest, a pair of joint-stools, a hinged table in the chimney-corner, and hung upon the wall the old soldier's armoury of bows and defensive armour. Hatch began to look about him curiously.

'Nick had money,' he said. 'He may have had three score pounds put by. I would I could light upon 't! When ye lose an old friend, Master Richard, the best consolation is to heir him. See, now, this chest. I would go a mighty wager there is a bushel of gold therein. He had a strong hand to get, and a hard hand to keep withal, had Appleyard the archer. Now may God rest his spirit! Near eighty year he was afoot and about, and ever getting; but now he's on the broad of his back, poor shrew, and no more lacketh; and if his chattels came to a good friend, he would be merrier, methinks, in heaven.'

'Come, Hatch,' said Dick, 'respect his stone-blind eyes. Would ye rob the man before his body? Nay, he would walk!'

Hatch made several signs of the cross; but by this time his natural complexion had returned, and he was not easily to be dashed from any purpose. It would have gone hard with the chest had not the gate sounded, and presently after the door of the house opened and admitted a tall, portly, ruddy, black-eyed man of near fifty, in a surplice and black robe.

'Appleyard,' the newcomer was saying, as he entered, but he stopped dead. 'Ave Maria!' he cried. 'Saints be our shield! What cheer is this?'

'Cold cheer with Appleyard, sir parson,' answered Hatch, with perfect cheerfulness. 'Shot at his own door, and alighteth even now at purgatory gates. Ay! there, if tales be true, he shall lack neither coal nor candle.'

Sir Oliver groped his way to a joint-stool, and sat down upon it, sick and white.

'This is a judgment! O, a great stroke!' he sobbed, and rattled off a leash of prayers.

Hatch meanwhile reverently doffed his salet and knelt down.

'Ay, Bennet,' said the priest, somewhat recovering, 'and what may this be? What enemy hath done this?'

'Here, Sir Oliver, is the arrow. See, it is written upon with words,' said Dick.

'Nay,' cried the priest, 'this is a foul hearing! John Amend-All! A right Lollardy word. And black of hue, as for an omen! Sirs, this knave arrow likes me not. But it importeth rather to take counsel. Who should this be? Bethink you, Bennet. Of so many black ill-willers, which should he be that doth so hardily outface us? Simnel? I do much question it. The Walsinghams? Nay, they are not yet so broken; they still think to have the law over us, when times change. There was Simon Malmesbury, too. How think ye, Bennet?'

'What think ye, sir,' returned Hatch, 'of Ellis Duckworth?'

'Nay, Bennet, never. Nay, not he,' said the priest. 'There cometh never any rising, Bennet, from below – so all judicious chroniclers concord in their opinion; but rebellion travelleth ever downward from above; and when Dick, Tom, and Harry take them to their bills, look ever narrowly to see what lord is profited thereby. Now, Sir Daniel, having once more joined him to the Queen's party, is in ill odour with the Yorkist lords. Thence, Bennet, comes the blow – by what procuring, I yet seek; but therein lies the nerve of this discomfiture.'

'An't please you, Sir Oliver,' said Bennet, 'the axles are so hot in this country that I have long been smelling fire.

So did this poor sinner, Appleyard. And, by your leave, men's spirits are so foully inclined to all of us, that it needs neither York nor Lancaster to spur them on. Hear my plain thoughts: You, that are a clerk, and Sir Daniel, that sails on any wind, ye have taken many men's goods, and beaten and hanged not a few. Y' are called to count for this; in the end, I wot not how, ye have ever the uppermost at law, and ye think all patched. But give me leave, Sir Oliver: the man that ye have dispossessed and beaten is but the angrier, and some day, when the black devil is by, he will up with his bow and clout me a yard of arrow through your inwards.'

'Nay, Bennet, y' are in the wrong. Bennet, ye should be glad to be corrected,' said Sir Oliver. 'Y' are a prater, Bennet, a talker, a babbler; your mouth is wider than your two ears. Mend it, Bennet, mend it.'

'Nay, I say no more. Have it as ye list,' said the retainer.

The priest now rose from the stool, and from the writing-case that hung about his neck took forth wax and a taper, and a flint and steel. With these he sealed up the chest and the cupboard with Sir Daniel's arms, Hatch looking on disconsolate; and then the whole party proceeded, somewhat timorously, to sally from the house and get to horse.

' 'Tis time we were on the road, Sir Oliver,' said Hatch, as he held the priest's stirrup while he mounted.

'Ay; but, Bennet, things are changed,' returned the parson. 'There is now no Appleyard – rest his soul! – to keep the garrison. I shall keep you, Bennet. I must have a good man to rest me on in this day of black arrows. "The arrow that flieth by day," saith the evangel; I have no mind of the context; nay, I am a sluggard priest, I am too deep in men's affairs. Well, let us ride forth, Master Hatch. The jackmen should be at the church by now.'

So they rode forward down the road, with the wind after them, blowing the tails of the parson's cloak; and behind them, as they went, clouds began to arise and blot out the sinking sun. They had passed three of the scattered houses that make up Tunstall hamlet, when, coming to a turn, they saw the church before them. Ten or a dozen

houses clustered immediately round it; but to the back
the churchyard was next the meadows. At the lych-gate,
near a score of men were gathered, some in the saddle,
some standing by their horses' heads. They were variously
armed and mounted; some with spears, some with bills,
some with bows, and some bestriding plough-horses, still
splashed with the mire of the furrow; for these were the
very dregs of the country, and all the better men and the
fair equipments were already with Sir Daniel in the field.

'We have not done amiss, praised be the cross of
Holywood! Sir Daniel will be right well content,' observed
the priest, inwardly numbering the troop.

'Who goes? Stand! if ye be true!' shouted Bennet.

A man was seen slipping through the churchyard among
the yews; and at the sound of this summons he discarded
all concealment, and fairly took to his heels for the forest.
The men at the gate, who had been hitherto unaware of
the stranger's presence, woke and scattered. Those who
had dismounted began scrambling into the saddle: the
rest rode in pursuit; but they had to make the circuit
of the consecrated ground, and it was plain their quarry
would escape them. Hatch, roaring an oath, put his horse
at the hedge, to head him off; but the beast refused, and
sent his rider sprawling in the dust. And though he was up
again in a moment, and had caught the bridle, the time
had gone by, and the fugitive had gained too great a lead
for any hope of capture.

The wisest of all had been Dick Shelton. Instead of
starting in a vain pursuit, he had whipped his cross-bow
from his back, bent it, and set a quarrel to the string; and
now, when the others had desisted, he turned to Bennet,
and asked if he should shoot.

'Shoot! shoot!' cried the priest, with sanguinary violence.

'Cover him, Master Dick,' said Bennet. 'Bring me him
down like a ripe apple.'

The fugitive was now within but a few leaps of safety; but
this last part of the meadow ran very steeply uphill, and the
man ran slower in proportion. What with the greyness of
the falling night, and the uneven movements of the runner,

it was no easy aim; and as Dick levelled his bow, he felt a kind of pity, and a half desire that he might miss. The quarrel sped.

The man stumbled and fell, and a great cheer arose from Hatch and the pursuers. But they were counting their corn before the harvest. The man fell lightly; he was lightly afoot again, turned and waved his cap in a bravado, and was out of sight next moment in the margin of the wood.

'And the plague go with him' cried Bennet. 'He has thieves' heels: he can run, by St Banbury! But you touched him, Master Shelton; he has stolen your quarrel, may he never have good I grudge him less!'

'Nay, but what made he by the church?' asked Sir Oliver. 'I am shrewdly afeared there has been mischief here. Clipsby, good fellow, get ye down from your horse, and search thoroughly among the yews.'

Clipsby was gone but a little while ere he returned, carrying a paper.

'This writing was pinned to the church door,' he said, handing it to the parson. 'I found naught else, sir parson.'

'Now, by the power of Mother Church,' cried Sir Oliver, 'but this runs hard on sacrilege! For the king's good pleasure, or the lord of the manor – well! But that every run-the-hedge in a green jerkin should fasten papers to the chancel door – nay, it runs hard on sacrilege, hard; and men have burned for matters of less weight! But what have we here? The light falls apace. Good Master Richard, y' have young eyes. Read me, I pray, this libel.'

Dick Shelton took the paper in his hand and read it aloud. It contained some lines of a very rugged doggerel, hardly even rhyming, written in a gross character, and most uncouthly spelt. With the spelling somewhat bettered, this is how they ran:—

> I had four blak arrows under my belt,
> Four for the greefs that I have felt,
> Four for the nomber of ill menne
> That have oppressid me now and then.

One is gone; one is wele sped;
Old Apulyaird is ded.

One is for Maister Bennet Hatch,
That burned Grimstone, walls and thatch.

One for Sir Oliver Oates,
That cut Sir Harry Shelton's throat.

Sir Daniel, ye shull have the fourt;
We shall think it fair sport.

Ye shull each have your own part,
A blak arrow in each blak heart.
Get ye to your knees for to pray:
Ye are ded theeves, by yea and nay!

JON AMEND-ALL
of the Green Wood,
And his jolly fellaweship.

Item, we have mo arrowes and goode hempen cord for otheres of your following.

'Now, well-a-day for charity and the Christian graces!' cried Sir Oliver, lamentably. 'Sirs, this is an ill world, and groweth daily worse. I will swear upon the cross of Holywood I am as innocent of that good knight's hurt, whether in act or purpose, as the babe unchristened. Neither was his throat cut; for therein they are again in error, as there still live credible witnesses to show.'

'It boots not, sir parson,' said Bennet. 'Here is unseasonable talk.'

'Nay, Master Bennet, not so. Keep ye in your due place, good Bennet,' answered the priest. 'I shall make mine innocence appear. I will upon no consideration lose my poor life in error. I take all men to witness that I am clear of this matter. I was not even in the Moat House. I was sent of an errand before nine upon the clock—'

'Sir Oliver,' said Hatch, interrupting, 'since it please you not to stop this sermon, I will take other means. Goffe, sound to horse.'

And while the tucket was sounding, Bennet moved close to the bewildered parson, and whispered violently in his ear.

Dick Shelton saw the priest's eye turned upon him for an instant in a startled glance. He had some cause for thought; for this Sir Harry Shelton was his own natural father. But he said never a word, and kept his countenance unmoved.

Hatch and Sir Oliver discussed together for awhile their altered situation; ten men, it was decided between them, should be reserved, not only to garrison the Moat House, but to escort the priest across the wood. In the meantime, as Bennet was to remain behind, the command of the reinforcement was given to Master Shelton. Indeed, there was no choice; the men were loutish fellows, dull and unskilled in war, while Dick was not only popular, but resolute and grave beyond his age. Although his youth had been spent in these rough country places, the lad had been well taught in letters by Sir Oliver, and Hatch himself had shown him the management of arms and the first principles of command. Bennet had always been kind and helpful; he was one of those who are cruel as the grave to those they call their enemies, but ruggedly faithful and well-willing to their friends; and now, while Sir Oliver entered the next house to write, in his swift, exquisite penmanship, a memorandum of the last occurrences to his master, Sir Daniel Brackley, Bennet came up to his pupil to wish him God-speed upon his enterprise.

'Ye must go the long way about, Master Shelton,' he said; 'round by the bridge, for your life! Keep a sure man fifty paces afore you, to draw shots; and go softly till y' are past the wood. If the rogues fall upon you, ride for 't; ye will do naught by standing. And keep ever forward, Master Shelton; turn me not back again, an ye love your life; there is no help in Tunstall, mind ye that. And now, since ye go to the great wars about the king, and I continue to dwell here in extreme jeopardy of my life, and the saints alone can certify if we shall meet again below, I give you my last counsels now at your riding. Keep an eye on Sir Daniel; he is unsure. Put not your trust in the jack-priest; he intendeth not amiss, but doth the will of others; it is a hand-gun for Sir Daniel! Get you good lordship where ye go; make you strong friends; look to it. And think ever a pater-noster-while on Bennet Hatch. There are worse rogues afoot than Bennet. So, Godspeed!'

'And Heaven be with you, Bennet!' returned Dick. 'Ye were a good friend to me-ward and so I shall say ever.'

'And, look ye, master,' added Hatch, with a certain embarrassment, 'if this Amend-All should get a shaft into me, ye might, mayhap, lay out a gold mark or mayhap a pound for my poor soul; for it is like to go stiff with me in purgatory.'

'Ye shall have your will of it, Bennet,' answered Dick. 'But, what cheer, man! we shall meet again, where ye shall have more need of ale than masses.'

'The saints so grant it, Master Dick!' returned the other. 'But here comes Sir Oliver. An he were as quick with the long-bow as with the pen, he would be a brave man-at-arms.'

Sir Oliver gave Dick a sealed packet, with this superscription: 'To my ryght worchypful master, Sir Daniel Brackley, knyght, be thys delyvered in haste.'

And Dick, putting it in the bosom of his jacket, gave the word and set forth westward up the village.

BOOK I

THE TWO LADS

CHAPTER ONE

At the Sign of the 'Sun' in Kettley

SIR DANIEL and his men lay in and about Kettley that night, warmly quartered and well patrolled. But the Knight of Tunstall was one who never rested from money-getting; and even now, when he was on the brink of an adventure which should make or mar him, he was up an hour after midnight to squeeze poor neighbours. He was one who trafficked greatly in disputed inheritances; it was his way to buy out the most unlikely claimant, and then, by the favour he curried with great lords about the king, procure unjust decisions in his favour; or, if that was too roundabout, to seize the disputed manor by force of arms, and rely on his influence and Sir Oliver's cunning in the law to hold what he had snatched. Kettley was one such place; it had come very lately into his clutches; he still met with opposition from the tenants; and it was to overawe discontent that he had led his troops that way.

By two in the morning, Sir Daniel sat in the inn room, close by the fireside, for it was cold at that hour among the fens of Kettley. By his elbow stood a pottle of spiced ale. He had taken off his visored headpiece, and sat with his bald head and thin, dark visage resting on one hand, wrapped warmly in a sanguine-coloured cloak. At the lower end of the room about a dozen of his men stood sentry over the door or lay asleep on benches; and, somewhat nearer hand, a young lad, apparently of twelve or thirteen, was stretched in a mantle on the floor. The host of the Sun stood before the great man.

'Now, mark me, mine host,' Sir Daniel said, 'follow but mine orders, and I shall be your good lord ever. I must have good men for head boroughs, and I will have Adam-a-More high constable; see to it narrowly. If other men be chosen, it shall avail you nothing; rather it shall be found to your sore cost. For those that have paid rent to Walsingham I shall take good measure – you among the rest, mine host.'

'Good knight,' said the host, 'I will swear upon the cross of Holywood I did but pay to Walsingham upon compulsion. Nay, bully knight, I love not the rogue Walsinghams; they were as poor as thieves, bully knight. Give me a great lord like you. Nay; ask me among the neighbours, I am stout for Brackley.'

'It may be,' said Sir Daniel, drily. 'Ye shall then pay twice.'

The innkeeper made a horrid grimace; but this was a piece of bad luck that might readily befall a tenant in these unruly times, and he was perhaps glad to make his peace so easily.

'Bring up yon fellow, Selden!' cried the knight.

And one of his retainers led up a poor, cringing old man, as pale as a candle, and all shaking with the fen fever.

'Sirrah,' said Sir Daniel, 'your name?'

'An't please your worship,' replied the man, 'my name is Condall – Condall of Shoreby, at your good worship's pleasure.'

'I have heard you ill reported on,' returned the knight. 'Ye deal in treason, rogue; ye trudge the country leasing; y' are heavily suspicioned of the death of severals. How, fellow, are ye so bold? But I will bring you down.'

'Right honourable and my reverend lord,' the man cried, 'here is some hodge-podge, saving your good presence. I am but a poor private man, and have hurt none.'

'The under-sheriff did report of you most vilely,' said the knight. '"Seize me," saith he, "that Tyndal of Shoreby."'

'Condall, my good lord; Condall is my poor name,' said the unfortunate.

'Condall or Tyndal, it is all one,' replied Sir Daniel, coolly. 'For, by my sooth, y' are here, and I do mightily suspect your honesty. If you would save your neck, write me swiftly an obligation for twenty pound.'

'For twenty pound, my good lord!' cried Condall. 'Here is midsummer madness! My whole estate amounteth not to seventy shillings.'

'Condall or Tyndal,' returned Sir Daniel, grinning, 'I will run my peril of that loss. Write me down twenty, and when I have recovered all I may, I will be good lord to you, and pardon you the rest.'

'Alas! my good lord, it may not be; I have no skill to write,' said Condall.

'Well-a-day!' returned the knight. 'Here then, is no remedy. Yet I would fain have spared you, Tyndal, had my conscience suffered. Selden, take me this old shrew softly to the nearest elm, and hang me him tenderly by the neck, where I may see him at my riding. Fare ye well, good Master Condall, dear Master Tyndal; y' are post-haste for Paradise; fare ye then well!'

'Nay, my right pleasant lord,' replied Condall, forcing an obsequious smile, 'an ye be so masterful, as doth right well become you, I will even, with all my poor skill, do your good bidding.'

'Friend,' quoth Sir Daniel, 'ye will now write two score. Go to!' y' are too cunning for a livelihood of seventy shillings. Selden, see him write me this in good form, and have it duly witnessed.'

And Sir Daniel, who was a very merry knight, none merrier in England, took a drink of his mulled ale, and lay back, smiling.

Meanwhile, the boy upon the floor began to stir, and presently sat up and looked about him with a scare.

'Hither,' said Sir Daniel; and as the other rose at his command and came slowly towards him, he leaned back and laughed outright. 'By the rood!' he cried, 'a sturdy boy!'

The lad flushed crimson with anger, and darted a look of hate out of his dark eyes. Now that he was on his legs, it was more difficult to make certain of his age. His face looked somewhat older in expression, but it was as smooth as a young child's; and in bone and body he was unusually slender, and somewhat awkward of gait.

'Ye have called me, Sir Daniel,' he said. 'Was it to laugh at my poor plight?'

'Nay, now, let laugh,' said the knight. 'Good shrew, let laugh, I pray you. An ye could see yourself, I warrant ye would laugh the first.'

'Well,' cried the lad, flushing, 'ye shall answer this when ye answer for the other. Laugh while yet ye may!'

'Nay, now, good cousin,' replied Sir Daniel, with some earnestness, 'think not that I mock at you, except in mirth, as between kinsfolk and singular friends. I will make you a marriage of a thousand pounds, go to! and cherish you exceedingly. I took you, indeed, roughly, as the time demanded; but from henceforth I shall ungrudgingly maintain and cheerfully serve you. Ye shall be Mrs Shelton – Lady Shelton, by my troth! for the lad promiseth bravely. Tut! ye will not shy for honest laughter; it purgeth melancholy. They are no rogues who laugh, good cousin. Good mine host, lay me a meal now for my cousin, Master John. Sit ye down, sweetheart, and eat.'

'Nay,' said Master John, 'I will break no bread. Since ye force me to this sin, I will fast for my soul's interest. But, good mine host, I pray you of courtesy give me a cup of fair water; I shall be much beholden to your courtesy indeed.'

'Ye shall have a dispensation, go to!' cried the knight. 'Shalt be well shriven, by my faith! Content you, then, and eat.'

But the lad was obstinate, drank a cup of water, and, once more wrapping himself closely in his mantle, sat in a far corner, brooding.

In an hour or two, there rose a stir in the village of sentries challenging and the clatter of arms and horses; and then a troop drew up by the inn door, and Richard Shelton, splashed with mud, presented himself upon the threshold.

'Save you, Sir Daniel,' he said.

'How!' Dickie Shelton!' cried the knight; and at the mention of Dick's name the other lad looked curiously across. 'What maketh Bennet Hatch?'

'Please you, sir knight, to take cognizance of this packet from Sir Oliver, wherein are all things fully stated,' answered Richard, presenting the priest's letter. 'And please you farther, ye were best make all speed to Risingham; for on the way hither we encountered one riding furiously with letters, and by his report, my Lord of Risingham was sore bested, and lacked exceedingly your presence.'

'How say you? Sore bested?' returned the knight. 'Nay, then, we will make speed sitting down, good Richard. As the world goes in this poor realm of England, he that rides softliest rides surest. Delay, they say, begetteth peril; but it is rather this itch of doing that undoes men; mark it, Dick. But let me see, first, what cattle ye have brought. Selden, a link here at the door!'

And Sir Daniel strode forth into the village street, and, by the red glow of a torch, inspected his new troops. He was an unpopular neighbour and an unpopular master; but as a leader in war he was well beloved by those who rode behind his pennant. His dash, his proved courage, his forethought for the soldiers' comfort, even his rough gibes, were all to the taste of the bold blades in jack and salet.

'Nay, by the rood!' he cried, 'what poor dogs are these? Here be some as crooked as a bow, and some as lean as a spear. Friends, ye shall ride in the front of the battle; I can spare you, friends. Mark me this old villain on the piebald! A two-year mutton riding on a hog would look more soldierly! Ha! Clipsby, are ye there, old rat? Y' are a man I could lose with a good heart; ye shall go in front of all, with a bull's-eye painted on your jack, to be the better butt for archery; sirrah, ye shall show me the way.'

'I will show you any way, Sir Daniel, but the way to change sides,' returned Clipsby, sturdily.

Sir Daniel laughed a guffaw.

'Why, well said!' he cried. 'Hast a shrewd tongue in thy mouth, go to! I will forgive you for that merry word. Selden, see them fed, both man and brute.'

The knight re-entered the inn.

'Now, friend Dick,' he said, 'fall to. Here is good ale and bacon. Eat, while that I read.'

Sir Daniel opened the packet, and as he read his brow darkened. When he had done he sat a little, musing. Then he looked sharply at his ward.

'Dick,' said he, 'y' have seen this penny rhyme?'

The lad replied in the affirmative.

'It bears your father's name,' continued the knight; 'and our poor shrew of a parson is, by some mad soul, accused of slaying him.'

'He did most eagerly deny it,' answered Dick.

'He did?' cried the knight, very sharply. 'Heed him not. He has a loose tongue; he babbles like a jack-sparrow. Some day, when I may find the leisure, Dick, I will myself more fully inform you of these matters. There was one Duckworth shrewdly blamed for it; but the times were troubled, and there was no justice to be got.'

'It befell at the Moat House?' Dick ventured, with a beating at his heart.

'It befell between the Moat House and Holywood,' replied Sir Daniel, calmly; but he shot a covert glance, black with suspicion, at Dick's face. 'And now,' added the knight, 'speed you with your meal; ye shall return to Tunstall with a line from me.'

Dick's face fell sorely.

'Prithee, Sir Daniel,' he cried, 'send one of the villains! I beseech you let me to the battle. I can strike a stroke, I promise you.'

'I misdoubt it not,' replied Sir Daniel, sitting down to write. 'But here, Dick, is no honour to be won. I lie in Kettley till I have sure tidings of the war, and then ride to join me with the conqueror. Cry not on cowardice; it is but wisdom, Dick; for this poor realm so tosseth with rebellion, and the king's name and custody so changeth hands, that no man may be certain of the morrow. Toss-pot and Shuttle-wit run in, but my Lord Good-Counsel sits o' one side, waiting.'

With that, Sir Daniel, turning his back to Dick, and quite at the farther end of the long table, began to write his letter, with his mouth on one side, for this business of the Black Arrow stuck sorely in his throat.

Meanwhile, young Shelton was going on heartily enough with his breakfast, when he felt a touch upon his arm, and a very soft voice whispering in his ear.

'Make not a sign, I do beseech you,' said the voice, 'but of your charity teach me the straight way to Holywood. Beseech you, now, good boy, comfort a poor soul in peril and extreme distress, and set me so far forth upon the way to my repose.'

'Take the path by the windmill,' answered Dick, in the same tone; 'it will bring you to Till Ferry; there inquire again.'

And without turning his head, he fell again to eating. But with the tail of his eye he caught a glimpse of the young lad called Master John stealthily creeping from the room.

'Why,' thought Dick, 'he is as young as I. "Good boy" doth he call me? An I had known, I should have seen the varlet hanged ere I had told him. Well, if he goes through the fen, I may come up with him and pull his ears.'

Half an hour later, Sir Daniel gave Dick the letter, and bade him speed to the Moat House. And again, some half an hour after Dick's departure, a messenger came, in hot haste, from my Lord of Risingham.

'Sir Daniel,' the messenger said, 'ye lose great honour, by my sooth! The fight began again this morning ere the dawn, and we have beaten their van and scattered their right wing. Only the main battle standeth fast. An we had your fresh men, we should tilt you them all into the river. What, sir knight! Will ye be the last? It stands not with your good credit.'

'Nay,' cried the knight, 'I was but now upon the march. Selden, sound me the tucket. Sir, I am with you on the instant. It is not two hours since the more part of my command came in, sir messenger. What would ye have? Spurring is good meat, but yet it killed the charger. Bustle, boys!'

By this time the tucket was sounding cheerily in the morning, and from all sides Sir Daniel's men poured into the main street and formed before the inn. They had slept upon their arms, with chargers saddled, and in ten minutes five-score men-at-arms and archers, cleanly equipped and briskly disciplined, stood ranked and ready. The chief part were in Sir Daniel's livery, murrey and blue, which gave the greater show to their array. The best armed rode first; and away out of sight, at the tail of the column, came the sorry reinforcement of the night before. Sir Daniel looked with pride along the line.

'Here be the lads to serve you in a pinch,' he said.

'They are pretty men, indeed,' replied the messenger. 'It but augments my sorrow that ye had not marched the earlier.'

'Well,' said the knight, 'what would ye? The beginning of a feast and the end of a fray, sir messenger;' and he mounted into his saddle. 'Why! how now!' he cried. 'John! Joanna! Nay, by the sacred rood! where is she? Host, where is that girl?'

'Girl, Sir Daniel?' cried the landlord. 'Nay, sir, I saw no girl.'

'Boy, then, dotard!' cried the knight. 'Could ye not see it was a wench? She in the murrey-coloured mantle – she that broke her fast with water, rogue – where is she?'

'Nay, the saints bless us! Master John, ye called him,' said his host. 'Well, I thought none evil. He is gone. I saw him – her – I saw her in the stable a good hour agone; 'a was saddling a grey horse.'

'Now, by the rood!' cried Sir Daniel, 'the wench was worth five hundred pound to me and more.'

'Sir knight,' observed the messenger, with bitterness, 'while that ye are here, roaring for five hundred pounds, the realm of England is elsewhere being lost and won.'

'It is well said,' replied Sir Daniel. 'Selden, fall me out with six cross-bowmen; hunt me her down. I care not what it cost; but, at my returning, let me find her at the Moat House. Be it upon your head. And now, sir messenger, we march.'

And the troop broke into a good trot, and Selden and his six men were left behind upon the street of Kettley, with the staring villagers.

CHAPTER TWO

In the Fen

IT was near six in the May morning when Dick began to ride down into the fen upon his homeward way. The sky was all blue; the jolly wind blew loud and steady; the windmill sails were spinning; and the willows over all the fen rippling and whitening like a field of corn. He had been all night in the saddle, but his heart was good and his body sound, and he rode right merrily.

The path went down and down into the marsh, till he lost sight of all the neighbouring landmarks but Kettley windmill on the knoll behind him, and the extreme top of Tunstall Forest far before. On either hand there were great fields of blowing reeds and willows, pools of water shaking in the wind, and treacherous bogs, as green as emerald, to tempt and to betray the traveller. The path lay almost straight through the morass. It was already very ancient; its foundation had been laid by Roman soldiery; in the lapse of ages much of it had sunk, and every here and there, for a few hundred yards, it lay submerged below the stagnant waters of the fen.

About a mile from Kettley, Dick came to one such break in the plain line of causeway, where the reeds and willows grew dispersedly like little islands and confused the eye. The gap, besides, was more than usually long; it was a place where any stranger might come readily to mischief; and Dick bethought him, with something like a pang, of the lad whom he had so imperfectly directed. As for himself, one look backward to where the windmill sails were turning black against the blue of heaven – one look forward to the high ground of Tunstall Forest, and he was sufficiently directed and held straight on, the water washing to his horse's knees, as safe as on a highway.

Half-way across, and when he had already sighted the path rising high and dry upon the farther side, he was aware of a great splashing on his right, and saw a grey horse, sunk to its belly in the mud, and still spasmodically struggling. Instantly, as though it had divined the neighbourhood of help, the poor beast began to neigh most piercingly. It rolled, meanwhile, a bloodshot eye, insane with terror; and as it sprawled wallowing in the quag, clouds of stinging insects rose and buzzed about it in the air.

'Alack!' thought Dick, 'can the poor lad have perished? There is his horse, for certain – a brave grey! Nay, comrade, if thou criest to me so piteously, I will do all man can to help thee. Shalt not lie there to drown by inches!'

And he made ready his crossbow, and put a quarrel through the creature's head.

Dick rode on after this act of rugged mercy, somewhat sobered in spirit, and looking closely about him for any sign of his less happy predecessor in the way.

'I would I had dared to tell him further,' he thought; 'for I fear he has miscarried in the slough.'

And just as he was so thinking, a voice cried upon his name from the causeway side, and, looking over his shoulder, he saw the lad's face peering from a clump of reeds.

'Are ye there?' he said, reining in. 'Ye lay so close among the reeds that I had passed you by. I saw your horse bemired, and put him from his agony; which, by my sooth! and ye had been a more merciful rider, ye had done yourself. But come forth out of your hiding. Here be none to trouble you.'

'Nay, good boy, I have no arms, nor skill to use them if I had,' replied the other, stepping forth upon the pathway.

'Why call me "boy"?' cried Dick. 'Y' are not, I trow, the elder of us twain.'

'Good Master Shelton,' said the other, 'prithee forgive me. I have none the least intention to offend. Rather I would in every way beseech your gentleness and favour, for I am now worse bested than ever, having lost my way, my cloak, and my poor horse. To have a riding-rod and spurs, and never a horse to sit upon! And before all,' he added, looking ruefully upon his clothes – 'before all, to be so sorrily besmirched!'

'Tut!' cried Dick. 'Would ye mind a ducking? Blood of wound or dust of travel – that's a man's adornment.'

'Nay, then, I like him better plain,' observed the lad. 'But, prithee, how shall I do? Prithee, good Master Richard, help me with your good counsel. If I come not safe to Holywood, I am undone.'

'Nay,' said Dick, dismounting, 'I will give more than counsel. Take my horse, and I will run awhile, and when I am weary we shall change again, that so, riding and running, both may go the speedier.'

So the change was made, and they went forward as briskly as they durst on the uneven causeway, Dick with his hand upon the other's knee.

'How call ye your name?' asked Dick.

'Call me John Matcham,' replied the lad.

'And what make ye to Holywood?' Dick continued.

'I see sanctuary from a man that would oppress me,' was the answer. 'The good Abbot of Holywood is a strong pillar to the weak.'

'And how came ye with Sir Daniel, Master Matcham?' pursued Dick.

'Nay,' cried the other, 'by the abuse of force! He hath taken me by violence from my own place; dressed me in these weeds; ridden with me till my heart was sick; gibed me till I could 'a' wept; and when certain of my friends pursued, thinking to have me back, claps me in the rear to stand their shot! I was even grazed in the right foot, and walk but lamely. Nay, there shall come a day between us; he shall smart for all!'

'Would ye shoot at the moon with a hand-gun?' said Dick. ''Tis a valiant knight, and hath a hand of iron. An he guessed I had made or meddled with your flight, it would go sore with me.'

'Ay, poor boy,' returned the other, 'y'are his ward, I know it. By the same token, so am I, or so he saith; or else he hath bought my marriage – I wot not rightly which; but it is some handle to oppress me by.'

'Boy again!' said Dick.

'Nay, then, shall I call you girl, good Richard?' asked Matcham.

'Never a girl for me,' returned Dick. 'I do abjure the crew of them!'

'Ye speak boyishly,' said the other. 'Ye think more of them than ye pretend.'

'Not I,' said Dick, stoutly. 'They come not in my mind. A plague of them, say I! Give me to hunt and to fight and to feast, and to live with jolly foresters. I never heard of a maid yet that was for any service, save one only; and she, poor shrew, was burned for a witch and the wearing of men's clothes in spite of nature.'

Master Matcham crossed himself with fervour, and appeared to pray.

'What make ye?' Dick inquired.

'I pray for her spirit,' answered the other, with a somewhat troubled voice.

'For a witch's spirit?' Dick cried. 'But pray for her, an ye list; she was the best wench in Europe, was this Joan of Arc. Old Appleyard the archer ran from her, he said, as if she had been Mahoun. Nay, she was a brave wench.'

'Well, but, good Master Richard,' resumed Matcham, 'an ye like maids so little, y' are no true natural man; for God made them twain by intention, and brought true love into the world, to be man's hope and woman's comfort.'

'Faugh!' said Dick. 'Y' are a milk-sopping baby, so to harp on women. An ye think I be no true man, get down upon the path, and whether at fists, backsword, or bow and arrow, I will prove my manhood on your body.'

'Nay, I am no fighter,' said Matcham eagerly. 'I mean no tittle of offence. I meant but pleasantry. And if I talk of women, it is because I heard ye were to marry.'

'I to marry!' Dick exclaimed. 'Well, it is the first I hear of it. And with whom was I to marry?'

'One Joan Sedley,' replied Matcham, colouring. 'It was Sir Daniel's doing; he hath money to gain upon both sides; and, indeed, I have heard the poor wench bemoaning herself pitifully of the match. It seems she is of your mind, or else distasted to the bridegroom.'

'Well! marriage is like death, it comes to all,' said Dick,

with resignation. 'And she bemoaned herself? I pray ye now, see there how shuttle-witted are these girls: to bemoan herself before that she had seen me! Do I bemoan myself! Not I. An I be to marry, I will marry dry-eyed! But if ye know her, prithee, of what favour is she? fair or foul? And is she shrewish or pleasant?'

'Nay, what matters it?' said Matcham. 'An y' are to marry, ye can but marry. What matters foul or fair? These be but toys. Y' are no milksop, Master Richard; ye will wed with dry eyes, anyhow.'

'It is well said,' replied Shelton. 'Little I reck.'

'Your lady wife is like to have a pleasant lord,' said Matcham.

'She will have the lord Heaven made her for,' returned Dick. 'I trow there be worse as well as better.'

'Ah, the poor wench!' cried the other.

'And why so poor?' asked Dick.

'To wed a man of wood,' replied his companion. 'O me, for a wooden husband!'

'I think I be a man of wood, indeed,' said Dick, 'to trudge afoot the while you ride my horse; but it is good wood, I trow.'

'Good Dick, forgive me,' cried the other. 'Nay, y' are the best heart in England; I but laughed. Forgive me now, sweet Dick.'

'Nay, no fool words,' returned Dick, a little embarrassed by his companion's warmth. 'No harm is done. I am not touchy, praise the saints.'

And at that moment the wind, which was blowing straight behind them as they went, brought them the rough flourish of Sir Daniel's trumpeter.

'Hark!' said Dick, 'the tucket soundeth.'

'Ay,' said Matcham, 'they have found my flight, and now I am unhorsed!' and he became pale as death.

'Nay, what cheer!' returned Dick. 'Y' have a long start, and we are near the ferry. And it is I, methinks, that am unhorsed.'

'Alack, I shall be taken!' cried the fugitive. 'Dick, kind Dick, beseech ye help me but a little!'

'Why, now, what aileth thee?' said Dick. 'Methinks I help

you very patently. But my heart is sorry for so spiritless a fellow! And see ye here, John Matcham – sith John Matcham is your name – I, Richard Shelton, tide what betideth, come what may, will see you safe in Holywood. The saints so do to me again if I default you. Come, pick me up a good heart, Sir White-face. The way betters here; spur me the horse. Go faster! faster! Nay, mind not for me; I can run like a deer.'

So, with the horse trotting hard, and Dick running easily alongside, they crossed the remainder of the fen, and came out upon the banks of the river by the ferryman's hut.

CHAPTER THREE

The Fen Ferry

THE river Till was a wide, sluggish, clayey water, oozing out of fens, and in this part of its course it strained among some score of willow-covered, marshy islets.

It was a dingy stream; but upon this bright, spirited morning everything was become beautiful. The wind and the martens broke it up into innumerable dimples; and the reflection of the sky was scattered over all the surface in crumbs of smiling blue.

A creek ran up to meet the path, and close under the bank the ferryman's hut lay snugly. It was of wattle and clay, and the grass grew green upon the roof.

Dick went to the door and opened it. Within, upon a foul old russet cloak, the ferryman lay stretched and shivering; a great hulk of a man, but lean and shaken by the country fever.

'Hey, Master Shelton,' he said, 'be ye for the ferry? Ill times, ill times! Look to yourself. There is a fellowship abroad. Ye were better turn round on your two heels and try the bridge.'

'Nay; time's in the saddle,' answered Dick. 'Time will ride, Hugh Ferryman. I am hot in haste.'

'A wilful man!' returned the ferryman, rising. 'An ye win safe to the Moat House, y' have done lucky; but I say no more.' And then catching sight of Matcham, 'Who be this?' he asked, as he paused, blinking, on the threshold of his cabin.

'It is my kinsman, Master Matcham,' answered Dick.

'Give ye good day, good ferryman,' said Matcham, who had dismounted, and now came forward, leading the horse. 'Launch me your boat, I prithee; we are sore in haste.'

The gaunt ferryman continued staring.

'By the mass!' he cried at length, and laughed with open throat.

Matcham coloured to his neck and winced; and Dick, with an angry countenance, put his hand on the lout's shoulder.

'How now, churl!' he cried. 'Fall to thy business, and leave mocking thy betters.'

Hugh Ferryman grumblingly undid his boat, and shoved it a little forth into the deep water. Then Dick led in the horse, and Matcham followed.

'Ye be mortal small made, master,' said Hugh, with a wide grin; 'something o' the wrong model, belike. Nay, Master Shelton, I am for you,' he added, getting to his oars. 'A cat may look at a king. I did but take a shot of the eye at Master Matcham.'

'Sirrah, no more words,' said Dick. 'Bend me your back.'

They were by that time at the mouth of the creek, and the view opened up and down the river. Everywhere it was enclosed with islands. Clay banks were falling in, willows nodding, reeds waving, martens dipping and piping. There was no sign of man in the labyrinth of waters.

'My master,' said the ferryman, keeping the boat steady with one oar, 'I have a shrewd guess that John-a-Fenne is on the island. He bears me a black grudge to all Sir Daniel's. How if I turned me up stream and landed you an arrow-flight above the path? Ye were best not meddle with John Fenne.'

'How, then? is he of this company?' asked Dick.

'Nay, mum is the word,' said Hugh. 'But I would go up water, Dick. How if Master Matcham came by an arrow?' and he laughed again.

'Be it so, Hugh,' answered Dick.

'Look ye, then,' pursued Hugh. 'Sith it shall so be, unsling me your cross-bow – so: now make it ready – good; place me a quarrel. Ay, keep it so, and look upon me grimly.'

'What meaneth this?' asked Dick.

'Why, my master, if I steal you across, it must be under force or fear,' replied the ferryman; 'for else, if John Fenne got wind of it, he were like to prove my most distressful neighbour.'

'Do these churls ride so roughly?' Dick inquired. 'Do they command Sir Daniel's own ferry?'

'Nay,' whispered the ferryman winking. 'Mark me! Sir Daniel shall down. His time is out. He shall down. Mum!' And he bent over his oars.

They pulled a long way up the river, turned the tail of an island, and came softly down a narrow channel next the opposite bank. Then Hugh held water in midstream.

'I must land you here among the willows,' he said.

'Here is no path but willow swamps and quagmires,' answered Dick.

'Master Shelton,' replied Hugh, 'I dare not take you nearer down, for your own sake now. He watcheth me the ferry, lying on his bow. All that go by and owe Sir Daniel goodwill, he shooteth down like rabbits. I heard him swear it by the rood. An I had not known you of old days – ay, and from so high upward – I would 'a' let you go on; but for old days' remembrance, and because ye had this toy with you that's not fit for wounds or warfare, I did risk my two poor ears to have you over whole. Content you; I can no more, on my salvation!'

Hugh was still speaking, lying on his oars, when there came a great shout from among the willows on the island, and sounds followed as of a strong man breasting roughly through the wood.

'A murrain!' cried Hugh. 'He was on the upper island all the while!' He pulled straight for shore. 'Threat me with your bow, good Dick; threat me with it plain,' he added. 'I have tried to save your skins, save you mine!'

The boat ran into a tough thicket of willows with a crash. Matcham, pale, but steady and alert, at a sign from Dick, ran along the thwarts and leaped ashore; Dick, taking the horse by the bridle, sought to follow, but what with the animal's bulk, and what with the closeness of the thicket, both stuck fast. The horse neighed and trampled; and the boat, which was swinging in an eddy, came on and off and pitched with violence.

'It may not be, Hugh; here is no landing,' cried Dick;

but he still struggled valiantly with the obstinate thicket and the startled animal.

A tall man appeared upon the shore of the island, a long-bow in his hand. Dick saw him for an instant, with the corner of his eye, bending the bow with a great effort, his face crimson with hurry.

'Who goes?' he shouted. 'Hugh, who goes?'

''Tis Master Shelton, John,' replied the ferryman.

'Stand, Dick Shelton!' bawled the man upon the island. 'Ye shall have no hurt, upon the rood! Stand! Back out, Hugh Ferryman.'

Dick cried a taunting answer.

'Nay, then, ye shall go afoot,' returned the man; and he let drive an arrow.

The horse, struck by the shaft, lashed out in agony and terror; the boat capsized, and next moment all were struggling in the eddies of the river.

When Dick came up, he was within a yard of the bank; and before his eyes were clear, his hand had closed on something firm and strong that instantly began to drag him forward. It was the riding-rod, that Matcham, crawling forth upon an overhanging willow, had opportunely thrust into his grasp.

'By the mass!' cried Dick, as he was helped ashore, 'that makes a life I owe you. I swim like a cannon-ball.' And he turned instantly towards the island.

Midway over, Hugh Ferryman was swimming with his upturned boat, while John-a-Fenne, furious at the ill-fortune of his shot, bawled to him to hurry.

'Come, Jack,' said Shelton, 'run for it! Ere Hugh can hale his barge across, or the pair of 'em can get it righted, we may be out of cry.'

And adding example to his words, he began to run, dodging among the willows, and in marshy places leaping from tussock to tussock. He had no time to look for his direction; all he could do was to turn his back upon the river, and put all his heart to running.

Presently, however, the ground began to rise, which showed him he was still in the right way, and soon after they came forth upon a slope of solid turf, where elms began to mingle with the willows.

But here Matcham, who had been dragging far into the rear, threw himself fairly down.

'Leave me, Dick!' he cried pantingly; 'I can no more.'

Dick turned, and came back to where his companion lay.

'Nay, Jack, leave thee!' he cried. 'That were a knave's trick, to be sure, when ye risked a shot and a ducking, ay, and a drowning too, to save my life. Drowning, in sooth; for why I did not pull you in along with me, the saints alone can tell!'

'Nay,' said Matcham, 'I would 'a' saved us both, good Dick, for I can swim.'

'Can ye so?' cried Dick, with open eyes. It was the one manly accomplishment of which he was himself incapable. In the order of things that he admired, next to having killed a man in single fight came swimming. 'Well,' he said, 'here is a lesson to despise no man. I promised to care for you as far as Holywood, and, by the rood, Jack, y' are more capable to care for me.'

'Well, Dick, we're friends now,' said Matcham.

'Nay, I never was unfriends,' answered Dick. 'Y' are a brave lad in your way, albeit something of a milksop, too. I never met your like before this day. But, prithee, fetch back your breath, and let us on. Here is no place for chatter.'

'My foot hurts shrewdly,' said Matcham.

'Nay, I had forgot your foot,' returned Dick. 'Well, we must go the gentlier. I would I knew rightly where we were. I have clean lost the path; yet that may be for the better, too. An they watch the ferry, they watch the path, belike, as well. I would Sir Daniel were back with two-score men; he would sweep me these rascals as the wind sweeps leaves. Come, Jack, lean ye on my shoulder, ye poor shrew. Nay, y' are not tall enough. What age are ye, for a wager? – twelve?'

'Nay, I am sixteen,' said Matcham.

'Y' are poorly grown to height, then,' answered Dick. 'But take my hand. We shall go softly, never fear. I owe you a life; I am a good repayer, Jack, of good or evil.'

They began to go forward up the slope.

'We must hit the road, early or late,' continued Dick; 'and then for a fresh start. By the mass! but y' 'ave a rickety hand, Jack. If I had a hand like that, I would think shame. I tell you,' he went on, with a sudden chuckle, 'I swear by the mass I believe Hugh Ferryman took you for a maid.'

'Nay, never!' cried the other, colouring high.

''A did, though, for a wager!' Dick exclaimed. 'Small blame to him. Ye look liker maid than man; and I tell you more – y' are a strange-looking rogue for a boy; but for a hussy, Jack, ye would be right fair – ye would. Ye would be well-favoured for a wench.'

'Well,' said Matcham, 'ye know right well that I am none.'

'Nay, I know that; I do but jest,' said Dick. 'Ye'll be a man before your mother, Jack. What cheer, my bully! Ye shall strike shrewd strokes. Now, which, I marvel, of you or me, shall be first knighted, Jack? for knighted I shall be, or die for 't. "Sir Richard Shelton, Knight," it soundeth bravely. But "Sir John Matcham" soundeth not amiss.'

'Prithee, Dick, stop till I drink,' said the other, pausing where a little clear spring welled out of the slope into a gravelled basin no bigger than a pocket. 'And O, Dick, if I might come by anything to eat! – my very heart aches with hunger.'

'Why, fool, did ye not eat at Kettley?' asked Dick.

'I had made a vow – it was a sin I had been led into,' stammered Matcham; 'but now, if it were but dry bread, I would eat it greedily.'

'Sit ye, then, and eat,' said Dick, 'while that I scout a little forward for the road.' And he took a wallet from his girdle, wherein were bread and pieces of dry bacon, and, while Matcham fell heartily to, struck farther forth among the trees.

A little beyond there was a dip in the ground, where a streamlet soaked among dead leaves; and beyond that, again, the trees were better grown and stood wider, and oak and beech began to take the place of willow and elm. The continuous tossing and pouring of the wind among the leaves sufficiently concealed the sound of his footsteps on the mast; it was for the ear what a moonless night is to the eye; but for all that Dick went cautiously, slipping from one big trunk to another, and looking sharply about him as he went. Suddenly a doe passed like a shadow through the underwood in front of him, and he paused, disgusted at the chance. This part of the wood had been certainly deserted, but now that the poor deer had run, she was like a messenger he should have sent before him to announce his coming; and instead of pushing farther, he turned him to the nearest well-grown tree, and rapidly began to climb.

Luck had served him well. The oak on which he had mounted was one of the tallest in that quarter of the wood, and easily out-topped its neighbours by a fathom and a half; and when Dick had clambered into the topmost fork and clung there, swinging dizzily in the great wind, he saw behind him the whole fenny plain as far as Kettley, and the Till wandering among woody islets, and in front of him, the white line of high-road winding through the forest. The boat had been righted – it was even now midway on the ferry. Beyond that there was no sign of man nor aught moving but the wind. He was about to descend, when, taking a last view, his eye lit upon a string of moving points about the middle of the fen. Plainly a small troop was threading the causeway, and that at a good pace; and this gave him some concern as he shinned vigorously down the trunk and returned across the wood for his companion.

CHAPTER FOUR

A Greenwood Company

MATCHAM WAS well rested and revived; and the two lads, winged by what Dick had seen, hurried through the remainder of the outwood, crossed the road in safety, and began to mount into the high ground of Tunstall Forest. The trees grew more and more in groves, with heathy places in between, sandy, gorsy, and dotted with old yews. The ground became more and more uneven, full of pits and hillocks. And with every step of the ascent the wind still blew the shriller, and the trees bent before the gusts like fishing-rods.

They had just entered one of the clearings, when Dick suddenly clapped down upon his face among the brambles, and began to crawl slowly backward towards the shelter of the grove. Matcham, in great bewilderment, for he could see no reason for this flight, still imitated his companion's course; and it was not until they had gained the harbour of a thicket that he turned and begged him to explain.

For all reply, Dick pointed with his finger.

At the far end of the clearing, a fir grew high above the neighbouring wood, and planted its black shock of foliage clear against the sky. For about fifty feet above the ground the trunk grew straight and solid like a column. At that level, it split into two massive boughs; and in the fork, like a mast-headed seaman, there stood a man in a green tabard, spying far and wide. The sun glistened upon his hair; with one hand he shaded his eyes to look abroad, and he kept slowly rolling his head from side to side, with the regularity of a machine.

The lads exchanged glances.

'Let us try to the left,' said Dick. 'We had near fallen foully, Jack.'

Ten minutes afterwards they struck into a beaten path.

'Here is a piece of forest that I know not,' Dick remarked. 'Where goeth me this track?'

'Let us even try,' said Matcham.

A few yards further, the path came to the top of a ridge and began to go down abruptly into a cup-shaped hollow. At the foot, out of a thick wood of flowering hawthorn, two or three roofless gables, blackened as if by fire, and a single tall chimney marked the ruins of a house.

'What may this be?' whispered Matcham.

'Nay, by the mass, I know not,' answered Dick. 'I am all at sea. Let us go warily.'

With beating hearts they descended through the hawthorns. Here and there, they passed signs of recent cultivation; fruit-trees and pot-herbs ran wild among the thicket; a sun-dial had fallen in the grass; it seemed they were treading what once had been a garden. Yet a little farther and they came forth before the ruins of the house.

It had been a pleasant mansion and a strong. A dry ditch was dug deep about it; but it was now choked with masonry, and bridged by a fallen rafter. The two farther walls still stood, the sun shining through their empty windows; but the remainder of the building had collapsed, and now lay in a great cairn of ruin, grimed with fire. Already in the interior a few plants were springing green among the chinks.

'Now I bethink me,' whispered Dick, 'this must be Grimstone. It was a hold of one Simon Malmesbury; Sir Daniel was his bane! 'Twas Bennet Hatch that burned it, now five years agone. In sooth, 'twas pity, for it was a fair house.'

Down in the hollow, where no wind blew, it was both warm and still; and Matcham, laying one hand upon Dick's arm, held up a warning finger.

'Hist!' he said.

Then came a strange sound, breaking on the quiet. It was twice repeated ere they recognised its nature. It was the sound of a big man clearing his throat; and just then a hoarse, untuneful voice broke into singing.

Then up and spake the master, the king of the outlaws:
'What make ye here, my merry men, among the greenwood
   shaws?'
And Gamelyn made answer – he looked never a down:
'O, they must need to walk in wood that may not walk in town!'

The singer paused, a faint clink of iron followed, and
then silence.

The two lads stood looking at each other. Whoever he
might be, their invisible neighbour was just beyond the
ruin. And suddenly the colour came into Matcham's face,
and next moment he had crossed the fallen rafter, and was
climbing cautiously on the huge pile of lumber that filled
the interior of the roofless house. Dick would have withheld
him, had he been in time; as it was, he was fain to follow.

Right in the corner of the ruin, two rafters had fallen
crosswise, and protected a clear space no larger than a pew
in church. Into this the lads silently lowered themselves.
There they were perfectly concealed, and through a narrow
loophole commanded a view upon the farther side.

Peering through this, they were struck stiff with terror at
their predicament. To retreat was impossible; they scarce
dared to breathe. Upon the very margin of the ditch, not
thirty feet from where they crouched, an iron cauldron
bubbled and steamed above a glowing fire; and close by,
in an attitude of listening, as though he had caught some
sound of their clambering among the ruins, a tall, red-faced,
battered-looking man stood poised, an iron spoon in his
right hand, a horn and a formidable dagger at his belt.
Plainly this was the singer; plainly he had been stirring the
cauldron, when some incautious step among the lumber
had fallen upon his ear. A little farther off another man lay
slumbering, rolled in a brown coat, with a butterfly hovering
above his face. All this was in a clearing white with daisies;
and at the extreme verge a bow, a sheaf of arrows, and part
of a deer's carcase, hung upon a flowering hawthorn.

Presently the fellow relaxed from his attitude of attention,
raised the spoon to his mouth, tasted its contents, nodded,
and then fell again to stirring and singing.

'O, they must need to walk in wood that may not walk in town,' he croaked, taking up his song where he had left it.

'O, sir, we walk not here at all an evil thing to do,
But if we meet with the good king's deer to shoot a shaft
into.'

Still as he sang, he took from time to time another spoonful of the broth, blew upon it, and tasted it, with all the airs of an experienced cook. At length, apparently, he judged the mess was ready, for taking the horn from his girdle, he blew three modulated calls.

The other fellow awoke, rolled over, brushed away the butterfly, and looked about him.

'How now, brother?' he said. 'Dinner?'

'Ay, sot,' replied the cook, 'dinner it is, and a dry dinner, too, with neither ale nor bread. But there is little pleasure in the greenwood now; time was when a good fellow could live here like a mitred abbot, set aside the rain and the white frosts; he had his heart's desire both of ale and wine. But now are men's spirits dead; and this John Amend-All, save us and guard us! but a stuffed booby to scare crows withal.'

'Nay,' returned the other, 'y' are too set on meat and drinking, Lawless. Bide ye a bit; the good time cometh.'

'Look ye,' returned the cook, 'I have even waited for this good time sith that I was so high. I have been a grey friar; I have been a king's archer; I have been a shipman, and sailed the salt seas; and I have been in greenwood before this, forsooth! and shot the king's deer. What cometh of it? Naught! I were better to have bided in the cloister. John Abbot availeth more than John Amend-All. By'r Lady! here they come.'

One after another, tall likely fellows began to stroll into the lawn. Each as he came produced a knife and a horn cup, helped himself from the cauldron, and sat down upon the grass to eat. They were very variously equipped and armed; some in rusty smocks, and with nothing but a knife and an old bow; others in the height of forest gallantry, all in Lincoln green, both hood and jerkin, with dainty peacock arrows in their belts, a horn upon a baldrick, and a sword and dagger at their sides. They came in the silence of hunger, and scarce growled a salutation, but fell instantly to meat.

There were, perhaps, a score of them already gathered, when a sound of suppressed cheering arose close by among the hawthorns, and immediately after five or six woodmen carrying a stretcher debouched upon the lawn. A tall, lusty fellow, somewhat grizzled, and as brown as a smoked ham, walked before them with an air of some authority, his bow at his back, a bright boar-spear in his hand.

'Lads!' he cried, 'good fellows all, and my right merry friends, y' have sung this while on a dry whistle and lived at little ease. But what said I ever? Abide Fortune constantly; she turneth, turneth swift. And lo! here is her little firstling – even that good creature, ale!'

There was a murmur of applause as the bearers set down the stretcher and displayed a goodly cask.

'And now haste ye, boys,' the man continued. 'There is work toward. A handful of archers are but now come to the ferry, murrey and blue is their wear; they are our butts – they shall all taste arrows – no man of them shall struggle through this wood. For, lads, we are here some fifty strong, each man of us most foully wronged; for some they have lost lands, and some friends; and some they have been outlawed – all oppressed! Who, then, hath done this evil? Sir Daniel, by the rood! Shall he then profit? shall he sit snug in our houses? shall he till our fields? shall he suck the bone he robbed us of? I trow not. He getteth him strength at law; he gaineth cases; nay, there is one case he shall not gain – I have a writ here at my belt that, please the saints, shall conquer him.'

Lawless the cook was by this time already at his second horn of ale. He raised it, as if to pledge the speaker.

'Master Ellis,' he said, 'y' are for vengeance – well it becometh you! – but your poor brother o' the greenwood, that had never lands to lose nor friends to think upon, looketh rather, for his poor part, to the profit of the thing. He had liever a gold noble and a pottle of canary wine than all the vengeances in purgatory.'

'Lawless,' replied the other, 'to reach the Moat House, Sir Daniel must pass the forest. We shall make that passage dearer, pardy, than any battle. Then, when he has got to earth with such ragged handful as escapeth us – all his great friends fallen and fled away, and none to give him aid – we shall beleaguer that old fox about, and great shall be the fall of him. 'Tis a fat buck; he will make a dinner for us all.'

'Ay,' returned Lawless, 'I have eaten many of these dinners beforehand; but the cooking of them is hot work, good Master Ellis. And meanwhile what do we? We make black arrows, we write rhymes, and we drink fair cold water, that discomfortable drink.'

'Y' are untrue, Will Lawless. Ye still smell of the Grey Friars' buttery; greed is your undoing,' answered Ellis. 'We took twenty pounds from Appleyard. We took seven marks from the messenger last night. A day ago we had fifty from the merchant.'

'And to-day,' said one of the men, 'I stopped a fat pardoner riding apace for Holywood. Here is his purse.' Ellis counted the contents.

'Five-score shillings!' he grumbled. 'Fool, he had more in his sandal, or stitched into his tippet. Y' are but a child, Tom Cuckow; ye have lost the fish.'

But, for all that, Ellis pocketed the purse with nonchalance. He stood leaning on his boar-spear, and looked round upon the rest. They, in various attitudes, took greedily of the venison pottage, and liberally washed it down with ale. This was a good day; they were in luck; but business pressed, and they were speedy in their eating. The first-comers had by this time even despatched their dinner. Some lay down upon the grass and fell instantly asleep, like boa-constrictors; others talked together, or overhauled their weapons; and one, whose humour was particularly gay, holding forth an ale-horn, began to sing:

> Here is no law in good green shaw,
>   Here is no lack of meat;
> 'Tis merry and quiet, with deer for our diet,
>   In summer, when all is sweet.
>
> Come winter again, with wind and rain –
>   Come winter, with snow and sleet,
> Get home to your places, with hoods on your faces,
>   And sit by the fire and eat.

All this while the two lads had listened and lain close; only Richard had unslung his cross-bow, and held ready in one hand the windac, or grappling-iron that he used to bend it. Otherwise they had not dared to stir; and this scene of forest life had gone on before their eyes like a scene upon a theatre. But now there came a strange interruption. The tall chimney which overtopped the remainder of the ruins rose right above their hiding-place. There came a whistle in the air, and then a sounding smack, and the fragments of a broken arrow fell about their ears. Some one from the upper quarters of the wood, perhaps the very sentinel they saw posted in the fir, had shot an arrow at the chimney-top.

Matcham could not restrain a little cry, which he instantly stifled, and even Dick started with surprise, and dropped the windac from his fingers. But to the fellows on the lawn, this shaft was an expected signal. They were all afoot together, tightening their belts, testing their bow-strings, loosening sword and dagger in the sheath. Ellis held up his hand; his face had suddenly assumed a look of savage energy; the white of his eyes shone in his sun-brown face.

'Lads,' he said, 'ye know your places. Let not one man's soul escape you. Appleyard was a whet before a meal; but now we go to table. I have three men whom I will bitterly avenge – Harry Shelton, Simon Malmesbury, and' – striking his broad bosom – 'and Ellis Duckworth, by the mass!'

Another man came, red with hurry, through the thorns. '"Tis not Sir Daniel!' he panted. 'They are but seven. Is the arrow gone?'

'It struck but now,' replied Ellis.

'A murrain!' cried the messenger. 'Methought I heard it whistle. And I go dinnerless!'

In the space of a minute, some running, some walking sharply, according as their stations were nearer or farther away, the men of the Black Arrow had all disappeared from the neighbourhood of the ruined house; and the cauldron, and the fire, which was now burning low, and the dead deer's carcase on the hawthorn, remained alone to testify they had been there.

CHAPTER FIVE

'Bloody as the Hunter'

THE lads lay quiet till the last footstep had melted on the wind. Then they arose, and with many an ache for they were weary with constraint, clambered through the ruins, and recrossed the ditch upon the rafter. Matcham had picked up the windac and went first, Dick following stiffly, with his cross-bow on his arm.

'And now,' said Matcham, 'forth to Holywood.'

'To Holywood!' cried Dick, 'when good fellows stand shot? Not I! I would see you hanged first, Jack!'

'Ye would leave me, would ye?' Matcham asked.

'Ay, by my sooth!' returned Dick. 'An I be not in time to warn these lads, I will go die with them. What! would ye have me leave my own men that I have lived among? I trow not! Give me my windac.'

But there was nothing further from Matcham's mind.

'Dick,' he said, 'ye sware before the saints that ye would see me safe to Holywood. Would ye be forsworn? Would you desert me – a perjurer?'

'Nay, I sware for the best,' returned Dick. 'I meant it too; but now! But look ye, Jack, turn again with me. Let me but warn these men, and, if needs must, stand shot with them; then shall all be clear, and I will on again to Holywood and purge mine oath.'

'Ye but deride me,' answered Matcham. 'These men ye go to succour are the same that hunt me to my ruin.'

Dick scratched his head.

'I cannot help it, Jack,' he said. 'Here is no remedy. What would ye? Ye run no great peril, man; and these are in the way of death. Death!' he added. 'Think of it! What a murrain do ye keep me here for? Give me the windac. Saint George! shall they all die?'

'Richard Shelton,' said Matcham, looking him squarely in the face, 'would ye, then, join party with Sir Daniel? Have ye not ears? Heard ye not this Ellis, what he said? or have ye no heart for your own kindly blood and the father that men slew? "Harry Shelton," he said; and Sir Harry Shelton was your father, as the sun shines in heaven.'

'What would ye?' Dick cried again. 'Would ye have me credit thieves?'

'Nay, I have heard it before now,' returned Matcham. 'The fame goeth currently, it was Sir Daniel slew him. He slew him under oath; in his own house he shed the innocent blood. Heaven wearies for the avenging on't; and you – the man's son – ye go about to comfort and defend the murderer!'

'Jack,' cried the lad, 'I know not. It may be; what know I? But, see here: This man hath bred me up and fostered me, and his men I have hunted with and played among; and to leave them in the hour of peril – O, man, if I did that, I were stark dead to honour! Nay, Jack, ye would not ask it; ye would not wish me to be base.'

'But your father, Dick?' said Matcham, somewhat wavering. 'Your father? and your oath to me? Ye took the saints to witness.'

'My father?' cried Shelton. 'Nay, he would have me go! If Sir Daniel slew him, when the hour comes this hand shall slay Sir Daniel; but neither him nor his will I desert in peril. And for mine oath, good Jack, ye shall absolve me of it here. For the lives' sake of many men that hurt you not, and for mine honour, ye shall set me free.'

'I, Dick? Never!' returned Matcham. 'An ye leave me, y' are forsworn, and so I shall declare it.'

'My blood heats,' said Dick. 'Give me the windac! Give it me!'

'I'll not,' said Matcham. 'I'll save you in your teeth.'

'Not?' cried Dick. 'I'll make you!'

'Try it,' said the other.

They stood, looking in each other's eyes, each ready for a spring. Then Dick leaped; and though Matcham turned instantly and fled, in two bounds he was overtaken, the windac was twisted from his grasp, he was thrown roughly

to the ground, and Dick stood across him, flushed and
menacing, with doubled fist. Matcham lay where he
had fallen, with his face in the grass, not thinking of
resistance.

Dick bent his bow.

'I'll teach you!' he cried fiercely. 'Oath or no oath, ye
may go hang for me!'

And he turned and began to run. Matcham was on his
feet at once, and began running after him.

'What d'ye want?' cried Dick, stopping. 'What make ye
after me? Stand off!'

'I will follow an I please,' said Matcham. 'This wood is
free to me.'

'Stand back, by'r Lady!' returned Dick, raising his
bow.

'Ah, y' are a brave boy!' retorted Matcham. 'Shoot!'

Dick lowered his weapon in some confusion.

'See here,' he said. 'Y' have done me ill enough. Go,
then. Go your way in fair wise; or, whether I will or not,
I must even drive you to it.'

'Well,' said Matcham, doggedly, 'y' are the stronger. Do
your worst. I shall not leave to follow thee, Dick, unless
thou makest me,' he added.

Dick was almost beside himself. It went against his heart
to beat a creature so defenceless; and, for the life of him, he
knew no other way to rid himself of this unwelcome and,
as he began to think, perhaps untrue companion.

'Y' are mad, I think,' he cried. 'Fool-fellow, I am hasting
to your foes; as fast as foot can carry me, go I thither.'

'I care not, Dick,' replied the lad. 'If y' are bound to die,
Dick, I'll die too. I would liever go with you to prison than
to go free without you.'

'Well,' returned the other, 'I may stand no longer prating.
Follow me, if ye must; but if ye play me false, it shall but
little advance you, mark ye that. Shalt have a quarrel in
thine inwards, boy.'

So saying, Dick took once more to his heels, keeping in
the margin of the thicket, and looking briskly about him as
he went. At a good pace he rattled out of the dell, and came
again into the more open quarters of the wood. To the left

a little eminence appeared, spotted with golden gorse, and crowned with a black tuft of firs.

'I shall see from there,' he thought, and struck for it across a heathy clearing.

He had gone but a few yards, when Matcham touched him on the arm, and pointed. To the eastward of the summit there was a dip, and, as it were, a valley passing to the other side; the heath was not yet out; all the ground was rusty, like an unscoured buckler, and dotted sparingly with yews; and there, one following another, Dick saw half a score green jerkins mounting the ascent, and marching at their head, conspicuous by his boar-spear, Ellis Duckworth in person. One after another gained the top, showed for a moment against the sky, and then dipped upon the further side, until the last was gone.

Dick looked at Matcham with a kindlier eye.

'So y' are to be true to me, Jack?' he asked. 'I thought ye were of the other party.'

Matcham began to sob.

'What cheer!' cried Dick. 'Now the saints behold us! would ye snivel for a word?'

'Ye hurt me,' sobbed Matcham. 'Ye hurt me when ye threw me down. Y' are a coward to abuse your strength.'

'Nay, that is fool's talk,' said Dick, roughly. 'Y' had no title to my windac, Master John. I would 'a' done right to have well basted you. If ye go with me, ye must obey me; and so, come.'

Matcham had half a thought to stay behind; but, seeing that Dick continued to scour full-tilt towards the eminence, and not so much as looked across his shoulder, he soon thought better of that, and began to run in turn. But the ground was very difficult and steep; Dick had already a long start, and had, at any rate, the lighter heels, and he had long since come to the summit, crawled forward through the firs, and ensconced himself in a thick tuft of gorse, before Matcham, panting like a deer, rejoined him, and lay down in silence by his side.

Below, in the bottom of a considerable valley, the short cut from Tunstall hamlet wound downwards to the ferry. It was well beaten, and the eye followed it easily from point to point. Here it was bordered by open glades; there the forest closed upon it; every hundred yards it ran beside an ambush. Far down the path, the sun shone on seven steel salets, and from time to time, as the trees opened, Selden and his men could be seen riding briskly, still bent upon Sir Daniel's mission. The wind had somewhat fallen, but still tussled merrily with the trees, and, perhaps, had Appleyard been there, he would have drawn a warning from the troubled conduct of the birds.

'Now, mark,' Dick whispered. 'They be already well advanced into the wood; their safety lieth rather in continuing forward. But see ye where this wide glade runneth down before us, and in the midst of it, these two-score trees make like an island? There were their safety. An they but come sound as far as that, I will make shift to warn them. But my heart misgiveth me; they are but seven against so many, and they but carry cross-bows. The long-bow, Jack, will have the uppermost ever.'

Meanwhile, Selden and his men still wound up the path, ignorant of their danger, and momently drew nearer hand. Once, indeed, they paused, drew into a group, and seemed to point and listen. But it was something from far away across the plain that had arrested their attention – a hollow growl of cannon that came, from time to time, upon the wind, and told of the great battle. It was worth a thought, to be sure; for if the voice of the big guns were thus become audible in Tunstall Forest, the fight must have rolled ever eastward, and the day, by consequence, gone sore against Sir Daniel and the lords of the dark rose.

But presently the little troop began again to move forward, and came next to a very open, heathy portion of the way, where but a single tongue of forest ran down to join the road. They were but just abreast of this, when an arrow shone flying. One of the men threw up his arms, his horse reared, and both fell and struggled together in a mass. Even from where the boys lay they could hear the rumour of the men's voices crying out; they could see the startled horses prancing, and, presently, as the troop began to recover from their first surprise, one fellow beginning to dismount. A second arrow from somewhat farther off glanced in a wide arch; a second rider bit the dust. The man who was dismounting lost hold upon the rein, and his horse fled galloping, and dragged him by the foot along the road, bumping from stone to stone, and battered by the fleeing hoofs. The four who still kept the saddle instantly broke and scattered; one wheeled and rode, shrieking, towards the ferry; the other three, with loose rein and flying raiment, came galloping up the road from Tunstall. From every clump they passed an arrow sped. Soon a horse fell, but the rider found his feet and continued to pursue his comrades till a second shot despatched him. Another man fell; then another horse; out of the whole troop there was but one fellow left, and he on foot; only, in different directions, the noise of the galloping of three riderless horses was dying fast into the distance.

All this time not one of the assailants had for a moment showed himself. Here and there along the path, horse or man rolled, undespatched, in his agony; but no merciful enemy broke cover to put them from their pain.

The solitary survivor stood bewildered in the road beside his fallen charger. He had come the length of that broad glade, with the island of timber, pointed out by Dick. He was not, perhaps, five hundred yards from where the boys lay hidden; and they could see him plainly, looking to and fro in deadly expectation. But nothing came; and the man began to pluck up his courage, and suddenly unslung and bent his bow. At the same time, by something in his action, Dick recognised Selden.

At this offer of resistance, from all about him in the covert of the woods there went up the sound of laughter. A score of men, at least, for this was the very thickest of the ambush, joined in this cruel and untimely mirth. Then an arrow glanced over Selden's shoulder; and he leaped and ran a little back. Another dart struck quivering at his heel. He made for the cover. A third shaft leaped out right in his face, and fell short in front of him. And then the laughter was repeated loudly, rising and re-echoing from different thickets.

It was plain that his assailants were but baiting him, as men, in those days, baited the poor bull, or as the cat still trifles with the mouse. The skirmish was well over; farther down the road, a fellow in green was already calmly gathering the arrows; and now, in the evil pleasure of their hearts, they gave themselves the spectacle of their poor fellow-sinner in his torture.

Selden began to understand; he uttered a roar of anger, shouldered his cross-bow, and sent a quarrel at a venture into the wood. Chance favoured him, for a slight cry responded. Then, throwing down his weapon, Selden began to run before him up the glade, and almost in a straight line for Dick and Matcham.

The companions of the Black Arrow now began to shoot in earnest. But they were properly served; their chance had passed; most of them had now to shoot against the sun; and Selden, as he ran, bounded from side to side to baffle and deceive their aim. Best of all, by turning up the glade he had defeated their preparations; there were no marksmen posted higher up than the one whom he had just killed or wounded; and the confusion of the foresters' counsels soon became apparent. A whistle sounded thrice, and then again twice. It was repeated from another quarter. The woods on either side became full of the sound of people bursting through the underwood; and a bewildered deer ran out into the open, stood for a second on three feet, with nose in air, and then plunged again into the thicket.

Selden still ran, bounding; ever and again an arrow followed him, but still would miss. It began to appear as if he might escape. Dick had his bow armed, ready to support him; even Matcham, forgetful of his interest, took sides at heart for the poor fugitive; and both lads glowed and trembled in the ardour of their hearts.

He was within fifty yards of them, when an arrow struck him, and he fell. He was up again, indeed, upon the instant; but now he ran staggering, and, like a blind man, turned aside from his direction.

Dick leaped to his feet and waved to him.

'Here!' he cried. 'This way! here is help! Nay, run, fellow – run!'

But just then a second arrow struck Selden in the shoulder, between the plates of his brigandine, and, piercing through his jack, brought him, like a stone, to earth.

'Oh, the poor heart!' cried Matcham, with clasped hands.

And Dick stood petrified upon the hill, a mark for archery.

Ten to one he had speedily been shot – for the foresters were furious with themselves, and taken unawares by Dick's appearance in the rear of their position – but instantly out of a quarter of the wood surprisingly near to the two lads, a stentorian voice arose, the voice of Ellis Duckworth.

'Hold!' it roared. 'Shoot not! Take him alive! It is young Shelton – Harry's son.'

And immediately after a shrill whistle sounded several times, and was again taken up and repeated farther off. The whistle, it appeared, was John Amend-All's battle trumpet, by which he published his directions.

'Ah, foul fortune!' cried Dick. 'We are undone. Swiftly, Jack, come swiftly!'

And the pair turned and ran back through the open pine clump that covered the summit of the hill.

CHAPTER SIX

To the Day's End

IT was, indeed, high time for them to run. On every side the company of the Black Arrow was making for the hill. Some, being better runners, or having open ground to run upon, had far outstripped the others, and were already close upon the goal; some, following valleys, had spread out to right and left, and outflanked the lads on either side.

Dick plunged into the nearest cover. It was a tall grove of oaks, firm under foot and clear of underbrush, and as it lay down hill, they made good speed. There followed next a piece of open, which Dick avoided, holding to his left. Two minutes after, and the same obstacle arising, the lads followed the same course. Thus it followed that, while the lads, bending continually to the left, drew nearer and nearer to the high road and the river which they had crossed an hour or two before, the great bulk of their pursuers were leaning to the other hand, and running towards Tunstall.

The lads paused to breathe. There was no sound of pursuit. Dick put his ear to the ground, and still there was nothing; but the wind, to be sure, still made a turmoil in the trees, and it was hard to make certain.

'On again!' said Dick; and, tired as they were, and Matcham limping with his injured foot, they pulled themselves together, and once more pelted down the hill.

Three minutes later, they were breasting through a low thicket of evergreen. High overhead, the tall trees made a continuous roof of foliage. It was a pillared grove, as high as a cathedral, and except for the hollies among which the lads were struggling, open and smoothly swarded.

On the other side, pushing through the last fringe of evergreen, they blundered forth again into the open twilight of the grove.

'Stand!' cried a voice.

And there, between the huge stems, not fifty feet before them, they beheld a stout fellow in green, sore blown with running, who instantly drew an arrow to the head and covered them. Matcham stopped with a cry; but Dick, without a pause, ran straight upon the forester, drawing his dagger as he went. The other, whether he was startled by the daring of the onslaught, or whether he was hampered by his orders, did not shoot: he stood wavering; and before he had time to come to himself, Dick bounded at his throat, and sent him sprawling backward on the turf. The arrow went one way and the bow another with a sounding twang. The disarmed forester grappled his assailant; but the dagger shone and descended twice. Then came a couple of groans, and then Dick rose to his feet again, and the man lay motionless, stabbed to the heart.

'On!' said Dick; and he once more pelted forward, Matcham trailing in the rear. To say truth, they made but poor speed of it by now, labouring dismally as they ran, and catching for their breath like fish. Matcham had a cruel stitch, and his head swam; and as for Dick, his knees were like lead. But they kept up the form of running with undiminished courage.

Presently they came to the end of the grove. It stopped abruptly; and there, a few yards before them, was the high road from Risingham to Shoreby, lying, at this point, between two even walls of forest.

At the sight Dick paused; and as soon as he stopped running, he became aware of a confused noise, which rapidly grew louder. It was at first like the rush of a very high gust of wind, but it soon became more definite, and resolved itself into the galloping of horses; and then, in a flash, a whole company of men-at-arms came driving round the corner, swept before the lads, and were gone again upon the instant. They rode as for their lives, in complete disorder; some of them were wounded; riderless horses galloped at their side with bloody saddles. They were plainly fugitives from the great battle.

The noise of their passage had scarce begun to die away towards Shoreby, before fresh hoofs came echoing in their

wake, and another deserter clattered down the road; this
time a single rider, and, by his splendid armour, a man
of high degree. Close after him there followed several
baggage-waggons, fleeing at an ungainly canter, the drivers
flailing at the horses as if for life. These must have run early
in the day; but their cowardice was not to save them. For just
before they came abreast of where the lads stood wondering,
a man in hacked armour, and seemingly beside himself with
fury, overtook the waggons, and with the truncheon of a
sword began to cut the drivers down. Some leaped from
their places and plunged into the wood; the others he sabred
as they sat, cursing them the while for cowards in a voice
that was scarce human.

All this time the noise in the distance had continued
to increase; the rumble of carts, the clatter of horses,
the cries of men, a great, confused rumour, came swell-
ing on the wind; and it was plain that the rout of
a whole army was pouring, like an inundation, down
the road.

Dick stood sombre. He had meant to follow the highway
till the turn for Holywood, and now he had to change his
plan. But above all, he had recognised the colours of Earl
Risingham, and he knew that the battle had gone finally
against the rose of Lancaster. Had Sir Daniel joined, and
was he now a fugitive and ruined? or had he deserted to
the side of York, and was he forfeit to honour? It was an
ugly choice.

'Come,' he said, sternly; and, turning on his heel, he
began to walk forward through the grove, with Matcham
limping in his rear.

For some time they continued to thread the forest in
silence. It was now growing late; the sun was setting in
the plain beyond Kettley; the tree-tops overhead glowed
golden; but the shadows had begun to grow darker and
the chill of the night to fall.

'If there was anything to eat!' cried Dick, suddenly,
pausing as he spoke.

Matcham sat down and began to weep.

'Ye can weep for your own supper, but when it was
to save men's lives, your heart was hard enough,' said

Dick, contemptuously. 'Y' 'ave seven deaths upon your conscience, Master John; I'll ne'er forgive you that.'

'Conscience!' cried Matcham, looking fiercely up. 'Mine! And ye have the man's red blood upon your dagger! And wherefore did ye slay him, the poor soul? He drew his arrow, but he let not fly; he held you in his hand, and spared you! 'Tis as brave to kill a kitten as a man that not defends himself.'

Dick was struck dumb.

'I slew him fair. I ran me in upon his bow,' he cried.

'It was a coward blow,' returned Matcham. 'Y' are but a lout and bully, Master Dick; ye but abuse advantages; let there come a stronger, we will see you truckle at his boot! Ye care not for vengeance, neither – for your father's death that goes unpaid, and his poor ghost that clamoureth for justice. But if there come but a poor creature in your hands that lacketh skill and strength, and would befriend you, down she shall go!'

Dick was too furious to observe that 'she.'

'Marry!' he cried, 'and here is news! Of any two the one will still be stronger. The better man throweth the worse, and the worse is well served. Ye deserve a belting, Master Matcham, for your ill-guidance and unthankfulness to me-ward; and what ye deserve ye shall have.'

And Dick, who, even in his angriest temper, still preserved the appearance of composure, began to unbuckle his belt.

'Here shall be your supper,' he said, grimly.

Matcham had stopped his tears; he was as white as a sheet, but he looked Dick steadily in the face, and never moved. Dick took a step, swinging the belt. Then he paused, embarrassed by the large eyes and the thin weary face of his companion. His courage began to subside.

'Say ye were in the wrong, then,' he said, lamely.

'Nay,' said Matcham, 'I was in the right. Come, cruel! I be lame; I be weary; I resist not; I ne'er did thee hurt; come, beat me – coward!'

Dick raised the belt at this last provocation; but Matcham winced and drew himself together with so cruel an apprehension, that his heart failed him yet again. The strap fell by his side, and he stood irresolute, feeling like a fool.

'A plague upon thee, shrew!' he said. 'An ye be so feeble of hand, ye should keep the closer guard upon your tongue. But I'll be hanged before I beat you!' and he put on his belt again. 'Beat you I will not,' he continued; 'but forgive you? – never. I knew ye not; ye were my master's enemy; I lent you my horse; my dinner ye have eaten; y' 'ave called me a man o' wood, a coward, and a bully. Nay, by the mass! the measure is filled, and runneth over. 'Tis a great thing to be weak, I trow: ye can do your worst, yet shall none punish you; ye may steal a man's weapons in the hour of need, yet may the man not take his own again; – y' are weak, forsooth! Nay, then, if one cometh charging at you with a lance, and crieth he is weak, ye must let him pierce your body through! Tut! fool words!'

'And yet ye beat me not,' returned Matcham.

'Let be,' said Dick – 'let be. I will instruct you. Y' 'ave been ill-nurtured, methinks, and yet ye have the makings of some good, and, beyond all question, saved me from the river. Nay, I had forgotten it; I am as thankless as thyself. But, come, let us on. An we be for Holywood this night, ay, or to-morrow early, we had best set forward speedily.'

But though Dick had talked himself back into his usual good-humour, Matcham had forgiven him nothing. His violence, the recollection of the forester whom he had slain – above all, the vision of the upraised belt, were things not easily to be forgotten.

'I will thank you, for the form's sake,' said Matcham. 'But, in sooth, good Master Shelton, I had liever find my way alone. Here is a wide wood: prithee, let each choose his path; I owe you a dinner and a lesson. Fare ye well!'

'Nay,' cried Dick, 'if that be your tune, so be it, and a plague be with you!'

Each turned aside, and they began walking off severally, with no thought of the direction, intent solely on their quarrel. But Dick had not gone ten paces ere his name was called, and Matcham came running after.

'Dick,' he said, 'it were unmannerly to part so coldly. Here is my hand, and my heart with it. For all that wherein you have so excellently served and helped me – not for the form, but from the heart, I thank you. Fare ye right well.'

'Well, lad,' returned Dick, taking the hand which was offered him, 'good speed to you, if speed you may. But I misdoubt it shrewdly. Y' are too disputatious.'

So then they separated for the second time; and presently it was Dick who was running after Matcham.

'Here,' he said, 'take my cross-bow; shalt not go unarmed.'

'A cross-bow!' said Matcham. 'Nay, boy, I have neither the strength to bend nor yet the skill to aim with it. It were no help to me, good boy. But yet I thank you.'

The night had now fallen, and under the trees they could no longer read each other's face.

'I will go some little way with you,' said Dick. 'The night is dark. I would fain leave you on a path, at least. My mind misgiveth me, y' are likely to be lost.'

Without any more words, he began to walk forward, and the other once more followed him. The blackness grew thicker and thicker; only here and there, in open places, they saw the sky, dotted with small stars. In the distance, the noise of the rout of the Lancastrian army still continued to be faintly audible; but with every step they left it farther in the rear.

At the end of half an hour of silent progress they came forth upon a broad patch of heathy open. It glimmered in the light of the stars, shaggy with fern and islanded with clumps of yew. And here they paused and looked upon each other.

'Y' are weary?' Dick said.

'Nay, I am so weary,' answered Matcham, 'that methinks I could lie down and die.'

'I hear the chiding of a river,' returned Dick. 'Let us go so far forth, for I am sore athirst.'

The ground sloped down gently; and, sure enough, in the bottom, they found a little murmuring river, running among willows. Here they threw themselves down together by the brink; and putting their mouths to the level of a starry pool, they drank their fill.

'Dick,' said Matcham, 'it may not be. I can no more.'

'I saw a pit as we came down,' said Dick. 'Let us lie down therein and sleep.'

'Nay, but with all my heart!' cried Matcham.

The pit was sandy and dry; a shock of brambles hung upon one edge, and made a partial shelter; and there the two lads lay down, keeping close together for the sake of warmth, their quarrel all forgotten. And soon sleep fell upon them like a cloud, and under the dew and stars they rested peacefully.

CHAPTER SEVEN

The Hooded Face

THEY AWOKE in the grey of the morning; the birds were
not yet in full song, but twittered here and there among
the woods; the sun was not yet up, but the eastern sky was
barred with solemn colours. Half starved and over-weary
as they were, they lay without moving, sunk in a delightful
lassitude. And as they thus lay, the clang of a bell fell
suddenly upon their ears.

'A bell!' said Dick, sitting up. 'Can we be, then, so near
to Holywood?'

A little after, the bell clanged again, but this time
somewhat nearer hand; and from that time forth, and
still drawing nearer and nearer, it continued to sound
brokenly abroad in the silence of the morning.

'Nay, what should this betoken?' said Dick, who was
now broad awake.

'It is some one walking,' returned Matcham, 'and the
bell tolleth ever as he moves.'

'I see that well,' said Dick. 'But wherefore? What maketh
he in Tunstall Woods? Jack,' he added, 'laugh at me an ye
will, but I like not the hollow sound of it.'

'Nay,' said Matcham, with a shiver, 'it hath a doleful
note. An the day were not come—'

But just then the bell, quickening its pace, began to ring
thick and hurried, and then it gave a single hammering
jangle, and was silent for a space.

'It is as though the bearer had run for a paternoster-while,
and then leaped the river,' Dick observed.

'And now beginneth he again to pace soberly forward,'
added Matcham.

'Nay,' returned Dick – 'nay, not so soberly, Jack. 'Tis a
man that walketh you right speedily. 'Tis a man in some

fear of his life, or about some hurried business. See ye not how swift the beating draweth near?'

'It is now close by,' said Matcham.

They were now on the edge of the pit; and as the pit itself was on a certain eminence, they commanded a view over the greater proportion of the clearing, up to the thick woods that closed it in.

The daylight, which was very clear and grey, showed them a riband of white footpath wandering among the gorse. It passed some hundred yards from the pit, and ran the whole length of the clearing, east and west. By the line of its course, Dick judged it should lead more or less directly to the Moat House.

Upon this path, stepping forth from the margin of the wood, a white figure now appeared. It paused a little and seemed to look about; and then, at a slow pace, and bent almost double, it began to draw near across the heath. At every step the bell clanked. Face, it had none; a white hood, not even pierced with eye-holes, veiled the head; and as the creature moved, it seemed to feel its way with the tapping of a stick. Fear fell upon the lads, as cold as death.

'A leper!' said Dick, hoarsely.

'His touch is death,' said Matcham. 'Let us run.'

'Not so,' returned Dick. 'See ye not? – he is stone-blind. He guideth him with a staff. Let us lie still; the wind bloweth towards the path, and he will go by and hurt us not. Alas, poor soul, and we should rather pity him!'

'I will pity him when he is by,' replied Matcham.

The blind leper was now about half-way towards them, and just then the sun rose and shone full on his veiled face. He had been a tall man before he was bowed by his disgusting sickness, and even now he walked with a vigorous step. The dismal beating of his bell, the pattering of the stick, the eyeless screen before his countenance, and the knowledge that he was not only doomed to death and suffering, but shut out for ever from the touch of his fellow-men, filled the lads' bosoms with dismay; and at every step that brought him nearer, their courage and strength seemed to desert them.

As he came about level with the pit, he paused, and turned his face full upon the lads.

'Mary be my shield! He sees us!' said Matcham, faintly.

'Hush!' whispered Dick. 'He doth but hearken. He is blind, fool!'

The leper looked or listened, whichever he was really doing, for some seconds. Then he began to move on again, but presently paused once more, and again turned and seemed to gaze upon the lads. Even Dick became dead-white and closed his eyes, as if by the mere sight he might become infected. But soon the bell sounded, and this time, without any further hesitation, the leper crossed the remainder of the little heath and disappeared into the covert of the woods.

'He saw us,' said Matcham. 'I could swear it!'

'Tut!' returned Dick, recovering some sparks of courage. 'He but heard us. He was in fear, poor soul! An ye were blind, and walked in a perpetual night, ye would start yourself, if ever a twig rustled or a bird cried "Peep".'

'Dick, good Dick, he saw us,' repeated Matcham. 'When a man hearkeneth, he doth not as this man; he doth otherwise, Dick. This was seeing; it was not hearing. He means foully. Hark, else, if his bell be not stopped!'

Such was the case. The bell rang no longer.

'Nay,' said Dick, 'I like not that. Nay,' he cried again, 'I like that little. What may this betoken? Let us go, by the mass!'

'He hath gone east,' added Matcham. 'Good Dick, let us go westward straight. I shall not breathe till I have my back turned upon that leper.'

'Jack, y'are too cowardly,' replied Dick. 'We shall go fair for Holywood, or as fair, at least, as I can guide you, and that will be due north.'

They were afoot at once, passed the stream upon some stepping-stones, and began to mount on the other side, which was steeper, towards the margin of the wood. The ground became very uneven, full of knolls and hollows; trees grew scattered or in clumps; it became difficult to choose a path, and the lads somewhat wandered. They were weary, besides, with yesterday's exertions and the lack of food, and they moved but heavily and dragged their feet among the sand.

Presently, coming to the top of a knoll, they were aware of the leper, some hundred feet in front of them, crossing the line of their march by a hollow. His bell was silent, his staff no longer tapped the ground, and he went before him with the swift and assured footsteps of a man who sees. Next moment he had disappeared into a little thicket.

The lads, at the first glimpse, had crouched behind a tuft of gorse; there they lay, horror-struck.

'Certain, he pursueth us,' said Dick – 'certain? He held the clapper of his bell in one hand, saw ye? that it should not sound. Now may the saints aid and guide us, for I have no strength to combat pestilence!'

'What maketh he?' cried Matcham. 'What doth he want? Who ever heard the like, that a leper, out of mere malice, should pursue unfortunates? Hath he not his bell to that very end, that people may avoid him? Dick, there is below this something deeper.'

'Nay, I care not,' moaned Dick; 'the strength is gone out of me; my legs are like water. The saints be mine assistance!'

'Would ye lie there idle?' cried Matcham. 'Let us back into the open. We have the better chance; he cannot steal upon us unawares.'

'Not I,' said Dick. 'My time is come; and peradventure he may pass us by.'

'Bend me, then, your bow!' cried the other. 'What! will ye be a man?'

Dick crossed himself. 'Would ye have me shoot upon a leper?' he cried. 'The hand would fail me. Nay, now,' he added – 'nay, now, let be! With sound men I will fight, but not with ghosts and lepers. Which this is, I wot not. One or other, Heaven be our protection!'

'Now,' said Matcham, 'if this be man's courage, what a poor thing is man! But sith ye will do naught, let us lie close.'

Then came a single, broken jangle on the bell.

'He hath missed his hold upon the clapper,' whispered Matcham. 'Saints! how near he is!'

But Dick answered never a word; his teeth were near chattering.

Soon they saw a piece of the white robe between some bushes; then the leper's head was thrust forth from behind a trunk, and he seemed narrowly to scan the neighbourhood before he once again withdrew. To their stretched senses the whole bush appeared alive with rustlings and the creak of twigs; and they heard the beating of each other's heart.

Suddenly, with a cry, the leper sprang into the open close by, and ran straight upon the lads. They, shrieking aloud, separated and began to run different ways. But their horrible enemy fastened upon Matcham, ran him swiftly down, and had him almost instantly a prisoner. The lad gave one scream that echoed high and far over the forest, he had one spasm of struggling, and then all his limbs relaxed, and he fell limp into his captor's arms.

Dick heard the cry and turned. He saw Matcham fall; and on the instant his spirit and his strength revived. With a cry of pity and anger, he unslung and bent his arblast. But ere he had time to shoot, the leper held up his hand.

'Hold your shot, Dickon!' cried a familiar voice. 'Hold your shot, mad wag! Know ye not a friend?'

And then laying down Matcham on the turf, he undid the hood from off his face, and disclosed the features of Sir Daniel Brackley.

'Sir Daniel!' cried Dick.

'Ay, by the mass, Sir Daniel!' returned the knight. 'Would ye shoot upon your guardian, rogue? But here is this—' And there he broke off, and pointing to Matcham, asked – 'How call ye him, Dick?'

'Nay,' said Dick, 'I call him Master Matcham. Know ye him not? He said ye knew him!'

'Ay,' replied Sir Daniel, 'I know the lad;' and he chuckled. 'But he has fainted; and, by my sooth, he might have had less to faint for. Hey, Dick? Did I put the fear of death upon you?'

'Indeed, Sir Daniel, ye did that,' said Dick, and sighed again at the mere recollection. 'Nay, sir, saving your respect, I had as lief 'a' met the devil in person; and to speak truth, I am yet all a-quake. But what made ye, sir, in such a guise?'

Sir Daniel's brow grew suddenly black with anger.

'What made I?' he said. 'Ye do well to mind me of it! What? I skulked for my poor life in my own wood of Tunstall, Dick. We were ill sped at the battle; we but got there to be swept among the rout. Where be all my good men-at-arms? Dick, by the mass, I know not! We were swept down; the shot fell thick among us; I have not seen one man in my own colours since I saw three fall. For myself, I came sound to Shoreby, and being mindful of the Black Arrow, got me this gown and bell, and came softly by the path for the Moat House. There is no disguise to be compared with it; the jingle of this bell would scare me the stoutest outlaw in the forest; they would all turn pale to hear it. At length I came by you and Matcham. I could see but evilly through this same hood, and was not sure of you, being chiefly, and for many a good cause, astonished at the finding you together. Moreover, in the open, where I had to go slowly and tap with my staff, I feared to disclose myself. But see,' he added, 'this poor shrew begins a little to revive. A little good canary will comfort the heart of it.'

The knight, from under his long dress, produced a stout bottle, and began to rub the temples and wet the lips of the patient, who returned gradually to consciousness, and began to roll dim eyes from one to another.

'What cheer, Jack!' said Dick. 'It was no leper, after all; it was Sir Daniel! See!'

'Swallow me a good draught of this,' said the knight. 'This will give you manhood. Thereafter, I will give you both a meal, and we shall all three on to Tunstall. For, Dick,' he continued, laying forth bread and meat upon the grass, 'I will avow to you, in all good conscience, it irks me sorely to be safe between four walls. Not since I backed a horse have I been pressed so hard; peril of life, jeopardy of land and livelihood, and to sum up, all these losels in the wood to hunt me down. But I be not yet shent. Some of my lads will pick me their way home. Hatch hath ten fellows; Selden, he had six. Nay, we shall soon be strong again; and if I can but buy my peace with my right fortunate and undeserving Lord of York, why, Dick, we'll be a man again and go a-horseback!'

And so saying, the knight filled himself a horn of canary, and pledged his ward in dumb show.

'Selden,' Dick faltered – 'Selden—' And he paused again.

Sir Daniel put down the wine untasted.

'How!' he cried, in a changed voice. 'Selden? Speak! What of Selden?'

Dick stammered forth the tale of the ambush and the massacre.

The knight heard in silence; but as he listened, his countenance became convulsed with rage and grief.

'Now here,' he cried, 'on my right hand, I swear to avenge it! If that I fail, if that I spill not ten men's souls for each, may this hand wither from my body! I broke this Duckworth like a rush; I beggared him to his door; I burned the thatch above his head; I drove him from this country; and now, cometh he back to beard me? Nay, but, Duckworth, this time it shall go bitter hard!'

He was silent for some time, his face working.

'Eat!' he cried, suddenly. 'And you here,' he added to Matcham, 'swear me an oath to follow straight to the Moat House.'

'I will pledge mine honour,' replied Matcham.

'What make I with your honour?' cried the knight. 'Swear me upon your mother's welfare!'

Matcham gave the required oath; and Sir Daniel re-adjusted the hood over his face, and prepared his bell and staff. To see him once more in that appalling travesty somewhat revived the horror of his two companions. But the knight was soon upon his feet.

'Eat with despatch,' he said, 'and follow me yarely to mine house.'

And with that he set forth again into the woods; and presently after the bell began to sound, numbering his steps, and the two lads sat by their untasted meal, and heard it die slowly away uphill into the distance.

'And so ye go to Tunstall?' Dick inquired.

'Yea, verily,' said Matcham, 'when needs must! I am braver behind Sir Daniel's back than to his face.'

They ate hastily, and set forth along the path through

the airy upper levels of the forest, where great beeches stood apart among green lawns, and the birds and squirrels made merry on the boughs. Two hours later, they began to descend upon the other side, and already, among the tree-tops, saw before them the red walls and roofs of Tunstall House.

'Here,' said Matcham, pausing, 'ye shall take your leave of your friend Jack, whom y'are to see no more. Come, Dick, forgive him what he did amiss, as he, for his part, cheerfully and lovingly forgiveth you.'

'And wherefore so?' asked Dick. 'An we both go to Tunstall, I shall see you yet again, I trow, and that right often.'

'Ye'll never again see poor Jack Matcham,' replied the other, 'that was so fearful and burthensome, and yet plucked you from the river; ye'll not see him more, Dick, by mine honour!' He held his arms open, and the lads embraced and kissed. 'And, Dick,' continued Matcham, 'my spirit bodeth ill. Y'are now to see a new Sir Daniel; for heretofore hath all prospered in his hands exceedingly, and fortune followed him; but now, methinks, when his fate hath come upon him, and he runs the adventure of his life, he will prove but a foul lord to both of us. He may be brave in battle, but he hath the liar's eye; there is fear in his eye, Dick, and fear is as cruel as the wolf! We go down into that house, Saint Mary guide us forth again!'

And so they continued their descent in silence, and came out at last before Sir Daniel's forest stronghold, where it stood, low and shady, flanked with round towers and stained with moss and lichen, in the lilied waters of the moat. Even as they appeared, the doors were opened, the bridge lowered, and Sir Daniel himself, with Hatch and the parson at his side, stood ready to receive them.

BOOK II

THE MOAT HOUSE

CHAPTER ONE

Dick Asks Questions

THE Moat House stood not far from the rough forest road. Externally, it was a compact rectangle of red stone, flanked at each corner by a round tower, pierced for archery and battlemented at the top. Within, it enclosed a narrow court. The moat was perhaps twelve feet wide, crossed by a single drawbridge. It was supplied with water by a trench, leading to a forest pool, and commanded, through its whole length, from the battlements of the two southern towers. Except that one or two tall and thick trees had been suffered to remain within half a bowshot of the walls, the house was in a good posture of defence.

In the court, Dick found a part of the garrison, busy with preparations for defence, and gloomily discussing the chances of a siege. Some were making arrows, some sharpening swords that had long been disused; but even as they worked, they shook their heads.

Twelve of Sir Daniel's party had escaped the battle, run the gauntlet through the wood, and come alive to the Moat House. But out of this dozen, three had been gravely wounded: two at Risingham in the disorder of the rout, one by John Amend-All's marksmen as he crossed the forest. This raised the force of the garrison, counting Hatch, Sir Daniel, and young Shelton, to twenty-two effective men. And more might be continually expected to arrive. The danger lay not, therefore, in the lack of men.

It was the terror of the Black Arrow that oppressed the spirits of the garrison. For their open foes of the party of York, in these most changing times, they felt but a far-away concern. 'The world,' as people said in those days, 'might change again' before harm came. But for their neighbours in the wood they trembled. It was not Sir Daniel alone who was a mark for hatred. His men, conscious of impunity, had carried themselves cruelly through all the country. Harsh commands had been harshly executed; and of the little band that now sat talking in the court, there was not one but had been guilty of some act of oppression or barbarity. And now, by the fortune of war, Sir Daniel had become powerless to protect his instruments; now, by the issue of some hours of battle, at which many of them had not been present, they had all become punishable traitors to the State, outside the buckler of the law, a shrunken company in a poor fortress that was hardly tenable, and exposed upon all sides to the just resentment of their victims. Nor had there been lacking grisly advertisements of what they might expect.

At different periods of the evening and the night, no fewer than seven riderless horses had come neighing in terror to the gate. Two were from Selden's troop; five belonged to men who had ridden with Sir Daniel to the field. Lastly, a little before dawn, a spearman had come staggering to the moat-side, pierced by three arrows; even as they carried him in, his spirit had departed; but by the words that he uttered in his agony, he must have been the last survivor of a considerable company of men.

Hatch himself showed, under his sun-brown, the pallor of anxiety; and when he had taken Dick aside and learned the fate of Selden, he fell on a stone bench and fairly wept. The others, from where they sat on stools or doorsteps in the sunny angle of the court, looked at him with wonder and alarm, but none ventured to inquire the cause of his emotion.

'Nay, Master Shelton,' said Hatch, at last – 'nay, but what said I? We shall all go. Selden was a man of his hands; he was like a brother to me. Well, he has gone second; well, we shall all follow! For what said their knave rhyme? – "A black arrow in each black heart." Was it not so it went? Appleyard, Selden, Smith, old Humphrey gone; and there lieth poor John Carter, crying, poor sinner, for the priest.'

Dick gave ear. Out of a low window, hard by where they were talking, groans and murmurs came to his ear.

'Lieth he there?' he asked.

'Ay, in the second porter's chamber,' answered Hatch. 'We could not bear him further, soul and body were so bitterly at odds. At every step we lifted him, he thought to wend. But now, methinks, it is the soul that suffereth. Ever for the priest he crieth, and Sir Oliver, I wot not why, still cometh not. 'Twill be a long shrift; but poor Appleyard and poor Selden, they had none.'

Dick stooped to the window and looked in. The little cell was low and dark, but he could make out the wounded soldier lying moaning on his pallet.

'Carter, poor friend, how goeth it?' he asked.

'Master Shelton,' returned the man, in an excited whisper, 'for the dear light of heaven, bring the priest. Alack, I am sped: I am brought very low down; my hurt is to the death. Ye may do me no more service; this shall be the last. Now, for my poor soul's interest, and as a loyal gentleman, bestir you; for I have that matter on my conscience that shall drag me deep.'

He groaned, and Dick heard the grating of his teeth, whether in pain or terror.

Just then Sir Daniel appeared upon the threshold of the hall. He had a letter in one hand.

'Lads,' he said, 'we have had a shog, we have had a tumble; wherefore, then, deny it? Rather it imputeth to get speedily again to saddle. This old Harry the Sixt has had the undermost. Wash we, then, our hands of him. I have a good friend that rideth next the duke, the Lord of Wensleydale. Well, I have writ a letter to my friend, praying his good lordship, and offering large satisfaction for the past and reasonable surety for the future. Doubt not but he will lend a favourable ear. A prayer without gifts is like a song without music: I surfeit him with promises, boys – I spare not to promise. What, then, is lacking? Nay, a great thing – wherefore should I deceive you? – a great thing and a difficult; a messenger to bear it. The woods – y' are not ignorant of that – lie thick with our ill-willers. Haste is most needful; but without sleight and caution all is naught. Which, then, of this company will take me this letter, bear it to my Lord of Wensleydale, and bring me the answer back?'

One man instantly arose.

'I will, an't like you,' said he. 'I will even risk my carcase.'

'Nay, Dicky Bowyer, not so,' returned the knight. 'It likes me not. Y' are sly indeed, but not speedy. Ye were a laggard ever.'

'An't be so, Sir Daniel, here am I,' cried another.

'The saints forfend!' said the knight. 'Y' are speedy, but not sly. Ye would blunder me head-foremost into John Amend-All's camp. I thank you both for your good courage; but, in sooth, it may not be.'

Then Hatch offered himself, and he also was refused.

'I want you here, good Bennet; y' are my right hand, indeed,' returned the knight; and then several coming forward in a group, Sir Daniel at length selected one and gave him the letter.

'Now,' he said, 'upon your good speed and better discretion we do all depend. Bring me a good answer back, and before three weeks, I will have purged my forest of these vagabonds that brave us to our faces. But mark it well, Throgmorton; the matter is not easy. Ye must steal forth under night, and go like a fox; and how ye are to cross Till I know not, neither by the bridge nor ferry.'

'I can swim,' returned Throgmorton. 'I will come soundly, fear not.'

'Well, friend, get ye to the buttery,' replied Sir Daniel. 'Ye shall swim first of all in nut-brown ale.' And with that he turned back into the hall.

'Sir Daniel hath a wise tongue,' said Hatch, aside, to Dick. 'See, now, where many a lesser man had glossed the matter over, he speaketh it out plainly to his company. Here is a danger, 'a' saith, and here difficulty; and jesteth in the very saying. Nay, by Saint Barbary, he is a born captain! Not a man but he is some deal heartened up! See how they fall again to work.'

This praise of Sir Daniel put a thought in the lad's head.

'Bennet,' he said, 'how came my father by his end?'

'Ask me not that,' replied Hatch. 'I had no hand nor knowledge in it; furthermore, I will even be silent, Master

Dick. For look you, in a man's own business, there he may speak; but of hearsay matters and of common talk, not so. Ask me Sir Oliver – ay, or Carter, if ye will; not me.'

And Hatch set off to make the rounds, leaving Dick in a muse.

'Wherefore would he not tell me?' thought the lad. 'And wherefore named he Carter? Carter – nay, then Carter had a hand in it, perchance.'

He entered the house, and passing some little way along a flagged and vaulted passage, came to the door of the cell where the hurt man lay groaning. At his entrance Carter started eagerly.

'Have ye brought the priest?' he cried.

'Not yet awhile,' returned Dick. 'Y' 'ave a word to tell me first. How came my father, Harry Shelton, by his death?'

The man's face altered instantly.

'I know not,' he replied, doggedly.

'Nay, ye know well,' returned Dick. 'Seek not to put me by.'

'I tell you I know not,' repeated Carter.

'Then,' said Dick, 'ye shall die unshriven. Here am I, and here shall stay. There shall no priest come near you, rest assured. For of what avail is penitence, an ye have no mind to right those wrongs ye had a hand in? and without penitence, confession is but mockery.'

'Ye say what ye mean not, Master Dick,' said Carter, composedly. 'It is ill threatening the dying, and becometh you (to speak truth) little. And for as little as it commends you, it shall serve you less. Stay, an ye please. Ye will condemn my soul – ye shall learn nothing! There is my last word to you.' And the wounded man turned upon the other side.

Now, Dick, to say truth, had spoken hastily, and was ashamed of his threat. But he made one more effort.

'Carter,' he said, 'mistake me not. I know ye were but an instrument in the hand of others; a churl must obey his lord; I would not bear heavily on such an one. But I begin to learn upon many sides that this great duty lieth on my youth and ignorance, to avenge my father. Prithee, then, good Carter, set aside the memory of my threatenings, and in pure goodwill and honest penitence, give me a word of help.'

The wounded man lay silent; nor, say what Dick pleased, could he extract another word from him.

'Well,' said Dick, 'I will go call the priest to you as ye desired; for howsoever ye be in fault to me or mine, I would not be willingly in fault to any, least of all to one upon the last change.'

Again the old soldier heard him without speech or motion; even his groans he had suppressed; and as Dick turned and left the room, he was filled with admiration for that rugged fortitude.

'And yet,' he thought, 'of what use is courage without wit? Had his hands been clean, he would have spoken; his silence did confess the secret louder than words. Nay, upon all sides, proof floweth on me. Sir Daniel, he or his men, hath done this thing.'

Dick paused in the stone passage with a heavy heart. At that hour, in the ebb of Sir Daniel's fortune, when he was beleaguered by the archers of the Black Arrow, and proscribed by the victorious Yorkists, was Dick, also, to turn upon the man who had nourished and taught him, who had severely punished, indeed, but yet unwearyingly protected his youth? The necessity, if it should prove to be one, was cruel.

'Pray Heaven he be innocent!' he said.

And then steps sounded on the flagging, and Sir Oliver came gravely towards the lad.

'One seeketh you earnestly,' said Dick.

'I am upon the way, good Richard,' said the priest. 'It is this poor Carter. Alack, he is beyond cure.'

'And yet his soul is sicker than his body,' answered Dick.

'Have ye seen him?' asked Sir Oliver, with a manifest start.

'I do but come from him,' replied Dick.

'What said he – what said he?' snapped the priest, with extraordinary eagerness.

'He but cried for you the more piteously, Sir Oliver. It were well done to go the faster, for his hurt is grievous,' returned the lad.

'I am straight for him,' was the reply. 'Well, we have all our sins. We must all come to our latter day, good Richard.'

'Ay, sir; and it were well if we all came fairly,' answered Dick.

The priest dropped his eyes, and with an inaudible benediction hurried on.

'He, too!' thought Dick – 'he, that taught me in piety! Nay, then, what a world is this, if all that care for me be blood-guilty of my father's death! Vengeance! Alas! what a sore fate is mine, if I must be avenged upon my friends!'

The thought put Matcham in his head. He smiled at the remembrance of his strange companion, and then wondered where he was. Ever since they had come together to the doors of the Moat House the younger lad had disappeared, and Dick began to weary for a word with him.

About an hour after, mass being somewhat hastily run through by Sir Oliver, the company gathered in the hall for dinner. It was a long, low apartment, strewn with green rushes, and the walls hung with arras in a design of savage men and questing bloodhounds; here and there hung spears and bows and bucklers; a fire blazed in the big chimney; there were arras-covered benches round the wall, and in the midst the table, fairly spread, awaited the arrival of the diners. Neither Sir Daniel nor his lady made their appearance. Sir Oliver himself was absent, and here again there was no word of Matcham. Dick began to grow alarmed, to recall his companion's melancholy forebodings, and to wonder to himself if any foul play had befallen him in that house.

After dinner he found Goody Hatch, who was hurrying to my lady Brackley.

'Goody,' he said, 'where is Master Matcham, I prithee? I saw ye go in with him when we arrived.'

The old woman laughed aloud.

'Ah, Master Dick,' she said, 'y' have a famous bright eye in your head, to be sure!' and laughed aloud.

'Nay, but where is he, indeed?' persisted Dick.

'Ye will never see him more,' she returned; 'never. It is sure.'

'An I do not,' returned the lad, 'I will know the reason why. He came not hither of his full free will; such as I am, I am his best protector, and I will see him justly used. There be too many mysteries; I do begin to weary of the game!'

But as Dick was speaking, a heavy hand fell on his shoulder. It was Bennet Hatch that had come unperceived behind him. With a jerk of his thumb, the retainer dismissed his wife.

'Friend Dick,' he said, as soon as they were alone, 'are ye a moonstruck natural? An ye leave not certain things in peace, ye were better in the salt sea than here in Tunstall Moat House. Y' have questioned me; y' have baited Carter; y' have frighted the jack-priest with hints. Bear ye more wisely, fool; and even now, when Sir Daniel calleth you, show me a smooth face, for the love of wisdom. Y'are to be sharply questioned. Look to your answers.'

'Hatch,' returned Dick, 'in all this I smell a guilty conscience.'

'An ye go not the wiser, ye will soon smell blood,' replied Bennet. 'I do but warn you. And here cometh one to call you.'

And indeed, at that very moment, a messenger came across the court to summon Dick into the presence of Sir Daniel.

CHAPTER TWO

The Two Oaths

SIR DANIEL was in the hall; there he paced angrily before the fire, awaiting Dick's arrival. None was by, except Sir Oliver, and he sat discreetly backward, thumbing and muttering over his breviary.

'Y' have sent for me, Sir Daniel?' said young Shelton.

'I have sent for you, indeed,' replied the knight.

'For what cometh to mine ears? Have I been to you so heavy a guardian that ye make haste to credit ill of me? Or sith that ye see me, for the nonce, some worsted, do ye think to quit my party? By the mass, your father was not so! Those he was near, those he stood by, come wind or weather. But you, Dick, y'are a fair-day friend, it seemeth, and now seek to clear yourself of your allegiance.'

'An't please you, Sir Daniel, not so,' returned Dick firmly. 'I am grateful and faithful, where gratitude and faith are due. And before more is said, I thank you, and I thank Sir Oliver; y' have great claims upon me, both none can have more; I were a hound if I forgot them.'

'It is well,' said Sir Daniel; and then, rising into anger: 'Gratitude and faith are words, Dick Shelton,' he continued; 'but I look to deeds. In this hour of my peril, when my name is attainted, when my lands are forfeit, when this wood is full of men that hunger and thirst for my destruction, what doth gratitude? what doth faith? I have but a little company remaining; is it grateful or faithful to poison me their hearts with your insidious whisperings? Save me from such gratitude! But, come, now, what is it ye wish? Speak; we are here to answer. If ye have aught against me, stand forth and say it.'

'Sir,' replied Dick, 'my father fell when I was yet a child. It hath come to mine ears that he was foully done by. It hath come to mine ears – for I will not dissemble – that ye had a hand in his undoing. And in all verity, – I shall not be at peace in mine own mind, nor very clear to help you, till I have certain resolution of these doubts.'

Sir Daniel sat down in a deep settle. He took his chin in his hand and looked at Dick fixedly.

'And ye think I would be guardian to the man's son that I had murdered?' he asked.

'Nay,' said Dick, 'pardon me if I answer churlishly; but indeed ye know right well a wardship is most profitable. All these years have ye not enjoyed my revenues, and led my men? Have ye not still my marriage? I wot not what it may be worth – it is worth something. Pardon me again; but if ye were base enough to slay a man under trust, here were, perhaps, reasons enough to move you to the lesser baseness.'

'When I was a lad of your years,' returned Sir Daniel, sternly, 'my mind had not so turned upon suspicions. And Sir Oliver here,' he added, 'why should he, a priest, be guilty of this act?'

'Nay, Sir Daniel,' said Dick, 'but where the master biddeth, there will the dog go. It is well known this priest is but your instrument. I speak very freely; the time is not for courtesies. Even as I speak, so would I be answered. And answer get I none! Ye but put more questions. I rede ye beware, Sir Daniel; for in this way ye will but nourish and not satisfy my doubts.'

'I will answer you fairly, Master Richard,' said the knight. 'Were I to pretend ye have not stirred my wrath, I were no honest man. But I will be just even in anger. Come to me with these words when y'are grown and come to man's estate, and I am no longer your guardian, and so helpless to resent them. Come to me then, and I will answer you as ye merit, with a buffet in the mouth. Till then ye have two courses: either swallow me down these insults, keep a silent tongue, and fight in the meanwhile for the man that fed and fought for your infancy; or else – the door standeth open, the woods are full of mine enemies – go.'

The spirit with which these words were uttered, the looks with which they were accompanied, staggered Dick;

and yet he could not but observe that he had got no answer.

'I desire nothing more earnestly, Sir Daniel, than to believe you,' he replied. 'Assure me ye are free from this.'

'Will ye take my word of honour, Dick?' inquired the knight.

'That would I,' answered the lad.

'I give it you,' returned Sir Daniel. 'Upon my word of honour, upon the eternal welfare of my spirit, and as I shall answer for my deeds hereafter, I had no hand nor portion in your father's death.'

He extended his hand, and Dick took it eagerly. Neither of them observed the priest, who, at the pronunciation of that solemn and false oath, had half risen from his seat in an agony of horror and remorse.

'Ah,' cried Dick, 'ye must find it in your great-heartedness to pardon me! I was a churl indeed to doubt of you. But ye have my hand upon it; I will doubt no more.'

'Nay, Dick,' replied Sir Daniel, 'y' are forgiven. Ye know not the world and its calumnious nature.'

'I was the more to blame,' added Dick, 'in that the rogues pointed, not directly at yourself, but at Sir Oliver.'

As he spoke, he turned towards the priest, and paused in the middle of the last word. This tall, ruddy, corpulent, high-stepping man had fallen, you might say, to pieces; his colour was gone, his limbs were relaxed, his lips stammered prayers; and now, when Dick's eyes were fixed upon him suddenly, he cried out aloud, like some wild animal, and buried his face in his hands.

Sir Daniel was by him in two strides, and shook him fiercely by the shoulder. At the same moment Dick's suspicions reawakened.

'Nay,' he said, 'Sir Oliver may swear also. 'Twas him they accused.'

'He shall swear,' said the knight.

Sir Oliver speechlessly waved his arms.

'Ay, by the mass! but ye shall swear,' cried Sir Daniel, beside himself with fury. 'Here, upon this book, ye shall swear,' he continued, picking up the breviary, which had fallen to the ground. 'What! Ye make me doubt you! Swear, I say; swear!'

But the priest was still incapable of speech. His terror of Sir Daniel, his terror of perjury, risen to about an equal height, strangled him.

And just then, through the high stained-glass window of the hall, a black arrow crashed, and struck, and stuck quivering in the midst of the long table.

Sir Oliver, with a loud scream, fell fainting on the rushes; while the knight, followed by Dick, dashed into the court and up the nearest corkscrew stair to the battlements. The sentries were all on the alert. The sun shone quietly on green lawns dotted with trees, and on the wooded hills of the forest which enclosed the view. There was no sign of a besieger.

'Whence came that shot?' asked the knight.

'From yonder clump, Sir Daniel,' returned a sentinel.

The knight stood a little, musing. Then he turned to Dick. 'Dick,' he said, 'keep me an eye upon these men; I leave you in charge here. As for the priest, he shall clear himself, or I will know the reason why. I do almost begin to share in your suspicions. He shall swear, trust me, or we shall prove him guilty.'

Dick answered somewhat coldly, and the knight, giving him a piercing glance, hurriedly returned to the hall. His first glance was for the arrow. It was the first of these missiles he had seen, and as he turned it to and fro, the dark hue of it touched him with some fear. Again there was some writing: one word – 'Earthed.'

'Ay,' he broke out, 'they know I am home, then. Earthed! Ay, but there is not a dog among them fit to dig me out.'

Sir Oliver had come to himself, and now scrambled to his feet.

'Alack, Sir Daniel' he moaned, 'y' 'ave sworn a dread oath; y' are doomed to the end of time.'

'Ay,' returned the knight, 'I have sworn an oath, indeed, thou chucklehead; but thyself shalt swear a greater. It shall be on the blessed cross of Holywood. Look to it; get the words ready. It shall be sworn to-night.'

'Now, may Heaven lighten you!' replied the priest; 'may Heaven incline your heart from this iniquity!'

'Look you, my good father,' said Sir Daniel, 'if y' are for piety, I say no more; ye begin late, that is all. But if y' are in any sense bent upon wisdom, hear me. This lad beginneth to irk me like a wasp. I have a need for him, for I would sell his marriage. But I tell you, in all plainness, if that he continue to weary me, he shall go join his father. I give orders now to change him to the chamber above the chapel. If that ye can swear your innocency with a good solid oath and an assured countenance, it is well; the lad will be at peace a little, and I will spare him. If that ye stammer or blench, or anyways boggle at the swearing, he will not believe you; and by the mass, he shall die. There is for your thinking on.'

'The chamber above the chapel!' gasped the priest.

'That same,' replied the knight. 'So if ye desire to save him, save him; and if ye desire not, prithee, go to, and let me be at peace! For an I had been a hasty man, I would already have put my sword through you, for your intolerable cowardice and folly. Have ye chosen? Say!'

'I have chosen,' said the priest. 'Heaven pardon me, I will do evil for good. I will swear for the lad's sake.'

'So is it best!' said Sir Daniel. 'Send for him, then, speedily. Ye shall see him alone. Yet I shall have an eye on you. I shall be here in the panel room.'

The knight raised the arras and let it fall again behind him. There was the sound of a spring opening; then followed the creaking of trod stairs.

Sir Oliver, left alone, cast a timorous glance upward at the arras-covered wall, and crossed himself with every appearance of terror and contrition.

'Nay, if he is in the chapel room,' the priest murmured, 'were it at my soul's cost, I must save him.'

Three minutes later, Dick, who had been summoned by another messenger, found Sir Oliver standing by the hall table, resolute and pale.

'Richard Shelton,' he said, 'ye have required an oath from me. I might complain, I might deny you; but my heart is moved toward you for the past, and I will even

content you as ye choose. By the true cross of Holywood,
I did not slay your father.'

'Sir Oliver,' returned Dick, 'when first we read John
Amend-All's paper, I was convinced of so much. But
suffer me to put two questions. Ye did not slay him;
granted. But had ye no hand in it?'

'None,' said Sir Oliver. And at the same time he began
to contort his face, and signal with his mouth and eyebrows,
like one who desired to convey a warning, yet dared not
utter a sound.

Dick regarded him in wonder; then he turned and looked
all about him at the empty hall.

'What make ye?' he inquired.

'Why, naught,' returned the priest, hastily smoothing
his countenance. 'I make naught; I do but suffer; I am
sick. I – I – prithee, Dick, I must begone. On the true
cross of Holywood, I am clean innocent alike of violence
or treachery. Content ye, good lad. Farewell!'

And he made his escape from the apartment with unusual
alacrity.

Dick remained rooted to the spot, his eyes wandering
about the room, his face a changing picture of various
emotions, wonder, doubt, suspicion, and amusement.
Gradually, as his mind grew clearer, suspicion took the
upper hand, and was succeeded by certainty of the worst.
He raised his head, and, as he did so, violently started.
High upon the wall there was the figure of a savage hunter
woven in the tapestry. With one hand he held a horn to
his mouth; in the other he brandished a stout spear. His
face was dark, for he was meant to represent an African.

Now, here was what had startled Richard Shelton. The
sun had moved away from the hall windows, and at the
same time the fire had blazed up high on the wide hearth,
and shed a changeful glow upon the roof and hangings. In
this light the figure of the black hunter had winked at him
with a white eyelid.

He continued staring at the eye. The light shone upon
it like a gem; it was liquid, it was alive. Again the white
eyelid closed upon it for a fraction of a second, and the
next moment it was gone.

There could be no mistake. The live eye that had been watching him through a hole in the tapestry was gone. The firelight no longer shone on a reflecting surface.

And instantly Dick awoke to the terrors of his position. Hatch's warning, the mute signals of the priest, this eye that had observed him from the wall, ran together in his mind. He saw he had been put upon his trial, that he had once more betrayed his suspicions, and that, short of some miracle, he was lost.

'If I cannot get me forth out of this house,' he thought, 'I am a dead man! And this poor Matcham, too – to what a cockatrice's nest have I not led him!'

He was still so thinking, when there came one in haste, to bid him help in changing his arms, his clothing, and his two or three books, to a new chamber.

'A new chamber?' he repeated. 'Wherefore so? What chamber?'

'' 'Tis one above the chapel,' answered the messenger.

'It hath stood long empty,' said Dick, musing. 'What manner of room is it?'

'Nay, a brave room,' returned the man. 'But yet' – lowering his voice – 'they call it haunted.'

'Haunted?' repeated Dick, with a chill. 'I have not heard of it. Nay, then, and by whom?'

The messenger looked about him; and then, in a low whisper, 'By the sacrist of St John's,' he said. 'They had him there to sleep one night, and in the morning – whew! – he was gone. The devil had taken him, they said; the more betoken, he had drunk late the night before.'

Dick followed the man with black forebodings.

CHAPTER THREE

The Room over the Chapel

FROM THE battlements nothing further was observed. The sun journeyed eastward, and at last went down; but to the eyes of all these eager sentinels, no living thing appeared in the neighbourhood of Tunstall House.

When the night was at length fairly come, Throgmorton was led to a room overlooking an angle of the moat. Thence he was lowered with every precaution; the ripple of his swimming was audible for a brief period; then a black figure was observed to land by the branches of a willow and crawl away among the grass. For some half-hour Sir Daniel and Hatch stood eagerly giving ear; but all remained quiet. The messenger had got away in safety.

Sir Daniel's brow grew clearer. He turned to Hatch.

'Bennet,' said he, 'this John Amend-All is no more than a man, ye see. He sleepeth. We will make a good end of him, go to!'

All the afternoon and evening Dick had been ordered hither and thither, one command following another, till he was bewildered with the number and the hurry of commissions. All that time he had seen no more of Sir Oliver, and nothing of Matcham; and yet both the priest and the young lad ran continually in his mind. It was now his chief purpose to escape from Tunstall Moat House as speedily as might be; and yet, before he went, he desired a word with both of these.

At length, with a lamp in one hand, he mounted to his new apartment. It was large, low, and somewhat dark. The window looked upon the moat, and although it was so high up, it was heavily barred. The bed was luxurious, with one pillow of down, and one of lavender, and a red coverlet worked in a pattern of roses. All about the walls were cupboards, locked and padlocked, and concealed from view by hangings of dark-coloured arras. Dick made the round, lifting the arras, sounding the panels, seeking vainly to open the cupboards. He assured himself that the door was strong, and the bolt solid; then he set down his lamp upon a bracket, and once more looked all around.

For what reason had he been given this chamber? It was larger and finer than his own. Could it conceal a snare? Was there a secret entrance? Was it indeed haunted? His blood ran a little chilly in his veins.

Immediately over him the heavy foot of a sentry trod the leads. Below him, he knew, was the arched roof of the chapel; and next to the chapel was the hall. Certainly there was a secret passage in the hall; the eye that had watched him from the arras gave him proof of that. Was it not more than probable that the passage extended to the chapel, and if so, that it had an opening in his room?

To sleep in such a place, he felt, would be foolhardy. He made his weapons ready, and took his position in a corner of the room behind the door. If ill was intended, he would sell his life dear.

The sound of many feet, the challenge, and the password sounded overhead along the battlements; the watch was being changed.

And just then there came a scratching at the door of the chamber; it grew a little louder; then a whisper.

'Dick, Dick, it is I!'

Dick ran to the door, drew the bolt, and admitted Matcham. He was very pale, and carried a lamp in one hand and a drawn dagger in the other.

'Shut me the door,' he whispered. 'Swift, Dick! This house is full of spies; I hear their feet follow me in the corridors; I hear them breathe behind the arras.'

'Well, content you,' returned Dick, 'it is closed. We are safe for this while, if there be safety anywhere within these walls. But my heart is glad to see you. By the mass, lad, I thought ye were sped. Where hid ye?'

'It matters not,' returned Matcham. 'Since we be met, it matters not. But, Dick, are your eyes open: Have they told you of to-morrow's doings?'

'Not they,' replied Dick. 'What make they tomorrow?'

'To-morrow, or to-night, I know not,' said the other; 'but one time or other, Dick, they do intend upon your life. I had the proof of it: I have heard them whisper; nay, they as good as told me.'

'Ay,' returned Dick, 'is it so? I had thought as much.'

And he told him the day's occurrences at length.

When it was done, Matcham arose and began, in turn, to examine the apartment.

'No,' he said, 'there is no entrance visible. Yet 'tis a pure certainty there is one. Dick, I will stay by you. An y' are to die, I will die with you. And I can help – look! I have stolen a dagger – I will do my best! And meanwhile, an ye know of any issue, any sally-port we could get opened, or any window that we might descend by, I will most joyfully face any jeopardy to flee with you.'

'Jack,' said Dick, 'by the mass, Jack, y' are the best soul, and the truest, and the bravest in all England! Give me your hand, Jack.'

And he grasped the other's hand in silence.

'I will tell you,' he resumed. 'There is a window out of which the messenger descended; the rope should still be in the chamber. 'Tis a hope.'

'Hist!' said Matcham.

Both gave ear. There was a sound below the floor; then it paused, and then began again.

'Some one walketh in the room below,' whispered Matcham.

'Nay,' returned Dick, 'there is no room below; we are above the chapel. It is my murderer in the secret passage. Well, let him come: it shall go hard with him!' And he ground his teeth.

'Blow me the lights out,' said the other. 'Perchance he will betray himself.'

They blew out both the lamps and lay still as death. The footfalls underneath were very soft, but they were clearly audible. Several times they came and went; and then there was a loud jar of a key turning in a lock, followed by a considerable silence.

Presently the steps began again, and then, all of a sudden,

a chink of light appeared in the planking of the room in a far corner. It widened; a trap-door was being opened, letting in a gush of light. They could see the strong hand pushing it up; and Dick raised his cross-bow, waiting for the head to follow.

But now there came an interruption. From a distant corner of the Moat House shouts began to be heard, and first one voice, and then several, crying aloud upon a name. This noise had plainly disconcerted the murderer, for the trap-door was silently lowered to its place, and the steps hurriedly returned, passed once more close below the lads, and died away in the distance.

Here was a moment's respite. Dick breathed deep, and then, and not till then, he gave ear to the disturbance which had interrupted the attack, and which was now rather increasing than diminishing. All about the Moat House feet were running, doors were opening and slamming, and still the voice of Sir Daniel towered above all this bustle, shouting for 'Joanna.'

'Joanna!' repeated Dick. 'Why, who the murrain should this be? Here is no Joanna, nor ever hath been. What meaneth it?'

Matcham was silent. He seemed to have drawn further away. But only a little faint starlight entered by the window, and at the far end of the apartment, where the pair were, the darkness was complete.

'Jack,' said Dick, 'I wot not where ye were all day. Saw ye this Joanna?'

'Nay,' returned Matcham, 'I saw her not.'

'Nor heard tell of her?' he pursued.

The steps drew nearer. Sir Daniel was still roaring the name of Joanna from the courtyard.

'Did ye hear of her?' repeated Dick.

'I heard of her,' said Matcham.

'How your voice twitters! What aileth you?' said Dick. ' 'Tis a most excellent good fortune, this Joanna; it will take their minds from us.'

'Dick,' cried Matcham, 'I am lost; we are both lost! Let us flee if there be yet time. They will not rest till they have found me. Or, see! let me go forth; when they have found me, ye may flee. Let me forth, Dick – good Dick, let me away!'

She was groping for the bolt, when Dick at last comprehended.

'By the mass!' he cried, 'y' are no Jack; y' are Joanna Sedley; y' are the maid that would not marry me!'

The girl paused, and stood silent and motionless. Dick, too, was silent for a little; then he spoke again.

'Joanna,' he said, 'y' 'ave saved my life, and I have saved yours; and we have seen blood flow, and been friends and enemies – ay, and I took my belt to thrash you; and all that time I thought ye were a boy. But now death has me, and my time's out, and before I die I must say this: Y' are the best maid and the bravest under heaven, and, if only I could live, I would marry you blithely; and, live or die, I love you.'

She answered nothing.

'Come,' he said, 'speak up, Jack. Come, be a good maid, and say ye love me!'

'Why, Dick,' she cried, 'would I be here?'

'Well, see ye here,' continued Dick, 'an we but escape whole, we'll marry; and an we're to die, we die, and there's an end on't. But now that I think, how found ye my chamber?'

'I asked it of Dame Hatch,' she answered.

'Well, the dame's staunch,' he answered; 'she'll not tell upon you. We have time before us.'

And just then, as if to contradict his words, feet came down the corridor, and a fist beat roughly on the door.

'Here!' cried a voice. 'Open, Master Dick; open!'

Dick neither moved nor answered.

'It is all over,' said the girl; and she put her arms about Dick's neck.

One after another, men came trooping to the door. Then Sir Daniel arrived himself, and there was a sudden cessation of the noise.

'Dick,' cried the knight, 'be not an ass. The Seven Sleepers had been awake ere now. We know she is within there. Open, then, the door, man.'

Dick was again silent.

'Down with it,' said Sir Daniel. And immediately his followers fell savagely upon the door with foot and fist. Solid as it was, and strongly bolted, it would soon have given way, but once more fortune interfered. Over the thunderstorm of blows the cry of a sentinel was heard; it was followed by another; shouts ran along the battlements, shouts answered out of the wood. In the first moment of alarm it sounded as if the foresters were carrying the Moat House by assault. And Sir Daniel and his men, desisting instantly from their attack upon Dick's chamber, hurried to defend the walls.

'Now,' cried Dick, 'we are saved.'

He seized the great old bedstead with both hands, and bent himself in vain to move it.

'Help me, Jack. For your life's sake, help me stoutly!' he cried.

Between them, with a huge effort, they dragged the big frame of oak across the room, and thrust it endwise to the chamber door.

'Ye do but make things worse,' said Joanna, sadly. 'He will then enter by the trap.'

'Not so,' replied Dick. 'He durst not tell his secret to so many. It is by the trap that we shall flee. Hark! The attack is over. Nay, it was none!'

It had, indeed, been no attack; it was the arrival of another party of stragglers from the defeat of Risingham that had disturbed Sir Daniel. They had run the gauntlet under cover of the darkness; they had been admitted by the great gate; and now, with a great stamping of hoofs and jingle of accoutrements and arms, they were dismounting in the court.

'He will return anon,' said Dick. 'To the trap!'

He lighted a lamp, and they went together into the corner of the room. The open chink through which some light still glittered was easily discovered, and, taking a stout sword from his small armoury, Dick thrust it deep into the seam, and weighed strenuously on the hilt. The trap moved, gaped a little, and at length came widely open. Seizing it with their hands, the two young folk threw it back. It disclosed a few steps descending, and at the foot of them, where the would-be murderer had left it, a burning lamp.

'Now,' said Dick, 'go first and take the lamp. I will follow to close the trap.'

So they descended one after the other, and as Dick lowered the trap, the blows began once again to thunder on the panels of the door.

CHAPTER FOUR

The Passage

THE passage in which Dick and Joanna now found themselves was narrow, dirty, and short. At the other end of it,
a door stood partly open; the same door, without doubt,
that they had heard the man unlocking. Heavy cobwebs
hung from the roof, and the paved flooring echoed hollow
under the lightest tread.

Beyond the door there were two branches, at right angles.
Dick chose one of them at random, and the pair hurried,
with echoing footsteps, along the hollow of the chapel roof.
The top of the arched ceiling rose like a whale's back in the
dim glimmer of the lamp. Here and there were spyholes,
concealed, on the other side, by the carving of the cornice;
and looking down through one of these, Dick saw the paved
floor of the chapel – the altar, with its burning tapers – and
stretched before it on the steps, the figure of Sir Oliver
praying with uplifted hands.

At the other end, they descended a few steps. The passage
grew narrower; the wall upon one hand was now of wood;
the noise of people talking, and a faint flickering of lights,
came through the interstices; and presently they came to
a round hole about the size of a man's eye, and Dick,
looking down through it, beheld the interior of the hall,
and some half a dozen men sitting, in their jacks, about
the table, drinking deep and demolishing a venison pie.
These were certainly some of the late arrivals.

'Here is no help,' said Dick. 'Let us try back.'

'Nay,' said Joanna; 'maybe the passage goeth farther.'

And she pushed on. But a few yards farther the passage
ended at the top of a short flight of steps; and it became
plain that, as long as the soldiers occupied the hall, escape
was impossible upon that side.

They retraced their steps with all imaginable speed, and set forward to explore the other branch. It was exceedingly narrow, scarce wide enough for a large man; and it led them continually up and down by little breakneck stairs, until even Dick had lost all notion of his whereabouts.

At length it grew both narrower and lower; the stairs continued to descend; the walls on either hand became damp and slimy to the touch; and far in front of them they heard the squeaking and scuttling of the rats.

'We must be in the dungeons,' Dick remarked.

'And still there is no outlet,' added Joanna.

'Nay, but an outlet there must be!' Dick answered.

Presently, sure enough, they came to a sharp angle, and then the passage ended in a flight of steps. On the top of that there was a solid flag of stone by way of trap, and to this they both set their backs. It was immovable.

'Some one holdeth it,' suggested Joanna.

'Not so,' said Dick; 'for were a man strong as ten, he must still yield a little. But this resisteth like dead rock. There is a weight upon the trap. Here is no issue; and, by my sooth, good Jack, we are here as fairly prisoners as though the gyves were on our ankle-bones. Sit ye then down, and let us talk. After a while we shall return, when perchance they shall be less carefully upon their guard; and who knoweth? we may break out and stand a chance. But, in my poor opinion, we are as good as shent.'

'Dick!' she cried, 'alas the day that ever ye should have seen me! For like a most unhappy and unthankful maid, it is I have led you hither.'

'What cheer!' returned Dick. 'It was all written, and that which is written, willy nilly, cometh still to pass. But tell me a little what manner of a maid ye are, and how ye came into Sir Daniel's hands; that will do better than to bemoan yourself, whether for your sake or mine.'

'I am an orphan, like yourself, of father and mother,' said Joanna; 'and for my great misfortune, Dick, and hitherto for yours, I am a rich marriage. My Lord Foxham had me to ward; yet it appears Sir Daniel bought the marriage of me from the king, and a right dear price he paid for it. So here was I, poor babe, with two great and rich men fighting which should marry me, and I still at nurse! Well, then the world changed, and there was a new chancellor, and Sir Daniel bought the warding of me over the Lord Foxham's head. And then the world changed again, and Lord Foxham bought my marriage over Sir Daniel's; and from then to now it went on ill betwixt the two of them. But still Lord Foxham kept me in his hands, and was a good lord to me. And at last I was to be married – or sold, if ye like it better. Five hundred pounds Lord Foxham was to get for me. Hamley was the groom's name, and to-morrow, Dick, of all days in the year, was I to be betrothed. Had it not come to Sir Daniel, I had been wedded, sure – and never seen thee, Dick – dear Dick!'

And here she took his hand, and kissed it, with the prettiest grace; and Dick drew her hand to him and did the like.

'Well,' she went on, 'Sir Daniel took me unawares in the garden, and made me dress in these men's clothes, which is a deadly sin for a woman; and, besides, they fit me not. He rode with me to Kettley, as ye saw, telling me I was to marry you; but I, in my heart, made sure I would marry Hamley in his teeth.'

'Ay!' cried Dick, 'and so ye loved this Hamley!'

'Nay,' replied Joanna, 'not I. I did but hate Sir Daniel. And then, Dick, ye helped me, and ye were right kind, and very bold, and my heart turned towards you in mine own despite; and now, if we can in any way compass it, I would marry you with right goodwill. And if, by cruel destiny, it may not be, still ye'll be dear to me. While my heart beats, it'll be true to you.'

'And I,' said Dick, 'that never cared a straw for any manner of woman until now, I took to you when I thought ye were a boy. I had a pity to you, and knew not why. When I would have belted you, the hand failed me. But when ye owned ye were a maid, Jack – for still I will call you Jack – I made sure ye were the maid for me. Hark!' he said, breaking off – 'one cometh.'

And indeed a heavy tread was now audible in the echoing passage, and the rats again fled in armies.

Dick reconnoitred his position. The sudden turn gave

him a post of vantage. He could thus shoot in safety from the cover of the wall. But it was plain the light was too near him, and, running some way forward, he set down the lamp in the middle of the passage, and then returned to watch.

Presently, at the far end of the passage, Bennet hove in sight. He seemed to be alone, and he carried in his hand a burning torch, which made him the better mark.

'Stand, Bennet!' cried Dick. 'Another step and y' are dead.'

'So here ye are,' returned Hatch, peering forward into the darkness. 'I see you not. Aha! y' 'ave done wisely, Dick; y' 'ave put your lamp before you. By my sooth, but, though it was done to shoot my own knave body, I do rejoice to see ye profit of my lessons! And now, what make ye? what seek ye here? Why would ye shoot upon an old, kind friend? And have ye the young gentlewoman there?'

'Nay, Bennet, it is I should question and you answer,' replied Dick. 'Why am I in this jeopardy of my life? Why do men come privily to slay me in my bed? Why am I now fleeing in mine own guardian's strong house, and from the friends that I have lived among and never injured?'

'Master Dick, Master Dick,' said Bennet, 'what told I you? Y' are brave, but the most uncrafty lad that I can think upon!'

'Well,' returned Dick, 'I see ye know all, and that I am doomed indeed. It is well. Here, where I am, I stay. Let Sir Daniel get me out if he be able!'

Hatch was silent for a space.

'Hark ye,' he began, 'I return to Sir Daniel, to tell him where ye are, and how posted; for, in truth, it was to that end he sent me. But you, if ye are no fool, had best be gone ere I return.'

'Begone!' repeated Dick. 'I would begone already, an' I wist how. I cannot move the trap.'

'Put me your hand into the corner, and see what ye find there,' replied Bennet. 'Throgmorton's rope is still in the brown chamber. Fare ye well.'

And Hatch, turning upon his heel, disappeared again into the windings of the passage.

Dick instantly returned for his lamp, and proceeded to act upon the hint. At one corner of the trap there was a deep cavity in the wall. Pushing his arm into the aperture, Dick found an iron bar, which he thrust vigorously upwards. There followed a snapping noise, and the slab of stone instantly started in its bed.

They were free of the passage. A little exercise of strength easily raised the trap; and they came forth into a vaulted chamber, opening on one hand upon the court, where one or two fellows, with bare arms, were rubbing down the horses of the last arrivals. A torch or two, each stuck in an iron ring against the wall, changefully lit up the scene.

CHAPTER FIVE

How Dick Changed Sides

DICK, BLOWING OUT his lamp lest it should attract attention, led the way upstairs and along the corridor. In the brown chamber the rope had been made fast to the frame of an exceedingly heavy and ancient bed. It had not been detached, and Dick, taking the coil to the window, began to lower it slowly and cautiously into the darkness of the night. Joan stood by; but as the rope lengthened, and still Dick continued to pay it out, extreme fear began to conquer her resolution.

'Dick,' she said, 'is it so deep? I may not essay it. I should infallibly fall, good Dick.'

It was just at the delicate moment of the operations that she spoke. Dick started; the remainder of the coil slipped from his grasp, and the end fell with a splash into the moat. Instantly, from the battlement above, the voice of a sentinel cried, 'Who goes?'

'A murrain!' cried Dick. 'We are paid now! Down with you – take the rope.'

'I cannot,' she cried, recoiling.

'An ye cannot, no more can I,' said Shelton. 'How can I swim the moat without you? Do ye desert me, then?'

'Dick,' she gasped, 'I cannot. The strength is gone from me.'

'By the mass, then, we are all shent!' he shouted, stamping with his foot; and then, hearing steps, he ran to the room door and sought to close it.

Before he could shoot the bolt, strong arms were thrusting it back upon him from the other side. He struggled for a second; then, feeling himself overpowered, ran back to the window. The girl had fallen against the wall in the embrasure of the window; she was more than half insensible; and when he tried to raise her in his arms, her body was limp and unresponsive.

At the same moment the men who had forced the door against him laid hold upon him. The first he poniarded at a blow, and the others falling back for a second in some disorder, he profited by the chance, bestrode the window-sill, seized the cord in both hands, and let his body slip.

The cord was knotted, which made it the easier to descend; but so furious was Dick's hurry, and so small his experience of such gymnastics, that he span round and round in mid-air like a criminal upon a gibbet, and now beat his head, and now bruised his hands, against the rugged stonework of the wall. The air roared in his ears; he saw the stars overhead, and the reflected stars below him in the moat, whirling like dead leaves before the tempest. And then he lost hold and fell, and soused head over ears into the icy water.

When he came to the surface his hand encountered the rope, which, newly lightened of his weight, was swinging wildly to and fro. There was a red glow overhead, and looking up, he saw, by the light of several torches and a cresset full of burning coals, the battlements lined with faces. He saw the men's eyes turning hither and thither in quest of him; but he was too far below, the light reached him not, and they looked in vain.

And now he perceived that the rope was considerably too long, and he began to struggle as well as he could towards the other side of the moat, still keeping his head above water. In this way he got much more than halfway over; indeed the bank was almost within reach, before the rope began to draw him back by its own weight. Taking his courage in both hands, he left go and made a leap for the trailing sprays of willow that had already, that same evening, helped Sir Daniel's messenger to land. He went down, rose again, sank a second time, and then his hand caught a branch, and with the speed of thought he had dragged himself into the thick of the tree and clung there, dripping and panting, and still half uncertain of his escape.

But all this had not been done without a considerable splashing, which had so far indicated his position to the men along the battlements. Arrows and quarrels fell thick around him in the darkness, thick like driving hail; and suddenly a torch was thrown down – flared through the air in its swift passage – stuck for a moment on the edge of the bank, where it burned high and lit up its whole surroundings like a bonfire – and then, in a good hour for Dick, slipped off, plumped into the moat, and was instantly extinguished.

It had served its purpose. The marksmen had had time to see the willow, and Dick ensconced among its boughs; and though the lad instantly sprang higher up the bank and ran for his life, he was yet not quick enough to escape a shot. An arrow struck him in the shoulder, another grazed his head.

The pain of his wounds lent him wings; and he had no sooner got upon the level than he took to his heels and ran straight before him in the dark, without a thought for the direction of his flight.

For a few steps missiles followed him, but these soon ceased; and when at length he came to a halt and looked behind, he was already a good way from the Moat House, though he could still see the torches moving to and fro along its battlements.

He leaned against a tree, streaming with blood and water, bruised, wounded, and alone. For all that, he had saved his life for that bout; and though Joanna remained behind in the power of Sir Daniel, he neither blamed himself for an accident that it had been beyond his power to prevent, nor did he augur any fatal consequences to the girl herself. Sir Daniel was cruel, but he was not likely to be cruel to a young gentlewoman who had other protectors, willing and able to bring him to account. It was more probable he would make haste to marry her to some friend of his own.

'Well,' thought Dick, 'between then and now will find me the means to bring that traitor under; for I think, by the mass, that I be now absolved from any gratitude or obligation; and when war is open, there is a fair chance for all.'

In the meanwhile, here he was in a sore plight.

For some little way farther he struggled forward through the forest; but what with the pain of his wounds, the darkness of the night, and the extreme uneasiness and confusion of his mind, he soon became equally unable to guide himself or to continue to push through the close undergrowth, and he was fain at length to sit down and lean his back against a tree.

When he awoke from something betwixt sleep and swooning, the grey of the morning had begun to take the place of night. A little chilly breeze was bustling among the trees, and as he still sat staring before him, only half awake, he became aware of something dark that swung to and fro among the branches, some hundred yards in front of him. The progressive brightening of the day and the return of his own senses at last enabled him to recognise the object. It was a man hanging from the bough of a tall oak. His head had fallen forward on his breast; but at every stronger puff of wind his body span round and round, and his legs and arms tossed, like some ridiculous plaything.

Dick clambered to his feet, and, staggering and leaning on the tree-trunks as he went, drew near to this grim object.

The bough was perhaps twenty feet above the ground, and the poor fellow had been drawn up so high by his executioners that his boots swung clear above Dick's reach; and as his hood had been drawn over his face, it was impossible to recognise the man.

Dick looked about him right and left; and at last he perceived that the other end of the cord had been made fast to the trunk of a little hawthorn which grew, thick with blossom, under the lofty arcade of the oak. With his dagger, which alone remained to him of all his arms, young Shelton severed the rope, and instantly, with a dead thump, the corpse fell in a heap upon the ground.

Dick raised the hood; it was Throgmorton, Sir Daniel's messenger. He had not gone far upon his errand. A paper, which had apparently escaped the notice of the men of the Black Arrow, stuck from the bosom of his doublet, and Dick, pulling it forth, found it was Sir Daniel's letter to Lord Wensleydale.

'Come,' thought he, 'if the world changes yet again, I may have here the wherewithal to shame Sir Daniel – nay, and perchance to bring him to the block.'

And he put the paper in his own bosom, said a prayer over the dead man, and set forth again through the woods.

His fatigue and weakness increased; his ears sang, his steps faltered, his mind at intervals failed him, so low had he been brought by loss of blood. Doubtless he made many deviations from his true path, but at last he came out upon the high-road, not very far from Tunstall hamlet.

A rough voice bid him stand.

'Stand?' repeated Dick. 'By the mass, but I am nearer falling.'

And he suited the action to the word, and fell all his length upon the road.

Two men came forth out of the thicket, each in green forest jerkin, each with long-bow and quiver and short sword.

'Why, Lawless,' said the younger of the two, 'it is young Shelton.'

'Ay, this will be as good as bread to John Amend-All,' returned the other. 'Though, faith, he hath been to the wars. Here is a tear in his scalp that must 'a' cost him many a good ounce of blood.'

'And here,' added Greensheve, 'is a hole in his shoulder that must have pricked him well. Who hath done this, think ye? If it be one of ours, he may all to prayer; Ellis will give him a short shrift and a long rope.'

'Up with the cub,' said Lawless. 'Clap him on my back.'

And then, when Dick had been hoisted to his shoulders, and he had taken the lad's arms about his neck, and got a firm hold of him, the ex-Grey Friar added—

'Keep ye the post, brother Greensheve. I will on with him by myself.'

So Greensheve returned to his ambush on the wayside, and Lawless trudged down the hill, whistling as he went, with Dick, still in a dead faint, comfortably settled on his shoulders.

The sun rose as he came out of the skirts of the wood

and saw Tunstall hamlet straggling up the opposite hill. All seemed quiet, but a strong post of some half a score of archers lay close by the bridge on either side of the road, and, as soon as they perceived Lawless with his burden, began to bestir themselves and set arrow to string like vigilant sentries.

'Who goes?' cried the man in command.

'Will Lawless, by the rood – ye know me as well as your own hand,' returned the outlaw, contemptuously.

'Give the word, Lawless,' returned the other.

'Now, Heaven lighten thee, thou great fool,' replied Lawless. 'Did I not tell it thee myself? But ye are all mad for this playing at soldiers. When I am in the greenwood, give me greenwood ways; and my word for this tide is, "A fig for all mock soldiery!"'

'Lawless, ye but show an ill example; give us the word, fool jester,' said the commander of the post.

'And if I had forgotten it?' asked the other.

'An ye had forgotten it – as I know y' 'ave not – by the mass, I would clap an arrow into your big body,' returned the first.

'Nay, an y' are so ill a jester,' said Lawless, 'ye shall have your word for me. "Duckworth and Shelton" is the word; and here, to the illustration, is Shelton on my shoulders, and to Duckworth do I carry him.'

'Pass, Lawless,' said the sentry.

'And where is John?' asked the Grey Friar.

'He holdeth a court, by the mass, and taketh rents as to the manner born!' cried another of the company.

So it proved. When Lawless got as far up the village as the little inn, he found Ellis Duckworth surrounded by Sir Daniel's tenants, and, by the right of his good company of archers, coolly taking rents, and giving written receipts in return for them. By the faces of the tenants, it was plain how little this proceeding pleased them; for they argued very rightly that they would simply have to pay them twice.

As soon as he knew what had brought Lawless, Ellis dismissed the remainder of the tenants, and, with every mark of interest and apprehension, conducted Dick into an inner chamber of the inn. There the lad's hurts were looked to; and he was recalled, by simple remedies, to consciousness.

'Dear lad,' said Ellis, pressing his hand, 'y' are in a friend's hands that loved your father, and loves you for his sake. Rest ye a little quietly, for ye are somewhat out of case. Then shall ye tell me your story, and betwixt the two of us we shall find a remedy for all.'

A little later in the day, and after Dick had awakened from a comfortable slumber to find himself still very weak, but clearer in mind and easier in body, Ellis returned, and, sitting down by the bedside, begged him, in the name of his father, to relate the circumstance of his escape from Tunstall Moat House. There was something in the strength of Duckworth's frame, in the honesty of his brown face, in the clearness and shrewdness of his eyes, that moved Dick to obey him; and from first to last the lad told him the story of his two days' adventures.

'Well,' said Ellis, when he had done, 'see what the kind saints have done for you, Dick Shelton, not alone to save your body in so numerous and deadly perils, but to bring you into my hands that have no dearer wish than to assist your father's son. Be but true to me – and I see y'are true – and betwixt you and me, we shall bring that false-heart traitor to the death.'

'Will ye assault the house?' asked Dick.

'I were mad, indeed, to think of it,' returned Ellis. 'He hath too much power; his men gather to him; those that gave me the slip last night, and by the mass came in so handily for you – those have made him safe. Nay, Dick, to the contrary, thou and I and my brave bowmen, we must all slip from this forest speedily, and leave Sir Daniel free.'

'My mind misgiveth me for Jack,' said the lad.

'For Jack!' repeated Duckworth. 'Oh, I see, for the wench! Nay, Dick, I promise you, if there come talk of any marriage we shall act at once; till then, or till the time is ripe, we shall all disappear, even like shadows at morning; Sir Daniel shall look east and west, and see none enemies; he shall think, by the mass, that he hath dreamed awhile, and hath now awakened in his bed. But our four eyes, Dick, shall follow him right close, and our four hands – so help us all the army of the saints! – shall bring that traitor low!'

Two days later Sir Daniel's garrison had grown to such a strength that he ventured on a sally, and, at the head of some two score horsemen, pushed without opposition as far as Tunstall hamlet. Not an arrow flew, not a man stirred in the thicket; the bridge was no longer guarded, but stood open to all comers; and as Sir Daniel crossed it, he saw the villagers looking timidly from their doors.

Presently one of them, taking heart of grace, came forward, and with the lowliest salutations, presented a letter to the knight.

His face darkened as he read the contents. It ran thus:

To the most untrue and cruel gentylman, Sir Daniel Brackley, Knyght, These:

I fynde ye were untrue and unkynd fro the first. Ye have my father's blood upon your hands; let be, it will not wasshe. Some day ye shall perish by my procurement, so much I let you to wytte; and I let you to wytte farther, that if ye seek to wed to any other the gentyl-woman, Mistresse Joan Sedley, whom that I am bound upon a great oath to wed myself, the blow will be very swift. The first step therinne will be thy first step to the grave.

RIC. SHELTON

BOOK III
MY LORD FOXHAM

CHAPTER ONE

The House by the Shore

MONTHS HAD passed away since Richard Shelton made his escape from the hands of his guardian. These months had been eventful for England. The party of Lancaster, which was then in the very article of death, had once more raised its head. The Yorkists defeated and dispersed, their leader butchered on the field, it seemed, for a very brief season in the winter following upon the events already recorded, as if the House of Lancaster had finally triumphed over its foes.

The small town of Shoreby-on-the-Till was full of the Lancastrian nobles of the neighbourhood. Earl Risingham was there, with three hundred men-at-arms; Lord Shoreby, with two hundred; Sir Daniel himself, high in favour and once more growing rich on confiscations, lay in a house of his own, on the main street, with three score men. The world had changed indeed.

It was a black, bitter cold evening in the first week of January, with a hard frost, a high wind, and every likelihood of snow before the morning.

In an obscure alehouse in a by-street near the harbour, three or four men sat drinking ale and eating a hasty mess of eggs. They were all likely, lusty, weather-beaten fellows, hard of hand, bold of eye; and though they wore plain tabards, like country ploughmen, even a drunken soldier might have looked twice before he sought a quarrel in such company.

A little apart before the huge fire sat a younger man, almost a boy, dressed in much the same fashion, though it was easy to see by his looks that he was better born, and might have worn a sword, had the time suited.

'Nay,' said one of the men at the table, 'I like it not. Ill will come of it. This is no place for jolly fellows. A jolly fellow loveth open country, good cover, and scarce foes; but here we are shut in a town, girt about with enemies; and, for the bull's-eye of misfortune, see if it snow not ere the morning.'

' 'Tis for Master Shelton there,' said another, nodding his head towards the lad before the fire.

'I will do much for Master Shelton,' returned the first; 'but to come to the gallows for any man – nay, brothers, not that!'

The door of the inn opened, and another man entered hastily and approached the youth before the fire.

'Master Shelton,' he said, 'Sir Daniel goeth forth with a pair of links and four archers.'

Dick (for this was our young friend) rose instantly to his feet.

'Lawless,' he said, 'ye will take John Capper's watch. Greensheve, follow with me. Capper, lead forward. We will follow him this time, an he go to York.'

The next moment they were outside in the dark street, and Capper, the man who had just come, pointed to where two torches flared in the wind at a little distance.

The town was already sound asleep; no one moved upon the streets, and there was nothing easier than to follow the party without observation. The two link-bearers went first; next followed a single man, whose long cloak blew about him in the wind; and the rear was brought up by the four archers, each with his bow upon his arm. They moved at a brisk walk, threading the intricate lanes and drawing nearer to the shore.

'He hath gone each night in this direction?' asked Dick, in a whisper.

'This is the third night running, Master Shelton,' returned Capper, 'and still at the same hour and with the same small following, as though his end were secret.'

Sir Daniel and his six men were now come to the outskirts of the country. Shoreby was an open town, and though the Lancastrian lords who lay there kept a strong guard on the main roads, it was still possible to enter or depart unseen by any of the lesser streets or across the open country.

The lane which Sir Daniel had been following came to an abrupt end. Before him there was a stretch of rough down, and the noise of the sea-surf was audible upon one hand. There were no guards in the neighbourhood, nor any light in that quarter of the town.

Dick and his two outlaws drew a little closer to the object of their chase, and presently, as they came forth from between the houses and could see a little farther upon either hand, they were aware of another torch drawing near from another direction.

'Hey,' said Dick, 'I smell treason.'

Meanwhile, Sir Daniel had come to a full halt. The torches were stuck into the sand, and the men lay down, as if to await the arrival of the other party.

This drew near at a good rate. It consisted of four men only – a pair of archers, a varlet with a link, and a cloaked gentleman walking in their midst.

'Is it you, my lord?' cried Sir Daniel.

'It is I, indeed; and if ever true knight gave proof I am that man,' replied the leader of the second troop; 'for who would not rather face giants, sorcerers, or pagans, than this pinching cold?'

'My lord,' returned Sir Daniel, 'beauty will be the more beholden, misdoubt it not. But shall we forth? for the sooner ye have seen my merchandise, the sooner shall we both get home.'

'But why keep ye her here, good knight?' inquired the other. 'An she be so young, and so fair, and so wealthy, why do ye not bring her forth among her mates? Ye would soon make her a good marriage, and no need to freeze your fingers and risk arrow-shots by going abroad at such untimely seasons in the dark.'

'I have told you, my lord,' replied Sir Daniel, 'the reason thereof concerneth me only. Neither do I purpose to explain it farther. Suffice it, that if ye be weary of your old gossip, Daniel Brackley, publish it abroad that y' are to wed Joanna Sedley, and I give you my word ye will be quit of him right soon. Ye will find him with an arrow in his back.'

Meantime the two gentlemen were walking briskly forward over the down; the three torches going before them, stooping against the wind and scattering clouds of smoke and tufts of flame, and the rear brought up by the six archers.

Close upon the heels of these, Dick followed. He had, of course, heard no word of this conversation; but he had recognised in the second of the speakers old Lord Shoreby himself, a man of an infamous reputation, whom even Sir Daniel affected, in public, to condemn.

Presently they came close down upon the beach. The air smelt salt; the noise of the surf increased; and here, in a large walled garden, there stood a small house of two storeys, with stables and other offices.

The foremost torch-bearer unlocked a door in the wall, and after the whole party had passed into the garden, again closed and locked it on the other side.

Dick and his men were thus excluded from any farther following, unless they should scale the wall and thus put their necks in a trap.

They sat down in a tuft of furze and waited. The red glow of the torches moved up and down and to and fro within the enclosure, as if the link-bearers steadily patrolled the garden.

Twenty minutes passed, and then the whole party issued forth again upon the down; and Sir Daniel and the baron, after an elaborate salutation, separated and turned severally homeward, each with his own following of men and lights.

As soon as the sound of their steps had been swallowed by the wind, Dick got to his feet as briskly as he was able, for he was stiff and aching with the cold.

'Capper, ye will give me a back up,' he said.

They advanced, all three, to the wall; Capper stooped, and Dick, getting upon his shoulders, clambered on to the cope-stone.

'Now, Greensheve,' whispered Dick, 'follow me up here; lie flat upon your face, that ye may be the less seen; and be ever ready to give me a hand if I fall foully on the other side.'

And so saying, he dropped into the garden.

It was all pitch dark; there was no light in the house. The

wind whistled shrill among the poor shrubs, and the surf
beat upon the beach; there was no other sound. Cautiously
Dick footed it forth, stumbling among bushes, and groping
with his hands; and presently the crisp noise of gravel
underfoot told him that he had struck upon an alley.

Here he paused, and taking his cross-bow from where he
kept it concealed under his long tabard, he prepared it for
instant action, and went forward once more with greater
resolution and assurance. The path led him straight to the
group of buildings.

All seemed to be sorely dilapidated: the windows of the
house were secured by crazy shutters; the stables were open
and empty; there was no hay in the hay-loft, no corn in
the corn-box. Anyone would have supposed the place to
be deserted; but Dick had good reason to think otherwise.
He continued his inspection, visiting the offices, trying all
the windows. At length he came round to the sea-side of the
house, and there, sure enough, there burned a pale light in
one of the upper windows.

He stepped back a little way, till he thought he could see
the movement of a shadow on the wall of the apartment.
Then he remembered that, in the stable his groping hand
had rested for a moment on a ladder, and he returned with
all despatch to bring it. The ladder was very short, but yet,
by standing on the topmost round, he could bring his hands
as high as the iron bars of the window; and, seizing these, he
raised his body by main force until his eyes commanded the
interior of the room.

Two persons were within: the first he readily knew to be
Dame Hatch; the second, a tall and beautiful and grave
young lady, in a long, embroidered dress – could that be
Joanna Sedley? his old wood-companion, Jack, whom he
had thought to punish with a belt?

He dropped back again to the top round of the ladder in a
kind of amazement. He had never thought of his sweetheart
as of so superior a being, and he was instantly taken with
a feeling of diffidence. But he had little opportunity for
thought. A low 'Hist!' sounded from close by, and he
hastened to descend the ladder.

'Who goes?' he whispered.

'Greensheve,' came the reply, in tones similarly guarded.

'What want ye?' asked Dick.

'The house is watched, Master Shelton,' returned the outlaw. 'We are not alone to watch it; for even as I lay on my belly on the wall I saw men prowling in the dark, and heard them whistle softly one to the other.'

'By my sooth,' said Dick, 'but this is passing strange! Were they not men of Sir Daniel's?'

'Nay, sir, that they were not,' returned Greensheve; 'for if I have eyes in my head, every man-Jack of them weareth me a white badge in his bonnet, something chequered with dark.'

'White, chequered with dark?' repeated Dick. 'Faith, 'tis a badge I know not. It is none of this country's badges. Well, an that be so, let us slip as quietly forth from this garden as we may; for here we are in an evil posture for defence. Beyond all question there are men of Sir Daniel's in that house, and to be taken between two 'shots is a beggarman's position. Take me this ladder; I must leave it where I found it.'

They returned the ladder to the stable, and groped their way to the place where they had entered.

Capper had taken Greensheve's position on the cope, and now he leaned down his hand, and, first one and then the other, pulled them up.

Cautiously and silently they dropped again upon the other side; nor did they dare to speak until they had returned to their old ambush in the gorse.

'Now, John Capper,' said Dick, 'back with you to Shoreby, even as for your life. Bring me instantly what men ye can collect. Here shall be the rendezvous; or if the men be scattered and the day be near at hand before they muster, let the place be something farther back, and by the entering in of the town. Greensheve and I lie here to watch. Speed ye, John Capper, and the saints aid you to despatch! And now, Greensheve, he continued, as soon as Capper had departed, "let thou and I go round about the garden in a wide circuit. I would fain see whether thine eyes betrayed thee."

Keeping well outwards from the wall, and profiting by every height and hollow, they passed about two sides, beholding nothing. On the third side the garden wall was built close upon the beach, and to preserve the distance necessary to their purpose, they had to go some way down upon the sands. Although the tide was still pretty far out, the surf was so high, and the sands so flat, that at each breaker a great sheet of froth and water came careering over the expanse, and Dick and Greensheve made this part of their inspection wading, now to the ankles, and now as deep as to the knees, in the salt and icy waters of the German Ocean.

Suddenly, against the comparative whiteness of the garden wall, the figure of a man was seen, like a faint Chinese shadow, violently signalling with both arms. As he dropped again to the earth, another arose a little farther on and repeated the same performance. And so, like a silent watchword, these gesticulations made the round of the beleaguered garden.

'They keep good watch,' Dick whispered.

'Let us back to land, good master,' answered Greensheve. 'We stand here too open; for, look ye, when the seas break heavy and white out there behind us, they shall see us plainly against the foam.'

'Ye speak sooth,' returned Dick. 'Ashore with us, right speedily.'

CHAPTER TWO

A Skirmish in the Dark

THOROUGHLY DRENCHED and chilled, the two adventurers returned to their position in the gorse. 'I pray Heaven that Capper make good speed!' said Dick. 'I vow a candle to St Mary of Shoreby if he come before the hour!'

'Y' are in a hurry, Master Dick?' asked Greensheve.

'Ay, good fellow,' answered Dick; 'for in that house lieth my lady, whom I love, and who should these be that lie about her secretly by night? Unfriends for sure!'

'Well,' returned Greensheve, 'an John come speedily, we shall give a good account of them. They are not two score at the outside – I judge so by the spacing of their sentries – and, taken where they are, lying so widely, one score would scatter them like sparrows. And yet, Master Dick, an she be in Sir Daniel's power already, it will little hurt that she should change into another's. Who should these be?'

'I do suspect the Lord of Shoreby,' Dick replied. 'When came they?'

'They began to come, Master Dick,' said Greensheve, 'about the time ye crossed the wall. I had not lain there the space of a minute ere I marked the first of the knaves crawling round the corner.'

The last light had been already extinguished in the little house when they were wading in the wash of the breakers, and it was impossible to predict at what moment the lurking men about the garden wall might make their onslaught. Of two evils, Dick preferred the least. He preferred that Joanna should remain under the guardianship of Sir Daniel rather than pass into the clutches of Lord Shoreby; and his mind was made up, if the house should be assaulted, to come at once to the relief of the besieged.

But the time passed, and still there was no movement.

From quarter of an hour to quarter of an hour the same signal passed about the garden wall, as if the leader desired to assure himself of the vigilance of his scattered followers; but in every other particular the neighbourhood of the little house lay undisturbed.

Presently Dick's reinforcements began to arrive. The night was not yet old before nearly a score of men crouched beside him in the gorse.

Separating these into two bodies, he took the command of the smaller himself, and entrusted the larger to the leadership of Greensheve.

'Now, Kit,' said he to this last, 'take me your men to the near angle of the garden wall upon the beach. Post them strongly, and wait till that ye hear me falling on upon the other side. It is those upon the sea front that I would fain make certain of, for there will be the leader. The rest will run; even let them. And now, lads, let no man draw an arrow; ye will but hurt friends. Take to the steel, and keep to the steel; and if we have the uppermost, I promise every man of you a gold noble when I come to mine estate.'

Out of the odd collection of broken men, thieves, murderers, and ruined peasantry, whom Duckworth had gathered together to serve the purposes of his revenge, some of the boldest and the most experienced in war had volunteered to follow Richard Shelton. The service of watching Sir Daniel's movements in the town of Shoreby had from the first been irksome to their temper, and they had of late begun to grumble loudly and threaten to disperse. The prospect of a sharp encounter and possible spoils restored them to good humour, and they joyfully prepared for battle.

Their long tabards thrown aside, they appeared, some in plain green jerkins, and some in stout leathern jacks; under their hoods many wore bonnets strengthened by iron plates; and for offensive armour, swords, daggers, a few stout boar-spears, and a dozen of bright bills, put them in a posture to engage even regular feudal troops. The bows, quivers, and tabards were concealed among the gorse, and the two bands set resolutely forward.

Dick, when he had reached the other side of the house, posted his six men in a line, about twenty yards from the garden wall, and took position himself a few paces in front. Then they all shouted with one voice, and closed upon the enemy.

These, lying widely scattered, stiff with cold, and taken at unawares, sprang stupidly to their feet, and stood undecided. Before they had time to get their courage about them, or even to form an idea of the number and mettle of their assailants, a similar shout of onslaught sounded in their ears from the far side of the enclosure. Thereupon they gave themselves up for lost and ran.

In this way the two small troops of the men of the Black Arrow closed upon the sea front of the garden wall, and took a part of the strangers, as it were, between two fires; while the whole of the remainder ran for their lives in different directions, and were soon scattered in the darkness.

For all that, the fight was but beginning. Dick's outlaws, although they had the advantage of the surprise, were still considerably outnumbered by the men they had surrounded. The tide had flowed in the meanwhile; the beach was narrowed to a strip; and on this wet field between the surf and the garden wall, there began, in the darkness, a doubtful, furious, and deadly contest.

The strangers were well armed; they fell in silence upon their assailants; and the affray became a series of single combats. Dick, who had come first into the mellay, was engaged by three; the first he cut down at the first blow, but the other two coming upon him hotly he was fain to give ground before their onset. One of these two was a huge fellow, almost a giant for stature, and armed with a two-handed sword, which he brandished like a switch. Against this opponent, with his reach of arm and the length and weight of his weapon, Dick and his bill were quite defenceless; and had the other continued to join vigorously in the attack, the lad must have indubitably fallen. This second man, however, less in stature and slower in his movements, paused for a moment to peer about him in the darkness, and to give ear to the sounds of the battle.

The giant still pursued his advantage, and still Dick fled before him, spying for his chance. Then the huge blade flashed and descended, and the lad, leaping on one side and running in, slashed sideways and upwards with his bill. A roar of agony responded, and before the wounded man could raise his formidable weapon, Dick, twice repeating his blow, had brought him to the ground.

The next moment he was engaged upon more equal terms with his second pursuer. Here there was no great difference in size, and though the man, fighting with sword and dagger against a bill, and being wary and quick of fence, had a certain superiority of arms, Dick more than made it up by his greater agility on foot. Neither at first gained any obvious advantage; but the older man was still insensibly profiting by the ardour of the younger to lead him where he would; and presently Dick found that they had crossed the whole width of the beach, and were now fighting above the knees in the spume and bubble of the breakers. Here his own superior activity was rendered useless; he found himself more or less at the discretion of his foe; yet a little, and he had his back turned upon his own men, and saw that this adroit and skilful adversary was bent upon drawing him farther and farther away.

Dick ground his teeth. He determined to decide the combat instantly; and when the wash of the next wave had ebbed and left them dry, he rushed in, caught a blow upon his bill, and leaped right at the throat of his opponent. The man went down backwards, with Dick still upon the top of him; and the next wave, speedily succeeding the last, buried him below a rush of water.

While he was still submerged, Dick forced his dagger from his grasp, and rose to his feet victorious.

'Yield ye!' he said. 'I give you life.'

'I yield me,' said the other, getting to his knees. 'Ye fight, like a young man, ignorantly and foolhardily; but, by the array of the saints, ye fight bravely!'

Dick turned to the beach. The combat was still raging doubtfully in the night; over the hoarse roar of the breakers steel clanged upon steel, and cries of pain and the shout of battle resounded.

'Lead me to your captain, youth,' said the conquered knight. 'It is fit this butchery should cease.'

'Sir,' replied Dick, 'so far as these brave fellows have

a captain, the poor gentleman who here addresses you is
he.'

'Call off your dogs, then, and I will bid my villains hold,'
returned the other.

There was something noble both in the voice and manner
of his late opponent, and Dick instantly dismissed all fears
of treachery.

'Lay down your arms, men!' cried the stranger knight.
'I have yielded me, upon promise of life.'

The tone of the stranger was one of absolute command,
and almost instantly the din and confusion of the mellay
ceased.

'Lawless,' cried Dick, 'are ye safe?'

'Ay,' cried Lawless, 'safe and hearty.'

'Light me the lantern,' said Dick.

'Is not Sir Daniel here?' inquired the knight.

'Sir Daniel?' echoed Dick. 'Now, by the road, I pray
not. It would go ill with me if he were.'

'Ill with *you*, fair sir?' inquired the other. 'Nay, then, if
ye be not of Sir Daniel's party, I profess I comprehend
no longer. Wherefore, then, fell ye upon mine ambush?
in what quarrel, my young and very fiery friend? to what
earthly purpose? and, to make a clear end of questioning,
to what good gentleman have I surrendered?'

But before Dick could answer, a voice spoke in the
darkness from close by. Dick could see the speaker's
black and white badge, and the respectful salute which
he addressed to his superior.

'My lord,' said he, 'if these gentlemen be unfriends to
Sir Daniel, it is a pity, indeed, we should have been at
blows with them; but it were tenfold greater that either
they or we should linger here. The watchers in the house –
unless they be all dead or deaf – have heard our hammering
this quarter-hour agone; instantly they will have signalled
to the town; and unless we be the livelier in our departure,
we are like to be taken, both of us, by a fresh foe.'

'Hawksley is in the right,' added the lord. 'How please
ye, sir? Whither shall we march?'

'Nay, my lord,' said Dick, 'go where you will for me. I
do begin to suspect we have some ground of friendship, and

if, indeed, I began our acquaintance somewhat ruggedly, I would not churlishly continue. Let us, then, separate, my lord, you laying your right hand in mine; and at the hour and place that ye shall name, let us encounter and agree.'

'Y' are too trustful, boy,' said the other; 'but this time your trust is not misplaced. I will meet you at the point of day at St Bride's Cross. Come, lads, follow?'

The strangers disappeared from the scene with a rapidity that seemed suspicious; and, while the outlaws fell to the congenial task of rifling the dead bodies, Dick made once more the circuit of the garden wall to examine the front of the house. In a little upper loophole of the roof he beheld a light set; and as it would certainly be visible in town from the back windows of Sir Daniel's mansion, he doubted not that this was the signal feared by Hawksley, and that ere long the lances of the Knight of Tunstall would arrive upon the scene.

He put his ear to the ground, and it seemed to him as if he heard a jarring and hollow noise from townward. Back to the beach he went hurrying. But the work was already done; the last body was disarmed and stripped to the skin, and four fellows were already wading seaward to commit it to the mercies of the deep.

A few minutes later, when there debouched out of the nearest lanes of Shoreby some two score horsemen, hastily arrayed and moving at the gallop of their steeds, the neighbourhood of the house beside the sea was entirely silent and deserted.

Meanwhile, Dick and his men had returned to the alehouse of the Goat and Bagpipes to snatch some hours of sleep before the morning tryst.

CHAPTER THREE

St Bride's Cross

ST BRIDE'S CROSS stood a little way back from Shoreby, on the skirts of Tunstall Forest. Two roads met: one, from Holywood across the forest; one, that road from Risingham down which we saw the wrecks of a Lancastrian army fleeing in disorder. Here the two joined issue, and went on together down the hill to Shoreby; and a little back from the point of junction, the summit of a little knoll was crowned by the ancient and weather-beaten cross.

Here, then, about seven in the morning, Dick arrived. It was as cold as ever; the earth was all grey and silver with the hoar-frost, and the day began to break in the east with many colours of purple and orange.

Dick set him down upon the lowest step of the cross, wrapped himself well in his tabard, and looked vigilantly upon all sides. He had not long to wait. Down the road from Holywood a gentleman in very rich and bright armour, and wearing over that a surcoat of the rarest furs, came pacing on a splendid charger. Twenty yards behind him followed a clump of lancers; but these halted as soon as they came in view of the trysting-place, while the gentleman in the fur surcoat continued to advance alone.

His visor was raised, and showed a countenance of great command and dignity, answerable to the richness of his attire and arms. And it was with some confusion of manner that Dick arose from the cross and stepped down the bank to meet his prisoner.

'I thank you, my lord, for your exactitude,' he said louting very low. 'Will it please your lordship to set foot to earth?'

'Are ye here alone, young man?' inquired the other.

'I was not so simple,' answered Dick; 'and, to be plain

with your lordship, the woods upon either hand of this cross lie full of mine honest fellows lying on their weapons.'

'Y' 'ave done wisely,' said the lord. 'It pleaseth me the rather, since last night ye fought foolhardily, and more like a savage Saracen lunatic than any Christian warrior. But it becomes not me to complain that had the undermost.'

'Ye had the undermost indeed, my lord, since ye so fell,' returned Dick; 'but had the waves not holpen me, it was I that should have had the worst. Ye were pleased to make me yours with several dagger marks, which I still carry. And in fine, my lord, methinks I had all the danger, as well as all the profit, of that little blind-man's medley on the beach.'

'Y' are shrewd enough to make light of it, I see,' returned the stranger.

'Nay, my lord, not shrewd,' replied Dick, 'in that I shoot at no advantage to myself. But when, by the light of this new day, I see how stout a knight hath yielded, not to my arms alone, but to fortune, and the darkness, and the surf – and how easily the battle had gone otherwise, with a soldier so untried and rustic as myself – think it not strange, my lord, if I feel confounded with my victory.'

'Ye speak well,' said the stranger. 'Your name?'

'My name, an't like you, is Shelton,' answered Dick.

'Men call me the Lord Foxham,' added the other.

'Then, my lord, and under your good favour, ye are guardian to the sweetest maid in England,' replied Dick; 'and for your ransom, and the ransom of such as were taken with you on the beach, there will be no uncertainty of terms. I pray you, my lord, of your goodwill and charity, yield me the hand of my mistress, Joan Sedley; and take ye, upon the other part, your liberty, the liberty of these your followers, and (if ye will have it) my gratitude and service till I die.'

'But are ye not ward to Sir Daniel? Methought, if y' are Harry Shelton's son, that I had heard it so reported,' said Lord Foxham.

'Will it please you, my lord, to alight? I would fain tell you fully who I am, how situate, and why so bold in my demands. Beseech you, my lord, take place upon these steps, hear me to a full end, and judge me with allowance.'

And so saying, Dick lent a hand to Lord Foxham to dismount; led him up the knoll to the cross; installed him in the place where he had himself been sitting; and, standing respectfully before his noble prisoner, related the story of his fortunes up to the events of the evening before.

Lord Foxham listened gravely, and when Dick had done, 'Master Shelton,' he said, 'ye are a most fortunate-unfortunate young gentleman; but what fortune y' 'ave had, that ye have amply merited; and what unfortune, ye have noways deserved. Be of a good cheer; for ye have made a friend who is devoid neither of power nor favour. For yourself, although it fits not for a person of your birth to herd with outlaws, I must own ye are both brave and honourable; very dangerous in battle, right courteous in peace; a youth of excellent disposition and brave bearing. For your estates, ye will never see them till the world shall change again; so long as Lancaster hath the strong hand, so long shall Sir Daniel enjoy them for his own. For my ward, it is another matter; I had promised her before to a gentleman, a kinsman of my house, one Hamley; the promise is old—'

'Ay, my lord, and now Sir Daniel hath promised her to my Lord Shoreby,' interrupted Dick. 'And his promise, for all it is but young, is still the likelier to be made good.'

' 'Tis the plain truth,' returned his lordship. 'And considering, moreover, that I am your prisoner, upon no better composition than my bare life, and over and above that, that the maiden is unhappily in other hands, I will so far consent. Aid me with your good fellows—'

'My lord,' cried Dick, 'they are these same outlaws that ye blame me for consorting with.'

'Let them be what they will, they can fight,' returned Lord Foxham. 'Help me, then; and if between us we regain the maid, upon my knightly honour, she shall marry you!'

Dick bent his knee before his prisoner; but he, leaping up lightly from the cross, caught the lad up and embraced him like a son.

'Come,' he said, 'an y' are to marry Joan, we must be early friends.'

CHAPTER FOUR

The 'Good Hope'

AN HOUR thereafter, Dick was back at the Goat and Bagpipes, breaking his fast, and receiving the report of his messengers and sentries. Duckworth was still absent from Shoreby; and this was frequently the case, for he played many parts in the world, shared many different interests, and conducted many various affairs. He had founded that fellowship of the Black Arrow, as a ruined man longing for vengeance and money; and yet among those who knew him best, he was thought to be the agent and emissary of the great King-maker of England, Richard, Earl of Warwick.

In his absence, at any rate, it fell upon Richard Shelton to command affairs in Shoreby; and, as he sat at meat, his mind was full of care, and his face heavy with consideration. It had been determined, between him and the Lord Foxham, to make one bold strike that evening, and, by brute force, to set Joanna free. The obstacles, however, were many; and as one after another of his scouts arrived, each brought him more discomfortable news.

Sir Daniel was alarmed by the skirmish of the night before. He had increased the garrison of the house in the garden; but not content with that, he had stationed horsemen in all the neighbouring lanes, so that he might have instant word of any movement. Meanwhile, in the court of his mansion, steeds stood saddled, and the riders, armed at every point, awaited but the signal to ride.

The adventure of the night appeared more and more difficult of execution, till suddenly Dick's countenance lightened.

'Lawless!' he cried, 'you that were a shipman, can ye steal me a ship?'

'Master Dick,' replied Lawless, 'if ye would back me, I would agree to steal York Minster.'

Presently after, these two set forth and descended to the harbour. It was a considerable basin, lying among sand hills, and surrounded with patches of down, ancient ruinous lumber, and tumble-down slums of the town. Many decked ships and many open boats either lay there at anchor, or had been drawn up on the beach. A long duration of bad weather had driven them from the high seas into the shelter of the port; and the great trooping of black clouds, and the cold squalls that followed one another, now with a sprinkling of dry snow, now in a mere swoop of wind, promised no improvement, but rather threatened a more serious storm in the immediate future.

The seamen, in view of the cold and the wind, had for the most part slunk ashore, and were now roaring and singing in the shoreside taverns. Many of the ships already rode unguarded at their anchors; and as the day wore on, and the weather offered no appearance of improvement, the number was continually being augmented. It was to these deserted ships, and, above all, to those of them that lay far out, that Lawless directed his attention; while Dick, seated upon an anchor that was half embedded in the stand, and giving ear, now to the rude, potent, and boding voices of the gale, and now to the hoarse singing of the shipmen in a neighbouring tavern, soon forgot his immediate surroundings and concerns in the agreeable recollection of Lord Foxham's promise.

He was disturbed by a touch upon his shoulder. It was Lawless, pointing to a small ship that lay somewhat by itself, and within but a little of the harbour mouth, where it heaved regularly and smoothly on the entering swell. A pale gleam of winter sunshine fell, at that moment, on the vessel's deck, relieving her against a bank of scowling cloud; and in this momentary glitter Dick could see a couple of men hauling the skiff alongside.

'There, sir,' said Lawless, 'mark ye it well! There is the ship for to-night.'

Presently the skiff put out from the vessel's side, and the

two men, keeping her head well to the wind, pulled lustily for shore. Lawless turned to a loiterer.

'How call ye her?' he asked, pointing to the little vessel.

'They call her the *Good Hope*, of Dartmouth,' replied the loiterer. 'Her captain, Arblaster by name. He pulleth the bow oar in yon skiff.'

This was all that Lawless wanted. Hurriedly thanking the man, he moved round the shore to a certain sandy creek, for which the skiff was heading. There he took up his position, and as soon as they were within earshot, opened fire on the sailors of the *Good Hope*.

'What! Gossip Arblaster!' he cried. 'Why, ye be well met; nay, gossip, ye be right well met, upon the rood! And is that the *Good Hope?* Ay, I would know her among ten thousand! – a sweet shear, a sweet boat! But marry come up, my gossip, will ye drink? I have come into mine estate which doubtless ye remember to have heard on. I am now rich; I have left to sail upon the sea; I do sail now, for the most part, upon spiced ale. Come, fellow; thy hand upon 't! Come, drink with an old shipfellow!'

Skipper Arblaster, a long-faced, elderly, weather-beaten man, with a knife hanging about his neck by a plaited cord, and for all the world like any modern seaman in his gait and bearing, had hung back in obvious amazement and distrust. But the name of an estate, and a certain air of tipsified simplicity and good-fellowship which Lawless very well affected, combined to conquer his suspicious jealousy; his countenance relaxed, and he at once extended his open hand and squeezed that of the outlaw in a formidable grasp.

'Nay,' he said, 'I cannot mind you. But what o' that? I would drink with any man, gossip, and so would my man Tom. Man Tom,' he added, addressing his follower, 'here is my gossip, whose name I cannot mind, but no doubt a very good seaman. Let's go drink with him and his shore friend.'

Lawless led the way, and they were soon seated in an alehouse, which, as it was very new, and stood in an exposed and solitary station, was less crowded than those nearer to the centre of the port. It was but a shed of timber, much like a block-house in the backwoods of to-day, and was coarsely furnished with a press or two, a number of naked benches, and boards set upon barrels to play the part of tables. In the middle, and besieged by half a hundred violent draughts, a fire of wreck-wood blazed and vomited thick smoke.

'Ay, now,' said Lawless, 'here is a shipman's joy – a good fire and a good stiff cup ashore, with foul weather without and an off-sea gale a-snoring in the roof! Here's to the *Good Hope*! May she ride easy!'

'Ay,' said Skipper Arblaster, ''tis good weather to be ashore in, that is sooth. Man Tom, how say ye to that? Gossip, ye speak well, though I can never think upon your name; but ye speak very well. May the *Good Hope* ride easy! Amen!'

'Friend Dickson,' resumed Lawless, addressing his commander, 'ye have certain matters on hand, unless I err? Well, prithee be about them incontinently. For here I be with the choice of all good company, two tough old shipmen; and till that ye return I will go warrant these brave fellows will bide here and drink me cup for cup. We are not like shore-men, we old, tough tarry-Johns!'

'It is well meant,' returned the skipper. 'Ye can go, boy; for I will keep your good friend and my good gossip company till curfew – ay, and by St Mary, till the sun get up again! For, look ye, when a man hath been long enough at sea, the salt getteth me into the clay upon his bones; and let him drink a draw-well, he will never be quenched.'

Thus encouraged upon all hands, Dick rose, saluted his company, and going forth again into the gusty afternoon, got him as speedily as he might to the Goat and Bagpipes. Thence he sent word to my Lord Foxham that, so soon as ever the evening closed, they would have a stout boat to keep the sea in. And then leading along with him a couple of outlaws who had some experience of the sea, he returned himself to the harbour and the little sandy creek.

The skiff of the *Good Hope* lay among many others, from which it was easily distinguished by its extreme smallness and fragility. Indeed, when Dick and his two men had taken their places, and begun to put forth out of the creek into the open harbour, the little cockle dipped into the swell and staggered under every gust of wind, like a thing upon the point of sinking.

The *Good Hope*, as we have said, was anchored far out, where the swell was heaviest. No other vessel lay nearer than several cables' length; those that were the nearest were themselves entirely deserted; and as the skiff approached, a thick flurry of snow and a sudden darkening of the weather further concealed the movements of the outlaws from all possible espial. In a trice they had leaped upon the heaving deck, and the skiff was dancing at the stern. The *Good Hope* was captured.

She was a good stout boat, decked in the bows and amidships, but open in the stern. She carried one mast, and was rigged between a felucca and a lugger. It would seem that Skipper Arblaster had made an excellent venture, for the hold was full of pieces of French wine; and in the little cabin, besides the Virgin Mary in the bulkhead which proved the captain's piety, there were many lockfast chests and cupboards, which showed him to be rich and careful.

A dog, who was the sole occupant of the vessel, furiously barked and bit the heels of the boarders; but he was soon kicked into the cabin, and the door shut upon his just resentment. A lamp was lit and fixed in the shrouds to mark the vessel clearly from the shore; one of the wine pieces in the hold was broached, and a cup of excellent Gascony emptied to the adventure of the evening; and then, while one of the outlaws began to get ready his bow and arrows and prepare to hold the ship against all comers, the other hauled in the skiff and got overboard, where he held on, waiting for Dick.

'Well, Jack, keep me a good watch,' said the young commander, preparing to follow his subordinate. 'Ye will do right well.'

'Why,' returned Jack, 'I shall do excellent well indeed, so long as we lie here; but once we put the nose of this poor ship outside the harbour—See, there she trembles! Nay, the poor shrew heard the words, and the heart misgave her in her oak-tree ribs. But look, Master Dick! how black the weather gathers!'

The darkness ahead was, indeed, astonishing. Great billows heaved up out of the blackness, one after another; and one after another the *Good Hope* buoyantly climbed, and giddily plunged upon the further side. A thin sprinkle of snow and thin flakes of foam came flying, and powdered the deck; and the wind harped dismally among the rigging.

'In sooth, it looketh evilly,' said Dick. 'But what cheer! 'Tis but a squall, and presently it will blow over.' But, in spite of his words, he was depressingly affected by the bleak disorder of the sky and the wailing and fluting of the wind; and as he got over the side of the *Good Hope* and made once more for the landing-creek with the best speed of oars, he crossed himself devoutly, and recommended to Heaven the lives of all who should adventure on the sea.

At the landing-creek there had already gathered about a dozen of the outlaws. To these the skiff was left, and they were bidden embark without delay.

A little further up the beach Dick found Lord Foxham hurrying in quest of him, his face concealed with a dark hood, and his bright armour covered by a long russet mantle of a poor appearance.

'Young Shelton,' he said, 'are ye for sea, then, truly?'

'My lord,' replied Richard, 'they lie about the house with horsemen; it may not be reached from the land side without alarum; and Sir Daniel once advertised of our adventure, we can no more carry it to a good end than, saving your presence, we could ride upon the wind. Now, in going round by sea, we do run some peril by the elements; but, what much outweigheth all, we have a chance to make good our purpose and bear off the maid.'

'Well,' returned Lord Foxham, 'lead on. I will, in some sort, follow you for shame's sake; but I own I would I were in bed.'

'Here, then,' said Dick. 'Hither we go to fetch our pilot.'

And he led the way to the rude alehouse where he had given rendezvous to a portion of his men. Some of these he found lingering round the door outside; others had pushed more boldly in, and, choosing places as near as possible to where they saw their comrade, gathered close about Lawless and the two shipmen. These, to judge by the distempered countenance and cloudy eye, had long since gone beyond the boundaries of moderation; and as Richard entered, closely followed by Lord Foxham, they were all three tuning up an old, pitiful sea-ditty, to the chorus of the wailing of the gale.

The young leader cast a rapid glance about the shed. The fire had just been replenished, and gave forth volumes of black smoke, so that it was difficult to see clearly in the further corners. It was plain, however, that the outlaws very largely outnumbered the remainder of the guests. Satisfied upon this point, in case of any failure in the operation of his plan, Dick strode up to the table and resumed his place upon the bench.

'Hey?' cried the skipper, tipsily, 'who are ye, hey?'

'I want a word with you without, Master Arblaster,' returned Dick; 'and here is what we shall talk of.' And he showed him a gold noble in the glimmer of the firelight.

The shipman's eyes burned, although he still failed to recognise our hero.

'Ay, boy,' he said, 'I am with you. Gossip, I will be back anon. Drink fair, gossip;' and, taking Dick's arm to steady his uneven steps, he walked to the door of the alehouse.

As soon as he was over the threshold, ten strong arms had seized and bound him; and in two minutes more, with his limbs trussed one to another, and a good gag in his mouth, he had been tumbled neck and crop into a neighbouring hay-barn. Presently, his man Tom, similarly secured, was tossed beside him, and the pair were left to their uncouth reflections for the night.

And now, as the time for concealment had gone by, Lord Foxham's followers were summoned by a preconcerted signal, and the party, boldly taking possession of as many boats as their numbers required, pulled in a flotilla for the light in the rigging of the ship. Long before the last man had climbed to the deck of the *Good Hope*, the sound of furious shouting from the shore showed that a part, at least, of the seamen had discovered the loss of their skiffs.

But it was now too late, whether for recovery or revenge. Out of some forty fighting men now mustered in the stolen ship, eight had been to sea, and could play the part of mariners. With the aid of these, a slice of sail was got upon her. The cable was cut. Lawless, vacillating on his feet, and still shouting the chorus of sea-ballads, took the long tiller in his hands: and the *Good Hope* began to flit forward into the darkness of the night, and to face the great waves beyond the harbour bar.

Richard took his place beside the weather rigging. Except for the ship's own lantern, and for some lights in Shoreby town, that were already fading to leeward, the whole world of air was as black as in a pit. Only from time to time, as the *Good Hope* swooped dizzily down into the valley of the rollers, a crest would break – a great cataract of snowy foam would leap in one instant into being – and, in an instant more, would stream into the wake and vanish.

Many of the men lay holding on and praying aloud; many more were sick, and had crept into the bottom, where they sprawled among the cargo. And what with the extreme violence of the motion, and the continued drunken bravado of Lawless, still shouting and singing at the helm, the stoutest heart on board may have nourished a shrewd misgiving as to the result.

But Lawless, as if guided by an instinct, steered the ship across the breakers, struck the lee of a great sandbank, where they sailed for a while in smooth water, and presently after laid her alongside a rude, stone pier, where she was hastily made fast, and lay ducking and grinding in the dark.

CHAPTER FIVE

The 'Good Hope' — continued

THE pier was not far distant from the house in which Joanna lay; it now only remained to get the men on shore to surround the house with a strong party, burst in the door and carry off the captive. They might then regard themselves as done with the *Good Hope*; it had placed them on the rear of their enemies; and the retreat, whether they should succeed or fail in the main enterprise, would be directed with a greater measure of hope in the direction of the forest and my Lord Foxham's reserve.

To get the men on shore, however, was no easy task; many had been sick, all were pierced with cold; the promiscuity and disorder on board had shaken their discipline; the movement of the ship and the darkness of the night had cowed their spirits. They made a rush upon the pier; my lord, with his sword drawn on his own retainers, must throw himself in front; and this impulse of rabblement was not restrained without a certain clamour of voices, highly to be regretted in the case.

When some degree of order had been restored, Dick, with a few chosen men, set forth in advance. The darkness on shore, by contrast with the flashing of the surf, appeared before him like a solid body; and the howling and whistling of the gale drowned any lesser noise.

He had scarce reached the end of the pier, however, when there fell a lull of the wind; and in this he seemed to hear on shore the hollow footing of horses and the clash of arms. Checking his immediate followers, he passed forward a step or two alone, even setting foot upon the down; and here he made sure he could detect the shape of men and horses moving. A strong discouragement assailed him. If their enemies were really on the watch, if they had beleaguered

the shoreward end of the pier, he and Lord Foxham were
taken in a posture of very poor defence, the sea behind, the
men jostled in the dark upon a narrow causeway. He gave
a cautious whistle, the signal previously agreed upon.

It proved to be a signal for more than he desired. Instantly
there fell, through the black night, a shower of arrows sent
at a venture; and so close were the men huddled on the
pier that more than one was hit, and the arrows were
answered with cries of both fear and pain. In this first
discharge, Lord Foxham was struck down; Hawksley had
him carried on board again at once; and his men, during the
brief remainder of the skirmish, fought (when they fought
at all) without guidance. That was perhaps the chief cause
of the disaster which made haste to follow.

At the shore end of the pier, for perhaps a minute, Dick
held his own with a handful; one or two were wounded upon
either side; steel crossed steel; nor had there been the least
signal of advantage, when in the twinkling of an eye the tide
turned against the party from the ship. Someone cried out
that all was lost; the men were in the very humour to lend an
ear to a discomfortable counsel; the cry was taken up. 'On
board, lads, for your lives!' cried another. A third, with the
true instinct of the coward, raised that inevitable report on
all retreats: 'We are betrayed!' And in a moment the whole
mass of men went surging and jostling backward down the
pier, turning their defenceless backs on their pursuers and
piercing the night with craven outcry.

One coward thrust off the ship's stern, while another still
held her by the bows. The fugitives leaped, screaming, and
were hauled on board, or fell back and perished in the sea.
Some were cut down upon the pier by the pursuers. Many
were injured on the ship's deck in the blind haste and
terror of the moment, one man leaping upon another,
and a third on both. At last, and whether by design or
accident, the bows of the *Good Hope* were liberated; and
the ever-ready Lawless, who had maintained his place at
the helm through all the hurly-burly by sheer strength of
body and a liberal use of the cold steel, instantly clapped
her on the proper tack. The ship began to move once more
forward on the stormy sea, its scuppers running blood, its

deck heaped with fallen men, sprawling and struggling in the dark.

Thereupon, Lawless sheathed his dagger, and turning to his next neighbour, 'I have left my mark on them, gossip,' said he, 'the yelping, coward hounds.'

Now, while they were all leaping and struggling for their lives, the men had not appeared to observe the rough shoves and cutting stabs with which Lawless had held his post in the confusion. But perhaps they had already begun to understand somewhat more clearly, or perhaps another ear had overheard the helmsman's speech.

Panic-stricken troops recover slowly, and men who have just disgraced themselves by cowardice, as if to wipe out the memory of their fault, will sometimes run straight into the opposite extreme of insubordination. So it was now; and the same men who had thrown away their weapons and been hauled, feet foremost, into the *Good Hope*, began to cry out upon their leaders, and demand that someone should be punished.

This growing ill-feeling turned upon Lawless.

In order to get a proper offing, the old outlaw had put the head of the *Good Hope* to seaward.

'What!' bawled one of the grumblers, 'he carrieth us to seaward!'

''Tis sooth,' cried another. 'Nay, we are betrayed for sure.'

And they all began to cry out in chorus that they were betrayed, and in shrill tones and with abominable oaths bade Lawless go about-ship and bring them speedily ashore. Lawless, grinding his teeth, continued in silence to steer the true course, guiding the *Good Hope* among the formidable billows. To their empty terrors, as to their dishonourable threats, between drink and dignity he scorned to make reply. The malcontents drew together a little abaft the mast, and it was plain they were like barnyard cocks, 'crowing for courage.' Presently they would be fit for any extremity of injustice or ingratitude. Dick began to mount by the ladder, eager to interpose; but one of the outlaws, who was also something of a seaman, got beforehand.

'Lads,' he began, 'y' are right wooden heads, I think. For

to get back, by the mass, we must have an offing, must we not? And this old Lawless—'

Someone struck the speaker on the mouth, and the next moment, as a fire springs among dry straw, he was felled upon the deck, trampled under the feet, and despatched by the daggers of his cowardly companions. At this the wrath of Lawless rose and broke.

'Steer yourselves,' he bellowed, with a curse; and, careless of the result, he left the helm.

The *Good Hope* was at that moment, trembling on the summit of a swell. She subsided, with sickening velocity, upon the farther side. A wave, like a great black bulwark, hove immediately in front of her; and, with a staggering blow, she plunged head-foremost through that liquid hill. The green water passed right over her from stem to stern, as high as a man's knees; the sprays ran higher than the mast; and she rose again upon the other side, with an appalling, tremulous indecision, like a beast that has been deadly wounded.

Six or seven of the malcontents had been carried bodily overboard; and as for the remainder, when they found their tongues again, it was to bellow to the saints and wail upon Lawless to come back and take the tiller.

Nor did Lawless wait to be twice bidden. The terrible result of his fling of just resentment sobered him completely. He knew, better than anyone on board, how nearly the *Good Hope* had gone bodily down below their feet; and he could tell, by the laziness with which she met the sea, that the peril was by no means over.

Dick, who had been thrown down by the concussion and half drowned, rose wading to his knees in the swamped well of the stern, and crept to the old helmsman's side.

'Lawless,' he said, 'we do all depend on you; y' are a brave, steady man, indeed, and crafty in the management of ships; I shall put three sure men to watch upon your safety.'

'Bootless, my master, bootless,' said the steersman, peering forward through the dark. 'We come every moment somewhat clearer of these sandbanks; with every moment, then, the sea packeth upon us heavier, and for all these whimperers, they will presently be on their backs. For, my master, 'tis a right mystery, but true, there never yet was a bad man that was a good shipman. None but the honest and the bold can endure me this tossing of a ship.'

'Nay, Lawless,' said Dick, laughing, 'that is a right shipman's byword, and hath no more of sense than the whistle of the wind. But, prithee, how go we? Do we lie well? Are we in good case?'

'Master Shelton,' replied Lawless, 'I have been a Grey Friar – I praise fortune – an archer, a thief, and a shipman. Of all these coats, I had the best fancy to die in the Grey Friar's, as ye may readily conceive, and the least fancy to die in John Shipman's tarry jacket; and that for two excellent good reasons: first, that the death might take a man suddenly; and second, for the horror of that great salt smother and welter under my foot here' – and Lawless stamped with his foot. 'Howbeit,' he went on, 'an I die not a sailor's death, and that this night, I shall owe a tall candle to our Lady.'

'Is it so?' asked Dick.

'It is right so,' replied the outlaw. 'Do ye not feel how heavy and dull she moves upon the waves? Do ye not hear the water washing in her hold? She will scarce mind the rudder even now. Bide till she has settled a bit lower; and she will either go down below your boots like a stone image, or drive ashore here, under our lee, and come all to pieces like a twist of string.'

'Ye speak with a good courage,' returned Dick. 'Ye are not then appalled?'

'Why, master,' answered Lawless, 'if ever a man had an ill crew to come to port with, it is I – a renegade friar, a thief, and all the rest on't. Well, ye may wonder, but I keep a good hope in my wallet; and if that I be to drown, I will drown with a bright eye, Master Shelton, and a steady hand.'

Dick returned no answer; but he was surprised to find the old vagabond of so resolute a temper, and fearing some fresh violence or treachery, set forth upon his quest for three sure men. The great bulk of the men had now deserted the deck, which was continually wetted with the flying sprays, and where they lay exposed to the shrewdness of the winter wind. They had gathered, instead, into the hold of the merchandise, among the butts of wine, and lighted by two swinging lanterns.

Here a few kept up the form of revelry, and toasted each other deep in Arblaster's Gascony wine. But as the *Good Hope* continued to tear through the smoking waves, and toss her stem and stern alternately high in air and deep into white foam, the number of these jolly companions diminished with every moment and with every lurch. Many sat apart, tending their hurts, but the majority were already prostrated with sickness, and lay moaning in the bilge.

Greensheve, Cuckow, and a young fellow of Lord Foxham's whom Dick had already remarked for his intelligence and spirit, were still, however, both fit to understand and willing to obey. These Dick set as a bodyguard about the person of the steersman, and then, with a last look at the black sky and sea, he turned and went below into the cabin, whither Lord Foxham had been carried by his servants.

CHAPTER SIX

The 'Good Hope' — concluded

THE moans of the wounded baron blended with the wailing of the ship's dog. The poor animal, whether he was merely sick at heart to be separated from his friends, or whether he indeed recognised some peril in the labouring of the ship, raised his cries, like minute-guns, above the roar of wave and weather; and the more superstitious of the men heard, in these sounds, the knell of the *Good Hope*.

Lord Foxham had been laid in a berth, upon a fur cloak. A little lamp burned dim before the Virgin in the bulk-head, and by its glimmer Dick could see the pale countenance and hollow eyes of the hurt man.

'I am sore hurt,' said he. 'Come near to my side, young Shelton; let there be one by me who, at least, is gentle born; for after having lived nobly and richly all the days of my life, this is a sad pass that I should get my hurt in a little ferreting skirmish, and die here, in a foul, cold ship upon the sea, among broken men and churls.'

'Nay, my lord,' said Dick, 'I pray rather to the saints that ye will recover you of your hurt, and come soon and sound ashore.'

'How?' demanded his lordship. 'Come sound ashore? There is, then, a question of it?'

'The ship laboureth – the sea is grievous and contrary,' replied the lad; 'and by what I can learn of my fellow that steereth us, we shall do well, indeed, if we come dryshod to land.'

'Ha!' said the baron, gloomily, 'thus shall every terror attend upon the passage of my soul! Sir, pray rather to live hard, that ye may die easy, than to be fooled and fluted all through life, as to the pipe and tabor, and, in the last hour, be plunged among misfortunes! Howbeit, I have that upon my mind that must not be delayed. We have no priest aboard?'

'None,' replied Dick.

'Here, then, to my secular interests,' resumed Lord Foxham: 'ye must be as good a friend to me dead, as I found you a gallant enemy when I was living. I fall in an evil hour for me, for England, and for them that trusted me. My men are being brought by Hamley – he that was your rival; they will rendezvous in the long room at Holywood; this ring from off my finger will accredit you to represent mine orders; and I shall write, besides, two words upon this paper, bidding Hamley yield to you the damsel. Will ye obey? I know not.'

'But, my lord, what orders?' inquired Dick.

'Ay,' quoth the baron, 'ay – the orders;' and he looked upon Dick with hesitation. 'Are ye Lancaster or York?' he asked, at length.

'I shame to say it,' answered Dick, 'I can scarce clearly answer. But so much I think is certain: since I serve with Ellis Duckworth, I serve the House of York. Well, if that be so, I declare for York.'

'It is well,' returned the other; 'it is exceeding well. For, truly, had ye said Lancaster, I wot not for the world what I had done. But sith ye are for York, follow me. I came hither but to watch these lords at Shoreby, while mine excellent young lord, Richard of Gloucester,[1] prepareth a sufficient force to fall upon and scatter them. I have made me notes of their strength, what watch they keep, and how they lie; and these I was to deliver to my young lord on Sunday, an hour before noon, at St Bride's Cross beside the forest. This tryst I am not like to keep, but I pray you, of courtesy, to keep it in my stead; and see that not pleasure, nor pain, tempest, wound, nor pestilence withhold you from the hour and place, for the welfare of England lieth upon this cast.'

'I do soberly take this upon me,' said Dick. 'In so far as in me lieth, your purpose shall be done.'

---

1. At the date of this story, Richard Crookback could not have been created Duke of Gloucester; but for clearness, with the reader's leave, he shall so be called.

'It is good,' said the wounded man. 'My lord duke shall order you farther, and if ye obey him with spirit and good-will, then is your fortune made. Give me the lamp a little nearer to mine eyes, till that I write these words for you.'

He wrote a note 'to his worshipful kinsman, Sir John Hamley'; and then a second, which he left without external superscription.

'This is for the duke,' he said. 'The word is "England and Edward," and the counter, "England and York."'

'And Joanna, my lord?' asked Dick.

'Nay, ye must get Joanna how ye can,' replied the baron. 'I have named you for my choice in both these letters; but ye must get her for yourself, boy. I have tried, as ye see here before you, and have lost my life. More could no man do.'

By this time the wounded man began to be very weary; and Dick, putting the precious papers in his bosom, bade him be of good cheer, and left him to repose.

The day was beginning to break, cold and blue, with flying squalls of snow. Close under the lee of the *Good Hope*, the coast lay in alternate rocky headlands and sandy bays; and further inland the wooded hill-tops of Tunstall showed along the sky. Both the wind and the sea had gone down; but the vessel wallowed deep, and scarce rose upon the waves.

Lawless was still fixed at the rudder; and by this time nearly all the men had crawled on deck, and were now gazing, with blank faces, upon the inhospitable coast.

'Are we going ashore?' asked Dick.

'Ay,' said Lawless, 'unless we get first to the bottom.'

And just then the ship rose so languidly to meet a sea, and the water weltered so loudly in her hold, that Dick involuntarily seized the steersman by the arm.

'By the mass!' cried Dick, as the bows of the *Good Hope* reappeared above the foam, 'I thought we had foundered, indeed; my heart was at my throat.'

In the waist, Greensheve, Hawksley, and the better men of both companies were busy breaking up the deck to build a raft; and to these Dick joined himself, working the harder to drown the memory of his predicament. But, even as he worked, every sea that struck the poor ship, and every one of her dull lurches, as she tumbled wallowing among the waves, recalled him with a horrid pang to the immediate proximity of death.

Presently, looking up from his work, he saw that they were close in below a promontory; a piece of ruinous cliff, against the base of which the sea broke white and heavy, almost overplumbed the deck; and, above that again, a house appeared, crowning a down.

Inside the bay, the seas ran gaily, raised the *Good Hope* upon their foam-flecked shoulders, carried her beyond the control of the steersman, and in a moment dropped her with a great concussion on the sand, and began to break over her, half-mast high, and roll her to and fro. Another great wave followed, raised her again, and carried her yet farther in; and then a third succeeded, and left her far inshore of the more dangerous breakers, wedged upon a bank.

'Now, boys,' cried Lawless, 'the saints have had a care of us, indeed. The tide ebbs; let us but sit down and drink a cup of wine, and before half an hour ye may all march me ashore as safe as on a bridge.'

A barrel was broached, and, sitting in what shelter they could find from the flying snow and spray, the ship-wrecked company handed the cup around, and sought to warm their bodies and restore their spirits.

Dick, meanwhile, returned to Lord Foxham, who lay in great perplexity and fear, the floor of his cabin washing knee-deep in water, and the lamp, which had been his only light, broken and extinguished by the violence of the blow.

'My lord,' said young Shelton, 'fear not at all; the saints are plainly for us; the seas have cast us high upon a shoal, and as soon as the tide hath somewhat ebbed, we may walk ashore upon our feet.'

It was nearly an hour before the vessel was sufficiently deserted by the ebbing sea, and they could set forth for the land, which appeared dimly before them through a veil of driving snow.

Upon a hillock on one side of their way a party of men lay

huddled together, suspiciously observing the movements of the new arrivals.

'They might draw near and offer us some comfort,' Dick remarked.

'Well, an they come not to us, let us even turn aside to them,' said Hawksley. 'The sooner we come to a good fire and a dry bed, the better for my poor lord.'

But they had not moved far in the direction of the hillock before the men, with one consent, rose suddenly to their feet, and poured a flight of well-directed arrows on the shipwrecked company.

'Back! back!' cried his lordship. 'Beware, in Heaven's name, that ye reply not!'

'Nay,' cried Greensheve, pulling an arrow from his leather jack. 'We are in no posture to fight, it is certain, being drenching wet, dog-weary, and three-parts frozen; but, for the love of old England, what aileth them to shoot thus cruelly on their poor country people in distress?'

'They take us to be French pirates,' answered Lord Foxham. 'In these most troublesome and degenerate days we cannot keep our own shores of England; but our old enemies, whom we once chased on sea and land, do now range at pleasure, robbing and slaughtering and burning. It is the pity and reproach of this poor land.'

The men upon the hillock lay, closely observing them, while they trailed upward from the beach and wound inland among desolate sand-hills; for a mile or so they even hung upon the rear of the march, ready, at a sign, to pour another volley on the weary and dispirited fugitives; and it was only when, striking at length upon a firm high-road, Dick began to call his men to some more martial order, that these jealous guardians of the coast of England silently disappeared among the snow. They had done what they desired; they had protected their own homes and farms, their own families and cattle; and their private interest being thus secured, it mattered not the weight of a straw to any one of them although the Frenchmen should carry blood and fire to every other parish in the realm of England.

BOOK IV
THE DISGUISE

CHAPTER ONE

The Den

THE PLACE where Dick had struck the line of a high road was not far from Holywood, and within nine or ten miles of Shoreby-on-the-Till; and here, after making sure that they were pursued no longer, the two bodies separated. Lord Foxham's followers departed, carrying their wounded master towards the comfort and security of the great abbey; and Dick, as he saw them wind away and disappear in the thick curtain of the falling snow, was left alone with near upon a dozen outlaws, the last remainder of his troop of volunteers.

Some were wounded; one and all were furious at their ill-success and long exposure; and though they were now too cold and hungry to do more, they grumbled and cast sullen looks upon their leaders. Dick emptied his purse among them, leaving himself nothing; thanked them for the courage they had displayed, though he could have found it more readily in his heart to rate them for poltroonery; and having thus somewhat softened the effect of his prolonged misfortune, despatched them to find their way, either severally or in pairs, to Shoreby and the Goat and Bagpipes.

For his own part, influenced by what he had seen on board of the *Good Hope*, he chose Lawless to be his companion on the walk. The snow was falling, without pause or variation, in one even, blinding cloud; the wind had been strangled, and now blew no longer; and the whole world was blotted out and sheeted down below that silent inundation. There was great danger of wandering by the way and perishing in drifts; and Lawless, keeping half a step in front of his companion, and holding his head forward like a hunting dog upon the scent, inquired his way of every tree, and studied out their path as though he were conning a ship among dangers.

About a mile into the forest they came to a place where several ways met, under a grove of lofty and contorted oaks. Even in the narrow horizon of the falling snow, it was a spot that could not fail to be recognised; and Lawless evidently recognised it with particular delight.

'Now, Master Richard,' said he, 'an y' are not too proud to be the guest of a man who is neither a gentleman by birth nor so much as a good Christian, I can offer you a cup of wine and a good fire to melt the marrow in your frozen bones.'

'Lead on, Will,' answered Dick. 'A cup of wine and a good fire! Nay, I would go a far way round to see them.'

Lawless turned aside under the bare branches of the grove, and, walking resolutely forward for some time, came to a steepish hollow or den, that had now drifted a quarter full of snow. On the verge a great beech-tree hung, precariously rooted; and here the old outlaw, pulling aside some bushy underwood, bodily disappeared into the earth.

The beech had, in some violent gale, been half-uprooted, and had torn up a considerable stretch of turf; and it was under this that old Lawless had dug out his forest hiding-place. The roots served him for rafters, the turf was his thatch; for walls and floor he had his mother the earth. Rude as it was, the hearth in one corner, blackened by fire, and the presence in another of a large oaken chest well fortified with iron, showed it at one glance to be the den of a man, and not the burrow of a digging beast.

Though the snow had drifted at the mouth and sifted in upon the floor of this earth-cavern, yet was the air much warmer than without; and when Lawless had struck a spark, and the dry furze bushes had begun to blaze and crackle on the hearth, the place assumed, even to the eye, an air of comfort and of home.

With a sigh of great contentment Lawless spread his broad hands before the fire, and seemed to breathe the smoke.

'Here, then,' he said, 'is this old Lawless's rabbit-hole;

pray Heaven there come no terrier! Far I have rolled hither
and thither, and here and about, since that I was fourteen
years of mine age and first ran away from mine abbey,
with the sacrist's gold chain and a mass-book that I
sold for four marks. I have been in England and France
and Burgundy, and in Spain, too, on a pilgrimage for
my poor soul; and upon the sea, which is no man's
country. But here is my place, Master Shelton. This is
my native land, this burrow in the earth. Come rain or
wind – and whether it's April, and the birds all sing,
and the blossoms fall about my bed, or whether it's
winter, and I sit alone with my good gossip the fire,
and robin redbreast twitters in the woods – here is my
church and market, my wife and child. It's here I come
back to, and it's here, so please the saints, that I would
like to die.'

''Tis a warm corner, to be sure,' replied Dick, 'and a
pleasant, and a well hid.'

'It had need to be,' returned Lawless, 'for an they found
it, Master Shelton, it would break my heart. But here,' he
added, burrowing with his stout fingers in the sandy floor,
'here is my wine cellar and ye shall have a flask of excellent
strong stingo.'

Sure enough, after but a little digging, he produced a big
leathern bottle of about a gallon, nearly three parts full of
a very heady and sweet wine; and when they had drunk to
each other comradely, and the fire had been replenished
and blazed up again, the pair lay at full length, thawing
and steaming, and divinely warm.

'Master Shelton,' observed the outlaw, 'y' 'ave had two
mischances this last while, and y'are like to lose the maid
– do I take it aright?'

'Aright!' returned Dick, nodding his head.

'Well now,' continued Lawless, 'hear an old fool that hath
been nigh-hand everything, and seen nigh-hand all! Ye go
too much on other people's errands, Master Dick. Ye go
on Ellis's; but he desireth rather the death of Sir Daniel.
Ye go on Lord Foxham's; well – the saints preserve him! –
doubtless he meaneth well. But go ye upon your own, good
Dick. Come right to the maid's side. Court her, lest that she

forget you. Be ready; and when the chance shall come, off with her at the saddlebow.'

'Ay, but, Lawless, beyond doubt she is now in Sir Daniel's own mansion,' answered Dick.

'Thither, then, go we,' replied the outlaw.

Dick stared at him.

'Nay, I mean it,' nodded Lawless. 'And if y' are of so little faith, and stumble at a word, see here!'

And the outlaw, taking a key from about his neck, opened the oak chest, and dipping and groping deep among its contents, produced first a friar's robe, and next a girdle of rope; and then a huge rosary of wood, heavy enough to be counted as a weapon.

'Here,' he said, 'is for you. On with them!'

And then, when Dick had clothed himself in this clerical disguise, Lawless produced some colours and a pencil, and proceeded, with the greatest cunning, to disguise his face. The eyebrows he thickened and produced; to the moustache, which was yet hardly visible, he rendered a like service; while, by a few lines around his eye, he changed the expression and increased the apparent age of this young monk.

'Now,' he resumed, 'when I have done the like, we shall make as bonny a pair of friars as the eye could wish. Boldly to Sir Daniel we shall go, and there be hospitably welcome for the love of Mother Church.'

'And how, dear Lawless,' cried the lad, 'shall I repay you?'

'Tut, brother,' replied the outlaw, 'I do naught but for my pleasure. Mind not for me. I am one, by the mass, that mindeth for himself. When that I lack, I have a long tongue and a voice like the monastery bell – I do ask, my son; and where asking faileth, I do most usually take.'

The old rogue made a humorous grimace; and although Dick was displeased to lie under so great favours to so equivocal a personage, he was yet unable to restrain his mirth.

With that, Lawless returned to the big chest, and was soon similarly disguised; but below his gown, Dick wondered to observe him conceal a sheaf of black arrows.

'Wherefore do ye that?' asked the lad. 'Wherefore arrows, when ye take no bow?'

'Nay,' replied Lawless, lightly, ''tis like there will be heads broke – not to say backs – ere you and I win sound from where we're going to; and if any fall, I would our fellowship should come by the credit on't. A black arrow, Master Dick, is the seal of our abbey; it showeth you who writ the bill.'

'An ye prepare so carefully,' said Dick, 'I have here some papers that, for mine own sake, and the interest of those that trusted me, were better left behind than found upon my body. Where shall I conceal them, Will?'

'Nay,' replied Lawless, 'I will go forth into the wood and whistle me three verses of a song; meanwhile, do you bury them where ye please, and smooth the sand upon the place.'

'Never!' cried Richard. 'I trust you, man. I were base indeed if I not trusted you.'

'Brother, y' are but a child,' replied the old outlaw, pausing and turning his face upon Dick from the threshold of the den. 'I am a kind old Christian, and no traitor to men's blood, and no sparer of mine own in a friend's jeopardy. But, fool, child, I am a thief by trade and birth and habit. If my bottle were empty and my mouth dry, I would rob you, dear child, as sure as I love, honour, and admire your parts and person! Can it be clearer spoken? No.'

And he stumped forth through the bushes with a snap of his big fingers.

Dick, thus left alone, after a wondering thought upon the inconsistencies of his companion's character, hastily produced, reviewed, and buried his papers. One only he reserved to carry along with him, since it in nowise compromised his friends, and yet might serve him, in a pinch, against Sir Daniel. That was the knight's own letter to Lord Wensleydale, sent by Throgmorton, on the morrow of the defeat at Risingham, and found next day by Dick upon the body of the messenger.

Then, treading down the embers of the fire, Dick left the den, and rejoined the old outlaw, who stood awaiting him under the leafless oaks, and was already beginning to be powdered by the falling snow. Each looked upon the other, and each laughed, so thorough and so droll was the disguise.

'Yet I would it were but summer and a clear day,' grumbled the outlaw, 'that I might see myself in the mirror of a pool. There be many of Sir Daniel's men that know me; and if we fell to be recognised, there might be two words for you, my brother, but as for me, in a paternoster while, I should be kicking in a rope's-end.'

Thus they set forth together along the road to Shoreby, which, in this part of its course, kept near along the margin of the forest, coming forth, from time to time, in the open country, and passing beside poor folks' houses and small farms.

Presently at sight of one of these, Lawless pulled up.

'Brother Martin,' he said, in a voice capitally disguised, and suited to his monkish robe, 'let us enter and seek alms from these poor sinners. *Pax vobiscum*! Ay,' he added, in his own voice, ''tis as I feared; I have somewhat lost the whine of it; and by your leave, good Master Shelton, ye must suffer me to practise in these country places, before that I risk my fat neck by entering Sir Daniel's. But look ye a little, what an excellent thing it is to be a Jack-of-all-trades! An I had not been a shipman, ye had infallibly gone down in the *Good Hope*; and I had not been a thief, I could not have painted me your face; and but that I had been a Grey Friar, and sung loud in the choir, and ate hearty at the board, I could not have carried this disguise, but the very dogs would have spied us out and barked at us for shams.'

He was by this time close to the window of the farm, and he rose on his tip-toes and peeped in.

'Nay,' he cried, 'better and better. We shall here try our false faces with a vengeance, and have a merry jest on Brother Capper to boot.'

And so saying he opened the door and led the way into the house.

Three of their own company sat at the table, greedily eating. Their daggers, stuck beside them in the board, and the black and menacing looks which they continued to shower upon the people of the house, proved that they owed their entertainment rather to force than favour. On the two monks, who now, with a sort of humble dignity, entered the kitchen of the farm, they seemed to turn with a particular resentment; and one – it was John Capper in person – who seemed to play the leading part, instantly and rudely ordered them away.

'We want no beggars here!' he cried.

But another – although he was as far from recognising Dick and Lawless – inclined to more moderate counsels.

'Not so,' he cried. 'We be strong men, and take: these be weak, and crave; but in the latter end these shall be uppermost and we below. Mind him not, my father; but come, drink of my cup, and give me a benediction.'

'Y' are men of a light mind, carnal and accursed,' said the monk. 'Now, may the saints forbid that ever I should drink with such companions! But here, for the pity I bear to sinners, here I do leave you a blessed relic, the which, for your soul's interest, I bid you kiss and cherish.'

So far Lawless thundered upon them like a preaching friar; but with these words he drew from under his robe a black arrow, tossed it on the board in front of the three startled outlaws, turned in the same instant, and, taking Dick along with him, was out of the room and out of sight among the falling snow before they had time to utter a word or move a finger.

'So,' he said, 'we have proved our false faces, Master Shelton. I will now adventure my poor carcass where ye please.'

'Good!' returned Richard. 'It irks me to be doing. Set we on for Shoreby!'

CHAPTER TWO

'In Mine Enemies' House'

SIR DANIEL'S residence in Shoreby was a tall, commodious, plastered mansion, framed in carven oak, and covered by a low-pitched roof of thatch. To the back there stretched a garden, full of fruit-trees, alleys, and thick arbours, and overlooked from the far end by the tower of the abbey church.

The house might contain, upon a pinch, the retinue of a greater person than Sir Daniel; but even now it was filled with hubbub. The court rang with arms and horseshoe-iron; the kitchen roared with cookery like a bees'-hive; minstrels, and the players of instruments, and the cries of tumblers, sounded from the hall. Sir Daniel, in his profusion, in the gaiety and gallantry of his establishment, rivalled with Lord Shoreby, and eclipsed Lord Risingham.

All guests were made welcome. Minstrels, tumblers, players of chess, the sellers of relics, medicines, perfumes and enchantments, and along with these every sort of priest, friar, or pilgrim, were made welcome to the lower table, and slept together in the ample lofts, or on the bare boards of the long dining-hall.

On the afternoon following the wreck of the *Good Hope*, the buttery, the kitchens, the stables, the covered cartshed that surrounded two sides of the court, were all crowded by idle people, partly belonging to Sir Daniel's establishment, and attired in his livery of murrey and blue, partly nondescript strangers attracted to the town by greed, and received by the knight through policy, and because it was the fashion of the time.

The snow, which still fell without interruption, the extreme chill of the air, and the approach of night, combined to keep them under shelter. Wine, ale, and money were all plentiful; many sprawled gambling in the straw of the barn, many were still drunken from the noontide meal. To the eye of a modern it would have looked like the sack of a city; to the eye of a contemporary it was like any other rich and noble household at a festive season.

Two monks – a young and an old – had arrived late, and were now warming themselves at a bonfire in a corner of the shed. A mixed crowd surrounded them – jugglers, mountebanks, and soldiers: and with these the elder of the two had soon engaged so brisk a conversation, and exchanged so many loud guffaws and country witticisms, that the group momentarily increased in number.

The younger companion, in whom the reader has already recognised Dick Shelton, sat from the first somewhat backward, and gradually drew himself away. He listened, indeed, closely, but he opened not his mouth; and by the grave expression of his countenance, he made but little account of his companion's pleasantries.

At last his eye, which travelled continually to and fro, and kept a guard upon all the entrances of the house, lit upon a little procession entering by the main gate and crossing the court in an oblique direction. Two ladies, muffled in thick furs, led the way, and were followed by a pair of waiting-women and four stout men-at-arms. The next moment they had disappeared within the house; and Dick, slipping through the crowd of loiterers in the shed, was already giving hot pursuit.

'The taller of these twain was Lady Brackley,' he thought; 'and where Lady Brackley is, Joan will not be far.'

At the door of the house the four men-at-arms had ceased to follow, and the ladies were now mounting the stairway of polished oak, under no better escort than that of the two waiting-women. Dick followed close behind. It was already the dusk of the day; and in the house the darkness of the night had almost come. On the stair-landings torches flared in iron holders; down the long tapestried corridors a lamp burned by every door. And where the door stood open, Dick could look in upon arras-covered walls, and rush-bescattered floors, glowing in the light of the wood-fires.

Two floors were passed and at every landing the younger
and shorter of the two ladies had looked back keenly at
the monk. He, keeping his eyes lowered, and affecting
the demure manners that suited his disguise, had but
seen her once, and was unaware that he had attracted
her attention. And now, on the third floor, the party
separated, the younger lady continuing to ascend alone,
the other, followed by the waiting-maids, descending the
corridor to the right.

Dick mounted with a swift foot, and, holding to the
corner, thrust forth his head and followed the three women
with his eyes. Without turning or looking behind them, they
continued to descend the corridor.

'It is right well,' thought Dick. 'Let me but know my
Lady Brackley's chamber, and it will go hard an I find not
Dame Hatch upon an errand.'

And just then a hand was laid upon his shoulder, and,
with a bound and a choked cry, he turned to grapple his
assailant.

He was somewhat abashed to find, in the person whom he
had so roughly seized, the short young lady in the furs. She,
on her part, was shocked and terrified beyond expression,
and hung trembling in his grasp.

'Madam,' said Dick, releasing her, 'I cry you a thousand
pardons; but I have no eyes behind, and, by the mass, I
could not tell ye were a maid.'

The girl continued to look at him, but, by this time,
terror began to be succeeded by surprise, and surprise by
suspicion. Dick, who could read these changes on her face,
became alarmed for his own safety in that hostile house.

'Fair maid,' he said, affecting easiness, 'suffer me to kiss
your hand, in token ye forgive my roughness, and I will
even go.'

'Y' are a strange monk, young sir,' returned the young
lady, looking him both boldly and shrewdly in the face;
'and now that my first astonishment hath somewhat passed
away, I can spy the layman in each word you utter. What do
ye here? Why are ye thus sacrilegiously tricked out? Come
ye in peace or war? And why spy ye after Lady Brackley
like a thief?'

'Madam,' quoth Dick, 'of one thing I pray you to be very sure: I am no thief. And even if I come here in war, as in some degree I do, I make no war upon fair maids, and I hereby entreat them to copy me so far, and to leave me be. For, indeed, fair mistress, cry out – if such be your pleasure – cry but once, and say what ye have seen, and the poor gentleman before you is merely a dead man. I cannot think ye would be cruel,' added Dick; and taking the girl's hand gently in both of his, he looked at her with courteous admiration.

'Are ye then a spy – a Yorkist?' asked the maid.

'Madam,' he replied, 'I am indeed a Yorkist, and in some sort, a spy. But that which bringeth me into this house, the same which will win for me the pity and interest of your kind heart, is neither of York nor Lancaster. I will wholly put my life in your discretion. I am a lover, and my name—'

But here the young lady clapped her hand suddenly upon Dick's mouth, looked hastily up and down and east and west, and, seeing the coast clear, began to drag the young man, with great strength and vehemence, upstairs.

'Hush!' she said, 'and come. Shalt talk hereafter.'

Somewhat bewildered, Dick suffered himself to be pulled upstairs, bustled along a corridor, and thrust suddenly into a chamber, lit, like so many of the others, by a blazing log upon the hearth.

'Now,' said the young lady, forcing him down upon a stool, 'sit ye there and attend my sovereign good pleasure. I have life and death over you, and I will not scruple to abuse my power. Look to yourself; y' 'ave cruelly mauled my arm. He knew not I was a maid, quoth he! Had he known I was a maid, he had ta'en his belt to me, forsooth!'

And with these words she whipped out of the room and left Dick gaping with wonder, and not very sure if he were dreaming or awake.

'Ta'en my belt to her!' he repeated. 'Ta'en my belt to her!' And the recollection of that evening in the forest flowed back upon his mind, and he once more saw Matcham's wincing body and beseeching eyes.

And then he was recalled to the dangers of the present. In the next room he heard a stir, as of a person moving;

then followed a sigh, which sounded strangely near; and then the rustle of skirts and tap of feet once more began. As he stood hearkening, he saw the arras wave along the wall; there was the sound of a door being opened, the hangings divided, and, lamp in hand, Joanna Sedley entered the apartment.

She was attired in costly stuffs of deep and warm colours, such as befit the winter and the snow. Upon her head, her hair had been gathered together and became her as a crown. And she, who had seemed so little and so awkward in the attire of Matcham, was now tall like a young willow, and swam across the floor as though she scorned the drudgery of walking.

Without a start, without a tremor, she raised her lamp and looked at the young monk.

'What make ye here, good brother?' she inquired. 'Ye are doubtless ill-directed. Whom do ye require?' And she set her lamp upon the bracket.

'Joanna,' said Dick; and then his voice failed him. 'Joanna,' he began again, 'ye said ye loved me; and the more fool I, but I believed it!'

'Dick!' she cried. 'Dick!'

And then, to the wonder of the lad, this beautiful and tall young lady made but one step of it, and threw her arms about his neck and gave him a hundred kisses all in one.

'Oh, the fool fellow!' she cried. 'Oh, dear Dick! Oh, if ye could see yourself! Alack!' she added, pausing, 'I have spoilt you, Dick! I have knocked some of the paint off. But that can be mended. What cannot be mended, Dick – or I much fear it cannot! – is my marriage with Lord Shoreby.'

'Is it decided, then?' asked the lad.

'To-morrow, before noon, Dick, in the abbey church,' she answered, 'John Matcham and Joanna Sedley both shall come to a right miserable end. There is no help in tears, or I could weep mine eyes out. I have not spared myself to pray, but Heaven frowns on my petition. And dear Dick – good Dick – but that ye can get me forth of this house before the morning, we must even kiss and say good-bye.'

'Nay,' said Dick, 'not I; I will never say that word. 'Tis like despair; but while there is life, Joanna, there is hope! Yet will I hope. Ay, by the mass, and triumph! Look ye, now, when ye were but a name to me, did I not follow – did I not rouse good men – did I not stake my life upon the quarrel? And now that I have seen you for what ye are – the fairest maid and stateliest of England – think ye I would turn? – if the deep sea were there, I would straight through it; if the way were full of lions, I would scatter them like mice.'

'Ay,' she said drily, 'ye make a great ado about a sky-blue robe!'

'Nay, Joan,' protested Dick, ''tis not alone the robe. But, lass, ye were disguised. Here am I disguised; and to the proof, do I not cut a figure of fun – a right fool's figure?'

'Ay, Dick, an' that ye do!' she answered smiling.

'Well, then!' he returned triumphant. 'So was it with you, poor Matcham, in the forest. In sooth, ye were a wench to laugh at. But now!'

So they ran on, holding each other by both hands, exchanging smiles and lovely looks, and melting minutes into seconds; and so they might have continued all night long. But presently there was a noise behind them; and they were aware of the short young lady, with her finger on her lips.

'Saints!' she cried, 'but what a noise ye keep! Can ye not speak in compass? And now, Joanna, my fair maid of the woods, what will ye give your gossip for bringing you your sweetheart?'

Joanna ran to her, by way of answer, and embraced her fierily.

'And you, sir,' added the young lady, 'what do ye give me?'

'Madam,' said Dick, 'I would fain offer to pay you in the same money.'

'Come then,' said the lady, 'it is permitted you.'

But Dick, blushing like a peony, only kissed her hand.

'What ails ye at my face, fair sir?' she inquired, curtseying to the very ground; and, then, when Dick had at length and most tepidly embraced her, 'Joanna,' she added, 'your sweetheart is very backward under your eyes; but I warrant you, when first we met, he was more ready. I am all black and blue, wench; trust me never, if I be not black and blue! And now,' she continued, 'have ye said your sayings! for I must speedily dismiss the paladin.'

But at this they both cried out that they had said nothing, that the night was still very young, and that they would not be separated so early.

'And supper?' asked the young lady. 'Must we not go down to supper?'

'Nay, to be sure?' cried Joan. 'I had forgotten.'

'Hide me, then,' said Dick, 'put me behind the arras, shut me in the chest, or what ye will, so that I may be here on your return. Indeed, fair lady,' he added, 'bear this in mind, that we are sore bested, and may never look upon each other's face from this night forward till we die.'

At this the young lady melted; and when, a little after, the bell summoned Sir Daniel's household to the board, Dick was planted very stiffly against the wall, at a place where a division in the tapestry permitted him to breathe the more freely, and even to see into the room.

He had not been long in this position when he was somewhat strangely disturbed. The silence in that upper storey of the house was only broken by the flickering of the flames and the hissing of a green log in the chimney; but presently, to Dick's strained hearing, there came the sound of some one walking with extreme precaution; and soon after the door opened, and a little black-faced, dwarfish fellow, in Lord Shoreby's colours, pushed first his head and then his crooked body into the chamber. His mouth was open as though to hear the better; and his eyes, which were very bright, flitted restlessly and swiftly to and fro. He went round and round the room, striking here and there upon the hangings; but Dick, by a miracle, escaped his notice. Then he looked below the furniture, and examined the lamp; and at last, with an air of cruel disappointment, was preparing to go away as silently as he had come, when down he dropped upon his knees, picked up something from among the rushes on the floor, examined it, and, with every signal of delight, concealed it in the wallet at his belt.

Dick's heart sank, for the object in question was a tassel from his own girdle; and it was plain to him that this dwarfish spy, who took a malign delight in his employment, would lose no time in bearing it to his master, the baron. He was half-tempted to throw aside the arras, fall upon the scoundrel, and, at the risk of his life, remove the tell-tale token. And while he was still hesitating, a new cause of concern was added. A voice, hoarse and broken by drink, began to be audible from the stair; and presently after, uneven, wandering, and heavy footsteps sounded without along the passage.

'What make ye here, my merry men, among the greenwood shaws?' sang the voice. 'What make ye here? Hey! sots, what make ye here?' it added, with a rattle of drunken laughter; and then once more breaking into song:

> If ye should drink the clary wine,
> Fat Friar John, ye friend o' mine—
> If I should eat, and ye should drink,
> Who shall sing the mass, d'ye think?

Lawless, alas! rolling drunk, was wandering the house, seeking for a corner wherein to slumber off the effects of his potations. Dick inwardly raged. The spy, at first terrified, had grown reassured as he found he had to deal with an intoxicated man, and now, with a movement of cat-like rapidity, slipped from the chamber, and was gone from Richard's eyes.

What was to be done? If he lost touch of Lawless for the night he was left impotent, whether to plan or carry forth Joanna's rescue. If, on the other hand, he dared to address the drunken outlaw, the spy might still be lingering within sight, and the most fatal consequences ensue.

It was, nevertheless, upon this last hazard that Dick decided. Slipping from behind the tapestry, he stood ready in the doorway of the chamber, with a warning hand upraised. Lawless, flushed crimson, with his eyes injected, vacillating on his feet, drew still unsteadily nearer.

At last he hazily caught sight of his commander, and, in despite of Dick's imperious signals, hailed him instantly and loudly by his name.

Dick leaped upon and shook the drunkard furiously.

'Beast!' he hissed – 'beast, and no man! It is worse than treachery to be so witless. We may all be shent for thy sotting.'

But Lawless only laughed and staggered, and tried to clap young Shelton on the back.

And just then Dick's quick ear caught a rapid brushing in the arras. He leaped towards the sound, and the next moment a piece of the wall-hanging had been torn down, and Dick and the spy were sprawling together in its folds. Over and over they rolled, grappling for each other's throat, and still baffled by the arras, and still silent in their deadly fury. But Dick was by much the stronger, and soon the spy lay prostrate under his knee, and, with a single stroke of the long poniard, ceased to breathe.

CHAPTER THREE

The Dead Spy

THROUGHOUT this furious and rapid passage, Lawless had looked on helplessly, and even when all was over, and Dick, already re-arisen to his feet, was listening with the most passionate attention to the distant bustle in the lower storeys of the house, the old outlaw was still wavering on his legs like a shrub in a breeze of wind, and still stupidly staring on the face of the dead man.

'It is well,' said Dick, at length; 'they have not heard us, praise the saints! But, now, what shall I do with this poor spy? At least, I will take my tassel from his wallet.'

So saying, Dick opened the wallet; within he found a few pieces of money, the tassel, and a letter addressed to Lord Wensleydale, and sealed with my Lord Shoreby's seal. The name awoke Dick's recollection; and he instantly broke the wax and read the contents of the letter. It was short, but, to Dick's delight, it gave evident proof that Lord Shoreby was treacherously corresponding with the House of York.

The young fellow usually carried his ink-horn and implements about him, and so now, bending a knee beside the body of the dead spy, he was able to write these words upon a corner of the paper:

My Lord of Shoreby, ye that writt the letter, wot ye why your man is ded? But let me rede you, marry not.

JON AMEND-ALL

He laid this paper on the breast of the corpse; and then Lawless, who had been looking on upon these last manœuvres with some flickering returns of intelligence, suddenly drew a black arrow from below his robe, and therewith pinned the paper in its place. The sight of this disrespect, or, as it almost seemed, cruelty to the dead, drew a cry of horror from young Shelton; but the old outlaw only laughed.

'Nay, I will have the credit for mine order,' he hiccupped. 'My jolly boys must have the credit on't – the credit, brother'; and then, shutting his eyes tight and opening his mouth like a precentor, he began to thunder, in a formidable voice:

If ye should drink the clary wine—

'Peace, sot!' cried Dick, and thrust him hard against the wall. 'In two words – if so be that such a man can understand me who hath more wine than wit in him – in two words, and, a-Mary's name, begone out of this house, where, if ye continue to abide, ye will not only hang yourself, but me also! Faith, then, up foot! be yare, or, by the mass, I may forget that I am in some sort your captain, and in some your debtor! Go!'

The sham monk was now, in some degree, recovering the use of his intelligence; and the ring in Dick's voice, and the glitter in Dick's eye, stamped home the meaning of his words.

'By the mass,' cried Lawless, 'an I be not wanted, I can go;' and he turned tipsily along the corridor and proceeded to flounder downstairs, lurching against the wall.

So soon as he was out of sight, Dick returned to his hiding-place, resolutely fixed to see the matter out. Wisdom, indeed, moved him to be gone; but love and curiosity were stronger.

Time passed slowly for the young man, bolt upright behind the arras. The fire in the room began to die down, and the lamp to burn low and to smoke. And still there was no word of the return of anyone to these upper quarters of the house; still the faint hum and clatter of the supper party sounded from far below; and still, under the thick fall of the snow, Shoreby town lay silent upon every side.

At length, however, feet and voices began to draw near upon the stair; and presently after several of Sir Daniel's guests arrived upon the landing, and, turning down the corridor, beheld the torn arras and the body of the spy.

Some ran forward, and some back, and all together began to cry aloud.

At the sound of their cries, guests, men-at-arms, ladies, servants, and, in a word, all the inhabitants of that great house, came flying from every direction, and began to join their voices to the tumult.

Soon a way was cleared, and Sir Daniel came forth in person, followed by the bridegroom of the morrow, my Lord Shoreby.

'My lord,' said Sir Daniel, 'have I not told you of this knave Black Arrow? To the proof, behold it! There it stands, and, by the rood, my gossip, in a man of yours, or one that stole your colours!'

'In good sooth, it was a man of mine,' replied Lord Shoreby, hanging back. 'I would I had more such. He was keen as a beagle and secret as a mole.'

'Ay, gossip, truly?' asked Sir Daniel, keenly. 'And what came he smelling up so many stairs in my poor mansion? But he will smell no more.'

'An 't please you, Sir Daniel,' said one, 'here is a paper written upon with some matter, pinned upon his breast.'

'Give it me, arrow and all,' said the knight. And when he had taken into his hand the shaft, he continued for some time to gaze upon it in sullen musing. 'Ay,' he said, addressing Lord Shoreby, 'here is a hate that followeth hard and close upon my heels. This black stick, or its just likeness, shall yet bring me down. And, gossip, suffer a plain knight to counsel you; and if these hounds begin to wind you, flee! 'Tis like a sickness – it still hangeth, hangeth upon the limbs. But let us see what they have written. It is as I thought, my lord; y' are marked, like an old oak, by the woodman; to-morrow or next day, by will come the axe. But what wrote ye in a letter?'

Lord Shoreby snatched the paper from the arrow, read it, crumpled it between his hands, and, overcoming the reluctance which had hitherto withheld him from approaching, threw himself on his knees beside the body and eagerly groped in the wallet.

He rose to his feet with a somewhat unsettled countenance.

'Gossip,' he said, 'I have indeed lost a letter here that much imported; and could I lay my hand upon the knave that took it, he should incontinently grace a halter. But let us, first of all, secure the issues of the house. Here is enough harm already, by St George!'

Sentinels were posted close around the house and garden; a sentinel on every landing of the stair, a whole troop in the main entrance-hall; and yet another about the bonfire in the shed. Sir Daniel's followers were supplemented by Lord Shoreby's; there was thus no lack of men or weapons to make the house secure, or to entrap a lurking enemy, should one be there.

Meanwhile, the body of the spy was carried out through the falling snow and deposited in the abbey church.

It was not until these dispositions had been taken, and all had returned to a decorous silence, that the two girls drew Richard Shelton from his place of concealment, and made a full report to him of what had passed. He, upon his side, recounted the visit of the spy, his dangerous discovery, and speedy end.

Joanna leaned back very faint against the curtained wall.

'It will avail but little,' she said. 'I shall be wed to-morrow, in the morning, after all!'

'What!' cried her friend. 'And here is our paladin that driveth lions like mice! Ye have little faith, of a surety – But come, friend lion-driver, give us some comfort; speak, and let us hear bold counsels.'

Dick was confounded to be thus outfaced with his own exaggerated words; but though he coloured, he still spoke stoutly.

'Truly,' said he, 'we are in straits. Yet, could I but win out of this house for half an hour, I do honestly tell myself that all might still go well; and for the marriage, it should be prevented.'

'And for the lions,' mimicked the girl, 'they shall be driven.'

'I crave your excuse,' said Dick. 'I speak not now in any boasting humour, but rather as one inquiring after help or counsel; for if I get not forth of this house through these sentinels, I can do less than naught. Take me, I pray you, rightly.'

'Why said ye he was rustic, Joan?' the girl inquired. 'I warrant he hath a tongue in his head; ready, soft, and bold is his speech at pleasure. What would ye more?'

'Nay,' sighed Joanna, with a smile, 'they have changed me my friend Dick, 'tis sure enough. When I beheld him, he was rough indeed. But it matters little; there is no help for my hard case, and I must still be Lady Shoreby!'

'Nay, then,' said Dick, 'I will even make the adventure. A friar is not much regarded; and if I found a good fairy to lead me up, I may find another belike to carry me down. How call they the name of this spy?'

'Rutter,' said the young lady; 'and an excellent good name to call him by. But how mean ye, lion-driver? What is in your mind to do?'

'To offer boldly to go forth,' returned Dick; 'and if any stop me, to keep an unchanged countenance, and say I go to pray for Rutter. They will be praying over his poor clay even now.'

'The device is somewhat simple,' replied the girl, 'yet it may hold.'

'Nay,' said young Shelton, 'it's no device, but mere boldness, which serveth often better in great straits.'

'Ye say true,' she said. 'Well, go, a-Mary's name, and may Heaven speed you! Ye leave here a poor maid that loves you entirely, and another that is most heartily your friend. Be wary, for their sakes, and make not shipwreck of your safety.'

'Ay,' added Joanna, 'go, Dick. Ye run no more peril, whether ye go or stay. Go; ye take my heart with you; the saints defend you!'

Dick passed the first sentry with so assured a countenance that the fellow merely fidgeted and stared; but at the second landing the man carried his spear across and bade him name his business.

'*Pax vobiscum*,' answered Dick. 'I go to pray over the body of this poor Rutter.'

'Like enough,' returned the sentry; 'but to go alone is not permitted you.' He leaned over the oaken balusters and

whistled shrill. 'One cometh!' he cried; and then motioned
Dick to pass.

At the foot of the stair he found the guard afoot and
awaiting his arrival; and when he had once more repeated
his story, the commander of the post ordered four men to
accompany him to the church.

'Let him not slip, my lads,' he said. 'Bring him to Sir
Oliver, on your lives!'

The door was then opened; one of the men took Dick
by either arm, another marched ahead with the link, and
the fourth, with bent bow and the arrow on the string,
brought up the rear. In this order they proceeded through
the garden, under the thick darkness of the night and the
scattering snow, and drew near to the dimly illuminated
windows of the abbey church.

At the western portal a picket of archers stood, taking
what shelter they could find in the hollow of the arched
doorways, and all powdered with the snow; and it was not
until Dick's conductors had exchanged a word with these
that they were suffered to pass forth and enter the nave of
the sacred edifice.

The church was doubtfully lighted by the tapers upon
the great altar, and by a lamp or two that swung from the
arched roof before the private chapels of illustrious families.
In the midst of the choir the dead spy lay, his limbs piously
composed, upon a bier.

A hurried mutter of prayer sounded along the arches;
cowled figures knelt in the stalls of the choir; and on the
steps of the high altar a priest in pontifical vestments
celebrated mass.

Upon this fresh entrance, one of the cowled figures arose,
and, coming down the steps which elevated the level of the
choir above that of the nave, demanded from the leader of
the four men what business brought him to the church.
Out of respect for the service and the dead, they spoke in
guarded tones; but the echoes of that huge, empty building
caught up their words, and hollowly repeated and repeated
them along the aisles.

'A monk!' returned Sir Oliver (for he it was), when he
had heard the report of the archer. 'My brother, I looked

not for your coming,' he added, turning to young Shelton. 'In all civility who are ye? and at whose instance do ye join your supplications to ours?'

Dick, keeping his cowl about his face, signed to Sir Oliver to move a pace or two aside from the archers; and, so soon as the priest had done so, 'I cannot hope to deceive you, sir,' he said. 'My life is in your hands.'

Sir Oliver violently started; his stout cheeks grew pale, and for a space he was silent.

'Richard,' he said, 'what brings you here, I know not; but I much misdoubt it to be evil. Nevertheless, for the kindness that was, I would not willingly deliver you to harm. Ye shall sit all night beside me in the stalls: ye shall sit there till my Lord of Shoreby be married, and the party gone safe home; and if all goeth well, and ye have planned no evil, in the end ye shall go whither ye will. But if your purpose be bloody, it shall return upon your head. Amen!'

And the priest devoutly crossed himself, and turned and louted to the altar.

With that, he spoke a few words more to the soldiers, and, taking Dick by the hand, led him up to the choir, and placed him in the stall beside his own, where, for mere decency the lad had instantly to kneel and appear to be busy with his devotions.

His mind and his eyes, however, were continually wandering. Three of the soldiers, he observed, instead of returning to the house, had got them quietly into a point of vantage in the aisle; and he could not doubt that they had done so by Sir Oliver's command. Here, then, he was trapped. Here he must spend the night in the ghostly glimmer and shadow of the church, and looking on the pale face of him he slew; and here, in the morning, he must see his sweetheart married to another man before his eyes.

But, for all that, he obtained a command upon his mind, and built himself up in patience to await the issue.

CHAPTER FOUR

In the Abbey Church

IN SHOREBY Abbey Church the prayers were kept up all
night without cessation, now with the singing of psalms,
now with a note or two upon the bell.

Rutter, the spy, was nobly waked. There he lay, meanwhile, as they had arranged him, his dead hands crossed
upon his bosom, his dead eyes staring on the roof; and
hard by, in the stall, the lad who had slain·him waited, in
sore disquietude, the coming of the morning.

Once only in the course of the hours, Sir Oliver leaned
across to his captive.

'Richard,' he whispered, 'my son, if ye mean me evil,
I will certify, on my soul's welfare, ye design upon an
innocent man. Sinful in the eye of Heaven I do declare
myself, but sinful as against you I am not, neither have
been ever.'

'My father,' returned Dick, in the same tone of voice,
'trust me, I design nothing; but as for your innocence, I
may not forget that ye cleared yourself but lamely.'

'A man may be innocently guilty,' replied the priest. 'He
may be set blindfolded upon a mission, ignorant of its true
scope. So it was with me. I did decoy your father to his
death; but as Heaven sees us in this sacred place, I knew
not what I did.'

'It may be,' returned Dick. 'But see what a strange web
ye have woven, that I should be, at this hour, at once your
prisoner and your judge; that ye should both threaten my
days and deprecate my anger. Methinks, if ye had been
all your life a true man and good priest, ye would neither
thus fear nor thus detest me. And now to your prayers. I
do obey you, since needs must; but I will not be burthened
with your company.'

The priest uttered a sigh so heavy that it had almost touched the lad into some sentiment of pity, and he bowed his head upon his hands like a man borne down below a weight of care. He joined no longer in the psalms; but Dick could hear the beads rattle through his fingers and the prayers a-pattering between his teeth.

Yet a little, and the grey of the morning began to struggle through the painted casements of the church, and to put to shame the glimmer of the tapers. The light slowly broadened and brightened, and presently through the south-eastern clerestories a flush of rosy sunlight flickered on the walls. The storm was over; the great clouds had disburdened their snow and fled farther on, and the new day was breaking on a merry winter landscape sheathed in white.

A bustle of church officers followed; the bier was carried forth to the deadhouse, and the stains of blood were cleansed from off the tiles, that no such ill-omened spectacle should disgrace the marriage of Lord Shoreby. At the same time, the very ecclesiastics who had been so dismally engaged all night began to put on morning faces, to do honour to the merrier ceremony which was about to follow. And further to announce the coming of the day, the pious of the town began to assemble and fall to prayer before their favourite shrines, or wait their turn at the confessionals.

Favoured by this stir, it was of course easily possible for any man to avoid the vigilance of Sir Daniel's sentries at the door; and presently Dick, looking about him wearily, caught the eye of no less a person than Will Lawless, still in his monk's habit.

The outlaw, at the same moment, recognised his leader, and privily signed to him with hand and eye.

Now, Dick was far from having forgiven the old rogue his most untimely drunkenness, but he had no desire to involve him in his own predicament; and he signalled back to him, as plain as he was able, to begone.

Lawless, as though he had understood, disappeared at once behind a pillar, and Dick breathed again.

What, then, was his dismay to feel himself plucked by the sleeve and to find the old robber installed beside him, upon the next seat, and, to all appearance, plunged in his devotions!

Instantly Sir Oliver arose from his place, and, gliding behind the stalls, made for the soldiers in the aisle. If the priest's suspicions had been so lightly wakened, the harm was already done, and Lawless a prisoner in the church.

'Move not,' whispered Dick. 'We are in the plaguiest pass, thanks, before all things, to thy swinishness of yestereven. When ye saw me here, so strangely seated, where I have neither right nor interest, what a murrain! could ye not smell harm and get ye gone from evil?'

'Nay,' returned Lawless, 'I thought ye had heard from Ellis, and were here on duty.'

'Ellis!' echoed Dick. 'Is Ellis then returned?'

'For sure,' replied the outlaw. 'He came last night, and belted me sore for being in wine – so there ye are avenged, my master. A furious man is Ellis Duckworth! He hath ridden me hotspur from Craven to prevent this marriage; and, Master Dick, ye know the way of him – do so he will!'

'Nay, then,' returned Dick, with composure, 'you and I, my poor brother, are dead men; for I sit here a prisoner upon suspicion, and my neck was to answer for this very marriage that he purposeth to mar. I had a fair choice by the rood! to lose my sweetheart or else lose my life! Well, the cast is thrown – it is to be my life.'

'By the mass,' cried Lawless, half arising, 'I am gone!'

But Dick had his hand at once upon his shoulder.

'Friend Lawless, sit ye still,' he said. 'An ye have eyes, look yonder at the corner by the chancel arch; see ye not that, even upon the motion of your rising, yon armed men are up and ready to intercept you? Yield ye, friend. Ye were bold aboard ship, when ye thought to die a sea-death; be bold again, now that y' are to die presently upon the gallows.'

'Master Dick,' gasped Lawless, 'the thing hath come upon me somewhat of the suddenest. But give me a moment till I fetch my breath again; and, by the mass, I will be as stout-hearted as yourself.'

'Here is my bold fellow!' returned Dick. 'And yet,

Lawless, it goes hard against the grain with me to die; but where whining mendeth nothing, wherefore whine?'

'Nay, that indeed!' chimed Lawless. 'And a fig for death, at worst! It has to be done, my master, soon or late. And hanging in a good quarrel is an easy death, they say, though I could never hear of any that came back to say so.'

And so saying the stout old rascal leaned back in his stall, folded his arms, and began to look about him with the greatest air of insolence and unconcern.

'And for the matter of that,' Dick added, 'it is yet our best chance to keep quiet. We wot not yet what Duckworth purposes; and when all is said, and if the worst befall, we may yet clear our feet of it.'

Now that they ceased talking, they were aware of a very distant and thin strain of mirthful music which steadily drew nearer, louder and merrier. The bells in the tower began to break forth into a doubling peal, and a greater and greater concourse of people to crowd into the church, shuffling the snow from off their feet, and clapping and blowing their hands. The western door was flung wide open, showing a glimpse of sunlit, snowy street, and admitting in a great gust the shrewd air of the morning; and in short, it became plain by every sign that Lord Shoreby desired to be married very early in the day, and that the wedding-train was drawing near.

Some of Lord Shoreby's men now cleared a passage down the middle aisle, forcing the people back with lance-stocks; and just then, outside the portal, the secular musicians could be descried drawing near over the frozen snow, the fifers and trumpeters scarlet in the face with lusty blowing, the drummers and the cymbalists beating as for a wager.

These, as they drew near the door of the sacred building, filed off on either side, and, marking time to their own vigorous music, stood stamping in the snow. As they thus opened their ranks, the leaders of this noble bridal train appeared behind and between them; and such was the variety and gaiety of their attire, such the display of silks and velvet, fur and satin, embroidery and lace, that the procession showered forth upon the snow like a flower-bed in a path or a painted window in a wall.

First came the bride, a sorry sight, as pale as winter, clinging to Sir Daniel's arm, and attended, as bridesmaid, by the short young lady who had befriended Dick the night before. Close behind, in the most radiant toilet, followed the bridegroom, halting on a gouty foot, and as he passed the threshold of the sacred building, and doffed his hat, his bald head was seen to be rosy with emotion.

And now came the hour of Ellis Duckworth.

Dick, who sat stunned among contrary emotions, grasping the desk in front of him, beheld a movement in the crowd, people jostling backward, and eyes and arms uplifted. Following these signs, he beheld three or four men with bent bows, leaning from the clerestory gallery. At the same instant they delivered their discharge, and before the clamour and cries of the astounded populace had time to swell fully upon the ear, they had flitted from their perch and disappeared.

The nave was full of swaying heads and voices screaming; the ecclesiastics thronged in terror from their places; the music ceased, and though the bells overhead continued for some seconds to clang upon the air, some wind of the disaster seemed to find its way at last even to the chamber where the ringers were leaping on their ropes, and they also desisted from their merry labours.

Right in the midst of the nave the bridegroom lay stone-dead, pierced by two black arrows. The bride had fainted. Sir Daniel stood, towering above the crowd in surprise and anger, a clothyard shaft quivering in his left forearm, and his face streaming blood from another which had grazed his brow.

Long before any search could be made for them, the authors of this tragic interruption had clattered down a turnpike stair and decamped by a postern door.

But Dick and Lawless still remained in pawn; they had indeed arisen on the first alarm, and pushed manfully to gain the door; but what with the narrowness of the stalls, and the crowding of terrified priests and choristers, the attempt had been in vain, and they had stoically resumed their places.

And now, pale with horror, Sir Oliver rose to his feet

and called upon Sir Daniel, pointing with one hand to Dick.

'Here,' he cried, 'is Richard Shelton – alas the hour! – blood guilty! Seize him! – bid him be seized! For all our lives' sakes, take him and bind him surely! He hath sworn our fall.'

Sir Daniel was blinded by anger – blinded by the hot blood that still streamed across his face.

'Where?' he bellowed. 'Hale him forth! By the cross of Holywood but he shall rue this hour.'

The crowd fell back, and a party of archers invaded the choir, laid rough hands on Dick, dragged him head foremost from the stall, and thrust him by the shoulders down the chancel steps. Lawless, on his part, sat as still as a mouse.

Sir Daniel, brushing the blood out of his eyes, stared blinkingly upon his captive.

'Ay,' he said, 'treacherous and insolent, I have thee fast; and by all potent oaths, for every drop of blood that now trickles in mine eyes, I will wring a groan out of thy carcase. Away with him!' he added. 'Here is no place! Off with him to my house. I will number every joint of thy body with a torture.'

But Dick, putting off his captors, uplifted his voice.

'Sanctuary!' he shouted. 'Sanctuary! Ho, there, my fathers! They would drag me from the church!'

'From the church thou hast defiled with murder, boy,' added a tall man, magnificently dressed.

'On what probation?' cried Dick. 'They do accuse me, indeed, of some complicity, but have not proved one tittle. I was, in truth, a suitor for this damsel's hand; and she, I will be bold to say it, repaid my suit with favour. But what then? To love a maid is no offence, I trow – nay, nor to gain her love. In all else, I stand here free from guiltiness.'

There was a murmur of approval among the bystanders, so boldly Dick declared his innocence; but at the same time a throng of accusers arose upon the other side, crying how he had been found last night in Sir Daniel's house, how he wore a sacrilegious disguise; and in the midst of the Babel, Sir Oliver indicated Lawless, both by voice and gesture, as accomplice to the fact. He, in his turn, was dragged from his seat and set beside his leader. The feelings of the crowd rose high on either side, and while some dragged the prisoners to and fro to favour their escape, others cursed and struck them with their fists. Dick's ears rang and his brain swam dizzily, like a man struggling in the eddies of a furious river.

But the tall man, who had already answered Dick, by a prodigious exercise of voice restored silence and order in the mob.

'Search them,' he said, 'for arms. We may so judge of their intentions.'

Upon Dick they found no weapon but his poniard, and this told in his favour, until one man officiously drew it from its sheath, and found it still uncleansed of the blood of Rutter. At this there was a great shout among Sir Daniel's followers, which the tall man suppressed by a gesture and an imperious glance. But when it came to the turn of Lawless, there was found under his gown a sheaf of arrows identical with those that had been shot.

'How say ye now?' asked the tall man, frowningly, of Dick.

'Sir,' replied Dick, 'I am here in sanctuary, is it not so? Well, sir, I see by your bearing that ye are high in station, and I read in your countenance the marks of piety and justice. To you, then, I will yield me prisoner, and that blithely, foregoing the advantage of this holy place. But rather than to be yielded into the discretion of that man – whom I do here accuse with a loud voice to be the murderer of my natural father and the unjust detainer of my lands and revenues – rather than that, I would beseech you, under favour, with your own gentle hand, to despatch me on the spot. Your own ears have heard him, how before that I was proven guilty he did threaten me with torments. It standeth not with your own honour to deliver me to my sworn enemy and old oppressor, but to try me fairly by the way of law, and, if that I be guilty indeed, to slay me mercifully.'

'My lord,' cried Sir Daniel, 'ye will not hearken to this wolf? His bloody dagger reeks him the lie into his face.'

'Nay, but suffer me, good knight,' returned the tall stranger; 'your own vehemence doth somewhat tell against yourself.'

And here the bride, who had come to herself some minutes past and looked wildly on upon this scene, broke loose from those that held her, and fell upon her knees before the last speaker.

'My Lord of Risingham,' she cried, 'hear me, in justice. I am here in this man's custody by mere force, reft from mine own people. Since that day I had never pity, countenance, nor comfort from the face of man – but from him only – Richard Shelton – whom they now accuse and labour to undo. My lord, if he was yesternight in Sir Daniel's mansion, it was I that brought him there; he came but at my prayer, and thought to do no hurt. While yet Sir Daniel was a good lord to him, he fought with them of the Black Arrow loyally; but when his foul guardian sought his life by practices, and he fled by night, for his soul's sake, out of that bloody house, whither was he to turn – he, helpless and penniless? Or if he be fallen among ill company, whom should ye blame – the lad that was unjustly handled, or the guardian that did abuse his trust?'

And then the short young lady fell on her knees by Joanna's side.

'And I, my good lord and natural uncle,' she added, 'I can bear testimony, on my conscience and before the face of all, that what this maiden saith is true. It was I, unworthy, that did lead the young man in.'

Earl Risingham had heard in silence, and when the voices ceased, he still stood silent for a space. Then he gave Joanna his hand to arise, though it was to be observed that he did not offer the like courtesy to her who had called herself his niece.

'Sir Daniel,' he said, 'here is a right intricate affair, the which, with your good leave, it shall be mine to examine and adjust. Content ye, then; your business is in careful hands; justice shall be done you; and in the meanwhile get ye incontinently home, and have your hurts attended. The air is shrewd, and I would not ye took cold upon these scratches.'

He made a sign with his hand; it was passed down the nave by obsequious servants, who waited there upon his smallest gesture. Instantly, without the church, a tucket sounded shrill, and through the open portal archers and men-at-arms, uniformly arrayed in the colours and wearing the badge of Lord Risingham, began to file into the church, took Dick and Lawless from those who still detained them, and, closing their files about the prisoners, marched forth again and disappeared.

As they were passing, Joanna held both her hands to Dick and cried him her farewell; and the bridesmaid, nothing downcast by her uncle's evident displeasure, blew him a kiss, with a 'Keep your heart up, lion-driver!' that for the first time since the accident called up a smile to the faces of the crowd.

CHAPTER FIVE

Earl Risingham

EARL RISINGHAM, although by far the most important person then in Shoreby, was poorly lodged in the house of a private gentleman upon the extreme outskirts of the town. Nothing but the armed men at the doors, and the mounted messengers that kept arriving and departing, announced the temporary residence of a great lord.

Thus it was that, from lack of space, Dick and Lawless were clapped into the same compartment.

'Well spoken, Master Richard,' said the outlaw; 'it was excellently well spoken, and, for my part, I thank you cordially. Here we are in good hands; we shall be justly tried, and some time this evening decently hanged on the same tree.'

'Indeed, my poor friend, I do believe it,' answered Dick.

'Yet we have a string to our bow,' returned Lawless. 'Ellis Duckworth is a man out of ten thousand; he holdeth you right near his heart, both for your own and for your father's sake; and, knowing you guiltless of this fact, he will stir earth and heaven to bear you clear.'

'It may not be,' said Dick. 'What can he do? He hath but a handful. Alack, if it were but to-morrow – could I but keep a certain tryst an hour before noon tomorrow – all were, I think, otherwise. But now there is no help.'

'Well,' concluded Lawless, 'an ye will stand to it for my innocence, I will stand to it for yours, and that stoutly. It shall naught avail us; but an I be to hang, it shall not be for lack of swearing.'

And then, while Dick gave himself over to his reflections, the old rogue curled himself down into a corner, pulled his monkish hood about his face, and composed himself

to sleep. Soon he was loudly snoring, so utterly had his
long life of hardship and adventure blunted the sense of
apprehension.

It was long after noon, and the day was already failing,
before the door was opened and Dick taken forth and led
upstairs to where, in a warm cabinet, Earl Risingham sat
musing over the fire.

On his captive's entrance he looked up.

'Sir,' he said, 'I knew your father, who was a man of
honour, and this inclineth me to be the more lenient; but
I may not hide from you that heavy charges lie against
your character. Ye do consort with murderers and robbers;
upon a clear probation ye have carried war against the
king's peace; ye are suspected to have piratically seized
upon a ship; ye are found skulking with a counterfeit
presentment in your enemy's house; a man is slain that
very evening—'

'An it like you, my lord,' Dick interposed, 'I will at once
avow my guilt, such as it is. I slew this fellow Rutter; and to
the proof' – searching in his bosom – 'here is a letter from
his wallet.'

Lord Risingham took the letter, and opened and read
it twice.

'Ye have read this?' he inquired.

'I have read it,' answered Dick.

'Are ye for York or Lancaster?' the earl demanded.

'My lord, it was but a little while back that I was asked
that question, and knew not how to answer it,' said Dick;
'but having answered once, I will not vary. My lord, I am
for York.'

The earl nodded approvingly.

'Honestly replied,' he said. 'But wherefore, then, deliver
me this letter?'

'Nay, but against traitors, my lord, are not all sides
arrayed?' cried Dick.

'I would they were, young gentleman,' returned the earl;
'and I do at least approve your saying. There is more youth
than guile in you, I do perceive; and were not Sir Daniel a
mighty man upon our side, I were half tempted to espouse
your quarrel. For I have inquired, and it appears that you

have been hardly dealt with, and have much excuse. But look ye, sir, I am, before all else, a leader in the queen's interest; and though by nature a just man, as I believe, and leaning even to the excess of mercy, yet must I order my goings for my party's interest, and to keep Sir Daniel, I would go far about.'

'My lord,' returned Dick, 'ye will think me very bold to counsel you: but do ye count upon Sir Daniel's faith? Methought he had changed sides intolerably often.'

'Nay, it is the way of England. What would ye have?' the earl demanded. 'But ye are unjust to the knight of Tunstall; and as faith goes, in this unfaithful generation, he hath of late been honourably true to us of Lancaster. Even in our last reverses he stood firm.'

'An it please you, then,' said Dick, 'to cast your eye upon this letter, ye might somewhat change your thought of him,' and he handed to the earl Sir Daniel's letter to Lord Wensleydale.

The effect upon the earl's countenance was instant; he lowered like an angry lion, and his hand, with a sudden movement, clutched at his dagger.

'Ye have read this also?' he asked.

'Even so,' said Dick. 'It is your lordship's own estate he offers to Lord Wensleydale.'

'It is my own estate, even as you say!' returned the earl. 'I am your bedesman for this letter. It hath shown me a fox's hole. Command me, Master Shelton; I will not be backward in gratitude, and to begin with, York or Lancaster, true man or thief, I do now set you at freedom. Go, a-Mary's name! But judge it right that I retain and hang your fellow Lawless. The crime hath been most open, and it were fitting that some open punishment should follow.'

'My lord, I make it my first suit to you to spare him also,' pleaded Dick.

'It is an old condemned rogue, thief, and vagabond, Master Shelton,' said the earl. 'He hath been gallows-ripe this score of years. And, whether for one thing or another, whether to-morrow or the day after, where is the great choice?'

'Yet, my lord, it was through love to me that he came

hither,' answered Dick, 'and I were churlish and thankless to desert him.'

'Master Shelton, ye are troublesome,' replied the earl severely. 'It is an evil way to prosper in this world. Howbeit, and to be quit of your importunity, I will once more humour you. Go then, together; but go warily, and get swiftly out of Shoreby town. For this Sir Daniel (whom may the saints confound!) thirsteth most greedily to have your blood.'

'My lord, I do now offer you in words my gratitude, trusting at some brief date to pay you some of it in service,' replied Dick, as he turned from the apartment.

CHAPTER SIX

Arblaster Again

WHEN DICK and Lawless were suffered to steal, by a back way, out of the house where Lord Risingham held his garrison, the evening had already come.

They paused in shelter of the garden wall to consult on their best course. The danger was extreme. If one of Sir Daniel's men caught sight of them and raised the view-hallo, they would be run down and butchered instantly. And not only was the town of Shoreby a mere net of peril for their lives, but to make for the open country was to run the risk of the patrols.

A little way off, upon some open ground, they spied a windmill standing; and, hard by that, a very large granary with open doors.

'How if we lay there until the night fall?' Dick proposed.

And Lawless having no better suggestion to offer, they made a straight push for the granary at a run, and concealed themselves behind the door among some straw. The daylight rapidly departed; and presently the moon was silvering the frozen snow. Now or never was their opportunity to gain the Goat and Bagpipes unobserved and change their tell-tale garments. Yet even then it was advisable to go round by the outskirts, and not run the gauntlet of the market-place, where, in the concourse of people, they stood the more imminent peril to be recognised and slain.

This course was a long one. It took them not far from the house by the beach, now lying dark and silent, and brought them forth at last by the margin of the harbour. Many of the ships, as they could see by the clear moonshine, had weighed anchor, and, profiting by the calm sky, proceeded for more distant parts; answerably to this, the rude alehouses along the beach (although, in defiance of the curfew law, they still shone with fire and candle) were no longer thronged with customers, and no longer echoed to the chorus of sea-songs.

Hastily, half-running, with their monkish raiment kilted to the knee, they plunged through the deep snow and threaded the labyrinth of marine lumber; and they were already more than half-way round the harbour when, as they were passing close before an alehouse, the door suddenly opened and let out a gush of light upon their fleeting figures.

Instantly they stopped, and made believe to be engaged in earnest conversation.

Three men, one after another, came out of the alehouse, and the last closed the door behind him. All three were unsteady upon their feet, as if they had passed the day in deep potations, and they now stood wavering in the moonlight, like men who knew not what they would be after. The tallest of the three was talking in a loud, lamentable voice.

'Seven pieces of as good Gascony as ever a tapster broached,' he was saying, 'the best ship out o' the port o' Dartmouth, a Virgin Mary parcel-gilt, thirteen pounds of good gold money—'

'I have bad losses, too,' interrupted one of the others. 'I have had losses of mine own, gossip Arblaster. I was robbed at Martinmas of five shillings and a leather wallet well worth ninepence farthing.'

Dick's heart smote him at what he heard. Until that moment he had not perhaps thought twice of the poor skipper who had been ruined by the loss of the *Good Hope*; so careless, in those days, were men who wore arms of the goods and interests of their inferiors. But this sudden encounter reminded him sharply of the high-handed manner and ill-ending of his enterprise; and both he and Lawless turned their heads the other way, to avoid the chance of recognition.

The ship's dog had, however, made his escape from the wreck and found his way back again to Shoreby. He was now at Arblaster's heels, and, suddenly sniffing and pricking his ears, he darted forward and began to bark furiously at the two sham friars.

His master unsteadily followed him.

'Hey, shipmates!' he cried. 'Have ye ever a penny piece for a poor old shipman, clean destroyed by pirates? I am a man that would have paid for you both o' Thursday morning; and now here I be o' Saturday night, begging for a flagon of ale! Ask my man Tom, if ye misdoubt me. Seven pieces of good Gascon wine, a ship that was mine own, and was my father's before me, a Blessed Mary of plane-tree wood and parcel-gilt, and thirteen pounds in gold and silver. Hey! what say ye? A man that fought the French, too; for I have fought the French; I have cut more French throats upon the high seas than ever a man that sails out of Dartmouth. Come, a penny piece.'

Neither Dick nor Lawless durst answer him a word, lest he should recognise their voices; and they stood there as helpless as a ship ashore, not knowing where to turn nor what to hope.

'Are ye dumb, boy?' inquired the skipper. 'Mates,' he added, with a hiccup, 'they be dumb. I like not this manner of discourtesy; for an a man be dumb, so be as he's courteous, he will still speak when he was spoken to, methinks.'

By this time the sailor Tom, who was a man of great personal strength, seemed to have conceived some suspicion of these two speechless figures; and, being soberer than his captain, stepped suddenly before him, took Lawless roughly by the shoulder, and asked him, with an oath, what ailed him that he held his tongue. To this the outlaw, thinking all was over, made answer by a wrestling feint that stretched the sailor on the sand, and, calling upon Dick to follow him, took to his heels among the lumber.

The affair passed in a second. Before Dick could run at all, Arblaster had him in his arms; Tom, crawling on his face, had caught him by one foot, and the third man had a drawn cutlass brandishing above his head.

It was not so much the danger, it was not so much the annoyance, that now bowed down the spirits of young

Shelton; it was the profound humiliation to have escaped Sir
Daniel, convinced Lord Risingham, and now fall helpless in
the hands of this old drunken sailor; and not merely helpless,
but, as his conscience loudly told him when it was too late,
actually guilty – actually the bankrupt debtor of the man
whose ship he had stolen and lost.

'Bring me him back into the alehouse, till I see his face,'
said Arblaster.

'Nay, nay,' returned Tom; 'but let us first unload his
wallet, lest the other lads cry share.'

But though he was searched from head to foot, not a
penny was found upon him; nothing but Lord Foxham's
signet, which they plucked savagely from his finger.

'Turn me him to the moon,' said the skipper; and taking
Dick by the chin, he cruelly jerked his head into the air.
'Blessed Virgin!' he cried, 'it is the pirate.'

'Hey!' cried Tom.

'By the Virgin of Bordeaux, it is the man himself!'
repeated Arblaster. 'What, sea-thief, do I hold you?' he
cried. 'Where is my ship? Where is my wine? Hey! have
I you in my hands? Tom, give me one end of a cord here;
I will so truss me this sea-thief, hand and foot together,
like a basting turkey – marry, I will so bind him up – and
thereafter I will so beat – so beat him!'

And so he ran on, winding the cord meanwhile about
Dick's limbs with the dexterity peculiar to seamen, and at
every turn and cross securing it with a knot, and tightening
the whole fabric with a savage pull.

When he had done, the lad was a mere package in his
hands – as helpless as the dead. The skipper held him at
arm's length, and laughed aloud. Then he fetched him a
stunning buffet on the ear; and then turned him about, and
furiously kicked and kicked him. Anger rose up in Dick's
bosom like a storm; anger strangled him, and he thought
to have died; but when the sailor, tired of this cruel play,
dropped him all his length upon the sand and turned to consult with his companions, he instantly regained command of
his temper. Here was a momentary respite; ere they began
again to torture him, he might have found some method
to escape from this degrading and fatal misadventure.

Presently, sure enough, and while his captors were still discussing what to do with him, he took heart of grace, and, with a pretty steady voice, addressed them.

'My masters,' he began, 'are ye gone clean foolish? Here hath Heaven put into your hands as pretty an occasion to grow rich as ever shipman had – such as ye might make thirty over-sea adventures and not find again – and, by the mass! what do ye? Beat me? – nay; so would an angry child! But for long-headed tarry-Johns, that fear not fire nor water, and that love gold as they love beef, methinks ye are not wise.'

'Ay,' said Tom, 'now y' are trussed ye would cozen us.'

'Cozen you!' repeated Dick. 'Nay, if ye be fools, it would be easy. But if ye be shrewd fellows, as I trow ye are, ye can see plainly where your interest lies. When I took your ship from you, we were many, we were well clad and armed; but now, bethink you a little, who mustered that array? One incontestably that hath made much gold. And if he, being already rich, continueth to hunt after more even in the face of storms – bethink you once more – shall there not be a treasure somewhere hidden?'

'What meaneth he?' asked one of the men.

'Why, if ye have lost an old skiff and a few jugs of vinegary wine,' continued Dick, 'forget them, for the trash they are; and do ye rather buckle to an adventure worth the name, that shall, in twelve hours, make or mar you for ever. But take me up from where I lie, and let us go somewhere near at hand and talk across a flagon, for I am sore and frozen, and my mouth is half among the snow.'

'He seeks but to cozen us,' said Tom contemptuously.

'Cozen! cozen!' cried the third man. 'I would I could see the man that could cozen me! He were a cozener indeed! Nay, I was not born yesterday. I can see a church when it hath a steeple on it; and for my part, gossip Arblaster, methinks there is some sense in this young man. Shall we go hear him, indeed? Say, shall we go hear him?'

'I would look gladly on a pottle of strong ale, good Master Pirret,' returned Arblaster. 'How say ye, Tom? But then the wallet is empty.'

'I will pay,' said the other – 'I will pay. I would fain see this matter out; I do believe, upon my conscience, there is gold in it.'

'Nay, if ye get again to drinking, all is lost!' cried Tom.

'Gossip Arblaster, ye suffer your fellow to have too much liberty,' returned Master Pirret. 'Would ye be led by a hired man? Fy, fy!'

'Peace, fellow!' said Arblaster, addressing Tom. 'Will ye put your oar in? Truly a fine pass, when the crew is to correct the skipper!'

'Well, then, go your way,' said Tom; 'I wash my hands of you.'

'Set him, then, upon his feet,' said Master Pirret. 'I know a privy place where ye may drink and discourse.'

'If I am to walk, my friends, ye must set my feet at liberty,' said Dick, when he had been once more planted upright like a post.

'He saith true,' laughed Pirret. 'Truly, he could not walk accoutred as he is. Give it a slit – out with your knife and slit it, gossip.'

Even Arblaster paused at this proposal; but as his companion continued to insist, and Dick had the sense to keep the merest wooden indifference of expression, and only shrugged his shoulders over the delay, the skipper consented at last, and cut the cords which tied his prisoner's feet and legs. Not only did this enable Dick to walk; but the whole network of his bonds being proportionately loosened, he felt the arm behind his back begin to move more freely, and could hope, with time and trouble, to entirely disengage it. So much he owed already to the owlish silliness and greed of Master Pirret.

That worthy now assumed the lead, and conducted them to the very same rude alehouse where Lawless had taken Arblaster on the day of the gale. It was now quite deserted; the fire was a pile of red embers, radiating the most ardent heat; and when they had chosen their places, and the landlord had set before them a measure of mulled ale, both Pirret and Arblaster stretched forth their legs and squared their elbows like men bent upon a pleasant hour.

The table at which they sat, like all the others in the alehouse, consisted of a heavy, square board, set on a pair of barrels; and each of the four curiously assorted cronies sat at one side of the square, Pirret facing Arblaster, and Dick opposite to the common sailor.

'And now, young man,' said Pirret, 'to your tale. It doth appear, indeed, that ye have somewhat abused our gossip Arblaster; but what then? Make it up to him – show him but this chance to become wealthy – and I will go pledge he will forgive you.'

So far Dick had spoken pretty much at random; but it was now necessary, under the supervision of six eyes, to invent and tell some marvellous story, and, if it were possible, get back into his hands the all-important signet. To squander time was the first necessity. The longer his stay lasted, the more would his captors drink, and the surer should he be when he attempted his escape.

Well, Dick was not much of an inventor, and what he told was pretty much the tale of Ali Baba, with Shoreby and Tunstall Forest substituted for the East, and the treasures of the cavern rather exaggerated than diminished. As the reader is aware, it is an excellent story, and has but one drawback – that it is not true; and so, as these three simple shipmen now heard it for the first time, their eyes stood out of their faces, and their mouths gaped like codfish at a fishmonger's.

Pretty soon a second measure of mulled ale was called for; and while Dick was still artfully spinning out the incidents a third followed the second.

Here was the position of the parties towards the end:

Arblaster, three-parts drunk and one-half asleep, hung helpless on his stool. Even Tom had been much delighted with the tale, and his vigilance had abated in proportion. Meanwhile, Dick had gradually wormed his right arm clear of its bonds, and was ready to risk all.

'And so,' said Pirret, 'y' are one of these?'

'I was made so,' replied Dick, 'against my will; but an I could but get a sack or two of gold coin to my share, I should be a fool indeed to continue dwelling in a filthy cave, and standing shot and buffet like a soldier. Here be we four; good! Let us, then, go forth into the forest to-morrow ere the sun be up. Could we come honestly by a donkey, it were better; but an we cannot, we have our four strong backs, and I warrant me we shall come home staggering.'

Pirret licked his lips.

'And this magic,' he said – 'this password, whereby the cave is opened – how call ye it, friend?'

'Nay, none know the word but the three chiefs,' returned Dick; 'but here is your great good fortune, that, on this very evening, I should be the bearer of a spell to open it. It is a thing not trusted twice a year beyond the captain's wallet.'

'A spell!' said Arblaster, half awakening, and squinting upon Dick with one eye. 'Aroint thee! no spells! I be a good Christian. Ask my man Tom, else.'

'Nay, but this is white magic,' said Dick. 'It doth naught with the devil; only the powers of numbers, herbs, and planets.'

'Ay, ay,' said Pirret; '’tis but white magic, gossip. There is no sin therein, I do assure you. But proceed, good youth. This spell – in what should it consist?'

'Nay, that I will incontinently show you,' answered Dick. 'Have ye there the ring ye took from my finger? Good! Now hold it forth before you by the extreme finger-ends, at the arm's length, and over against the shining of these embers. 'Tis so exactly. Thus, then, is the spell.'

With a haggard glance, Dick saw the coast was clear between him and the door. He put up an internal prayer. Then, whipping forth his arm, he made but one snatch of the ring, and at the same instant, levering up the table, he sent it bodily over upon the seaman Tom. He, poor soul, went down bawling under the ruins; and before Arblaster understood that anything was wrong, or Pirret could collect his dazzled wits, Dick had run to the door and escaped into the moonlit night.

The moon, which now rode in the mid-heavens, and the extreme whiteness of the snow, made the open ground about the harbour bright as day; and young Shelton leaping, with kilted robe, among the lumber, was a conspicuous figure from afar.

Tom and Pirret followed him with shouts; from every drinking-shop they were joined by others whom their cries aroused; and presently a whole fleet of sailors was in full pursuit. But Jack ashore was a bad runner, even in the fifteenth century, and Dick, besides, had a start, which he rapidly improved, until, as he drew near the entrance of a narrow lane, he even paused and looked laughingly behind him.

Upon the white floor of snow, all the shipmen of Shoreby came clustering in an inky mass, and tailing out rearward in isolated clumps. Every man was shouting or screaming; every man was gesticulating with both arms in air; some one was continually falling; and, to complete the picture, when one fell, a dozen would fall upon the top of him.

The confused mass of sound which they rolled up as high as to the moon was partly comical and partly terrifying to the fugitive whom they were hunting. In itself, it was impotent, for he made sure no seaman in the port could run him down. But the mere volume of noise, in so far as it must awake all the sleepers in Shoreby, and bring all the skulking sentries to the street, did really threaten him with danger in the front. So, spying a dark doorway at a corner, he whipped briskly into it, and let the uncouth hunt go by him, still shouting and gesticulating, and all red with hurry, and white with tumbles in the snow.

It was a long while, indeed, before this great invasion of the town by the harbour came to an end, and it was long before silence was restored. For long, lost sailors were still to be heard pounding and shouting through the streets in all directions and in every quarter of the town. Quarrels followed, sometimes among themselves, sometimes with the men of the patrols; knives were drawn, blows given and received, and more than one dead body remained behind upon the snow.

When, a full hour later, the last seaman returned grumblingly to the harbour side and his particular tavern, it may fairly be questioned if he had ever known what manner of man he was pursuing, but it was absolutely sure that he had now forgotten. By next morning there were many strange stories flying; and a little while after, the legend of the devil's nocturnal visit was an article of faith with all the lads of Shoreby.

But the return of the last seaman did not, even yet, set free young Shelton from his cold imprisonment in the doorway.

For some time after, there was a great activity of patrols; and special parties came forth to make the round of the place and report to one or other of the great lords, whose slumbers had been thus unusually broken.

The night was already well spent before Dick ventured from his hiding-place and came, safe and sound, but aching with cold and bruises, to the door of the Goat and Bagpipes. As the law required, there was neither fire nor candle in the house; but he groped his way into a corner of the icy guest-room, found an end of a blanket, which he hitched round his shoulders, and, creeping close to the nearest sleeper, was soon lost in slumber.

BOOK V
CROOKBACK

CHAPTER ONE

The Shrill Trumpet

VERY EARLY the next morning, before the first peep of the day, Dick arose, changed his garments, armed himself once more like a gentleman, and set forth for Lawless's den in the forest. There, it will be remembered, he had left Lord Foxham's papers; and to get these and be back in time for the tryst with the young Duke of Gloucester could only be managed by an early start, and the most vigorous walking.

The frost was more rigorous than ever; the air windless and dry, and stinging to the nostril. The moon had gone down, but the stars were still bright and numerous, and the reflection from the snow was clear and cheerful. There was no need for a lamp to walk by; nor, in that still but ringing air, the least temptation to delay.

Dick had crossed the greater part of the open ground between Shoreby and the forest, and had reached the bottom of the little hill, some hundred yards below the Cross of St Bride, when, through the stillness of the black morn, there rang forth the note of a trumpet, so shrill, clear, and piercing, that he thought he had never heard the match of it for audibility. It was blown once, and then hurriedly a second time; and then the clash of steel succeeded.

At this young Shelton pricked his ears, and, drawing his sword, ran forward up the hill.

Presently he came in sight of the cross, and was aware of a most fierce encounter raging on the road before it. There were seven or eight assailants, and but one to keep head against them; but so active and dexterous was this one, so desperately did he charge and scatter his opponents, so deftly keep his footing on the ice, that already, before Dick could intervene, he had slain one, wounded another, and kept the whole in check.

Still, it was by a miracle that he continued his defence, and at any moment, any accident, the least slip of foot or error of hand, his life would be a forfeit.

'Hold ye well, sir! Here is help!' cried Richard; and forgetting that he was alone, and that the cry was somewhat irregular, 'To the Arrow! to the Arrow!' he shouted, as he fell upon the rear of the assailants.

These were stout fellows also, for they gave not an inch at this surprise, but faced about, and fell with astonishing fury upon Dick. Four against one, the steel flashed about him in the starlight; the sparks flew fiercely; one of the men opposed to him fell — in the stir of the fight he hardly knew why; then he himself was struck across the head, and though the steel cap below his hood protected him, the blow beat him down upon one knee, with a brain whirling like a windmill sail.

Meanwhile the man whom he had come to rescue, instead of joining in the conflict, had, on the first sign of intervention, leaped back and blown again, and yet more urgently and loudly, on that same shrill-voiced trumpet that began the alarm. Next moment, indeed, his foes were on him, and he was once more charging and fleeing, leaping, stabbing, dropping to his knees, and using indifferently sword and dagger, foot and hand, with the same unshaken courage and feverish energy and speed.

But that ear-piercing summons had been heard at last. There was a muffled rushing in the snow; and in a good hour for Dick, who saw the sword-points glitter already at his throat, there poured forth out of the wood upon both sides a disorderly torrent of mounted men-at-arms, each cased in iron, and with visor lowered, each bearing his lance in rest, or his sword bared and raised, and each carrying, so to speak, a passenger, in the shape of an archer or page, who leaped one after another from their perches, and had presently doubled the array.

The original assailants, seeing themselves outnumbered and surrounded, threw down their arms without a word.

'Seize me these fellows!' said the hero of the trumpet;

and when his order had been obeyed, he drew near to Dick and looked him in the face.

Dick, returning this scrutiny, was surprised to find in one who had displayed such strength, skill and energy, a lad no older than himself – slightly deformed, with one shoulder higher than the other, and of a pale, painful, and distorted countenance.[1] The eyes, however, were very clear and bold.

'Sir,' said this lad, 'ye came in good time for me, and none too early.'

'My lord,' returned Dick, with a faint sense that he was in the presence of a great personage, 'ye are yourself so marvellous a good swordsman that I believe ye had managed them single-handed. Howbeit, it was certainly well for me that your men delayed no longer than they did.'

'How knew ye who I was?' demanded the stranger.

'Even now, my lord,' Dick answered, 'I am ignorant of whom I speak with.'

'Is it so?' asked the other. 'And yet ye threw yourself head first into this unequal battle.'

'I saw one man valiantly contending against many,' replied Dick, 'and I had thought myself dishonoured not to bear him aid.'

A singular sneer played about the young nobleman's mouth as he made answer:

'These are very brave words. But to the more essential – are ye Lancaster or York?'

'My lord, I make no secret; I am clear for York,' Dick answered.

'By the mass!' replied the other, 'it is well for you.'

And so saying, he turned towards one of his followers.

'Let me see,' he continued, in the same sneering and cruel tones – 'let me see a clean end of these brave gentlemen. Truss me them up.'

There were but five survivors of the attacking party. Archers seized them by the arms; they were hurried to the borders of the wood, and each placed below a tree of suitable

1. Richard Crookback would have been really far younger at this date.

dimensions; the rope was adjusted; an archer, carrying the end of it, hastily clambered overhead, and before a minute was over, and without a word passing upon either hand, the five men were swinging by the neck.

'And now,' cried the deformed leader, 'back to your posts, and when I summon you next, be readier to attend.'

'My lord duke,' said one man, 'beseech you, tarry not here alone. Keep but a handful of lances at your hand.'

'Fellow,' said the duke, 'I have forborne to chide you for your slowness. Cross me not, therefore. I trust my hand and arm, for all that I be crooked. Ye were backward when the trumpet sounded: and ye are now too forward with your counsels. But it is ever so; last with the lance and first with tongue. Let it be reversed.'

And with a gesture that was not without a sort of dangerous nobility, he waved them off.

The footmen climbed again to their seats behind the men-at-arms, and the whole party moved slowly away and disappeared in twenty different directions, under the cover of the forest.

The day was by this time beginning to break, and the stars to fade. The first grey glimmer of dawn shone upon the countenances of the two young men, who now turned once more to face each other.

'Here,' said the duke, 'ye have seen my vengeance, which is, like my blade, both sharp and ready. But I would not have you, for all Christendom, suppose me thankless. You that came to my aid with a good sword and a better courage – unless that ye recoil from my misshapenness – come to my heart.'

And so saying, the young leader held out his arms for an embrace.

In the bottom of his heart Dick already entertained a great terror and some hatred for the man whom he had rescued; but the invitation was so worded that it would not have been merely discourteous, but cruel, to refuse or hesitate, and he hastened to comply.

'And now, my lord duke,' he said, when he had regained his freedom, 'do I suppose aright? Are ye my Lord Duke of Gloucester?'

'I am Richard of Gloucester,' returned the other. 'And you – how call they you?'

Dick told him his name, and presented Lord Foxham's signet, which the duke immediately recognised.

'Ye come too soon,' he said; 'but why should I complain? Ye are like me, that was here at watch two hours before the day. But this is the first sally of mine arms; upon this adventure, Master Shelton, shall I make or mar the quality of my renown. There lie mine enemies, under two old, skilled captains, Risingham and Brackley, well posted for strength, I do believe, but yet upon two sides without retreat, enclosed betwixt the sea, the harbour, and the river. Methinks, Shelton, here were a great blow to be stricken, an we could strike it silently and suddenly.'

'I do think so, indeed,' cried Dick, warming.

'Have ye my Lord Foxham's notes?' inquired the duke.

And then Dick, having explained how he was without them for the moment, made himself bold to offer information, every jot as good, of his own knowledge.

'And for mine own part, my lord duke,' he added, 'an ye had men enough, I would fall on even at this present. For, look ye, at the peep of day the watches of the night are over; but by day they keep neither watch nor ward – only scour the outskirts with horsemen. Now, then, when the night-watch is already unarmed, and the rest are at their morning cup – now were the time to break them.'

'How many do ye count?' asked Gloucester.

'They number not two thousand,' Dick replied.

'I have seven hundred in the woods behind us,' said the duke; 'seven hundred follow from Kettley, and will be here anon; behind these, and farther, are four hundred more; and my Lord Foxham hath five hundred half-a-day from here, at Holywood. Shall we attend their coming, or fall on?'

'My lord,' said Dick, 'when ye hanged these five poor rogues ye did decide the question. Churls although they were, in these uneasy times they will be lacked and looked for, and the alarm be given. Therefore, my lord, if ye do count upon the advantage of a surprise, ye have not, in my poor opinion, one whole hour in front of you.'

'I do think so indeed,' returned Crookback. 'Well, before

an hour, ye shall be in the thick on't, winning spurs. A swift man to Holywood, carrying Lord Foxham's signet; another along the road to speed my laggards! Nay, Shelton, by the rood, it may be done!'

Therewith he once more set his trumpet to his lips and blew.

This time he was not long kept waiting. In a moment the open space about the cross was filled with horse and foot. Richard of Gloucester took his place upon the steps, and despatched messenger after messenger to hasten the concentration of the seven hundred men that lay hidden in the immediate neighbourhood among the woods; and before a quarter of an hour had passed, all his dispositions being taken, he put himself at their head, and began to move down the hill towards Shoreby.

This plan was simple. He was to seize a quarter of the town of Shoreby lying on the right hand of the high-road, and make his position good there in the narrow lanes until his reinforcements followed.

If Lord Risingham chose to retreat, Richard would follow upon his rear, and take him between two fires; or, if he preferred to hold the town, he would be shut in a trap, there to be gradually overwhelmed by force of numbers.

There was but one danger, but that was imminent and great – Gloucester's seven hundred might be rolled up and cut to pieces in the first encounter, and, to avoid this, it was needful to make the surprise of their arrival as complete as possible.

The footmen, therefore, were all once more taken up behind the riders, and Dick had the signal honour meted out to him of mounting behind Gloucester himself. For as far as there was any cover the troops moved slowly, and when they came near the end of the trees that lined the highway, stopped to breathe and reconnoitre.

The sun was now well up, shining with a frosty brightness out of a yellow halo, and right over against the luminary, Shoreby, a field of snowy roofs and ruddy gables, was rolling up its columns of morning smoke.

Gloucester turned round to Dick.

'In that poor place,' he said, 'where people are cooking

breakfast, either you shall gain your spurs and I begin a life of mighty honour and glory in the world's eye, or both of us, as I conceive it, shall fall dead and be unheard of. Two Richards are we. Well then, Richard Shelton, they shall be heard about, these two! Their swords shall not ring more loudly on men's helmets than their names shall ring in people's ears.'

Dick was astonished at so great a hunger after fame expressed with so great vehemence of voice and language; and he answered very sensibly and quietly that, for his part, he promised he would do his duty, and doubted not of victory if everyone did the like.

By this time the horses were well breathed, and the leader holding up his sword and giving rein, the whole troop of chargers broke into the gallop and thundered, with their double load of fighting men, down the remainder of the hill and across the snow-covered plain that still divided them from Shoreby.

CHAPTER TWO

The Battle of Shoreby

THE whole distance to be crossed was not above a quarter of a mile. But they had no sooner debouched beyond the cover of the trees than they were aware of people fleeing and screaming in the snowy meadows upon either hand. Almost at the same moment a great rumour began to arise, and spread and grow continually louder in the town; and they were not yet half-way to the nearest house before the bells began to ring backward from the steeple.

The young duke ground his teeth together. By these so early signals of alarm he feared to find his enemies prepared; and if he failed to gain a footing in the town, he knew that his small party would soon be broken and exterminated in the open.

In the town, however, the Lancastrians were far from being in so good a posture. It was as Dick had said. The night-guard had already doffed their harness; the rest were still hanging – unlatched, unbraced, all unprepared for battle – about their quarters; and in the whole of Shoreby there were not, perhaps, fifty men full armed, or fifty chargers ready to be mounted.

The beating of the bells, the terrifying summons of men who ran about the streets crying and beating upon the doors, aroused in an incredibly short space at least two score out of that half hundred. These got speedily to horse, and, the alarm still flying wild and contrary, galloped in different directions.

Thus it befell that, when Richard of Gloucester reached the first house of Shoreby, he was met in the mouth of the street by a mere handful of lances, whom he swept before his onset as the storm chases the bark.

A hundred paces into the town, Dick Shelton touched

the duke's arm; the duke, in answer, gathered his reins, put the shrill trumpet to his mouth, and blowing a concerted point, turned to the right hand out of the direct advance. Swerving like a single rider, his whole command turned after him, and, still at the full gallop of the chargers, swept up the narrow by-street. Only the last score of riders drew rein and faced about in the entrance; the footmen, whom they carried behind them, leapt at the same instant to the earth, and began, some to bend their bows, and others to break into and secure the houses upon either hand.

Surprised at this sudden change of direction, and daunted by the firm front of the rear-guard, the few Lancastrians, after a momentary consultation, turned and rode farther into town to seek for reinforcements.

The quarter of the town upon which, by the advice of Dick, Richard of Gloucester had now seized, consisted of five small streets of poor and ill-inhabited houses, occupying a very gentle eminence, and lying open towards the back.

The five streets being each secured by a good guard, the reserve would thus occupy the centre, out of shot, and yet ready to carry aid wherever it was needed.

Such was the poorness of the neighbourhood that none of the Lancastrian lords, and but few of their retainers, had been lodged therein; and the inhabitants, with one accord, deserted their houses and fled, squalling, along the streets or over garden walls.

In the centre, where the five ways all met, a somewhat ill-favoured alehouse displayed the sign of the Chequers; and here the Duke of Gloucester chose his headquarters for the day.

To Dick he assigned the guard of one of the five streets. 'Go,' he said, 'win your spurs. Win glory for me; one Richard for another. I tell you, if I rise, ye shall rise by the same ladder. Go,' he added, shaking him by the hand.

But, as soon as Dick was gone, he turned to a little shabby archer at his elbow.

'Go, Dutton, and that right speedily,' he added. 'Follow that lad. If ye find him faithful, ye answer for his safety, a head for a head. Woe unto you, if ye return without him!

But if he be faithless – or, for one instant, ye misdoubt him – stab him from behind.'

In the meanwhile Dick hastened to secure his post. The street he had to guard was very narrow, and closely lined with houses, which projected and overhung the roadway; but narrow and dark as it was, since it opened upon the market-place of the town, the main issue of the battle would probably fall to be decided on that spot.

The market-place was full of townspeople fleeing in disorder; but there was as yet no sign of any foeman ready to attack, and Dick judged he had some time before him to make ready his defence.

The two houses at the end stood deserted, with open doors, as the inhabitants had left them in their flight, and from these he had the furniture hastily tossed forth and piled into a barrier in the entry of the lane. A hundred men were placed at his disposal, and of these he threw the more part into the houses, where they might lie in shelter and deliver their arrows from the windows. With the rest, under his own immediate eye, he lined the barricade.

Meanwhile the utmost uproar and confusion had continued to prevail throughout the town; and what with the hurried clashing of bells, the sounding of trumpets, the swift movement of bodies of horse, the cries of the commanders, and the shrieks of women, the noise was almost deafening to the ear. Presently, little by little, the tumult began to subside; and soon after, files of men in armour and bodies of archers began to assemble and form in line of battle in the market-place.

A large portion of this body were in murrey and blue, and in the mounted knight who ordered their array Dick recognised Sir Daniel Brackley.

Then there befell a long pause, which was followed by the almost simultaneous sounding of four trumpets from four different quarters of the town. A fifth rang in answer from the market-place, and at the same moment the files began to move, and a shower of arrows rattled about the barricade, and sounded like blows upon the walls of the two flanking houses.

The attack had begun, by a common signal, on all the

five issues of the quarter. Gloucester was beleaguered upon every side; and Dick judged, if he would make good his post, he must rely entirely on the hundred men of his command.

Seven volleys of arrows followed one upon the other, and in the very thick of the discharges Dick was touched from behind upon the arm, and found a page holding out to him a leathern jack, strengthened with bright plates of mail.

'It is from my Lord of Gloucester,' said the page. 'He hath observed, Sir Richard, that ye went unarmed.'

Dick, with a glow at his heart at being so addressed, got to his feet and, with the assistance of the page, donned the defensive coat. Even as he did so, two arrows rattled harmlessly upon the plates, and a third struck down the page, mortally wounded, at his feet.

Meantime the whole body of the enemy had been steadily drawing nearer across the market-place; and by this time were so close at hand that Dick gave the order to return their shot. Immediately, from behind the barrier and from the windows of the houses, a counterblast of arrows sped, carrying death. But the Lancastrians, as if they had but waited for a signal, shouted loudly in answer; and began to close at a run upon the barrier, the horsemen still hanging back, with visors lowered.

Then followed an obstinate and deadly struggle, hand to hand. The assailants, wielding their falchions with one hand, strove with the other to drag down the structure of the barricade. On the other side, the parts were reversed; and the defenders exposed themselves like madmen to protect their rampart. So for some minutes the contest raged almost in silence, friend and foe falling one upon another. But it is always the easier to destroy; and when a single note upon the tucket recalled the attacking party from this desperate service, much of the barricade had been removed piecemeal, and the whole fabric had sunk to half its height, and tottered to a general fall.

And now the footmen in the market-place fell back, at a run, on every side. The horsemen, who had been standing in a line two deep, wheeled suddenly, and made their flank into their front; and as swift as a striking adder, the long, steel-clad column was launched upon the ruinous barricade.

Of the first two horsemen, one fell, rider and steed, and was ridden down by his companions. The second leaped clean upon the summit of the rampart, transpiercing an archer with his lance. Almost in the same instant he was dragged from the saddle and his horse despatched.

And then the full weight and impetus of the charge burst upon and scattered the defenders. The men-at-arms, surmounting their fallen comrades, and carried onward by the fury of their onslaught, dashed through Dick's broken line and poured thundering up the lane beyond, as a stream bestrides and pours across a broken dam.

Yet was the fight not over. Still, in the narrow jaws of the entrance, Dick and a few survivors plied their bills like woodmen; and already, across the width of the passage, there had been formed a second, a higher, and a more effectual rampart of fallen men and disembowelled horses, lashing in the agonies of death.

Baffled by this fresh obstacle, the remainder of the cavalry fell back; and as, at the sight of this movement, the flight of arrows redoubled from the casements of the houses, their retreat had, for a moment, almost degenerated into flight.

Almost at the same time, those who had crossed the barricade and charged farther up the street, being met before the door of the 'Chequers' by the formidable hunchback and the whole reserve of the Yorkists, began to come scattering backward, in the excess of disarray and terror.

Dick and his fellows faced about, fresh men poured out of the houses; a cruel blast of arrows met the fugitives full in the face, while Gloucester was already riding down their rear; in the inside of a minute and a half there was no living Lancastrian in the street.

Then, and not till then, did Dick hold up his reeking blade and give the word to cheer.

Meanwhile Gloucester dismounted from his horse and came forward to inspect the post. His face was as pale as linen; but his eyes shone in his head like some strange jewel, and his voice, when he spoke, was hoarse and broken

with the exultation of battle and success. He looked at the
rampart, which neither friend nor foe could now approach
without precaution, so fiercely did the horses struggle in
the throes of death, and at the sight of that great carnage
he smiled upon one side.

'Despatch these horses,' he said; 'they keep you from
your vantage. Richard Shelton,' he added, 'ye have pleased
me. Kneel.'

The Lancastrians had already resumed their archery, and
the shafts fell thick in the mouth of the street; but the duke,
minding them not at all, deliberately drew his sword and
dubbed Richard a knight upon the spot.

'And now, Sir Richard,' he continued, 'if that ye see Lord
Risingham, send me an express upon the instant. Were it
your last man, let me hear of it incontinently. I had rather
venture the post than lose my stroke at him. For mark me,
all of ye,' he added, raising his voice, 'if Earl Risingham
fall by another hand than mine, I shall count this victory
a defeat.'

'My lord duke,' said one of his attendants, 'is your grace
not weary of exposing his dear life unneedfully? Why tarry
we here?'

'Catesby,' returned the duke, 'here is the battle, not
elsewhere. The rest are but feigned onslaughts. Here
must we vanquish. And for the exposure – if ye were
an ugly hunchback, and the children gecked at you upon
the street, ye would count your body cheaper, and an
hour of glory worth a life. Howbeit, if ye will, let us
ride on and visit the other posts. Sir Richard here, my
namesake, he shall still hold this entry, where he wadeth
to the ankles in hot blood. Him can we trust. But mark it,
Sir Richard, ye are not yet done. The worst is yet to ward.
Sleep not.'

He came right up to young Shelton, looking him hard
in the eyes, and taking his hand in both of his, gave it
so extreme a squeeze that the blood had nearly spurted.
Dick quailed before his eyes. The insane excitement, the
courage, and the cruelty that he read therein, filled him
with dismay about the future. This young duke's was
indeed a gallant spirit, to ride foremost in the ranks of

war; but, after the battle, in the days of peace and in the circle of his trusted friends, that mind, it was to be dreaded, would continue to bring forth the fruits of death.

CHAPTER THREE

The Battle of Shoreby — concluded

DICK, ONCE MORE left to his own counsels, began to look about him. The arrow-shot had somewhat slackened. On all sides the enemy were falling back; and the greater part of the market-place was now left empty, the snow here trampled into orange mud, there splashed with gore, scattered all over with dead men and horses, and bristling thick with feathered arrows.

On his own side the loss had been cruel. The jaws of the little street and the ruins of the barricade were heaped with the dead and dying; and out of the hundred men with whom he had begun the battle, there were not seventy left who could still stand to arms.

At the same time the day was passing. The first reinforcements might be looked for to arrive at any moment; and the Lancastrians, already shaken by the result of their desperate but unsuccessful onslaught, were in an ill-temper to support a fresh invader.

There was a dial in the wall of one of the two flanking houses; and this, in the frosty, winter sunshine, indicated ten of the forenoon.

Dick turned to the man who was at his elbow, a little insignificant archer, binding a cut in his arm.

'It was well fought,' he said, 'and, by my sooth, they will not charge us twice.'

'Sir,' said the little archer, 'ye have fought right well for York, and better for yourself. Never hath man in so brief space prevailed so greatly on the duke's affections. That he should have entrusted such a post to one he knew not is a marvel. But look to your head, Sir Richard! If ye be vanquished – ay, if ye give way one foot's breadth – axe or cord shall punish it; and I am set, if ye do aught doubtful, I will tell you honestly, here to stab you from behind.'

Dick looked at the little man in amaze.

'You!' he cried. 'And from behind!'

'It is right so,' returned the archer; 'and because I like not the affair I tell it you. Ye must make the post good, Sir Richard, at your peril. O, our Crookback is a bold blade and a good warrior; but whether in cold blood or in hot, he will have all things done exact to his commandment. If any fail or hinder, they shall die the death.'

'Now, by the saints!' cried Richard, 'is this so? And will men follow such a leader?'

'Nay, they follow him gleefully,' replied the other; 'for if he be exact to punish, he is most open-handed to reward. And if he spare not the blood and sweat of others, he is ever liberal of his own, still in the first front of battle, still the last to sleep. He will go far, will Crookback Dick o' Gloucester!'

The young knight, if he had been before brave and vigilant, was now all the more inclined to watchfulness and courage. His sudden favour, he began to perceive, had brought perils in its train. And he turned from the archer, and once more scanned anxiously the market-place. It lay empty as before.

'I like not this quietude,' he said. 'Doubtless they prepare us some surprise.'

And, as if in answer to his remark, the archers began once more to advance against the barricade, and the arrows to fall thick. But there was something hesitating in the attack. They came not on roundly, but seemed rather to await a further signal.

Dick looked uneasily about him, spying for a hidden danger. And sure enough, about half-way up the little street, a door was suddenly opened from within, and the house continued, for some seconds, and both by door and window, to disgorge a torrent of Lancastrian archers. These, as they leaped down, hurriedly stood to their ranks, bent their bows, and proceeded to pour upon Dick's rear a flight of arrows.

At the same time, the assailants in the market-place

redoubled their shot, and began to close in stoutly upon the barricade.

Dick called down his whole command out of the houses, and facing them both ways, and encouraging their valour both by word and gesture, returned as best he could the double shower of shafts that fell about his post.

Meanwhile house after house was opened in the street, and the Lancastrians continued to pour out of the doors and leap down from the windows, shouting victory, until the number of enemies upon Dick's rear was almost equal to the number in his face. It was plain that he could hold the post no longer; what was worse, even if he could have held it, it had now become useless; and the whole Yorkist army lay in a posture of helplessness upon the brink of a complete disaster.

The men behind him formed the vital flaw in the general defence; and it was upon these that Dick turned, charging at the head of his men. So vigorous was the attack, that the Lancastrian archers gave ground and staggered, and, at last, breaking their ranks, began to crowd back into the houses from which they had so recently and so vaingloriously sallied.

Meanwhile the men from the market-place had swarmed across the undefended barricade, and fell on hotly upon the other side; and Dick must once again face about, and proceed to drive them back. Once again the spirit of his men prevailed; they cleared the street in a triumphant style, but even as they did so the others issued again out of the houses, and took them, a third time, upon the rear.

The Yorkists began to be scattered; several times Dick found himself alone among his foes and plying his bright sword for life; several times he was conscious of a hurt. And meanwhile the fight swayed to and fro in the street without determinate result.

Suddenly Dick was aware of a great trumpeting about the outskirts of the town. The war-cry of York began to be rolled up to heaven, as by many and triumphant voices. And at the same time the men in front of him began to give ground rapidly, streaming out of the street and back upon the market-place. Some one gave the word to fly.

Trumpets were blown distractedly, some for a rally, some to charge. It was plain that a great blow had been struck, and the Lancastrians were thrown, at least for the moment, into full disorder, and some degree of panic.

And then, like a theatre trick, there followed the last act of Shoreby Battle. The men in front of Richard turned tail, like a dog that has been whistled home, and fled like the wind. At the same moment there came through the market-place a storm of horsemen, fleeing and pursuing, the Lancastrians turning back to strike with the sword, the Yorkists riding them down at the point of the lance.

Conspicuous in the mellay, Dick beheld the Crookback. He was already giving a foretaste of that furious valour and skill to cut his way across the ranks of war, which, years afterwards upon the field of Bosworth, and when he was stained with crimes, almost sufficed to change the fortunes of the day and the destiny of the English throne. Evading, striking, riding down, he so forced and so manœuvred his strong horse, so aptly defended himself, and so liberally scattered death to his opponents, that he was now far ahead of the foremost of his knights, hewing his way, with the truncheon of a bloody sword, to where Lord Risingham was rallying the bravest. A moment more and they had met; the tall, splendid, and famous warrior against the deformed and sickly boy.

Yet Shelton had never a doubt of the result; and when the fight next opened for a moment, the figure of the earl had disappeared; but still, in the first of the danger, Crookback Dick was launching his big horse and plying the truncheon of his sword.

Thus, by Shelton's courage in holding the mouth of the street against the first attack, and by the opportune arrival of his seven hundred reinforcements, the lad, who was afterwards to be handed down to the execration of posterity under the name of Richard III, had won his first considerable fight.

CHAPTER FOUR

The Sack of Shoreby

THERE WAS not a foe left within striking distance; and Dick, as he looked ruefully about him on the remainder of his gallant force, began to count the cost of victory. He was himself, now that the danger was ended, so stiff and sore, so bruised and cut and broken, and, above all, so utterly exhausted by his desperate and unremitting labours in the fight, that he seemed incapable of any fresh exertion.

But this was not yet the hour for repose. Shoreby had been taken by assault; and though an open town, and not in any manner to be charged with the resistance, it was plain that these rough fighters would be not less rough now that the fight was over, and that the more horrid part of war would fall to be enacted. Richard of Gloucester was not the captain to protect the citizens from his infuriated soldiery; and, even if he had the will, it might be questioned if he had the power.

It was, therefore, Dick's business to find and to protect Joanna; and with that end he looked about him at the faces of his men. The three or four who seemed likeliest to be obedient and to keep sober he drew aside; and promising them a rich reward and a special recommendation to the duke, led them across the market-place, now empty of horsemen, and into the streets upon the farther side.

Every here and there small combats of from two to a dozen still raged upon the open street; here and there a house was being besieged, the defenders throwing out stools and tables on the heads of the assailants. The snow was strewn with arms and corpses; but except for these partial combats the streets were deserted, and the houses, some standing open, and some shuttered and barricaded, had for the most part ceased to give out smoke.

Dick, threading the skirts of these skirmishers, led his followers briskly in the direction of the abbey church; but when he came the length of the main street a cry of horror broke from his lips. Sir Daniel's great house had been carried by assault. The gates hung in splinters from the hinges, and a double throng kept pouring in and out through the entrance, seeking and carrying booty. Meanwhile, in the upper storeys, some resistance was still being offered to the pillagers; for just as Dick came within eyeshot of the building, a casement was burst open from within, and a poor wretch in murrey and blue, screaming and resisting, was forced through the embrasure and tossed into the street below.

The most sickening apprehension fell upon Dick. He ran forward like one possessed, forced his way into the house among the foremost, and mounted without pause to the chamber on the third floor where he had last parted from Joanna. It was a mere wreck; the furniture had been overthrown, the cupboards broken open, and in one place a trailing corner of the arras lay smouldering on the embers of the fire.

Dick, almost without thinking, trod out the incipient conflagration, and then stood bewildered. Sir Daniel, Sir Oliver, Joanna, all were gone; but whether butchered in the rout or safe escaped from Shoreby, who should say?

He caught a passing archer by the tabard.

'Fellow,' he asked, 'were ye here when this house was taken?'

'Let be,' said the archer. 'A murrain! let be, or I strike.'

'Hark ye,' returned Richard, 'two can play at that. Stand and be plain.'

But the man, flushed with drink and battle, struck Dick upon the shoulder with one hand, while with the other he twitched away his garment. Thereupon the full wrath of the young leader burst from his control. He seized the fellow in his strong embrace, and crushed him on the plates of his mailed bosom like a child; then, holding him at arm's length, he bid him speak as he valued life.

'I pray you mercy!' gasped the archer. 'An I had thought

ye were so angry I would 'a' been charier of crossing you. I was here indeed.'

'Know ye Sir Daniel?' pursued Dick.

'Well do I know him,' returned the man.

'Was he in the mansion?'

'Ay, sir, he was,' answered the archer; 'but even as we entered by the yard gate he rode forth by the garden.'

'Alone?' cried Dick.

'He may 'a' had a score of lances with him,' said the man.

'Lances! No women, then?' asked Shelton.

'Troth, I saw not,' said the archer. 'But there were none in the house, if that be your quest.'

'I thank you,' said Dick. 'Here is a piece for your pains.' But, groping in his wallet, Dick found nothing. 'Inquire for me to-morrow,' he added – 'Richard Shel—Sir Richard Shelton,' he corrected, 'and I will see you handsomely rewarded.'

And then an idea struck Dick. He hastily descended to the courtyard, ran with all his might across the garden, and came to the great door of the church. It stood wide open; within, every corner of the pavement was crowded with fugitive burghers, surrounded by their families and laden with the most precious of their possessions, while, at the high altar, priests in full canonicals were imploring the mercy of God. Even as Dick entered, the loud chorus began to thunder in the vaulted roofs.

He hurried through the groups of refugees, and came to the door of the stair that led into the steeple. And here a tall churchman stepped before him and arrested his advance.

'Whither, my son?' he asked, severely.

'My father,' answered Dick, 'I am here upon an errand of expedition. Stay me not. I command here for my Lord of Gloucester.'

'For my Lord of Gloucester?' repeated the priest.

'Hath, then, the battle gone so sore?'

'The battle, father, is at an end, Lancaster clean sped, my Lord of Risingham – heaven rest him! – left upon the field. And now, with your good leave, I follow mine affairs.' And thrusting on one side the priest, who seemed stupefied at the news, Dick pushed open the door and rattled up the stairs four at a bound, and without pause or stumble, till he stepped upon the open platform at the top.

Shoreby Church tower not only commanded the town, as in a map, but looked far, on both sides, over sea and land. It was now near upon noon; the day exceeding bright, the snow dazzling. And as Dick looked around him, he could measure the consequences of the battle.

A confused, growling uproar reached him from the streets, and now and then, but very rarely, the clash of steel. Not a ship, not so much as a skiff remained in harbour; but the sea was dotted with sails and row-boats laden with fugitives. On shore, too, the surface of the snowy meadows was broken up with bands of horsemen, some cutting their way towards the borders of the forest, others, who were doubtless of the Yorkist side, stoutly interposing, and beating them back upon the town. Over all the open ground there lay a prodigious quantity of fallen men and horses, clearly defined upon the snow.

To complete the picture, those of the foot soldiers as had not found place upon a ship still kept up an archery combat on the borders of the port, and from the cover of the shoreside taverns. In that quarter, also, one or two houses had been fired, and the smoke towered high in the frosty sunlight, and blew off to sea in voluminous folds.

Already close upon the margin of the woods, and somewhat in the line of Holywood, one particular clump of fleeing horsemen riveted the attention of the young watcher on the tower. It was fairly numerous; in no other quarter of the field did so many Lancastrians still hold together; thus they had left a wide, discoloured wake upon the snow, and Dick was able to trace them step by step from where they had left the town.

While Dick stood watching them, they had gained, unopposed, the first fringe of the leafless forest, and a little from their direction, the sun fell for a moment full on their array, as it was relieved against the dusky wood.

'Murrey and blue!' cried Dick. 'I swear it – murrey and blue!'

The next moment he was descending the stairway.

It was now his business to seek out the Duke of Gloucester, who alone, in the disorder of the forces, might be able to supply him with a sufficiency of men. The fighting in the main town was now practically at an end; and as Dick ran hither and thither, seeking the commander, the streets were thick with wandering soldiers, some laden with more booty than they could well stagger under, others shouting drunk. None of them, when questioned, had the least notion of the duke's whereabouts; and, at last, it was by sheer good fortune that Dick found him, where he sat in the saddle, directing operations to dislodge the archers from the harbour side.

'Sir Richard Shelton, ye are well found,' he said. 'I owe you one thing that I value little, my life; and one that I can never repay you for, this victory. Catesby, if I had ten such captains as Sir Richard, I would march forthright on London. But now, sir, claim your reward.'

'Freely, my lord,' said Dick, 'freely and loudly. One hath escaped to whom I owe some grudges, and taken with him one whom I owe love and service. Give me, then, fifty lances, that I may pursue; and for any obligation that your graciousness is pleased to allow, it shall be clean discharged.'

'How call ye him?' inquired the duke.

'Sir Daniel Brackley,' answered Richard.

'Out upon him, double-face!' cried Gloucester. 'Here is no reward, Sir Richard; here is fresh service offered, and, if that ye bring his head to me, a fresh debt upon my conscience. Catesby, get him these lances; and you, sir, bethink ye, in the meanwhile, what pleasure, honour, or profit it shall be mine to give you.'

Just then the Yorkist skirmishers carried one of the shoreside taverns, swarming in upon it on three sides, and driving out or taking its defenders. Crookback Dick was pleased to cheer the exploit, and, pushing his horse a little nearer, called to see the prisoners.

There were four or five of them – two men of my Lord Shoreby's and one of Lord Risingham's among the number, and last, but in Dick's eyes not least, a tall, shambling, grizzled old shipman, between drunk and sober, and with a dog whimpering and jumping at his heels.

The young duke passed them for a moment under a severe review.

'Good,' he said. 'Hang them.'

And he turned the other way to watch the progress of the fight.

'My lord,' said Dick, 'so please you, I have found my reward. Grant me the life and liberty of yon old shipman.'

Gloucester turned and looked the speaker in the face.

'Sir Richard,' he said, 'I make not war with peacocks' feathers, but steel shafts. Those that are mine enemies I slay, and that without excuse or favour. For, bethink ye, in this realm of England, that is so torn in pieces, there is not a man of mine but hath a brother or a friend upon the other party. If, then, I did begin to grant these pardons, I might sheathe my sword.'

'It may be so, my lord; and yet I will be overbold, and, at the risk of your disfavour, recall your lordship's promise,' replied Dick.

Richard of Gloucester flushed.

'Mark it right well,' he said, harshly. 'I love not mercy, nor yet mercymongers. Ye have this day laid the foundations of high fortune. If ye oppose to me my word, which I have plighted, I will yield. But, by the glory of heaven, there your favour dies!'

'Mine is the loss,' said Dick.

'Give him his sailor,' said the duke; and wheeling his horse, he turned his back upon young Shelton.

Dick was nor glad nor sorry. He had seen too much of the young duke to set great store on his affection; and the origin and growth of his own favour had been too flimsy and too rapid to inspire much confidence. One thing alone he feared – that the vindictive leader might revoke the offer of the lances. But here he did justice neither to Gloucester's honour (such as it was) nor, above all, to his decision. If he had once judged Dick to be the right man to pursue Sir Daniel, he was not one to change; and he soon proved it by shouting after Catesby to be speedy, for the paladin was waiting.

In the meanwhile, Dick turned to the old shipman, who

had seemed equally indifferent to his condemnation and to his subsequent release.

'Arblaster,' said Dick, 'I have done you ill; but now, by the rood, I think I have cleared the score.'

But the old skipper only looked upon him dully and held his peace.

'Come,' continued Dick, 'a life is a life, old shrew, and it is more than ships or liquor. Say ye forgive me; for if your life is worth nothing to you, it hath cost me the beginnings of my fortune. Come, I have paid for it dearly; be not so churlish.'

'An I had had my ship,' said Arblaster, 'I would 'a' been forth and safe upon the high seas – I and my man Tom. But ye took my ship, gossip, and I'm a beggar; and for my man Tom, a knave fellow in russet shot him down. "Murrain!" quoth he, and spake never again. "Murrain" was the last of his words, and the poor spirit of him passed. 'A will never sail no more, will my Tom.'

Dick was seized with unavailing penitence and pity; he sought to take the skipper's hand, but Arblaster avoided his touch.

'Nay,' said he, 'let be. Y' have played the devil with me, and let that content you.'

The words died in Richard's throat. He saw, through tears, the poor old man, bemused with liquor and sorrow, go shambling away, with bowed head, across the snow, and the unnoticed dog whimpering at his heels; and for the first time began to understand the desperate game that we play in life, and how a thing once done is not to be changed or remedied by any penitence.

But there was no time left to him for vain regret. Catesby had now collected the horsemen; and riding up to Dick he dismounted, and offered him his own horse.

'This morning,' he said, 'I was somewhat jealous of your favour; it hath not been of a long growth; and now, Sir Richard, it is with a very good heart that I offer you this horse – to ride away with.'

'Suffer me yet a moment,' replied Dick. 'This favour of mine – whereupon was it founded?'

'Upon your name,' answered Catesby. 'It is my lord's

chief superstition. Were my name Richard, I should be an earl to-morrow.'

'Well, sir, I thank you,' returned Dick; 'and since I am little likely to follow these great fortunes, I will even say farewell. I will not pretend I was displeased to think myself upon the road to fortune; but I will not pretend, neither, that I am over-sorry to be done with it. Command and riches, they are brave things, to be sure; but a word in your ear – yon duke of yours, he is a fearsome lad.'

Catesby laughed.

'Nay,' said he, 'of a verity he that rides with Crooked Dick will ride deep. Well, God keep us all from evil! Speed ye well.'

Thereupon Dick put himself at the head of his men, and giving the word of command, rode off.

He made straight across the town, following what he supposed to be the route of Sir Daniel, and spying around for any signs that might decide if he were right.

The streets were strewn with the dead and wounded, whose fate, in the bitter frost, was far more pitiable. Gangs of the victors went from house to house, pillaging and stabbing, and sometimes singing together as they went.

From different quarters, as he rode on, the sounds of violence and outrage came to young Shelton's ears; now the blows of the sledge-hammer on some barricaded door, and now the miserable shrieks of women.

Dick's heart had just been awakened. He had just seen the cruel consequences of his own behaviour; and the thought of the sum of misery that was now acting in the whole of Shoreby filled him with despair.

At length he reached the outskirts, and there, sure enough, he saw straight before him the same broad, beaten track across the snow that he had marked from the summit of the church. Here, then, he went the faster on; but still, as he rode, he kept a bright eye upon the fallen men and horses that lay beside the track. Many of these, he was relieved to see, wore Sir Daniel's colours, and the faces of some, who lay upon their back, he even recognised.

About half-way between the town and the forest, those whom he was following had plainly been assailed by archers;

for the corpses lay pretty closely scattered, each pierced by an arrow. And here Dick spied among the rest the body of a very young lad, whose face was somehow hauntingly familiar to him.

He halted his troop, dismounted, and raised the lad's head. As he did so, the hood fell back, and a profusion of long brown hair unrolled itself. At the same time the eyes opened.

'Ah! lion-driver!' said a feeble voice. 'She is farther on. Ride – ride fast!'

And then the poor young lady fainted once again.

One of Dick's men carried a flask of some strong cordial, and with this Dick succeeded in reviving consciousness. Then he took Joanna's friend upon his saddle-bow, and once more pushed towards the forest.

'Why do ye take me?' said the girl. 'Ye but delay your speed.'

'Nay, Mistress Risingham,' replied Dick. 'Shoreby is full of blood and drunkenness and riot. Here ye are safe; content ye.'

'I will not be beholden to any of your faction,' she cried; 'set me down.'

'Madam, ye know not what ye say,' returned Dick. 'Y' are hurt—'

'I am not,' she said. 'It was my horse was slain.'

'It matters not one jot,' replied Dick. 'Ye are here in the midst of open snow, and compassed about with enemies. Whether ye will or not, I carry you with me. Glad am I to have the occasion; for thus shall I repay some portion of our debt.'

For a little while she was silent. Then, very suddenly, she asked:

'My uncle?'

'My Lord Risingham?' returned Dick. 'I would I had good news to give you, madam, but I have none. I saw him once in the battle, and once only. Let us hope the best.'

CHAPTER FIVE

Night in the Woods: Alicia Risingham

IT WAS almost certain that Sir Daniel had made for the Moat House; but, considering the heavy snow, the lateness of the hour, and the necessity under which he would lie of avoiding the few roads and striking across the wood, it was equally certain that he could not hope to reach it ere the morrow.

There were two courses open to Dick; either to continue to follow in the night's trail, and, if he were able, to fall upon him that very night in camp, or to strike out a path of his own, and seek to place himself between Sir Daniel and his destination.

Either scheme was open to serious objection, and Dick, who feared to expose Joanna to the hazards of a fight, had not yet decided between them when he reached the borders of the wood.

At this point Sir Daniel had turned a little to his left, and then plunged straight under a grove of very lofty timber. His party had then formed to a narrower front, in order to pass between the trees, and the track was trod proportionately deeper in the snow. The eye followed it, under the leafless tracery of the oaks, running direct and narrow; the trees stood over it, with knotty joints and the great, uplifted forest of their boughs; there was no sound, whether of man or beast – not so much as the stirring of a robin; and over the field of snow the winter sun lay golden among netted shadows.

'How say ye,' asked Dick of one of the men, 'to follow straight on, or strike across for Tunstall?'

'Sir Richard,' replied the man-at-arms, 'I would follow the line until they scatter.'

'Ye are doubtless right,' returned Dick; 'but we came

right hastily upon the errand, even as the time commanded. Here are no houses, neither for food nor shelter, and by the morrow's dawn we shall know both cold fingers and an empty belly. How say ye, lads? Will ye stand a pinch for expedition's sake, or shall we turn by Holywood and sup with Mother Church? The case being somewhat doubtful, I will drive no man; yet if ye would suffer me to lead you, ye would choose the first.'

The men answered, almost with one voice, that they would follow Sir Richard where he would.

And Dick, setting spurs to his horse, began once more to go forward.

The snow in the trail had been trodden very hard, and the pursuers had thus a great advantage over the pursued. They pushed on, indeed, at a round trot, two hundred hoofs beating alternately on the dull pavement of snow, and the jingle of weapons and the snorting of horses raising a warlike noise along the arches of the silent wood.

Presently, the wide slot of the pursued came out upon the high-road from Holywood; it was there, for a moment, indistinguishable; and, where it once more plunged into the unbeaten snow upon the farther side, Dick was surprised to see it narrower and lighter trod. Plainly, profiting by the road, Sir Daniel had begun already to scatter his command.

At all hazards, one chance being equal to another, Dick continued to pursue the straight trail; and that, after an hour's riding, in which it led into the very depths of the forest, suddenly split, like a bursting shell, into two dozen others, leading to every point of the compass.

Dick drew bridle in despair. The short winter's day was near an end; the sun, a dull red orange, shorn of rays, swam low among the leafless thickets; the shadows were a mile long upon the snow; the frost bit cruelly at the finger-nails; and the breath and steam of the horses mounted in a cloud.

'Well, we are outwitted,' Dick confessed. 'Strike we for Holywood, after all. It is still nearer us than Tunstall – or should be by the station of the sun.'

So they wheeled to their left, turning their backs on the

red shield of sun, and made across country for the abbey. But now times were changed with them; they could no longer spank forth briskly on a path beaten firm by the passage of their foes, and for a goal to which that path itself conducted them. Now they must plough at a dull pace through the encumbering snow, continually pausing to decide their course, continually floundering in drifts. The sun soon left them; the glow of the west decayed; and presently they were wandering in a shadow of blackness, under frosty stars.

Presently, indeed, the moon would clear the hill-tops, and they might resume their march. But till then, every random step might carry them wider of their march. There was nothing for it but to camp and wait.

Sentries were posted; a spot of ground was cleared of snow, and after some failures a good fire blazed in the midst. The men-at-arms sat close about this forest hearth, sharing such provisions as they had, and passing about the flask; and Dick, having collected the most delicate of the rough and scanty fare, brought it to Lord Risingham's niece, where she sat apart from the soldiery against a tree.

She sat upon one horse-cloth, wrapped in another, and stared straight before her at the firelit scene. At the offer of food she started, like one awakened from a dream, and then silently refused.

'Madam,' said Dick, 'let me beseech you, punish me not so cruelly. Wherein I have offended you, I know not; I have, indeed, carried you away, but with a friendly violence; I have, indeed, exposed you to the inclemency of night, but the hurry that lies upon me hath for its end the preservation of another, who is no less frail and no less unfriended than yourself. At least, madam, punish not yourself; and eat, if not for hunger, then for strength.'

'I will eat nothing at the hands that slew my kinsman,' she replied.

'Dear madam,' Dick cried, 'I swear to you upon the rood I touched him not.'

'Swear to me that he still lives,' she returned.

'I will not palter with you,' answered Dick. 'Pity bids me to wound you. In my heart I do believe him dead.'

'And ye ask me to eat!' she cried. 'Ay, and they call you "sir"! Y' have won your spurs by my good kinsman's murder. And had I not been fool and traitor both, and saved you in your enemy's house, ye should have died the death, and he – he that was worth twelve of you – were living.'

'I did but my man's best, even as your kinsman did upon the other party,' answered Dick. 'Were he still living – as I vow to Heaven I wish it! – he would praise, not blame me.'

'Sir Daniel hath told me,' she replied. 'He marked you at the barricade. Upon you, he saith, their party foundered; it was you that won the battle. Well, then, it was you that killed my good Lord Risingham, as sure as though ye had strangled him. And ye would have me eat with you – and your hands not washed from killing? But Sir Daniel hath sworn your downfall. He 'tis that will avenge me!'

The unfortunate Dick was plunged in gloom. Old Arblaster returned upon his mind, and he groaned aloud.

'Do ye hold me so guilty?' he said; 'you that defended me – you that are Joanna's friend?'

'What made ye in the battle?' she retorted. 'Y' are of no party; y' are but a lad – but legs and body, without government of wit or counsel! Wherefore did ye fight? for the love of hurt, pardy!'

'Nay,' cried Dick, 'I know not. But as the realm of England goes, if that a poor gentleman fight not upon the one side, perforce he must fight upon the other. He may not stand alone; 'tis not in nature.'

'They that have no judgment should not draw the sword,' replied the young lady. 'Ye that fight but for a hazard, what are ye but a butcher? War is but noble by the cause, an y' have disgraced it.'

'Madam,' said the miserable Dick, 'I do partly see mine error. I have made too much haste; I have been busy before my time. Already I stole a ship – thinking, I do swear it, to do well – and thereby brought about the death of many innocent, and the grief and ruin of a poor old man whose face this very day hath stabbed me like a dagger. And for this morning, I did but design to do myself credit and get fame to marry with, and, behold! I have brought about the death of your dear kinsman that was good to me. And what besides, I know not. For, alas! I may have set York upon the throne, and that may be the worser cause, and may do hurt to England. O, madam, I do see my sin. I am unfit for life. I will, for penance sake and to avoid worse evil, once I have finished this adventure, get me to a cloister. I will forswear Joanna and the trade of arms. I will be a friar, and pray for your good kinsman's spirit all my days.'

It appeared to Dick, in this extremity of his humiliation and repentance, that the young lady had laughed.

Raising his countenance, he found her looking down upon him, in the fire-light, with a somewhat peculiar but not unkind expression.

'Madam,' he cried, thinking the laughter to have been an illusion of his hearing, but still, from her changed looks, hoping to have touched her heart— 'madam, will not this content you? I give up all to undo what I have done amiss; I make heaven certain for Lord Risingham. And all this upon the very day that I have won my spurs, and thought myself the happiest young gentleman on ground.'

'O, boy,' she said— 'good boy!'

And then, to the extreme surprise of Dick, she first very tenderly wiped the tears away from his cheeks, and then, as if yielding to a sudden impulse, threw both her arms about his neck, drew up his face, and kissed him. A pitiful bewilderment came over simple-minded Dick.

'But come,' she said, with great cheerfulness, 'ye that are a captain, ye must eat. Why sup ye not?'

'Dear Mistress Risingham,' replied Dick, 'I did but wait first upon my prisoner; but, to say truth, penitence will no longer suffer me to endure the sight of food. I were better to fast, dear lady, and to pray.'

'Call me Alicia,' she said; 'are we not old friends? And now, come, I will eat with you, bit for bit and sup for sup; so if ye eat not, neither will I; but if ye eat hearty, I will dine like a ploughman.'

So there and then she fell to; and Dick, who had an excellent stomach, proceeded to bear her company, at first with great reluctance, but gradually, as he entered into the spirit, with more and more vigour and devotion;

until, at last, he forgot even to watch his model, and most heartily repaired the expenses of his day of labour and excitement.

'Lion-driver,' she said, at length, 'ye do not admire a maid in a man's jerkin?'

The moon was now up; and they were only waiting to repose the wearied horses. By the moon's light, the still penitent but now well-fed Richard beheld her looking somewhat coquettishly down upon him.

'Madam—' he stammered, surprised at this new turn in her manners.

'Nay,' she interrupted, 'it skills not to deny; Joanna hath told me; but come, Sir Lion-driver, look at me – am I so homely – come!'

And she made bright eyes at him.

'Ye are something smallish, indeed—' began Dick.

And here again she interrupted him, this time with a ringing peal of laughter that completed his confusion and surprise.

'Smallish!' she cried. 'Nay, now, be honest as ye are bold; I am a dwarf, or little better; but for all that – come, tell me! – for all that, passably fair to look upon; is't not so?'

'Nay, madam, exceedingly fair,' said the distressed knight, pitifully trying to seem easy.

'And a man would be right glad to wed me?' she pursued.

'O, madam, right glad!' agreed Dick.

'Call me Alicia,' said she.

'Alicia,' quoth Sir Richard.

'Well, then, lion-driver,' she continued, 'sith that ye slew my kinsman, and left me without stay, ye owe me, in honour, every reparation; do ye not?'

'I do, madam,' said Dick. 'Although, upon my heart, I do hold me but partially guilty of that brave knight's blood.'

'Would ye evade me?' she cried.

'Madam, not so. I have told you; at your bidding, I will even turn me a monk,' said Richard.

'Then, in honour, ye belong to me?' she concluded.

'In honour, madam, I suppose—' began the young man.

'Go to!' she interrupted; 'ye are too full of catches. In honour do ye belong to me, till ye have paid the evil?'

'In honour I do,' said Dick.

'Hear, then,' she continued. 'Ye would make but a sad friar, methinks; and since I am to dispose of you at pleasure, I will even take you for my husband. Nay, now, no words!' cried she. 'They will avail you nothing. For see how just it is, that you who deprived me of one home should supply me with another. And as for Joanna, she will be the first, believe me, to commend the change; for, after all, as we be dear friends, what matters it with which of us ye wed? Not one whit!'

'Madam,' said Dick, 'I will go into a cloister, an ye please to bid me; but to wed with anyone in this big world besides Joanna Sedley is what I will consent to neither for man's force nor yet for lady's pleasure. Pardon me if I speak my plain thoughts plainly; but where a maid is very bold, a poor man must even be the bolder.'

'Dick,' she said, 'ye sweet boy, ye must come and kiss me for that word. Nay, fear not, ye shall kiss me for Joanna, and when we meet, I shall give it back to her, and say I stole it. And as for what ye owe me, why, dear simpleton, methinks ye were not alone in that great battle; and even if York be on the throne, it was not you that set him there. But for a good, sweet, honest heart, Dick, y' are all that; and if I could find it in my soul to envy your Joanna anything, I would even envy her your love.'

CHAPTER SIX

Night in the Woods — concluded:
Dick and Joan

THE HORSES had by this time finished the small store of provender, and fully breathed from their fatigues. At Dick's command, the fire was smothered in snow; and while his men got once more wearily to saddle, he himself, remembering, somewhat late, true woodland caution, chose a tall oak, and nimbly clambered to the topmost fork. Hence he could look far abroad on the moonlit and snow-paven forest. On the south-west, dark against the horizon, stood those upland heathy quarters where he and Joanna had met with the terrifying misadventure of the leper. And there his eye was caught by a spot of ruddy brightness no bigger than a needle's eye.

He blamed himself sharply for his previous neglect. Were that, as it appeared to be, the shining of Sir Daniel's camp-fire, he should long ago have seen and marched for it; above all, he should, for no consideration, have announced his neighbourhood by lighting a fire of his own. But now he must no longer squander valuable hours. The direct way to the uplands was about two miles in length; but it was crossed by a very deep, precipitous dingle, impassable to mounted men; and for the sake of speed, it seemed to Dick advisable to desert the horses and attempt the adventure on foot.

Ten men were left to guard the horses; signals were agreed upon by which they could communicate in case of need; and Dick set forth at the head of the remainder, Alicia Risingham walking stoutly by his side.

The men had freed themselves of heavy armour, and left behind their lances; and they now marched with a very good spirit in the frozen snow, and under the exhilarating lustre of the moon. The descent into the dingle, where a stream strained sobbing through the snow and ice, was effected with silence and order; and on the further side, being then within a short half-mile of where Dick had seen the glimmer of the fire, the party halted to breathe before the attack.

In the vast silence of the wood, the lightest sounds were audible from far; and Alicia, who was keen of hearing, held up her finger warningly, and stooped to listen. All followed her example; but besides the groans of the choked brook in the dingle close behind, and the barking of a fox at a distance of many miles among the forest, to Dick's acutest hearkening not a breath was audible.

'But yet, for sure, I heard the clash of harness,' whispered Alicia.

'Madam,' returned Dick, who was more afraid of that young lady than of ten stout warriors, 'I would not hint ye were mistaken; but it might well have come from either of the camps.'

'It came not thence. It came from westward,' she declared.

'It may be what it will,' returned Dick; 'and it must be as Heaven please. Reck we not a jot, but push on the livelier, and put it to the touch. Up, friends – enough breathed.'

As they advanced, the snow became more and more trampled with hoof-marks, and it was plain that they were drawing near to the encampment of a considerable force of mounted men. Presently they could see the smoke pouring from among the trees, ruddily coloured on its lower edge and scattering bright sparks.

And here, pursuant to Dick's orders, his men began to open out, creeping stealthily in the covert, to surround on every side the camp of their opponents. He himself, placing Alicia in the shelter of a bulky oak, stole straight forth in the direction of the fire.

At last, through an opening of the wood, his eye embraced the scene of the encampment. The fire had been built upon a heathy hummock of the ground, surrounded on three sides by thicket, and it now burned very strong, roaring aloud and brandishing flames. Around it there sat not quite a dozen people, warmly cloaked; but though the neighbouring snow was trampled down as by a regiment, Dick looked in vain for any horse. He began to have a terrible misgiving that he was out-manœuvred. At the same time, in a tall man with a steel salet, who was spreading his hands before the blaze, he recognised his old friend and still kindly enemy, Bennet Hatch; and in two others, sitting a little back, he made out, even in their male disguise, Joanna Sedley and Sir Daniel's wife.

'Well,' thought he to himself, 'even if I lose my horses, let me get my Joanna, and why should I complain?'

And then, from the further side of the encampment, there came a little whistle, announcing that his men had joined, and the investment was complete.

Bennet, at the sound, started to his feet; but ere he had time to spring upon his arms, Dick hailed him.

'Bennet,' he said – 'Bennet, old friend, yield ye. Ye will but spill men's lives in vain if ye resist.'

' 'Tis Master Shelton, by St Barbary!' cried Hatch. 'Yield me. Ye ask much. What force have ye?'

'I tell you, Bennet, ye are both outnumbered and begirt,' said Dick. 'Cæsar and Charlemagne would cry for quarter. I have two score men at my whistle, and with one shoot of arrows I could answer for you all.'

'Master Dick,' said Bennet, 'it goes against my heart; but I must do my duty. The saints help you!' And therewith he raised a little tucket to his mouth and wound a rousing call.

Then followed a moment of confusion; for while Dick, fearing for the ladies, still hesitated to give the word to shoot, Hatch's little band sprang to their weapons and formed back to back as for a fierce resistance. In the hurry of their change of place, Joanna sprang from her seat and ran like an arrow to her lover's side.

'Here, Dick!' she cried, as she clasped his hand in hers.

But Dick still stood irresolute; he was yet young to the more deplorable necessities of war, and the thought of old Lady Brackley checked the command upon his tongue. His own men became restive. Some of them cried on him by name; others, of their own accord, began to shoot; and at the first discharge poor Bennet bit the dust. Then Dick awoke.

'On!' he cried. 'Shoot boys, and keep to cover. England and York!'

But just then the dull beat of many horses on the snow suddenly arose in the hollow ear of the night, and, with incredible swiftness, drew nearer and swelled louder. At the same time, answering tuckets repeated and repeated Hatch's call.

'Rally, rally!' cried Dick. 'Rally upon me! Rally for your lives!'

But his men – afoot, scattered, taken in the hour when they had counted on an easy triumph – began instead to give ground severally, and either stood wavering or dispersed into the thickets. And when the first of the horsemen came charging through the open avenues and fiercely riding their steeds into the underwood, a few stragglers were overthrown or speared among the brush, but the bulk of Dick's command had simply melted at the rumour of their coming.

Dick stood for a moment, bitterly recognising the fruits of his precipitate and unwise valour. Sir Daniel had seen the fire; he had moved out with his main force, whether to attack his pursuers or to take them in the rear if they should venture the assault. His had been throughout the part of a sagacious captain; Dick's the conduct of an eager boy. And here was the young knight, his sweetheart, indeed, holding him tightly by the hand, but otherwise alone, his whole command of men and horse dispersed in the night and the wide forest, like a paper of pins in a hay barn.

'The saints enlighten me!' he thought. 'It is well I was knighted for this morning's matter; this doth me little honours.'

And thereupon, still holding Joanna, he began to run.

The silence of the night was now shattered by the shouts of the men of Tunstall, as they galloped hither and thither, hunting fugitives; and Dick broke boldly through the underwood and ran straight before him like a deer. The silver clearness of the moon upon the open snow increased, by contrast, the obscurity of the thickets; and the extreme dispersion of the vanquished led the pursuers into widely divergent paths. Hence, in but a little while, Dick and

Joanna paused, in a close covert, and heard the sounds of the pursuit, scattering abroad, indeed, in all directions, but yet fainting already in the distance.

'An I had but kept a reserve of them together,' Dick cried, bitterly, 'I could have turned the tables yet! Well, we live and learn; next time, it shall go better, by the rood.'

'Nay, Dick,' said Joanna, 'what matters it? Here we are together once again.'

He looked at her, and there she was – John Matcham; as of yore, in hose and doublet. But now he knew her; now, even in that ungainly dress, she smiled upon him, bright with love; and his heart was transported with joy.

'Sweetheart,' he said, 'if ye forgive this blunderer, what care I? Make we direct for Holywood; there lieth your good guardian and my better friend, Lord Foxham. There shall we be wed; and whether poor or wealthy, famous or unknown, what matters it? This day, dear love, I won my spurs; I was commended by great men for my valour; I thought myself the goodliest man of war in all broad England. Then, first, I fell out of my favour with the great; and now have I been well thrashed, and clean lost my soldiers. There was a downfall for conceit! But, dear, I care not – dear, if ye still love me and will wed, I would have my knighthood done away, and mind it not a jot.'

'My Dick!' she cried. 'And did they knight you?'

'Ay, dear, ye are my lady now,' he answered fondly; 'or ye shall, ere noon to-morrow – will ye not?'

'That will I, Dick, with a glad heart,' she answered.

'Ay, sir? Methought ye were to be a monk!' said a voice in their ears.

'Alicia!' cried Joanna.

'Even so,' replied the young lady, coming forward.

'Alicia, whom ye left for dead, and whom your lion-driver found, and brought to life again, and, by my sooth, made love to, if ye want to know.'

'I'll not believe it,' cried Joanna. 'Dick!'

'Dick!' mimicked Alicia. 'Dick, indeed! Ay, fair sir, and ye desert poor damsels in distress,' she continued, turning to the young knight. 'Ye leave them planted behind oaks. But they say true – the age of chivalry is dead.'

'Madam,' cried Dick, in despair, 'upon my soul I had forgotten you outright. Madam, ye must try to pardon me. Ye see, I had new found Joanna!'

'I did not suppose that ye had done it o' purpose,' she retorted. 'But I will be cruelly avenged. I will tell a secret to my Lady Shelton – she that is to be,' she added, curtseying. 'Joanna,' she continued, 'I believe, upon my soul, your sweetheart is a bold fellow in a fight, but he is, let me tell you plainly, the softest-hearted simpleton in England. Go to – ye may do your pleasure with him! And now, fool children, first kiss me, either one of you, for luck and kindness; and then kiss each other just one minute by the glass, and not one second longer; and then let us all three set forth for Holywood as fast as we can stir; for these woods, methinks, are full of peril and exceeding cold.'

'But did my Dick make love to you?' asked Joanna, clinging to her sweetheart's side.

'Nay, fool girl,' returned Alicia; 'it was I made love to him. I offered to marry him, indeed; but he bade me go marry with my likes. These were his words. Nay, that I will say: he is more plain than pleasant. But now, children, for the sake of sense, set forward. Shall we go once more over the dingle, or push straight for Holywood?'

'Why,' said Dick, 'I would like dearly to get upon a horse; for I have been sore mauled and beaten, one way and another, these last days, and my poor body is one bruise. But how think ye? If the men, upon the alarm of the fighting, had fled away, we should have gone about for nothing. 'Tis but some three short miles to Holywood direct; the bell hath not beat nine; the snow is pretty firm to walk upon, the moon clear; how if we went even as we are?'

'Agreed,' cried Alicia; but Joanna only pressed upon Dick's arm.

Forth, then, they went, through open leafless groves and down snow-clad alleys, under the white face of the winter moon; Dick and Joanna walking hand in hand and in a heaven of pleasure; and their light-minded companion, her own bereavements heartily forgotten, followed a pace or two behind, now rallying them upon their silence,

and now drawing happy pictures of their future and
united lives.

Still, indeed, in the distance of the wood, the riders of
Tunstall might be heard urging their pursuit; and from time
to time cries or the clash of steel announced the shock of
enemies. But in these young folk, bred among the alarms of
war, and fresh from such a multiplicity of dangers, neither
fear nor pity could be lightly wakened. Content to find the
sounds still drawing farther and farther away, they gave up
their hearts to the enjoyment of the hour, walking already as
Alicia put it, in a wedding procession; and neither the rude
solitude of the forest nor the cold of the freezing night had
any force to shadow or distract their happiness.

At length, from a rising hill, they looked below them
on the dell of Holywood. The great windows of the forest
abbey shone with torch and candle; its high pinnacles and
spires arose very clear and silent, and the gold rood upon
the topmost summit glittered brightly in the moon. All
about it, in the open glade, camp-fires were burning, and
the ground was thick with huts; and across the midst of
the picture the frozen river curved.

'By the mass,' said Richard, 'there are Lord Foxham's
fellows still encamped. The messenger hath certainly miscarried. Well, then, so better. We have power at hand to
face Sir Daniel.'

But if Lord Foxham's men still lay encamped in the
long holm at Holywood, it was from a different reason
from the one supposed by Dick. They had marched,
indeed, for Shoreby; but ere they were half-way thither,
a second messenger met them, and bade them return to
their morning's camp, to bar the road against Lancastrian
fugitives, and to be so much nearer to the main army of
York. For Richard of Gloucester, having finished the battle
and stamped out his foes in that district, was already on
the march to rejoin his brother; and not long after the
return of my Lord Foxham's retainers, Crookback himself
drew rein before the abbey door. It was in honour of this
august visitor that the windows shone with lights; and at
the hour of Dick's arrival with his sweetheart and her
friend, the whole ducal party was being entertained in the

refectory with the splendour of that powerful and luxurious monastery.

Dick, not quite with his goodwill, was brought before them. Gloucester, sick with fatigue, sat leaning upon one hand with his white and terrifying countenance; Lord Foxham, half recovered from his wound, was in a place of honour on his left.

'How, sir?' asked Richard. 'Have ye brought me Sir Daniel's head?'

'My lord duke,' replied Dick, stoutly enough, but with a qualm at heart, 'I have not even the good fortune to return with my command. I have been, so please your grace, well beaten.'

Gloucester looked upon him with a formidable frown.

'I gave you fifty lances,[1] sir,' he said.

'My lord duke, I had but fifty men-at-arms,' replied the young knight.

'How is this?' said Gloucester. 'He did ask me fifty lances.'

'May it please your grace,' replied Catesby smoothly, 'for a pursuit we gave him but the horsemen.'

'It is well,' replied Richard, adding, 'Shelton, ye may go.'

'Stay!' said Lord Foxham. 'This young man likewise had a charge from me. It may be he hath better sped. Say, Master Shelton, have ye found the maid?'

'I praise the saints, my lord,' said Dick; 'she is in this house.'

'Is it even so? Well, then, my lord the duke,' resumed Lord Foxham, 'with your goodwill, to-morrow, before the army march, I do propose a marriage. This young squire—'

'Young knight,' interrupted Catesby.

'Say ye so, Sir William?' cried Lord Foxham.

'I did myself, and for good service, dub him knight,' said Gloucester. 'He hath twice manfully served me. It is not valour of hands, it is a man's mind of iron, that he lacks. He will not rise, Lord Foxham. 'Tis a fellow that

---

1. Technically, the term 'lance' included a not quite certain number of foot soldiers attached to the man-at-arms.

will fight indeed bravely in a mellay, but hath a capon's heart. Howbeit, if he is to marry, marry him in the name of Mary, and be done!'

'Nay, he is a brave lad – I know it,' said Lord Foxham. 'Content ye, then, Sir Richard. I have compounded this affair with Master Hamley, and to-morrow ye shall wed.'

Whereupon Dick judged it prudent to withdraw; but he was not yet clear of the refectory, when a man, but newly alighted at the gate, came running four stairs at a bound, and brushing through the abbey servants, threw himself on one knee before the duke.

'Victory, my lord,' he cried.

And before Dick had got to the chamber set apart for him as Lord Foxham's guest, the troops in the holm were cheering around their fires; for upon that same day, not twenty miles away, a second crushing blow had been dealt to the power of Lancaster.

CHAPTER SEVEN

Dick's Revenge

THE NEXT morning Dick was afoot before the sun, and having dressed himself to the best advantage, with the aid of Lord Foxham's baggage, and got good reports of Joan, he set forth on foot to walk away his impatience.

For some while he made rounds among the soldiery, who were getting to arms in the wintry twilight of the dawn and by the red glow of torches; but gradually he strolled further afield, and at length passed clean beyond the outpost, and walked alone in the frozen forest, waiting for the sun.

His thoughts were both quiet and happy. His brief favour with the duke he could not find it in his heart to mourn; with Joan to wife, and my Lord Foxham for a faithful patron, he looked most happily upon the future; and in the past he found but little to regret.

As he thus strolled and pondered, the solemn light of the morning grew more clear, the east was already coloured by the sun, and a little scathing wind blew up the frozen snow. He turned to go home; but even as he turned, his eye lit upon a figure behind a tree.

'Stand!' he cried. 'Who goes?'

The figure stepped forth and waved its hand like a dumb person. It was arrayed like a pilgrim, the hood lowered over the face, but Dick, in an instant, recognised Sir Daniel.

He strode up to him, drawing his sword; and the knight, putting his hand in his bosom, as if to seize a hidden weapon, steadfastly awaited his approach.

'Well, Dickon,' said Sir Daniel, 'how is it to be? Do ye make war upon the fallen?'

'I made no war upon your life,' replied the lad; 'I was your true friend until ye sought for mine; but ye have sought for it greedily.'

'Nay – self-defence,' replied the knight. 'And now, boy, the news of this battle, and the presence of yon crooked devil here in mine own wood, have broken me beyond all help. I go to Holywood for sanctuary; thence overseas, with what I can carry, and to begin life again in Burgundy or France.'

'Ye may not go to Holywood,' said Dick.

'How! May not?' asked the knight.

'Look ye, Sir Daniel, this is my marriage morn,' said Dick; 'and yon sun that is to rise will make the brightest day that ever shone for me. Your life is forfeit – doubly forfeit, for my father's death and your own practices to me-ward. But I myself have done amiss; I have brought about men's deaths; and upon this glad day I will be neither judge nor hangman. An ye were the devil, I would not lay a hand on you. An ye were the devil, ye might go where ye will for me. Seek God's forgiveness; mine ye have freely. But to go on to Holywood is different. I carry arms for York, and I will suffer no spy within their lines. Hold it, then, for certain, if ye set one foot before another, I will uplift my voice and call the nearest post to seize you.'

'Ye mock me,' said Sir Daniel. 'I have no safety out of Holywood.'

'I care no more,' returned Richard. 'I let you go east, west, or south; north I will not. Holywood is shut against you. Go, and seek not to return. For, once ye are gone, I will warn every post about this army, and there will be so shrewd a watch upon all pilgrims that, once again, were ye the very devil, ye would find it ruin to make the essay.'

'Ye doom me,' said Sir Daniel, gloomily.

'I doom you not,' returned Richard. 'If it so please you to set your valour against mine, come on; and though I fear it be disloyal to my party, I will take the challenge openly and fully, fight you with mine own single strength, and call for none to help me. So shall I avenge my father, with a perfect conscience.'

'Ay,' said Sir Daniel, 'y' have a long sword against my dagger.'

'I rely upon Heaven only,' answered Dick, casting his sword some way behind him on the snow. 'Now, if

your ill-fate bids you, come; and, under the pleasure
of the Almighty, I make myself bold to feed your bones
to foxes.'

'I did but try you, Dickon,' returned the knight, with
an uneasy semblance of a laugh. 'I would not spill your
blood.'

'Go, then, ere it be too late,' replied Shelton. 'In five
minutes I will call the post. I do perceive that I am too
long-suffering. Had but our places been reversed, I should
have been bound hand and foot some minutes past.'

'Well, Dickon, I will go,' replied Sir Daniel. 'When we
next meet, it shall repent you that ye were so harsh.'

And with these words, the knight turned and began to
move off under the trees. Dick watched him with strangely
mingled feelings, as he went, swiftly and warily, and ever
and again turning a wicked eye upon the lad who had
spared him, and whom he still suspected.

There was upon one side of where he went a thicket,
strongly matted with green ivy, and, even in its winter
state, impervious to the eye. Herein, all of a sudden,
a bow sounded like a note of music. An arrow flew,
and with a great, choked cry of agony and anger, the
Knight of Tunstall threw up his hands and fell forward
in the snow.

Dick bounded to his side and raised him. His face desperately worked; his whole body was shaken by contorting
spasms.

'Is the arrow black?' he gasped.

'It is black,' replied Dick, gravely.

And then, before he could add one word, a desperate
seizure of pain shook the wounded man from head to foot,
so that his body leaped in Dick's supporting arms, and with
the extremity of that pang his spirit fled in silence.

The young man laid him back gently in the snow and
prayed for that unprepared and guilty spirit, and as he
prayed the sun came up at a bound, and the robins began
chirping in the ivy.

When he rose to his feet, he found another man upon his
knees but a few steps behind him, and, still with uncovered
head, he waited until that prayer also should be over. It

took long; the man, with his head bowed and his face covered with his hands, prayed like one in a great disorder or distress of mind; and by the bow that lay beside him, Dick judged that he was no other than the archer who had laid Sir Daniel low.

At length he also rose, and showed the countenance of Ellis Duckworth.

'Richard,' he said, very gravely, 'I heard you. Ye took the better part and pardoned; I took the worse, and there lays the clay of mine enemy. Pray for me.'

And he wrung him by the hand.

'Sir,' said Richard, 'I will pray for you, indeed; though how I may prevail I wot not. But if ye have so long pursued revenge, and find it now of such a sorry flavour, bethink ye, were it not well to pardon others? Hatch – he is dead, poor shrew! I would have spared a better; and for Sir Daniel, here lies his body. But for the priest, if I might anywise prevail, I would have you let him go.'

A flash came into the eyes of Ellis Duckworth.

'Nay,' he said, 'the devil is still strong within me. But be at rest; the Black Arrow flieth nevermore – the fellowship is broken. They that still live shall come to their quiet and ripe end, in Heaven's good time, for me; and for yourself, go where your better fortune calls you, and think no more of Ellis.'

CHAPTER EIGHT

Conclusion

ABOUT NINE IN the morning, Lord Foxham was leading his ward, once more dressed as befitted her sex, and followed by Alicia Risingham, to the church of Holywood, when Richard Crookback, his brow already heavy with cares, crossed their path and paused.

'Is this the maid?' he asked; and when Lord Foxham had replied in the affirmative, 'Minion,' he added, 'hold up your face until I see its flavour.'

He looked upon her sourly for a little.

'Ye are fair,' he said at last, 'and, as they tell me, dowered. How if I offered you a brave marriage, as became your face and parentage?'

'My lord duke,' replied Joanna, 'may it please your grace, I had rather wed with Sir Richard.'

'How so?' he asked harshly. 'Marry but the man I name to you, and he shall be my lord, and you my lady, before night. For Sir Richard, let me tell you plainly, he will die Sir Richard.'

'I ask no more of Heaven, my lord, than but to die Sir Richard's wife,' returned Joanna.

'Look ye at that, my lord,' said Gloucester, turning to Lord Foxham. 'Here be a pair for you. The lad, when for good services I gave him his choice of my favour, chose but the grace of an old, drunken shipman. I did warn him freely, but he was stout in his besottedness. "Here dieth your favour," said I; and he, my lord, with a most assured impertinence, "Mine be the loss," quoth he. It shall be so, by the rood!'

'Said he so?' cried Alicia. 'Then well said, lion-driver!'

'Who is this?' asked the duke.

'A prisoner of Sir Richard's,' answered Lord Foxham; 'Mistress Alicia Risingham.'

'See that she be married to a sure man,' said the duke.

'I had thought of my kinsman, Hamley, an it like your grace,' returned Lord Foxham. 'He hath well served the cause.'

'It likes me well,' said Richard. 'Let them be wedded speedily. Say, fair maid, will you wed?'

'My lord duke,' said Alicia, 'so as the man is straight—' And there, in a perfect consternation, the voice died on her tongue.

'He is straight, my mistress,' replied Richard, calmly. 'I am the only crookback of my party; we are else passably well-shapen. Ladies, and you, my lord,' he added, with a sudden change to grave courtesy, 'judge me not too churlish if I leave you. A captain, in the time of war, hath not the ordering of his hours.'

And with a very handsome salutation he passed on, followed by his officers.

'Alack,' cried Alicia, 'I am shent!'

'Ye know him not,' replied Lord Foxham. 'It is but a trifle; he hath already clean forgot your words.'

'He is, then, the very flower of knighthood,' said Alicia.

'Nay, he but mindeth other things,' returned Lord Foxham. 'Tarry we no more.'

In the chancel they found Dick waiting, attended by a few young men; and there were he and Joan united. When they came forth again, happy and yet serious, into the frosty air and sunlight, the long files of the army were already winding forward up the road; already the Duke of Gloucester's banner was unfolded and began to move from before the abbey in a clump of spears; and behind it, girt by steel-clad knights, the bold, black-hearted, and ambitious hunchback moved on towards his brief kingdom and his lasting infamy. But the wedding-party turned upon the other side, and sat down, with sober merriment, to breakfast. The father cellarer attended on their wants, and sat with them at table. Hamley, all jealousy forgotten, began to ply the nowise loth Alicia with courtship. And there, amid the sounding of tuckets and the clash of armoured soldiery and horses continually moving forth, Dick and Joan sat side by side, tenderly held hands, and looked, with ever-growing affection, in each other's eyes.

Thenceforth the dust and blood of that unruly epoch passed them by. They dwelt apart from alarms in the green forest where their love began.

Two old men in the meanwhile enjoyed pensions in great prosperity and peace, and with perhaps a superfluity of ale and wine, in Tunstall hamlet. One had been all his life a shipman, and continued to the last to lament his man Tom. The other, who had been a bit of everything, turned in the end towards piety, and made a most religious death under the name of Brother Honestus in the neighbouring abbey. So Lawless had his will, and died a friar.

The Song of the Morrow

The Song of the Morrow

THE King of Duntrine had a daughter when he was old, and she was the fairest King's daughter between two seas; her hair was like spun gold, and her eyes like pools in a river; and the King gave her a castle upon the sea beach, with a terrace, and a court of the hewn stone, and four towers at the four corners. Here she dwelt and grew up, and had no care for the morrow, and no power upon the hour, after the manner of simple men.

It befell that she walked one day by the beach of the sea, when it was autumn, and the wind blew from the place of rains; and upon the one hand of her the sea beat, and upon the other the dead leaves ran. This was the loneliest beach between two seas, and strange things had been done there in the ancient ages. Now the King's daughter was aware of a crone that sat upon the beach. The sea foam ran to her feet, and the dead leaves swarmed about her back, and the rags blew about her face in the blowing of the wind.

'Now,' said the King's daughter, and she named a holy name, 'this is the most unhappy old crone between two seas.'

'Daughter of a King,' said the crone, 'you dwell in a stone house, and your hair is like the gold: but what is your profit? Life is not long, nor lives strong; and you live after the way of simple men, and have no thought for the morrow, and no power upon the hour.'

'Thought for the morrow, that I have,' said the King's daughter; 'but power upon the hour, that have I not.' And she mused with herself.

Then the crone smote her lean hands one within the other, and laughed like a sea-gull. 'Home!' cried she. 'O daughter of a King, home to your stone house; for the longing is come upon you now, nor can you live any more after the manner of simple men. Home, and toil and suffer, till the gift come that will make you bare, and till the man come that will bring you care.'

The King's daughter made no more ado, but she turned about and went home to her house in silence. And when she was come into her chamber she called for her nurse.

'Nurse,' said the King's daughter, 'thought is come upon me for the morrow, so that I can live no more after the manner of simple men. Tell me what I must do that I may have power upon the hour.'

Then the nurse moaned like a snow wind. 'Alas!' said she, 'that this thing should be; but the thought is gone into your marrow, nor is there any cure against the thought. Be it so, then, even as you will; though power is less than weakness, power shall you have; and though the thought is colder than winter, yet shall you think it to an end.'

So the King's daughter sat in her vaulted chamber in the masoned house, and she thought upon the thought. Nine years she sat; and the sea beat upon the terrace, and the gulls cried about the turrets, and wind crooned in the chimneys of the house. Nine years she came not abroad, nor tasted the clean air, neither saw God's sky. Nine years she sat and looked neither to the right nor to the left, nor heard speech of any one, but thought upon the thought of the morrow. And her nurse fed her in silence, and she took of the food with her left hand, and ate it without grace.

Now when the nine years were out, it fell dusk in the autumn, and there came a sound in the wind like a sound of piping. At that the nurse lifted up her finger in the vaulted house.

'I hear a sound in the wind,' said she, 'that is like the sound of piping.'

'It is but a little sound,' said the King's daughter, 'but yet is it enough for me.'

So they went down in the dusk to the doors of the house, and along the beach of the sea. And the waves beat upon the one hand, and upon the other the dead leaves ran; and the clouds raced in the sky, and the gulls flew widdershins. And when they came to that part of the beach where strange things had been done in the ancient ages, lo, there was the crone, and she was dancing widdershins.

'What makes you dance widdershins, old crone?' said the King's daughter; 'here upon the bleak beach, between the waves and the dead leaves?'

'I hear a sound in the wind that is like a sound of piping,' quoth she. 'And it is for that that I dance widdershins. For the gift comes that will make you bare, and the man comes that must bring you care. But for me the morrow is come that I have thought upon, and the hour of my power.'

'How comes it, crone,' said the King's daughter, 'that you waver like a rag, and pale like a dead leaf before my eyes?'

'Because the morrow has come that I have thought upon, and the hour of my power,' said the crone; and she fell on the beach, and, lo! she was but stalks of the sea tangle, and dust of the sea sand, and the sand lice hopped upon the place of her.

'This is the strangest thing that befell between two seas,' said the King's daughter of Duntrine.

But the nurse broke out and moaned like an autumn gale. 'I am weary of the wind,' quoth she; and she bewailed her day.

The King's daughter was aware of a man upon the beach; he went hooded so that none might perceive his face, and a pipe was underneath his arm. The sound of his pipe was like singing wasps, and like the wind that sings in windlestraw; and it took hold upon men's ears like the crying of gulls.

'Are you the comer?' quoth the King's daughter of Duntrine.

'I am the comer,' said he, 'and these are the pipes that a man may hear, and I have power upon the hour, and this is the song of the morrow.' And he piped the song of the morrow, and it was as long as years; and the nurse wept out aloud at the hearing of it.

'This is true,' said the King's daughter, 'that you pipe the song of the morrow; but that ye have power upon the hour, how may I know that? Show me a marvel here upon the beach, between the waves and the dead leaves.'

And the man said, 'Upon whom?'

'Here is my nurse,' quoth the King's daughter. 'She is weary of the wind. Show me a good marvel upon her.'

And, lo! the nurse fell upon the beach as it were two handfuls of dead leaves, and the wind whirled them widdershins, and the sand lice hopped between.

'It is true,' said the King's daughter of Duntrine; 'you are the comer, and you have power upon the hour. Come with me to my stone house.'

So they went by the sea margin, and the man piped the song of the morrow, and the leaves followed behind them as they went. Then they sat down together; and the sea beat on the terrace, and the gulls cried about the towers, and the wind crooned in the chimneys of the house. Nine years they sat, and every year when it fell autumn, the man said, 'This is the hour, and I have power in it'; and the daughter of the King said, 'Nay, but pipe me the song of the morrow.' And he piped it, and it was long like years.

Now when the nine years were gone, the King's daughter of Duntrine got her to her feet, like one that remembers; and she looked about her in the masoned house; and all her servants were gone; only the man that piped sat upon the terrace with the hand upon his face; and as he piped the leaves ran about the terrace and the sea beat along the wall. Then she cried to him with a great voice, 'This is the hour, and let me see the power in it.' And with that the wind blew off the hood from the man's face, and, lo! there was no man there, only the clothes and the hood and the pipes tumbled one upon another in a corner of the terrace, and the dead leaves ran over them.

And the King's daughter of Duntrine got her to that part of the beach where strange things had been done in the ancient ages; and there she sat her down. The sea foam ran to her feet, and the dead leaves swarmed about her back, and the veil blew about her face in the blowing of the wind. And when she lifted up her eyes, there was the daughter of a King come walking on the beach. Her hair was like the spun gold, and her eyes like pools in a river, and she had no thought for the morrow and no power upon the hour, after the manner of simple men.

CANONGATE CLASSICS

Books listed in alphabetical order by author.

The Bruce John Barbour
The Land of the Leal James Barke
Farewell Miss Julie Logan: A Barrie Omnibus (*Little White Bird, Twelve Pound Look, Farewell Miss Julie Logan*) J. M. Barrie
The Wallace Harry Blind
The Scottish Enlightenment: An Anthology Edited by Alexander Broadie
The House with the Green Shutters George Douglas Brown
Magnus George Mackay Brown
The Leithen Stories John Buchan
The Watcher by the Threshold John Buchan
Witch Wood John Buchan
The Canongate Burns Robert Burns, edited by Andrew Noble and Patrick Scott Hogg
Sartor Resartus Thomas Carlyle
Lying Awake Catherine Carswell
Open the Door Catherine Carswell
The Life of Robert Burns Catherine Carswell
The Triumph Tree Edited by Thomas Owen Clancy
The Complete Brigadier Gerard Sir Arthur Conan Doyle
The Exploits of Brigadier Gerard Sir Arthur Conan Doyle
20th Century Scottish Drama Edited by Cairns Craig and Randall Stevenson
The Raiders Samuel R. Crockett
Two Worlds: An Edinburgh Jewish Childhood David Daiches
The Man Who Wanted to Smell Books and Other Stories Elspeth Davie
Divided Loyalties: A Scotswoman in Occupied France Janet Du Cros Teissier
The Golden Bough J. G. Frazer
A Glasgow Trilogy (*The Boy Who Wanted Peace, Mr Alfred, M.A., Grace, Miss Patridge*) George Friel
Mr Alfred, M.A. George Friel
Dance of the Apprentices Edward Gaitens
Ringan Gilhaize John Galt
The Member and *The Radical* John Galt
A Scots Quair (*Sunset Song, Cloud Howe, Grey Granite*) Lewis Grassic Gibbon
Cloud Howe Lewis Grassic Gibbon
Grey Granite Lewis Grassic Gibbon
Smeddum: A Lewis Grassic Gibbon Anthology Lewis Grassic Gibbon

Sunset Song Lewis Grassic Gibbon
Memoirs of a Highland Lady (Vols I and II)
    Elizabeth Grant of Rothiemurchus
The Highland Lady in Ireland Elizabeth Grant of Rothiemurchus
1982, Janine Alasdair Gray
Lanark Alasdair Gray
Unlikely Stories, Mostly Alasdair Gray
Highland River Neil M. Gunn
Sun Circle Neil M. Gunn
The Key of the Chest Neil Gunn
The Serpent Neil M. Gunn
The Well at World's End Neil M. Gunn
Gillespie J. Macdougall Hay
The Private Memoirs and Confessions of a Justified Sinner James Hogg
The Three Perils of Man James Hogg
A Caledonian Feast Annette Hope
Flemington and Tales From Angus Violet Jacob
Fergus Lamont Robin Jenkins
Just Duffy Robin Jenkins
The Changeling Robin Jenkins
The Cone Gatherers Robin Jenkins
*Journey to the Hebrides (A Journey to the Western Isles of Scotland, The
    Journal of a Tour to the Hebrides)* Samuel Johnson & James Boswell
*Household Ghosts: A James Kennaway Omnibus (Tunes of Glory, Household
    Ghosts, Silence)* James Kennaway
Tunes of Glory James Kennaway
Wisdom, Madness and Folly R. D. Laing
A Voyage to Arcturus David Lindsay
Ane Satyre of the Thrie Estaitis David Lindsay
The Haunted Woman David Lindsay
Magnus Merriman Eric Linklater
Private Angelo Eric Linklater
The Dark of Summer Eric Linklater
The New Testament in Scots William L. Lorimer
Scottish Ballads Edited by Emily Lyle
Modern Scottish Gaelic Poems / Nua-Bhardachd Gaidhlig
    Donald Macaulay / Domhnall MacAmhlaigh
The Early Life of James McBey James McBey
And the Cock Crew Fionn MacColla
The Devil and the Giro: The Scottish Short Story
    Edited by Carl MacDougall
St Kilda: Island on the Edge of the World Charles MacLean
Linmill Stories Robert McLellan

Modern Scottish Women Poets Dorothy McMillan
The Silver Bough Florence Marian McNeill
Before Burns Christopher Maclachlan
Wild Harbour Ian Macpherson
A Question of Loyalties Allan Massie
The Death of Men Allan Massie
A Childhood In Scotland Christian Miller
The Blood of the Martyrs Naomi Mitchison
The Corn King and the Spring Queen Naomi Mitchison
The Gowk Storm Nancy Brysson Morrison
An Autobiography Edwin Muir
Growing Up in the West John Muir
My First Summer in the Sierra John Muir
The Story of My Boyhood and Youth John Muir
*Wilderness Journeys (The Story of My Boyhood and Youth, A Thousand
    Mile Walk to the Gulf, My First Summer in the Sierra, Travels in Alaska,
    Stickeen)* John Muir
Imagined Corners Willa Muir
*Imagined Selves (Imagined Corners, Mrs Ritchie, Mrs Grundy in Scotland,
    Women: An Inquiry, Women in Scotland)* Willa Muir
A Beleaguered City and Other Tales of the Seen and Unseen
    Margaret Oliphant
Homeward Journey John MacNair Reid
A Twelvemonth and a Day Christopher Rush
The End of an Old Song J. D. Scott
The Journal of Sir Walter Scott Sir Walter Scott
*The Grampian Quartet (The Quarry Wood, The Weatherhouse, A Pass in the
    Grampians, The Living Mountain)* Nan Shepherd
The Quarry Wood Nan Shepherd
The Weatherhouse Nan Shepherd
Consider the Lilies Iain Crichton Smith
Listen to the Voice: Selected Stories Iain Crichton Smith
Queen of Science Mary Somerville
Diaries of a Dying Man William Soutar
Catriona Robert Louis Stevenson
Island Landfalls: Reflections from the South Seas Robert Louis Stevenson
Kidnapped Robert Louis Stevenson
Markheim, Jekyll and the Merry Men Robert Louis Stevenson
Shorter Scottish Fiction Robert Louis Stevenson
*Tales of Adventure (Black Arrow, Treasure Island, The Sire de Malétroit's
    Door and other stories)* Robert Louis Stevenson
Tales of the South Seas (Island Landfalls, The Ebb-Tide, The Wrecker)
    Robert Louis Stevenson

The Master of Ballantrae Robert Louis Stevenson
*The Scottish Novels (Kidnapped, Catriona, The Master of Ballantrae, Weir of
   Hermiston)* Robert Louis Stevenson
The Man Who Counted Malba Tahan
The Makars Jacqueline Tasioulas
The Bad Sister: Emma Tennant Omnibus Emma Tennant
The People of the Sea David Thomson
City of Dreadful Night James Thomson
Three Scottish Poets: MacCaig, Morgan, Lochhead
   Edited by Roderick Watson
Black Lamb and Grey Falcon Rebecca West
The King and the Lamp: Scottish Traveller Tales Duncan Williamson